PRAISE FOR
MARGARET MILLAR

Mystery Writers of America Grand Master
Winner of the Edgar® Award for Best Novel
***Los Angeles Times* Woman of the Year**

"One of the most original and vital voices in all of American crime fiction."
—Laura Lippman

"No woman in twentieth-century American mystery writing is more important than Margaret Millar."
—H.R.F. Keating

"I long ago changed my writing name to Ross Macdonald for obvious reasons."
—Kenneth Millar (Ross Macdonald), in a letter to the *Toronto Saturday Night* newspaper

"Very Original."
—Agatha Christie

"Stunningly original."
—Val McDermid

"She has few peers, and no superior in the art of bamboozlement."
—Julian Symons

"Written with such complete realization of every character that the most bitter antagonist of mystery fiction may be forced to acknowledge it as a work of art."
—Anthony Boucher reviewing *Beast in View* for the *New York Times*

"Margaret Millar can build up the sensation of fear so strongly that at the end it literally hits you like a battering ram."
—BBC

"Wonderfully ingenious."
—*The New Yorker*

"Brilliantly superlative . . . One of the most impressive additions to mystery literature—and the word "literature" is used in its fullest sense."
—*San Francisco Chronicle*

"In the whole of crime fiction's distinguished sisterhood, there is no one quite like Margaret Millar."
—*The Guardian*

"She writes minor classics."
—*Washington Post*

"Mrs. Millar doesn't attract fans she creates addicts."
—Dilys Winn, namesake of the Dilys Award

COLLECTED MILLAR

THE TOM ARAGON NOVELS

COLLECTED MILLAR

COLLECTED MILLAR

THE TOM ARAGON NOVELS

INCLUDING

ASK FOR ME TOMORROW
THE MURDER OF MIRANDA
MERMAID

MARGARET
MILLAR

SYNDICATE BOOKS
NEW YORK

Ask for Me Tomorrow © 1976 The Margaret Millar Charitable Unitrust
The Murder of Miranda © 1979 The Margaret Millar Charitable Unitrust
Mermaid © 1982 The Margaret Millar Charitable Unitrust

This volume published in 2016 by Syndicate Books

www.syndicatebooks.com

Distributed by
Soho Press, Inc.
853 Broadway
New York, NY 10003

Library of Congress Cataloging-in-Publication Data is available

ISBN: 978-1-68199-029-3
Ask for Me Tomorrow eISBN: 978-1-68199-005-7
The Murder of Miranda eISBN: 978-1-68199-006-4
Mermaid eISBN: 978-1-68199-007-1

Cover and interior design by Jeff Wong

Printed in the United States of America

10 9 8 7 6 5 4 3 2 1

TABLE OF CONTENTS

ASK FOR ME TOMORROW

To Charles Barton Clapp

Ask for me tomorrow and you shall find me a grave man.
Romeo and Juliet
Act III, Scene I

1

IT WAS LATE afternoon. As Marco dozed in his wheelchair the long lazy rays of the sun touched the top of his head and stroked the sparse grey hairs of his good arm and fell among the folds of his lap robe. Gilly stood in the doorway and watched her husband, waiting for some sign that he was aware of her presence.

"Marco? Can you hear me?"

Only a few parts of his body were capable of movement and none of them moved. No spasm of the fingers of his right hand which operated the controls of his wheelchair, no twitch of one side of his mouth, no flutter of his right eyelid, which was the one that opened and closed normally. The other eye remained as it always did, the lid half open and half closed, the pupil dead center. Even when he was awake no one could be sure exactly what he was looking at or how much he saw. Sometimes Gilly thought the eye was accusatory, staring directly at her, and sometimes it seemed amused as if it were focused on some wry joke in the past or bit of fun in the future. "It sees nothing," the doctor had told her. "But I'm sure you're mistaken, Doctor. It *looks* at things." "The eye is dead."

The dead eye that saw nothing watched Gilly cross the room. She made no noise. The carpet was silent as grass.

"You're pretending to be asleep to get rid of me, aren't you, Marco? Well, I won't go. I won't go, see?"

See? The dead eye didn't, the live one stayed hidden under its lid.

Gilly touched her husband's forehead. It was scarred with wrinkles as if some cannibal had started to eat the flesh, had dug his nails across it leaving tracks like a fork.

"It makes me nervous when people pretend," Gilly said. "I think I'll scream."

She didn't, though. Whenever she screamed, Marco's nurse, Reed, came running and the gardener's Airedale started to howl and Violet Smith, the housekeeper, had a sinking spell. One of Violet Smith's sinking spells was as memorable as the *Titanic's*.

"Violet Smith says we eat too much meat, so it's fish again tonight." That ought to do it. He hated fish. "Marco?"

Neither the threat of screams nor fish disturbed the rhythm of his breathing.

3

Gilly waited. It was hot and she would have liked to sit outside on the patio for a little while to catch the breeze that started blowing in from the ocean nearly every afternoon at this time. But the patio belonged entirely to Marco. Though she was the one who'd had it designed and built, she didn't feel at ease there. She blamed it on the plants. They were all over the place, growing in stone urns and redwood boxes on the deck, and hanging from the rafters in terra-cotta pots and moss pouches held together by wire and baskets of sea grass and palm fibers.

Marco could maneuver his wheelchair among them quite easily, but Gilly was always bumping her shins on tubs of fuchsias and getting her hair caught in the tentacles of the spider plant. Marco's patio was comfortable only for people in wheelchairs, or children or dwarfs. Full-grown upright people found it hazardous. Marco's nurse, Reed, cursed when he was ambushed by the hidden barbs of the asparagus fern or the vicious spikes of the windmill palm, and even Violet Smith, who never swore, used a borderline phrase when she stepped into the lily pond while trying to avoid the soft seductive ruffles of the polypody.

For dwarfs, for children, for cripples like himself, Marco's patio was a place of fun where grownups could be booby-trapped and ordinary people made to look foolish and awkward. No child ever saw it, of course. No dwarf, either. Just Gilly and Reed and Violet Smith and occasionally the doctor, who didn't say or do much because there wasn't much to say or do once he'd taught Gilly how to give injections. (She had practiced on oranges until it became quite natural for her to plunge the needle into something both soft and resistant. "As the Lord is my Savior," Violet Smith said, "that is a silly thing to do, wasting valuable oranges when you could just as easy practice on yourself." "Shut up or I'll practice on you," Gilly said.)

The sliding glass door to the patio was open and there were little rustles and stirrings among the plants as if they were whispering among themselves. They might have been fussing about the smell of fish drifting across the lawn from the kitchen. They were Marco's plants, maybe they didn't like fish any more than he did and their protests were as weak and difficult to understand as his. Not that protests would have done much good: Violet Smith had recently joined the Holy Sabbathians and each week she seemed to acquire a new conviction. This week it was fish.

"She'll be here with your dinner in a few minutes, Marco."

His rate of respiration had increased and she knew for sure now that he was awake and simply didn't want to be bothered either with food or with her.

"If you don't like it, I'll bring you something else after Violet Smith leaves for her meeting. Are you hungry?"

One side of his mouth moved and a noise came out. It didn't sound like an animal or even like one of the plants outside on the patio. It was a vegetable sound coming from a vegetable. "He's a sorrowful figure," Violet Smith often said in Marco's presence as if the stroke that had paralyzed his vocal cords and most of his body had also deafened him. This wasn't true. He had, as Gilly was well aware, ears like a fox. She and Reed had to be very cautious and time their meetings according to Marco's pills and injections.

"How would you like to eat in your Ferrari tonight?" Gilly always referred to the wheelchair as some kind of sports car. It was intended partly to amuse him and partly to soften, for her, the constant and imposing reality of it. Reed supplied her with names, most of which were unfamiliar to her—Maserati, Lotus Europa, Aston Martin, Lamborghini, Jensen-Healey.

He opened his right eye slowly and with difficulty, as if the lid had been glued shut during his afternoon sleep. It was impossible to tell from the eye's expression whether he was amused or not. Probably not. It was a very small joke and he was a very sick man. But Gilly could not help trying. Trying was part of her nature, just as giving up was part of Marco's. He had given up long before the stroke. It was merely a punctuation mark, a period at the end of a sentence.

"Okay, so it's the Ferrari. The Lamborghini's in the garage, anyway, having a tune-up . . . Eat a little fish to keep your strength up . . . Do you have to go to the john?"

The fingers of his right hand dismissed the idea.

"The doctor thinks you should drink more water if you can."

He couldn't. He wouldn't. He had given up. His hunger was only for pills, his thirst only for the fluid in the hypodermic needle.

Violet Smith came into the room with the tray, using her bony butt to close the door behind her. She was a tall, light-skinned Indian from South Dakota, Oklahoma, Michigan, Arizona, depending on her mood and whichever state happened to be in the headlines at the time. A severe tornado in Oklahoma was likely to elicit stories of a childhood spent in constant danger darting from storm cellar to storm cellar. At these times her dull brown eyes would start gleaming like polished bronze and her smooth solemn face would crack up with excitement. She forgot all about the forms she'd filled out at the employment agency which had sent her out to Gilly less than a year ago. The information was simple: Violet Smith, now forty-two, had been born and raised, educated and employed, in Los Angeles. Gilly suspected that she'd never been east of Disneyland or north of right where she was now, Santa Felicia.

"I bought this red snapper out on the wharf this morning, fresh caught." Violet Smith held the silver-lidded tray in front of her like a shield, half proudly, half defensively. "We should eat what the Lord provides for us in His seas and rivers instead of deliberately raising a bunch of cows and pigs and then slaughtering them."

"Don't proselytize," Gilly said.

"I can't do it if I don't know what it means."

"The hell you can't."

"Was I doing that what she said, Mr. Decker? Was I? . . . No? No. Mr. Decker says I wasn't doing it. He shows good judgment. What a pity he can't read. It diminishes a man not to be able to read his Bible."

"He doesn't own one."

"It's not too late. He could be saved in the nick of time like I was, Jesus be praised."

"Just put the tray down and shut up."

"I think he could be saved."

"All right, work on it tonight at church. But kindly don't use our real name. I won't have a bunch of lunatics raving and ranting in public about us needing to be saved for committing God knows what sins. People might think this is a house full of thieves, crooks, murderers."

"We are all flawed," Violet Smith said coldly. "Just look who's prosetizing now."

"Proselytizing. And that's not what it means."

"Meaning is in the eye of the beholder. I think you were doing what you thought I was doing. Isn't that right, Mr. Decker? Yes? He says yes."

"Hurry up, you'll be late for your meeting."

Gilly looked at her wristwatch, noting with surprise how thin and wrinkled her arms were getting, as if her body were shrinking and aging in sympathy with Marco's no matter how much food she ate or how many times Reed assured her she was still young. "You don't look a day over forty," Reed would say. "That's because I'm not a day over forty, I'm ten years over forty." "Oh, can that crap. Who counts, anyway?" She counted. He counted. Everybody counted, whether they admitted it or not. Age was the second thing a child learned. What's your name, little girl? How old are you? . . . Gilda Grace Decker. I'm fifty.

Violet Smith put the tray on the adjustable metal table beside Marco's chair and cranked the table to the correct height. "I forgot to give you Mr. Smedler's message. He said eleven o'clock tomorrow morning in his office will be okay."

"Thanks."

"Some of these lawyers' secretaries can be very snippy."

"Yes, they can. Good night, Violet Smith."

"Good night, Mrs. Decker. And you, too, Mr. Decker. I'll be praying for you both."

Gilly waited until the door closed behind her. Then she said to Marco, trying to sound quite casual, "It's nothing for you to worry about, dear. I have to talk to Smedler about stocks, bonds, trusts, that sort of thing. Very dull, lawyerish stuff."

It wasn't dull, it wasn't lawyerish, but this was not the time to tell her husband. He had to be told gradually and gently so he would understand that it wasn't just a whim on her part. She had been thinking about it, no, planning it, for several months now. Each day it seemed more and more the right thing to do until now it was more than right. It was inevitable.

2

THE WIND HAD come up during the night, a Santa Ana that brought with it sand and dust from the desert on the other side of the mountain. By midmorning the city was stalled as if by a blizzard. People huddled in doorways shielding their faces with scarves and handkerchiefs. Cars were abandoned in parking lots, and here and there news racks had overturned and broken and their contents were blowing down the street, rising and falling like battered white birds.

Smedler's office was in a narrow three-story building in the center of the city a block from the courthouse. The lesser members of the firm shared the two bottom floors. Smedler, who owned the building, kept the third floor for himself. After an earthquake a few years ago he'd remodeled it so that the only inside access to his office was by a grille-fronted elevator. The arrangement gave Smedler a great deal of privacy and power, since the circuit breaker that controlled the electric current was beside his desk. If an overwrought or otherwise undesirable client was on the way up, Smedler could, by the mere thrust of a handle, cut off the electricity and allow the client time to acquire new insights on the situation while trapped between floors.

Gilly knew nothing about the circuit breaker but she had a morbid fear of elevators, which seemed to her like little prisons going up and down. Instead she used the outside entrance, a very steep narrow staircase installed as a fire escape to appease the building-code inspector. The door at the top was locked and Gilly had to wait for Smedler's secretary, Charity Nelson, to open it.

Charity made much the same use of the bolt as Smedler did of the current breaker. "Who's there?"

"Mrs. Decker."

"Who?"

"Decker. *Decker.*"

"What do you want?"

"I have an appointment with Mr. Smedler at eleven o'clock."

"Why didn't you use the elevator?"

"I don't like elevators."

"Well, I don't like taxes but I pay them."

Charity unlocked the door. She was a short wiry woman past sixty with thick grey eyebrows so lively compared to the rest of her face that they seemed controlled by some outside force. She wore a pumpkin-colored wig, not for the purpose of fooling anyone—she frequently removed it if her scalp itched or if the weather turned warm or if she was especially busy— but because orange was her favorite color. She had been with Smedler for thirty years through five marriages, two of her own, three of his.

"Really, Mrs. Decker, I wish you'd use the elevator like everyone else. It would save me getting up from my desk, walking all the way across the room to unlock the door and then walking all the way back to my desk."

"Sorry I inconvenienced you."

"It's such a lovely little elevator and it would save you all that huffing and puffing. I bet you're a heavy smoker, aren't you?"

"I don't smoke."

"Just out of shape, eh? You should try jogging."

"Karate appeals to me more at the moment," Gilly said.

She wondered why so many employees these days acted as though they worked for the government and were not obliged to show respect to anyone. Charity's general attitude indicated that she was in the pay of the IRS, CIA and FBI and possibly God, in addition to Smedler, Downs, Castleberg, MacFee and Powell.

"Smedler's waiting for you in his office." Charity pressed a buzzer. "And Aragon will be up in a few minutes."

"Who's Aragon?"

"He's your boy. You did specify a bilingual. N'est-ce pas?"

"N'est-ce pas. In a private, personal call to Mr. Smedler."

"All of Smedler's calls go through me. I am his confidential secretary."

"You're also a smart-ass. N'est-ce pas?"

Charity's bushy eyebrows scurried up into her wig and hid for a moment under the orange curls like startled mice. When they reappeared they looked smaller, as if stunted by the experience. "Crude."

"Effective, though."

"We'll see."

Gilly went into Smedler's office. He rose from behind his desk and came to greet her, a tall handsome man in his late fifties. He had known Gilly for thirteen years, since the day she married B. J. Lockwood. An old school chum of B. J.'s, Smedler had been an usher at both of his weddings. He could barely recall the first—to a socialite named Ethel—but he often thought of the second with a considerable degree of amazement. Gilly wasn't young or especially pretty, but on that day, in her long white lace gown and veil, she'd looked radiant. She was madly in love. B. J. was short and fat and freckled and nobody had ever taken him seriously before. Yet there was Gilly, well over thirty and certainly old enough to know better, iridescing like a hummingbird whenever she looked at him. Smedler decided later that her appearance was, had to be, simply a matter of make-up, a dash of pink here, a silver gleam there, French drops to intensify the blue of her eyes. (He was frequently heard to remark during the next dozen years that it was not politics which made strange bedfellows, it was marriage.)

Except for an occasional business meeting or football game, Smedler saw very little of Gilly and B. J. after the marriage. The divorce eight years ago had been handled by an out-of-town firm, and the only inside story on it had come to Smedler from Charity: B. J. had run away with a young girl. Gilly was rumored to have taken the divorce very hard, though not all the effects were on the bad side. B. J., evidently suffering from guilt as well as his usual poor business judgment, had been very generous in dividing the community property.

"Sit down, my dear, sit down. Here, you'll be more comfortable in the striped chair."

He told her she looked lovely (false), that her beige silk and linen suit was very chic (true) and that he was happy to see her (a little of both).

He was, in fact, more puzzled than either happy or unhappy. Her phone call the day before had provided few details: she wanted to hire a young man who could speak Spanish and was trustworthy, to do a job for her, probably in Mexico. Why *probably?* Smedler wondered. And what kind of job? She had no business interests south of the border or even outside the country, except for a small money-hungry gold mine in northern Canada. But he had been a lawyer too long to go directly to the point.

"And how is Mr. Decker?"

7

"The same."

"There is still no hope?"

"Well, my housekeeper prayed for him last night at church. That's something, I suppose, when you're as hard up for hope as I am."

It had been three months or so since Smedler had seen her and she had aged considerably in such a short time. The results weren't all negative, though. There seemed to be a new strength in her face and more assurance in her manner. She'd also lost quite a lot of weight. Smedler had always admired her sense of style—no matter what costume she wore, it was difficult to imagine it suiting anyone else—and the weight loss emphasized her individuality.

"About your call yesterday," Smedler said. "It was rather enigmatic."

"It was meant to be, in case anyone was listening in on my phone or yours."

"Don't worry about mine. I have no secrets from Charity."

"I have."

"She's very discreet."

"As my housekeeper would say, discretion is in the eye of the beholder."

"Yes. Well."

"Tell me about the young man."

"His name's Aragon. Tom Aragon. He's twenty-five, bright, personable, speaks Spanish like a native, graduated from law school last spring. I find him a bit pedantic, though that could be simply his manner with me, since I'm the boss. Technically, anyway."

"How much do I pay him?"

"That depends entirely on what you want him to do. We estimate the time of a recent graduate to be worth so much an hour."

"Paying by the hour would be too complicated in this case. I'll need his total services for—well, two or three weeks, perhaps longer. What's Aragon's monthly salary?"

"I don't know for sure. Let's call Charity and—"

"No. Negative no."

"I think you may be doing Charity an injustice."

"More likely I'm doing her a justice," Gilly said. "Suppose I pay your office the amount of his salary plus a commission for the use of his services. Then I'll make separate financial arrangements with Aragon. They'll be strictly between him and me."

"Why all the secrecy, my dear?"

"If I told you anything further, you'd try and talk me out of it."

"Perhaps not. Give me a chance."

"No."

They stared at each other for a minute in silence, not hostile, but not friendly either. Then Smedler, sighing, got up and walked over to the main window. Clouds were parading across the sky like a procession of spaceships. On the earthbound street below, traffic remained sparse and sluggish. Smedler didn't look either up or down. *This is a damn stubborn woman. Okay, I can be a damn stubborn man.*

"You were B. J.'s friend," Gilly said. "But you always had a pretty low opinion of him. You treated him like a nice jolly little fellow without a brain in his head."

"Now what in hell—I mean, what brought that on? What's it got to do with anything? Even if it were true, which it isn't—"

"Oh, it's true. You made it quite obvious and it hurt. I guess it hurt me worse than it did B. J. because he never had any more faith in himself and his ability than you did. I *did.* I was *full* of faith."

"Dammit, Gilly. Get to the point."

"It's simple. If I told you what I want Aragon to do, you'd just call me a fool."

"Try me."

"No."

"Negative no?"

She didn't answer.

"By God," Smedler said. "I need a drink."

Tom Aragon closed the iron-grilled elevator door behind him and approached Charity's desk. He was a tall thin young man with horn-rimmed glasses that gave him a look of continual surprise. He'd come to Smedler's firm straight out of law school, so most of the time he was in fact surprised. The jobs assigned to him so far didn't often involve the third floor or the woman who ran it. There was a rumor, though, that she had a sense of humor if it could be found and excavated.

She must have heard the elevator door clank open and shut, but Charity didn't look up from the papers on her desk or indicate in any way that she was aware of someone else in the room.

"Hey," Aragon said. "Remember me?"

She raised her head. "Ah so. The new boy from the bottom of the bottom floor. Rather cute. Well, don't try any of the cutes on me. What do you want?"

"The boss said you'd clue me in."

"On the world in general or did you have something specific in mind?"

"This Mrs. Decker, what's she like?"

"You'd better not ask *my* opinion. She just called me a smartass. What do you think of that?"

"I think that's a leading question which in a court of law I wouldn't be required to answer."

"This isn't a court of law. It's a nice cozy little office with only two people in it, and one of them just asked a question and the other is going to answer."

"Very well. Mrs. Decker could be right. You and I haven't been acquainted long enough for me to judge."

Charity pushed aside her wig and scratched the lobe of her left ear in a contemplative way. "The junior members of this firm, especially the junior juniors, are usually careful to show me some respect, even a little hard homage around Christmas."

"Christmas is a long way off. Maybe I'll work up to it by then."

"I hope so."

"Now back to Mrs. Decker."

"Gilda. Gilda Grace Lockwood Decker. Lockwood was her first husband, a funny little man, looked like a drunken cherub even when he was cold sober. She married him for his money, of course, though Smedler doesn't think so. Smedler's an incurable romantic, considering the business he's in and the number of marriages he's had. Anyway, Lockwood's long gone . . . Gilly did a lot of traveling after her divorce and there was talk of various affairs in different parts of the world. Nothing really serious until she met this guy Marco Decker in Paris. Then it was clang clang, wedding bells again. She wired Smedler to send her money in care of American Express for her trousseau. Some trousseau. She must have bought half the night-gowns and perfume in France. I guess it was too much for poor old Decker. He had a stroke while they were honeymooning at Saint-Tropez. So there was Gilly, stuck with a paralyzed bridegroom in the midst of all those lovely naked young Frenchmen."

"Why were the Frenchmen naked?"

"My dear boy, it was Saint-Tropez. That's why people visit there, to see other people naked."

"It seems like a long way to go to see somebody naked."

"Well, of course only the 'in' people go to Saint-Tropez. The 'out' people like you and me, we just take off our clothes and stand in front of a mirror . . . Well, that's the sad story of Gilly. She brought Decker home, installed a lot of expensive equipment so she could keep him there and hired a male nurse to help look after him. Et cetera."

"What's included in the et cetera?"

"You can bet your life she's not wasting all those Paris nightgowns. Any more questions?"

"One," Aragon said.

"Okay, shoot."

"What joker gave you the name Charity?"

3

THE SWIMMING POOL in the middle of the patio was larger than the one at the YMCA where Aragon had learned to swim as a boy. At the bottom lay a ceramic mermaid which no YMCA would have tolerated. She wore nothing but a smirk.

A dark-haired good-looking man in very brief tight swim trunks was cleaning the pool with a vacuum. His movements were tense and angry. He pushed the vacuum back and forth across the mermaid's face as though trying to obliterate her smirk. At the same time he was conducting a monologue which Aragon assumed was aimed at him.

"Nobody manages this place. It's simply not *managed*. Take a look around, just look. Disgusting."

Aragon looked. The early-morning wind from the desert had thrown a film of dust across the water and littered it with pine needles and the petals of roses and jacarandas and cypress twigs and eucalyptus pods, all the leaves and loves and leavings of plants.

"We have two daily gardeners, a cleaning woman, a day maid, a pool boy who comes twice a week and a handyman living over the garage. So what happens? The handyman has arthritis, the gardeners say it's not their job, the day maid and cleaning woman can't be trusted with anything more complicated than a broom, and the pool boy has a term paper in biology due this week. Guess who's left? Reed. Good old Reed. That's me."

"Hello, good old Reed."

"Who are you?"

"Tom Aragon. I have an appointment with Mrs. Decker."

"Aragon. There was a fighter named Aragon once. Remember him?"

"No."

"Too young, eh? Actually, so am I. My mother told me about him. She was a fight fan. I'll never forget her actually, really—can you beat it?—putting on the gloves with me when I was six or seven years old. She was one weird old lady."

He thrust the vacuum across the mermaid's face again, then suddenly dropped it in the pool and continued his monologue. "It's only the middle of October. How could the kid have a term paper due the second week of school? And the handyman with his arthritis— hell, I'm a registered nurse, I know an arthritis case when I see it. There are over eighty different kinds and he hasn't got any of them. What he's got is a hangover, same as he had yesterday and the day before and last month and last year. If this place were *managed*, he'd be kicked out. What's behind the whole thing is this—I'm the one who uses the pool most, so if I want it clean I better bloody well clean it myself."

He was beginning to sound like a querulous old man. Aragon guessed that he was no more than thirty-five. He also guessed that Reed's bad mood hadn't much connection with merely cleaning the pool. Reed confirmed this indirectly: "Gilly told me to stick around till you got here. I had to give up my five o'clock cooking class. I was going to do beef Wellington with spinach soufflé orien-tale. The food around here is vile. If you're invited for dinner, split fast. Gilly hired this crazy cook who keeps getting hyped on various diets. We haven't been served any decent red meat for a week . . . I don't know what Gilly expects me to do, size you up, maybe. She can be so *obscure*."

"Well, size me up."

Reed stared. He had green murky eyes like dirty little ponds. "You look okay."

"Thanks."

"Of course, it's hard to tell nowadays. I had my wallet lifted last Thursday by two of the most innocent-faced chicks you ever saw . . . Go right across the patio to the glass door and shake the wind chimes good and hard. She's in Marco's room. If I hurry, maybe I can catch at least the soufflé part of my class."

"Good luck."

"A soufflé is more a matter of correct temperature and timing than luck. Do you cook?"

"Peanut butter sandwiches."

"You might *enjoy* the food around here," Reed said and disappeared around the side of the house.

It wasn't necessary for Aragon to shake the wind chimes. Gilly was waiting for him inside the door of what seemed to be a family recreation room. Its focus was a round barbecue pit level with the floor and made of used brick. The steel grill in the pit was spotless, and underneath it there were no ashes from yesterday's fire and no charcoal for tomorrow's. Only a few stains indicated the pit had been used. Above it was a huge copper hood which reflected everything in the room distorted in various degrees, much like the convex mirrors utilized in stores to spot shoplifters.

Aragon saw himself in the copper hood, a bit taller and thinner and a great deal more mysterious than he looked in the mirror of the men's room at the office. The lenses of his horn-rimmed glasses seemed almost opaque, as though they'd been designed to disguise his appearance rather than to improve his vision. He might have been a college professor who did a little spying on the side, or a spy who taught a few classes as a cover.

Gilly, too, looked different. Instead of the beige suit she'd worn earlier she had on a pink cotton dress a couple of sizes too large and espadrilles with frayed rope soles. Only the faintest coating of make-up remained on her face. The rest had disappeared, the mascara blinked off, the blushes rubbed off, the lipstick smiled or talked off. Or perhaps it had all simply been washed away in a deluge of tears. She was carrying a large manila envelope with some letters hand-printed across the front in black ink.

"Your name's Tom, isn't it?"

"Yes."

"I suppose you're curious about why I dragged you all the way out here."

"It's not far."

"Now, that's a nice evasive response. You should make a fine lawyer."

"Well, okay. I *am* curious."

"I couldn't talk to you freely this morning because I didn't want Smedler or that witch in his office to overhear." A smile swept across her face like a summer storm, leaving it refreshed, softer. "The old devil has the place bugged, you know. What did he tell you about me?"

"Very little." *Go along with her, Smedler had said. I'm sure she won't ask you to do anything too indiscreet. And whatever it is, you'll get some money and some experience out of it and we hang on to her business. She's one of our golden oldies.* "I don't think he has his office bugged, by the way."

"No? Why not?"

"It wouldn't be ethical."

"Tell that to Smedler sometime when I'm around. I'd love to watch his face come unglued." She put the manila envelope on a leather-topped table. Then she sat down in one of the four matching chairs and motioned for him to sit opposite her. "I've played a lot of games at this table, bridge, Scrabble, backgammon, Monopoly. This one will be new."

"What's the name of it?"

"See for yourself." She turned the manila envelope so he could read the letters, printed on the front: B. J. PHOTOGRAPHS. CERTIFICATES, ET CETERA. "Let's just call it B. J., for short."

"And the rules?"

"We make them up as we go along . . . Did Smedler tell you about B. J.?"

"No."

"Did anyone?"

"Charity mentioned him."

"I have to watch you, you really are evasive. What did she say?"

"That he was your first husband, B. J. Lockwood, and that he was long gone."

"Long gone. Yes, he's long gone," she repeated, almost as if she were tasting the words to identify their flavor. Spinach soufflé? Peanut butter sandwiches? Sour grapes? It was impossible for an observer to judge from her expression. "Eight years, to be precise. We'd been married five years and things were going along fine. Maybe not storybook peachy keen—we weren't kids, he'd been married before and I'd been around here and there—but certainly a whole lot better than average. At least, I thought so."

"What changed your mind?"

"He did. He took off with one of the servants, a Mexican girl no more than fifteen years old. She was pregnant. B. J. always wanted a child and I refused for a number of reasons. His family had a history of diabetes and frankly my side of it wasn't too hot either. Besides, you don't start having kids when you're in your late thirties, not unless your maternal instincts are a hell of a lot stronger than mine."

"What was the girl's name?"

"Tula Lopez. Whether B. J. was the father of her child or not, she persuaded him he was and he did the honorable thing. B. J. always did honorable things, impulsive, stupid, absurd, but honorable. So off the two of them rode into the sunset. It was what they rode in that burns me up—the brand-new motor home I'd just bought for us to go on a vacation to British Columbia. I was crazy about that thing. Dreamboat, I called it. On the first night it was delivered here to the house B. J. and I actually slept in it, and the next morning I made our breakfast in the little kitchen, orange juice and Grapenuts. A week later it was goodbye Dreamboat, B. J., Tula and the rest of the box of Grapenuts."

"What do you want me to do, get back the rest of the Grapenuts?"

She didn't smile. She merely looked pensive as if she was seriously considering the proposition. "It's hard for me to make you understand the position I'm in. How can you?—You're young, you have choices ahead of you, alternatives. Nothing's final. You get sick, you get well again. You lose a job or a girl, okay, you find another job, another girl. Right?"

"In a general way, yes."

"Well, I'm fifty. That's not very old, of course, but it cuts down on your alternatives, narrows your choices. There are more goodbyes and not so many hellos. Too many of the goodbyes are final. And the hellos—well, they've become more and more casual . . . I've lost one husband and I'm about to lose another. I'm depressed, scared, sitting in that room with Marco, listening to his breathing and waiting for it to stop. When it does stop, I'll be alone. Alone, period. I have no relatives and no friends I haven't bought."

"I'm sorry."

"Good. It will help motivate you."

"To do what?"

She ran her fingers across the letters on the manila envelope as if it had turned into a Ouija board and she were receiving a message. "I'd like to see B. J. again. I think—I have this strong feeling he'd like to see me, too."

"And my job is to go looking for him?"

"Yes."

"You don't even know if he's still alive."

"No."

"Or whether he'd want to contact you if he is alive."

"No."

"He and the girl, Tula, may in fact be living happily ever after with half a dozen kids."
"No." She moved her head back and forth, slowly, as if her neck had suddenly become stiff. "They only had one, a boy. He was born crippled."
"Where did you hear that?"
"B. J. wrote me a letter five years ago."
"Do you still have it?"
"It's in here."
She opened the envelope and shook out the contents on the table, snapshots, photographs, newspaper clippings, notarized documents, a bunch of letters tied together, a single one by itself.
The largest photograph was that of a bride and groom: Gilly, in a white lace gown and veil, carrying a tiny bouquet of lilies of the valley. Her expression was mischievous and girlish, as if the photographer had caught her between giggles. B. J., in morning coat and striped trousers, seemed to be sharing the joke and trying hard to keep from laughing. He had a small round face, very red, as though the strain of suppressing his laughter had sent the blood rushing to his head and the tight collar had trapped it there. He looked like a kind man who wished other people well and expected nothing but kindness from them in return. Aragon wondered how often he'd been surprised.
Gilly stared at the photograph for a long time. "We were very happy."
"I can see you were."
"Naturally he won't look like that anymore. The picture was taken thirteen years ago when he was forty-one. Maybe we've both changed so much we wouldn't even recognize each other."
"You haven't changed much—some loss of weight, hair not so brown, laugh lines a little deeper."
"Those aren't laugh lines, Aragon, they're cry lines. And they're deeper, all right. They're etched all the way through to the back of my head . . . Well, anyway, I wanted to show you a picture of him as he was in his prime. I thought he was simply beautiful. I see now, of course, that he wasn't. In the cold light of an eight-year separation he may even look a little silly, don't you think?"
"No."
"No, neither do I, really." The pitch of her voice altered like an instrument suddenly gone flat. "I was crazy about him. I'm not the kind of woman who attracts men without any effort. I'm not pretty enough or tactful enough or whatever enough. I had to fight like hell to land B. J. He was married when I met him. So was Marco. I often wonder if it isn't some kind of retribution that I should lose them both."
"I don't believe in retribution."
"You haven't met Violet Smith." She put the wedding portrait back in the manila envelope, her hands trembling slightly. "You'll need some pictures of him with you when you go."
"Exactly where and when am I going?"
"When is as soon as you can get ready and we can agree on terms. Where I'm not sure . . . There are several good snapshots of B. J. Here's the last one. I took it myself. And I know it's the last because by the time the negative was developed and returned to me, B. J. was gone."
The snapshot showed B. J. behind the wheel of an elaborate new motor home. The fancy gold script across the door identified it as Dreamboat.
B. J. needed no identification. He hadn't changed much in the five years since the wedding portrait was taken. His face was still plump and ruddy, and he wore a placid smile as if nothing whatever was bothering him, least of all the fact that he was about to run away with a pregnant fifteen-year-old girl. Obviously B. J. was expecting pleasant things ahead. He may have been imagining himself in the new role of father, helping his son learn to walk,

taking him to parks and zoos, teaching him to play ball, swim, sail a boat, telling him about the birds and the bees and how a little sister would be arriving, or a little brother . . . *They didn't live happily ever after with half a dozen kids. They only had one, a boy. He was born crippled.*

Aragon said, "Do you have a picture of the girl, Tula Lopez?"

"Why should I? She was a servant, not a member of the family. In fact, she was only employed here for about six months. She proved incompetent and lazy. But she must have been a fast worker in her off hours. By the time I decided to fire her, the decision had been made for me."

"How did you hire her in the first place?"

"Stupidly. There was a sob story in the local newspaper about some illegal aliens who were going to be sent back to Mexico if they weren't sponsored and given jobs. B. J. and I offered to help. He had a soft heart and I had a soft head, or maybe it was vice versa. Anyhow, for a couple of softies we did some pretty hard damage." She added cryptically, "The whole thing was like a war—nobody won."

Aragon set aside the pictures he wanted to take with him: the one of B. J. in Dreamboat, another of him sitting on the edge of the pool with his feet dangling in the water, a couple of full-face Polaroid shots and a copy of his passport photo. In all of them, even the passport, he looked pretty much the same, rather homely in a pleasant way, the kind of man who posed no threat to anyone and offered no challenge. Only a woman Gilly's age could have considered him beautiful; a fifteen-year-old would see him more clearly.

Gilly picked up the letter that was separate from the others and handed it to Aragon. It was heavy. The envelope—addressed to G. G. Lockwood, 1020 Robinhood Road, Santa Felicia, California—was expensive bond paper, engraved *Jenlock Haciendas, Bahía de Ballenas, Baja California Sur.* The grade of paper and the engraving were obviously meant to impress, but the handwriting inside ruined the effect. It was like that of a child not accustomed to the use of pen and ink or the discipline of forming letters.

Aragon said, "Are you sure this is B. J.'s handwriting?"

"Pretty sure. He never learned to write decently and he forgot to take along his typewriter." She smiled wryly. "I guess it's one of the things you tend to overlook under the circumstances . . . Can you make it out?"

"I think so."

"Read it aloud."

"Why?"

"I'd like to hear how it sounds coming from a stranger. Maybe it'll give me a few laughs."

"If it's very personal, you might want to reconsider your decision."

"There are no torrid passages, if that's what's worrying you."

"I'm not worried exactly. I'd simply like to spare you any embarrassment."

"Is that what they teach you in law school, not to *embarrass* people? Don't be such a stuffed shirt."

"Smedler, Downs, Castleberg, McFee and Powell," Aragon said, "only hire stuffed shirts."

"Really?"

"To protect their image."

"Well, I don't give a cow chip about their image. And you won't either when you find out what it is."

He already had and already didn't, but he wasn't eager to admit it, especially to one of Smedler's golden oldies.

"Why are you staring at me?" she said, frowning. "Haven't you ever heard the word 'cow chip' before?"

"Sure. About every half-hour from my old man, only he said *caca de toro.* Otherwise my old lady wouldn't have understood. She never learned English."

"Where do you come from?"

"Here. I was born in the barrio on lower Estero Street."

"What's a barrio?"

"A Mexican ghetto."

"Good. You'll be able to deal with these people on their own level."

"And what level are *these people* on, Mrs. Decker?"

"Oh hell, don't get fussed up over some silly little remark. The Tula Lopez incident gave me kind of a prejudiced view of her whole race."

"I'll try to correct that," Aragon said. "I think we'll get along fine."

"What makes you think so?"

"I'm being paid to think so."

"Why, that's downright cynical. Did you learn such stuff in your boy scout manual? That's what Smedler called you, you know, a real boy scout."

"It's an improvement over some of the things I've called him. In private, of course, like between you and me."

"I see. The lawyer-client relationship works both ways."

"Ideally, yes."

"Smedler also told me you were a very nice young man. That worried me because I'm not a very nice old lady. I wonder if we'll have any common ground. Do you have a sense of humor?"

"Sometimes."

"Well, read B. J.'s letter and let's have a few laughs. Or didn't you believe that about me getting some laughs out of it?"

"No."

"You could be wrong. Laughter, as Violet Smith says, is in the eye of the beholder. Maybe this time I'll behold it funny. Go ahead, read it."

4

Dear Gilly:

You're probably surprised to be hearing from me after all this time. I'd like to think you're even a little bit pleased, too, but how could you be after the crazy way I ran out on you like that. Honestly I didn't have much control over the situation. A man has to do the right thing under certain circumstances and I did it. You know Gilly I wanted to say goodbye in a civilized manner but I was just plain scared of you. I mean how you'd take it etc. And Tula kept saying hurry up, hurry up, as if the baby was going to be born any minute. (It wasn't born for 6 months, I guess she was just anxious to get away from the immigration authorities and back to her own family.)

Anyway here I am in this place that's hard to describe. Do you remember that time we went to a football game at the college stadium with Dave Smedler and his wife (I forget which one). Suddenly somebody yelled Whales! and we all looked out over the ocean and there they were, 5 or 6 grey whales migrating through the channel just beyond the kelp beds. It was some sight, blowing and leaping in the air and submerging again. Well Gilly you'd never guess where they were headed. Here. Right here a few hundred yards from where I sit writing this letter. Bahía de Ballenas is on a lovely little bay (it means Bay of Whales) and the grey whales come down here from California to have their calves etc. I never knew this before I got here. In fact I never thought of whales as doing much along that line but naturally they do. They're human just like us.

The water in the bay is very blue, as blue as your eyes used to be, G. G. I guess they still are, why not? I keep thinking it's such a long time since I've seen you

15

but it really hasn't been 3 years. It seems longer to me because this place is so foreign and the people live so different. I haven't caught on to the lingo or the way they can ignore dirt and bugs and things. I often think of how you used to take 3 showers a day. You certainly were a clean person.

" 'You certainly were a clean person,' " Gilly said. "I behold that funny, don't you, Aragon?"

"Yes."

"I'm a clean person with eyes as blue as the bay where a herd of whales go to copulate and calve. What a great compliment."

"I've heard worse."

She walked over to the barbecue pit and stood for a while staring down into it as if at the ashes of old forgotten fires. "I never took three showers a day. Where'd he dredge up that idea?" She turned back with a sudden explosive sound that seemed to come all the way from her bowels. "*Ethel!* By God, he got me mixed up with *Ethel.* How do you like that? He not only can't remember which of Smedler's wives went with us to the football stadium, he can't even remember which of his own wives took three showers a day."

"The letter's been in your possession for five years. It's a little late to fuss about it now."

"She's just the type to take three showers a day. And who's fussing?"

"The evidence indicates you are."

"Okay, you want to play lawyer, define your terms."

"Fussing is an unnecessary futile display of irritability that stops short of loss of temper."

"All right, I was fussing, dammit."

"Shall I go on reading?"

"Yes."

Now G. G. don't misunderstand what I wrote. I find the people here peculiar, who wouldn't, but the place itself is simply terrific, blue water, blue skies, no rain. It's sort of a piece of California desert like Yucca Valley for instance only it's right beside the ocean like Santa Felicia. A winning combination as you can well imagine which is why I'm betting on it. I've bet my shirt if you want the truth!

I know how businesslike and practical you are so I'll stop beating around the bush and come right out and state the purpose of this letter. Did you notice the letterhead? In case you missed the connection it has part of my name in it, the 'lock' in Jenlock is me. Me and a fellow called Jenkins (he's awfully smart, cram full of bright ideas) are in this project together. It's cost me a mint so far. But as Jenkins says Rome wasn't built in a day for 50 pesos and you have to spend money to get money. I enclose a brochure about Jenlock Haciendas. We're going to have a lot more printed when cash becomes available. Quite a few have already been mailed to interested parties.

"Where's the brochure?" Aragon said.

"I tore it up."

"Why?"

"I have a short fuse."

"So what lit it?"

"The thing was such an obvious come-on, the high-flown descriptions of a marina, a social center, a golf course, the haciendas themselves, when all they really had was a hunk of desert and a bunch of whales. I felt like going to Smedler with the brochure and asking him to investigate. Instead, I just tore it up. As I said, I have a short fuse. I'm also pretty tight with a buck."

"B. J. asked you for money?"

"Did he ever. Read on."

I need $100,000. Actually I need more but with that much I can at least cover current expenses and some past bills which are mounting up. Please don't think I'm just asking for that amount of money. I'm merely offering you the opportunity to invest in what I consider a truly promising venture. Or if you prefer instead to make me a straight loan at current interest rates that would be all right, too. The former suits me better personally. We would be sort of partners again. No matter which way you send it G. G. please send it, I really desperately need it.

I hope you won't think I'm begging for money. (Sounded like it there for a minute didn't it?) This is a very fine investment. I consider myself lucky to be in on the ground floor so to speak. But any kind of development takes a great deal more money than a person realizes in the beginning and Jenlock Haciendas is not your average development. It has class. Once the Americans get word of it we expect to be deluged with offers—retired people sick of smog and sportsmen looking for a vacation home (the fishing is great especially from May to September) or just plain nature lovers wanting to renew their contact with wildlife. Getting the word out, that's one of the problems we need money to solve, buying up lists of names and taking out ads in newspapers and magazines, perhaps a few T. V. spots. That would stimulate plenty of action. When you answer this (either way, yes or no, please answer) would you send it by registered mail? The other kind may take weeks or months or forever.

I've thought a whole lot about you and me G. G. and what happened. I did so many dumb things I'm sorry about now like taking Dreamboat. I'm truly sorry for that because I know you'd made a lot of vacation plans etc. But Tula said we wouldn't have any place to live otherwise and she was right. When we got here there were just a lot of old shacks and people were already crammed in them like sardines. I never thought human beings could live like that but here I am doing it myself. Tula's family gradually moved in with us and I'm a sardine like the rest of them. Of course that's only temporary. When Jenlock Haciendas gets into the construction phase I intend to occupy the first one finished as a combination office and dwelling. You know I've never been in business before and I'm looking forward to trying my wings. Please answer this soon G. G.

Hopefully, with affection, with regrets,

B. J.

P.S. It's terribly important for me to make good on this not just for me personally but for the boy. Unless I leave him provided for Pablo is in for a hard time. He was born crippled. You were right not to want children by me. I have rotten blood . . .

For a minute neither of them spoke. The room seemed to be silenced by the ghosts of a long-gone man, a crippled child, a dream. Then Gilly said, "He not only had rotten blood, he had rotten judgment. I didn't send him a nickel."

"Did you answer his letter?"

"No. He didn't want an answer. He wanted the *right* answer and I wasn't prepared to give it to him. Sure, I've often felt guilty about it. After all, every cent I own was his to begin with."

"What happened to Jenlock Haciendas?"

"I don't know. Once in a while I'd look in the real-estate section of the *Los Angeles Times* and occasionally I'd buy a San Diego paper, but I never found any mention of Jenlock Haciendas or Bahía de Ballenas. That doesn't prove anything, of course. He may have gotten the money from some place else and the project is a big success. It's possible, isn't it?"

17

"Yes."

"So I'm hiring you to go down and see. Hell, maybe he's struck it rich and *I'll* touch *him* for a hundred thousand dollars."

"You must consider other possibilities, Mrs. Decker. He may have left there by now. Or he may be dead."

"In either case I want to know. I also want to know what's happened to the boy."

So that's it, Aragon thought, the kid. She's rich and getting old, she has no relatives and pretty soon when Decker dies she'll be alone. A kid would bring life to the house again.

She said, "He's half Mexican, sure, but he's also half B. J., which makes him sort of related to me. Doesn't it?"

"Not legally, no."

"Who cares about the law? I'm talking about *feelings*."

"All right. Feeling-wise, he's sort of related to you. But please bear in mind that he has a mother and that Mexicans are very much family-oriented. There's also the possibility that the child may be dead, depending, among other things, on the degree of his congenital impairment. I realize that you're living under great stress right now, and people in such circumstances sometimes make plans based on an unrealistic assessment of the facts."

"You realize that, eh? Well, I realize that lawyers often like to use twenty words when one will do."

"How about two?"

"All right."

"Cool it."

"What does that mean exactly?"

"Even if I find the kid he won't be for sale."

She looked almost stunned for a moment. "Perhaps we should go back to the twenty-word system."

"It has certain advantages."

"Your style takes a little getting used to, Aragon, but then, so does mine. We might be able to work together satisfactorily. What do you think?"

"I don't pick the clients," Aragon said. "They have to pick me."

"Okay . . . I pick you."

"Fine."

She had a check ready for him, $2,500 made out to Tomás Aragon and marked "Legal Services."

"This should cover your airfare, car rental, living expenses, and of course, bribes. If anyone asks you, you can say you work for the local police. They may not believe you but they'll believe the money. Are you familiar with Baja California?"

"I've been to Tijuana."

"Then the answer is no. I've done a little research on my own. You can fly down as far as Rio Seco and rent a car there. It has the last car-rental agency until the southernmost tip of Baja. Bahía de Ballenas is roughly halfway between. It's not marked on most maps. Just keep driving south until you come to it. There's a new road that goes part of the way along the coast. They call it a highway but you'd better not expect too much."

Aragon put the check in his wallet and then returned the letter from B. J. to its envelope. "Do you mind if I keep this for a while? The references might be useful."

"Take it. By the way, let's get something clear. I could hire any investigator for a job like this a lot cheaper than you're going to cost me."

"Why don't you?"

"I'm paying for discretion, for the privacy of a lawyer-client relationship. You're not to tell anyone the nature of our business, not Smedler, not the authorities, not even your wife. Do you have a wife?"

"Yes. I haven't been seeing much of her, though. She's in her first year of residency in pediatrics at a hospital in San Francisco."

"Smart, eh?"

"Yes."

"What's her name?"

"Laurie Macgregor."

"Why didn't she take your name?"

"She already had one of her own."

"All very modern and with it. I see . . . I bet she's pretty."

"I think so."

"Describe her, nonlawyer style."

"Nonlawyer style, she's a dynamite chick."

Gilly was staring pensively at her image in the copper hood of the barbecue pit. "I wonder, if I were in my twenties again, would anyone call me a dynamite chick?"

"On the evidence presented so far I would assume that you were and that you would be so designated."

"Hey, that's nice, Aragon. You and I are going to be pals. You know what else? You'll make a very good lawyer."

"Well, if I don't, I hope I'll be married to a very good pediatrician."

Aragon hadn't intended it to be funny, but she laughed as if he'd made the joke of the century. He suspected that the dynamite-chick business had left his new pal, Gilly, a little intoxicated.

5

VIOLET SMITH PICKED her way carefully around the side of the house past the thorns of the carissa and the spiked leaves of the century plants and the gopher holes in the lawn. She had seen Aragon's car parked in the driveway and had been on her way to the barbecue room in the hope of overhearing something interesting when Mr. Decker's bell rang. Reed was off duty and the day girl had already left, so it was Violet Smith's Christian obligation to answer the bell. Mr. Decker had to go to the bathroom, which was messy and took forever, so that by the time she finished cleaning up, twenty minutes or more had elapsed.

Crossing the patio, she stooped to retrieve a stray leaf caught between two flagstones. Out of the corner of her eye she could see Mrs. Decker talking to a strange man. She couldn't make out the words but they must certainly have been funny because Mrs. Decker suddenly began laughing like some giddy young girl. Violet Smith transferred the leaf to the apron pocket of her uniform and slid open the screen door.

Mrs. Decker immediately sobered up and looked her age again. "You can see I'm busy, Violet Smith."

"Mr. Decker is agitated. I think he heard a strange car come up the driveway and wants to know what is it doing here."

"It's waiting for Mr. Aragon," Gilly said brusquely.

"Do I go back and tell him?"

"No. No, I'll do it . . . Aragon, please stay here for a minute while I check my husband, will you?"

"Don't hurry," Aragon said. "I have lots of time."

'After she'd gone Violet Smith studied Aragon carefully and at length. "How come you have lots of time? Don't you work?"

"I'm working now."

"You give a good impression of just standing around."

"Practice, Miss Smith. Years of practice . . . Mrs. Smith?"

"Violet Smith is my true name, both here and There. When people don't call me that, I pay them no mind. I figure they might be talking to someone else. There are millions of Smiths."

She had a point and Aragon guessed that she would cling to it even if it impaled her. He said, "I hope I haven't disturbed Mr. Decker."

"He's *agitated*. That could be good or bad, depending. I never know. I can't understand those monkey noises of his, meaning no disrespect. He heard a strange car and we don't get many strangers around here."

"Why not?"

"Mrs. Decker had Reed put up a lot of signs to scare people off, like NO PEDDLERS, NO TRESPASSING, PRIVATE PROPERTY, BEWARE OF DOGS. We don't even have a dog, except one of the gardeners brings his Airedale along in the truck which howls. The gardeners are both long-haired heathens . . . Have you been saved?"

"I think so."

"Aren't you sure?"

"It's not the sort of thing one can be sure about until—well, until later."

"If you think there's any doubt, it would be better to find out now than then."

"Yes, I guess it would."

"You know, you kind of remind me of my son. I don't see much of him anymore. I never raised a hand to that boy until the day he vilified the Lord. He diminished Jesus and I had to slug him. My hand pained me for several weeks. I could hardly hold my Bible."

She began dusting the glass table with a piece of tissue which she produced from one of the half-dozen pockets of her uniform. It was apparent from her vigorous movements that her slugging hand had been completely cured and that Violet Smith was ready for another round at the sound of the bell. She was a powerful woman with thick wrists, and shoulders as wide as Aragon's.

He said, "Why does Mrs. Decker want to scare people off?"

"They might disturb Mr. Decker. He's pretty far gone, a real sorrowful figure. I overheard Reed asking the doctor one day if it wouldn't be more humane to pull out the plugs. I couldn't understand what they were talking about until the doctor used the word, 'euthanasia.' Then I stepped right up and said I was against it. The doctor was polite enough, but oh, that Reed has a dirty tongue in his head. I felt duty-bound to report the incident to Mrs. Decker. Maybe I shouldn't have."

"Why not?"

"Wow, she threw a terrible fit, crying and carrying on and screaming how she wanted to have her plugs pulled out, too. Then she drank a lot of booze. I told her, 'You can't drown your troubles, Mrs. Decker, because troubles can swim.' *Well.* If you think Reed has a dirty tongue in his head you should have heard *her.* My ears cringed. 'Sticks and stones,' I said to her, 'sticks and stones can break my bones but words will never hurt me.' She told me what I could do with every stick and stone between here and Seattle."

"It wasn't one of your more popular nights, apparently."

"Oh, I forgave her. I knew she was just scared like everybody else who won't accept Jesus. Scared of the old man dying and leaving her alone, and scared of dying herself. I'm used to her bad language, anyway. She's not a true-born lady like the first Mrs. Lockwood. Mrs. Decker was the second Mrs. Lockwood."

"You're acquainted with the first?"

"I see her at church twice a week. We often share the same hymn book. She's a soprano but not one of those screechy ones, just soft and ladylike as befits her birth."

"Is she aware that you work for Mrs. Decker?"

"Sure. At our regular evening meetings we're encouraged to stand up and talk out our predicaments and troubles. Then afterwards we all sit around and help each other."

"Or not."

"Or not," Violet Smith agreed crisply. "We aren't *geniuses,* you know. It's the feeling that counts, the realizing you're not alone, someone else cares and wants to help."

"Your church meetings sound very interesting."

"Oh, they are. They're what really converted me. I didn't mind giving up carnality, jewelry and red meat in return for comradeship and an afterlife."

"I think you made the right decision."

"You do?"

"Yes."

"You're not being sarcastic like Reed or Mrs. Decker?"

"No."

"I'm glad. You know, when you're stuck in a place like this most of the time, you've got to have something lively, something hopeful, going on outside. The death house—that's what some of the employees call it. All the pretty flowers and trees, the sun shining, the pool, the birds singing, none of it makes any difference when you're waiting for someone to die. You want to tell the birds to shut up and the sun to drop down and the flowers to fold their petals and blow away. Imagine telling a bird to shut up. But I did one day. There was this little red-headed creature singing on top of the T. V. antenna and I screamed at him, 'Stop it, shut up, don't you know someone's dying down here?' "

"Did you ever express these feelings at any of your church meetings?"

"No. They'd think I was a loony . . . Listen, I hear Mrs. Decker coming back. She's suspicious. Pretend I never said a word, not one word, agreed?"

"Agreed."

Gilly re-entered the room through the inside door that connected it with the main part of the house. She looked flushed, as though she'd been engaged in some strenuous physical or emotional exertion. She said, "I suppose Violet Smith has talked your ear off."

"No."

"That's peculiar. She does it to everyone else."

"Oh, I do not," Violet Smith said coldly and went outside, pushing the screen door shut behind her as hard as she could.

Gilly waited for her to disappear around the side of the house. "My husband's all right. He sometimes reacts badly when Reed goes off duty or when something unusual happens."

"And I'm an unusual happening?"

"To Marco, yes. I'd like you to meet him. He sees the same people day after day and I'm sure he'd enjoy some different company for a change. No matter what impression Violet Smith gave you, Marco can hear and often understand as well—or almost as well—as you and I can."

"It might be better for me to see him some other time."

"This is the time I want you to see him, right now. I have my reasons."

"Very well, Mrs. Decker. You're the boss."

Gilly spoke his name softly. "Marco?"

Nothing happened for a minute. Then the wheelchair, which had been facing the patio, suddenly and noiselessly turned and Aragon had his first glimpse of Marco Decker. He seemed a little smaller than life. His face was pale and shriveled, and around his head there was a fringe of sparse silky hair like a baby's. Under the lap robe his knees showed almost as thin and sharp as elbows. A mohair shawl was wrapped around his shoulders and fastened at the front with a safety pin, the extra-large size used for diapers. It heightened the image of an old man returning through the maze of years to his infancy.

This was Aragon's first time in the presence of a terminally ill person and he understood more clearly what Violet Smith had been talking about. The imminence of death altered the meaning of things. The plants outside the window looked too grotesquely healthy, the hummingbirds among the fuchsia blossoms were too lively and brilliant, the warmth of the sun useless, even offensive. Aragon felt the reaction of his own body, the increased flow of adrenaline that increased his heartbeat and signaled his muscles to fight or flight. *Run away, man. Drop down, sun. Shut up, bird.*

"Marco dear, this is Tom Aragon, the young man from the lawyer's office."

"How do you do, Mr. Decker," Aragon said.

The fingers of one of Marco's hands twitched slightly in acknowledgment of the greeting.

Gilly said, "I thought I'd introduce Aragon to you and tell you exactly why I sent for him, Marco. I'd rather have kept it secret to spare you any worry, but I know you're bound to hear hints about it from Reed or Violet Smith or one of the maids, or even from me unintentionally. When very little occurs in a house, whatever does occur is repeated and blown up out of proportion. This is a small thing, actually."

Marco's right eye blinked. The movement was slow and labored but the expression in the eye itself was clear: *Hurry up, get on with it, I haven't much time.*

"I won't tell you if you're going to fuss about it because it isn't that important."

Hurry, hurry, giddyap, giddyap.

"Now, don't be upset . . . I've often talked to you about B. J., haven't I? And I've told you what happened. We have no secrets from each other. Well, I've been thinking, what if B. J. struck it rich, down in Mexico, I mean *rich* rich. Some of these developers rake in millions and millions, and while he was always a lousy businessman, maybe this time he struck it lucky. I talked to Smedler. He said I'd be a fool not to try and cash in on it if really big money is involved. He said I should make an effort to find B. J."

Aragon stared at her. There wasn't the subtlest change of expression on her face or the slightest quaver in her voice to indicate that she'd just told three lies in three sentences.

"Well, now you know what Mr. Aragon is doing here. He's collecting material on B. J. so he'll know where to look first, and so on. I showed him some pictures of B. J. and also the last letter I received from him five years ago. There now. That shouldn't upset you, should it?"

Marco's paralyzed eye remained half open but the good one was closed. He might have gone to sleep out of weariness or boredom; he might have died.

"Don't do that. Don't pretend you're sleeping when you're not, Marco, just to make me go away. I'll go away in a minute when I've finished explaining to you . . . Listen, he treated me badly, he almost destroyed me. It was a long time ago and everything ought to be forgotten and forgiven by now. But it's not. He *owes* me. I want to see him pay a few more damages."

The wheelchair turned, as it had before, without a sound and faced the patio again, the plants, the birds, the sun.

"All right, Marco, I'm leaving. I won't bother you anymore." She opened the door and went out into the corridor. With a final glance at the man in the wheelchair, Aragon followed her. "Perhaps I shouldn't have told him but I felt I'd better. He'll be quite reasonable once he gets used to the idea. If he is or isn't, I must go ahead with the project anyway. I've been considering it a long time and I have no intention of giving it up. You think—you may think I'm doing all this out of revenge."

"I may."

"In fact you do."

"Well, I was just wondering what the going price is for a pound of flesh."

"The same as it's always been," Gilly said quietly. "A pound of flesh."

Outside, the wind had gone down and all the billowy clouds had broken up and were strung across the sky in shreds. The plastic hose of the pool vacuum was floating in the water where Reed had dropped it. It looked like a giant white sea snake coiled to strike.

Later in the evening he called his wife, Laurie, at the hospital in San Francisco. The background noises and her crisp confident voice indicated she was on ward duty. It was the professional voice she used to intimidate germs and head nurses and to calm frightened children and their parents.

"Dr. Macgregor speaking."

"Tom Aragon here. Remember him?"

"Vaguely. Describe him."

"Dark-haired, kind of funny-looking, pale, could probably use some medical attention."

"Sorry, that's not the Tom Aragon I know who happens to be very handsome, well-built, healthy, intelligent—"

"Listen, we're in the money, Laurie."

"You robbed a bank."

"No."

"Blackmailed an old lady."

"Close. One of Smedler's clients wants me to find her first husband, who's somewhere in Baja California. I'm not sure why, exactly. She's given half a dozen reasons, which is five too many. But I took the job—and her money—and I'm leaving for Rio Seco tomorrow morning."

"When was your last smallpox vaccination?"

"I don't recall."

"Better check it out. You had a tetanus booster this summer after you swam into the jellyfish, so that's okay."

"Laurie, for Pete's sake, you're not going into your mother-hen routine?"

She ignored the question. "It's no joke about the water in Mexico. Don't drink it. Don't even brush your teeth with it. Use beer."

"I never heard of brushing teeth with beer."

"You could start a trend."

"Hey, I miss you."

"Save the soft talk for later. Now, don't even look at any vegetable that's not cooked or fruit that's not peeled. *Turista* is bad enough—you can pick up some Lomotil to take care of that—but infectious hepatitis is worse, in fact it's sometimes fatal . . . I miss you, too . . . Did you know there's a place in Mexico where Hansen's disease is endemic?"

"What's Hansen's disease? On second thought—"

"Leprosy."

"Don't tell me any more or I'll quit right now and send all the money back to Mrs. Decker."

"*No.* I mean, we can use it. Just be careful. Hansen's disease isn't contagious, but pick up some halazone tablets to put in water in case of emergency. Have you any antibiotics to take with you?"

"I don't know."

"Check the medicine cabinet for tetracycline or ampicillin. Also insect repellent, especially one containing D.E.E.T. And you'd better have your hair cut very short. There'll be less chance of pediculosis."

"I hesitate to ask—"

"Head lice."

"*Head lice?*"

"Well, you're not going to be staying at the Ritz, you know. Now, do you think you can remember all the things I've told you?"

"Sure. Absolutely. I'm making notes."

She laughed. "You're not really, are you?"

"I would be if I happened to have a pencil and some paper and knew how to spell tetracycline and ampicillin and Lomotil . . . How's the job going?"

"Fine. Long hours, hard work, lethal food. But the kids are great. I've got one on my lap right this minute, a Vietnamese orphan. He's a very sick little boy, but as long as someone is carrying him around or holding him he's perfectly quiet. Do you suppose we'll ever have any kids, Tom?"

"Under present circumstances it seems unlikely."

"Circumstances change."

"The decision will be yours, anyway. My minimal role merits only a fraction of a vote."

"What would it be, though?"

"I'm not sure I want to take a chance on any kid inheriting my myopia or your tendency to cry at movies."

"I don't cry at movies anymore."

"Why not?"

"I don't get a chance to see any. On my off-hours I sleep. I just plain sleep."

"You could never sleep plain, Laurie. You sleep very, very pretty."

"What are you trying to do, make me quit my job and come running?"

"Not on your life," he said soberly. "I may need somebody to support me."

"It'll be fun, won't it, when I hang up my shingle and you hang up your shingle."

"At least our shingles will be together. Maybe they'll have little shingles."

"Tom, you're not really beefing, are you?"

"No."

"Honestly?"

"I'm not beefing. I just happen to miss you and wish you were here or I was there and the hell with Mrs. Decker's first husband."

"I love you, too. Listen, I have to go, they're paging my number. Take care of yourself. Promise?"

"I promise to brush my teeth with beer and avoid head lice and lepers. Tell the little guy on your lap good night for me."

"I will. Good night, Tom. I think you're terribly nice."

After he hung up he sat staring at the phone as though he half expected it to ring again. No matter how often or how long he and Laurie talked to each other, the conversation always seemed unfinished. He wanted to pick up the phone and call her back, but he thought of the kids waiting for her on the ward and how tired she'd sounded under the cool professional voice and how selfish he'd be to make things tougher by leaning on her.

He went to the refrigerator and poured himself a glass of beer out of a recapped quart bottle. It was a little flat, the kind good for cleaning teeth. He swished some around in his mouth by way of practice.

6

ONCE HE GOT off the plane in Rio Seco, Aragon lapsed naturally into Spanish. It was the language of his boyhood, his family and friends, the streets where he'd played, even his school at recess and before and after classes. During classes the official language was English. *You are in the United States of America, children, and you are expected to speak the language of the United States of America.* They did, when teacher was listening. When she wasn't, the younger children said, *Qué mujer tan fea,* and the older ones, *Chinga tu madre.*

The car that he'd reserved by phone from Los Angeles was waiting for him, a compact Ford that looked older than its odometer indicated. When he checked it over, he found the oil gauge registered low, two of the tires needed air and the gas tank was only half filled. The man who seemed to be in charge at the rental agency, Zalamero, assured him that in all his years of experience in the business, almost one, such oversights had never before been detected. Zalamero spoke a mixture of Spanish and English slang sometimes called Spanglish. Aragon asked him for directions to Bahía de Ballenas.

"Bahía de Ballenas, why are you going there? It's an el dumpo."

"I'm thinking of buying some property."

"My wife's cousin has some super-duper property near here that he's willing to sell cheap, so cheap you wouldn't believe."

"That's right, I wouldn't," Aragon said. "Now, about Bahía de Ballenas."

"Okey-dokey, you drive south two hundred kilometers or so until the road turns inland. You stop. You're at a place called Viñadaco, another el dumpo, but they have tourist cabins, cafés, gas pumps. Get some gas and more water and start up again. Now you drive slow, very slow, in second gear, because the highway is going *east* and you are going *west.*"

"Are there any road signs?"

"No, no, no. You ask a person. This person answers and you have a nice talk, maybe a cup of coffee, a little social life. It's much better than signs."

Aragon tried to imagine the effect of this kind of social life on the Hollywood Freeway. After the initial chaos it might be quite pleasant for those who weren't going anywhere in a hurry.

Zalamero said anxiously, "You won't tattletale the agency in the U.S. about the oil and tires?"

"No, but you should be more careful."

"Yes, yes, yes, you bet I will be. I will personally inspect every part of every car every day."

"Your social life is bound to suffer."

"You've convinced me I have a duty to my customers. Besides, I can talk while I inspect. All Zalameros can do two things at once . . . How soon will you bring the car back?"

"A week, perhaps less."

"Go with God."

"Thanks."

He paid a deposit on the Ford and a week's rental in advance. It was nearly two o'clock when he started the engine.

For about twenty kilometers beyond Rio Seco the road continued to be fairly good. Then gradually it began to deteriorate, as if the surveyors and the foreman and the key workers had lost interest and dropped out, one by one.

The traffic was heavier than Aragon had expected but still sparse: dilapidated pickups and compacts and subcompacts with Mexican license plates, and newer vehicles mostly from the Western states, vans, trucks with cabover campers and complete houses on wheels like Dreamboat. The road hadn't been built with Dreamboats or highway speeds in mind. It was narrow, the curves were poorly banked and the roadbed inadequately compacted. Drivers accustomed to American standards of engineering took the curves and unexpected dips too fast in vehicles that were too wide and heavy. The accident rate, according to a safety pamphlet distributed on the plane by an insurance company, was extremely high.

He began to understand why his rented Ford looked old for its age. Sand blew across the roadway from the low barren hills to the east and the coastal dunes to the west, pitting the car's finish and burrowing its way through the closed windows. At times it was so fine and white that it swept past like a blizzard of talcum powder. Aragon could feel it clinging to the roof of his mouth and the membranes of his nose. It scratched the inside of his eyelids and mixed with the sweat of his palms on the steering wheel to form a sticky film of clay. The cars and vans and campers heading north were suddenly all white. They passed like ghosts of accidents. A few kilometers farther, the powder turned to sand again. *If I were going in the opposite direction, I'd be halfway to San Francisco by now. Laurie might manage a couple of days off and we could splurge and stay at the Clift. Just stay. No night clubs, no theaters, no fancy dinners . . .*

He braked to avoid a jackrabbit leaping across the road. Except for an occasional gull soaring overhead, the rabbit was the only sign of wildlife he'd seen. It was an inhospitable countryside. Clumps of creosote bushes and spindly spikes of cholla were the main vegetation, with here and there some mesquite or a palo triste like a billow of grey smoke.

Just short of two hundred kilometers the landscape suddenly changed, indicating the presence of fresh water and some kind of irrigation system. Fields of beans and chili peppers alternated with groves of palm trees. An abandoned sugar mill overlooked a scattering of adobe houses with children playing outside, and chickens and goats and burros wandering loose among them. This, according to a sign on the gas pump where Aragon stopped, was the village of Viñadaco.

The gas pump was operated by an entire family. While the man filled the tank, his wife cleaned the front windshield and a couple of small girls cleaned the back. A boy no more than five wiped off the headlights with the torn sleeve of his shirt while two teenagers lifted the hood and stared expertly at the engine without doing anything. They were mestizos, half-Indians, copper-skinned and thin-featured, with black eyes and straight black hair. Their solemn dignity reminded Aragon of Violet Smith.

He asked the woman for directions to Bahía de Ballenas.

"Nobody goes there."

"I do."

"But the road turns the other way towards the gulf. And it's late, it will soon be dark. You might get stuck in the sand or lost."

They were valid reasons but not the real one: she happened to have a vacant cabin which she rented out to tourists. Nothing fancy, of course, no running water or electricity, but a nice clean bed. For this nice clean bed the asking price was about the same as for a suite at the Beverly Hilton. The señora admitted that the price was high, but she didn't offer to change it and Aragon didn't argue. It was Gilly's money. If she wanted to come down here and haggle over it, let her. He was tired and hungry.

He ate at the nearest place, a shoebox-sized cafe overlooking a pond where a dozen or so coots were floating on the water and foraging on the banks. When he was a child he'd often eaten coot, which his mother called black mallard. This sounded better but didn't improve the taste or texture. As he ate the *machaca* he was served, a kind of hash, he tried to identify its contents. Coot maybe, dried goat meat probably, and chilis unmistakably, the small green innocent-looking kind that lit up his mouth and throat and brought tears to his eyes to put out the fire. Dessert was a dish of fried beans and a cactus fruit with sweet juicy pulp. He drank two bottles of beer and bought two extra to take with him in case his teeth were extra dirty.

He returned to the gas pump and the Viñadaco Hilton. The señora had left a kerosene lamp burning for him, and a basin with a pitcher of water and two small towels. After he'd stripped and washed he sat down to drink some beer. Almost immediately he discovered that the Viñadaco Hilton had one other thing which the Beverly Hilton didn't—mosquitoes. The first bite coincided with the first twinge in his stomach. He went to sleep trying to remember some of the things Laurie had urged him to take along—*antibiotics . . . head lice . . . tooth beer . . . Laurie, I miss you . . .*

He woke up at dawn. So did every man, woman, child and beast in the village. Children chanted, donkeys brayed, roosters crowed, dogs barked. Aragon got up and opened the door. The sun was shining and a cool moist wind was blowing steadily in from the sea. It was the kind of day he wanted to rush out to meet.

During the night the señora's conscience must have been bothering her: she appeared at the door with a cup of coffee and two tortillas rolled up with guava jelly and a pot of hot water.

"Are you hungry?"

"Yes."

"And you want hot water. Why do Americans always want hot water?"

"To shave."

"You have hardly anything to shave. And who is going to see you in *that* forsaken place? I've never been there myself but I hear the people are very dark-skinned and ignorant."

While he shaved she gave him directions to Bahía de Ballenas and even borrowed his pen to draw him a little map. He didn't put much faith in the map—she held the pen as though it were the first one she'd ever used.

Also during the night someone—probably the two teenaged boys who were now leaning casually against the gas pump—had washed the Ford. He appreciated the gesture, but unfortunately the car was now parked in the middle of a large puddle of water. He took off his shoes and socks, waded through the puddle and climbed in behind the wheel. His feet felt pleasantly refreshed. People checking out of the Beverly Hilton might have their cars waiting at the front door, but they didn't get guava jelly tortillas, farewell footbaths and all the fresh air they could breathe.

He stopped at the café where he'd eaten dinner the previous evening and picked up a dozen bottles of beer. If the señora's prediction came true and he was going to get lost, he might as well do it in style. He was on a little dirt road a couple of miles south of Viñadaco when he stopped to consult the map and discovered that the señora had neglected to return his pen. He might ask for it on the way back, assuming he arrived at any place to come back from. Or, better yet, he would put it down as a business expense, Gilly's small and undoubtedly grudging contribution toward international relations. She was, in her own words, pretty tight with a buck.

The road climbed uphill along a cliff for a while, then dropped down again between sand dunes, sometimes disappearing entirely, only to reappear a few yards farther on like a magician's scarf. At one point there was a fork not indicated on the map. The east branch showed signs of more frequent use than the west. If the señora was correct in claiming that no one went to Bahía de Ballenas, then the west branch seemed the better choice. He took it.

The sun, which had seemed so gentle and friendly at dawn, was turning into a monster that couldn't be pacified or controlled. He wasn't sure at what point or why the Ford's air conditioner blew out, but he suddenly became aware that he was riding in an oven with the heat turned on full and that he'd better do something about it fast. He stopped in the meager shade of some mesquite, opened all the car windows and two of the bottles of beer. The beer had been in the oven with him and did nothing to quench his thirst, but it improved his general outlook from terrible to bad. He was, if not lost, certainly misplaced. The road, which had never been more than a series of tire tracks, was now visible only at times when the capricious wind deposited the sand short of it or beyond it. He wondered how B. J. had ever maneuvered a vehicle the size of Dreamboat as far as Bahía de Ballenas. Of course the girl, Tula, had lived in this area with her relatives and was familiar with it. She would have known which road to avoid, and this was undoubtedly it.

A mixed flock of gulls and smaller, more agile sea birds often flew low over the car like an advance patrol. They had a cool confident air as if they knew exactly what they were doing. Aragon started the engine again and followed them.

At the top of the next sand dune Bahía de Ballenas came into view, a half circle of sparkling blue water surrounded by desert. A few small fishing boats were tied up at a battered pier. The only other boat visible rode at anchor in the middle of the bay, a grey sloop sleek as a dolphin. It was flying both American and Mexican ensigns, a purple-and-white yacht-club burgee and an officers' flag. At the water's edge were some salt-water conversion tanks, an old fish cannery that looked abandoned and half a dozen wooden shacks. On higher ground stood the crumbling remains of a small adobe mission. Between the mission and the shacks was the inevitable collection of children and chickens and dogs and goats all covered with dust. An invisible and insurmountable barrier seemed to separate the clean clear water of the bay from the dirty little village and its people.

The children, ranging in age from a baby barely able to walk to a twelve-or thirteen-year-old girl, were ragged and shoeless, like the mestizos of Viñadaco, but different in appearance. These were darker-skinned, with rounded features and soft expressive brown eyes. Under their grimy clothes their bodies looked well-nourished and healthy except for one boy who had a withered left leg.

Aragon addressed the girl. "Hello."

"Hello."

"Is this place Bahía de Ballenas?"

She nodded. The other children broke into giggles as if they'd never before heard such a funny question. Was this place Bahía de Ballenas? Of course. It had to be. There wasn't any other place.

"What's your name?"

"Valeria. What's your name?"

"Tomás."

"I have a chicken named Tomás. He doesn't lay eggs and he's mean."

"Boys don't lay eggs."

"Chickens do."

"Boy chickens don't."

"I know *that*. I just *told* you he doesn't."

"Okay, okay. Whatever game we're playing, you win."

She accepted her victory with the equanimity of a champion. "I'm grown up. Next year I might marry my cousin Raul. He lives in a real house beyond that hill over there."

She pointed. Aragon couldn't see any house and there were half a dozen hills all exactly the same. He turned his attention to the boy with the withered leg. "What's your name?"

"Okay okay."

"Is that what they call you?"

"Okay okay."

Suddenly the boy thrust his hand in the window of the car and honked the horn. The children began running away, shrieking with laughter, followed by their squawking barking baaing retinue of animals. He got out of the car intending to follow them, but a voice stopped him, the high cracked voice of someone very old: "Good morning. Is there anything I can do for you?"

Aragon turned. A man was standing in the doorway of the crumbling mission. He wore a straw hat and the remnants of a brown priest's robe tied at the waist with a piece of rope. He was tiny and shriveled as though he'd been left too long in the sun. One of his eyes was bloodshot and dripped tears that ran down the deepest groove in his cheek. Flecks of salt from previous tears glistened on his face when he pushed back his hat.

"Are you lost, friend?"

"This is Bahía de Ballenas?"

"Yes."

"Then I'm not lost. I've been looking for it."

"Not many people look for us. This is a pleasant surprise. What is your name?"

"Tomás Aragon."

"Everyone calls me padre. I once had a real name, but it slips my mind now and then. No matter. Such things are not important where everybody knows everybody. Will you come inside where it's cool?"

"Thank you, padre."

"Padre is a courtesy title only. I have long since left the Church, but it has not left me. I am allowed to live here. The villagers and I have mutual respect. I give them comfort when I can and take it when I must."

The doorway was so low that Aragon had to stoop to enter. The man noticed his hesitation.

"Have no fear for your safety, friend. These walls will last beyond my time and yours. Adobe is a very fine building material in a climate like this. It is strong. And more, it is friendly, absorbing heat during the day and giving it back during the night."

The room was only a little larger than the cabin Aragon had occupied the previous night at Viñadaco, but it was cool and comfortable, furnished with a cot, a table and chairs and an adobe bench in front of the altar. Dwarfing the room and its contents was a life-sized and extremely ugly statue of the Virgin Mary. It was all grey like an angel of death.

The padre looked up at her with affection. "I made her myself. The original statue fell and broke during an earthquake, so I spent some years, ten, perhaps twelve or thirteen—*tempus fugit*—fashioning a replacement. It is the only gift I will leave behind for the villagers when I die."

"It's very impressive."

"Yes. Yes, I think so. Inside, to hold her together, I piled stones which the children helped me collect. And the sculpting material is what we use to make our cooking stoves, water poured over hot ashes and mixed into a paste. Each day, every time I had a fire, I added a little, and there she is." He crossed himself. "Now I don't have to worry so much that the villagers will lose touch with God after I'm gone. They will have the Blessed Virgin to remind them . . . I was about to eat my midday meal. Will you be my guest?"

"Thanks."

"Simple fare, a bit of mullet I cooked this morning and some pitahaya. The Americans in La Paz used to call it organ-pipe cactus, so it seems most fitting to serve it in my little church, doesn't it?"

"Yes."

"I'm sorry, I've forgotten your name. My memory has dulled with age."

"Tomás Aragon."

"Would it be suitable if I called you Tomás?"

"I'd be pleased."

The two men sat down facing each other across the wooden table. The padre blessed the piece of mullet on the battered tin plate and waved away the flies buzzing around it. Though the fish had a slight greenish iridescence, it tasted all right, and the pitahaya was similar to what he'd been served at the café in Viñadaco, only sweeter and juicier. After the meal Aragon went out to the car and brought in several bottles of beer.

"My saints and sinners," the padre said. "This is a great surprise."

"It's very warm, if you don't mind . . ."

"Oh, no no no. I like it any way at all. Tecate. I haven't tasted that for a long time. This is an occasion, Tomás, yes, a celebration. We ought to make a toast. What do you suggest?"

"To your health, padre."

"To your safe journey, Tomás."

"To your village and the future of its children."

"That's the best toast. To their future."

The two men drank. The beer was the temperature of restaurant tea.

"One of the girls has her future planned," Aragon said. "She will marry her cousin Raul and live in a real house."

"That would be Valeria. Always planning, already like a woman."

"I haven't seen any real houses in Bahía de Ballenas. Perhaps she is dreaming."

"Perhaps. Now if you will excuse me for a few minutes, I'll go and bury the remains of our meal."

"Let me help."

"No. No, it won't take long. Sit and contemplate the Blessed Virgin."

It would have been difficult in that small room to contemplate anything else, so Aragon did as he was told. In spite of the strong beer, the statue of the Virgin remained ugly. There was a frightening determination about her face that reminded him of Violet Smith. It was now Sunday afternoon. In a few hours Violet Smith would be setting out for church to sing hymns—sharing her hymn book with B. J.'s first wife, Ethel—and stand up afterward in front of the assemblage to voice her problems and concerns. Perhaps she would tell about the young man who was hired by B. J.'s second wife to go on a confidential mission, giving names and places and dates and whatever other details she might have wormed out of Gilly or Reed, or overheard on an extension phone or through a thin closed door.

When the padre returned, his breath was wheezing in and out of his lungs like the air through an old leaky accordion.

Aragon said, "Do you teach the children?"

"Whatever and whenever possible."

"I noticed one of the boys has a deformed leg and acts retarded."

"A child of God."

"His skin seems somewhat lighter than that of the others. His parents—"

"He is an orphan."

"Where does he live?"

"In Mexico all people love children. Pablo can live anywhere."

"But where *does* he live?"

"It would break hearts if he were ever taken away. If you have any such thought, any reason—"

"No. None."

"He is much beloved, a child marked by God." The padre crossed himself, then frowned briefly through the open door at the sky as if for a fraction of a second he was questioning God's common sense. "He lives with his grandparents and aunts and uncles and cousins. A happy family. It would be a pity to disturb their tranquility."

"Where are his parents?"

"Gone. They left here years ago. They couldn't take the boy along because the authorities wouldn't allow it. You yourself are not from them, from the authorities?"

"No."

"Then I don't think I should answer any more questions. It might appear to be gossiping . . . When tragedy strikes, everyone likes to talk about it, that's human nature. But it all happened in the distant past. Pablo doesn't remember his mother. To him everything is ten minutes ago, or an hour, or at most, yesterday. Even if he were normal, no one would remind him of her. She fell from grace."

"Does she communicate with the family?"

"No. She wouldn't want to, anyway, but even if she did, we have no telephones or mail service. There was talk of mail service once when someone was going to build here. Nothing came of either the building or the service. No matter, we survive."

"What about the boy's father?"

The padre considered the question in silence, squinting out at the sky again, this time for guidance. "He was an American. You see, Tula went away for a while to America. She had an unexpected opportunity to make a fortune. A fortune around here is very little, and when Tula saw her chance to go and get a job in America, she reached out and grabbed it."

"Who gave her the chance?"

"One Christmas a couple came along in a truck loaded with old clothes and bedding and things like soap and canned goods to distribute to the more remote villagers in Baja. Tula persuaded the couple to take her back with them. She was very pretty, not too smart, but she could talk the ears off a donkey. So the people agreed and off she went. We heard nothing from her for a year or more. Then she came back married to a rich American and riding in a veritable chariot. My saints and sinners, what a vision she was, dressed like a princess and waving from the window of the chariot. Some of the women began screaming. They thought Tula had died and gone to heaven and this was her spirit. Oh, it was a great day. Everybody got drunk."

"What happened to the chariot?"

The padre's excitement faded. The great day was finished, everybody was sober, the chariot in ruins and the princess a long time missing.

"It never moved again. Its wheels got stuck in the sand and the engine broke down and there was no fuel anyway."

"And now it's the 'real house' the girl Valeria referred to in her marriage plans?"

"Yes. But you mustn't go there, you will disturb the family's tranquility."

"Does Pablo live with them?"

"You most certainly can't talk to him. He doesn't understand. He is like a parrot, only repeating noises he hears. And the family will not want to discuss Tula, because she fell from grace . . . But I can see you're not hearing me, Tomás."

"I'm hearing you, padre," Aragon said. "I just can't afford to listen."

7

ONLY A FEW letters of the name still faintly visible on one side identified the ravaged hulk as Gilly's Dreamboat. The wheels had disappeared into the ground and most of the windows were broken. The paint had been scratched by chollas and creosote bushes, rusted by fog and salt air, blasted off by wind-driven sand.

On the roof was an old sun-bleached, urine-stained mattress. A lone chicken sat in the middle of it, casually pecking out the stuffing. It was the only living thing in sight. Yet Aragon was positive that there were people inside watching his approach with quiet hostility as if they'd already found out the purpose of his visit. It seemed impossible, though he knew it wasn't. In places where more sophisticated forms of communication were lacking, the grapevine was quick and efficient, and the fact that he'd seen no one outside the mission while he was talking to the padre meant nothing.

"Hello? Hello, in there! Can you hear me?"

He didn't expect an answer and none came. But he kept trying.

"Listen to me. I came from the United States looking for Mr. Lockwood, Byron James Lockwood. Can anyone give me some information about him or about Tula?"

If they could, they didn't intend to. The silence seemed even more profound: Tula's fall from grace had evidently been far and final.

"The padre will tell you that I mean no harm. And I'm offering money in return for information. Doesn't anyone want money?"

No one did. Money was of little value to people without a place to spend it or a desire to change their lot.

He waited another five minutes. The chicken pecking at the mattress stuffing remained the only sign of life.

The padre was waiting for him. He had opened another bottle of beer and his color was high and his eyes slightly out of focus.

"You're back very soon, Tomás."

"Yes."

"Our people are normally very friendly to strangers. If you were the exception, I apologize."

"I was, and thanks."

"You remind them of bad things and they're afraid. I am perhaps a little afraid myself. You're searching for the American, Lockwood?"

"Yes."

"Why?"

"Because Lockwood's wife wants him found." Lockwood's wife wasn't too accurate a description of Gilly but it served its purpose.

The padre looked shocked. "I thought Tula was—I didn't know he had another wife."

"Two other wives. Only one of them wants him found."

"Then Pablo is illegitimate?"

"Yes."

"All the more he is a child of God," the padre said, but he sounded shaken. "Of course, we will not tell any of the villagers about this. It would serve no purpose and the little boy might suffer unnecessarily. It is not easy being a child of God."

"How long did Lockwood stay here in the village?"

"Some four years or so. He was a nice man, kind to all the little ones and very fond of his son. He pretended the boy was normal, perhaps even to himself he pretended, I'm not sure."

"No, he knew the facts. The second Mrs. Lockwood had a letter from him referring to the boy."

"Then all the more he was a nice man, don't you think?"

"I think he must have been. Everyone I've talked to seems to have liked him." With the exception of Smedler, who didn't count because he never liked anybody. "Was he happy here, living under what for him were certainly primitive conditions?"

"But he was going to *change* the conditions. He had great plans for the village, great dreams. The mission would be restored, haciendas built, and a town square and a new pier to attract tourists in big boats. Also streets would be put in, real streets with beautiful names carved on stone pillars. The streets were laid out and some of the pillars already carved when the authorities arrived. Then suddenly it was all over."

"What happened?"

"He was arrested along with his partner, Jenkins, who was the real villain. But the authorities didn't bother to apportion blame on a percentage basis, eighty percent Jenkins, twenty percent Lockwood. No, they arrested them both equally."

"What was the charge?"

"It seems a lot of people were cheated. They sent money to buy lots on which haciendas were to be built, Jenlock Haciendas."

"A real estate swindle."

"I couldn't believe Mr. Lockwood deliberately swindled anyone. But what I believed was unimportant . . . The whole village came here to church to say farewell prayers for him. He was all dressed up for the occasion in his best suit and tie with a diamond tiepin in it, his fancy wristwatch and gold wedding ring and the ruby ring he wore on his little finger. He looked very splendid, like the day he arrived in the chariot. No one would have imagined he was being arrested, perhaps he could not really imagine it himself. Is this possible?"

"Yes."

"They took him away in a dirty old vehicle something like a bus with bars across the windows, a far cry from a chariot. When the bus left, he and Jenkins sat quietly, but Tula kept waving at us from the window precisely the way she'd waved on the day she and Lockwood arrived."

"Why did Tula go along?"

"I think to get away from the village, which bored her, and the child she was ashamed of, not so much to be with Lockwood."

"She couldn't be with him anyway, could she, if he was being sent to jail?"

"Oh yes, if she really wanted to. The jail in Rio Seco is very different from American jails I have seen in the cinema in Ensenada. Sometimes whole families live together, inside the walls. Or a prisoner, if he can afford it, may have his meals brought to him from outside or be visited by night ladies. The latter I don't approve. But the other thing—what harm is done? It is a more humane way to conduct a prison than the American way, don't you agree?"

32

"I agree that it's more humane for the prisoner, not necessarily for his family."

"Bear in mind that many of the men in prison have committed no crime, they are simply waiting for their cases to be heard. For most offenses no bail is allowed because under Mexican law there is no presumption of innocence such as in your country. Quite the contrary. A man is presumed guilty and is not entitled to a jury trial. His guilt or innocence, and his sentence, is decided by a magistrate. He can be kept in jail for a whole year before his case is even heard. This is very sad for the poor, who can't afford to pay bribes, but everyone expected when Mr. Lockwood was taken away that he would be back any week. We thought he still had some money, or that he could at least borrow some from his American friends in order to pay the magistrate for a favorable verdict. Perhaps he did. Perhaps he was released from prison and simply chose not to return here. We never heard from him again."

"Or from the girl?"

"No. A funny thing happened, though. Last fall, about a year ago, a sports fishing boat came down from the north coast and anchored in the bay. A man rowed ashore in a dinghy and left some boxes for the children containing clothes and toys and chewing gum and vitamin pills."

"Could they have been sent by Lockwood?"

"Possibly, though I would think he'd have included some more useful things. The children broke the toys in a week and fed the vitamin pills to the goats."

"Didn't you ask the man in the dinghy who sent him?"

"He couldn't speak Spanish and my English is very bad. We have been the recipients of charity before—remember the truck which carried Tula to America?—so perhaps it was merely a coincidence that the boxes came to us."

"Coincidences happen, of course," Aragon said. "But in my profession they're usually viewed with suspicion."

"In my profession, also." The padre's smile was merely a further deepening of the grooves around his mouth. "So we view with suspicion, you and I. I wish it were not so."

"What happened to Jenkins?"

"No one knows or is in any hurry to find out. He had a bad effect on Mr. Lockwood. He would drive down to the village in a jeep, bringing rum and tequila and a briefcase full of drawings and blueprints and newspapers. Then after a few days he'd disappear again with more of Mr. Lockwood's money. Anyone but Mr. Lockwood would have perceived Jenkins' true character. He cared nothing about the villagers. He couldn't conceal how much he despised the people who couldn't read or write and didn't care. And to me, who could read and write on a higher level than his own, he made unkind remarks about being kicked out of the Church. I was never kicked out. I left. I left voluntarily because I committed a carnal sin."

The padre covered his face with his sleeve and Aragon wasn't sure whether he was wiping away tears or sweat, or whether he was attempting to hide his shame.

"Now I have told you everything, Tomás, more than you asked. I'm a silly old man full of beer and gossip."

"You've been a great help."

"I hope so. I'd like very much to see Mr. Lockwood again. We had many pleasant conversations and we used to listen to his radio until the batteries wore out. Will you give him a message for me? Tell him he is missed. Tell him— No, that will be enough. He is missed. I wouldn't really want him to know how much, it might make him feel bad if circumstances won't permit him to come back."

"You mean if he's still in jail?"

"Oh, I'm sure he won't be, a man of his worth, both moral and financial."

"I'm in no position to judge his moral worth," Aragon said. "However, I know that five years ago he needed money very badly. 'Desperately' was the word he used."

"But he had friends, did he not—rich American friends?"

"Rich American friends are hard to come by, especially when you're in trouble."

"You said he had a wife. She is also American?"

"Yes."

"And rich?"

"Yes."

"Perhaps he—"

"No. He didn't. She refused to send him any."

"That *is* a shame." The padre sighed, and wiped at his face again. "So you will go first to the Rio Seco jail to look for him. And if he's not there?"

"They must keep records."

"Oh, Tomás, you're a dreamer. Records of what? Of who paid how much to which magistrate?"

"The girl is the only lead I have."

"So off you go. When?"

"I should get back to Rio Seco late tonight. Right now I'd like to look around the village."

"I would accompany you, Tomás, but I'm a little unsteady on my feet and this is siesta time. The sun is very hot. Do you have a hat to wear?"

"No."

"Here, you can have mine."

"No," Aragon said. "No thank you." It would be unfair to the gentle little man to be reminded of him by a case of head lice.

"Have a safe journey, Tomás. Our visit has been so enjoyable I hate to see it end. Will you ever come back?"

"Not likely."

"I've reached the age where anyone who lets me talk seems like an old friend. By listening to my memories, you have become part of them. I hope you don't mind."

"I like the idea very much."

"Goodbye, friend."

"Good health and God's blessing, padre."

The two men shook hands. Then Aragon started walking down toward the pier and the row of shacks beside the abandoned fish cannery.

The severity of the sun had closed the village down as completely as if a bad storm had struck or an epidemic of plague. There was no sign of activity anywhere, even on the sloop riding at anchor in the bay. Only the sound of a crying child from inside one of the shacks indicated that they were occupied.

Beyond the shacks, on a knoll overlooking the bay, he found what he was looking for, the beginning—and the ending—of Jenlock Haciendas. "Streets would be put in," the padre had said, "real streets with beautiful names carved on stone pillars." The streets, if they had ever existed, were buried under sand, but the identifying pillars remained unchanged. The same wind that blasted the paint off Dreamboat had merely kept the pillars wiped as clean as tombstones in a carefully tended cemetery. Each way was a dead end, avenues east and west, streets north and south: Calle Jardin Encanto, Calle Paloma de Paz, Avenida Cielito Verde, Avenida Corona de Oro, Avenida Gilda.

"Avenida Gilda." He repeated the name aloud as if the sound of it might make it more believable. The stone was perfectly symmetrical and the carving done with great care and skill in Gothic letters.

He went back to his car. Through the open door of the mission he could hear the padre snoring. He took the remaining bottles of beer inside and left them on the table. The Blessed Virgin gave him one fierce final stare.

He reached Rio Seco about one o'clock in the morning and checked into a hotel. It was too late to phone Gilly. Besides, he had very little to tell her and nothing she'd like to hear: B. J.

and his partner, Jenkins, had been taken to jail; the boy, Pablo, was not only crippled but retarded; and in the middle of a couple of billion cubic feet of sand was a tombstone with her name carved on it.

He went to bed.

8

THE JAIL WAS in the center of Rio Seco as if it had been the first structure and the rest of the city had been built around it. It was shaped like a roundhouse and circled by stone walls twenty-five or thirty feet high which gave it its name: the stone quarry. LA CANTERA, PENITENCIARIA DEL ESTADO was carved above the main entrance where Aragon stood with the other people waiting to be admitted.

In spite of the earliness of the hour, traffic was heavy and the crowd outside the jail was large—a few men of varying ages, but mostly women carrying babies and straw bags and packages wrapped in newspaper, and a handful of prostitutes in miniskirts and maxiwigs. Children played in the street, oblivious to the honking of horns and squealing of tires, or ran up the stone steps and slid down the iron banisters. Apart from the crowd an older American couple, neatly dressed and quiet, stood with their arms locked as if they were holding each other up.

One of the three guards on duty, a young man wearing a cowboy hat and oversized boots that looked like hand-me-downs from a bigger brother, fielded questions: "Ten more minutes, I don't make the rules, señora . . . Carlos Gonzalez got out last week . . . Café opens at nine . . . You can go home, girls, it's too early. Give the boys a chance to wash up . . . If Gonzalez left a message, I don't know about it . . . Anyone want a shouter? Ten cents for a shouter, fifteen cents for a first-class shouter."

The American man held up his hand. "Yes. Please."

"How much?"

"Fifteen cents."

"Name?"

"Sandra Boyd."

"Sandra Boyd. Okay, anyone else? . . . Ten cents for Cecilio Martinez . . . Five cents for Manuel Ysidro. That's a whisper, maybe you don't want him to hear . . . Ten for Fernando Escobar . . . Ten, Inocente Santana. We got a lot of Inocentes in this place. Not a guilty in sight, ha ha . . . Carlos Gonzalez. You're wasting your money, señora. I told you, he's gone. Okay, ten for Gonzalez."

"Lockwood," Aragon said. "B. J. Lockwood and Harry Jenkins."

"That's two names."

"Yes."

"You can't have one shouter for two names. You must have one shouter for each name."

"All right, thirty cents."

At eight thirty the gates of the Quarry opened and the crowd surged inside. No attempt was made to question or search anyone or to examine packages. It would have been impossible under the circumstances. The pushing and shoving and screaming reminded Aragon of doorbuster sales at some of the stores back home.

Within the walls, similar high-pressure merchandising was taking place. The prison peddlers began hawking their wares: pottery, leatherwork, novelties, food and drink, children's toys. A trio of *mariachis* singing "Guadalajara, Guadalajara," gave a fiesta atmosphere to the scene.

The *mariachis* picked Aragon as their first mark of the morning.

"You want to hear a special song, señor?"

"No thanks."

"We sing anything you say."

"Not right now."

"We know a hundred songs."

Aragon paid twenty-five cents not to hear any of them.

The cellblocks were built in a circle around a huge recreation yard, where a soccer game was in progress. While he waited in line at the iron-grilled information window, he watched the soccer game. Both sides were dressed alike, so it was difficult to follow. But it was a very lively spectacle, since there were no referees.

Guadalajara, Guadalajara.

You buy a taco, señor? An empanada?

Real, hand-tooled leather purses and belts at prices so low it is a crime.

Balloons, dolls, madonnas, bracelets, cigarettes.

A fight broke out between two men peddling identical calfskin wallets. Compared to the soccer game, it was dull and half-hearted and attracted little attention. Obviously the inmates had more interest in soccer than in fistfights that consisted mainly of loud words and soft blows.

The shouters were already at work:

"*Oswaldo Fernandez, hey, Oswaldo Fernandez, hey, Fernandez.*"

"*Cruz Rivera, ay ay Cruz, ay ay Rivera, ay ay ay ay Cruz Rivera.*"

"*B. J. Lockwood . . . Lock—wood.*"

"*Harry Jenkins . . . You are wanted, Harry Jenkins.*"

"*Juanita Maria Placencia, come here, Jua—ni—ta!*"

"*Sandra Boyd, if you please . . . Sandra Boyd . . . Sandra Boyd.*"

"*Amelio Gutierrez, answer to your name.*"

When Aragon's turn came he presented his credentials to the uniformed man at the information window. After consulting with his colleagues, the man sent a runner to summon the assistant to the assistant to the warden himself.

The new arrival introduced himself as Superintendent Perdiz. "These two Americans you are asking about, I never heard of them. It would be better for you to come back later when the warden is here."

"How much later?"

"Wednesday. He works very hard and needs long weekends to recuperate at his beach house."

"Who's in charge when the warden's away?"

"The assistant warden. He'll be back tomorrow, Tuesday. He doesn't need such long weekends because his responsibilities are not so great."

"He's got a beach house, too, I suppose."

"No. He likes to go to the mountains. The air is more invigorating. Here in Rio Seco we have bad air. Do you smell it? Phew!"

Aragon smelled it. Traffic odors, people odors, jail odors, exhaust fumes, sweat, garlic, urine, cigarette smoke, antiseptic.

"Phew," Perdiz said again. "Don't you think so?"

"Yes."

"Then you understand the need for long weekends out of town?"

"Of course."

"So now we are in complete agreement. A man, even one in a lowly position like mine, needs a country house for a breath of sea or mountain air on the weekends. I'd like to buy such a place but my salary won't allow it."

"Would ten dollars help?"

"A little more might inspire me to go and search the files personally. What do you think my personal attention is worth?"

"Fifteen dollars."

"That's most kind of you."

Perdiz accepted the bribe with solemn dignity. After all, it was part of the system, paying a *mordida* to *influyentes*, and he was an *influyente*. "You wait here."

Aragon waited. He watched the soccer game some more and bought a wallet from the loser of the fistfight, a can of ginger ale and a doll made of two withered oranges with cloves marking its features and dried red chiles for arms and legs. He didn't know why he'd bought such a ridiculous thing until he held it in his hand and studied it for a while: it looked like Pablo, round-eyed and vacant-faced, untouched, untouchable.

The shouters were still at work. At least one of them had brought results—the American couple were talking to a pale stringy-haired young woman wearing a ragged poncho that reached almost to her ankles. The man was doing most of the talking, the older woman was crying, the younger one looked bored.

Perdiz returned. Nowhere in the files was there any mention of B. J. Lockwood.

"You should have some record of him," Aragon said. "He was arrested."

"How do you know he was arrested?"

"I was told."

"Who told you?"

"A priest."

"A priest. Then it's very likely true that he was arrested. But maybe it was a mistake. Maybe he didn't do anything wrong, so they let him go. If we kept records on everyone who never did anything wrong, we'd have a jail full of paper. A paper jail, isn't that a funny idea?"

"A real rib-tickler," Aragon said. Gilly was now an unofficial contributor to a beach house or maybe a mountain cabin, but she wasn't any closer to B. J. "What about Harry Jenkins?"

"I could find nothing concerning him either. Truthfully—you want truthfully?"

"Yes."

"All right, truthfully. We don't like to keep records on Americans. It's bad for international relations. Consider which is more important, a few pieces of paper or a great war between nations."

"I don't think anyone would start even a very small war over Harry Jenkins."

"One never knows. Peace today, war tomorrow."

"Yes. Well, thank you for your trouble, Perdiz." *And may your beach house be swept away by a tidal wave and your mountain cabin buried under an avalanche.*

He began pushing his way through the crowd in the direction of the main gate. When he passed the American couple he saw that both the man and the older woman were now crying, but the girl hadn't changed expression. She was absently tying, untying and retying a couple of strands of her hair. On impulse Aragon handed her the dried orange-and-chili doll that looked like Pablo. She immediately picked out the cloves that were his eyes and popped them in her mouth. Nobody said anything.

He had almost reached the main gate when he felt a hand touch his back between his shoulder blades. He turned abruptly, expecting to catch an inept pickpocket. Instead, he saw a Mexican woman about thirty, with dark despondent eyes and wiry black hair that seemed to have sprung out of her scalp in revolt. Her arms and hands were covered with scars of various sizes and shapes and colors, as if the wounds had occurred at different times under different circumstances.

Her voice had the hoarseness of someone who talked too loud and too long. "I heard a shouter calling for Harry Jenkins. I said, 'Who hired you?' and he said, 'An American with big glasses and a blue striped shirt.' That's you."

"That's me. Tomás Aragon."

"Why do you want to see Harry?"

"Why do you want to know why I want to see Harry?"

"I'm Emilia, Harry's good friend. Very good, special. Someday we will be married in the church but that must wait. Right now I am in and he is out. Before that, I was out and he was in, and before that, we were both in. What did Harry do to you?"

"Nothing."

"Then why are you looking for him?"

"Actually I'm looking for a friend of his. I thought Harry might give me—or sell me—some information."

"You buy information?"

"Sometimes."

Her lips parted enough to reveal two slightly protruding front teeth. It was the closest Emilia ever came to a smile. "I have information."

"What kind?"

"All kinds. The best. I've been around the Quarry off and on since I was fifteen. When I go away they beg me, 'Emilia Ontiveros, come back, come back.' If I say no, they invent charges to force me to come back because I am such a fine cook. I am the head cook in the Quarry café."

That explained the scars. They were burns and cuts accumulated throughout the years.

"Do you have information about Harry Jenkins, Emilia?"

"He is a snake. That much I give you free. The rest will be more expensive."

"I'd like to talk to you. Isn't there some place we could have a little more privacy?"

"There's a talking room. It will cost you money, fifty cents. But a dollar would be better."

It was probably the primary law of the Quarry: a dollar was better than fifty cents but not as good as two dollars, which was vastly inferior to ten.

For a dollar they were given a couple of wooden stools in the corner of a room half filled with people, most of them in the fifty-cent, or standing, class. Emilia sat with her scarred hands clenched in her lap.

"A snake," she repeated. "Though you would never guess it to look at him. Such honest blue eyes, such even teeth."

"Do you know where he's living?"

"Ha! I have people keeping track of him every day, every minute. I know what clothes he wears, what he eats for breakfast. He can't buy a pack of cigarettes without me finding out. What a fool he was to think he could leave me cold after I paid good money for his release. When I leave this place again, I'm going to mash him like a turnip."

"I thought you intended to get married in the church."

"First I mash him like a turnip. *Then* we get married."

She was unmistakably serious. No matter where he was, Harry's future didn't look too bright.

"Marriage might improve my temper," she added thoughtfully. "I lose it at the stove, at the pots and pans, because they burn me. Then I throw them and they burn me again, and on it goes, back and forth. Do you think marriage has an improving effect?"

"Occasionally."

"How much are you planning to pay me?"

"You haven't told me anything useful yet."

"What do you want to know?"

"You said you and Jenkins served time together."

"That's how we met. These two Americans were brought in one day and as soon as I saw Harry my insides started spinning."

"The other American was Lockwood?"

Emilia nodded. "Him, what a crybaby, always fussing about this and that. The guards had to give him stuff to shut him down. Harry was a real man, pretending he didn't care what the authorities did to him or how long they kept him there."

"What was the charge against him?"

"Something silly like cheating. It's the custom. Somebody cheats you, you cheat somebody else."

"How did Jenkins get out?"

"Me. I had some money saved—the head cook's pay is pretty good and there's nothing pretty to spend it on in this place. When I finished serving my sentence I rented a nice apartment and then I went and paid Harry's fine and we set up housekeeping. For a while we had a rosy time. But my rosy times never last. As soon as the money ran out, so did Harry. Or tried to. I caught him packing and beat him up, not bad, just enough to put him in the hospital. He didn't squeal on me—he knew he had it coming—but the doctor at the hospital reported me to the police and they brought me back here to the Quarry. Everybody was glad to see me, of course, because my tamale pie is the best in town . . . How much are you going to pay me?"

"For telling me your tamale pie is the best in town? Nothing. It's not the kind of information that's worth anything to me."

"What kind do you want? You name it, it's yours. See, I'm saving up so I can buy my way out of this place and go back with Harry."

"And mash him like a turnip."

"Maybe not. Maybe my heart will melt when I see him again."

Aragon wouldn't have bet a nickel on it. Emilia's temper probably had a lower boiling point than her heart. "Is Jenkins still living in the apartment you rented?"

"How could he afford an apartment without my help? No, he has a little room over the shoemaker's shop, Reynoso's, on Avenida Gobernador. It's a low neighborhood, lots of thieves and prostitutes, but Harry hasn't anything to steal and the prostitutes don't bother him, because he's broke. How am I sure? My spies are here, there and everywhere, watching. Right this minute he is"—Emilia consulted a man's wristwatch which she fished out of the front of her dress—"sleeping. That's Harry for you. Everybody else running around working and Harry in bed snoring his head off."

"What does he do when he's not sleeping?"

"Hangs out at bars and cafés, especially the places where Americans go, El Domino, Las Balatas, El Alegre. He's not a drunk, liquor's not one of his weaknesses, he goes there on business."

"What kind of business?"

"Whatever he thinks of. He's very smart but he has bad luck. And tourists aren't as easy as they used to be in the old days when all he had to do was make up a few little stories. Expenses keep going up and up, and tourists keep getting more and more suspicious and stingy."

Aragon thought of the Hilton price he'd paid for the shack at Viñadaco and he wasn't surprised that the tourists were getting more wary of Harry's little stories.

He said, "What happened to Lockwood?"

"I don't know. Suddenly he left. That was long before I paid Harry's fine and got him out."

"Did he come back to visit Jenkins?"

"Why should he? They weren't friends, they were partners. He blamed Harry for leading him into trouble. How can you lead someone who doesn't want to go?"

"Did you notice whether Lockwood had any visitors?"

"There are always Americans shut up in this place, and the American consulate sends somebody over to check on them from time to time. Maybe it was one of the consulate that got Lockwood released."

"Did his case ever come to trial?"

"It was a single case, him and Harry together, when they were brought in. But when the magistrate finally heard it, there was just Harry. Lockwood had disappeared."

"Do you think he died?"

"A lot of people do," Emilia said philosophically. "He was an old man, anyway, more than fifty, always throwing up from his stomach."

"Didn't Jenkins try to find out what happened to him?"

"If he did he never told me. We had more interesting things to talk about in our rosy times. In the not-so-rosy we didn't speak to each other at all."

She repeated Jenkins' address, Avenida Gobernador above the shop of Reynoso the shoemaker. Aragon thanked her and gave her ten dollars. She didn't seem too pleased at the amount, but at least she didn't try to mash him like a turnip.

NINE

HE RETURNED TO the Hotel Castillo, stopping at the desk for his key and a map of the city, the kind which gas stations back home used to give away free. The map cost two dollars, the key was free. From his room he tried, for the second time that day, to put through a call to Gilly. All the lines were in use, on business, the *telefonista* implied, much more urgent than his.

Over lunch and beer at the hotel café he studied the map of Rio Seco. Avenida Gobernador was within walking distance and he would have liked to walk, both for exercise and to avoid the insanities of the city traffic. (One of the oddities of the automotive age was how such good-natured, slow-moving people could become irascible speed freaks behind the wheel of a car.) But the Avenida paralleled the course of the river for several miles and he had no way of knowing on what part of it Reynoso's shop was located. It was not in the telephone directory or on the hotel's list of shops and services.

He found out why when he reached it. It was hardly more than a hole in the wall on the edge of the red-light district where porno bars alternated with the rows of prostitutes' cubicles. The neighborhood was quiet and Reynoso's place closed. Sex as well as shoemakers took a siesta.

A boy about Pablo's age offered to watch his car to make sure nobody stole the hub caps and windshield wipers and radio antenna. "Hey, man, watch your car? One quarter for watching your car, man."

"Who's going to watch you?" Aragon said.

He meant it as a joke but the boy took it seriously. "My brother José. He's working the other side of the street."

"Why aren't you in school?"

"It's a holiday."

"What holiday?"

"I don't know. Somebody just told me, 'Hey, man, you don't got to go to school today, it's a holiday.' Watch your car for a quarter?"

"All right."

He paid the money. The boy climbed on the hood of the car, leaned back against the windshield and lit the butt of a cigar he'd picked up from the road.

Aragon said, "You watch cars around here all the time?"

"Sure, man."

"I bet you know a lot of people in the neighborhood."

"I got eyes, don't I?"

"I'm looking for an American named Harry Jenkins. I was told he lives in a room above Reynoso's."

"Whoever told you's got eyes, too. That's where he lives, Harry Jenkins. Some cheapskate. Never gave me a dime."

"Reynoso's shop is closed."

"Yeah, I know."

"For one of the dimes Jenkins never gave you, will you tell me how I can get up to his room?"

"You a hustler, man?"

"Let's just say that the members of my profession are sometimes called hustlers."

"Yeah? Okay, then. There's an alley four, five doors down, takes you straight to Reynoso's outside stairs."

The boy pocketed the dime and settled back against the windshield to enjoy the final inch of the cigar.

Jenkins' door was locked. When Aragon knocked on it, it felt flimsy as though it would collapse like cardboard if he leaned against it too heavily. He wrote a note and pushed it underneath the door:

Mr. Jenkins:

I am offering a fair price for any information you might have about B. J. Lockwood. If you are interested, please contact me at the Hotel Castillo.

T. C. Aragon

He returned to the hotel and tried for the third time to put through a call to Gilly. The *telefonista* must have had a refreshing siesta, she sounded almost human: "You wish to speak personally to Mrs. Marco Decker, is that correct?"

"Yes."

"I may have a line for you now. Hold on."

After about five minutes of back-and-forth chatter in two languages, a man answered the phone. "Hello." A certain note of petulance in the man's tone identified him as Reed Robertson, Marco Decker's nurse.

"I have a person-to-person call for Mrs. Marco Decker. Is Mrs. Decker there?"

"Hold on." Reed raised the pitch of his voice about an octave. "This is Mrs. Decker, operator. I'll take the call."

"Your party is on the line, sir. Go ahead."

"Hello, Reed."

"That you, Aragon?"

"Yes."

"She's in the pool. Violet Smith just took her out a robe, so she'll be here in a minute. Listen, amigo, she's burned up because she hasn't heard from you."

"She burns easy. It's only Monday."

"Any trace of B. J.?"

" 'Trace' just about covers it. I found his ex-partner, though."

"Harry Jenkins."

"I gather Mrs. Decker has confided in you."

"The old girl has to talk to somebody. It was a toss-up between me and Violet Smith. I won. If you want to call it winning."

"What do you call it?"

"I call it a living," Reed said. "Speaking of living, where's Jenkins doing his, in some castle in the sky?"

"Over Reynoso's shoemaking shop on Avenida Gobernador. I might say he's on his uppers if I went in for bad puns."

"So Jenlock Haciendas never got off the ground."

"No. All the other news is bad, too."

"How bad?"

Gilly came on the line. "Aragon? What's this about bad? Have you found B. J.?"

41

"No."

"That's not exactly bad, is it? I mean, it's just nothing. How is that bad?"

"B. J. seems to have disappeared."

"From where?"

"The jail in Rio Seco."

"Did you say *jail*?"

"Yes."

"What was he doing in jail?"

"Like all the others in there, he was waiting to get out."

"Don't get sharp with me, dammit."

"I'm trying not to," Aragon said. "I don't like delivering news like this any more than you like receiving it."

"Why was he sent to jail? B. J. wouldn't hurt a fly."

"Flies don't invest money in real estate developments. People do, and when they discover they've been swindled they complain to the police. B. J. and Jenkins were picked up in Bahía de Ballenas. While they were waiting trial B. J. disappeared. One of the other inmates told me he'd been ill and upset and the guards had to give him stuff to calm him down. 'Stuff' was the word used. It could have been anything."

"Oh God, poor B. J."

She began to cry. Aragon could hear Reed trying to soothe her: *Buck up, old girl. Stop it now. Here, here's a drink. That's a good girl . . .*

When things quieted down, Aragon continued, "I may get more information tonight or tomorrow. I haven't talked to Harry Jenkins, but I found out where he's living and left a note for him."

"Left a *note*? You should have waited for him, camped on his doorstep if necessary."

"He didn't have a doorstep. He didn't even have much of a door."

"Give me his phone number. I want to talk to him myself."

"I guess I'm not getting through to you, Mrs. Decker. Jenkins is broke. That's the main reason I expect to hear from him. I offered him money for information about B. J."

There was a long interval of silence. Then, "Where's the girl, Tula?"

"I have no recent news about her. When the two men were arrested she went with them to Rio Seco. The word is that she wanted to get away from Bahía de Ballenas and the child, too."

"Away from her own child?"

"He's retarded as well as crippled, Mrs. Decker . . . Now don't start crying again. The boy's safe, he's being looked after by relatives. Mexican families are very close-knit, as I mentioned to you before, and retarded children aren't considered undesirable."

"Have you nothing decent, nothing pleasant to tell me?"

"I think it's both decent and pleasant that Pablo is being taken care of. He's luckier in many ways than his American cousins."

"How long ago did they leave him there?"

"Four years. He's eight now, chronologically. Mentally, perhaps three. There is no way he could fit into your life, Mrs. Decker."

"I never thought he could," she said quietly. "I just hoped a little bit. If it were only a matter of his being crippled, I could have paid for doctors, operations . . . Now, of course, I realize that it's impossible. I wish I'd never been told of his existence. Maybe B. J. told me deliberately to rouse my sympathy so I'd send him the money he asked for. If I could believe that, it would make it easier for me to accept—what I'm afraid you're going to find out."

"Which is?"

"That he's dead, he died in jail and they dragged him out and buried him like a common criminal." He heard her take a long deep breath as if to regain control of herself. "Okay, all the news is bad so far. What's the next step?"

"I'll talk to Jenkins."

"Suppose he doesn't know anything?"

"Then I'd better quit wasting your money and come home."

"Call me after you've seen him. And thanks, by the way, for leveling with me, even though I didn't like it. The truth hurts... I wonder who first discovered that."

"Probably Adam."

"The little boy, does he seem happy?"

"He seems not unhappy. He gets affection and enough food to eat, and he has children to play with who aren't much more advantaged than he is. You could present a bigger problem to him than any he has now, Mrs. Decker."

"Yes, I see. It was really stupid of me after all this time to get the idea that—well, anyway, thanks again. And call me."

"I will."

She hung up. Reed was leaning against the wall with his arms crossed on his chest, watching her. She had never realized before what cruel little eyes he had. They didn't match the rest of his face, which smiled a lot.

"You were practically screaming at one point," Reed said. "Women should learn to modulate their voices."

"Why?"

"So people will assume they're ladies. Also to make it harder for eavesdroppers like Violet Smith to hear everything. Violet Smith is ninety-eight percent ears and mouth and two percent common sense. She could be dangerous."

"I didn't say anything she can't broadcast to the world if she wants to."

"Fear not, she'll want to. Wait until the next show-and-tell meeting at her church—you and B. J. will be the star attractions, with the kid thrown in for a touch of pathos. By the way, you're not fooling me for a minute. And if Aragon weren't such a boy scout, you wouldn't be fooling him, either."

"How am I trying to fool anyone?"

"The kid. You wouldn't touch him with a ten-foot pole even if he had a perfect physique and an IQ of a hundred and fifty."

"You're malicious, you're really malicious."

"That's why we get along so well. Malice is something we both understand. Now, Violet Smith isn't malicious. She's just dumb and self-righteous, which is a lot harder to cope with. You'd better go and have a talk with her right now. Lay it on the line but keep it light, casual. Don't let on that it matters too much."

"*You're* giving *me* orders?"

"Suggestions."

"They sounded like orders."

"No, my orders sound quite different," Reed said. "You may find that out."

The cleaning woman and day maid had left and Violet Smith was alone in the kitchen, cooking dinner and watching T. V.

"Turn that thing off," Gilly said.

"I'm in the middle of a murder."

"Turn it off."

"My stars, you needn't shout. I didn't know this was top priority."

"You do now."

Violet Smith turned off the set, grumbling. "My programs are always being interrupted, phones ringing, Mr. Decker buzzing—"

"Speaking of phones, did you listen in on the extension to my conversation with Mr. Aragon?"

"I told you, I'm in the middle of a murder, which is a heap more interesting than anything Mr. Aragon has to say."

"Answer the question. Did you listen in?"

"No. Honest injun, though I'm not supposed to say that. It's ethnic. I heard all about ethnic from a black man at church. People shouldn't use ethnic expressions like 'eeny meeny miney mo, catch a nigger by the toe,' or—"

"At these church meetings of yours, what do you talk about when it's your turn?"

"My life."

"Including the part of it that takes place here?"

"Here it's your life, not mine."

"Then you wouldn't mention my personal affairs in front of the group?"

"No."

"That's good. Because what goes on in this house is my own business and I don't care to have any of it repeated in the name of the Lord or soul cleansing or mental health or any damn thing at all. Understand?"

Violet Smith stood mute as marble.

"Do you understand?"

"I'd like to get back to my murder now, if you don't mind."

"Do that."

"Thank you," said Violet Smith.

She waited until she heard Gilly go down the hall and open the door of her husband's room. Then she picked up the phone and dialed the number she had just checked in the directory. The voice that answered was one Violet Smith greatly admired, so soft and sweet and the opposite of Gilly's.

"Hello?"

"Is that Mrs. Lockwood?"

"Yes. Who's this?"

"Violet Smith, your friend from church."

"Oh, of course."

"You said you'd like me to come over sometime for a little chat."

"Yes."

"Well, I think this is the time, Mrs. Lockwood."

It took Marco an hour to eat a meal that would hardly have nourished a sparrow.

Sometimes Gilly sat with him in silence, feeding him his sparrow-sized bites and watching him chew so slowly and awkwardly that she felt her own teeth grinding in frustration. Sometimes she turned on the T. V., which Marco didn't like because he had trouble seeing with only one functioning eye; and sometimes she just talked, dipping into the present or cutting up the past into small digestible pieces.

Consciously or not, she left out a few things about her past and added a few. In the main, though, it was pretty straight talk. During the months of her husband's illness she'd covered a great many of her fifty years, but more and more her conversation was about those she'd spent with B. J. For the past week it had been almost exclusively about B. J. She talked of falling in love with him right away, bingo, at first sight. She never believed such a thing could happen, to her of all people. He wasn't much to look at, he had no line of fast talk, he couldn't play games or dance very well or any of the things that might draw a woman's attention. And he was married. Happily married, or so his wife claimed when she came to Gilly and told her to leave him alone. Leave him alone. How could she? As long as B. J. was alive in this world she could never have left him alone.

The sick man listened. He had no way of stopping her except by going to sleep or pretending to, and he seldom did either. Gilly had such an impassioned way of talking that she could make a visit from the plumber sound like an earthshaking event. Gilly's plumber wouldn't be handsome or witty or charming, but he would have an indefinable irresistible something. She couldn't bear to let him go—but at twenty bucks an hour she had to.

"I'm giving Reed a few days off," she said. "He's getting restless and bossy, he needs a change. I've put in a call for a substitute nurse. I'll ask for two if you think you need them."

The forefinger of his right hand moved. *One would be enough.*

"Just one then. We can manage. I usually give you your shots, anyway. Do you need another right now or can you wait?"

Now.

She was very expert at it, better than Reed, who was inclined to hurry, as though he had a ward full of patients waiting for him.

"There. That will help you chew. Let's try the fish. It might be better tonight. I asked Violet Smith to pour a lot of booze on it . . . When Reed gets like this, you know, sort of pushy and insolent, a little holiday snaps him back . . . B. J. and I were going on a holiday when— But I've bored you with that story a dozen times, haven't I?"

Yes.

"I went out and bought this marvelous motor home as a surprise for his birthday so the two of us could drive up to British Columbia, where my folks came from. I called it Dreamboat and I had the name printed on it as a custom touch. Well, you know what happened, don't you? B. J. added a custom touch of his own. Tula her name was, not as pretty as Dreamboat. Neither was she. All I can really remember about her is a lot of black bushy hair and greasy skin. Oh yes, and her fingernails. She kept them painted bright-red but her hands were always grimy. How she got to B. J. I don't know. The why was easy enough. She was hungry. She wanted to live like in the movies and there was only one way to do it. So she did it. In the end she lost him, too, not to another woman but to a con man named Harry Jenkins, can you beat it?"

No, he couldn't beat it, or tie it, or come close. He could only listen.

"It's funny when you think about it—Henry Jenkins took B. J. from Tula the way she took him from me and I took him from Ethel. We just sort of passed him along from one to another like a used car. Even Ethel, Ethel the Good, she probably took him from somebody else. There was always someone waiting, wanting to use B. J. Where did it all start? The day he was born, the day the car came off the assembly line . . . Come on, try the mashed potatoes. Violet Smith makes them with real cream."

He wouldn't. She didn't.

"I think B. J.'s real weakness was the way he had of living completely in the present, never looking back to learn from experience, never looking ahead to see consequences. Somebody like Harry Jenkins could have picked him out of a crowd in half a minute. By the way, Aragon has found out where Jenkins is living in Rio Seco. He'll be talking to him tonight or tomorrow. The trail's getting really hot now. Isn't that exciting? Aren't you excited?"

I am afraid.

He stopped chewing. He refused to swallow. He closed his eye.

10

ABOUT THE TIME Aragon would be thinking of going to bed back home, Rio Seco was just opening up for the night. From the window of his hotel room he watched the street below. There were crowds of people, including whole families, in the cafés and markets and in a long line in front of the cinema. The curio and art dealers, the silversmiths and street vendors and sandal makers were starting the real business of the day.

Except for an hour off for dinner, Aragon had spent the evening waiting to hear from Harry Jenkins. He'd written a long letter to his wife and a short note to Smedler. He read the evening paper, *La Diaria,* and twice he went down to the desk to ask for messages. There were none. A third time he went down for a can of insecticide to get rid of the mosquitoes. What might have been an unusual request in most hotels was taken for granted at the Castillo. The insecticide was provided by the night clerk free of charge. "We have this problem with the bugs, sir. When we kill them, they come back. When we don't kill them, they don't go away."

"I understand."

The clerk looked surprised. "You do?"

"I'm a lawyer."

"That's it, then. Lawyers understand everything, even bugs, yes?"

"Especially bugs," Aragon said. "Good night."

He sprayed the room until the mosquitoes were all dead. Then he had to open the window to get rid of the fumes, and a whole new swarm of mosquitoes entered. He settled down with some beer to match them, pint for pint. For every pint they took from him, he drank a pint to replace the fluid.

The din from the street below increased in volume. He almost missed hearing the knock on his door shortly after midnight.

He unlocked the door. "Mr. Jenkins?"

"That's me, Harry Jenkins."

"I'm Tom Aragon. Come in, won't you?"

"Don't mind if I do, seeing as you offered some reimbursement for my time and trouble. That's correct, isn't it?"

"Yes."

Jenkins closed the door behind him. He was a small thin man in his mid-forties, dressed in a dark-blue suit frayed at the cuffs and so shiny across the seat of his pants that he looked as though he'd slipped in a pool of melted wax. "So you want to talk about B. J., right?"

"No. I want you to talk about him."

"Same difference, like they say. After I read your note I sat me down to do some thinking. Here's how it came out. One of B. J.'s old big-shot friends got a pang of conscience for not helping him out before and now he, or she, wants to buy a little peace of mind."

"Go on."

"Any damn fool knows that that's the only piece of something not for sale in the world. So I figure it has to be a she, since they don't go by the rules of reason. The question is, 'What she?' "

"I thought the question was, 'How much do you know and what is it worth?' "

"You have yourself a point there, laddie."

Jenkins moved quickly and gracefully across the room, balancing on the balls of his feet like a featherweight boxer between punches. Everything about him seemed to be in motion except his eyes. They had no more life in them than patches of grey suede.

"If you read my note this afternoon," Aragon said, "what took you so long to get here?"

"A place like this cramps my style. I don't even have the clothes for it. I had to borrow the suit from a friend. It's not much of a suit, but then, he's not much of a friend, either."

"Clothes don't matter much anymore."

"They do in my business."

"What's your business, Mr. Jenkins?"

"It varies. Right now things are slow, but I'm tossing a few ideas back and forth." He smoothed his thinning hair across the bald spot on top of his head as if to protect the source of the ideas. "I can't work at an ordinary job. Don't have the stomach for it. Or the papers. The immigration boys are a nervous bunch. One little mistake and they jump you."

"Jenlock Haciendas was more than a little mistake, wouldn't you say?"

"I'd be the first to say it. I got in over my head. My other business ventures are less ambitious."

"Sit down, will you?"

"Thanks."

"Join me in a beer?"

"Might as well, I guess." Jenkins stood at the window looking down at the street. "I'd like to get out of this crappy town."

"Why don't you?"

"There was a little episode in Albuquerque and maybe a couple of other places. Not everybody shares my philosophy of forgive and forget . . . How'd you track me down, anyway?"

"Went to the Quarry and hired a shouter. One of the inmates came over to talk to me."

"Emilia."

"Yes."

"What'd she tell you?"

"That when she's released she's going to mash you like a turnip."

"She will, too," Jenkins said gloomily. "Unless I get out before she does. I always had a weakness for fiery women, but now I think I'm over it." He took a sip of beer, grimacing, as though the stuff had the bitter taste of regrets. "I have to shake this town. The cops, the immigration boys, Emilia's relatives—I can't walk around the block without being hassled. My only chance is meeting up with a well-heeled sucker at one of the American bars. Funny how Americans who wouldn't give each other the time of day in Chicago or Louisville become bosom pals over a couple of drinks at the Domino Club. Well, all I need is the right bosom." Jenkins turned and studied Aragon carefully for a moment. "It's too bad we know each other. It cramps my style. I prefer to deal with strangers."

"I bet you do."

"Friends are murder in this business . . . I wouldn't mind another beer if you were offering any, laddie."

"I'm offering." Aragon opened another can. "How did you get mixed up in something as big as the Jenlock Haciendas project?"

"Innocent-like. I mean, I didn't walk into it. I just stood there and it grew up around me."

"Is that what you told the magistrate?"

"I tried to. My Spanish isn't too good. Maybe he didn't understand me."

"Or maybe he did."

"It was true, so help me. I'd been hearing plenty of talk about how Baja was due for a big boom as soon as the new highway was finished. I borrowed some money, rented a jeep and went down to have a look-see. Well, the boom's on now and it's big, so I was right about that. The wrong part was the location and B. J. . . . . To this day I don't know how I managed to get lost. But I did. And that's how I arrived at Bahía de Ballenas. Ever hear of it?"

"I've heard of it."

"Well, there was B. J., living in a super-deluxe motor home and looking like money. A bunch of money. It went to my head. No drink ever invented could go to my head like that. It wasn't like getting drunk alone and sleeping it off. B. J. stayed right with me. Every idea I came up with, he came up with an improvement. Then I improved on the improvement, until finally there it was, Jenlock Haciendas, bigger than both of us. I didn't have sense enough to be scared. I was not only out of my league, I didn't even know what game I was playing."

"It's called fraud."

"Wouldn't have mattered, anyway. Me, Harry Jenkins, who never wrote on anything he didn't swipe from a hotel lobby, suddenly had his name on a fancy letterhead. Me, who never had more than a couple of hundred bucks in his pocket, was suddenly throwing money around like there was no tomorrow. It was the longest drunk a man's ever been on—and not a drop of liquor, so to speak."

"What sobered you up?"

"Tomorrow," Jenkins said. "Tomorrow came. If it was the longest drunk, it sure as hell brought the biggest hangover. I won't be over it until I get out of this place."

"Where's B. J. now?"

"I don't know."

"Take a guess."

"I'm a lousy guesser. Look at my record."

"Try."

"I kind of guess he's dead."

"Why?"

"Some people make out okay in the Quarry but B. J. wasn't the type. First off, he was the wrong nationality. He kept demanding his rights and bail and habeas corpus and a bunch of stuff they never heard of in this country and wouldn't care if they had. Second off, he was a rich boy, spoiled rotten. He never had anything but the best all his life, and suddenly there he was with nothing but the worst. There we *both* were, only with me it didn't matter so much. If sheepshead is all they give me to eat—hell, I eat it. B. J. threw up just looking at it. Oversensitive he was, and then some. Bled like a stuck pig if he got the slightest scratch. And scratch he did, laddie, scratch he did. The mosquitoes had a banquet on him every night. You could hear them flying around laughing as soon as the sun went down. Call it buzzing, humming, hissing, whatever. Down here they laugh." He added with a touch of nostalgia, "One thing you could say about Jenlock Haciendas, we never had any mosquitoes there."

"Why not?"

"No water. Tons of sea water but no drink water."

"You should have thought of that before you started thinking of building a bunch of haciendas."

"Oh, we did. B. J. said it was no problem. All we had to do was build a desalinization plant to take the salt out of the sea water. He put up the money, and I mean large money. He wanted the best. Me, I never heard of a desalinization plant before, but by God, suddenly there I was with the wherewithal, so I started building one. You know what I'd do if I had it to do all over again, laddie?"

"Tell me."

"I'd take every penny and lam out of there. Nasty, you say? Not a bit of it. I would have been doing both of us a favor, like putting a plug in a sink where a heap of money was going down the drain. Down the drain, that's how it was. Before you could say 'desalinization,' things began going wrong. The boom started and the price of everything doubled, tripled, quadrupled. Supplies had to come by boat, and mostly they didn't. Work crews had to be trucked in, and so did water. Maybe one arrived, maybe the other, maybe neither. And all the time the government was making up new rules about building on the coast. Boy, I wouldn't go through that again for a million dollars." He added wistfully, "Which is roughly what I expected to make."

"That much."

"I told you, I was drunk, crazy drunk, without touching a drop. Well, at least I didn't lose much except time. B. J. lost everything, shirt, pants and shoelaces. Funny about that man. He must have been over fifty then, but I swear he was like a five-year-old kid believing in everything, Santa Claus, the Easter bunny, the tooth fairy."

"I don't see you as a tooth fairy, Jenkins, though you'd be pretty good at extractions."

Jenkins made a small sound like a mosquito's laugh. "So I didn't fit the role. Well, I never asked for it, either. I got sucked into somebody else's dream. B. J. really *believed* in Jenlock Haciendas. In his mind's eye the whole project was built and operating, the haciendas occupied, people playing on the golf course, swimming in the pool, sailing around the marina, even flushing their toilets. Sure, they sent both of us to jail for fraud, but with B. J. there actually was no fraud, just a big fat dumb dream . . . Well, that's all over now and good riddance." For the first time since he entered the room, Jenkins' eyes brightened. "I've been thinking, if I could lay my hands on enough cash, I'd open up a fried chicken business here. Quality stuff only, both table and takeout service."

"I don't think you have the beard for it, Jenkins."

"You may be missing out on a fortune. Mexicans are crazy about chicken and if we coated it with corn meal it would be sort of like a chicken tortilla. Roll that around on your tongue. Savor it. How does it taste?"

"It tastes like one of the residents of Jenlock Haciendas just tried to flush his toilet."

"Hell, you probably don't have the money, anyway. That's a cheap suit you're wearing."

"J. C. Penney's."

"You got to think bigger than J. C. Penney's, laddie. With a well-tailored suit you could make a pretty good appearance, sort of the ambitious but honest type."

"Thanks. I'll try it someday."

"Nothing too extreme, remember. People distrust extremities. One of my own weaknesses was Hawaiian shirts. I should have known better. Who's going to trust a man in a Hawaiian shirt with anything but a ukulele concession? Nobody. Not even B. J."

"Would you like another beer?"

"I better be moseying along to the Domino Club or El Alegre. This is the best time of night for new contacts."

"Suckers."

Jenkins shrugged. "Same difference. I got to live, don't I? And if the tourists didn't have money to spare they wouldn't be here, so it's not like robbing orphans and widows . . . Oh hell, let the suckers wait. One more beer would be nice considering how we're down to brass tacks, you and me. I don't often get to the brass-tacks stage with people. I hope it doesn't become a habit."

"I don't think you have to worry."

The third beer increased Jenkins' spirit of camaraderie. "Laddie me lad, what do you want to know? Name it. What's mine is yours—for a small stipend, of course."

"So you think B. J. died in jail."

"He was a sick man, I told you. Cried a lot, couldn't eat, shriveled up like a prune. The guards kept him pretty well doped so he'd be quiet and wouldn't bother anyone."

"Suppose he didn't die but simply served his time and was released. Where would he be likely to go?"

"If he didn't have a habit, back to Bahía de Ballenas, maybe. Only he had a habit, a big one. You can't feed a habit by holing up in a little Mexican village. You got to get out and fight, hustle, beg, steal. Poor B. J. He was soft as a marshmallow; none of that would come natural to him."

"Perhaps he had someone who'd do it for him."

"You mean Tula?"

"It's possible, isn't it?"

"Oh, she could do it, all right. She was hustling a couple of weeks after she hit town. But I doubt that a nickel of the money she picked up went to B. J. She was a taker, not a giver."

"Why do you say *was*?"

"I don't know whether she *is* or not. So to me she's *was* until I find out for sure."

"Can you find out?"

"Maybe. I never tried. Me and Tula weren't real buddy-buddy. Know what she used to call me? Uncle Harry. Me, half a dozen years younger than her husband and still in the prime, so to speak."

"What was her attitude toward B. J.?"

"As long as the money held out, she put on a show of affection. She even came to see him in jail a few times for what they call in polite society 'connubial privileges.' That's probably where she got the idea of taking up the work professionally. On visiting days the hustlers flock around the jail like starlings. Tula just naturally followed the flock. There wasn't much else she was prepared to do, she couldn't read or write. I used to see her once in a while, all gussied up hanging around the cheap bars. She pretended not to recognize me. Good old Uncle Harry found himself de-uncled."

"You don't think she might have paid B. J.'s fine, or put up bail or bribe money?"

"Not in a million years would be my guess. But what's that worth? Women are not reasonable creatures, so how can a reasonable man like me tell what they're going to do?"

"Let's assume," Aragon said, "that Tula is still in town and you have the right connections for finding her."

"Consider it assumed. And then?"

"I'd like to ask her some questions. Given enough time, I might be able to find her myself. But I don't know the city, what name she's using, where her hangouts are, or even what she looks like."

"So how much is it worth to you if I ask around?"

"Two hundred dollars."

Jenkins ran an expert eye up and down the J. C. Penney suit, the Sears, Roebuck shirt and the orange birthday tie from his cousin Sandoval, who was color-blind.

"You can't afford that kind of money, laddie, unless the job is real important. Two hundred is pretty small potatoes for something real important. Let's raise the ante to three hundred, fifty in advance."

The deal was settled at $250. Gilly might squawk, but Aragon had the feeling that if she and Jenkins ever met, at the Domino Club or El Alegre, they would understand each other immediately.

Jenkins put the bills Aragon gave him in his coat pocket. "I could walk out of here with this fifty and you might never see me again. Did that occur to you?"

"Certainly. You won't do it, though. You need the rest of the money to help you get out of town. There's Emilia and the turnip mashing, remember?"

"Hell, how could I forget. One of those relatives of hers is probably standing right outside the hotel this very minute waiting for me to come out. It's not fair. Me, I don't have a relative in the world unless it's a kid some place where I got careless . . . Did you know B. J. and Tula had a kid?"

"I've heard of him."

"Crazy as a coot. Makes funny noises."

"We all make funny noises. Some may be just a little funnier."

"Is that philosophy or bullshit, laddie?"

"A little of both."

"No matter. I try to avoid stepping in either." Jenkins stood up. He was unsteady on his feet, and small round patches of red had appeared at the tip of his nose and on both cheekbones like the make-up of a circus clown. "I'd better start to work. That two fifty ought to set me up in Mexicali. Mexicali's full of tourists, it'll be a gold mine."

"Stay out of real estate."

"Oh, I can't truly regret Jenlock Haciendas. It was a great place while it lasted." It sounded like a fitting epitaph.

Aragon said, "Suppose you come back here tomorrow night and give me a progress report."

"If that's how you want it."

"I'll be waiting for you. Good night, Jenkins."

"I have a nice feeling about you, laddie. You're going to bring me luck."

11

TWENTY-FOUR HOURS later Aragon was still waiting in his hotel room to hear from Harry Jenkins. It was after eleven when the phone finally rang.

"It's me, laddie."

"Where are you?"

"Never mind about that. Listen, I said you were going to bring me luck, and by God, you did. I met this pigeon. He came down to Mexico to scout around for investment opportunities and I happen to have one for him. Me."

"I've already invested in you, fifty bucks, two hundred more coming. I'm expecting a report."

"All in good time. This other matter is more urgent. The pigeon's due to leave town pretty soon and I'm trying to nail him down."

"What are you nailing him to?"

"The chicken tortilla business. He thinks it's a winner."

"How many drinks has he had?"

"That's not a nice implication," Jenkins said reproachfully. "But I won't hold a grudge. Maybe you got something against chickens, maybe you just lack financial vision."

"Did you find Tula?"

"I'm on her heels. By tomorrow night I'll be able to take you straight to her."

"Why not tonight?"

"I told you, tonight I'm involved in a new business venture."

"Where are you?"

"Now, why do you want to know that?"

"Because wherever it is, I'm coming. I want to protect my investment."

"Oh hell, laddie, don't do that. You'll blow it for me. This may be my chance of a lifetime. He's fat and juicy and ready for plucking."

"Let's get back to Tula."

"Sure, sure, whatever you say. Only I'm in kind of a hurry."

"I think you're bulling me," Aragon said. "You already know where the girl is, don't you?"

"Even if I told you, you couldn't find her. It's not like she has an ordinary job with a real address and maybe even a telephone. Looking for customers while dodging the police, that takes moving around, see?"

"Where are you, Jenkins?"

"I asked you not to press me, laddie," Jenkins said and hung up.

Aragon put the phone back on the hook. It was late and he was tired. He would have liked to go to bed and forget about Jenkins for the night, but the conversation had made him uneasy on two counts. The first was the possibility that if Jenkins plucked enough feathers out of his new pigeon, he wouldn't wait around town for Gilly's extra two hundred. He'd be in Mexicali by morning.

The second possibility was in a sense more disturbing. Rich, drunk, gullible tourists were not uncommon in Rio Seco, but the fact that Jenkins found one so quickly and easily was suspicious. Nobody was easier to con than a con man, and Jenkins would be easier than most. He seemed to have the same kind of basic innocence he'd criticized in B. J. If B. J. believed in Santa Claus and the tooth fairy, Jenkins believed in rainbows with pots of gold. The only thing that would protect him from being taken was that he had nothing much to take, only the fifty dollars he'd received in advance for locating Tula.

Aragon was almost certain that Jenkins had found out where the girl lived and that the reason he'd refused to give more information over the phone was his fear of not being paid the extra two hundred. For someone in Jenkins' position it was a natural enough fear. He'd probably cheated and been cheated hundreds of times. Now that he had something real to sell he would deliver it in person, for cash and in his own time. Meanwhile, some half-soused American tourist was hearing a lot about chicken tortillas.

As he put on his coat and tie Aragon thought back over the conversation. Jenkins had not, in fact, mentioned the word "American," only a pigeon ready for plucking. The pigeon could be an Eskimo or an Algerian, but the odds were against it. Emilia had named three places as Jenkins' favorite hangouts because they catered to American tourists, and Jenkins had referred to two of them the previous night, El Alegre and the Domino Club.

Aragon combed his hair and straightened his tie in front of the bureau mirror. "You're going out on the town, laddie."

El Alegre was in a new section of town that was already beginning to look old and in another few years would be just another addition to the slums. Right now business was booming. A fleet of taxicabs was double-parked outside the entrance vying with each other for the attention of the hustlers. Jenkins had compared the girls hanging around outside the jail to a flock of starlings. That was how they looked now as they gathered on the sidewalk in front of the club, like starlings getting ready to roost for the night, twittering, fluttering, fidgeting, grumbling.

A teenager wearing a high-rise platinum wig and four-inch cork wedgies attached herself to Aragon's coat sleeve and spoke to him in English. "Hey, gringo, you and me make fun. What kind of fun? You name it. You tiger, me pussycat, me tiger, you pussycat."

"I'm here on business."

"Okey-dokey, we do business."

"No thank you."

"No okey-dokey?"

"No okey-dokey."

"Son a bitch cheapskate." She returned to the flock, twitching her tail and smoothing her ruffled feathers. She was about fifteen, the age Tula had been when she'd gone to work as a maid in Gilly's house.

Aragon looked over the girl's companions, wondering if Tula was one of them. No, they were all too young. Tula would be twenty-three by now, young by the standards of an ordinary middle-class American, old for a prostitute in Rio Seco.

"Hey, gringo, lotsa fun. Play games. Hot stuff."

The Domino Club was on the other side of the bridge crossing the seasonally dry river that gave the city its name. It was October and the rainy season was late starting. The *rio* was *seco* after months of drought, just as the wells in the higher sections of the city were drying up and those nearer the sea were turning to salt.

In earlier days a narrow wooden bridge had divided the slums and squatters from the residential areas of the more prosperous merchants and professional men. With the building of the new bridge over the new concrete lining of the riverbed, the two sections of town were becoming indistinguishable. Thousands of cars and pedestrians crossed the steel arch every day. The wealthier citizens resented the intrusion and escaped to the hills and the privacy of iron gates and chain-link fences. Their deserted houses were torn down for apartments or rebuilt into stores or night clubs like the Domino.

Several coats of black paint decorated with white polka dots, a black-and-white marquee topped by a neon sign indicated that the Domino catered to a better class of clientele than El Alegre. A uniformed doorman kept the hustlers on the opposite side of the street, the taxicabs in single file and the cigarette butts swept into the gutter. Otherwise things were much the same, including the fact that Harry Jenkins wasn't in sight.

Aragon was on the point of leaving when he noticed a small man in a blue suit slumped over the table in the end booth. He thought of Emilia at the jail talking about Jenkins: *He's not a drunk, liquor's not one of his weaknesses.*

Tonight was the exception. Jenkins reeked of whiskey as though he'd spilled it all over himself. His head lay sideways on the table at an awkward angle looking detached from the rest of his body. Though his eyes were open, they were as unfocused and unblinking as a dead man's. One of his hands was curled around an empty bottle of beer.

"Jenkins? Hey, are you all right?"

Jenkins' mouth moved in response to his name, but the only thing to come out of it were some bubbles of saliva that slid down his chin. Aragon took out his handkerchief and attempted to wipe off the saliva. Jenkins' whole face, his hair, his shirt and tie, even the shoulders of his suit coat were soaking wet. Instead of merely spilling some whiskey on himself, he seemed to have been the target of a whole glass of it, as though someone had thrown it at him in a rage.

"Jenkins, can you hear me?"

He moaned.

"What happened to you? Are you sick?"

One of the bartenders came over, a young man with a moist red face like underdone beef. He spoke English with a New York accent. "This a friend of yours?"

"I know him."

"That's good enough. Get him out of here. I don't want him puking up the place."

"I think he's sick."

"I don't care why he's doing it, just let him do it some other place."

"Help me lift him and I'll put him in a cab."

"I got a hernia."

"How can you have a hernia when you're all heart?"

"Just lucky, I guess. Use the back door."

Aragon managed to get his hands under Jenkins' armpits and pull him to his feet. "Come on, Jenkins, wake up. Wake up and see the birdie."

"Chicken birdie?"

"Chicken birdie it is. Can you walk?"

"I can *fly*."

"Good. Let's fly home to roost."

Jenkins' eyes were coming back into focus. The pupils were so dilated that only a tiny rim of iris was left around them. He stood up, holding on to the table for support. "Who—are you?"

"I'm laddie. Remember?"

"Oh, I feel funny, laddie—help me, help."

"You'll be all right. Come along."

They walked arm in arm with a kind of awkward dignity out the back door and into a dimly lit area that had once been somebody's walled garden. A water-boy fountain, the pitcher on his shoulder long since dry, stood in the middle of dusty dying weeds. The only living relic of the garden was a half-naked tamarisk tree.

Aragon put the sick man down on the concrete bench that circled the fountain. Jenkins' forehead was hot and the pulse in his throat very rapid and irregular.

"Listen now, Jenkins. Wait here and I'll go line up a taxi and come back for you. Have you got that? I'm coming back for you, so *wait here.* Do you understand me?"

It was apparent even in the dim light that Jenkins was incapable of understanding. His eyes had glazed over, vomit was bubbling down both sides of his mouth, and he was alternately chewing and spitting out chunks of sentences. His symptoms didn't fit those of an ordinary drunk. He'd had a few moments of lucidity when his speech was clear and unslurred, and he recognized Aragon as a friend. Now he seemed to have slipped once again into a state of delirium.

"Big bird, fly me golden . . . help B. J., he's sick . . . must go home . . . takeout and delivery . . . fry me to the moon, Emilia . . . bad bird boy . . . where are you, laddie? Get me a drink. Water. *Water.*"

"I'm right here. I'm going away for a few minutes, then I'm coming back to take you home. Are you listening, Jenkins? You stay where you are. Don't move. I'm going for help."

"Where's laddie? Water. Drink."

Jenkins reached out and clutched the marble water boy with both hands. Aragon left him like that, hanging on to the statue as if it were still pouring out the stuff of life.

Aragon returned through the bar to the front of the building. He gave one of the taxi drivers waiting at the curb five dollars to come and help him with Jenkins. The two men were just starting toward the club when Jenkins himself came staggering out through the front door, his head lowered as if he were about to charge some unseen unknown enemy.

Aragon shouted at him, "Jenkins, wait for me. Hey, hold it!"

Jenkins turned and began running toward the bridge, dodging between pedestrians and around passing cars. He was small and agile, and whatever illness he was suffering from hadn't affected his speed. By the time he reached the bridge he was ahead of Aragon by a hundred yards or more. He started to cross the bridge, his arms flapping like the clipped wings of a chicken. Then, about a third of the way across, he suddenly stopped and clutched his stomach as though he was going to be sick again.

He leaned over the railing. People paid no attention to him. They were like travelers on the deck of a ship politely ignoring a fellow passenger who was seasick. Five seconds later he had disappeared into the concrete darkness below the bridge.

A woman screamed. A crowd gathered. People peered down into the darkness to see if anything exciting was going on. It wasn't. They walked on by.

Aragon stood at the railing. Beads of sweat rolled down his face, as cold and heavy as hailstones. *I have a nice feeling about you, laddie. You're going to bring me luck.*

"God Almighty," he whispered. "I'm sorry, Jenkins, I'm sorry."

A short fat young man stopped beside him. He wore a striped serape over his work clothes, and his hair was greased back over his head so that it looked like a black plastic cap. He had a wheezy worried voice: "Did you push him?"

"*Push* him? For Christ's sake, he was a friend of mine."

"Then why were you chasing him?"

"I was trying to help him."

"Why was he running away from you?"

"I don't know. Now will you please—"

"Pretty soon the police will arrive. Already I hear the sirens."

Aragon heard them, too.

"They'll be nasty," the man said. "They always are when such a serious crime is committed."

"There was no crime."

"They arrest everyone in sight, helter-skelter. They have to act fast because corpses are usually buried the next day . . . What story will you give them?"

"No story. Just the truth. I was trying to save him, to take him home because he was sick."

"It didn't look that way to me. You were chasing him and he was trying to escape from you. The police don't like it when Americans come here to murder each other. It gives our country a bad reputation."

"Oh, for God's sake."

"And if the Americans also swear and blaspheme—"

"Okay, okay. How much?"

"Twenty dollars seems a small price to stay out of our jail. We have a very poor jail."

Aragon gave him a twenty-dollar bill and the man disappeared into the crowd as quickly as Jenkins had disappeared into the darkness below the bridge.

The sirens were getting closer. He started walking as fast as he could back toward the Domino Club. His legs felt rubbery and the sweat was still pouring down his face.

12

THE BACK BOOTH at the Domino Club where Jenkins had been sitting was cleaned up and smelled of disinfectant. The cleanup even included the young bartender who'd spoken to him previously. He wore a freshly laundered white jacket with the name Mitchell stitched across the breast pocket.

Aragon sat down in the booth. About three minutes later Mitchell joined him, bringing along a cup of coffee. He didn't offer Aragon either the coffee or anything else.

"How's your friend?"

"Dead."

"Yeah? Well, when you gotta go, you gotta go."

"His name was Harry Jenkins," Aragon said quietly. "He wasn't a bad man, just unlucky. He had the wrong kind of friends."

"There's a right kind? Show me."

"What was he drinking?"

"Beer. I took the empty bottle away myself before I had one of the boys tidy the place up."

"Your boys are very thorough tidy-uppers. Do they always use a gallon of disinfectant after each customer?"

"The booth stank of puke and whiskey."

"You said Jenkins was drinking beer."

"I removed an empty beer bottle from this table. I didn't smell it to see what had been in it. I figured a beer bottle would contain beer. Anyway, that was his usual drink. He often came in and ordered a beer. He'd nurse a single bottle along for half the night, waiting around for a touch or whatever he had in mind. How come all this fuss over one little dead man?"

"I think he was poisoned."

"You think funny. Go home. Sleep it off."

Aragon looked at his watch. It was twenty after one. "Jenkins called me about two hours ago at my hotel. He was completely sober and in good spirits. Yet forty-five minutes and one bottle of beer later, he was so stoned out of his head that he went and jumped off a bridge. Does that make sense?"

"My business is to make money, not sense. And you know how I do it? I keep my nose clean and out of other people's affairs. I also stay away from booze."

"Jenkins told me on the phone that he was with somebody, an American."

"He wasn't an American."

"What was he?"

"Like I said, I mind my own affairs. But I couldn't help noticing that he was dark-skinned and wearing the usual Mexican work clothes, half native, half cowboy."

"How old was he?"

"They never show their age. I hired one last year, thought he was about thirty, until suddenly he dropped dead of old age. It's all that grease in their skin, keeps the wrinkles away."

"Did Jenkins and his companion seem friendly?"

"There was no quarrel, no fuss, no nothing, until you showed up."

"When I showed up, Jenkins was alone and you seemed pretty anxious to get rid of him."

"I hate pukers."

"You hate a lot of people, don't you, Mitchell?"

"In this business you see their worst side, until pretty soon you forget they have a better one. And ten chances to one they haven't, anyway. Any more questions?"

"What happened to Jenkins between the time he phoned me and the time I arrived?"

"Nothing happened to him. He got drunk, took a walk to sober up, fell off a bridge. Period." Mitchell finished his coffee. "So don't throw any wild statements around. Our club has a good reputation, the best that money can buy. When a little trouble comes along, zap, it goes away again. The police are very understanding."

"How much are cops selling for these days?"

"They're dirt cheap. Which is what dirt ought to be, cheap."

"That's not much of a tribute to your protectors."

"I pay them, I don't have to kiss their asses," Mitchell said. "Now, if it will shut you up and make you feel any better, I'm sorry about your friend."

It was the first human remark Mitchell had made. "The coffee must be getting to you," Aragon said. "For a minute there I thought I heard the faint beating of a heart."

"I have the hiccups."

Aragon drove to the police station and waited around for the rest of the night. At seven in the morning he was informed that Jenkins' body had been examined, and death was declared the result of injuries received in an accidental fall. Fifty dollars was found in his pocket, enough for funeral expenses. In Rio Seco, funerals were cheap, since there was no embalming, and quick if there were no survivors to wait for and the weather was hot. The body was removed to an undertaking parlor, a priest was notified, and Jenkins' funeral service was scheduled for six o'clock that night.

Death was always sad, the undertaker told Aragon. "But one must be realistic. The new bridge is good for business. More than thirty people have already jumped from it."

"The police said Jenkins' death was accidental."

"Such a verdict makes it easier for them. Also for the Church. The Church frowns on suicide."

"I think Jenkins was drugged, which makes it murder not accident or suicide."

"Oh no, no no. The bridge is a magnet for troubled souls seeking oblivion or what not. You have one like it in San Francisco, the Golden Gate. I read in the newspaper that more than five hundred people have jumped from it. Is this true?"

"I don't know."

"Newspapers tell the truth, certainly?"

"When they recognize it and when they want to, like you and me. The truth about Jenkins is that he was murdered."

"God must decide such things," the undertaker said. "He is the Final Judge."

The funeral service was held in the cemetery in a mixture of Spanish and Latin, and Jenkins' name was pronounced Arry Yen-keen. The only other mourner was the fat young man in the striped serape who'd accosted Aragon on the bridge. When their eyes met across the open grave, he pretended not to recognize Aragon. But as soon as the service was over and the priest had departed, the man spoke: "We meet again."

"Yes. I hope it doesn't become a habit. I can't afford it."

"You mean the money?" He pulled a twenty-dollar bill out of his pocket. "I didn't want this for myself. It's for my sister, Emilia Ontiveros, to buy a mourning dress and to light candles. She is stricken with grief."

Aragon thought of the jailed woman with her scarred hands and arms and her despairing eyes. In a crude sense she was lucky: her grief would be less caustic this way than the way Jenkins had planned.

"It was a great love," Ontiveros said. "A little more so on her part, naturally, because he was a man and men meet more temptations. Harry was always meeting temptations, especially when Emilia wasn't around to head them off. Lighting candles for him is a waste of good money—he wasn't even a Catholic. But Emilia is beyond reason. She can't see how much better off she'll be with him gone. He roused her to terrible angers. Without these angers she'd be safe at home, leading a nice normal life."

"What did you tell her about this death?"

"That he drank too much, lost his balance and fell over the railing. She didn't believe it."

"Why not?"

"Harry didn't get drunk. In all their good and bad times together she never once saw him drunk. She told me that B. J. must have pushed Harry over the railing."

"Who is B. J.?"

"An American, somebody Harry knew in the old days. Harry was responsible for him being sent to jail. B. J. swore he'd get even. Maybe it's true. I've never met this man,

B. J., he may be very bad, very vengeful, but I can't always take Emilia's word for things. Her great passion makes fires in her mind and you can't poke around until the ashes cool." Ontiveros ran the back of his hand across his forehead as though he felt the sudden heat of one of Emilia's fires. "I'm the oldest son in the family. It's my duty to look after Emilia and maybe someday to find her a real husband. This will be easier with Harry gone."

It was getting late. No workmen had appeared to fill in the grave, as though they were in no hurry to appear for such a cheap funeral of such an unimportant man.

"You were on the bridge," Aragon said. "You saw what happened."

"Not everything. It was night and there were many people. One of them could have been B. J. It wouldn't have been hard to do. Harry was a small man and not a worker in strong condition like myself—he would need only a little push, so quick, so natural."

Aragon stared down into the open grave with its plain pine box. Had B. J. long since been put into one like it? Or could he still be alive and here in Rio Seco? Suppose he'd found out that Gilly was looking for him. Suppose he wanted to avoid her as much as Harry Jenkins had wanted to avoid Emilia.

"For all I know," Ontiveros said, "*you* might be B. J."

"No, I'm looking for him."

"Why?"

"His wife would like to see him again."

"She has great passion like Emilia?"

"She had at one time."

"And fires in the mind?"

"Yes, I think so."

"Such women are a nuisance. Day in, day out, the family nags at me to find Emilia a husband. I might be able to do it finally now that Harry's gone. If I had some way of collecting a little money for her dowry—"

"No."

"No?"

"No."

"Then I might as well be going." Ontiveros picked up a handful of earth, threw it on top of the coffin and crossed himself. "That's from Emilia."

He walked away, his serape flapping around his knees. The sun was setting, expanding into an improbably brilliant flame-red ball. It looked like one of the fires in Emilia's mind. Or Gilly's. In ten minutes it had fallen into ashes below the horizon.

13

HE CALLED GILLY that night after dinner. He had nothing better to tell her this time than last time, so he poured himself a double Scotch before he tried to contact her. He got his message across in a hurry: Jenkins was dead and buried, Tula still missing, and the search for B. J. had come to a halt.

Her reaction was unexpected—no shock, no anger. She merely sounded depressed. "We've lost."

"Yes."

"You might as well come home."

"All right."

There was a long silence, then a sudden burst of words. "I can't—I *can't* let it go like this. I can't leave him in a dreary foreign prison."

He didn't say what he thought: *You could and you did, Gilly. Your grief may be genuine but it's years too late, miles too short.*

She said, "Jenkins at least had a decent burial, yet it was all his fault. He dragged B. J. down into the gutter."

"B. J. dragged easy, Mrs. Decker. Let's call it a *folie a deux*. Neither man would have gotten into such a crazy predicament without the other."

"You've turned against B. J.. Jenkins won you over."

"Let's not make this a personal thing, Mrs. Decker."

"It's personal to *me*. Not to you, naturally. I never met a lawyer yet who had any more feeling than a dead mackerel."

Gilly was returning to normal.

"And you can quote me to that pompous old boss of yours, Smedler. Tell him the whole damn Bar Association hasn't enough heart for a single baboon."

"He won't be surprised," Aragon said. "Now that your opinion of lawyers has been clarified, I'll continue my report."

"Why did you let Jenkins get away from you?"

"That's not quite accurate, Mrs. Decker. When he refused to tell me over the phone where Tula was, I went after him and found him. But someone else got to him first and slipped something into the bottle of beer he was drinking. Whether it was intended to kill him, I don't know."

"Something like what?"

"I don't know that either."

"And why?"

"A possible motive might have been to prevent him from giving out any more information, either about B. J. or about Tula."

"Maybe it was a simple robbery."

"He had fifty dollars on him when he was found, enough for his funeral. It was your fifty, by the way."

"So the funeral was my treat." She let out a small brittle laugh. "If life is funny, how about death? It's a real scream."

"It was for Jenkins. He screamed all the way down."

Another silence. "Why do—why do you tell me things like that?"

"Because I'm a lawyer, I like to make people feel rotten."

"You're an extremely unpleasant young man."

"Right now I'm not so crazy about you either. And I'm damn glad I'm through working for you."

"What makes you think you're through working for me?"

"You said I was to come home."

"So I did. But at the moment—between insults—you're still on the job, giving me your report. You may continue."

Aragon swallowed a chunk of pride, washing it down with a second glass of Scotch. "When Jenkins called me here late last night he was pretty high, not on drugs or alcohol, on hope and anticipation. He said he had a pigeon. I don't think so. I think he *was* the pigeon. The only description I could get of his companion was that he was wearing the clothes of an ordinary Mexican workingman. This doesn't jibe with what Jenkins told me, that the meeting offered him the chance of a lifetime, that his so-called pigeon had come down to Mexico—note the word 'down'—to scout around for investment opportunities and that he was ready to put money into the chicken tortilla business which Jenkins was touting. We're faced with quite a few contradictions if we look at Jenkins' death from only one viewpoint."

"I have only one viewpoint," Gilly said. "My own."

"I'm aware of that, Mrs. Decker. But others do exist. Jenkins had a pretty shady past and he's undoubtedly been involved in dozens of scams in the past couple of years. That was the way he lived. Maybe it was the way he died, and B. J. and Tula and you and I had nothing to do with it."

"Naturally, I like the idea. I don't want a man's death on my conscience if I can help it."

"Let's leave it at that, then. Jenkins had other enemies."

"What do you mean by other?"

"Other than B. J."

"B. J. wasn't his enemy. That was the trouble—he should have been. B. J. was nobody's enemy."

Emilia has a different idea, Aragon thought. *But she's in jail and crazy with grief and crazy without it. Nobody will believe her. Except me, dammit. Except me.*

"Tell me about the girl, Tula," Gilly said. "Though she isn't a girl anymore, is she? That's some consolation, I guess."

"When B. J. was arrested she followed him to Rio Seco."

"How touchingly faithful."

"Not exactly. She went into business for herself."

"What kind of business, a taco stand or something?"

"She's a hooker."

Her little gasp of surprise sounded genuine. "I—I'm sorry. I didn't expect—I didn't want that kind of fate for her."

"People's fates don't depend on what you want, Mrs. Decker, not even your own."

"I wish you'd have something nice to tell me for once instead of all this ugliness and death and dirt."

"You gave me a dirty job," Aragon said. "I'm glad it's over."

"Wait a minute, don't hang up. Reed's here trying to—*I wish you'd stop interrupting, I can't listen to two people at once. All right, I'll ask him*—Reed wants to know if you've been to the American consulate."

"No."

"They often get information about American citizens which the Mexican authorities don't have or won't admit having. Reed thinks you should go there and ask questions before you come home."

"It's a good idea."

"Will you do it?"

"Yes."

"That means you're still working for me?"

"I guess I am."

"Try sounding a little happier about it."

"Yippee," Aragon said and hung up.

Ordinarily it was Reed who put Marco to bed after dinner. Tonight Gilly did it herself. She gave him a sponge bath, then she rubbed his back with alcohol and dusted it with baby powder. She cleaned his teeth and applied moisturizing cream to his lips and drops to lubricate the eye that never closed. She gave him his shots, one to help him sleep, another to keep him free of pain for a few hours. She wasn't as quick or thorough as Reed and she did some things the hard way, like the bath in the wheelchair instead of on a rubber sheet on the bed. But in the end everything was done and Gilly had a real sense of accomplishment. She'd always been full of natural energy and it was a relief to use some of the surplus on a constructive task.

Violet Smith came to say good night before she left for her evening meeting at the church of the Holy Sabbathians. She assisted Gilly in lifting Marco out of his chair and into the bed. He was very light and brittle, like a hollow glass child.

"Upsy-daisy," Violet Smith said cheerfully. "My stars, he's getting skinny. It casts a reflection on my cooking."

"Why shouldn't it?" Gilly said. "You're not a very good cook."

"I never claimed I was. Anyway, *cordon bleu* would be wasted in this house, what with sickness and booze and that fancy-pantsy male nurse who thinks he's Mr. Wonderful. I do good plain cooking for good plain folks." She emphasized the word "good." It might not help, but it certainly wouldn't hurt. "Nighty-night, Mr. Decker. We'll all be praying for you at the meeting."

Gilly waited until Violet Smith was out of earshot. "Reed thinks we should try and stop her from going to these meetings. He doesn't trust her discretion. What do you think?"

She often asked his opinion to make him feel he had a hand in running the house. She even waited a few seconds after each question as though giving him a chance to consider and to answer. He had no answer. If he had, he couldn't have spoken it, and if he could have spoken it, he wouldn't. Answers were useless when there were no issues left to be resolved, only time to be put in.

"She and Reed are beginning to feud over everything. Someday when you're better I'll fire both of them, and you and I will take a long trip together. Maybe I'll buy another home on wheels like Dreamboat . . . Just think, if B. J. and I had gone away together in Dreamboat the way I'd planned, none of these terrible things would have happened. He wouldn't have deserted me for Tula and wouldn't have gotten involved with Harry Jenkins and been sent to jail. Tula wouldn't be walking the streets in Rio Seco, and Jenkins himself would be alive. You've often heard me talk about Jenkins, B. J.'s old partner in crime."

She watched the fingers of his right hand to see if he raised them to indicate interest. They didn't move. Perhaps the sleeping hypo had already taken effect; perhaps he couldn't remember Jenkins and didn't want to. She went on talking anyway. Nothing could have stopped her now.

"Jenkins died last night and was buried late this afternoon. They bury people as soon as possible in Mexico, I'm not sure why. The funeral only cost fifty dollars, imagine that. In this town they don't even allow you to look at a coffin for fifty dollars. Since he's already buried, there won't be an autopsy and probably nobody will ever know for sure what killed him. Aragon thinks some kind of drug was slipped into his drink. He didn't say so directly but he gave the impression that he suspects B. J. did it. That's rather funny, isn't it?"

He didn't think it was funny. Laughter had been lost longer and farther back in his brain than speech.

"Naturally, I told Aragon the idea was ridiculous. I'm not so sure it was, though. Oh, I know B. J. could never have done anything *violent*. But merely putting something in a drink, that's such a quiet little crime, hardly more than running off with one of the servants."

He willed her to stop talking and go away. It was useless. His will had no more power than the rest of him. He could only listen and wish he was deaf and hope for an earthquake, a thunderstorm, the ringing of a phone, a dog barking, the sound of a car in the driveway, a low-flying plane. *Shut up and leave me alone, leave me be.*

"And Tula," she said. "Poor little Tula. I drove down to Rio Seco years ago before B. J. and I were married. It was an evil place. You could smell it rotting, the garbage, the sewage in the streets, the decadence and decay. What a strange fate for such a pretty young girl. A 'nymphet' I believe they'd call her nowadays. You know what a nymphet is? I looked it up in the encyclopedia. It's a young nymph. And a nymph is like a larva and a larva is sort of a worm. Wormlet— that doesn't sound quite so flattering or mysterious, does it? Wormlet. It describes her perfectly." Her brief laugh was more like a cough. "If the worm turns, I wonder if the wormlet makes a turnlet. B. J. would have thought that was funny. He had a nice sense of humor."

I don't. Go away.

She pulled the woolen blanket up around his shoulders. "B. J.'s women, Ethel, me, Tula— they're the only ones I know of for sure—none of us have had happy lives. I'm not claiming it was his fault, it's just a fact. Maybe he wrecked things for people, maybe he chose people who were bound to wreck things for themselves. Anyway, Tula's life is finished and Ethel has lost herself in some weird religious group. That leaves me. I might still have a chance . . . Yes, the more I think about it, the more the idea appeals to me of buying another motor home like Dreamboat. I won't be able to get one exactly like it because that was eight years ago, they've probably changed quite a few things about it. But basically it will be Dreamboat, and I'll have the name painted on it just the same way. Then when you're better, you and I will go on a vacation together."

She smiled down at him. It was a stage smile that, seen at a distance, might have projected warmth and good cheer. Close up, it chilled him. Her mouth was cold red wax, her teeth were dwarf tombstones, the dimple in her cheek was a hole made by an icepick.

"You and I, dearest," she said, "you and I will go on a long vacation."

It was the night Ethel Lockwood was scheduled to address her fellow Sabbathians. The group leader for the occasion had been a poor choice, a nervous young man who stammered and was attempting to overcome his affliction by making protracted speeches in public.

"And so in c-c-conclusion, let me w-w-welcome our f-f-f-friend in need and our f-f-f-friend in deed, Ethel."

"Thank you, George," Ethel said, wishing they hadn't picked such an incompetent boob to introduce her, "for the long long long introduction."

It was too late now for her to read the pages of blank verse she'd written as a tribute to the Holy Sabbathians and their evenings of cleansing and healing. It would have been a shame to omit any of it, so she decided to save it for next time. Sin and sickness were very dependable: there would always be a next time.

Ethel's outfit had been purchased for the occasion at a thrift shop. The ivory-colored chiffon dress looked gauzy and spiritual and floated around her like ectoplasm.

"Thank you also, sisters and brothers, for giving me this opportunity." To match her dress she wore her best voice, so delicate it seemed to emanate from another world.

"Speak up, I can't hear you," Violet Smith said from the back row.

"I came here this evening not for myself but for the sake of a very ill and helpless man. He is at the mercy of a merciless woman. I have known her for many years and I repeat, she is without mercy. I beg the Lord to intercede on his behalf."

"Wh-wh-what is the p-p-p-problem, sister?"

"I wish you wouldn't interrupt me any further, George. I am about to state the problem. This woman I referred to has engaged a man to find her first husband. If and when he is found, I have reason to believe that the second husband, the sick man, will be—I hesitate to say such a word, to think such a thought, but even the most devout Christian must sometimes entertain unchristian thoughts."

"Entertain" seemed exactly the right word. The audience stirred in anticipation. Ethel's previous confessions had been dull and her illnesses commonplace: eating red meat, loss of temper, sinusitis and impacted wisdom teeth.

"What I'm afraid of," Ethel said, "is that this poor old man will be murdered."

She went on speaking. Every now and then she raised her arms, and from her angel-wing sleeves would come the scent of gardenias to sweeten the poisoned air.

"Violet Smith is late getting home tonight," Gilly said. "It must be a very interesting meeting."

14

IT WAS ALMOST midnight when Aragon's call to his wife in San Francisco was finally put through. Once the connection to the hospital was made, he had to hang on the line for another five minutes while Laurie was tracked down and brought to a phone.

She sounded breathless. "Hello, Tom?"

"How did you know it was me?"

"The operator told me. She recognized your voice. She thinks it's cute."

"Well?"

"Well what?"

"What do you think?"

"You roll your r's a bit too much."

"Rrrrreally?"

"I don't mind. I roll mine, too, being Scottish."

"Let's roll our r's together."

"That sounds dirty," Laurie said. "I'm sure you didn't mean it that way."

"Are you?"

"Well, sort of sure. Tom, have you been drinking?"

"Just enough to ease the pain of reporting in to Gilly, the Dragon Lady."

"Is she that bad?"

"I don't know. And the more I talk to her, the more I don't know."

"You *have* been drinking. In fact, it sounds as if you're at a party. Are you?"

"I may be the only person in Rio Seco who isn't," Aragon said. "This is when all the natives start whooping it up. Men, women, children, dogs, donkeys, anything that can move is out moving."

"Would you like to be whooping it up with them?"

"No. I prefer to sit and talk to my beautiful wife who rolls her r's."

"I think you're a dirty young man."

"You should know, lassie."

"That's the first time you've ever called me lassie," she said. "You sound sort of funny, Tom. What's the matter?"

"It's a long story, involving someone I liked . . . I have a medical question to ask you. Can you spare a minute?"

"Ten or so. I'm on my break, in the interns' lounge."

"What do you know about hallucinogenic drugs?"

"More than I want to, in one way. Not enough, in another. We've had kids brought in here so stoned we thought they were hopeless mental cases until the stuff wore off. Sometimes it didn't. Last month an eight-year-old boy died of respiratory failure after an overdose of mescaline. He was never able to tell us how much he took or where he got it. His parents are both users, involved in some kind of consciousness-raising meditation, but neither of them would admit anything. In fact, they threatened to sue the hospital . . . Exactly what do you want me to tell you?"

"Just keep talking."

"The trouble is that so many new hallucinogens are available now in addition to old stand-bys like hashish and LSD. Their street names are often enticing—Cherry Velvet, Angel Dust, China Dolls. The lethal doses vary tremendously and there is no real antidote. If the victims are in a state of great excitement, we calm them down with tranquilizers or barbituric acid derivatives, or pump their stomachs if there's a chance some of the drug hasn't been absorbed into the system. Ordinarily, though, we simply provide custodial care until the effects wear off. Does this sound like a lecture?"

"I asked for it. Go on."

"In addition to the new drugs, we're faced with combinations of old ones, or mixtures of old and new, which can be lethal. A tolerable amount of cocaine taken at the same time as a tolerable amount of methedrine becomes intolerable . . . This someone you liked, is he dead?"

"He was killed in a fall from a bridge. The police claim it was an accident. In a broad sense they're right. If someone tampered with the brakes of my car and I couldn't stop in time to avoid a collision with a truck, it would be an accident. I think someone tampered with

Jenkins' brakes. About forty-five minutes before I found him, he called me from a nightclub to postpone a date we'd made. He said he'd met someone with money to invest in Mexico and that he'd sold him the idea of investing in a chicken tortilla business. I was skeptical. I knew Jenkins was anxious to leave town before his girlfriend got out of jail and I didn't want him to leave until he gave me the rest of the information he'd promised me. I went to the nightclub and found Jenkins in pretty bad shape. He was vomiting, sweating profusely and breathing very rapidly. He seemed to be out of his head. Or rather, in and out, mainly out. He recognized me briefly and talked to me."

"Did he ask you for anything?"

"Help. He asked me for help and I couldn't—"

"I meant something specific, a drink of water, perhaps."

"He asked me for some water. He even tried to get some for himself out of a fountain. The fountain was dry."

"Go on."

"I went to find help for him," Aragon said. "I thought he'd stay there at the fountain until I came back. He didn't. He started running away when he saw me again as if he was trying to escape from an enemy. I ran after him. He was probably heading for home, he lived on the other side of the bridge. Well, he didn't make it. Suddenly he went to the railing, leaned over and fell."

"Did he seem dizzy?"

"Crazy, dizzy, how do you tell the difference?"

"Vertigo and disorientation are both signs of LSD poisoning. So are the other symptoms you mentioned—profuse sweating, very rapid pulse, nausea and vomiting, dryness of the mouth, dilation of the pupils. An autopsy might reveal traces of LSD in the urine."

"There won't be an autopsy. He's already buried. And the bottle he was drinking from is in a pile of rubbish with a hundred other bottles like it, and the man he was drinking with can't be identified, let alone questioned."

"Is your story the only evidence of foul play?"

"My story is not evidence. Even if it were, even if the police were certain that Jenkins was murdered, it wouldn't concern them much. He was unimportant, an ex-convict with no money and a warrant waiting for him in Albuquerque and maybe a dozen other places. He was low man on the totem pole. There was no way up, no way down. The only way was out, to grow wings and fly out." *I met this pigeon . . . the chicken tortilla business is a winner . . . the hustlers flock around the jail like starlings . . . I'm chicken birdie, lean fly.* "He talked a lot about birds. I mean, they came naturally into his conversation more than into most people's. He may even have been trying to fly when he went off the bridge."

"That's not uncommon with LSD."

Aragon heard a faint tap-tap-tap on the line and he knew Laurie was drumming her fingers on the table or desk the way she did when something was bothering her and she was trying to straighten it out in her mind. He said, "Okay, what's the matter?"

"The man who gave Jenkins the LSD, or whatever, had no way of predicting that Jenkins would either attempt to fly or suffer an attack of vertigo just as he happened to be crossing a bridge. He was betting on a very, very long shot. That's dumb."

"So we have a dumb murderer. They're not, as a class, noted for brains."

"Or else the bridge thing wasn't actually necessary and the man was sure Jenkins had already ingested a lethal dose. He could have been waiting around for Jenkins to pass out when you appeared at the club and scared him off . . . You have to consider a third possibility, too."

"Such as?"

"There wasn't any murder or any murderer. A couple of guys were getting their kicks by mixing drinks and drugs, like the housewife taking her Valium with a glass of muscatel or the high school kid carrying a flask of vodka to wash down the rainbows he can buy in the hall for a quarter apiece. Alcohol is usually half of the lethal mixtures in the cases that come our way."

"Jenkins was drinking beer—"

"Mild, but still alcohol. Drink enough and you're drunk."

"—and only one bottle, according to the bartender. The man with him was someone Jenkins hoped to con out of enough money to get him to Mexicali. He needed all his wits about him. He wasn't likely, under the circumstances, to mess around with any drugs or to break his pattern of nursing along one beer for a whole evening."

"So where are we?"

"Nowhere," he said. "I'll be going back to Santa Felicia either tomorrow or Friday. The Dragon Lady has asked me to check the American consulate here for any record of her ex-husband. After that I'll head for home and forget all about Jenkins and bridges and B. J. and Tula, the whole enchilada."

"No, you won't."

"How do you know I won't?"

"You've always liked enchiladas."

"I can take them or leave them."

"You'd better leave this one," she said. "I mean that seriously, Tom. You should be in court handling a complicated tax case or somebody's nice messy divorce."

"This *is* somebody's messy divorce, or was at the beginning. Now it's something even messier, something weird, crazy. I'm getting bad vibes."

"I speak as a doctor—there's nothing you can do for bad vibes except walk away from their source. So start walking."

"Tomorrow. Friday at the latest. May I ask you one more question?"

"You will, anyway."

"Is LSD readily accessible?"

"Here in San Francisco you can practically buy it over the counter if you go to the right counter. In Mexico, the whole drug situation is pretty murky. Officially, narcotics and hallucinogens are illegal. Yet it's well known that mescal buttons and high-grade marijuana are widely grown. Less well known is the fact that opium poppies are cultivated just as successfully as they are in Turkey. The heroin extracted from them is not white like the stuff grown in Turkey. It's a peculiar color, that's why they call it Mexican Brown. It's equally strong, and a hundred times more dangerous because it's so much easier to smuggle into the country. There are nearly two thousand miles of border, most of it unguarded . . . But I haven't really answered your question. Maybe I was just postponing admitting that I don't know how accessible LSD is in Rio Seco. My guess is, not very. It's a product of labs, not fields. An American like Jenkins would be more likely than a Mexican to know about it and buy it."

"Good."

"Why good?"

"It fits in with what I've thought since the beginning, that the man with Jenkins at the Domino Club was an American and the bartender's description of him was phony. I'd better go and pay another call on Mitchell. He plays bartender, but I'm pretty sure he's part owner of the club."

"It's terribly late. And if Mitchell lied before, why shouldn't he lie again? You can't choke the truth out of him."

"He was bribed. I'll rebribe him."

"Tom, I hate the idea of your mingling with people like that in a place like that."

"I grew up in a barrio with people like that. I didn't even know there were any other kinds until I reached high school."

"Don't give me any of that *macho* bull."

"Okay, cut out the maternal bit. Bargain?"

"Some bargain," she said. "You do what you want and I'm too far away to stop you."

"How would you stop me, fair means or foul?"

"Diseases aren't the only things you learn about in med school. Definitely foul."

"I'll take you up on that some time."

"Tom, listen—"

"Stop worrying about me. I haven't been in a fight for ten years. Or five, anyway. I promise to be sensible, cautious, alert, et cetera, et cetera, et cetera."

"It would have been more reassuring without all those et ceteras," she said coolly. "And if you bring up that barrio stuff once again, I'll scream."

"You can't. You'll scare your patients."

"There aren't any patients in here. Just a couple of interns so tired they wouldn't wake up if a bomb exploded."

"Anyway, thanks for the information about drugs. I truly appreciate it."

"How truly?"

"I'll bring you a present, a great big sombrero to hide all those brains of yours. Us *macho* men like dumb dames."

"Go back to your enchilada. I hope you get heartburn."

"I love you, too."

It was one o'clock, the peak of the evening in the Domino Club district. Before going inside, Aragon stopped to talk to the hustlers waiting across the street. There were about half a dozen left by this time. Most of them merely looked blank when Aragon mentioned the name, Tula Lopez. Only one, a girl about seventeen, said she used to know a Tula years ago when she first went into the racket. The Tula she knew must be very old by now, maybe twenty-five, and surely Aragon wouldn't be interested in such a hag.

"I just want to talk to her about a family matter. Can you put out the word?"

"How much word?"

"Twenty dollars. My name is Aragon and I'm staying at the Hotel Castillo."

"Sure, okay."

"What's your name?"

"Blondie."

"Blondie?"

The girl had jet-black hair reaching to her waist. "Why do you look funny? Don't you like that name?"

"I like it fine."

"So do all the other men. They laugh, it makes them feel good, I don't know why. But they give me more money when they laugh and feel good. How about you?"

"We agreed on a price."

When she opened her purse to deposit the twenty-dollar bill Aragon gave her, he saw the gleam of a knife. Blondie wasn't taking any chances on a customer getting away without paying.

He went inside the club. Mitchell saw him coming. He wasn't happy about it: "I thought you left town."

"I stayed around to pick up some loose ends."

"Loose ends is what we got plenty of. Take your pick."

"You lied to me, Mitchell."

"I lie a lot," Mitchell said. "I took a course."

"How much were you paid?"

"What for? Who by?"

65

"The American with Jenkins last night. How much did he pay you to forget he was here?"

"Nobody has to pay me to forget. I took a course in that, too. It's called Elementary Survival. I recommend it to you."

"Maybe I could hire you as a tutor. What do you charge?"

"Don't waste your money. You'd flunk the first lesson, how not to ask questions. The second lesson's even harder—how to spot a rat fink, get rid of him and stay in business. Adios, amigo, nice knowing you. Don't hurry back."

15

THE AMERICAN CONSULATE was located in one of the older sections of the city, the Colonia Maciza. The formidable stone building reminded Aragon of the Quarry and he soon discovered another similarity. The consul and the assistant consul, like the warden and his assistant, believed in long weekends. They had, he was told by a receptionist, gone on a deep-sea fishing trip and wouldn't return until Monday afternoon. Possibly Tuesday. If there was a storm at sea, Wednesday. If the boat sank, never.

The consul's executive secretary sat behind a large mahogany desk with a name plate identifying her as Miss Eckert. She was fat as a robin, and she held her head on one side as if she were listening for a worm. Aragon did his best to provide a substitute by giving her his card, Tomás Aragon, Attorney-at-Law, Smedler, Downs, Castleberg, McFee and Powell.

Miss Eckert put on a pair of steel-rimmed spectacles, glanced at the card and then dropped it quickly into the wastebasket as though she'd detected a lethal fungus somewhere between Smedler and Powell.

"Is this a confidential matter, Mr. Aragon?"

"Yes."

"Then close the door. A man has been hanging around the corridor all week. I suspect he may be CIA. You're not by any chance CIA?"

"Now, would I tell you if I were?"

"I don't know. I've never asked anyone before."

"The answer is no. But I may be lying."

Miss Eckert was not amused. She leaned back in her chair with a little sigh. "I gather your business concerns an American citizen in Baja."

"He came to Baja eight years ago. I'm not certain he's still here or if he's still alive. His family would like to find out."

"Name, please?"

"Byron James Lockwood."

"Last reported address?"

"The Quarry."

"The Quarry. That's the penitentiary."

"Lockwood was arrested on a charge of fraud involving some real estate in Bahía de Ballenas. I wasn't allowed access to the files at the Quarry. I was assured, however, that they contain no record of Lockwood's arrest or release."

"Are you sure he was taken there?"

"Positive. His partner in the fraud, Harry Jenkins, served time with him. I talked to Jenkins on Monday and again on Tuesday. On Wednesday I attended his funeral."

"Was he sick?—I refer to Monday and Tuesday, of course."

"No."

"This is beginning to sound," Miss Eckert said carefully, "like the kind of thing I would rather not hear."

"Better listen anyway. Jenkins told me—and this was confirmed by someone still in the jail—that Lockwood was ill and frequently disturbed and the guards used drugs to keep him from making trouble. Maybe in the beginning they gave him something like paregoric or laudanum to quiet him, but he eventually became drug dependent. He was wearing quite a bit of expensive jewelry when he left Bahía de Ballenas. He probably used it to purchase narcotics from, or through, the guards at the jail."

"Narcotics?" The word brought Miss Eckert's chair upright with a squawk of dismay. "What kind of narcotics?"

"I'm not certain."

"Oh, I knew, I *knew* this was going to be a rotten day. My horoscope said, stay home and attend to family affairs. I thought it couldn't apply to me because I don't have a family. I should have taken the advice. It meant me, all right—*me*."

"What's your sign?"

"Scorpio."

"That's the sign of a person who always copes, no matter how difficult the situation."

"I thought Scorpios were supposed to be creative."

"When they're not coping, they're creative."

"If you're trying to be funny," Miss Eckert said, "I may as well warn you that I have a very poor sense of humor. Especially when certain subjects are brought up. Poppies. Back home in Bakersfield I used to love poppies. Here it's a dirty word, and of course, a different kind of poppy, or *Papaver somniferum*."

"Why? I mean, why is it a dirty word?"

"We—meaning all the U.S. government employees in this country—are in quite a delicate position right now. There are diplomatic negotiations going on between the two governments. Our government is well aware that illegal poppy fields are sprouting up all over the Sierra Madre, particularly the slopes on the Pacific side. It wants them destroyed. The Mexican government has pledged its cooperation and has actually burned off a few of the fields. But we're asking for more widespread and more complete destruction, such as Army helicopters spraying the fields with herbicides. Certainly we know that something must be done quickly. The last samplings of heroin picked up in L. A. showed that all of it, one hundred percent, came from Mexico. And the last New York samplings were eighty-five percent Mexican. The stuff which is grown in Turkey and processed in Marseilles has been drawing everyone's attention, while the Mexican stuff has been taking over the market. It's processed in mobile labs around Culiacan, north of Mazatlan. Law enforcement officials refer to Culiacan as the new Marseilles. You see the problem?"

"Clearly."

"Now the question is, what do we do about it? Obviously we can't tell the Mexican government officials to spray the fields or else. We must ask. Politely. That's called negotiating."

"And while these negotiations are taking place you want to avoid any international incidents."

"Yes."

"Such as might be caused by a prominent American citizen becoming a narcotics addict while confined in a Mexican jail unfairly if not illegally."

Miss Eckert looked grim. "That's what we want to avoid. Exactly."

"So let's you and I do a little negotiating of our own."

"I would rather not."

"The Mexican government would rather not destroy the poppy fields, and the United States government would rather they did."

"Which government am I supposed to be?"

"Take your pick."

"Swiss."

"Ah, you *do* have a sense of humor, Miss Eckert. Swiss. Ha ha."

"Ha ha," Miss Eckert said. "What are your terms?"

"I'll keep quiet about Lockwood, and you use some of your consular clout to find out if and when he was released from jail. Somebody must have a record of him—the state or local police, the jail officials, the immigration department, the coroner. You can open doors that are closed to me. So you open doors, I shut my mouth." Aragon took another card from his wallet and printed on it the address of his office and the telephone number. "You can write to me here, or if you want to phone, leave a message for me any time. There's an answering service after business hours."

"The consul should *be* here instead of out chasing fish or whatever. I can't decide something like this alone."

"Scorpios usually make quick decisions."

"That's what you want, is it—a quick decision? All right, here it is. I'm not going to break down doors trying to find traces of some junkie."

"You're not negotiating, Miss Eckert."

"I don't have to," Miss Eckert said. "I'm Swiss."

He flew back to Santa Felicia that afternoon. He found his car at the airport where he'd left it, the hubcaps and radio antenna still in place, the windows and tires undamaged. Even the battery was in working order: the engine turned over after only three attempts. He took all this as a good omen.

He picked up a quarter-pounder and fries at a McDonald's near the airport and ate them on the way home. It was ten o'clock when he called Gilly's house.

Violet Smith answered. "Good evening. Praise the Lord."

"Praise the Lord."

"Who's this?"

"Tom Aragon."

"Oh. Wait till I get a pencil and paper. She's not here. I'm supposed to write down whatever you say."

"But I haven't anything that important to—"

"Okay, I'm ready. You can say something."

"Where is she?"

"*Where . . . is . . . she.*"

"You don't have to write that down, for Pete's sake. This is personal, between you and me, like 'How are you.' "

"*Asked . . . regarding . . . health.*"

"Knock it off. All you have to write down is that I'm back in town and I'll talk to her tomorrow morning. There's nothing further to report, anyway."

"You didn't find Mr. Lockwood?"

"No."

"I must admit that's a load off my mind."

"Why must you admit that?"

Violet Smith made a number of small peculiar noises that sounded as though she might be wrestling with her conscience. "I just better not speak too freely over the telephone. You never know who might be listening in."

"Who else is there to listen in?"

"A new nurse, for one, Mrs. Morrison. She was hired so Reed could take a couple of days off this week, and Mrs. Decker decided to keep her on for a while until Reed's disposition improves. She's a nasty old thing, all starch and steel, not a human bone in her body."

"If she's listening in, she's certainly getting an earful."

"It won't come as a surprise. I made my feelings toward her quite clear, especially after they gave her the guest room. It's the best room in the house, a view of the ocean, a Beautyrest mattress and a pink velvet chaise. Pink velvet, and her an ordinary nurse."

Aragon said, "Where did Mrs. Decker go?"

"To the movies with Reed. Reed told her if she didn't get out of this house once in a while, she'd have a nervous breakdown. I felt like saying, maybe she already has one. But I didn't. My car's not paid for and my left back molar needs a new crown. There are also spiritual considerations."

"What kind of spiritual considerations?"

"The church needs money. Did you hear a click on the line just then?"

"I accidentally touched the phone with my glass."

"Your glass. What are you drinking?"

He lied a little. "Soda water."

"Reed has been drinking hard liquor lately and far too much of it. His eyes get all bleary and he talks fresh to Mrs. Decker. If I talked fresh to her with bleary eyes, I wouldn't get away with it, no sir. She'd up and—"

"Violet Smith."

"—fire me like a shot. She allows Reed to—"

"Violet Smith, I'm tired. I want to go to bed."

"What time is it?"

"A quarter after ten."

"Went . . . to . . . bed . . . ten fifteen."

16

"WELL, HERE HE is, our wandering boy, fresh from foreign soil." Charity Nelson pushed back her orange wig so she could get a better view of him. "You've only been gone a week but I detect a certain new maturity about you, Aragon. What happened?"

"Nothing much."

"Did you miss me?"

"I thought of you a few times."

"I thought of you, too. Especially when the answering service woke me up at six thirty this morning to read me a night letter addressed to you."

"A night letter?"

"From Rio Seco. Want me to read it to you? Better say yes, I took it down in my own version of shorthand."

"Yes."

"Please."

"Please."

"Please. Hasn't that word got a nice ring to it? I can't recall ever hearing it around this office before."

"You've put a very funny act together, Miss Nelson."

"There's more."

"Spare me. Double please."

"Okay." She consulted a piece of paper which she took from the top drawer of her desk. "It's signed 'Scorpio.' That sounds like a code name. In fact, the whole thing sounds as though it might be in code. You're not a spy, are you?"

"Yes."

"No kidding. Whose side are you on?"

"What sides are there? Pick one and read the letter."

" 'Swiss connection reports penetrating paper doors at the stone quarry'—I think that's what the operator said, 'stone quarry.' Does that make sense?"

"Yes."

" 'Records indicate Byron James Lockwood was released three years ago by Magistrate Guadalupe Hernandez. Exact circumstances of Lockwood's release unavailable and current whereabouts unknown. Hernandez contacted by phone but refused to give additional information. Home address, Camino de la Cima. Try Mordida.' Who's Mordida?"

"It's not a who, it's a what. A bite. A bribe."

"What a shame. I thought it was a girl, some gorgeous brunette who's a double or triple agent—you know, the usual thing."

Smedler came out of his office to pick up his mail. He appeared a little too perfectly groomed, as if he'd just been given the full treatment in a beauty salon or a mortician's prep room. "Good morning, Aragon. Great weather, isn't it? On these crisp fall days you can feel the old corpuscles moving right along."

"Yes, sir. It's nice to be back."

Smedler looked surprised. "Have you been away? . . . Has he been away, Miss Nelson?"

"Yes, Mr. Smedler. On a personal mission for Mrs. Decker."

"Ah yes. How'd it go, Aragon?"

"Fine."

"Fine. Now *that's* the kind of answer I appreciate. Pour him a cup of coffee on the house, Miss Nelson."

Smedler returned to his office while Charity put fifteen cents in the coffee machine and extracted a cup of semihot, semicreamed, semicoffee.

"Oh, you shouldn't, Miss Nelson," Aragon said. "This is too much, it's beyond the call of duty. You really shouldn't."

"Okay, I won't," she said and drank the coffee herself. "I can type this letter up for you, if you like. How many copies do you need?"

"One."

"One? Nobody ever needs just one. Since this concerns Mrs. Decker, you'll want to give her the ribbon copy and keep a few others for your private files."

"Why will I want to do that?"

"It's standard practice," Charity said. "Don't fight it."

"I have no private files."

"You shouldn't admit anything like that. You'll never get to first base in this business without the basics. Rule one: always have plenty of copies made of everything. The less important the matter is, the more copies you ask for."

"But I only need one. In fact, I don't really need that. Mrs. Decker probably hasn't any files either."

"As a businesswoman I don't know how to deal with people who won't obey the ordinary commonsense business rules."

"I'll tell you how," Aragon said. "Leave us alone. Forget the night letter. It never happened."

"You're getting weird, Aragon. I don't think being a spy agrees with you. Maybe you should try some other line of work, something that keeps you out in the fresh air and sunshine, like a forest ranger. I can picture you ranging the forest in cute little green shorts to match all those leaves . . . Don't dash off. I have lots of other suggestions."

"Make twenty copies of each and file them."

The week since he'd first arrived at the house and seen Reed cleaning the pool seemed like a month, and the patio itself was a world or two away from the squalid streets of Rio Seco. Camellias were starting to bloom, pink and perfect in their marble tubs, and the nandina leaves were already tipped with autumn bronze. Reflections of royal blue princess flowers moved back and forth in the sky blue water, rippling the outlines of the ceramic mermaid and softening her tile smirk. She looked real, like a child playing a game of drowning.

Reed was sitting at a glass and aluminum table that was set for two. He wore his working uniform, slacks and a short-sleeved cotton jacket buttoned at the throat. As usual, he wasted no time on amenities. "Sit down. You're early. I can guess why. After a week of the food you get down there, you're half starved."

"I was brought up on that kind of food."

"Yeah? You'll probably have ulcers by the time you're thirty. Do you know how those terribly hot spices came to be used? They were meant to cover the smell and taste of putrescent fish, fowl and animal flesh."

"You're a bundle of information, Reed."

"I know . . . The old girl will be out in a few minutes. She's getting herself all dolled up. What did you tell her? She hasn't fussed like this about her appearance for months. I hope she's not building up to a letdown. Her letdowns are rough on the hired help."

"Are you classed as one of the hired help?"

"Not for long."

"What does that mean?"

"Nothing lasts forever. Right? Sit down, be cool. I made the lunch myself so you wouldn't have to eat the local swill, an austere little casserole of artichoke hearts and eggs in a Ceylonese coconut-milk sauce. I had to break open four coconuts to get the right amount of milk. Violet Smith is having fits about what to do with all the coconut meat. I told her what she could do with all the coconut meat, but she didn't buy the idea. Some people aren't open to suggestion."

"I can see why."

Reed laughed, a bubbly mischievous sound that might have come from the mermaid at the bottom of the pool. "Violet Smith and I are on different wavelengths. To be frank, she doesn't fit into the household. I want Gilly to fire her."

"Gilly?"

"Everybody calls her by her first name—behind her back, anyway. You can't behave the way she behaves and expect to be treated like Queen Elizabeth. Queen Elizabeth doesn't get looped and loud, or exchange insults and jokes with the staff. I don't intend this as criticism of Gilly—it's just her way of dealing with the tremendous emotional strain of Decker's illness."

Feathery scraps of pampas grass drifted across the flagstones and caught in the spikes of the firethorn bushes. The berries were ripe and ready for the winter birds.

Aragon said, "What brought you here in the first place, Reed?"

"I worked in the private hospital where Decker was a patient after his stroke. He took a fancy to me."

"And Mrs. Decker?"

"She also took a fancy to me. Women do. Strange, isn't it, since the fancy can hardly be called mutual. Gilly's a nice old girl, if you like nice and old. And if you like girls."

"You reassure me."

"How come?"

"I've had the notion of something going on between you and Mrs. Decker, that you might even be thinking of marriage after Decker dies and providing B. J. doesn't turn up."

"Oh, come now. Why would I want to get married?"

"To enjoy an early retirement."

"I don't believe in early retirements or marriage. That puts two holes in your theory, enough to kill it, right?"

Aragon brushed some scraps of pampas grass off the tablecloth. They shone in the sun like golden feathers. He said, "I'm beginning to doubt very seriously that B. J. will turn up, either because he can't or because he doesn't want to. As for Decker, I gather he's not going to survive."

"None of us is going to survive, amigo. Decker's number is coming up sooner than most, is all."

"What do you expect will be the actual cause of death?"

"Kidney failure, cerebral hemorrhage, heart congestion, who knows? He's in bad shape in every department. He has only one thing going for him. Gilly. She works her tail off to keep him alive. She won't give up and she won't let him give up. He doesn't really want to live. She's *making* him do it."

"Why?"

"She's a very loyal woman. Stubborn, too. She thinks fate handed Decker a bum deal and she's fighting back. She's a great believer in fair play, justice, all that kind of crap." Reed got up, straightening the jacket of his uniform as if he were going on duty. "I'd better check the casserole. What did you tell Gilly on the phone?"

"That B. J. was released from jail three years ago by a magistrate named Guadalupe Hernandez."

"So at least he didn't leave feet first."

"Not according to the records anyway. Hernandez wouldn't give Miss Eckert of the consulate any details, so she suggests trying a little bribery. Or a lot. No sum was specified, but a great many officials lead high lives on low wages, so somebody must be paying."

"And now it's Gilly's turn."

"If she's willing."

"She'll be willing, bet on it. I told you she has this thing about justice and fair play. Well, all her money—except what she gets from Decker—was B. J.'s to begin with. She'll spend every cent of it on him if she has to, the way she spends every ounce of her energy and will on Decker. Probably with the same result. Zero."

The artichoke hearts and eggs lay untouched on Gilly's plate.

"How much?"

"I don't know," Aragon said. "I've never bribed a judge."

"You claim a lot of them live high. How high? Like this, for instance—this house, the servants?"

"I think so."

"Offer him a thousand to start. Be prepared to raise the price as much as you have to."

"You assume I'm going back."

"Of course you're going back. Don't you want to?"

"No."

"You're quitting," she said. "Just when the case is beginning to open up, you're quitting."

"No, I'm not. You asked if I wanted to go back and I said no. I have the feeling someone is following me around down there, watching every move I make."

"You're getting paranoid."

"If you prefer to use that word, fine. I'm a paranoid with someone following me around, watching every—"

"You must admit it doesn't sound reasonable, Aragon. I expect a lawyer, even a novice like you, to have a certain objectivity. Someone who's behind you and headed in the same direction as you are isn't necessarily following you. Now, are you going back or aren't you?"

"I am."

"Right away. This afternoon or tonight."

He shook his head. "Sorry. I need a day off to catch up on my mail, my laundry, some—"

"Laundry, mail, all that can wait. You're not helpless. Can't you rinse out your own socks?"

"Yes, dammit, I can rinse out my own socks."

"Then do it. And please try to work up a little enthusiasm for your job."

"I'm trying," he said grimly.

"As for the business about someone tailing you, it's probably a mistake. He may think you're someone else."

"I'm beginning to think the same thing."

"In any case, the solution is very simple. Next time it happens, all you have to do is turn around and confront him—or her—and identify yourself. That ought to solve the problem."

"Or create new ones."

"Please try to take a more positive attitude. I'm trying. I'm trying very, very hard to keep my—well, we won't go into that. You'll need extra money."

"Not yet. Wait until I talk to Hernandez."

"All right." She glanced down at her plate. "What's this crud taste like?"

"I can't describe the taste exactly, but it feels kind of slippery."

"Slippery. Christ." She got up and dumped the contents of her plate in one of the marble tubs containing a camellia bush. The leaves covered the evidence. A dog or cat might smell it out or a bird discover it while searching for insects, but Reed would never see it.

When she returned to the table with the empty plate she looked suddenly old and sick, as if the dumping of the food had been a symbolic gesture, a rejection of life itself.

"You shouldn't go without lunch," Aragon said. "Let me take you out for a burger, guaranteed not slippery."

"That's nice of you, Aragon. I really appreciate it, I'd love a burger and fries, a whole bunch of nice greasy fries. But I can't leave Marco. He's not used to the new nurse yet. I can tell by his pulse that she makes him nervous. It's too bad. Mrs. Morrison has excellent references and Marco has to get used to someone else besides me and Reed. Reed could quit any time. He has no contract, and I have no guarantee that I'll last longer than my husband. It's likely but not certain. I must prepare for every contingency. I promised him he'd never be left alone."

Mrs. Morrison's voice was as crisp and starched as the small pleated white cap which sat on top of her head like a crown. No matter how vigorously she moved her head, the crown remained firmly attached as though she'd been born wearing it and entitled to all the privileges it bestowed.

"I have studied your charts with some care, Mr. Decker," she said regally, "and I have reached the conclusion that the amount of brain damage you have sustained will not prevent us from communicating with each other, at least on an elementary level. Such communication can be arranged in a fairly simple manner. Have you ever played twenty questions? Of course you have. Very well. I will ask you only questions which can be answered by yes or no. You will then raise one finger of your right hand for yes, and two for no. Or if you prefer, blink your right eyelid instead, once for yes, twice for no. Think you can do that?"

He didn't move. He had so much to say that the sheer bulk of it overwhelmed him. His fingers were icicles inside their warm blanket of flesh, and his eyelid felt as though someone had sewn it shut.

"Come, come, you're not going to be uncooperative just because we're strangers, are you? I am your *nurse*. You should trust me to practically the same degree that you trust your doctor or your wife. I am with you, Mr. Decker, *with* you. Let's try a few basic questions for practice. Wait now, did I say one finger or one blink for yes, and two for no, or was it two fingers or two blinks for yes, and one for no? We'd better start over. I think we'll say two fingers or two blinks for yes, and one finger or one blink for no. Ready to begin?"

He opened his right eye and gave her a look of such terrible loathing that even Mrs. Morrison, who was not noted for sensitivity, felt a certain coolness in the air.

"We must *communicate*, Mr. Decker. I'm not a mind reader and you're not a vegetable, appearances to the contrary. Let's make that a test question: Are you a vegetable?"

He wasn't.

"There, that's better, you are not a vegetable. Is your name Marco Decker? No? Are you being deliberately perverse or are you just stupid? This is a serious matter. Is the sun shining? Yes, it *is*, so I want two, *two* for yes. Do you understand me? Another yes, two fingers or two blinks."

All of his powers of concentration and will were gathered now to move his hand.

"Why, you old goat, I do believe that's an obscene gesture."

He blinked twice.

17

ARAGON HAD BEEN half hoping he wouldn't be able to find it, but he could hardly have missed. It was the only house on Camino de la Cima, an oiled dirt road southeast of the city. The long winding driveway that led up to it was lined with silver-leaved eucalyptus trees that tossed and trembled at the slightest hint of wind.

The whole hillside was enclosed by hurricane fencing with half a dozen rows of barbed wire along the top. At the entrance the double iron-grilled gates were open, and so was the door of the gatehouse itself. The small building had been constructed like a miniature mission with sand-colored adobe walls and red tile roof. It reminded Aragon of the abandoned church in Bahía de Ballenas where the padre lived, but there was a couple of hundred years' difference in age. Another and more important difference quickly became apparent. Instead of a kindly old padre coming to the door, there were two young men wearing uniforms and holsters. One of them also carried a rifle.

They watched with polite interest as Aragon parked his car and approached the gatehouse. Then the man with the rifle nodded and his companion went over to the car. He opened the right front door and looked through the glove compartment and under the seat. Then he took out the ignition keys, unlocked the trunk and searched it. He closed it again and replaced the ignition keys. Hernandez was taking good care of his past *mordidas*.

Aragon said, "Is this the residence of Magistrate Guadalupe Hernandez?"

The man with the rifle did the talking, in a professional monotone. "You have business with the magistrate?"

"Yes. My name is Aragon."

"It is Saturday afternoon, surely not your ordinary business hours, Mr. Aragon."

"This was the only time I could get here. I just arrived from Los Angeles and I was hoping Mr. Hernandez would give me an appointment this afternoon."

"The matter you wish to see him about must be of grave importance."

"No. I simply thought if I could contact him now, I'd be able to go back home tomorrow."

"You don't like our city?"

"It's fine."

"Very fine, I think."

"Yes."

"Finer than Los Angeles?"

"I'll have to consider that for a while."

"Take your time." He dropped his rifle against the gatehouse door. Then he leaned against the wall with his arms crossed on his chest. "I am in no hurry. Salazar, my assistant, is in no hurry either. Are you, Salazar?"

"No, sir," the younger man said. "I am on duty."

"Where would you go if you weren't on duty?"

"To the jai alai games."

"I prefer the bullfights. You don't have bullfights in Los Angeles, Mr. Aragon?"

"No."

"Jai alai. Do you have jai alai?"

"Not to my knowledge."

"What do you do for amusement?"

"Punch out old ladies, kick dogs, stuff like that."

"Ah, most uncivilized."

"Yes."

"So you must come here for amusement . . . He won't find the magistrate very amusing today, will he, Salazar?"

"No, sir."

"Certainly I've heard no one laughing."

"Neither have I, sir."

"Perhaps you'd better drive our American visitor up to the house to discover why no one is laughing."

"I'm not sure that would be wise, sir."

"You never do foolish things, Salazar? Then you must start by taking Mr. Aragon up to see Magistrate Hernandez."

"Yes, sir."

The blacktop road that led to the house was about half a mile long. Salazar drove it as though he were practicing for the Indianapolis 500 in low gear. He stopped at the entrance to a carport on the east side of the house. There was space for four cars but only one was in it at the moment, a late-model jeep station wagon.

"Thank you, Salazar," Aragon said. "That was a very interesting ride."

"I am a fine driver, do you think?"

"You are a very fine driver." *Like Rio Seco is a very fine city and your boss is a very fine man.*

Salazar took the keys out of the ignition and handed them to Aragon with a solemn nod of the head. "I have only driven twice before. I guess it is a natural talent."

The main house was a combination of mission and ranch style. Under the wide beamed overhang of the tile roof, about an acre of patio circled the house. It was furnished with dark heavy wooden benches and decorated with glazed clay pots painted in such vivid colors that the plants they contained looked drab by contrast and secondary in importance. Many of the plants were dead or dying, as if the effort of competing with the pots had been too much of a strain.

Under the arch of the main entrance, two Cadillac limousines and a Jensen Interceptor were parked with a chauffeur behind the wheel of each. The three chauffeurs and Salazar were the only people in sight, and the only sound was Salazar's voice: "Someday when I attain a position of importance, I will buy a big car like one of those. Meanwhile I will practice by going to the cinema and watching carefully how they are driven. The important thing is aim."

"Aim?"

"Like a rifle. You aim it just so and it shoots in that direction just so."

Aragon hoped he wouldn't be in the vicinity when Salazar bought his big car and aimed it just so.

An older man came out of one of the side doors. Like Salazar and the gatekeeper, he was in uniform. Either the uniform had been too small to begin with or he'd grown fat in the wearing of it. He was stuffed into it like a sausage balancing on two toothpick legs.

He said to Salazar, "Who is this person?"

"An American who flew in from Los Angeles this afternoon. His name is Aragon."

"Does he speak Spanish?"

"Yes, Superintendent. Very well."

"What does he want?"

"To see Magistrate Hernandez."

"I'm sorry I barged in like this," Aragon said. "If Mr. Hernandez is in the middle of an emergency, I can wait for a later appointment."

The superintendent gazed at him pensively. "Oh no. The emergency has passed."

"Is something the matter around here?"

"Why do you think something is the matter?"

"The security precautions seem excessive."

"Excessive for what?"

"The house of an ordinary magistrate."

"Magistrates have great power in this part of the world. Where there is great power, there are many enemies."

"I assure you I'm not one of them."

"I thought not," the superintendent said. "Enemies don't usually appear at the front gate and give their names. Unless, of course, they're subtle. Which you are not. I consider myself an excellent judge of character and you appear to me a heavy young man—heavy-handed, heavy-footed, heavy-minded. Is this correct?"

"It may be a trifle too flattering."

"Your tone indicates that I hit a nerve. Which nerve?"

"I ran the mile in four ten in college."

"That's good?"

"Yes."

"Very well, we'll take out the heavy-footed. The rest stays. Come inside."

He led the way through a long narrow room that looked like a combination of art gallery, church and library. The books were leatherbound copies of English classics translated into Spanish. The pictures, in ornate gilt frames, were of a religious nature—madonnas, crucifixions, resurrections—except for one large oil painting of a man wearing a magnificent scarlet uniform with gold epaulettes and silver scabbard and sword. A dozen or more candles burned in silver candelabra below the painting and on the altar at the far end of the room.

The superintendent surveyed the room proudly as if it were his own and the man in the scarlet uniform were an earlier self, or at least a relative. "The *galleria* is most impressive, don't you agree, Mr. Aragon?"

"Yes." *I hope this agreeing business starts getting easier. I may have to do a hell of a lot more of it.* "Most impressive."

"But I detect a certain hesitancy in your manner. You're not a religious man, perhaps?"

"Perhaps not."

"Religion can be a great solace for people in trouble."

"Are you implying that I'm in some kind of trouble, Superintendent?"

"What kind of trouble could you be in when you only arrived in Rio Seco this afternoon? You've hardly had time to go out looking for it. Perhaps I can help. Come, I'll show you the magistrate's office."

Beyond the altar was a massive, elaborately carved oak door with iron hinges which creaked a warning when the superintendent pushed the door open.

The room inside was in sharp contrast to the *galleria*. Except for a picture window which offered a view of the main entrance to the house, this was strictly an office, with fluorescent lighting, a mahogany desk with a leather swivel chair, and floor-to-ceiling shelves and files. Nearly every drawer in the desk and the files was open and spilling paper, folders, cards, manila envelopes, letters. A painting hiding a small safe had been pushed aside, but the door of the safe remained closed. In one corner of the room was a small table with two wine glasses and a bottle of Beaujolais on it. The bottle was still full, but it had been uncorked. The cork was lying on the tray with the forced-air opener still stuck in it like a hypodermic needle.

A middle-aged man sitting behind the desk rose when the superintendent and Aragon entered and immediately took Aragon's picture with a Polaroid camera. The pictures he'd already taken were scattered on the desk in front of him. They seemed to be mainly various angles of the disarray in the room.

The superintendent said, "I assume you don't mind having your picture taken."

"That depends on what you're going to do with it."

"I may keep it in my wallet. Then again, I may not. Let's see how it turned out . . . Not bad. Certain physiological characteristics are obscured, others are emphasized. It all balances out, wouldn't you say?"

The superintendent held up the picture and Aragon glanced at it. He hardly recognized himself. The young man in the picture looked confident, almost cocky. He didn't feel either.

"You may have deduced, Mr. Aragon, that someone paid a call on Magistrate Hernandez while he was working. He liked to catch up on his work at night whenever possible so he could spend more of the daylight hours with his children . . . Obviously the call wasn't a friendly one, or at least it didn't end up that way. Kindly remove your spectacles. I believe Ganso here would like another shot."

"Do I have a choice?"

"Of course not."

He removed his spectacles. The second picture showed a little more of the truth. He looked scared. "I hope you don't think I had anything to do with all this. I told you, I just arrived in town."

"But you have been here before in our city?"

"Yes."

"When?"

"I—well, at the beginning of the week. I left Thursday afternoon."

"This is only Saturday afternoon. What made you leave and come back so soon?"

"I received word at my office that Magistrate Hernandez might have news of someone I've been searching for on behalf of a client. I'm a lawyer."

"So? The last man I arrested was a lawyer. His interpretation of the law didn't quite coincide with mine." The superintendent went and stood by the window with the view of the front entrance. "Presumably your client has a name."

"That's privileged information."

"In your country, yes. In mine, no. It's one of the basic differences in our legal systems. Now, the name of your client, please."

"Gilda Grace Decker."

"And she hired you to find someone who also has a name."

"Byron James Lockwood, her former husband."

"How does Magistrate Hernandez fit into all this?"

"Lockwood was serving time in the Quarry for a real estate swindle and Hernandez was responsible for his release three years ago. No one has seen Lockwood since."

"Perhaps," the superintendent said dryly, "Mr. Lockwood doesn't wish to be seen."

"It's possible."

"It is, then, possible that he took steps to make sure he is not seen?"

"What kind of steps?"

"He may have come here to the house, for instance, to destroy some records pertaining to him. That would have been stupid enough, he being an ex-convict and the magistrate an important person. But what followed was surely the ultimate in stupidity . . . Step over here for a minute. I want you to see something."

Aragon went to the window. Some people were coming out of the front door, three men, a stout woman, heavily veiled, leaning on the arm of a fourth man, and half a dozen children ranging in age from five to midteens. The woman and the man escorting her got into the first limousine, and the children into the second. The rest of the group entered the Jensen and all the cars began moving slowly down the driveway.

"See those people," the superintendent said. "Where do you think they are going?"

"I don't know."

"How are they dressed?"

"In black."

"Like mourners, would you say?"

"Yes."

"Where would they be going, dressed like mourners?"

"To a funeral," Aragon said.

18

FOR THE NEXT three hours Aragon answered questions, many of them repetitious: What was he doing in Rio Seco? What was he actually doing? What was he *really* actually doing? Who was Lockwood? Had he ever met him? What kind of man was he?

"It's unlikely he could have committed any crime of violence," Aragon said. "He was, by all accounts, a very gentle person."

"A lot of gentle persons go into the Quarry and come out not so gentle. You speak of yesterday, I must think of now and tomorrow. Lockwood could be a changed man. You agree?"

"Yes." *I agree again. This time it's real.*

"As you can see"— the superintendent pointed to the table with the opened bottle of wine and the two glasses— "Hernandez was preparing to offer his visitor a drink. Which indicates that either he was a friend or he had come on a friendly mission such as bringing Hernandez something, a gift, say."

"Say a *mordida*."

"All right, a *mordida*. I don't like the word but it is a fact of life so we'll use it. Certainly we can assume that Hernandez was expecting someone, if not this particular person, because he left the gate open and no one is on duty in the gatehouse at night except on special occasions. So the caller arrived. Let's call him Lockwood."

"Let's not."

"Very well—Mr. Mordida, then. How's that?"

"Better."

"Mr. Mordida drove up to the house and Hernandez let him in. It was obviously an informal visit. Hernandez was wearing a paisley print robe over white silk pajamas. He brought Mr. Mordida here into the office and opened a bottle of wine. Up to this point the meeting was amicable. What happened to change it, I don't know. The children and servants occupy another wing of the house and most of them were sleeping. Mrs. Hernandez heard nothing, no car driving up, no sounds of quarreling or of the office being ransacked. This isn't surprising, since the adobe walls are a foot thick and she was in the bedroom watching television. Shortly after ten o'clock she came to say good night to her husband and found him dead and the room looking like this. She telephoned the doctor, who in turn called me. I came right out with Ganso, my photographer, and several other men. I've been on duty ever since, both here and at the hospital where Hernandez's body was taken to determine the cause of death. There were no marks on him, he gave every evidence of having died naturally of a heart attack or a stroke. Except for the condition of the room, we might have left it at that. Would you like to see some of the pictures Ganso took of the body?"

"Not particularly."

"Ganso likes to take pictures of everything. No one ever looks at them, which is a shame because the film is expensive. Are you sure you—?"

"I'm sure."

"Very well, I'll proceed. When Hernandez's robe was removed at the hospital I noticed a very small spot of blood on the back of his pajama top. It seemed a peculiar place for a bloodstain. If it had been on the front it could have passed as the result of a shaving nick or even a dribble of red wine which, as you can see, Hernandez fancied. After I drew the doctor's attention to the spot he examined Hernandez's back very carefully and found, under the left shoulder blade, a puncture wound made by an extremely thin sharp instrument, something in the nature of an icepick. But I don't believe it was an icepick. You see the forced-air opener still in the cork of the wine bottle over there? I think before it was inserted in the cork, it was inserted in Hernandez. The wound was so small that the skin closed over it almost immediately and all the bleeding, except for that one drop, took place internally. Death occurred fairly quickly, since the weapon penetrated the heart and the pressure of blood in the pericardial sac caused the heart to stop beating. I'm not a medical expert, I'm merely repeating roughly what the doctor told me. Whoever struck the blow was either very lucky or very skillful."

"Lockwood was neither," Aragon said. "All his luck was bad and his only skill seems to have been attracting women."

"That sounds to me like good luck."

"Not for him."

"I could use such luck, call it good or bad." The superintendent stared down at his belly as if he were wondering how it got there. "This Lockwood, he was probably thin?"

"No. In the only pictures I saw of him he was quite fat."

"Tall?"

"No."

"But very handsome?"

"No."

"That's most encouraging, a small fat homely man attracting many women. Yes, I like that very much, it tempts me to view you in a much friendlier light. But such a thing would be unprofessional. I am always professional."

"I can see you are."

"It shows, then?"

"It shows."

The superintendent sat down in the swivel chair behind the desk and Ganso immediately took a picture of him. There was complete silence while the film was developing. The finished product showed a small homely fat man.

The superintendent gazed at it soberly. "I must keep reminding myself of Lockwood and all those women. Were they nice sensible women, the kind a man would choose to marry and to bear his children?"

"I only know one of them. She's—" He wasn't sure that "nice" and "sensible" were the right words to describe Gilly. "She's very interesting."

"Why has she not formed an attachment to some other man?"

"She did. Or at any rate she married him."

"How is it, then, that she wants you to find Lockwood?"

"Her present husband is dying. I think she is afraid of being left alone."

"How old is she?"

"About fifty."

"I am not interested in any woman beyond childbearing age."

"Naturally not." *Poor Gilly will be heartbroken.* "One of the other women is still young, only twenty-three."

"That is much better. And she likes fat homely men?"

"Her personal preferences don't matter. She's a hustler here in Rio Seco. You might know her. In a professional way, of course—your profession, not hers."

"We have a great many hustlers in Rio Seco. Most of their customers are American tourists who drive down for the races or the bullfights, Navy men who drive by the busload from San Diego and Marines from Camp Pendleton."

"Her name is Tula Lopez."

The superintendent shook his head. "The hustlers don't come up to me on the street and introduce themselves. If I were a private citizen and wanted to find a particular young woman, I'd put her name on the grapevine and offer a sum of money for information."

"Or hire a shouter."

"So you have been to the Quarry. Good. That will give you some idea of what happens to people who don't watch their behavior . . . Do you know a man named Jenkins?"

"Jenkins is a common name in my country."

"In my country it's most unusual. Thus, when someone named Jenkins performs an unusual act like jumping off our new bridge, it arouses my curiosity and wonderment. Do you have much wonderment, Mr. Aragon?"

"Enough."

"Then let's wonder together about various coincidences. Mr. Jenkins and your friend, Lockwood, were both Americans. Jenkins served time in the Quarry for the same offense that Lockwood did. You tell me that Lockwood was released by Magistrate Hernandez after a payment of some kind. Now I tell you that Jenkins also was released by this same Magistrate Hernandez after paying a fine. What do you make of all this?"

"That Hernandez had ways of supplementing his income."

"His income wouldn't have bought the rug on this floor. Our public servants are very poorly paid, that is why they become private bosses. A little *mordida* here, and a little there, keeps them from starving."

"Hernandez was about as far from starving as I am from being named to the Supreme Court."

"*Mordida* is part of your system, too, so I hope you didn't come riding across the border on a white horse."

"I don't ride a horse of any color," Aragon said. "Just a ten-speed bicycle."

"I dislike all forms of exercise except that of the imagination. From the neck up I am very athletic. I am like a greyhound chasing a mechanical rabbit at the dog track. Only *I* catch the rabbit . . . You smile, I see, because I don't look like a greyhound. Well, you don't look like a rabbit. But here we both are."

Aragon had already stopped smiling. "I'm not sure what a greyhound would do to a real rabbit if he caught one."

"Probably nothing. The chase is what matters to him. But the rabbit doesn't know that. What matters to him is escape. Sometimes he makes a serious error and runs into a hole which has no exit. That's what you did. You ran right up that driveway and into this house."

"My coming here was a coincidence."

"I can swallow only a certain number of coincidences. Then I start to upchuck. So let's eliminate some of these coincidences, shall we?"

"I don't know how."

"We'll begin once more at the beginning."

The superintendent got up, walked around the room quite rapidly as if his athletic imagination were chasing him, then sat down again in the swivel chair. Aragon stared out the window, but it was dark. All he could see was the reflection of the room itself, the fat man in uniform behind the desk, the middle-aged man with the camera poking around in the clutter of ransacked papers, and the young man standing at the window peering through his hornrimmed glasses like a rabbit that had entered a hole with no exit.

"No, Mr. Aragon, tell me frankly, what brought you here this afternoon?"

"A telegram from someone at the U.S. consulate who found out that Lockwood had been released from prison by Magistrate Hernandez."

"Did you expect to see the magistrate?"

"Yes."

"And to ask him questions?"

"Yes."

"And to receive answers?"

"Yes."

"*Mordidas*," the superintendent said, "do not appear in filing cabinets or record books. Or magistrates' answers."

"I thought it was worth a try, since my previous attempts to find Lockwood failed."

"Now this one has also failed. What will be your next step?"

"I think I'll go home."

"But there is still the girl. Aren't you going to look for her?"

"No."

"Why not?"

"I'm afraid to."

"Afraid? You're strong, young—"

"I'm not afraid for myself. I do all right. I don't back into sharp instruments or fall off bridges."

"So . . ." The superintendent leaned his elbows on the desk and the tips of his fingers came together to frame an arch like a bridge. "So you *did* know Jenkins."

"I never said I didn't."

"You implied as much."

"I evaded the question. I wanted to make sure you were an intelligent and reasonable man."

"And now that you've made sure, you will tell me everything?"

"Everything isn't much," Aragon said. "First I got Jenkins' address from his girlfriend in the Quarry."

"Her name, please."

"Emilia Ontiveros."

"Why is she in the Quarry?"

"For assault. Assault on Jenkins."

"This Jenkins apparently didn't have a way with women like Lockwood."

"It wouldn't have mattered. Miss Ontiveros is the jealous type. Anyway, Jenkins claimed that he'd lost contact with Lockwood and had no idea where he was. For a sum of money he agreed to find Tula Lopez for me. I think he found her, but he never had a chance to tell me and to collect the rest of his money. I had paid him fifty dollars in advance and promised him two hundred more for Tula Lopez. She'd borne Lockwood a child. I figured there might still be some kind of bond between them and she could possibly put me in touch with him if he's alive, or tell me what happened to him if he's dead."

"Two hundred dollars to find a hustler in these parts, that's real inflation for you. They used to be a dime a dozen, and for fifty cents they'd throw in a free case of V.D. They're somewhat cleaner now. The tourists were complaining. *Turista* in Rio Seco did not always involve the digestive track . . . Tell me more about Jenkins."

"The fifty dollars was found in his pocket when they picked up the pieces. It paid for his funeral. It wasn't much of a funeral—I'm sure Hernandez did better."

Aragon thought of the mourning party leaving the house in the Cadillacs and Jensen, the black-veiled widow with her starched and scrubbed children, the dignified, formally dressed men. They hadn't yet returned. They were probably still at church, praying for Hernandez's soul and paying for the candles with some of his *mordidas*.

"I am still upchucking coincidences," the superintendent said. "A little wine might help settle my stomach. Would you care for some?"

Aragon glanced over at the table with the bottle of wine on it and the impaled cork. "From that bottle?"

"Certainly. Red wine should always be served at room temperature."

"What I meant was, I thought it would be considered evidence."

"I see no harm in drinking a little of the evidence. There'll be enough left." The superintendent poured two glasses of wine, gave one to Aragon and raised the other in a toast. "To crime. Without it we'd both be unemployed. Drink up."

"I prefer not to."

"Squeamish?"

"I was imagining what would happen to me back home if I were found drinking some of the evidence in a murder case."

"A bad thing would happen?"

"Very bad. Maybe terminal."

"Ah well, we're more civilized here. A little evidence is just as good as a lot." He drank both glasses of wine, pronounced it mediocre, wished aloud for some bleu cheese to go with it, poured a third glass and settled back in the swivel chair again. "This client of yours, the lady who is about fifty and likes fat homely men, she must be rich."

"Yes."

"Is she Catholic?"

"No."

"I can be ecumenical when necessary. Is she really very rich, do you suppose?"

"Yes."

"You know, Aragon, I could change my mind about wanting a family. After all, it might be a mistake for a man my age to start a family if he has the opportunity to marry a mature rich woman. This line of thought appeals to me suddenly. What do you think?"

"I think no."

"Why no?"

"For starters, Mrs. Decker is already married, she doesn't speak Spanish, she has strong opinions and states them bluntly, and she's pretty tight with a buck."

"But as her husband I would control her money."

"No."

"I would be boss."

"No."

"Ah well, there are other fish in the sea," the superintendent said.

He postponed his report to Gilly until after he'd had dinner and some tequila in the form of three margaritas. He decided to make the call as brief as possible in the hope of avoiding any histrionics, recriminations, hindsights or whatever she was offering, so after a brief exchange of amenities he said, "There's an item in tonight's newspaper. You'd better hear it."

"No. Wait. Maybe I'd rather not. Your voice sounds funny."

"I've been talking for four hours."

"What about? No, don't tell me. There's something wrong, of course. There always is when the phone rings late at night like this and it's you on the line."

He didn't say anything.

"Aragon? Operator, I think I've been cut off. Aragon, are you there? What are you doing?"

"Waiting for you to shut up."

"That's rude," Gilly said. "That's damn bloody rude."

"I know."

"Aren't you going to apologize?"

"Not unless I have to."

"I don't believe in *forced* apologies. What good are *forced* apologies?"

"Beats me."

"You've been drinking again. It's obvious from your impertinence."

"I'm having my third margarita."

"You'll turn into a lush if you keep this up. Does alcoholism run in your family?"

"Shucks, no. There was just Mom and Dad, and my grandparents on both sides, and my uncles Manuel and Reginato, and my Aunt Maya—she could really belt the booze—"

"Oh, shut up."

"I will if you will."

She did, for a minute. "Is it—do you have bad news?"

"It was bad for Hernandez and not so good for me. Are you ready to listen now?"

"Yes."

"Okay. 'Magistrate Guadalupe Hernandez, well-known in Rio Seco legal circles, died last night of a stab wound inflicted during an attempted burglary of his foothill residence. Magistrate Hernandez maintained an office in his home and it was in this room that the crime occurred. It is not known what was stolen from the ransacked office. No suspects have been arrested, but Superintendent Playa of the Police Department is following several important leads. The magistrate's survivors include his wife, Carmela Maria Espinosa, six children, three brothers and a sister. Requiem high mass will be recited Sunday evening at Her Lady of Sorrows Church.' That's it, Mrs. Decker."

"Does this mean you never even talked to him?"

"It means," Aragon said, "that someone reached him before I did. Any man who lives the way he lived makes enemies. Maybe one of them tried to get his *mordida* back."

"'Ransacked office.' What was ransacked?"

"Desk drawers, filing cabinets, everything. Even if Hernandez were alive to supervise the work, it would take a week to put things together again. As matters stand now, it will probably never be known for sure if any particular file is missing, such as one about B. J. and the circumstances of his release and his present whereabouts."

"How do you know such a file ever existed?"

"I don't. It probably didn't, and even more probably doesn't."

"So we've come to another dead end."

"Dying, anyway."

"How I hate those words, 'dead,' 'dying.' But God knows I should be used to them by now."

"Please," Aragon said, "don't go into a poor-little-me routine. I've been on the grill a long time tonight and I still have some sore spots. Which is better than being in jail."

"Did they put you in jail?"

"Almost."

"What crime did you commit?"

"I didn't commit anything. You don't have to commit anything to land in jail here. You just have to look as though you did or might or could."

"I never thought you looked especially criminal," Gilly said. "Perhaps a little on the sly side at times. You know, cunning, crafty. Maybe it's your glasses. Do you have to wear them?"

"No, I wear them for fun."

"You don't have to sound so mad. It was a perfectly simple question. Everyone seems awfully touchy tonight. Reed got mad at me because I refused to fire Marco's new nurse. He's jealous. She's a good nurse and I enjoy talking to her. He won't admit that I have to see other people for a change instead of spending all my time listening to him yak about food and Violet Smith about religion. Poor Reed. I think he'd like to marry me, but someone got his bootees mixed up in the nursery."

"Marry you?"

"Not me as in me, me as in money."

"How do you feel about it?"

"He's a boy. Boys are for girls. Or in Reed's case, for other boys. If he should ever become insistent, I'll give him a nice bonus and tell him to get lost. He'll be leaving eventually, anyway, when Marco—" The sentence dangled unfinished like a half-knotted noose. "All right, your job's over, Aragon. You might as well come home."

"My other trip home lasted less than forty-eight hours."

"This one will be permanent. I'm tired, you're tired."

"I have to stay here awhile."

"You're to come back now," she said sharply. "We'll settle the account. It's probably cost me a bundle already, bribing half the people in Baja and paying for all the margaritas you've been swilling."

"Margaritas don't swill easy. I charge extra."

"By the way, I intend to go over your expense account line by line."

"Do that. I'll submit it to you when I return."

"Which will be tomorrow."

"No."

"You're not hearing me, Aragon. I said—"

"I heard you and I said no. I'm going to stay here and look for the girl."

"Wait. Listen to me—"

"Good night, Gilly."

He put down the phone and ordered another margarita to see if it could be swilled. It couldn't. He used it to clean his teeth— it had a very stimulating effect on the gums—and went to bed.

19

IT WAS SUNDAY.

The fog of the previous night had been driven back to sea by the sun. The wet leaves of the camellias were dark-green mirrors, and the cypress trees were covered with drops of water that caught the sun and looked like tiny glass Christmas balls.

"A beautiful day," Gilly told Marco when she brought his breakfast. "It's so clear, the mountains look as though you could reach out and touch them. When Mrs. Morrison gets here she'll wheel you around to the front of the house so you can see them for yourself . . . I know you don't like her, but you will. And Reed can't work every day. He went to see his mother at a rest home in Oxnard; she's a little balmy. That's his story, anyway. Actually, I'm not even sure he has a mother. But he must have had at one time or another, so what does it matter?"

He stared, one-eyed, at the ceiling.

"The sky? There's not a cloud in sight and it's very blue, like cornflowers. Remember the cornflowers I wore at our wedding? I wanted to keep them but you said not to bother, there'd be a thousand others. But I've never seen any since that were quite that blue."

He was sorry.

"Oh well, they'd be faded by this time, anyway. It's not important. I must keep reminding myself to separate what's important from what isn't." She pulled open the drapes. Beyond the tips of his pygmy forest of plants, the sea shimmered like molten silver. "The kelp beds look purple . . . I wonder why they call that war decoration the Purple Heart. Do you know?"

He didn't know. He'd almost forgotten there was such a thing. What else had he forgotten? A minute here, a week there, or great whole chunks of time? Things were moving inside his head, in directions he could no longer control. Sometimes they met and merged, or they broke off and parts disappeared.

Years flowed in and flowed out of his mind like tides, leaving pools of memories full of small living things. Sometimes the tides stopped, the pools dried up and nothing lived in them any longer. A strange man came and helped him move his bowels. A strange woman sat beside him, claiming to be his wife. Another strange woman had been sent by the Lord to save him, but he didn't know from what. Strangers walked in and out while Gilly and

Violet Smith and Reed hid behind clouds or in forests under snow, disappeared around corners and below horizons.

But today was very clear. It was today. The woman was Gilly, his wife. Soldiers got Purple Hearts for being wounded in action. Purpleheart was also a timber from South America named for its color. Masses of kelp looked purple from a distance; close up they were copper-colored and the leaves felt slimy when you swam over them. The woman with the morning newspaper and the glass of orange juice with the plastic tube in it was his wife, Gilly. She was a little balmy, like Reed's mother.

She cranked up his bed and put the plastic tube in his mouth. "Drink up."

He drank. He would have liked to tell her about the timber purpleheart, but she probably wouldn't consider it important. Now that she was dividing things up into important and nonimportant, he wondered where he belonged. Maybe in the middle, leaning toward the non.

"That's a good boy," she said when he finished the orange juice. "Are you hungry this morning?"

No. But he let the egg slither down his throat.

"Violet Smith made you some of her special Sunday toast."

The toast was cut into cubes, soaked in warm milk and sprinkled with cinnamon and sugar and wheat germ. She spooned it into his mouth, giving him several minutes to swallow each spoonful. During these intervals she read aloud items from the newspaper.

Threat of a local bus strike was now believed ended. A government building on Downing Street had been bombed by the IRA. Dow-Jones went up twenty-four points during the past week. Heavy rains in Northern California were expected to hit the lower part of the state late tomorrow or Tuesday. Nine students were shot a few miles from Buenos Aires. A Los Angeles woman was found guilty of embezzling thirty thousand dollars from Crocker National Bank. The Coast Guard rescued a young couple becalmed five miles from shore in a small sailboat.

"I don't see anything in the paper about the magistrate who was murdered in Rio Seco. Aragon told me about it last night on the phone. Hernandez I believe his name was. It's a funny coincidence, isn't it, that he was the magistrate who took a bribe to release B. J. from jail. What a vicious man he must have been, allowing people to rot in jail until they got enough money to buy their way out. He deserved to be murdered, don't you think so, dear?"

He went on swallowing Violet Smith's special Sunday toast. It tasted like Monday morning.

Violet Smith came for the tray. She was dressed for church in a brown suit with an elaborate feathered hat given to her by a former employer. She talked across and around Marco almost as if he'd died during the night and no one had bothered to move the body.

"Did he like the toast, Mrs. Decker?"

"He didn't complain," Gilly said dryly.

"What do you think of my hat, is it too dressy?"

"No."

"Since I'm not allowed to wear jewelry anymore, I thought a few feathers would liven things up . . . Is he through?"

"Yes."

"Poor soul, I hope he can't taste too good. That wheat-germ stuff is nauseous. Reed bought it for his virility last week." Violet Smith picked up the tray. "I wonder if I could speak to you in private for a minute. I don't want him to hear. He has enough trouble already."

"I've told you before, Mr. Decker doesn't like to be talked about as if he's not here."

"Well, he's not really *here*, is he?"

"He's here, dammit."

He was there. It was today. The bickering women were Violet Smith and his wife, Gilly. He wished they'd go away and come in again as two strangers. Strangers were easier to bear.

They talked in the hall, with Marco's door closed. Rays of the sun slanted through the skylight, and the feathers in Violet Smith's hat iridesced and looked alive.

"I've been turning this over and over in my mind," she said, "until I'm on the verge of a sinking spell. I'm not sure what's right and what's not. There's such a thing as minding your own business and then there's such a thing as avoiding your responsibility."

"Get to the point."

"You told me I was never to talk in church about any of the things that happen here at the house—Mrs. Lockwood and all that hanky-panky—and I never did. I never so much as mentioned Mr. Lockwood. *She* did."

"Who?"

"Ethel Lockwood, his first wife. She brought up the subject at the last meeting. I tried to stop her." She couldn't recall saying from the back of the room, *Speak up, I can't hear you.* And if such a memory had struggled its way into her conscious mind, she would have disowned it. "Mrs. Lockwood was determined to continue."

"I can't prevent her from talking," Gilly said. "About Mr. Lockwood or anything else."

"But she's saying bad things."

"How bad?"

Violet Smith's wooden face was splintered by uncertainty. "We're honor-bound not to tell outsiders what goes on at the meetings and I'm scared. He is listening Up There. You better go and see Mrs. Lockwood for yourself."

"I don't want to. I haven't seen her in years."

"You better, anyway. She's a little odd, which aren't we all, but she knows something you don't and you ought to."

"Concerning B. J.?"

"Yes."

"Is it important?"

"I wouldn't be standing here talking like this with Him listening Up There if it wasn't important." Violet Smith's feathers were quivering. "Do you want me to tell you her address?"

"I know her address," Gilly said. "Ethel and I are old friends."

20

SHE REMEMBERED THE last time she'd seen the house.

B. J. was waiting to let her in. His face was flushed with excitement and anticipation.

"We'll have the whole house to ourselves for a week. Ethel's gone to visit her sister in Tucson and I'm supposed to be staying at the University Club while she's away. Isn't that marvelous?"

It was marvelous.

They used the guest room, which had a king-size bed with a blue silk spread that wrinkled. Afterward B. J., still naked, tried to iron out the wrinkles with his hands. He looked foolish and helpless. She loved him desperately.

"Next time," she said, "we'll take the spread off."

"Next time?" He couldn't cope with this time, let alone think about a next time. He glanced over at the suitcase she'd brought as if he couldn't recall carrying it upstairs for her and putting it on the rack at the foot of the bed. "Maybe you shouldn't actually move in, G. G. It might be better if we met at a motel."

"I want to stay here. I love this room. I love you."

"That damn spread, it'll be the first thing she notices. Why couldn't she have picked some material that doesn't wrinkle?"

"You mustn't be afraid of her."

"She might faint. She faints a lot."

"What if *I* fainted? Right this minute?"

"Oh hell, G. G., you wouldn't. I mean... would you?"

"I guess not. I'm trying, but I can't seem to get the hang of it."

She sat down on the bed again, deliberately, heavily.

"For God's sake," he said. "Get off there."

"No."

"You don't *realize*—"

"I realize. I just want you to love me so much that you don't care about anything else in the world."

"That's crazy."

"So I'm crazy. Do you love me anyway?"

"Sure I do. But Ethel brought that spread all the way from Hong Kong."

"Maybe if we're lucky she'll take it back to Hong Kong."

He began to laugh in spite of himself at the image of Ethel dragging the spread all the way back to Hong Kong.

Later he was sober again, and scared. Gilly wasn't. "I don't care," she said, "if Ethel walks in right this minute." She didn't. She walked in five days later. She and her sister had an argument and Ethel came home early. She was shocked, disgusted, reproachful. She sobbed, she fainted, she screamed. Then she went back to her sister's in Tucson to think things over.

B. J. thought things over, too. "She doesn't really like me, you know. I don't blame her. I'm no prize."

"You are to me," Gilly said.

"You weren't kidding when you said you were crazy. Me a prize. That's a laugh."

"It's true."

"What do you suppose I should do now?"

"Get a divorce and marry me."

"Is this—are you *proposing* to me?"

"Yes."

"Women aren't supposed to do that, G. G. They're supposed to wait to be asked."

"I waited. You never asked."

"How could I? I'm married."

"I'm not. So I'll do the asking. Will you marry me?"

"Well, for Christ's sake—"

"Leave Christ out of it. It's you and me, B. J."

B. J. consulted a lawyer and moved to the University Club. Ethel sent the bedspread to the dry cleaner. Gilly started shopping for a trousseau. If a shadow of remorse appeared now and then, she closed her eyes or turned her back. *It's you and me, B. J.*

From a distance the big white stucco house looked the same. But as she approached, Gilly saw that the paint was peeling off the walls and the window frames. The trees in the courtyard had turned brown from lack of water and were dropping their leaves in the dry birdbath and the empty lily pond. A black cat crouched on top of the wall as if he were waiting for Halloween or for the birdbath to be filled. It watched with green-eyed interest as Gilly walked through the courtyard and pressed the chime of the front door.

This time it was Ethel who let her in.

"I've been expecting you," she said. "Violet Smith called to tell me you were on your way."

"I don't know exactly what I'm doing here."

"You will. Come inside."

"We can talk out here."

"Are you afraid I've arranged some kind of trap for you? How quaint. I assure you I bear no grudges and I have forgiven all my enemies. Come, you'll want to see the changes in the house."

Gilly went inside, wondering about the changes and whether the blue silk bedspread had been one of them. Probably the first.

The living room was lavishly furnished, but it had the pervasive chill of a place that was never used. A layer of dust covered everything, like a family curse, the red velvet chairs and marble-topped tables, the gilt-framed portraits of plump gentle women and stiff-necked men. Silver vases for rosebuds, and crystal bowls made to float camellias, were empty. Spiderwebs hung undisturbed across the chandeliers, and there were cracks in the plaster of the ceiling as though the house had been shaken by a series of explosions.

There were matching cracks in Ethel's face, dividing it into sections like a relief map. She was very thin. Everything about her was thin, her arms and legs, her greying hair, even her skin looked transparent. The blue veins in her temples seemed barely covered.

"It's rude to stare." She spoke just above a whisper, hissing slightly over the *s* sounds. The effect was soft and deadly like escaping gas. "I told you there were changes. I can't afford to keep the place up."

"B. J. left you well provided for."

"He did. But times change—increasing taxes, inflation, some bad investments, a loan to an old friend. No wild extravagances, simply normal living, yet in a few years a house begins to look like this. B. J. would be distressed to see it."

"Don't worry, he won't see it."

"No? You might be wrong."

"What makes you say that?"

"ESP, perhaps. Perhaps something a good deal more practical . . . Gracious, I'm forgetting my manners. Please sit down. The wing chairs by the fireplace are very comfortable, but then, you know that, don't you? Now, how shall I address you? I don't believe it would be quite appropriate to call you Gilly or G. G., as B. J. did. B. J. and G. G. How sweet."

"My name is Mrs. Decker. I prefer to stand."

"Very well." She herself sat down in one of the wing chairs and began stroking its red velvet upholstery very gently as though soothing an elderly family pet. "You mustn't think Violet Smith has been indulging in idle gossip. She felt compelled to tell me certain facts."

"Such as?"

"That you were attempting to locate B. J. and the trail ended in the Rio Seco jail, where he is believed to have died."

"And why did Violet Smith feel compelled to tell you all this?"

"Because your facts and mine don't agree. That loan to an old friend I mentioned a few minutes ago, it wasn't actually for an old friend."

"It was for B. J.?"

"Yes."

"When?"

"Three years ago. He didn't die in jail. I paid ten thousand dollars to get him out of there. It wasn't easy to collect that much extra cash. I sold some of my antiques and borrowed the rest from my sister. I know the money arrived safely. He wrote me a thank you note after his release, just a line or two, without any return address. I didn't keep it. I guess I was piqued because it was so short, so—almost ungracious. I don't think he'd ever accepted money from a woman before and perhaps it hurt his pride." There was a ragged edge of doubt in her voice. "I still have the first letter, though, the one where he asked for the money. That was gracious, oh yes, very gracious indeed. I want you to read it."

"Why?"

"So you won't have to take my word for anything."

"I take it."

"Don't you think it would be better if you took his? Here."

The letter Gilly had received five years before had been written on heavy bond, engraved JENLOCK HACIENDAS, BAHÍA DE BALLENAS, BAJA CALIFORNIA SUR. This one was on a kind of onionskin paper Gilly hadn't seen since she was a child. It was postmarked Rio Seco and the return address was the Quarry: LA CANTERA, PENITENCIARIA DEL ESTADO.

> *Dear Ethel:*
>
> *I don't know how to start this letter because I shouldn't be writing it—not to you of all people. I treated you rotten. You have every right and reason to tear this up before you go any further. But please don't. I haven't anyone else to turn to. I am locked in this terrible place which is so terrible you couldn't bear to come inside the gate. I remember that day we went to the pound to claim Angel, how you cried just seeing the animals locked up. Well now I'm one of them . . .*

Gilly said, "Who was Angel?"

"Our Yorkshire terrier."

"I didn't know B. J. ever had a dog." It was such a small thing, completely unimportant, but it bothered her. It made her realize that he'd had a whole life before she even met him, that he'd been married to Ethel twice as long as to her.

> *I'm in this filthy cage Ethel and I didn't do anything to hurt people. I just thought it was a good idea to bring some prosperity to that God forsaken village I was stuck in. Why am I always being stuck in places? It must be lack of character like you told me once. It really hurt me your saying that. I was never sure what character was so how could I get any.*
>
> *I keep wishing I could start over or at least go back to the point where I began making bad mistakes. You are the only woman I ever truly loved and admired and respected. I could never live up to your standards. None of the other women had class like you Ethel. That's why they appealed to me I guess because they were no better than I was which wasn't much . . .*

Gilly's hands had begun to tremble. The paper made little rustling sounds like evil whispers. "He was desperate. People tell lies when they're desperate."

"Or truths."

"There's not a word of truth in—"

"Go on reading."

> *I don't understand how it all happened between Gilly and me. She was a lot of fun and we had some laughs but then suddenly she was expecting me to marry her. She asked me to, I'm not kidding. I was flattered. I had to really talk fast to get you even to consider marrying me and here was this other woman anxious to have me. I'm not making excuses Ethel. I just want you to realize that often things just happen to people like me. Ordinary people must see things coming and duck maybe, or fight back or run away. But there are some of us who don't see what's coming and we end up in a place like this. I won't try to describe it for you. You wouldn't believe it anyway being you're so clean in mind and body. Do you still take all those showers every day? My God what I'd give for a long hot shower right now. To be clean again what a luxury that would be. Everybody and everything at the Quarry is slimy. It's funny how the people in the U.S. have so many nicknames for prison like it was kind of a joke—pokey, slammer, clink, brig, cooler, tank etc. Here nobody ever calls it anything but the Quarry. It's too serious to have a nickname. I must get out. I must.*

Ethel you are the only hope I have left. One of the guards told me that my case is finally coming up next month. I can't explain how this crazy system works but it's not the way ours does with a jury, etc. The man who is the magistrate assigned to me will decide my fate. Word from the grapevine is that he charges a fixed price to release Americans $10,000. Guilt and innocence and justice they're only words here. No matter what I did nor didn't do, for $10,000 I can get out of this place.

Please help me. Please for the love of God help me Ethel. I'm going to die here unless you get me out. I am filthy. My clothes, my cot, the food I eat, it's all filthy. My teeth are rotting and my hair is falling out and my eyes are so bad I can hardly see what I'm writing. I've paid a hundred times for every hurt I've done anyone. I can't take it much longer. I am at your mercy Ethel.

B. J.

Gilly folded the letter and put it back in the envelope very quickly so that Ethel might not notice how badly her hands were trembling. She felt sick, as if someone had struck her a mortal blow in the stomach, and the lump in her throat was so large and heavy that she was afraid her voice couldn't push past it: "Why did you ask me to read this?"

"So you'd understand how useless it is for you to go on searching for B. J. Even if you found him, he wouldn't want to live with you anyway. He turned to *me* in his hour of need, not you. It's all there in the letter. I am the only woman he ever loved and admired and respected."

"Shut up, damn you! Shut your vicious mouth, you—"

"B. J. was right," Ethel said softly. "You have no class."

During the afternoon Gilly cried, sometimes for B. J., sometimes for herself. Mrs. Morrison gave her two pills and Violet Smith brought her the kind of drink Violet Smith had often made for her own consumption before she'd taken the pledge.

When she finally ran out of tears she used eyedrops to clear her eyes, and witch hazel pads to reduce the swelling, and make-up to obscure the lines of grief around her mouth. Then she walked across the hall to her husband's room.

She said, without looking at him, "I went to see Ethel Lockwood this morning. She showed me the letter she got from B. J. in prison."

He moved his head. He didn't want to hear about it. Everything was far away and long ago. Who was Ethel?

"The letter had a number of interesting things in it, personal things about me. The consensus of opinion is that I have no class. Imagine that. I always thought I was such a classy dame. Didn't you?"

He knew what was coming.

"Also, I'm dirty. I don't stand around in the shower all day, so I'm dirty."

He could hear the note in her voice that meant she was going to throw a fit and nothing and nobody could stop her. Not even Mrs. Morrison, who thrust her head inside the door and asked if there was anything she could do.

"Yes," Gilly said. "You can drop dead."

"I told you to lie down and rest after taking those pills. I naturally assumed—"

"You can assume right up your ass to your armpits."

"Your knowledge of anatomy is rather meager." Mrs. Morrison turned her attention to the wheelchair. "I'll be out in the hall if you need me, Mr. Decker. Press the buzzer and I'll hear it. I'll probably hear a great many other things as well, but it is my duty to stick with my patient in fair weather *or* foul. Press your buzzer. Have you got that, Mr. Decker? Signify that you understand me by raising two fingers of your right hand for yes. Or did we agree on one finger for yes and two for no? I'm not sure. No matter. Buzz."

"You buzz," Gilly said. "Buzz off."

"I shall be in the hall, Mr. Decker. Listening."

He lay silent and motionless, wishing all the women would go away and never come back, Mrs. Morrison and Violet Smith and Gilly, and now this other one, Ethel. Who was Ethel?

Gilly described her briefly. Ethel was a vicious-tongued, sanctimonious snotty old bitch.

"Where'd she get the right to criticize me? I have as much class as she has. Goddamn it, I'm a classy dame. Are you listening? Do you hear that, you nosy parker out in the hall? I'm a classy dame!"

She began to cry again.

"You know what it said in the letter? It said, 'I don't understand how it all happened between Gilly and me. She was a lot of fun and we had some laughs, but then suddenly she was expecting me to marry her. She asked me to.' That's what it said in the letter, making it sound like I begged, like I was lower than low."

Tears and more tears.

He wished he could offer her some comfort or explanation, anything to stop the deluge that threatened to wash them both out to sea. *We are drowning, Gilly and I, we are drowning together.*

21

ARAGON SPENT SUNDAY driving the rutted roads and walking the dusty streets of Rio Seco. He began near the shoemaker's shop where Jenkins had lived and worked his way past the tinsmiths and weavers and potters and wood-carvers into the red-light district of sleazy bars and sin shows and cubicles where the prostitutes lived and worked and died. He talked to peddlers, cabbies, hookers, *mariachis*. None of them had heard of Tula Lopez.

At eight o'clock he returned to his hotel to have dinner. The clerk on duty at the desk when he stopped to pick up his room key was the same elderly man who'd given him the insecticide on the first night of his stay. He looked nervous. "You like it here at our hotel, sir?"

"It's fine."

"No more mosquitoes?"

"Nothing I can't handle." *I drink beer and the mosquitoes siphon it off before it can damage my liver. It's a pretty fair system.*

"I was telling Superintendent Playa what a quiet and polite young man you were for an American."

"And why did you tell the superintendent that?"

"Because he asked."

"That seems like a good reason."

"I thought so." Some crazy insect was hurling itself at the light above the desk, and the clerk watched it for a while with a kind of detached interest. "*Why* the superintendent asked, I don't know. But you will certainly find out."

"Certainly?"

"Oh yes. He's waiting for you in the dining room. Since seven o'clock. Already he's eaten one dinner and may have finished a second by this time. Naturally, we cannot present him with a check. It would be unwise. Yet it hardly seems fair that the hotel should pay, since the reason he's here is you. Once in a while a policeman comes to the hotel, but never so important a one and never one with such a huge appetite."

"Put his dinners on my bill."

"What if you are not available later to pay the bill? Possibly you would like to settle your account tonight."

"No, I wouldn't like that."

"What if I insist?"

"I wouldn't like that, either."

"Perhaps you are not so polite an American as I thought," the clerk said and grabbed at the insect that was attacking the light over the desk. He missed. Aragon left the two of them battling it out.

Superintendent Playa, wearing civilian clothes, sat in a corner of the dining room behind a potted palm as though he were in hiding. But there was too much of him to hide, and it seemed inevitable that more of him was on its way. He was eating flan with whipped cream, and drinking something thick and yellowish out of a glass mug.

"Oh, Mr. Aragon. Good evening."

"Good evening, Superintendent."

"I've been waiting for you, passing the time with a bite to eat. Please sit down."

"All right."

"Join me in a *rompope*. It's an eggnog flavored with rum. Quite delicious."

"No thanks."

"Very well, we'll get down to business." The superintendent unbuckled the belt of his trousers, and his stomach ballooned out between him and the table like an air safety bag inflating on impact. "The word is that you've been searching for the girl Tula Lopez all over town."

"Yes."

"You still want to see her?"

"Very much."

"Perhaps I can arrange it. Yes, I think it would be quite possible."

"You know where she is?"

"I know. Come along, we'll pay her a call."

"I haven't had any dinner."

"I ate for both of us to save time."

"That's very good of you."

"You might really believe that, a little later on. If one is going to feel squeamish, it is better to do so on an empty stomach." He rose with some difficulty and pushed his own stomach back into the captivity of its belt. Then he called for his check.

Aragon said, "I told the clerk to add it to my bill."

"Why would you do such a thing? Have you a guilty conscience?"

"No."

"Are you attempting to influence my judgment?"

"No."

"Then why should you pay for my dinner as if I'd been your invited guest?"

"I—"

"Unless, of course, you invited me and the invitation failed to reach me in time. Could that be true?"

"It could."

"Then I accept your hospitality. Many of my invitations arrive late or never. Our local system of communications is poor, though I believe you and I are communicating quite nicely, are we not?"

"I think so."

"Then let us proceed on our way."

The superintendent was driving his personal car, a Toyota not much bigger than he was. He handled it as though it were his alter ego, with courteous attention and respect. Other motorists honked at him from behind, put their heads out windows to curse him as they passed, looked back and shook their fists. The superintendent didn't let it bother him.

"Peasants," he said amicably. "I save my wrath for more significant occasions. Besides, I have a full stomach. There is nothing more soothing than a good meal, isn't that correct?"

"I don't remember. I haven't had one lately."

"Try not to be waspish, Mr. Aragon. I am, after all, doing you a favor. You could have spent a week, even a month, searching for this girl, and I found her for you. You must learn the art of gratitude."

"I don't want to be grateful until I know what I'm being grateful for."

They had reached the bridge. The superintendent was driving very slowly in spite of the pressure of traffic. "Let's see now. It was right about here, from this spot, that your friend Harry Jenkins jumped. No manner of death is pleasant but it seems to me Jenkins picked, or was granted, one of the better ones, leaping out into the air like a bird, then dropping into oblivion. Magistrate Hernandez had no choice, no such beautiful moment of flying. It was quick, though. Others are not so lucky."

She had put up a struggle.

For Tula, there'd been no easy bird flight, no sudden halt of the heart. Deep-purple bruises covered her face and arms and throat. A patch of her hair had been pulled out by the roots and was caught in the splinters of a shattered chair, like a thick black spiderweb. Two of her front teeth were missing and her neck was broken.

The room was like a cage for animals, but it smelled of people, of human wastes and wasting.

"She's been dead since early this morning," the superintendent said. "As is usual in a neighborhood like this, nobody saw anything, nobody heard anything. She was conducting her ordinary business. Only this one particular client wasn't ordinary. He was—what would you call him in English?"

"Kinky."

"So we have a dead whore, murdered by a kinky client. That certainly seems reasonable, doesn't it?"

"I don't know. Whatever you say. I'd like to get out of here."

"Why? You wanted to see her. Well, here she is, take a look . . . What's the matter, do you feel squeamish?"

"Yes."

"I knew you were the type. At least be glad you didn't pay for a nice big dinner which you would only upchuck. As it is, you have nothing to upchuck."

Aragon went outside and proved him wrong. The air was fresh, straight from the sea, but all he could smell was the little room and the dead girl and his own vomit.

The superintendent followed him out. "You're becoming a problem, Mr. Aragon. Don't I have enough trouble without a squeamish American on my hands?"

"I think it's a touch of—it must be *turista.*"

"Nonsense. It's murder. You are revolted at the sight of murdered girls. I too am revolted, being a man of sensitivity, but it is my profession to look at them. The eye, the digestive system, the mind, they all make the necessary adjustments. Death is a fact of life."

Aragon leaned against the wall of the building, which was covered with graffiti, mainly in English. The first one he read when his eyes came back into focus was *You were on Canit Camera dummy haha Speedo Martinelli Newark NJ USA.*

"Are you feeling better, Mr. Aragon?"

"No."

"You have stopped upchucking."

"I ran out of chuck. I—may I go and sit in the car?"

"Very well. We can talk there."

They returned to the superintendent's Toyota. Even inside the car with the windows rolled up, Aragon could smell the cage that was Tula's room, and with his eyes closed he could see the wall that had served as the community's bulletin board: *This a hell hol . . . Chinga tu madre . . . Viva Echeveria . . . Freddy from Chi . . . Hi Freddy . . . God Forgive all Sinners . . . Constancia 3349 . . . Repent . . . Lolita esta pinchincha!*

"Three deaths," the superintendent said. "And you appear to be the common denominator. You come to Rio Seco to talk to Jenkins and suddenly he is leaping from a bridge. You go away and come back, this time to see Magistrate Hernandez, and lo, he is stabbed by a burglar. You look for Tula Lopez and here she is, beaten and strangled."

"I barely knew Jenkins, I never met Hernandez and I just saw Tula Lopez for the first time."

"But someone knew all those people."

"Yes."

"Someone didn't want any of them discussing him, perhaps telling you where he is. Would you call that a fair assumption?"

"Yes."

"This Lockwood, we must find him."

"Yes."

"Because he is a murderer, a madman."

Aragon stared, heavy-eyed, into the night. The Lockwood Gilly knew no longer existed. He had died somewhere in the years between Dreamboat and the Quarry, and a violent stranger now walked around in his body.

"No. No, I can't believe—"

"You must," the superintendent said quietly. "I think it would be wise for you to leave Rio Seco as soon as possible. It is an ugly place to die, especially at this time of year. Spring would be better, when the flowers are in bloom after the winter rains. But one doesn't have a choice of season when one is dealing with a madman. Lockwood doesn't intend to let you find him. That surely is clear to you by now, isn't it?"

"I guess so."

"Naturally, you hate to fail in your mission and thus disappoint your client, but you're young, you have much to live for. Are you married?"

"Yes."

"Your wife is expecting you back?"

"Yes."

"In a box?"

"If you're trying to scare me, don't bother. I'm already scared."

Instinctively, he looked back over his shoulder. The streets were crowded. Rio Seco was opening up for the night.

"No, no," the superintendent said. "Don't look back. He's not there. He hasn't been following you. He's been ahead of you, waiting behind every corner you turn."

"How could he know what I was going to do?"

"I don't mean to be unduly critical, Mr. Aragon, but your actions seem most predictable. That's to say, you're an amateur. Lockwood is a graduate of the Quarry."

Lockwood had learned well—how to con a con man, how to stab as expertly as a surgeon, how to beat up women. *Summa cum laude.*

"I must return you to your hotel and get to work," the superintendent said. "By the way, have you talked to your rich lady client since our last meeting?"

"Yes."

"You didn't by any chance mention me as a likely prospect for her?"

"No."

"No, of course not. The situation was too delicate. But now you may proceed with a clear conscience, since Lockwood is out of the picture and the situation is no longer delicate. There are a number of facts you might tell her about me which are perhaps not apparent on the surface. For instance, I have never once accepted a *mordida*, or at any rate nothing more than a few cases of liquor. That ought to impress her, yes?"

"Possibly."

"I am a man of honor. I have all my own teeth. Also, I have an independent income, my mother gives me a small allowance. I wouldn't want your client to think I was interested only in her money, when the truth is, I have a very romantic nature. Be sure to mention that."

"I'll mention it," Aragon said. Gilly would need all the laughs she could get after she heard his report: *Your precious B. J. is a nut who kills people, but there's this other guy waiting in the wings with an allowance from his mother and a very romantic nature. How's that for a joke, Gilly?*

"You look peculiar, Mr. Aragon. If you're going to upchuck again, kindly open the window."

He opened the window.

22

"WELL, THIS IS it," Violet Smith said. "It really is *it*, isn't it?"

Reed yawned, stretched and opened the two top buttons of his uniform. "There's not much point in standing around talking about it. Make yourself useful. Or scarce."

"I'm afraid. I never saw anyone die before."

"So don't look."

"It's different with you, being a nurse. You've probably seen people die all over the place."

"Usually in bed."

"What's it like, watching somebody die?"

"Great fun. Gives me the jollies. Ho ho ho."

"Our minister says there's a moment when the soul leaves the body. When it happens, can you feel it? I mean, is there kind of like a draft as the soul goes up?"

"Who says it goes up? Decker's may be going down."

"Oh no."

"Some go up, some go down, some may even go sideways. Mine is definitely going down."

"You can't be sure."

"Sure I'm sure."

"Why? Are you a terrible sinner?"

"You bet your butt," Reed said, yawning again. "I want to catch half an hour's sleep out on the patio. Wake me if the old girl starts flinging herself around."

He had been up since four o'clock when Gilly called him and told him her husband was dying. She'd done the same thing a dozen times in the past few months and Reed didn't take it seriously until the doctor came and said it was true. There was talk of moving him into a hospital but Gilly refused. What could they do for him in a hospital—stick tubes up his nose and needles into his veins to prolong his suffering? So he stayed home and she stayed with him.

"He will die in my arms, where he belongs," Gilly told Reed.

"It will be messy."

"Surely you, of all people, should be able to put up with a little mess."

"I'm able. Are you able?"

"Oh God, he's trying to *talk*. I can't stand it. I can't stand his torture."

"See what I mean?" Reed said. "Messy."

Aragon picked up his car at the airport and drove directly to Gilly's house. He wasn't sure how much of the truth he was going to tell her or even how much of the truth he actually knew. With the death of Tula Lopez, B. J.'s last tracks had been obliterated.

He crossed the patio. Reed was lying on a chaise beside the pool, sleeping. In spite of the fatigue circles under his eyes he looked very young and innocent, like a cherub who'd been up all night doing good deeds. Aragon spoke his name and Reed was instantly awake, his voice alert: "What are you doing here?"

"I came to give Mrs. Decker my report."

"Bad timing. The old boy's about to meet his maker. If there's anything she should know, tell me and I'll pass it along to her between fits."

"Tula Lopez is dead."

"Yeah? Too bad."

"She was beaten and strangled."

"That's one of the hazards of her profession."

"I wonder why anyone would bother killing a down-and-out prostitute like Tula."

"For kicks."

"Or money. A nice secure future, let's say."

"You say. I'm going back to sleep." Reed closed his eyes as if he intended to keep his word, but Aragon noticed that the muscles in his forearms were flexed and his jaw was set too tight. "Listen, Aragon, we're all under a strain here right now. Why don't you get lost for a few days?"

"I've been lost. I think I'm on the verge of finding myself."

"Do it someplace else."

"No. This is the place I was last seen."

Reed opened his eyes and sat up. "You're talking kind of weird, you know that?"

"I'm feeling kind of weird," Aragon said. "Like a patsy, for instance."

"Yeah? Well, life makes patsies of us all, as my old lady used to say before someone did her a favor and ran over her with a truck. Did I ever tell you about my old lady? She was a fight fan, used to put on the gloves with me when I was six, seven years old."

"You learned early."

"Everybody learns early when they get the hell knocked out of them if they don't."

Aragon watched the plumes of pampas grass bending toward the sun like gilded birds. "It's funny how everyone I was hired to find turned up dead."

"Yeah, that's a real chuckle."

"It would have been simpler and safer if she hadn't hired me in the first place. Why did she?"

"She had to. You speak Spanish, you see, and I don't, except for a couple of words like 'amigo.' Now, I couldn't have gone around looking for Harry Jenkins just saying 'amigo,' could I, amigo?" Reed lay down again, shielding his eyes with his right arm. "Don't worry about anything. I'm not. The Mexican police aren't likely to sweat over the murders of a hustler and a broken-down con man and a crooked judge. They certainly aren't going to bother extraditing anybody. So cheer up. You did a job, earned your money and came out cleaner than Snow White."

"Is that all you have to say?"

"Maybe I'll think of something else later on. Right now I'm tired and need a little rest. It's a strain waiting for someone to die, even when you don't give a damn about him."

"Do you give a damn about anyone, Reed?"

"Sure I do, amigo. Me."

The drapes were closed, but enough sunlight filtered through so Aragon could see that the oxygen tank beside the bed had been disconnected. Gilly was bending over her husband, her cheek against his. Tears had turned her eyes red and left the lids like transparent blisters.

Violet Smith stood beside the door in her black uniform looking smaller and more subdued than he remembered her. She said, "This is no place for strangers."

"I'll leave if Mrs. Lockwood wants me to."

"This is a sacred moment when the soul—"

"Be quiet," Gilly whispered. "He's trying to talk again. He's saying something . . . What is it, darling? Please, what is it?"

The dying man's mouth was moving and little noises were coming out, wordless croaks and whimpers, and finally, an identifiable sound: "Gee—gee—gee—"

Violet Smith clapped her hands. "Praise the Lord, he's been saved. He's trying to say 'Jesus.'"

"No," Gilly said. "Not Jesus. G. G. He always called me G. G."

"I distinctly heard 'Jesus.'"

"All right."

"I'll go and pray for his soul. O praise the Lord!"

"Yes."

Gilly had not yet given any indication that she was conscious of Aragon's presence.

"Mrs. Lockwood?"

She turned her head slightly in his direction. "They're all dead, aren't they?"

"Yes."

"Do you hear that, B. J.? They're all dead, just like I promised you, like I planned it." There was a long silence, then, "He came back across the border a year ago in a vanload of wetbacks. He was destitute and sick and on drugs. He didn't even have a wallet, but I found an old clipping in his pocket about Jenlock Haciendas, how it was going to be a great step forward for Baja. On the other side of the clipping there was a story about a Marco Decker winning the National Lottery. It seemed a lucky name. He couldn't use his own name, he'd done too many things against the law. So I set up a new identity for him, Marco Decker, and a new marriage for myself, complete with honeymoon in France. I let the word go out, through Smedler and others, that I'd met an eligible man in Europe and intended to marry him. I even arranged for Smedler to send me trousseau money in care of American Express. They sent it back to me in Los Angeles, where I was staying with B. J. in a private hospital. I arranged everything except the stroke. That was real, that was fate."

"Mrs. Lockwood, you don't have to tell me all this."

"You're my lawyer. I'm supposed to be able to tell you everything. Isn't that right?"

"Yes."

"And you're supposed to be able to keep it to yourself. I figured on that from the beginning when I chose you . . . One of the nurses in the private hospital was Reed. I hired him to help me bring B. J. home and take care of him. The three of us became not friends exactly, more like allies, allies against fate, against injustice. Reed had had a bum deal, too. He fitted in."

She got up and opened one of the drapes slightly. A shaft of sun struck the dying man across his chest.

"There was nothing I could do for B. J. except watch him die, moment by moment, inch by inch. I had such a terrible feeling of helplessness until it occurred to me one day, I don't even remember when, that there was something I could do, after all. I could find the people who corrupted him, who destroyed him, and make sure that they died, too. Tula, Jenkins, the judge, they had to die, and they had to die before he did, so I could tell him about it and he would know he was avenged. I told him. He knew."

"Maybe he didn't want to know. Maybe he didn't even like the idea of vengeance. It was your idea, wasn't it?"

"Yes."

"And Reed's work."

"Yes."

"You fed Reed the information I passed on to you. You alibied him by pretending he was here with you when I called from Rio Seco."

There was a sudden movement on the bed, a small final spasm as if the shaft of sun had hit its target.

"He's dead." She sounded a little surprised. "My husband has just died."

He knew she was wrong. B. J. had died a long time ago, in the years between Dreamboat and the Quarry.

THE MURDER OF MIRANDA

To my grandson, Jim Pagnusat

While the physical situation of the Penguin Club bears certain resemblances to that of various actual clubs on the California coast, the characters who populate it refer to no actual persons living or dead. Both the characters and the events are wholly imaginary.

Part I

MR. VAN EYCK had a great deal of money which he didn't want to spend, and a great deal of time which he didn't know how to spend. On sunny days he sat on the club terrace writing anonymous letters.

Bent over the glass and aluminum table he looked dedicated, intense. He might have been composing a poem about the waves that were crashing against the sea wall below him or about the gulls soaring high overhead reflected in the depths of the pool like languid white fish. But Mr. Van Eyck was oblivious to the sound of the ocean or the sight of birds. The more benign the weather, the more vicious the contents of his letters became. His pen glided and whirled across the paper like an expert skater across ice.

> *. . . You miserable, contemptible old fraud. Everyone is on to what you do in the shower room . . .*

His attention was not distracted by the new assistant lifeguard sitting on the mini-tower above the pool. She was a bony redhead whose biceps outmeasured her breasts and Van Eyck's taste still ran to blondes with more conventional anatomy. Nor was he paying, at the moment, any attention to the other club members, who dozed on chaises, gossiped in deck chairs, read under umbrellas, swam briefly in the pool. Wet or dry, they presented to the public a dull front.

Viewed from different, more personal angles they were far from dull. Van Eyck was in a position to know this. He had, in fact, made it his business as well as his hobby. He spent his time shuffling along the dimly lit corridors that led to the secluded cabanas. He wandered in and out of the sauna and massage department on the roof, the wine cellar in the basement, the boiler room and, if it wasn't locked, the office marked Private, Keep Out, which belonged to Henderson, the manager.

Locks and bolts and signs like Keep Out didn't bother Van Eyck, since he assumed they must be meant for other people, passing strangers, new members, crooked employees. As a result of this casual attitude, he had acquired a basic knowledge of vintage wines, therapeutic massage, Henderson's relationship with his bookie, the heating and chlorination of swimming pools and human nature in general.

> . . . *You are weaving a tangled web and you will be caught in it, blundering spider that you are . . .*

Van Eyck had another advantage in his pursuit of knowledge. He frequently pretended to be hard of hearing. He looked blank, shook his head sadly, cupped his ears: "Eh? What's that? Speak up!" So people spoke up, often saying highly interesting things both in front of and behind him. He grabbed at every morsel like a hungry squirrel and stored the lot of them away in the various hollows in his head. When he was bored he brought them out to chew and finally spit out on paper.

> . . . *You must be incredibly stupid to think you can keep your evil ways hidden from an intelligent woman like me . . .*

Van Eyck reread the sentence. Then, very lightly, he struck out woman and substituted man, leaving the original word easily legible. It was one of his favorite stratagems, to toss in small false clues and allow the reader to lead himself astray, up and down blind alleys, far from the center of the maze where Van Eyck sat secure, anonymous, shrouded in mystery, like a Minotaur.

He leaned back and took off his glasses, wiped them on the sleeve of his Polynesian print shirt and smiled at the bony redhead across the pool. No one would ever suspect that such a kindly old man, hard of hearing and seeing, was a Minotaur.

"He's at it again," Walter Henderson told Ellen, his secretary. "Don't give him any more club stationery."

"How can I refuse?"

"Say no. Like in N-O."

"We haven't had any complaints. Whoever he addresses the letters to can't be club members or we'd have heard about it before this."

"Suppose he's sending threats to the President. On *our* stationery."

"Oh, he wouldn't. I mean, why should he?"

"Because he needs a keeper," Henderson said gloomily. "They *all* need keepers . . . Ellen, sane people like you and me don't belong in a place like this. I think we should run away together. Wouldn't that be fun?"

Ellen shook her head.

"You don't consider me a fun person, is that what you're trying to tell me? Very well. But bear in mind that you've seen me only in these non-fun circumstances. After five I can be awfully amusing . . . It's that lifeguard, Grady, isn't it? Ellen, Ellen, you're making a most grievous error. He's a creep . . . Now, what were we talking about?"

"Stationery."

"A very non-fun subject. However, let us proceed. In the future club stationery is to be used exclusively for club business."

"When members ask for some stationery it's hard to refuse," Ellen said. "It's their club, they pay my salary."

"When they joined they signed an agreement to abide by the rules."

"But we have no rule concerning stationery."

"Then make one and post it on the bulletin board."

"Don't you think it would be more appropriate if you made it, since you're the manager?"

"No. And remember to keep it simple, most of them can't read. Perhaps you should try to get the message across in pictures or sign language."

Ellen couldn't tell by looking at him whether he was serious or not. He wore Polaroid sunglasses which hid his eyes and reflected Ellen herself, twin Ellens that stared back at her in miniature as if from the wrong end of a telescope. Henderson's glasses needed cleaning, so that in addition to being miniature, the twin Ellens were fuzzy and indefinite, two vague pale faces with short brownish hair balanced on top like inverted baskets. Sometimes, deep inside, she felt quite interesting and vivacious and different. It was always a shock to run into her real self in Henderson's glasses.

"Why are you peering at me, Ellen?"

"I wasn't, sir. I was just thinking there isn't any room on the bulletin board since you put up all those pictures your nephew took of sunsets."

"What's the matter with sunsets?"

"Nothing."

"And by the way, I wish you'd stop calling me sir. I am forty-nine, hardly old enough to be called sir by a mature woman of—"

"Twenty-seven."

"I made it quite clear on my arrival how the various echelons are to address me. Let me repeat. To the maintenance men and busboys I am boss. Waiters and lifeguards are to call me sir, and the engineer and catering manager, Mr. Henderson. To you I am Walter, or perhaps some simple little endearment." He smiled dreadfully. "Sweetie-pie, love-bunny, angel-face, something on that order."

"Really, Mr. Henderson," Ellen said, but the reproof sounded mild. Henderson's lechery was, in fact, so fainthearted and spasmodic that Ellen considered it one of the lesser burdens of the job. She didn't expect him to be around long anyway. He was the seventh club manager since she'd worked there, and though he was competent enough and had arrived with excellent references, his temperament seemed ill-suited to dealing with the wide variety of emergencies that came with the territory.

The current emergency involved the plumbing in the men's shower room.

One of the toilets had been plugged with a pair of sneakers and a T-shirt. All three objects, in spite of their prolonged soaking, were still clearly inked Frederic Quinn and the nine-year-old was confronted with the evidence. He was then locked in the first-aid room to ponder his crime by Grady, the head lifeguard.

Little Frederic, who went to an exclusive boys' school and knew obscenities in several languages, needed only one: "You can't keep me a prisoner, you pig frig, you didn't read me my rights."

"Okay, here are your rights," Grady said. "You've got a right to stay in there until hell freezes."

"There is no hell, everybody knows that."

"Or until a tidal wave washes away the club."

"The correct word is *tsunami*, not tidal wave."

"Or an earthquake destroys the entire city."

"Let me out, goddammit."

"Sorry, it's time for my lunch break."

"I'll tell everybody you beat me up."

But Grady was already on his way to his locker to get his sandwiches and Thermos.

Left to his own devices little Frederic poured a bottle of Mercurochrome over his head to simulate blood and painted himself two black eyes with burnt match tips. Once his creativity was activated, it was hard to stop. He added a mustache, a Vandyke beard, sideburns and a giant mole in the center of his forehead. Then he redirected his attention to the problem of getting out:

"Help! May Day! Police! Paramedics!"

If some of the members heard him, they paid no attention. There was a strong tradition of status quo at the club as well as the vaguely religious notion that somewhere, somehow, someone was taking care of things.

Miranda Shaw lay on a chaise beside the pool, shielded from the sun by a beach towel, a straw hat, an umbrella and several layers of an ointment imported for her from Mexico. She had no way of knowing that she was the subject of Mr. Van Eyck's current literary project.

. . . What a fraud you are, acting so refined in public and doing all those you-know-what things in private. I can see behind those baby-blue eyes of yours. You ought to be ashamed. Poor Neville was a good husband to you and he is barely cold in his grave and already you're ogling young men like Grady. Grady is hardly more than a boy and you are an old bat who's had your face, fanny and boobs lifted. Now if you could only lift your morals . . .

Miranda was beginning to feel uncomfortable, and there seemed to be no particular reason why. The sound of the waves was soothing, the sun's rays were not too warm and the humidity registered forty percent, exactly right for the complexion. *It must be the new ointment working, she thought, rejuvenating the cells by stimulating the nerve endings. Oh God, I hope it doesn't hurt. I can't stand any more pain.*

She twitched, coughed, sat up.

Van Eyck was staring at her from the other side of the pool, smiling. At least she thought he was smiling. She had to put on her glasses to make sure. When she did, Van Eyck raised his free hand and waved at her. It was a lively gesture, youthful and mischievous compared to the rest of him, which had been sobered and slowed and soured by age. *He must be eighty; Neville was almost eighty when he died last spring—*

She gave her head a quick hard shake. She must stop thinking of age and death. Dr. Ortiz insisted that his patients should picture in their minds only pleasant gentle things like flowers and birds and happy children and swaying trees. Nothing too amusing. Laughter stretched the muscles around the eyes and mouth.

She attempted to picture happy children, but unfortunately little Frederic Quinn was screaming again.

Since his cries for help had gone unanswered, little Frederic was resorting to threats.

"My father's going to buy me a fifty-thousand-volt Taser stun gun and I'm going to point it at you and shock you right out of your pants. How will you like that, Grady, you creep?"

"It'll be okay for starters," Grady said, finishing his second peanut butter and jelly sandwich. "Then what?"

"You'll fall motionless to the ground and go into convulsions."

"How about that."

"And maybe die."

"What if your father doesn't want you running around loose with a stun gun?"

"My brother Harold can get one for me," Frederic said. "IIe has Mafia connections at school."

"No kidding."

"I told you that before."

"Well, I didn't believe you before. Now I don't believe you again."

"It's true. Harold's best friend is Bingo Firenze whose uncle is a hit man. Bingo's teaching Harold a lot of things and Harold's going to teach me."

"You could probably teach both of them. And the uncle."

"What a heap of crap. I'm just a kid, an innocent little kid who was molested in the locker room by the head lifeguard. How will *that* sound to Henderson when I tell him?"

"Like music. He'll probably give me a medal."

"You're a mean bastard, Grady."

"You bet."

Happy children, swaying trees, birds, flowers—Miranda couldn't keep her mind on any of them. Her discomfort was increasing. The doctor had assured her that the new ointment wasn't just another peeling treatment, but it felt the same as the last time, like acid burning off the top layers of skin, dissolving away the wrinkles, the age spots, the keratoids. *He promised no pain. He said I'd hardly be aware of the stuff. Perhaps I used too much. Oh God, let me out of here. I must wash it off.*

She didn't allow her panic to show. She rose, draped the beach towel around her with careless elegance and headed toward the shower room. She walked the way the physical therapist at the clinic had taught her to walk, languidly, as if she were moving through water. The instruction manual advised clients to keep an aquarium and observe how even the ugliest fish was a model of grace in motion. Miranda had an aquarium installed in the master bedroom but Neville had complained that all that swimming around kept him awake. The fish solved the problem by dying off rather quickly, with, Miranda suspected, some help from Neville, because the water had begun to look murky and smell of Scotch.

She moved through an imagined aqueous world, a creature of grace. Past the lifeguard eating a peanut butter sandwich, past the young sisters squabbling over a magazine, and into the corridor, where she met Charles Van Eyck.

"Good morning, good morning, Mrs. Shaw. You are looking very beautiful today."

"Oh, Mr. Van Eyck, I'm not. Really I'm not."

"Have it your way," Van Eyck said and shuffled into the office to get some more stationery. It was fine sunny weather. His venomous juices were flowing like sap through a maple tree.

The episode left Miranda so shaken that she forgot all about fish and aquariums and broke into a run for the showers. Van Eyck watched her with the detachment of a veteran coach: Miranda was still frisky and the fanny surgeon had done a nice job.

"No, Mr. Van Eyck," Ellen said. "Absolutely no. It has the club letterhead on it and must be used only for official business."

"I can cut the letterhead off."

"It could still be identified."

"By whom?"

"The police."

"Now why would the police want to identify our club stationery?" Van Eyck said reasonably. "Has there been any embezzlement, murder, interesting stuff like that?"

"No."

"Then why should the police be concerned?" He peered at her over the top of his rimless half-glasses. "Aha. *Aha.* I'm catching on."

"If only you'd just take no for an answer, Mr. Van Eyck."

"When you crossed the terrace you peeked over my shoulder."

"Not really. And I couldn't help-"

"Yes really. And you could help. What did you *see?*"

"You. That's all. The word you."

"You and then what?"

"You—well, then maybe a couple of adjectives or so. Also, maybe a noun."

Van Eyck shook his head gravely. "I consider this a serious breech of club etiquette, Ellen. However, I will overlook it in exchange for a few sheets of notepaper. That's fair, isn't it?"

"Not for me. I have strict orders from Mr. Henderson. If I don't obey them I might get fired."

"Nonsense. You'll outlast a dozen Hendersons. Be a good girl and rustle me up that paper. Half a dozen sheets will do for the time being."

Little Frederic was trying a new ploy.

"Grady, sir, will you please unlock this door?"

"Can't. I swallowed the key."

"Hey man, that's great. You can sue the club and I'll act as your lawyer. We can gross maybe a couple-—"

"No."

"Okay, just let me out of here and we'll press the flesh and forget the whole thing."

Grady peeled a banana and took a two-inch bite. "What whole thing?"

"You know. The toilet bit."

"Are you confessing, Quinn?"

"Hell no. Why would I pull a dumb trick like plug a toilet with my own clothes? I'm a smart kid. I was framed."

"If you're so smart," Grady said, "how come you're always being framed?"

"Someone is out to get me."

"I have news for you, Quinn. *Everybody* is out to get you."

"Tell them my father is buying me a stun gun."

"Okay, I'll spread the word right now."

"Where are you going?"

"To the office. They should be the first to know."

Before he left, Grady combed his hair in front of the mirror in the cubbyhole that served as the lifeguards' dressing room. He knew Ellen was interested in him and there was always a chance that some day he might get interested back. She was a nice sensible girl with a steady job and great-looking legs. He could do better but he'd often done a lot worse.

"We can't expel Frederic," Ellen said. "He's already expelled."

"Then how come he's here?"

"He must have climbed over the back fence."

"There are four rows of barbed wire on top."

"The engineer reported yesterday that his wire cutters were missing from the storage shed."

"The kid's a genius," Grady said. "I wish we could think of something constructive for him to be a genius at."

"You can handle him. Opinion among the members is that you're very good with children. They seem to like you—the children, I mean."

"What about the other people?"

"What other people?"

"The ones who aren't children."

"Oh, I'm sure everyone likes you."

"Does that include you?"

She fixed her eyes at a point on the wall just over his left shoulder. "It's against the rules for you to come into the office wearing only swim trunks. You're supposed to put on your warm-up suit."

"I'm not cold," Grady said. "Are you?"

"Stop the cute act."

"What kind of act would you like? I'm versatile."

"I bet you are. But don't waste any of it on me."

He sat on the edge of the desk swinging one leg and admiring the way the sun had tanned the skin while bleaching the hair to a reddish gold. Then he turned his attention back to Ellen. Under ordinary circumstances he wouldn't have bothered making a pass, but right now the pickings were poor. Club members were off limits, especially the teenagers who'd hung around him during the summer indicating their availability in ways that would have shocked their parents as thoroughly as little Frederic's projected stun gun. Anyway, it was fall and they were back in school. Ellen was still here.

He said, "You sure play hard to get. What's the point?"

"And speaking of rules, tell your girlfriends not to phone here for you. Mr. Henderson doesn't approve of personal calls at the office."

"Hey, you're laying it on me pretty heavy. Lighten up, will you? I'm not your run-of-the-mill rapist."

"You could have fooled me."

"What are you so mad about, anyway?"

"I'm not mad, merely observant. I've watched you spreading the charm around for your fourteen-year-old groupies all summer and—"

"I like your eyes when you're mad, they're light bright green. Like emeralds. Or 7-Up bottles."

"Yours are grey. And strictly granite."

"I didn't know you were such a mean-type lady."

"I didn't know either." Ellen sounded a little surprised. "I guess it takes a mean-type man to bring it out in me."

"Okay, let's start over. I come into the office to report that I'm having some trouble with one of the kids. And you say we can't expel him because he's already expelled. Then I say—Oh hell, I forget what I said. You really do have pretty eyes, Ellen. They're emeralds. Forget the 7-Up bottles, I just tossed them in to make you laugh. Only you didn't."

"It wasn't funny."

"In fact, you never laugh at anything I say anymore." The telephone rang and she was about to pick it up when he reached across the desk and stopped her by grabbing her arm. "I notice you kidding around with some of the members and the engineer and even Henderson. Why the sudden down on me?"

"It's not sudden. It's been coming on for some time."

"Why? I didn't do anything to you. I thought we were friends, you know, on the same side but cool."

"Is that your definition of friends, on the same side but cool?"

"What's the matter with it?"

"It seems to leave out a few essentials."

"Put them in and we're still friends. Aren't we?" The phone had stopped ringing. Neither of them noticed. Grady said again, "Aren't we?"

"No."

"Why not . . . ? Oh hell, don't answer that. I wouldn't make much of a friend anyhow. Want to hear something funny? I must have had friends all along the line—I've got a lot going for me—but I don't remember them. I remember the places, none of them amounting to a hill of beans, but I forget the people. They walked away or I walked away. Same difference. They're gone like they died on me."

"This sounds like a pitch for sympathy."

"Sympathy? Why would I want sympathy? I'm on top of the world."

"Fine. How's the view?"

"Right now it's not so bad."

A woman was coming down the corridor toward the office and he liked the way she moved, kind of slow and waltzing like a bride walking down the aisle. She wore a long silky robe that clung to her thighs. Her blonde hair had been twisted into a single braid that fell over one shoulder and was fastened with a pink flower. With every step she took, the pink flower brushed her left breast. This seemed guileless, but Grady knew enough about women to be pretty sure it wasn't.

He said, "Who's the lady?"

"Mrs. Shaw."

"She looks rich."

"I guess she is."

"Very rich?"

"I don't know. How do you tell the difference between rich and very rich?"

"Easy. The very rich count their money, then put it in a bank and throw away the key. The rich spend theirs. They drive it, fly it, eat it, wear it, drink it."

"Mrs. Shaw put hers on her face."

"That's not a bad choice."

Ellen's voice was cold. "I can understand a glandular type like you getting excited about some teenage groupies. But a fifty-year-old widow, that's overdoing it a bit, isn't it? She's fifty-two, in fact. When her husband died a few months ago I had to look up their membership application to write an obit for the club bulletin. He was a very sweet old man nearly eighty."

"What's her first name?"

"Why?"

"I just want to know. You make it sound like a crime no matter what I say or do."

"Her name is Miranda. But you'd better stick to Mrs. Shaw if you know what's good for you."

"Can't I even ask a question without you getting all torqued up?"

"Mr. Henderson has a strict rule prohibiting fraternization between members and employees. You were warned about it several times last summer, remember? Frederic's sister, April, the Peterson girl, Cindy Kellogg—"

"What's to remember? Nothing happened."

"Nothing?"

"Practically nothing."

"Sometime when I have a week to spare you'll have to tell me what 'practically nothing' covers."

He hesitated for a moment, then leaned across the desk and patted her lightly on the top of her head. Her hair was very soft, like the feathers of a baby duck he'd found on a creek bank when he was a boy. The duck had died in his hands. "Hey, stop fighting me. I'm not so bad. What's so bad about me?" For no reason that he could see or figure out, the duck had died in his hands. Maybe it was because he touched it. Maybe there were soft delicate things that should never be touched.

He straightened up, crossing his arms over his chest as though he was suddenly conscious of his nakedness. "I like the girls and the girls like me. Why would you want to change that? It's normal."

"So it's normal. Hurray."

"Don't you like normal?"

"I like normal."

"But not in me," Grady said. "I wish we were friends, Ellen, I honest to God do. You seem to be friends with everyone else around here. What's so bad about me?"

With the ointment washed off her face and replaced with moisturizer and makeup, Miranda felt a little calmer. But each minute had its own tiny nucleus of panic. There was a new brownish patch on her forehead, the mole on her neck appeared to be enlarging, and the first ominous ripples of cellulite were showing on her upper arms and thighs. She missed Neville to tell her that the mole and the brown patch were her special beauty spots and the ripples of cellulite existed only in her imagination. Not that she would have believed him. She knew they were real, that it was time to go back to the clinic in Mexico for more injections.

She couldn't leave immediately or even make a reservation. Her lawyer had advised her to stay in town until Neville's will was probated. When she asked for a reason he'd been evasive, as if he knew something she didn't and wouldn't want to. His attitude worried her, especially since there was a story going around that Neville's son by his first marriage was planning to contest the will. She would have liked to question Ellen about it—Ellen might know the truth, people were always confiding in her—but when Miranda went into the office the lifeguard was there and Ellen looked a little flustered.

Miranda said, "I'm expecting to hear from my lawyer, Mr. Smedler. Has he called?"

"No, Mrs. Shaw."

"When he does, have someone bring me the message, will you please? I'll be in the snack bar."

She hadn't looked at Grady yet, or even in his direction, but he was well aware that she'd seen him. She'd been watching him off and on all morning from under the floppy straw hat and behind the oversized amber sunglasses.

She turned toward him, taking off the glasses very slowly, like a professional stripper. "You're the lifeguard, aren't you?"

"Yes, ma'am. Grady."

"Pardon?"

"That's my name. Grady Keaton."

"Oh. Well, there seems to be a child screaming somewhere."

"Yes, ma'am. It's the Quinn kid, Frederic."

"Can you do something about it?"

"Probably not."

"You might at least try. It sounds as though he's suffering."

"He'd be suffering a lot more right now if his father didn't have ten million dollars. Or maybe twenty. After the first million who counts?"

Her smile was so faint it was hardly more than a softening of the expression in her eyes. "Everybody counts, Grady. You must be new around here if you haven't learned that."

"I'm a slow learner. I may need some private tutoring."

"Indeed. Well, I'm sure Ellen would be willing to acquaint you with some basics."

"Ellen and I don't agree on basics. That presents kind of a problem."

"Then perhaps you'd better concentrate on more immediate problems, like Frederic Quinn."

She meant to put him in his place by sounding severe, but she couldn't quite manage it. During the years of her marriage to Neville she'd never had occasion to use her voice to exert authority or raise it in anger. Everything was arranged so she'd have no reason to feel dissatisfied or insecure. Her only bad times were at the clinic in Mexico when she'd screamed during the injections. Even then the screams had seemed to be coming from someone else, a shrill, undisciplined stranger, some poor scared old woman: *"Stop, you're killing me."* — *"The Señora will be young again!"* — *"For God's sake, please stop."* — *"The Señora will be twenty-five . . . "*

For the first time she looked directly and carefully at Grady. He had a small golden mustache that matched his eyebrows, and a scar on his right cheek like a dimple. He was no more than twenty-five. She felt a sudden sharp pain between her breasts like a needle going through the skin and right into the bone. *"Stop, you're killing me."* — *"The Señora will be twenty-five."*

She took a deep breath. "You'd better attend to the boy."

"Yes, ma'am."

"I may be able to help. I haven't had much experience with children but I like them."

"I don't," Grady said.

"You must like some of them, surely."

"Not a damn one."

"They don't all act like Frederic."

"They would if their fathers had ten million dollars."

"So here we are back at the ten million. It's quite pervasive, isn't it, like a smell."

"Yes, ma'am. Like a smell."

"Well, the boy can't be allowed to suffer simply because his father has a great deal of money. That would hardly be fair. Come on, I'll go with you and help you quiet him down."

"That won't be necessary, Mrs. Shaw," Ellen said. "Grady can handle the situation himself."

"Of course he can. I'll just tag along to see how it's done . . . if Grady doesn't mind. Do you mind, Grady?"

Grady didn't mind at all.

Ellen stood and watched the two of them walk down the hall side by side. She wanted to turn and busy herself at her desk with her own work but she couldn't take her eyes off them. In an odd disturbing way they looked exactly right together, as if they'd been matched up in a toy store and sold as a pair.

Having secured his notepaper, Mr. Van Eyck decided to drop by Mr. Henderson's private office to thank him.

Henderson was glancing through a week-old *Wall Street Journal* while he ate his lunch, a pint of cottage cheese which he spooned into his mouth with dip chips. He preferred to read with his meals, on the theory that his gastric juices flowed more freely when they were not interrupted by the conversation of nincompoops.

What he read was not important, was not, in fact, even his own choice. After the swimming area of the club closed for the day he went around gathering up all the reading material that had been abandoned or forgotten—paperback books, newspapers, travel brochures, medical journals, airplane schedules, magazines, even the occasional briefcase with interesting contents like the top-secret financial report of an oil company, or complete plans for an air-sea attack on Mogadishu drawn up by retired Rear Admiral Cooper Young. Henderson had no idea where Mogadishu was, but it was reassuring to know that if and when such an attack proved necessary, Admiral Young would be ready to take care of the situation.

Economics, war, politics, porn, pathology—Henderson devoured them all while his gastric juices flowed on like some good old dependable river that never spilled or went dry. But even the best-behaved river could be dammed.

"Very decent of you, Henderson, to lend me this stuff," Van Eyck said.

"What?"

"The notepaper. If you hadn't lent it, I'd have pinched it of course, but this way is preferable." The old man cleared his throat. "You will be able to take credit for making some small contribution to the cause of world literature."

"What?"

"I'm writing a novel."

"On our club paper?"

"Oh, don't thank me yet, Henderson, it's a bit premature for that. But some day a single page of this stuff might be worth a fortune."

"What?"

"You keep repeating *what*. Is there something the matter with your hearing?"

Henderson dipped a chip in his cottage cheese but he couldn't swallow, his mouth was dry. The good old dependable river had stopped flowing at its source. "This writing you're doing on our club paper, you claim it will be worth a fortune?"

"Oh yes."

"To whom?"

"Posterity. All those people out there. In a figurative sense."

In a less figurative sense Henderson pictured all the people out there as a line of attorneys waiting to file suit against the club for libel, character assassination and malicious mischief. He went over to the water cooler and poured himself a drink. Perhaps he would buy a ticket to Mogadishu. If there was going to be a war there, he might be lucky enough to become one of the first casualties.

"By the way," Van Eyck said, "to facilitate my research you might tell me how the club got its name."

"The birds."

"What birds?"

"All those penguins out there diving for fish."

"Those are pelicans. The nearest penguin is ten thousand miles away. They're an antarctic species."

"There must be a penguin around here some place," Henderson said quickly. "How else did the club get its name?"

"My dear chap, that's what *I* asked *you.*"

"Ten thousand miles?"

"Approximately."

"This puts me in an intolerable position. I've been telling everyone those little beasts are penguins, and now they aren't."

"They never were."

"You're sure?"

"Positive. But go on lying if you like. No law against it."

Van Eyck returned to his table on the terrace. There seemed little doubt that Henderson was getting peculiar, exactly like every other manager before him. In the next few weeks the same symptoms would emerge, a tendency to twitch, to smile at inappropriate moments, to mutter to himself. *A pity,* Van Eyck thought, taking up his pen. *He's not really a bad sort in spite of all that money he owes his bookie.*

Admiral Young's battle plans for Mogadishu were of no concern to his two daughters, who were busy conducting a war of their own in the snack bar. Their weapons were simple, their attacks direct. Cordelia hit Juliet over the head with a piece of celery, and as she was running for the door to avoid retaliation Juliet caught her on the ear with a ripe olive. The incident was reported to Ellen, who in turn telephoned Admiral Young and advised him to come and take the girls home.

Within a few minutes Young drove up in his vintage Rolls-Royce. Though he'd been retired for a number of years, he still moved like one of his own battleships, with a complete confidence that the way ahead was clear, and if the seas got rough the stabilizers were in operational order. His thick white hair was kept in the Annapolis crew cut of his youth, so that from a distance he looked like a bald man who'd been caught in a light flurry of snow.

He parked the Rolls-Royce in the No Parking zone outside the front door where his daughters were waiting with Ellen.

"Now, girls, what's this Ellen tells me about your fighting? Surely you're old enough to know better."

"*She* knows better," Juliet said. "She's older than I am."

"Only two years," Cordelia said.

"Which means you were talking and walking when I was born."

"Well, I *wasn't* learning *not* to fight."

"You should have been. Here you are all grown up and you haven't learned yet."

"Dear me," the Admiral said mildly. "Are you really all grown up, Cordelia?"

"You should know. Mrs. Young sent you a cable when I was born. You were in Hong Kong."

"I don't recall that it was Hong Kong."

"It was. She tried to get there but she had to stop off in Manila to have me. There were a lot of rats around the hospital."

"So one more wouldn't matter." Juliet laughed so hard at her own joke that her head, with its short brown hair, shook like a mop and she almost lost her balance.

"You mustn't tease your sister, Juliet," Admiral Young said mildly. "It's unkind."

"Well, she's unkinder than I am, she's had two more years of practice. I've got to catch up. It's only fair I should have a chance to catch up."

"Nobody has a guarantee that life will be fair, girls. We're lucky to get justice, let alone mercy."

"Oh, Pops, don't start throwing that bull at us," Cordelia said.

"Save it for the ensigns," Juliet added.

"Or second looies."

"We're *your* daughters."

"Serves you right, too."

"We're *your* fault."

"Think about it, Pops. If you hadn't—"

"But you *did*."

"So here we are."

And there they were, a problem not covered in the Navy rule book, yet to a certain extent a product of it.

They'd been brought up all over the world. At the language academy in Geneva they learned enough French and Italian to order a meal and summon a taxi or policeman. They attended finishing schools in London, Rome and Paris, with no visible results except to the teachers. At the music academy in Austria, during the periods set aside for Cordelia to practice the violin and Juliet the flute, they listened to Elvis Presley records in the basement and went to old Hollywood movies dubbed in German. At the American school in Singapore most of their time was spent tearing through the streets in a jeep, Cordelia having learned to drive somewhere between Sydney and Tokyo. The effect of this cosmopolitan background had been not to make them more sophisticated and at ease with people but to isolate them. While the real world expanded around them their personal world grew smaller and tighter. No matter who was present on social occasions, they talked to or at each other, as if they were surrounded by foreigners, interchangeable and of no importance. They had become immune to people as beekeepers do to stings.

"I never really liked this club," Cordelia said. "Did you?"

Juliet pursed her lips as though she were pondering the subject. There was no need to ponder, of course. If Cordelia didn't like the club, neither did she. "Never. Never ever."

"Let's go home."

"We'd better say goodbye to Ellen."

"Why?"

"*Noblesse oblige.*"

"That's French. I don't recognize French rules in the U.S.A."

"Pops is giving us an executive look."

"Oh, all right. Goodbye, Ellen."

"Goodbye, Ellen."

"Goodbye, girls," Ellen said.

Nearly everyone called them girls. Cordelia was thirty-five, Juliet thirty-three.

From his carefully chosen position on the terrace Van Eyck had an unobstructed view of what was happening at the entrance to the club. With a kind of detached loathing he watched his brother-in-law, Admiral Young, drive off in the Rolls-Royce with the two girls.

Van Eyck had strong feelings about the military and for a number of years he'd been working out plans for bringing it under control. His ideas, though varying in emphasis from time to time, remained basically the same. Salaries must be immediately and drastically reduced, especially at the upper levels. Pensions should begin no earlier than age seventy and continue only for a prudent and reasonable time. The brass should not be encouraged to live longer than necessary at taxpayers' expense. Wars should be confined to countries with unpronounceable names and severe climates—the former would prevent television and newsmen from mentioning them, the latter would keep foreign correspondents to a minimum.

Most important of all, uniforms were to be abolished or simplified, with no more fancy hats or tailored jackets with gold braid and rows of ribbons.

If it hadn't been for the uniform, his sister Iris wouldn't have looked twice at Cooper Young. It was the second look that did it. Until then Iris was a nice intelligent girl, expected to marry a nice intelligent man who would put her fortune to good use and sire three or four sons to carry on with it. Instead she fell for a uniform, gave birth to two half-witted daughters and became a sour, sick old woman. Poor Iris. The crowning irony was that the Admiral retired and now wore his uniform only once a year at the Regimental Ball. Van Eyck didn't enjoy music or dancing, and he certainly didn't spend money lightly, but he never missed a Regimental Ball. Each one produced a yearly renewal of his anger against the military.

Van Eyck took up his pen and a sheet of the paper Ellen had given him.

Secretary of Defense, The Pentagon, Washington, D.C.

Sir:

Overspend is overkill. Explore the following ways to cut your preposterous budget:
Reduce salaries.
Begin pensions later, terminate sooner.
Dispense with all uniforms.
Eliminate commissaries and personnel, R & R stations, free transportation to and from battles.
Avoid wars. If this is impossible, put them on a paying basis with T. V. and publishing rights, et cetera.
Reform, retrench or resign, sir.

John Q. Public

Van Eyck reread the letter, making only one change. He underlined *dispense with all uniforms* and added an exclamation point. Once uniforms were abolished, the other reforms would automatically occur sooner or later.

He heard someone yell *fire* but he didn't bother looking around. If there was, in fact, a fire, it seemed silly to yell about it instead of calling the fire department.

There was, in fact, a fire.

Little Frederic Quinn, acting on the advice of his older brother, Harold, who was taking the advice of his best friend, Bingo Firenze, whose uncle was a hit man for the Mafia, always carried a packet of matches even though he had given up smoking when he was seven. Bingo had figured it out. Fire was the best attention-getter in the world and no matter where you were something was flammable, not merely the more obvious things like paper and wood, but stuff like Grady's polyester warm-up suit hanging on a hook in the first-aid room. It took nearly all the matches in the packet before the warm-up suit finally ignited.

"Ha ha, Grady," Frederic said just before he passed out from smoke inhalation.

In the excitement following the discovery of the fire nobody could find the key to the first-aid room. Grady tried to pick the lock with a nail file. When that failed, the engineer pried the door open with a hatchet and put out the fire by tossing Grady's warm-up suit into the pool.

Frederic was given artificial respiration, and in a few minutes he was conscious again and coughing up the pizza, doughnuts and potato chips he'd had for breakfast.

Miranda Shaw knelt beside him and pressed a wet towel to his forehead. "Poor child, what happened? Are you all right?"

"I want a chocolate malted cherry Coke."

"A glass of milk would be more—"

"I want a chocolate malted cherry Coke."

"Of course, dear. Stay quiet and someone will bring you one. How did the fire start?"

"I don't know," Frederic said. "I got amnesty."

"What's that?"

"I can't remember."

"The little bastard set it himself," Grady said. "And I'm going to kick his butt in as soon as his pulse is normal. Give me the rest of the matches, Frederic."

"What matches? I don't remember any matches. I got amnesty."

"You're going to need amnesty, kid, if you don't hand over the evidence."

"I want a lawyer."

"A lawyer?" Miranda repeated. "Why would a child want a lawyer?"

"I'm pleading not guilty and taking the Fifth."

"A fifth of what, dear? I don't understand."

"Hey, Grady, this is a far-out chick."

Miranda stood up, looking helplessly at Grady and holding the wet towel at arm's length as if it had turned into a snake. "He seems to be acting so strangely. Do you suppose he could be delirious?"

"No, ma'am. He always acts like this."

"When I get my lawyer," Frederic said, "I'm going to sue you both for libel."

Miranda's silk robe was stained with smoke as well as the remains of Frederic's breakfast, and the flower had fallen out of her hair. Grady picked it up. Some of the petals came loose in his hand and drifted down onto the tile floor. He hadn't realized until then that the flower was genuine and perishable. He thought of the baby duck that had died in his hands and all the soft delicate things that shouldn't be touched.

"I'm sorry," Grady said. "I didn't mean to wreck it like that."

"It's not your fault."

"I thought the thing was—oh, plastic or something you can't wreck."

"Forget about it, please. It simply happened."

"Like the fire," Frederic said. "Honest to God, Grady, one minute I was sitting there doing my transcendental meditation and the next minute I was surrounded by leaping flames."

"There were no leaping flames."

"*I* saw leaping flames. I must have been delirious."

"No flames, no delirium. Just a little creep with some matches, and a smoldering warm-up suit which will cost the club twenty-five bucks to replace. A new door lock will bring the tab to two hundred, and cleaning and painting, fifty extra. Maybe I should add ten bucks for my medical services. I saved your life."

"Who asked you to?"

"Nobody. People were on their knees begging me to let you croak. But I have a kind heart."

"Yeah? Well, bring me a chocolate malted cherry Coke, double whipped cream."

"Get it yourself," Grady said.

"I can't."

"Try."

"I bet you want me to split so you can come on with the chick. Well, ha ha, I'm not going."

"You just changed your mind, Frederic." Grady grabbed him under the arms and jerked him to his feet. "Ha ha, you're going."

"All right, I'm going, I'm going. Only don't pull any of the mucho macho stuff till I get back, will you? It's time I started my education. The kids depend on me for info."

Miranda leaned against the wall, watching Frederic skip down the corridor toward the snack bar. Her braid was half-unraveled and her face had already started to sunburn.

"He's a very strange little boy," she repeated. "I find it difficult to understand what he's talking about, don't you?"

"No, I don't."

"What did he mean when he called me a chick?"

"A girl."

"A *girl*." Involuntarily she reached up and touched her face, as if to cover the tiny scars left by the last knife. "How nice. Though I'm afraid it's not very accurate."

"Accurate enough."

"You're kidding me."

Sure I am, lady. But that's the way you want it.

"Let me get this straight, Ellen." Mr. Henderson closed his eyes and pressed his fingertips very tightly together. This was supposed to set up a magnetic current which had soothing and curative powers. "The door to the first-aid room has been burned."

"Yes, Mr. Henderson."

"Perhaps you mean singed or scorched, requiring a few touches of paint here and there?"

"Burned," Ellen said. "Also, the lock's broken."

"I don't understand, it doesn't make sense, how such peculiar things happen to *me*."

"Frederic Quinn was playing with matches."

"In the first-aid room?"

"Yes."

"Why?"

"Grady had locked him in there to teach him not to plug toilets."

"And while he was being taught not to plug toilets he was learning how to set fire to things."

"He already knew. Last year it was a bunch of towels on the beach. He was cremating a dead gull."

Henderson loosened his fingers, which were beginning to ache. No magnetic current had manifested itself, certainly not one that was soothing or curative. He felt the same vague pervasive dissatisfaction. A little here, a little there, life was letting him down. There were plus factors—he had a pleasant apartment and a job with some prestige, his ex-wife had given up her alimony by remarrying, he picked an occasional long shot at the track—but the minuses were increasing. The long shots were getting longer and the neighbors complained about his new stereo system. There were aggravations at work, members with overdue bar bills, Van Eyck's anonymous letters, and Frederic's parents, whose passionate quarrels and no less passionate reconciliations—Frederic, Harold, Foster, April and Caroline—posed daily and debilitating problems.

"Obviously Grady showed poor judgment in locking the boy up," Henderson said. "He should have sent him to me."

"He sent him to you last week. You sent him back. You told him he should handle situations like that by himself. How can you blame him?"

"Easy. *I* didn't lock the little bastard in a closet."

"I heard you give Grady orders to use his own judgment in the future. Well, the future arrived and he did. Maybe the results weren't too good, but he tried."

"You are becoming," Henderson said, "increasingly transparent. Do you know what I mean, Ellen?"

"No."

"Let us have a moment's silence while you think about it."

Henderson's office was decorated with pictures of airplanes left over from an aeronautical engineers' convention. Henderson had hung them himself. He had no interest in planes or engines of any kind. But he liked the pictures because they were non-human. He didn't have to wonder what the expression in an eye meant, or what a mouth might have been on the verge of saying, or what a pair of ears had heard. Nobody had to wonder what an airplane had done or was going to do next. It went up and came down again.

"Transparent as glass," Henderson said. "I have been in, what you might call, the people business for twenty-five years. I know them. So let me give you some advice, Ellen. Don't waste your time on Grady. He has no character, no staying power. Not much of a future, in fact, unless he hits it lucky, and that's a longer shot than any I've ever hit on."

"Why are you telling me? I don't—"

"You do. All the girls do. Getting a crush on the lifeguard is part of growing up. But you're already grown up . . . Ah well, I suppose it's too late, isn't it? Advice usually is."

In the parking lot south of the club Miranda couldn't get her car started, and she sent one of the gardeners to bring someone out to help her.

The car, a gift from Neville on her last birthday, bore special license plates, U R 52, and it was as black and cumbersome as the joke itself. She hated it and intended to get rid of it at the first opportunity. But like the house and furniture of the condominium in Palm Springs, the car was considered part of the estate and couldn't be sold until Neville's will was probated. "You will be provided with a small widow's allowance," Smedler, the lawyer, had said. "In the meantime everything must be kept intact. Shall I explain to you what frozen assets are, Mrs. Shaw?"

"No, thank you, Mr. Smedler. I know . . . " She knew very well. Hers had been frozen for years.

Grady came out the back door of the club, barefooted but wearing jeans over his swim trunks and a T-shirt with a picture of a surfer printed on it. He seemed surprised to see her. Perhaps this was where his girlfriends waited for him and he was expecting one of them. Or two or a dozen.

"Oh, it's you, Mrs. Shaw." He smiled, showing teeth that were small and even but not very clean. "The gardener told me some lady wanted to see me. He was right, You are some lady."

"I didn't want to—to see you."

"Oh. Sorry."

"I mean, not personally. It's simply that I can't start this engine."

The car was parked in full sun, and its black paint and black leather upholstery had absorbed the heat and turned the interior into a furnace. *"I really wanted a light-colored car, Neville, they're so much cooler."* — *"Black has more dignity, Miranda."*

She sat, faint with heat and dignity.

"Are you all right, Mrs. Shaw?"

"I—it's very warm in here."

"Get out and stand in the shade. Come on, I'll help you."

"I can manage, thank you."

"Leave the key in the ignition."

She got out and he took her place behind the wheel. The engine turned over on his second attempt. He liked the sound of it, soft, powerful, steady.

"Here you are, all set to go, Mrs. Shaw."

"What was wrong?"

"You probably flooded it. If it happens again, push the accelerator to the floorboard and let it up slowly. Or if you're not in a hurry, wait a few minutes."

"I'm never in a hurry. I have nothing to do."

She didn't know why she said it. Neither did he, obviously. He looked puzzled and a little embarrassed, as though she'd made a very personal remark and he wasn't sure how to respond.

"I meant nothing important," she added. "The way you have, with your job."

"There's nothing important about my job. I put in time, I get paid. That's all."

"You save lives. You saved Frederic's only half an hour ago."

"He'd have come around eventually. Don't blame me for saving his life . . . And as far as the pool is concerned, there hasn't been a near-drowning, or even a nearly near, since I was hired. Which is fine with me, since I'm not even sure what I'd do if somebody yelled for help. Maybe I'd walk away and let him drown."

"You mustn't say that. Someone might take it seriously."

"Don't you?"

"Of course not."

"I hope you're a good swimmer."

They'd been talking above the noise of the engine. He reached over and switched it off. Then he got out, wiping the sweat from his forehead with the back of his hand. "Okay. It's all yours, Mrs. Shaw."

"Why didn't you leave the engine running?"

"Causes pollution, wastes gas. You can start it again when you're ready to leave."

They stood beside the long black car, almost touching but not looking at each other, like strangers at a funeral.

She said, "It's a very ugly car, don't you agree? Such a lot of bulk and horsepower merely to take someone like me from the house to the club to the market and back to the house. My husband gave it to me on my last birthday. Did you see the license plate?"

"Not well enough to remember."

"It's U R 52. Neville did it as a joke so I couldn't lie about my age. He didn't mean to be cruel, he adored me, he would never have been deliberately cruel. He simply considered it funny."

"Next year when you're fifty-three the laugh will be on him. Hang on to the car for ten or fifteen years and you can have yourself a real chuckle."

"No," she said sharply. "I'm going to get rid of it as soon as they give me permission."

"They?"

"The lawyers who are handling my husband's estate. Of course, if something *happened* to the car they'd have to give me permission, wouldn't they?"

"Happened like what?"

"I don't know exactly, but there are lots of stories in the newspapers about people having paint sprayed all over their cars or their windows damaged or their tires slashed."

"If that's what you want," Grady said, "maybe I can arrange it for you. I've got some rough pals."

"Do you? Have rough pals, I mean."

"I know a lot of crummy people."

She glanced up at him with an anxious little smile. "You mustn't take it seriously, what I said about something happening to the car. It was pretty crazy. I can't understand why I suddenly had such a wild idea. I'm not a violent person."

"You don't look it."

"Honestly I'm not."

"I believe you, I believe you."

"Why do you say it twice like that? It makes it sound as if you don't really believe me." She crossed her arms over her breasts as if for protection. Her skin was very white, and the veins so close to the surface they looked like routes of rivers on a map. "How can you think I'm a violent person?"

"Oh, come on now, Mrs. Shaw," Grady said. "You're having a bad day. Go home and pour yourself a drink."

"I can't drink alone."

"Then take a couple of aspirins. Or don't you do that alone either?"

She lowered her head as if it had suddenly become too heavy for her neck to support. "That wasn't a kind thing to say. You may be right about yourself, Grady. Perhaps if someone were drowning, you'd just walk away."

"Now wait a minute. What's the matter with you, anyway?"

"I'm drowning," she said. "You're not a very good lifeguard if you can't tell when people are drowning."

Little Frederic Quinn was hiding behind a eucalyptus tree in the middle of the parking lot. So far the conversation had been dumb and the action nil, so he decided to liven things up by revealing his presence.

He stepped out from his cover. The burnt-match Deco work had been scrubbed off his face but most of the Mercurochrome remained, leaving his hair streaked pink and his skin interestingly diseased-looking.

"Hey, Grady, how're you doing?"

"Beat it, you little bastard," Grady said.

"Using foul language in front of a lady, that's a misdemeanor."

"What is it when a kid is hacked to pieces and thrown off the wharf to feed the sharks?"

"Why are you so torqued up? Lost the old macho magic? Wait till I tell the kids, ha ha."

"You didn't hear me, Quinn. I said beat it."

"All right."

"Now."

"All right. I'm going, I'm going. I'm on my way. I'm—Help! Police! May Day! May Day!"

Admiral Cooper Young was returning to the club to pick up the handbag Cordelia had left in the snack bar. It was such a pleasant day he'd rolled one window down, though his wife, Iris, would be sure to notice the dust on the dashboard and complain about it. As he passed the parking lot he heard the May Day call.

"I do believe I hear someone crying for help."

"Then shut the window," Juliet said.

"Just because a person is crying for help," Cordelia added reasonably, "is no reason why you should listen. You're not in the Navy anymore. Besides, we have to hurry. There's a one-hundred-dollar-bill in my handbag."

The Admiral's grip on the steering wheel tightened perceptibly. "Now where did you get a one-hundred-dollar bill, Cordelia?"

"Mrs. Young. Your wife."

"Why did she give it to you?"

"Bribery."

"She gave me one, too," Juliet said, "though I wouldn't call it bribery exactly, Cordelia."

"I would. It was. Her instructions were to stay away from the house until the club closed because she was going to take a backgammon lesson."

The May Day calls had ceased.

"I didn't know your mother played backgammon," the Admiral said.

"She doesn't," Cordelia said. "Yet. She's taking a course."

"I see."

The Admiral did indeed see. There'd been other courses, dozens, but none of them seemed to satisfy his poor Iris. She'd been cheated and she was unable to think of any way to cheat back.

The crisis in the parking lot was altered by the sudden appearance of Mr. Tolliver, headmaster of the school Frederic more or less attended. Having learned during lunch hour that the surf was up, Mr. Tolliver shrewdly connected this information with the large number of absentees that morning. As a result he was patrolling the beach areas, armed with a pair of well-used binoculars and an officer's swagger stick left over from his Canadian army days.

Frederic Quinn was his first trophy. The boy was given a swat on the behind with the swagger stick and the promise of two hundred demerits. He was then locked in what the students called the cop cage, the rear of the school station wagon separated from the driver's seat by heavy canvas webbing.

Frederic proved a docile prisoner. He was tired, for one thing, and consequently, running short of ideas. For another, the new batch of demerits put him one hundred and fifteen ahead of Bingo Firenze for the current school championship. This was not a paltry achievement, in view of Bingo's superior age and connections with the Mafia, and Frederic leaned back smiling in anticipation of a hero's welcome.

Mr. Tolliver peered at his trophy through the canvas webbing. "Well, Quinn, what have you got to say for yourself?"

"Mea culpa."

"So you are admitting your guilt."

"Nolo contendere," Frederic said. "It doesn't matter anyway. I've already been punished."

"That's what *you* think, kiddo."

The hundred-dollar bill was still in Cordelia's handbag, much to her disappointment. She didn't need the money as much as she needed the attention she would have gotten if the bill had been missing. She thought of all the excitement, cops arriving at the club with sirens wailing, Henderson rounding up the employees for questioning, newsmen, photographers, maybe even an ambulance if she could have managed to faint . . .

"Oh hell, it's right where I left it."

Cordelia climbed into the back seat of the Rolls-Royce for the second time that day while her father said his second courteous farewells to Mr. Henderson and Ellen. He also wished them a Happy Thanksgiving, adding a little joke about turkeys which Ellen didn't understand and Henderson didn't hear.

"Thanksgiving is more than a month away," Henderson said as the Rolls moved majestically into the street. "Was he being sarcastic, do you suppose? If he was, I should have countered with something about Pearl Harbor. 'Happy Pearl Harbor to you, Admiral.' *That's* what I should have said . . . Speaking of turkeys, which I hadn't planned on doing and don't want to, you'd better have the catering manager come to the office to discuss the Thanksgiving menu. Thanksgiving. My God, I'm still recuperating from Labor Day and the Fourth of July. Will I make it to Christmas? Will I, Ellen?"

"I don't know," Ellen said.

"And you don't care, either. I hear it in your voice, that I-don't-care note. It's cruel."

"Sorry. But there've been so many managers, Mr. Henderson. I'd have been done in years ago if I'd allowed myself to care. I must maintain the proper emotional distance."

"Don't give me that crap."

"You asked for it."

Admiral Cooper Young lived with his wife, Iris, and the girls in a massive stone house on what had once been the most fashionable street in town.

The ride home was short and silent. It was only toward the end that Cordelia spoke in an uncharacteristically gloomy voice: "Mrs. Young's not going to like this. She might even force us to give the money back to her."

"She can't if we won't," Juliet said. "And let's not. Let's stand fast."

"She'll think of something. You know the mean way she stops payment on checks."

"This isn't like that. It's hard cash. Good as gold. Coin of the realm. And we can hide it in our bras."

"Even so . . . Pops, we don't really have to go home yet, do we?"

"Yes, girls, I think we do." The Admiral cleared his throat. "You see, your exclusion from the club was intended to teach you a lesson, and you can't be taught a lesson without suffering a bit."

"Oh, I hate suffering," Juliet said passionately. "It makes me throw up. If I throw up in the car, plus we arrive home three hours early, Mrs. Young will be *really* mad."

"Now, now, now. Don't borrow trouble, girls. Your mother will be just as glad to see you as she usually is."

And she was.

"I told you two to stay at the club until five o'clock," Iris Young said. "What happened?"

Cordelia answered first. "We got bounced."

"Dishonorably discharged," Juliet added.

"For conduct unbecoming."

Iris banged her cane on the floor. A tall athletic woman in her younger days, she was now stooped and misshapen. Her broad sallow face seldom changed expression and the hump she carried between her shoulder blades was a backpack of resentments that grew heavier each year.

She looked at her husband not in order to see him but to make sure he was seeing her and her displeasure. "You didn't have to bring them home, Cooper. You could have dropped them off at the zoo."

"We were at the zoo yesterday," Juliet said. "What's so great about being stared at by a bunch of animals?"

"The object of going to a zoo is to stare *at* the animals."

"You taught us not to stare because it's impolite. We never ever stare, do we, Cordelia?"

"Oh God," Iris said, but as usual He wasn't paying any attention.

The girls finally went out to the kitchen to make some butterscotch coconut pecan cookies and Iris was left alone with her husband in the small bright room she used both as an office and a refuge.

Here Iris spent most of her time with her books and stereo, a tiny champagne-colored poodle, Alouette, and an assortment of miniature chess sets. She played chess by mail with people she'd met in other parts of the world: a diplomat's wife in Bogotá, a medical missionary assigned to a hospital in Jakarta, a professor at the University of Tokyo, a petroleum engineer in Tabriz. She wasn't completely crippled and could have gone places if she'd wanted to, but she'd already been everywhere and her increasing deafness made communication with strangers difficult.

She sat by the window with the elderly poodle in her lap, leaning toward the sun as if its rays could rejuvenate both of them.

"Cooper."

"Yes, Iris."

"The girls aren't improving."

"I don't believe they are."

"Can't we do something, anything? I've been reading in the newspapers and magazines about vitamin E. Do you suppose if we put some in their food—?"

"No."

"We could give it a try, couldn't we?"

"No, I think not."

The little dog began to whimper in his sleep. Iris patted his woolly head and whispered in his ear, "Wake up, Alouette. Nothing's wrong, it's only a dream."

Cooper listened, sighing, wishing nothing was wrong, it was only a dream. Even the dog wasn't fooled. He woke up with a snort and cast a melancholy look around the room. He had eyes like bitter chocolate.

"Did you say something, Cooper?"

"No."

"I thought I heard—"

"No."

"We hardly ever talk these days."

"It's difficult to find anything new to say." And to say it loudly enough and enunciate clearly enough. "Iris, you promised me you'd ask the doctor about a hearing aid. I hate to press the point."

"Then don't."

He didn't. Besides the fact that he knew further argument would be useless, the Admiral was not combative on a person-to-person level. When his wife and the girls started fighting he got as far away as he could, usually withdrawing to his tiny hideaway in the bell tower, reached by a ladder which Iris couldn't climb and filled with squeals and scurryings which intimidated the girls. Here, where a century ago there had been a bell to proclaim peace and good will, the Admiral sat and planned wars.

They were not the ordinary kind found in history books. They were small interesting gentlemen's wars played under the old rules, captain against captain, plane against plane. And when they ended they left no poverty or desolation or bitterness. Everyone simply rallied round and got ready for the next one. A few people had to die, of course, but when they did, it was bravely, almost apologetically: "Sorry to let you down, old chap. I must—go—now—"

He didn't tell his wife about these private little wars. She was too serious. A mere look from her could cripple a tank or send a platoon into disorderly retreat or bring down a plane. Iris would be no fun in battle—she would insist on winning.

"Are you paying attention to me, Cooper?"

"Certainly, certainly I am."

"My brother Charles called to wish you a happy birthday. Is it your birthday?"

"No."

"Good. I didn't buy you anything . . . Charles must have had some reason for calling. Perhaps it's *his* birthday and this was a subtle way of reminding me. Would you check the birthday book in the top drawer of my desk?"

The desk, like the other furniture in the room, was an antique. Iris had no real interest in antiques. She'd bought the house furnished when Cooper retired because she and Cooper had never lived more than a couple of years in one place and it pleased her to own a house that looked and felt and even smelled ancestral.

Cooper said, "Is Charles listed under Charles or Van Eyck?"

"Van Eyck."

"Yes. Here it is. His birthday's next week, he'll be seventy-five."

"So I was right. He meant the phone call as a hint. Well, perhaps we should celebrate in some way, since he probably won't be around much longer. What do you think of a small dinner party?"

Cooper thought nothing at all of it but he didn't say so. He knew perfectly well that his opinion was not being asked, Iris was merely talking to herself.

"The trouble with a dinner party is that we'll have to invite some woman for Charles to escort. He's alienated so many people, I wonder who's left. Remember Mrs. Roffman who inherited all that meat money? I haven't heard of her dying, have you?"

"No."

"Then she's probably still alive. We could try her."

"Mrs. Roffman is nearly eighty. Charles prefers younger women."

"She used to be quite beautiful."

"I doubt that he'd take that into consideration."

"If you're just going to be negative about the whole thing, forget it."

"I'm not being negative, Iris. I want you to enjoy yourself."

"*Enjoy* myself?" The little dog jumped off her lap and darted across the room to hide under the desk. "*Enjoy* myself? Are you insane? Look at me, stuck here day after day, hardly able to move, worrying myself sick over the girls, wondering what will become of them, of me, of—"

"A small dinner party would be very nice," Cooper said. "Very nice. As for a partner for Charles, what about Neville's widow?"

"Who?"

"Miranda Shaw. I had a glimpse of her today at the club, so she's obviously over her period of mourning. She might be pleased to get back in circulation even if it means sitting next to Charles."

"I've never really liked Miranda Shaw," Iris said, "but I can't think of anyone else offhand."

Part II

It was only the second time since he'd worked for Smedler's law firm that Tom Aragon had been summoned by Smedler himself up to the penthouse office.

The penthouse wasn't far in terms of distance. The city of Santa Felicia had a building code limiting the height of buildings, so Smedler's office was in fact only three stories from the sidewalk. But in terms of accessibility it might as well have been a mile. It was serviced by an elevator whose movements could be controlled by Smedler through a circuit breaker beside his desk. There were, of course, little buttons in the elevator for clients to press, giving them the comfortable feeling of being in command of the situation, but a few minutes trapped between floors, or behind a door that wouldn't open, left them with reasonable doubts.

Smedler's secretary, Charity Nelson, wearing her orange wig slightly askew, was gluing on her fingernails for the day. She said, without looking up, "Aragon, you're late."

"Sorry."

"We expect our junior employees to be like the Boy Scouts, trustworthy, loyal, helpful, friendly, punctual—"

"Punctual is not part of the Boy Scout creed."

"Let's add it right now. Punctual."

"I couldn't get the elevator moving," Aragon said. "It happens all the time. The air conditioners and electric machines still function and the lights are on, but the elevator won't work."

"Electricity is a very mysterious thing."

"Not all that mysterious. I was the assistant manager of an apartment house when I went to law school. If I could take a look at the transformer—"

"Well, you're not the assistant manager here, so mind your own business. Sit down. Smedler's on the phone." Charity filed the glue and the rest of the fingernails under B for bite. "Did he tell you what he wanted?"

"No."

"Maybe he asked for you specifically because you did such a bang-up job on the Lockwood case. By the way, we're still waiting for Mrs. Lockwood to pay up. But that's a mere trifle, forget it. We can't have you worrying your pretty little head about anything as crass as money, can we? No indeedy."

Aragon sat down in a leather swivel chair facing Charity's desk. Though it was late October and only ten thirty in the morning, the room was uncomfortably warm and humid. Charity had turned off the air conditioner to protect her house plants, massed like a bonsai jungle in the east corner of the room. The plants didn't like air conditioning, and she felt the same maternal obligation to them that she would have to a child or pet, rejoicing in their growth and good health and fighting off their enemies like aphids and mealybugs and red spider mites.

Aragon looked at one of the plants, wondering if Charity talked to it, and if she did, why it hadn't shriveled up and blown away.

"You want to know why I believe you'll make it as a lawyer, Aragon?"

"Not particularly."

"You look dumb. Not dumb dumb, more innocent-like dumb. Any judge or jury would feel sorry for you seeing those calf eyes peering from behind those horn-rimmed glasses. Juries hate a smart-looking lawyer who dresses well."

"Do you talk to your plants, Miss Nelson?"

"No."

"I thought not."

"I'm not a loony. What in hell would I say to a plant?"

"Oh, something soothing, pleasant, complimentary—you know, the way you talk to the new employees."

"I don't talk like that to *any* employees. You trying to come on funny, junior? Better think twice."

Aragon thought twice and changed the subject. "What does Smedler want?"

"What he always wants, *everything.*"

"I meant from me."

"The file sent up was from Probate, so don't expect any fun and games like last time. Probates are ho hum." A light flashed on the intercom. "Okay, he's off the phone. You can go in."

Even on Monday morning Smedler looked fit and vigorous. Though office rumors had him spending every weekend fighting with his third wife at the country club, he showed no signs of injury, physical or mental. He wore a vested pin-striped suit, a Dartmouth tie and a small permanent smile unrelated to anything he happened to be saying. His admirers, mostly female, thought this smile made him look inscrutable and they were always disappointed to find out how scrutable he actually was.

"This matter is more of a nuisance than a problem," Smedler said. "So far, anyway. The reason I called you in is because I hear you get along well with women. Is this correct?"

"It depends on the circ—"

"Yes. Well, anyway, to get down to business, I have some probate papers that must be signed. An elderly man, Neville Shaw, died last spring, leaving his wife, Miranda, as the administrator and sole beneficiary of his estate. I made it clear to Mrs. Shaw that probate was often long and involved and that she'd better keep in touch with me, since there'd be matters coming up from time to time which would require her notarized signature. Well, matters have come up, a lot of them, but the past week I haven't been able to contact her. There's no answer when I call her house, she doesn't respond to messages left at her club, and two registered letters have been returned to the office undelivered. Even with her full cooperation, probate may drag on for months. So find her."

"I'll try."

"You shouldn't have much trouble. I'm sure this isn't a deliberate evasion on her part—she's a nice little woman, a good deal younger than her husband, well-bred, pretty, not too bright, always acts somewhat scared. In this case she has damned good reason to be scared."

There was a long pause, which Aragon recognized as a standard courtroom tactic: dangling question, delayed answer. He said nothing.

Smedler looked annoyed. "Don't you want to know *why*?"

"I figured you'd tell me."

"Of course I'll tell you. The problem is how much. It's important not to start any more rumors about Neville Shaw's will. There are enough already. He was nearly eighty when he died, and the fact is the estate should have had a conservator for the last few years of his life. He was getting senile, making a lot of crazy purchases and investments, highly speculative stocks, foreign currency, real estate syndicates. He even put up his house as down payment on a stud farm in Kentucky. I didn't know any of this was happening—and merely acted as his attorney when he made his will a dozen years ago—but I found out in a hurry. When the routine notice to creditors was published, they began coming out of the woodwork: brokers, bankers, developers, even the real estate hustler who'd handled the Kentucky transaction. To put it briefly, the creditors outnumber the credits. Shaw died broke."

"And Mrs. Shaw doesn't know this?"

"No."

"That seems peculiar for this day and age."

"The Shaws didn't live in this day and age."

"When are you going to bring her up to date?"

"The first step is yours, Aragon. Now, here's the address and phone number of her residence and her club. When you contact her, inform her firmly that she must come to my office to sign some papers. After that, I'll—well, I'll simply tell her that she's not quite as rich as she was at one time and that she'll have to make substantial reductions in her standard of living."

"Maybe you'd better tell her the truth; that she's broke."

"You don't tell women the truth," Smedler said. "Not all at once anyway, and certainly not a woman like Mrs. Shaw who's been protected and insulated from the world. My God, she might scream or cry or faint. She might even shoot me."

"If Mrs. Shaw is as insulated from the world as you claim she is, why would she be carrying a gun?"

"I only meant there's no way of predicting how a woman will act when she's *in extremis*. And believe me, that's what she is going to be. If nothing else does it, the stud farm in Kentucky will."

"It's a nice Freudian touch."

Smedler went over to the water cooler and poured himself a drink in a clear plastic cup. The water looked slightly murky and when he drank it he winced. "Ever taste this stuff, Aragon? It's lethal. I often suspect my secretary of trying to poison me. The only reason I survive is because I've gradually built up an immunity. Have some?"

"No, thank you."

"Better start working on your immunity. The water situation is not likely to improve. In fact, I predict that some day the world will dry up and blow away. There'll be no nonsense about floods and arks, just a whole lot of dust. Think about it."

"Yes, sir." Aragon thought about it and concluded that Smedler's weekend bash with his wife must have been worse than usual.

Smedler returned to his desk. "I was your age, Aragon, when I passed my bar exams and assumed I was about to enter the practice of law. What I actually entered was the practice of people. To put it another way, anyone can memorize the criminal code, but what's important is the code of criminals."

"That's very good, sir."

"I know. I've used it in a dozen speeches. Well, you have work to do, I won't keep you."

The Penguin Club was a long blue one-and-a-half-story building built on a narrow strip of land between the road and the sea. To passersby, it presented a windowless front except for a series of shuttered air ducts that peeked out from beneath the roof like half-closed eyes. In spite of the club's reputation as a gathering place for the very rich, the cars in the parking lot were the same size and brand as the ones found outside a supermarket or a laundromat. The only difference was that there were fewer of them—less than a quarter of the slots were occupied. In a time and place of abundance, space was the only real luxury left.

Tom Aragon hadn't been inside the Penguin Club since the night he and some of his high school friends had come up from the beach to scale the back fence and swim in the pool. Before they even hit the water the lights went on, every light in the place—at the entrance and inside the office, along the corridors and the terrace, under the water and from the depths of shrubbery, the tops of palm trees, the interiors of cabanas. A uniformed security guard appeared, his gun drawn. "Back to the barrio, you bobos!"

This time he was ten years older and went to the front entrance. For the first few seconds he felt nervous, as if the same security guard was going to be on duty and might recognize him.

The fancy gold lettering on the door didn't soften its message: Members and Guests Only. No Trespassing. Dress Code Enforced. He went inside. No one recognized him or even noticed him. In the office, on the other side of the waist-high counter, only one person was visible, a young woman sitting at a desk with a pencil behind her ear. She didn't seem to be doing anything except possibly thinking.

Aragon was the first to speak. "Miss?"

She removed the pencil and came over to the counter. She was tall and on the verge of being pretty, with dark hair and serious green eyes. The lids were pink, as if, not too long ago, she'd been crying. He wondered why, estimating his chance of finding out as very slight.

"May I help you?" The hoarseness of her voice tied in with the pink eyelids. "I'm Miss Brewster, the club secretary."

He gave her one of his business cards: Tomás Aragon, Attorney, Smedler, Downs, Castleberg, McFee, Powell. "I'm trying to locate one of our clients, Mrs. Miranda Shaw. I understand she's a member of this club."

"Yes."

"There are some important papers for her to sign and Mr. Smedler hasn't been able to contact her at her house. He thought she might be here."

"I haven't seen her."

"Does that mean she's not here?"

"Not necessarily. She might have come in while I was on my coffee break or before I arrived. I was late this morning. My car wouldn't start and I had to ride my bicycle."

"What kind of bicycle?"

"What difference does it make what *kind* of bicycle?"

"No difference. I was merely putting in time until you decide to tell me about Mrs. Shaw."

She took a deep breath. It seemed to hurt her. She began coughing, holding on hard to her throat.

He waited, looking toward the pool. A couple of swimmers were doing laps and half a dozen women were taking part in an exercise class at the shallow end. On the terrace an elderly man wearing a tennis visor sat at a table, writing. Most of the deck chairs on the opposite side of the pool were empty.

The lifeguard tower interested Aragon most. It was occupied by a red-haired boy about eight or nine looking through a pair of outsized binoculars. Aragon had the impression that they were focused on him. To test this he smiled and waved, and immediately the binoculars were lowered and the boy climbed down from the tower and disappeared.

The young woman had finished coughing. "We're not allowed to give out information about our members. It's in the rule book. Practically everything is, including fraternization."

She gave the word a certain bitter emphasis which he didn't understand. "I— Look, I'm having a bad morning. You'd better talk to the manager, Mr. Henderson. Wait here and I'll see if he's busy."

"Sure. Sorry about the bad morning. By noon things may be better."

"Or worse."

"Or worse," Aragon said. There was no point in wasting happy talk on Miss Brewster. She wasn't in a receptive mood.

Neither was Mr. Henderson.

Henderson had been going over the delinquent-dues list, trying to decide whether to take the drastic step of posting it on the main bulletin board or merely to keep a copy in strategic areas like the card and game room. There was the added decision of which names should be removed.

Each case had to be judged on its individual merits, or lack of them. The Whipples, for example, were traveling in the Orient and probably hadn't received the notice that the rent on their cabana was overdue. Billy Parr Davis had run up a two-thousand-dollar bill at his sixtieth birthday party, but it was only a matter of time before his mother sent a check to cover it as usual. The Redferns were in the throes of a divorce and custody of the club membership hadn't yet been determined, so it was unreasonable to expect payment from either of them. Mr. and Mrs. Quinn were protesting the charges for damages little Frederic had done to the first-aid station and the plumbing in the men's locker room. Mrs. Guinevere had gone to a fat farm to lose fifty pounds and her bill would be paid when the remaining two hundred returned.

There were, of course, the usual deadbeats, some, like Charles Van Eyck, very wealthy and intent on staying that way, others obviously having a hard time keeping up with inflation and the Joneses. Henderson was checking the list a final time when Ellen opened the door of his office.

He looked up, frowning. "You didn't knock. I've told you—"

"Sorry. Knock, knock."

"Come in and be brief."

"Yes, sir. There's a Tomás Aragon here. He's a lawyer. I think you'd better talk to him."

"Is he applying for membership?"

"No. He wants some information about Mrs. Shaw."

"That's a funny coincidence." Henderson sounded uneasy. He didn't like coincidences. Through some obscure mechanism they usually ended up working against him. "I was just going to ask you about her myself. Her name's been crossed off the delinquent list."

"She paid up," Ellen said. "In cash."

"Her bill's been outstanding for some time. I haven't pressed the matter because I wanted to give her a chance to get over the loss of her husband."

"Well, I guess she got over it."

"Why cash, I wonder. Nobody around here pays cash. It's a dirty word . . . This lawyer, Aragon, what sort of information is he after?"

"He's trying to find Mrs. Shaw so she can sign some legal papers."

"That sounds plausible to me," Henderson said. "What's he like?"

"Young, dark-haired, horn-rimmed glasses, rather appealing."

"I meant inside."

"I can't see his inside. Outside he looks honest enough."

"Then there's no reason to be secretive about it. Tell him Mrs. Shaw is not here. Unless, of course, she is?"

"I haven't seen her."

"Neither have I. Odd, she was coming every day for a while. Mr. Van Eyck used to stare at her across the pool. I sensed a possible romance between two lonely people. That would have been good for the club—we could have held a lovely wedding reception in the ballroom, with white cymbidiums and silver ribbon and podocarpus instead of ferns. Ferns are common . . . When's the last time you saw Mrs. Shaw at the club?"

"I don't remember exactly," Ellen said. She did, though. Exactly, to the minute. *"Goodbye, Ellen. Hasn't it been lovely weather? I must fly now. See you tomorrow."*

She went back into the corridor. On one of the rattan settees placed at intervals along the wall, Admiral Young's two daughters sat in identical postures. They looked so stiff and self-conscious that Ellen knew they'd been eavesdropping. Cordelia's face was sallow, as usual, but Juliet's cheeks and chin and the tip of her nose were pink with suppressed excitement.

Ellen tried to brush past them but they rose simultaneously and blocked her way.

"Sorry, girls, I haven't time to talk to you right now."

"You were talking to *him,*" Cordelia said.

"And that other him," Juliet added. "We think something's wrong. I smelled disaster the instant I heard Miranda Shaw's name."

"Juliet's no magna cum laude," her sister explained. "But she has very keen senses."

Juliet lowered her eyes modestly. "I really do, don't I, Cordelia?"

"I already said so. Now get on with the story."

"Why don't *you* tell it if you're in such a bloody hurry?"

"No. You tell, I'll edit."

"Oh, I hate being edited," Juliet cried. "Oh God, I hate it, it makes me throw up."

Cordelia did her Rhett Butler imitation, *Frankly, my dear, I don't give a damn,* which put Juliet in a good mood again and she was able to continue her narrative: "This year Mrs. Young had the peculiar idea of giving her brother, our Uncle Charley Van Eyck, a birthday party."

"Why you didn't smell *that* disaster, I'd like to know."

"Heavens to horehound, I can't smell them all . . . The trouble with Mrs. Young's idea was fixing Uncle Charley up with a dinner partner because he's such a weirdo. She decided to try Miranda Shaw, probably because Miranda doesn't know Uncle Charley very well. Mrs. Young kept phoning and phoning, and when she couldn't get an answer she gave us the job of coming down here every day to keep an eye out for Miranda so we could pass along the invitation when she showed up. Only she never did and the party was last week."

Cordelia started to describe the party, how Uncle Charley got drunk and dressed up in one of the Admiral's old uniforms and sang "Anchors Aweigh" with dirty lyrics, but Ellen interrupted.

"Thank you for your information, girls. Don't worry about Mrs. Shaw, I'm sure she's quite all right."

"You are very unworldly, Ellen," Cordelia said. "Things *happen* to women."

Juliet nodded. "Even to us. Once in Singapore we were escorted by—"

"Shut up. The Singapore incident is nobody's business."

"Well, you told everybody at the time. You could hardly wait to spread it around the yacht club."

"This isn't Singapore and Mrs. Shaw wasn't accosted," Ellen said. *And if she was, she accosted right back.* "Mrs. Shaw probably decided to take a vacation."

She told Aragon the same thing, while the girls stood in the background listening, Cordelia rolling her eyes in a pantomime of disbelief, Juliet waving one hand back and forth across her face as if fanning away a bad smell.

Aragon said, "Mrs. Shaw didn't actually mention taking a vacation?"

"No. Some of our members talk about their trips for six months in advance and six months afterwards, but Mrs. Shaw is the quiet type."

"I see. Well, if you happen to hear from her, please let me know. You have my card."

"Yes." She had thrown the card away immediately, without even stopping to think about it. "I'm terribly sorry I couldn't be of more help."

As he went out the door Aragon wondered why someone who was so terribly sorry didn't look even a little bit sorry.

In the parking lot he found his car already occupied. Sitting behind the wheel was the red-haired boy he'd seen on the lifeguard's tower. He wore a T-shirt with a picture of a surfer on it and the advice Make Waves, but he looked as if he didn't need the advice.

He slid across the seat to make room for Aragon. "You should lock your heap, man. These old-model Chevs are very big."

"Thanks for telling me."

"I *showed* you, man, I didn't tell you. Nobody learns by being told."

"All right, thanks for showing me."

"No sweat. It's because of the ignition."

"What is?"

"The reason the old Chevs are being ripped off. They're easy to start without a key. Let me show you."

"Don't bother," Aragon said. "I have a key."

"Yeah, but suppose you lose it and—"

"The only thing I ever lose is my temper."

The boy studied his fingernails, found them uninteresting, jammed his hands into the rear pockets of his jeans. The resulting posture made him look as though he'd been strapped in a strait jacket. "I suppose you're wondering who I am."

"It crossed my mind."

"I am Frederic Marshall Quinn the Third, *numero tres*."

"I figure you're also a smart-ass *numero uno*."

Frederic acknowledged the compliment with a worldly little shrug. "Sure, man. Why not? I got to survive."

"Haven't you heard, Freddy? Smart-asses are the first to go."

"In your day, maybe. Times have changed." His hands came out of his pockets and his fingernails were reexamined. "I heard you talking about Mrs. Shaw. You a lawyer?"

"Yes."

"I may need a lawyer someday so I thought I'd do you a favor, then you'll owe me one. Right?"

"I'll consider it," Aragon said.

"That's not good enough. Let's make it a real deal here and now. We're both in the same boat, see, on account of I'm looking for somebody, too."

"Sure you are."

"Honest. There's this lifeguard, Grady. He's okay. I mean, he's kind of like my friend. I've been learning about macho from him so I can pass the info to some of the kids at school. Only just when I was catching on to a few tricks, he split. Didn't say goodbye or where he was going or when he'd be back, didn't even wait for his paycheck."

"How do you know all this?"

"I heard Ellen talking to Henderson about it, wondering where to send Grady's paycheck. She got mad because it would screw up the bookkeeping if Grady didn't cash his check. She was even crying about it. She cries easy. Really gross."

"Who was Grady practicing his macho on?"

"That's the favor I'm doing you, man. Her, Mrs. Shaw. She was his new chick."

Aragon watched in silence as a fat brown bird landed on the hood of his car, hopped over to the windshield and picked a bug off one of the wipers. "You wouldn't make up a story like that, would you?"

"Sure I would, but I didn't. It was right here in the parking lot that I first saw them together. Grady was using a different technique, high class, no hands, lots of talk and eye contact. Then they drove off in her car, a custom-job black Lincoln Continental. What about our deal?"

"It's on. I owe you one. When you need my services, give me a call. Here's my card."

Frederic shook his head. "I already got your card. I picked it out of the wastebasket where Ellen threw it."

"All right, Frederic, now I owe you two."

"Two? How come?"

"It's a personal thing."

"I like personal things."

"So do I," Aragon said. *But not this one. She threw it in the wastebasket because she had no intention of telling me anything. The conversation was a cover-up, hocus pocus.* "The girl in the front office, Ellen you called her, what's she like?"

"She loses her cool and chews me out about once a day, but she's not on my H list."

"What's your H list, Frederic?"

"H for hate."

"Is this a real list or do you merely keep it in your head?"

"Real, man. Lots of people on it, too. I added one today, that old creep Van Eyck. He told me he was going to string me up by my thumbs in the boiler room. Imagine saying that to a kid."

"I'm trying to imagine what the kid said first."

"I only asked him if he was queen of the fairies."

"That's not an endearing question, Frederic."

Frederic looked up into the sun, squinting. "How am I going to learn things without asking? If he isn't queen of the fairies, he could have answered no. And if he is, well, we live in an enlightened society."

"Don't bet your thumbs on it, kid."

"It wasn't even my idea in the first place. The two flakies, those sisters that are always hanging around, they were talking about it. You know, hormones. They decided if the old man's trouble was hormones it could be corrected, but if it was genes it couldn't and they were stuck with it. Would you care to know what *I* think?"

"I don't believe I would, no."

"Van Eyck has blue genes." The boy doubled up with laughter and his tomato-red face looked ready to burst its skin. "That's a joke I heard at school. Blue genes, see? Hey, man, don't you have a sense of humor?"

"It's been temporarily deactivated," Aragon said. "Now let's leave it at that and you go back to school and I'll go back to the office."

"No. No, you can't. You have to look for Grady. I got everything figured out for you—find Mrs. Shaw and Grady will be with her. They're probably just shacked up in her house making macho and not answering the phone."

"How many times have you called there, Frederic?"

"Six, seven. Why shouldn't I? I mean, Grady and me, we're like friends almost. When he's not around I don't have anyone to talk to."

"You could attend classes once in a while. They have people there you can talk to called teachers."

"Don't lecture me, man. Every time I go near a grownup I get a lecture. Except Grady."

"And what do you get from Grady?"

"Action. Anyway, he can't afford to give me a lecture. He dropped out of the tenth grade and has been maxing it ever since."

"Maxing?"

"Living up to his maximum potential, like doing what he wants to without being caught."

Aragon watched the brown bird hop across the hood and down to the ground, thinking that Mrs. Shaw was an unlikely choice for Grady's maxing. "Listen, Frederic, are you sure Mrs. Shaw is Grady's new chick? She's an older woman, a widow with a refined background—"

"Where have you been all these years? Backgrounds don't matter anymore unless they're real special like Bingo Firenze's. His uncle is a hit man for the Mafia. Now *that* matters . . . Are you going to find Grady for me?"

"I'm going to keep looking for Mrs. Shaw. If Grady's with her, fine. I can't guarantee anything beyond that."

"Why are you after Mrs. Shaw, anyway?"

"There are some probate papers for her to sign. Know what probate means?"

"Sure," Frederic said. "It's when a person dies and everybody's fighting for the money that's left and a judge decides who gets it."

"Close enough."

"I hope Mrs. Shaw gets the money. Grady needs it. He's always scrounging. Last month he borrowed twenty dollars from my sister, April, just before they sent her away to riding school in Arizona. Grady doesn't know it yet but April gave me the IOU so I could collect. I'm saving it to use sort of like blackmail when I need a very important favor."

"Bingo Firenze's uncle would be proud of you, kid."

"Sure." Frederic opened the car door. "Listen, when you see Grady don't tell him it was me who sent you. I wouldn't want him to think I care what he does or anything like that. Deal?"

"Deal."

They shook hands. It was a solemn occasion: Aragon had acquired his first private client.

Leaving the parking lot, he drove past the front entrance of the club. The two sisters were standing outside the door looking as though they were expecting something or someone. He hoped he wasn't it.

"That's him, all right," Cordelia said. "Did you notice how he stepped on the accelerator the instant he spotted us? Very odd, don't you think?"

"Well, a lot of people do it," Juliet said wistfully.

"A lot of people have reason to because they know us. But this young man doesn't know us, so *that* can't be the reason."

"He has rather a pleasant face."

"You gullible idiot, they're the worst kind. Believe me, he's up to no good. You mustn't be taken in by appearances, Juliet."

"I'll try not."

"They mean nothing."

"I know. But wouldn't it be nice to be pretty, Cordelia? Just for a little while, even a few days?"

"Oh, shut up." Cordelia gave her sister a warning pinch on the arm. "We are us and that's that. Don't go dreaming."

"I won't. Still, it would be nice, just for a few—"

"All right, it would be nice. But it's not going to happen, never ever, so forget it."

Juliet's eyes were moist, partly from the pinch, partly from the *never ever,* which was even more final than plain *never.* Through the moisture, however, she could see the Admiral's Rolls-Royce approaching, as slow and steady as a ship nearing port. "Here comes Pops."

"Maybe we should tell him."

"What about?"

"The disaster," Cordelia said, frowning. "You told Ellen you distinctly smelled disaster the instant you heard Miranda Shaw's name."

"I did smell it, I really did. Unless it was my depilatory."

"Oh, for God's sakes, there you go ruining things again."

"I can't help it. I only this minute remembered using the depilatory, which has a peculiar odor, kind of sulphurous, like hellfire. I'm sorry, Cordelia."

"You damn well should be, blowing the whole bit like this."

"It's still very *possible* that something awful happened to her. We saw her and that lifeguard looking at each other and it was *that kind* of look, like in Singapore."

The mention of Singapore inspired Cordelia to new heights. It was her opinion that Grady had lured Mrs. Shaw up into the mountains, stripped her of her clothes, virtue, cash and jewels, probably in that order, and left her there to perish.

Juliet contemplated this in silence for a moment. Then she said cheerfully, "So it wasn't my depilatory after all."

The Admiral had agreed, after a somewhat one-sided discussion with his wife, Iris, to forgo the football game on T. V. and take the girls downtown for lunch at a cafeteria. They both loved cafeterias and selected so many things to eat that they had to use an extra tray to hold the desserts. After consuming as much as they could, they packed the rest into doggy bags and took them down to the bird refuge to feed the geese and gulls and coots. The gulls and coots ate anything, but the geese were choosy, preferring mixed green salad and apple pie.

The Admiral parked the Rolls, then moved to the rear to open the door for his daughters like a salaried chauffeur. "Are you ready for lunch?"

"I guess," Juliet said.

"You *guess*? Dear me, that doesn't sound like one of my girls talking. What about you, Cordelia?"

Cordelia didn't waste time on amenities. "Pops, did you ever know anyone who was murdered?"

"Now that depends on your definition of murder. During the Second World War and the Korean conflict I saw many of my—"

"Oh, not that kind of murder, it's so ordinary. I meant the real thing, with real motives and everything."

"What's the point of such a question, Cordelia?"

"Miranda Shaw has disappeared."

"Vanished," Juliet added.

"We think she's been murdered."

"Done in."

"Come, come," the Admiral said mildly. "Miranda Shaw isn't the kind of person who gets murdered. She's a fine lady with many womanly virtues."

"Ah so," Cordelia said. "And what are womanly virtues, Pops?"

"My dear, I should have thought your mother would have told you by this time."

"Maybe nobody told *her*."

"Yes, I see. Well, I can't speak for all men, of course, but among the traits I consider desirable in a woman are kindness, gentleness, loving patience."

They both stared at him for a few seconds before Cordelia spoke again. "Then what made you pick Mrs. Young?"

"That's a very rude question, Cordelia. I shall do my best to forget it was ever asked."

"Oh bull. You always say that when you don't know the answer to something."

"Most likely," Juliet said, "he didn't pick her, she picked him. Ten to one it happened like that. Didn't it, Pops?"

The Admiral cleared his throat. "I wish you girls could manage to show more respect towards your parents."

"We're trying, Pops."

"But remember, you're not in the Navy anymore," Cordelia said briskly. "We're not ensigns or junior looies. Are we, Juliet?"

"Not on your poop deck," Juliet said.

Aragon left his car on the street at the bottom of the Shaws' driveway.

It was an area of huge old houses build on large multiple acreages when land was cheap, and surrounded by tall iron or stone fences constructed when labor was cheap. Most of the residences had gatehouses, some not much larger than the gondolas of a ski lift, others obviously intended as living quarters for servants. The Shaws' gatehouse had Venetian blinds on the largest window and a well-used broom propped outside the front door.

Aragon pressed the button that was supposed to activate the squawk box connecting the gate to the main residence. Nothing happened. The squawk box was either out of order or disconnected. He waited several minutes, trying to decide what to do next. The gate was iron grillwork ten feet high. It would be possible to scale it, as he'd once scaled the Penguin Club fence, but the results might be more severe—a couple of police cars instead of a lone security guard.

He was turning to leave when he noticed that two slats of the blind on the gatehouse window had been parted and a pair of eyes was staring at him. They were small and dark and liquid, like drops of strong coffee.

"Hello," Aragon said. "Are you in charge here?"

"Nobody in charge. Nobody home. All gone, gone away." The man's accent sounded Mexican but there were Oriental inflections in his voice. "Maybe *you* are in charge?"

"No. I just want to see Mrs. Shaw."

"Me too. I need my truck."

"Mrs. Shaw took your truck?"

"You bet not. I have the keys. How could the Missus take my truck?"

"All right, let's start over. And it might make it easier if we didn't have to talk through the window. Why don't you come out?"

"Sure." The door of the gatehouse opened and a tiny man stepped out, moving briskly in spite of his age. He was so shriveled and hairless that he looked as though he'd fallen into a tanning vat and emerged a leather doll. "See, I can go in and out, out and in, easy for me. But for my truck to go in and out, out and in, I need to use the gate, and it won't work."

"Why not?"

"It is an electric gate and there is no electric."

"Why is there no electric?"

"Missus forgot to pay, I guess. A man came and shut it off. I said you can't do that, Missus is important rich lady. He said, the hell I can't. And he did."

"That's too bad."

"Very bad, yes. He wouldn't wait for me to get my truck onto the driveway, so it is still up there behind the garage with all my tools in it. I can't earn a living without my truck and tools. Here, see who I am." The old man showed Aragon his business card, so dirty and dilapidated that the printing was scarcely legible: Mitsu Hippollomia, Tree Care, Clean Up, Hauling, Reasonable Rates. "I can't leave without my truck, so I stay here in the gatehouse waiting for the electric and keeping my eye out for truck thieves."

"How long have you been living in the gatehouse?"

Hippollomia, having no clock or calendar, didn't know for sure. Nor did he care much. He was enjoying the closest thing to a holiday he'd ever had, with plenty of rest and food. He went to bed when it was dark and got up when it was light. He ate the avocados and persimmons that were ripening on the trees, and tomatoes reddening on the vines. From the storage room beside the main kitchen he had canned goods and preserves off the shelves, and melted ice cream out of the freezer. Besides such physical luxuries, he had the satisfaction of knowing he was doing an important job, protecting his livelihood.

Aragon said, "Do you mind if I come in and take a look around the property?"

"Why do you want to do that?"

"I work for Mrs. Shaw's attorney. There are some papers for her to sign and he hasn't been able to get in touch with her."

"She's not here."

"Have you been inside the house?"

"Not so much."

"How much is that?"

"Only in the storage room off the kitchen. I take a little food now and then."

"How do you get in?"

"There are a whole bunch of keys on nails in the garage," the old man said. "But I didn't need any of them. Missus isn't too careful about locking the house because the electric gate keeps strangers out."

"You found the back door open, Mr. Hippollomia?"

"Not open, unlocked."

"And it's unlocked now?"

"Yes."

"Would you have any objection to my going in?"

"It's not my house. I have no say-so."

"You're the only one on the premises," Aragon said. "That more or less puts you in charge."

The old man's shoulders twitched inside his oversized work shirt. "You go when you want, you do whatever, I'm out of it. I wait here."

"I'd like to make sure Mrs. Shaw left the house of her own free will. By the way, do you work for her on a regular basis?"

"Yes."

"Every day?"

"No. Twice a week I clip hedges and mow the lawn and haul away clippings."

"Are there live-in servants?"

"No more. The fat lady who cooks, the college girl who vacuums and cleans, the handyman living in the room over the garage, I don't see them for a long time. What do you think?"

"I think," Aragon said, "Missus forgot to pay."

The size and beauty of the place made its neglect more apparent. There was a sixty-foot white-tiled pool with a Jacuzzi at one end, but the water had turned green with algae and the weir was clogged with leaves and a dead gopher. Across a corner of the patio a dripping faucet had left a trail of rust like last year's blood. A marble birdbath was filled with the needles and sheathed pods of cypress. Pollen from the jellicoe trees had sifted the flour over the glass-topped tables and latticed chairs.

Inside, the house was dusty but very neat. Two living rooms, a library and a formal dining room all had fireplaces scrubbed as clean as the ovens in the kitchen. Upstairs there was a sitting room and half a dozen bedrooms, the largest of which was obviously Miranda Shaw's. It was here that Aragon found the only disorder in the house. The covers of the canopy bed had been pulled up over the pillows but the blue velvet spread was still draped across a matching chaise. Clothes were bulging out of one of the sliding doors of the closet. Beside the picture window a plant that looked like a refined cousin of marijuana was dying from lack of water. Some of its leaves had turned black and were curled up like charred Christmas ribbons.

In the adjoining bathroom used towels had been thrown into the pink porcelain tub. The chrome toothbrush holder was empty. So was the monogrammed silver tray made to hold a conventional hairbrush-comb-hand-mirror set.

Hippollomia was waiting at the kitchen door where Aragon had left him.

"Missus has taken a trip?"

"It looks that way."

"I hope she comes back soon and pays the electric. I want to go home. All the ice cream is gone."

"When I get back to my office I'll call the company and see if I can arrange to have your truck released."

"Why?"

"Because I feel that an injustice was done, probably due to a misunderstanding between you and the man who—"

"Misunderstanding," Hippollomia said. "I laugh. Ha ha."

It was noon when Aragon returned to the office. Smedler was busy on the phone, so Aragon made his report to Smedler's secretary, Charity Nelson.

She didn't like it. "What do you mean Mrs. Shaw went away?"

"Like in sayonara, auf Wiedersehen, adios."

"Where did you get your information?"

"Various sources. First, a kid told me."

"A what?"

"A child," Aragon said. "And an old man, a Filipino, I think."

Charity leaned back in her swivel chair, so that her orange-colored wig slid forward on her head and she had to peer out at Aragon through a fringe of bangs that looked like shredded pumpkin. "Smedler's not going to like this, one of his attorneys prying information out of children and old men."

"I didn't pry and it wasn't an ordinary child. It wasn't an ordinary old man either. He's waiting to get his truck out of Mrs. Shaw's driveway. I promised to help him, so if you don't mind I'd like to use your phone."

"I mind."

"Don't you want to help an old man?"

"How old?"

"About seventy or seventy-five."

"Sorry, I don't help anyone under eighty," Charity said pleasantly. "It's one of my rules."

Smedler came out of his office straightening his tie and smoothing his hair like a man who'd just been in a scuffle. He stared at Aragon the way he usually did, as though he wasn't quite sure of his identity. "Did you arrange for Mrs. Shaw to come in and sign the papers?"

"No, sir. I couldn't find her."

"Why not?"

"She wasn't where I looked."

"That answer will be stricken from the record as frivolous and non-responsive. Better try again."

Aragon tried again. "She left town."

"Go after her."

"I'm not even sure which direction she went, let alone—"

"Mrs. Shaw is not one of these modern flyaway women you find hanging around bars in San Francisco or blackjack tables in Las Vegas. If she left town she's probably visiting some elderly relative in Pasadena. Miss Nelson, check and see if Mrs. Shaw has an elderly relative in Pasadena or thereabouts."

"She ran off with a lifeguard," Aragon said.

"This seems to be your day for making funnies . . . It *is* a funny, of course?

"No, sir. His name's Grady and he's broke. That's about all I can tell you. I'm not even sure whether Grady's a first or last name."

"Find out and go after him."

"The staff at the Penguin Club aren't eager to give out information, especially the girl in the front office."

"So make yourself charming."

"That wasn't part of my contract with you, Mr. Smedler."

"It is now," Smedler said and went back into his office.

The conversation, which seemed to depress Smedler, had the opposite effect on his secretary. Her normally flat eyes looked round as marbles.

"A lifeguard yet," Charity said. "I wonder if she had to fake a drowning in order to make contact."

"Probably not. Lifeguards are usually quite accessible."

"Were you ever a lifeguard, Aragon?"

"No."

"Too bad. I bet you'd look cute in one of those teeny-weeny Mark Spitz numbers."

"Irresistible."

"What a shame you're married. I could arrange marvelous little office romances. I could anyway, of course, since your wife lives in San Francisco and you live here. That's a terribly funny arrangement, by the way."

"I'm glad it amuses you."

"Don't you get, well, you know?"

"I get you know," Aragon said. "But San Francisco is where my wife was offered a residency in pediatrics and she took it like a nice sensible girl. Like a nice sensible guy I approved."

Charity frowned. "I hate all that much sense. Takes the fun out of life . . . This Grady, I suppose he's years younger that Miranda Shaw. She's over fifty and there aren't many fifty-year-old lifeguards around. By that time they're gone on to better things."

"Or worse."

"Whatever. Actually, Mrs. Shaw looks marvelous for her age. In a nice dark restaurant she could pass for thirty-five. It can be done if you've got the money, the time, the motivation, the right doctor and lots of luck."

"That's a heap of ifs."

"I know. I've only got one of them, motivation. But I wouldn't want to spend the rest of my life sitting around dark restaurants anyway." Charity glanced toward Smedler's door as if to confirm that it was closed. "I heard a rumor about Miranda Shaw which I would like to repeat, I really would."

"Force yourself."

"Okay. I heard she gets injections made from the glands of unborn goats."

"Where does she get these injections?"

"In the butt, probably."

"No, no. I meant, does she go to a local doctor, a hospital, a clinic?"

"The rumor didn't cover details, but it doesn't sound like the sort of thing you could have done locally. Santa Felicia is a conservative city. Unborn goats get born, not injected."

"Where did you hear this about Mrs. Shaw?"

"Smedler. His wife picked it up at the country club. The injections are supposed to start working right away. You know, I wouldn't mind having a face lift if it didn't hurt too much and the results were guaranteed. But goat glands, that's positively obscene. Though if I had to keep up with a young lifeguard, maybe I wouldn't think so." Charity was sixty. In a nice dark restaurant she could pass for fifty-nine. "What's your opinion?"

"My opinion," Aragon said, "is that you are a fund of information and I'd like to take you to lunch."

Her eyebrows climbed up and hid briefly under her bangs. "Yeah? When?"

"Now."

"Have you flipped? You can't afford it on your salary."

"We can go to some simple little place. Do you like chili burgers?"

"No."

"Tacos? Burritos? Enchiladas?"

"No, no and no. I'm not a fun date at lunch anyway," Charity added. "I have an ulcer."

From his shoebox-sized office in the basement Aragon called the electric company and arranged to have Hippollomia's truck released. Then he phoned the Penguin Club and was told Ellen Brewster had gone into town on an errand and was expected back about two o'clock. He didn't leave a name, number or message; anticipating another visit from him probably wouldn't improve Miss Brewster's attitude.

He picked up a burger and fries at a fast food and ate them on his way to the public library.

The young woman on duty at the reference desk looked surprised when he asked for material on current methods of rejuvenation. "Starting early, aren't you?"

"A stitch in time."

"If we don't have the information you need, you might try the medical library at Castle Hospital."

"I just want a general idea of what's being done in the field."

"Okay. Be right back."

She disappeared in the stacks and emerged a few minutes later carrying a magazine. "You're in luck. The subject was researched a couple of months ago by one of the women's magazines. It's sketchy but it looks like the straight dope."

"Thanks."

"I get paid."

"Not enough."

"Now how did you know that?"

"A wild guess," Aragon said, wondering if he would ever meet anyone who admitted being paid enough.

During the next half-hour he learned some of the hard facts and fiction about growing old and how to prevent it.

At the Institute of Geriatrics in Bucharest a drug called KH-3 was administered to cure heart disease, arthritis, impotence, wrinkles and grey hair.

In Switzerland injections of live lamb embryo glands were available to revitalize the body and prevent disease by slowing down the aging process.

A villa outside Rome offered tours of the countryside alternating with periods of deep sleep induced by a narcotic banned in the United States.

A Viennese clinic guaranteed loss of ugly cellulite, and not so ugly money, by means of hypnotherapy and massive doses of vitamins.

In the Bahamas the Center for Study and Application of Revitalization Therapies promised to help the mature individual counteract the pressures of contemporary life, and overcome sleeplessness, fatigue, loss of vigor, frigidity, impotence, poor muscle and skin tone, problems of weight, anxiety and premature aging. Many different techniques were used, including lamb-cell therapy, but here the cells were freeze-dried.

At an experimental lab in New York volunteer patients underwent plasmapheresis, a process in which a quantity of their blood was removed, the plasma taken out and the blood put back. The fresh new plasma which the body then created was the stuff of youth and supposed to make the patients look better, feel stronger and heal faster.

Nowhere in the article was there any mention of goats.

Aragon called Charity Nelson from the pay phone beside the checkout desk.

She wasn't thrilled. "Oh, it's you."

"Listen, that rumor you heard about Mrs. Shaw, are you sure it was goats?"

"It was goats. What difference does it make? Where are you, anyway?"

"The library."

"Wise up. You're not going to find Mrs. Shaw at any library. She's not the type."

"I'm working on a hunch."

"Well, don't tell Smedler. He lost two grand playing one last week. Hunches won't be popular around here until he figures out a way to deduct it from his income tax."

"Will he?"

"Bet on it, junior."

He reached the parking lot of the Penguin Club as Ellen Brewster was getting out of her car. It was a fairly new Volkswagen but it already had a couple of body dents that were beginning to rust in the sea air.

She didn't notice, or at least acknowledge, his presence until he spoke.

"I see you got your car started."

"Yes. The garage man came out and charged the battery."

"Good."

"Yes."

"It could have been something more serious."

"I suppose." She pushed her hair back from her forehead with an impatient gesture. She had nice features. He wondered why they didn't add up to make her a pretty woman. "Are you coming or going, Mr. Aragon?"

"A question I often ask myself."

"Try answering."

"I'm arriving. Is that all right with you, Miss Brewster?"

"It depends on what you want. If it's the same thing you wanted this morning, I really can't help you now any more than I could then. Really I can't."

"That's one too many reallys."

"It's a speech habit I picked up from all the teenagers around this summer. You know, like you know."

"I went to Mrs. Shaw's house," Aragon said. "It seems she took off in a hurry, didn't even bother to lock the doors. What concerns my boss is that she was aware of the important papers she had to sign but she made no attempt to do it. Naturally there's some question of whether she left voluntarily."

"That's a joke."

"Is it private or do I get to laugh, too?"

"The question is not whether *she* left voluntarily but whether *he* did."

The afternoon wind had begun blowing in from the sea, carrying the smell of tar from the underwater oil wells. It was a faint pervasive smell like a hint of doomsday.

"Forget I said that," she added. "I'm not supposed to gossip about the members."

"This ranks as a little more than gossip, Miss Brewster. I learned the man's name this morning. Grady. He's a friend of yours, isn't he?"

"Did you learn that this morning, too?"

"Yes."

"You were misinformed. He's no friend of mine."

She turned and walked away. He followed her. She was almost as tall as he was and their steps exactly matched, so they looked as though they were marching in single file.

"Miss Brewster."

"If you already know so much, why did you come back here?"

"What's his full name?"

"Grady Keaton."

"Has he worked at the club long?"

"About six months."

"Can you tell me something of his background?"

"He didn't talk much about himself. Not to me anyway. Maybe to fifty other women."

"Why fifty?"

"Why not? One thing I can tell you about Grady is his philosophy—*why not?*"

They had reached the front door of the club but neither of them made any move to open it.They stood facing each other, almost eye to eye. Hers were green and very solemn. His were obscured by horn-rimmed glasses which needed cleaning.

Aragon said, "A minute ago you made it sound as though Mrs. Shaw had kidnapped an innocent lad. Now he's not such a lad and not so innocent, and Mrs. Shaw had to take a number and wait in line. Which version are you sticking with?"

"Are you going to make trouble for him?"

"I might. It's not my main objective, though. All I really want is Mrs. Shaw's signature on some legal documents."

"Why keep coming back here?"

"This is where she's known, where her friends are."

"I'm not sure she has friends at the club. She and her husband sort of dropped out of things when he began showing signs of senility, and after his death she didn't come around for ages. When she finally did she talked to me more than anyone else, mostly chitchat about the weather, food, clothes. Nothing heavy or even interesting."

"What makes you dislike her?"

"That's pretty strong. Let's just say I disapprove."

"Of what?"

"Her vanity," Ellen said. "She probably had reason to be vain some time ago. But at her age she should be able to pass a mirror without stopping to adore herself."

"Or criticize herself?"

"Whatever she's doing, the key word is *herself*. No matter how big the universe is it has to have a center, and Miranda decided long ago that she's it."

"Do you call her by her first name?"

"She asked me to. I don't, though. Mr. Henderson wouldn't like it."

"She must consider you a friend."

"I—well, I'm not. It's part of my job to act friendly toward the members and I do it. But when some of them expect or demand too much, that's their problem. I couldn't help them even if I wanted to. Mr. Henderson has rules about the staff becoming involved with any of the members."

"Evidently Mrs. Shaw wasn't aware of the rules."

"Grady was. But then, rules aren't exactly his strong suit."

A small plane passed very low along the edge of the sea as though it was searching for something washed up by the tide. She shielded her eyes to watch it until it disappeared behind a row of eucalyptus trees.

"You'd better come into the office," she said. "If people see us talking outside like this, some of them might think I'm carrying on an illicit affair. That wouldn't bother me but I don't suppose your wife would approve. You *are* married, of course."

"How did you know?"

"Intuition. Extrasensory perception."

"I don't buy those."

"Okay. How about research? The City Directory lists a Tomás Aragon, 203 Ramitas Road. Occupation, attorney. Wife, Laurie MacGregor, M.D."

"No age, weight, political party?"

"I'll have to guess about those. Twenty-seven, a hundred and eighty pounds, and a Democrat."

"You're very good, Miss Brewster. I wish you were on my side."

"I might be when I figure out what game we're playing."

The door opened and a tall elderly woman came out, leaning heavily on a cane. In her free hand she carried a small red leather case with a snap fastener. She had short thick grey hair and colorless lips so thin they looked glued together. They came apart only slightly when she spoke. "There you are, Ellen. I've been asking for you."

"Sorry, Mrs. Young. I had to—"

"My daughter Juliet has been complaining of burning eyes after swimming, so I brought over my own testing kit. It turns out Juliet is not imagining things, as she often does. Your chlorine registers too high and your pH too low."

"I'll tell the engineer."

"He'll deny it, of course, but I have the evidence." She shook the red leather case vigorously. "Considering the dues we pay, I should think the club would be able to afford a competent engineer."

"We try."

For the first time, Iris Young acknowledged Aragon's presence with a brief glance. Then she turned back to Ellen. "Who's he?"

"Mr. Aragon is a lawyer."

"I hope he's not applying for membership."

"I don't think so, Mrs. Young."

"Good. The club has too many lawyers as it is, sitting around encouraging people to sue each other. By the way, I expected to find the girls here. The Admiral brought them down this morning before his golf game."

"They left some time ago," Ellen said. "The Ingersolls gave them a lift into town."

"I've instructed them not to accept rides from strangers."

"The Ingersolls aren't exactly stra—"

"Too late to fuss now. The whole problem will be resolved as soon as Cordelia gets her driver's license back and I can buy her a new car, something more conventional. That Jaguar she had was a bad influence. It practically demanded to be driven at excessive speeds. It was too stimulating."

"A Jaguar would certainly stimulate me."

"I'm glad you agree."

Ellen wasn't entirely sure what she'd agreed about, but Mrs. Young seemed satisfied.

She crossed the road to her own car, a chauffeur-driven Mercedes, walking as if every step was painful. The chauffeur helped her into the back seat and put a blanket over her legs.

In Ellen's absence Mr. Henderson had taken charge of the office, a job he despised, since it nearly always involved complaints ranging from errors in billing to the fat content of the hamburgers in the snack bar. Neither of these extremes, and very little in between, interested him. He thought of himself as creative, a man of ideas. His latest idea, closing the club one day a week in order to conduct a bus tour to Santa Anita, Hollywood Park or Agua Caliente, had been poorly received by the membership. It was noted in the club newsletter that plans for a weekly Racing Revel had been indefinitely postponed. So were plans for a Blackjack Bash, which violated a local ordinance, and a Saturday Cinema for Stags, sabotaged by does, who outnumbered stags four to one.

Henderson kept right on trying. When Ellen entered he was, in fact, sketching out in his mind a Garden of Eden Ball.

People were tired of costume parties and the main attraction of the ball was certain to be its lack of costumes—except a figleaf or three. There would be some opposition, of course, from the elderly and fat, but in the long run the ball seemed destined to be a rousing success, the stuff of memories.

Ellen said, "Mr. Henderson."

He kept his eyes fixed on the ceiling and the future. The waitresses and busboys would be dressed as serpents, and from the chandeliers, just out of reach, would hang huge red paper apples. When the more athletic merrymakers succeeded in breaking the apples, confetti would come flying out with sinful abandon. Beautiful, beautiful.

"Mr. Henderson."

Henderson dragged himself rather irritably out of the Garden of Eden. "Welcome back, Miss Brewster. Did you have a nice vacation?"

"I was only gone for two hours."

"Two hours can be an eternity in this madhouse. The Admiral's wife was just in here complaining that we have too much chlorine in the pool and not enough pH. What the hell is pH? When you find out, buy some and pour it in."

"Mr. Henderson, this is Mr. Aragon."

"I can't help that. My God, people expect me to solve all their problems."

"I don't expect you to do anything about mine," Aragon said.

"You don't. Good. Stout fella. Now if you'll pardon me, I have important work to do, pH and all that."

"I understand."

"Of course, of course you do. Very understanding face you have there. Not many of them around these days."

Henderson departed, wondering why he was always meeting such odd people. Perhaps it was a family curse.

"We keep two files on each member," Ellen told Aragon. "One is for regular office use: address, phone number, occupation, names of family members, and so on. The other is private, to be used only by Mr. Henderson and the executive committee. It contains each member's original application for membership and the names and comments of their sponsors, letters of resignation and reinstatement, pertinent financial records, lists of other clubs they belong to. Some of this is useful, but mainly the file is a hodgepodge that should be cleaned out or updated."

"What's your definition of hodgepodge?"

"Oh, complaints from one person about another person, perhaps one or both of them long since dead, old newspaper clippings covering social events, divorces, scandals and the like; cards from members traveling abroad; photographs, many of them unidentified and unidentifiable."

"Apparently you have access to the file."

"Only when Mr. Henderson wants me to look something up," Ellen said. "He keeps the key."

"But you can ask him for it any time."

"Yes."

"Will you?"

"I'm supposed to have a good reason."

"Mrs. Shaw skipped town under unusual circumstances. That good enough?"

"We'll see if Mr. Henderson thinks so."

While she went to get the key Aragon stood at the door and watched the people. There were about twice as many of them as there had been during the morning. Several small groups were having late lunch on the terrace and most of the chaises on the opposite side of the pool were occupied. The water of the pool itself was being churned up by half a dozen earnest swimmers doing laps to a pace clock. On the lifeguard tower an ivory-haired young man was picking absently at his chest, peeling away the dead skin of his latest sunburn.

The elderly man in shorts and tennis visor was still busy writing but he had changed his position from the terrace to a chair under a cypress tree at the corner of the fence. The tree was bent and twisted by the wind and salt air. It seemed a good place for him.

Ellen came back carrying the key and looking a little embarrassed, as though Henderson might have given her a reprimand or a warning.

Her voice was subdued. "Listen, I'm sorry I said some of those things about Mrs. Shaw and Grady."

"Why?"

"Because I don't know for sure whether they're together or not. They both left at approximately the same time but that may be only a coincidence. She takes trips every now and then, cruises and stuff like that. As for Grady, lifeguards come and go around here like the tides. It's a boring job and the salary's lousy, that's why we mostly have to hire college kids who are subsidized by their families. Grady isn't a kid and he has no family. We all knew he wouldn't last."

"It's funny he didn't last long enough to pick up his paycheck."

"Where—how did you find that out?"

"Frederic told me."

"What else did he tell you?"

"He had the idea," Aragon said carefully, "that Mrs. Shaw was, in his words, Grady's new chick."

She looked down at the key in her hands, turning it over and over as if she was trying to remember what lock it fitted. "So even the kids were talking about it."

"Or kid. And he's not exactly typical."

"They probably all knew before I did, everyone in the club. What a prize cluck that makes me. I never even suspected her because she's so much older, and that day in the office they both pretended to be meeting for the first time."

"Some first meetings can be quite electric," Aragon said. The word reminded him of Hippollomia and his truck trapped behind Mrs. Shaw's locked gate. *"There is no electric . . . Missus forgot to pay."*

She said, "Afterward I watched them walk down the corridor together. There was something about them, something inevitable, fated. I couldn't describe it but I knew Grady was walking out of my life before he was even in it." She turned away with a shrug. "So scratch one lifeguard. He won't be back."

"Not even for his paycheck?"

"He won't need it. Miranda Shaw is a very wealthy woman."

He didn't correct her.

The files took up half the width of one wall of the office. They were painted pastel blues and pinks and mauves to help conceal their purpose. They still looked like files. Ellen unlocked the blue one.

The material on the Shaws was sparse. Attached to an application form dated twenty years previously were enthusiastic comments from the Shaws' sponsors, Mr. and Mrs. Edgar Godwit, and their seconders, Dr. Franklin Spitz and Mrs. Ada Cottam, and a card with a single word printed on it and underlined: *OIL*. Whether it was the *OIL* or the enthusiastic support, the Shaws were admitted to membership in the Penguin Club the following month, paid the initiation fee and a year's dues in advance and rented cabana number 22. Neville Shaw's other affiliations included the University Forum, the Greenhills Country Club, Turf and Tanbark, Rancheros Felicianos and the Yale Club.

An old letter from Shaw addressed to the manager and the Executive Committee deplored the kind of music played at the New Year's Eve Ball. A later one canceled the rental of cabana number 22, citing excessive noise from 21 and 23. To the bottom of this someone had added a brief comment in ink: Party Pooper!

There were only two recent items in the file, a copy of a delinquent-dues notice signed by Walter Henderson, and a greeting card bearing an indecipherable postmark and addressed to Miss Ellen Brewster, in care of Penguin Club, Santa Felicia, California.

"Go ahead, read it," Ellen said. "It's not personal. She wrote cards like that to a lot of people. I think she was homesick, she didn't enjoy traveling, especially in Mexico."

"Where was she in Mexico when she wrote this?"

"Pasoloma."

He had never heard of it.

Dear Ellen: Heavenly weather, blue sea, blue sky. Only fly in ointment is more like a mosquito or flea, what the tourists call no-see-ums. My husband is off on a 3-week fishing trip but I get seasick so I'm here on the beach, scratching. By the way, a mistake must have been in our last billing. I'm sure my husband paid it promptly as usual. Regards, Miranda Shaw

"She didn't like Pasoloma," Ellen said. "There's nothing to do except surf and fish, she told me. Yet she kept going back."

"Did her husband always go with her?"

"As far as Pasoloma. Then he'd charter a fishing boat for two or three weeks and do his thing while she did hers."

"That doesn't sound like the sort of vacation a rich beautiful woman would plan for herself."

"Not unless she liked surfing. Or surfers. Anyway, she went."

"When she came back," Aragon said, "did she look like a woman who'd just spent a couple of weeks lying on a beach?"

"No. She avoids the sun and salt water because they dry the skin. Even when she sits on the terrace here she hides under an umbrella and a wide-brimmed hat and a robe big enough for three Arabs and a camel."

"You're sure about the camel?"

She smiled faintly. "All right, scratch the camel and one Arab. The general picture remains the same."

"Where is Pasoloma?"

"I looked for it on the map once and couldn't find it. But I think it's fairly close to the border because they always took their car and Mr. Shaw refused to drive long distances."

He figured that would put it somewhere in the northern part of Baja California. During the Lockwood case, he'd covered the area by car and he couldn't recall even a small village by that name. Either Ellen Brewster had made a mistake—which seemed unlikely—or else Pasoloma wasn't a geographical location at all but merely the name of a resort where people went to swim in the surf or lie on the beach or charter a boat for deep-sea fishing. If so, it was a peculiar choice for a woman who didn't like any of those things. Maybe Pasoloma offered other enticements Mrs. Shaw hadn't mentioned to anyone at the Penguin Club.

Aragon said, "Is there a phone booth around?"

"At the south end of the corridor. But you can use the phone on my desk if it's for a local call."

"It's not."

"Oh. Well." She looked slightly annoyed, as though she considered listening to other people's talk a privilege that came with her territory.

"I am going to call my wife," Aragon said. "She works at a hospital in San Francisco and the call will be put through a switchboard. The operators all know my voice and are certain to monitor the conversation, so it won't be very interesting."

"Why tell me?"

"I wouldn't want you to think you're missing anything."

The switchboard operator at the hospital recognized his voice.

"Dr. MacGregor's on Ward C right now, Mr. Aragon. You want me to page her?"

"Please."

"Hold on. Won't take a minute."

The minute dragged out to three. He put in four more quarters, and as the last one clanked into its slot he heard Laurie's voice.

"Tom?"

"Hi."

There was a silence, the kind there often was at the beginning of their calls, as if they were trying to bridge the distance between them and it seemed, for a time, impossible.

Then, "Laurie, are you there?"

"Yes."

"Can we talk?"

"Business-type stuff only. I'm on duty."

"This is a business call."

"Really?"

"You've just been appointed my special assistant in charge of regenerative processes."

"What's the salary?"

"It's a purely honorary position."

"I figured it would be," she said. "You're a terrible tightwad."

"Of course, if you're not interested, there's a roster of beautiful blondes whose qualifications I've been studying."

"Tell them to get lost. Now, what exactly do you mean by regenerative processes?"

"I've been doing a rundown on rejuvenation clinics. Most of them operate outside the country because they use illegal drugs or unorthodox methods, shots of KH-3, monkey and lamb embryo glands, hypnotherapy, plasmapheresis, deep sleep, et cetera."

"So?"

He hesitated. "I'd like you to find out if there's one that uses goat glands."

"Goat glands? *Now* what have you got yourself into?"

"The story's kind of long and I'm running out of change. Will you do it?"

"I guess so. How do you know such a place exists?"

"Smedler's wife heard about it at the country club. Do you think you can find out by tonight? I'll be at the apartment from six—"

There was a sudden click and the long-distance operator's voice: "Your time is up. Please deposit another twenty-five cents."

"All I've got is two dimes. Will you—?" She wouldn't. The line went dead. He spoke into it anyway. "Hey Laurie, I forgot to tell you I love you."

The Admiral's daughters came charging through the front door, pursued by the dust devils that were whirling down the road behind them.

Neither wind nor sun had affected Cordelia's face, which remained as sallow and somber as usual, but Juliet had turned pink from her forehead all the way down to the pearl choker that emphasized the neckline of her favorite thrift shop dress. Everything about her seemed to be in motion at the same time, as though one of the dust devils had caught her and infected her with frenzy. She shook her head and giggled and moved her arms around so that her bracelets kept jangling, clank, clank, clank. Cordelia didn't have on as many bracelets but she wore a ruby and silver necklace, jade earrings, a pair of ruby-eyed owl pins, a diamond-studded pendant watch, a gold wristwatch and half a dozen rings.

Cordelia gave her sister a kick on the ankle to calm her down and said to Ellen, "We are back. Notice anything different about us?"

"Your mother was here," Ellen said. "She left half an hour ago."

"You're avoiding the subject. Besides, she never comes to this place anymore. She hates it."

"Considers it gross," Juliet added. "Hoi polloi."

"You must notice *something* different about us. If you don't, you're not trying. Concentrate. Use your eyes."

"And ears. That's a clue. Use your ears. Listen."

Ellen listened and heard clank, clank, clank, clank. "The bracelets? Has it anything to do with the bracelets?"

"Not just the bracelets," Cordelia said sharply. "Everything. We've changed our image."

"Cordelia read about it in a magazine."

"I thought about it before I ever read it in a magazine. That was merely the clincher, an article on How to Change Your Image in Twenty-Four Hours. So we went down to the bank this morning and took our jewelry out of the safe-deposit box and we're going to wear it from now on, everywhere we go, night and day, even in bed. We are sick of being *plain*."

"*No more plain*."

"You are looking at the new us."

"The new us." Beneath the excitement there was a note of anxiety in Juliet's voice. "In *bed*, Cordelia? My earrings hurt already and I'm not even lying down yet."

"Stop fussing. Nobody gets a new image for nothing."

"Well, I don't see why it has to hurt. Are you sure the article specified in *bed*?"

"It did."

"I'm going to hate that part. It's fine for you, you sleep flat on your back like you're on an operating table having your gall bladder out. But I'm a side sleeper."

"You'll have to change. That's what this is all about, change. You're the new you now, so act like it."

The new Juliet nodded. The old Juliet simply decided to cheat. Instead of wearing the earrings at night, she would keep them on her bedside table so that in case of an earthquake or fire she could put them on in a hurry. No one would be any the wiser, unless Cordelia got scared by a strange noise and came barging into her room in the middle of the night. Anyway, the new Cordelia might not be scared of strange noises.

Cordelia fingered the ruby and silver necklace. "You don't recognize this, do you, Ellen? Ha, I knew you wouldn't. You're not a noticer the way I am."

"And I," Juliet said. "I'm a noticer, too. In fact, *I* recognized it first. She wore it to the club's open house at Christmas with a green dress. Red and green, it looked very Christmasy."

"Are you telling this, Juliet, or am I?"

"You are, Cordelia."

"Then let me proceed. We went to an auction last week and saw this necklace with a matching bracelet that was to be sold as a set. I wanted both, but there's a limit on my charge card so I bought the necklace and Juliet bought the bracelet."

"Wait a minute," Ellen said. " *Who* wore it at the Christmas open house?"

"Mrs. Shaw," Cordelia said.

"She looked very Christmasy," Juliet said.

Ellen caught up with Aragon in the corridor. "Admiral Young's daughters are here. They have some information which may or may not be accurate, but I think you should talk to them."

The two girls were half hidden behind the door of Ellen's office like children ready to pop out and say boo when a grownup came along. Aragon smiled at them in a friendly way but they didn't respond.

"Why, it's him," Cordelia said. "The man who was staring at us this morning. Like in Singapore, that kind of stare."

"Singapore? I'm sure you're mistaken." But Juliet glanced nervously around the room as though planning an escape if one proved necessary. Cordelia was very frequently right. "Why, this is our very own club and we're just as safe here as—"

"Pops had two ensigns following us around Singapore, and what good did that do?"

145

Juliet couldn't remember the ensigns and had only the vaguest recollection of ever being in Singapore, let alone of what had actually happened. But she was too sensible to admit this to Cordelia, who would merely take it as additional proof of Juliet's inferiority.

"Stop this nonsense, girls," Ellen said briskly. "I want you to tell Mr. Aragon what you told me."

Cordelia came out from behind the door, her arms crossed on her chest in a defensive posture. "Why does he want to know?"

"He's a lawyer."

"We are not talking to any lawyer unless our lawyer is also present. Everybody who watches television knows that."

"Oh, Cordelia," Juliet said with a touch of sadness. "We don't have a lawyer."

"We'll get one immediately."

"Very well, you get one, but I refuse to pay for my half of him. He'll be entirely on your charge card."

"Wait a minute," Aragon said. "We should be able to settle this quite simply. You hire me and I'll waive the fee for my services."

"What does that mean?"

"I'm free."

"Bull," Cordelia said.

"No bull."

"I never heard of a free lawyer."

"There aren't many of us around. Business is good but the pay's lousy."

"The arrangement seems rather loose, but it's not costing us anything, so all right, you're hired."

Aragon congratulated himself. Not every young lawyer could afford to acquire in a single day such clients as the Admiral's daughters and little Frederic Quinn. If the trend continued, it would be very handy, probably downright necessary, to have a working wife.

The girls had a whispered conference behind the door, punctuated by the clank of Juliet's bracelets and the bronchial wheeze she developed when she became excited. Then Cordelia approached Aragon, licking her thin pale lips.

"No one could possibly connect us with Miranda Shaw's disappearance. We didn't get hold of her necklace and bracelet until a week ago when we spotted them at an auction. It wasn't a regular auction, more of a small estate sale where the prices are set ahead of time. There's this nice quiet young man who sells valuables other people want to get rid of for one reason or another."

"We think he's a fence," Juliet said.

Cordelia silenced her sister with a jab in the ribs. "He seems to be a perfectly legitimate businessman who conducts auctions, the refined low-key kind. Most auctioneers are such screamers. Mr. Tannenbaum never raises his voice. Every now and then when we're downtown we pop into his establishment to see what's available."

"Sometimes we buy, sometimes we spy," Juliet said.

"We don't actually spy, we just look around with our eyes wide open. I mean, you can never be *sure*, can you, Mr. Aragon?"

Aragon agreed that you could never be sure, at the same time feeling a twinge of sympathy for the unfortunate Tannenbaum. It was not an enviable fate, being the target of the girls' suspicions, the recipient of their pop-ins, the focus of their wide-opens. He hoped the occasional sale recompensed Tannenbaum to some degree.

He said, "Was the jewelry expensive?"

"It's crude to ask the price of things," Cordelia reminded him.

"Yes. However—"

"A mark of ill-breeding."

"Right. But I'd still like to know. It may be important."

Juliet let out an anxious little wheeze. "You hear that, Cordelia? He said—"

"I heard him."

"We've never done anything the least bit important in our whole lives."

"Oh, we have so. We were born, weren't we? And Mrs. Young's often told us how much it changed her life. That's important, changing someone's life."

"She didn't *mean* it nice."

"Important things aren't necessarily nice."

"I still don't see what harm would come from answering the man's question about the jewelry."

"Mind your own business, sister."

"It's half my business," Juliet said. "The bracelet was put on *my* charge card. If I want to tell someone what's on my own charge card, I can. It's a free country."

"You shut up."

"Fifteen hundred dollars. So there, ha ha! Fifteen hundred dollars."

Tannenbaum's place of business was on Estero Street in the lower part of the city. Two blocks to the east was the barrio where Aragon had been born and raised and gone to schools where English was in reality, if not in theory, a second language. The barrio was gradually filling up with the debris of poverty: pieces of abandoned cars, tires and doors and twisted bumpers, broken wine jugs and baby strollers, fallen branches of half-dead trees, disemboweled sofas and dismembered chairs.

Estero Street, at one time almost part of the barrio, had been salvaged by a downtown rehabilitation plan. Its two- and three-story redwood houses, built before the turn of the century, had been carefully restored and painted. Yards were tended, hedges clipped, lawns raked and clusters of birds-of-paradise and lilies-of-the-Nile bloomed under neat little windmill palms. The upper floors of the houses had been made into apartments, and the ground floors into small offices occupied by a travel agent, a chiropractor, a realtor, a bail bondsman, an attorney, an art dealer, a watch repairman.

In the window of what had once been somebody's parlor was a small discreet sign: R. Tannenbaum, Estate Sales and Appraisals. An old-fashioned bell above the front door announced Aragon's entrance. He found himself in a hall whose walls were hung with tapestries, some large enough to be used as rugs, some so small they were framed under glass. In a single spotlighted display case a collection of miniature musical instruments was arranged in a semicircle on a red velvet stage: a golden harp, an ivory grand piano, violins and cellos with silver strings fine as spider silk, trumpets and French horns carved from amethyst and woodwinds from tourmaline. No prices were shown. Tannenbaum's merchandise—if the tapestries and miniatures were typical—was not that of an ordinary fence doing business in a small city like Santa Felicia. Fences gravitated south to Los Angeles and San Diego or north to San Francisco.

A large black and brown mongrel came loping down the hall like an official greeter, and behind him, Tannenbaum himself. He was a tall angular man about forty, wearing a beard and rimless glasses and formally dressed in a dark vested suit and tie, white shirt with cuff links and carefully polished black oxfords.

Putting his hand on the dog's head, he said, "My partner, Rupert, likes you."

"Tell Rupert I like him back."

"He knows. In our profession we develop a sixth sense about people. At least in my case it's sixth, in Rupert's it's probably first. Perhaps a very long time ago it was our first, too, and our initial reaction to the approach of a stranger was, is this a friend or an enemy? It remains a good question. You are—" Tannenbaum narrowed his eyes to concentrate their focus— "I'd guess somewhere in between, leaning a bit towards friend, right?"

"Well . . ."

"I see you were admiring my miniatures. Or perhaps admire isn't quite the word. I don't care for miniatures myself, life is small and meager enough. A sculpture by Henry Moore, that's what I covet, though my mean little hall here is hardly the place for one."

Tannenbaum had a soft pleasant voice which made what he had to say seem more interesting than it actually was. He went on to describe the particular Henry Moore he would have liked to own, now in a private collection in Paris. Evidently Rupert had heard it all before. He went back to his rug at the rear of the hall, leaving the practical end of the business to his partner.

The dog's action seemed to remind Tannenbaum of his duties. He said, "What can I do for you?"

Aragon presented his card, which Tannenbaum glanced at briefly before putting it in his inside breast pocket. The pocket was already bulging, Aragon noticed, as if Tannenbaum's collections were not confined to valuables like tapestries and miniatures.

"Are you buying or selling, Mr. Aragon?"

"I'm asking."

"You want information?"

"Yes."

"My profit on information will never buy me a Henry Moore. However, in the interests of good will and that sort of thing, I'll try to oblige. What's on your mind?"

"Our office is holding some important legal documents which must be signed by one of our clients. I have cause to believe she's also one of yours, Miranda Shaw, Mrs. Neville Shaw."

"So?"

"Mrs. Shaw has, for all practical purposes, disappeared."

"Well, I haven't got her," Tannenbaum said reasonably. "My partner wouldn't approve. Rupert took an immediate dislike to her. Probably her perfume—too much and too musky. Rupert has such a sensitive nose it sometimes affects his judgment. I myself found her attractive, though a bit over the hill, wouldn't you say?"

"I might, but the fact is I've never met her."

"You should."

"My boss thinks I should, too, and the sooner the better."

Tannenbaum brushed a piece of lint off one of the tapestries. His movements were quick and precise, as if even the least important of them was thought out in advance for maximum efficiency. "Mrs. Shaw is not one of my regular customers. She came in about three weeks ago with a number of things she wanted to sell me then and there. I explained to her that my business is usually done on consignment and there would be a delay in payment. Some of the stuff might go immediately—for example, I've had a buyer waiting a long time for a coin collection like Shaw's. But other items, like the antique silver chess set and the jewelry, would have to wait for the right buyers. Mrs. Shaw was anxious to avoid a delay, so she offered to take whatever I was willing to pay her on the spot. I gave her what I believed to be a fair price considering the financial risk I was assuming. Actually, the deal's turning out better than I expected—some of the jewelry has been sold already. I included it in an estate auction which I conducted last week and the right buyers came along."

"Admiral Young's daughters."

"Why, yes. You know them?"

"Slightly," Aragon said. Even slightly seemed like a lot.

"The girls come in here quite often looking for a bargain. They never find any, of course—it's my business to see that people don't get bargains—but they think they do, so they make a purchase now and then, usually a rather small one. The ruby necklace and bracelet set was more expensive than anything they'd previously bought. They took a fancy to it for some reason."

"Juliet recognized it as Mrs. Shaw's."

"I see." Tannenbaum took off his glasses and rubbed the bridge of his nose where the frame had carved a red arc. "Or rather, I don't see. Surely you can't believe they bought the set for sentimental reasons?"

"It's possible."

"Oh, come now, Mr. Aragon. The Admiral's daughters aren't given to sentiment. Behind all that moronic conversation they're as hard-headed and hard-nosed as a pair of old Navy chiefs."

"I think they're pathetic."

"Are they clients of yours?"

"Yes."

"Wait till they try to beat you out of your fee. They won't seem quite so pathetic."

"The fee's already been settled."

"Well. You must have a way with you."

Aragon resisted the urge to tell the truth. Smedler wouldn't be too happy if word got out that one of his employees had, twice in the same day, offered his services free. "It's a gift," he said, more or less accurately. "What can you tell me about Mrs. Shaw?"

Tannenbaum replaced his glasses and looked toward the rear of the hall as if seeking the advice of his partner. Rupert was asleep and snoring. "She puzzled me, that much I can tell you. Many of my first-time customers act the way she did, nervous and ill at ease, but there was something contradictory about her, an air of excitement I couldn't figure out. It was the watch that clued me in."

"What kind of watch?"

"A man's wristwatch, a gold Swiss Jubilee. Very sophisticated and classy, with a face that shows the time only when viewed from a certain angle. I picked it up to examine it for an on-the-spot appraisal, but she asked for it back, said she'd changed her mind and wanted to hold on to it as a memento of her late husband. This is a common enough practice, for a bereaved person to hold on to a watch and keep it running and ticking like a heartbeat. I didn't believe her, though. Still don't."

"What do you believe?"

"A watch like that," Tannenbaum said, "would make a very nice gift."

Aragon was eating dinner, a barely warm pizza with mozzarella that clung in strings to the roof of his mouth and had to be dislodged with beer. He'd placed the phone on the table in front of him and every now and then he stared at it as though it was a stubborn little beast that needed to be urged into action. It rang, finally, shortly after seven-thirty and he answered on the first ring.

"Hello, Laurie."

"Tom." She sounded pleased. "How did you know it was me?"

"Just a lucky guess."

"What a liar you are. You were thinking about me."

"Yes."

"Good things?"

"The best."

"Me, too. Listen, Tom, we'll see each other at Thanksgiving. That's not too far away and I get three whole days off."

"The last time you had three whole days off you slept two and a half of them."

"I remember the other half-day very well," Laurie said. "Do you?"

"Vaguely. I may have to refresh my memory at Thanksgiving."

"That's a lovely idea."

"I hope so. It's the only one I have at the moment."

"Oh, *Tom*." There was a silence. "We'd better change the subject. This one is getting us nowhere and costing twenty-four cents a minute. Let's talk about goats."

"I don't want to talk about goats."

"Yes, you do. You appointed me your assistant in charge of regenerative process, goat division . . . Well, I found out from a geriatric specialist at the County Medical Association that there are a couple of places where people can get injections of goat embryo glands to stay young. One is in Hungary, and that's the extent of the information I could get on it. The other's in Mexico, run by a Dr. Manuel Ortiz. Ortiz doesn't advertise, but the word has spread around youth-oriented places like Beverly Hills. His clinic's main attractions seem to be that it guarantees immediate results and costs a lot of money."

"That's the attraction?"

"It is for wealthy people who have only one thing left to spend their money on, turning back the clock."

"Where does this Dr. Ortiz turn back the clock?"

"The clinic is a converted ranch in a small seaside village south of Ensenada."

"Pasoloma."

"That's it. How did you know?"

"Just another lucky guess."

"Come on, tell me."

"It's kind of complicated," Aragon said. "And as you mentioned a while ago, this conversation is costing twenty-four cents a minute. I figure we should save our money so that when you're old and grey we'll be able to send you down to Pasoloma for some of Dr. Ortiz's goat glands."

"How thoughtful of you."

"I come from a long line of thinkers."

"Tom, you're not going to tell me a thing, are you?"

"Just the usual. I love you."

"Well, I love you, too, but it doesn't prevent me from wondering why you're suddenly interested in rejuvenation. Did Smedler put you on a case involving Pasoloma?"

"I don't know yet," he said. "Honest."

"The last time you went to Mexico you got in all kinds of trouble."

"Other people got in trouble. I didn't."

"The Mexican police aren't normally interested in such fine distinctions."

"Laurie, dear, I can't tell you any more than I already have because I don't know any more. I'm working on a hunch and it may be miles off the track. You've been a great help finding out about Dr. Ortiz. Tomorrow morning I'll get Smedler's secretary to call Ortiz's clinic and see if our client is there. If she is, I'll take the papers down to her for her signature and come home, mission accomplished. If she isn't there, I'll start thinking up another angle."

It sounded logical, straightforward, easy. He wondered why he didn't feel better about it.

Aragon arrived at the office shortly before nine o'clock and took up a strategic position at the door of Smedler's private elevator. He was beginning to know Charity Nelson's weaknesses and strengths, and one of them was punctuality. The bell in the City Hall tower across the street was striking the hour when she came in. In addition to her handbag, she was carrying a large canvas tote fully packed and showing a number of interesting lumps and bumps. Her wig had been anchored with a scarf tied so tightly under her jaw that her lips could scarcely move when she spoke: "Whatever you want, no."

"I wasn't asking for anything," Aragon said. "I'm just reporting in."

"Like on what?"

"Mrs. Shaw."

"You found her."

"No."

"Then there's nothing to report."

"There may be."

"Listen, junior, this isn't the best time to mess around. Smedler spent the night in his office because he had a fight with his wife and he'd like her to believe he killed himself, which may not be such a bad idea, but who am I to suggest it. In here"—she indicated the canvas tote—"is his breakfast. Also mine. One thing Smedler and I have in common, we don't like problems before breakfast, so bug off."

Charity pressed the button and the little iron-grilled elevator came down from the top floor with the majestic dignity of a vehicle intended only for royalty.

When the door opened Charity said, "You'd better not come up yet, junior."

"That canvas bag looks heavy. Let me carry it for you."

"Okay. But don't say I didn't warn you."

Once in her office Charity untied the scarf anchoring her wig and filled the glass coffeepot from the water cooler. Then she began unpacking the canvas tote Aragon had put on her desk: cans of tomato juice, some fresh pears and oranges, a bag from a local doughnut shop, a plastic container of plant food, a bottle of leaf polish and a jar of instant coffee.

"I have to make a long-distance call to a place in Mexico," Aragon said. "I thought you'd want me to do it from here."

"Why should I?"

"Because it involves Mrs. Shaw."

He explained. In spite of the early hour and lack of breakfast, she was pleased with his theory. It fitted not only the rumors she'd heard but also her own picture of Miranda Shaw as the kind of vain, stupid woman who would go to a clinic in Mexico to buy back her youth. Charity didn't consider her own youth worth buying back.

She put the call in herself. Whether it was her crisp voice or just plain luck, the call was relayed through Tijuana to Pasoloma within five minutes. Almost immediately a woman answered in Spanish, switching to heavily accented English in response to Charity's question. Yes, this was the Clinica Pasoloma but no Mrs. Shaw was registered.

Charity held her hand over the mouthpiece. "The lady says Mrs. Shaw is not there. That blows your theory, junior."

"Let me talk to her." He took over the phone and spoke in Spanish. But Mrs. Shaw wasn't there in Spanish any more than she'd been in English.

The clinic, in fact, did not give out names or any other information over the telephone except to the proper authorities. Though Aragon tried to convince her that he was, as Mrs. Shaw's lawyer, a proper authority, she didn't wait for him to finish.

"You struck out," Charity said. "Admit it."

"Not yet. The woman was just following orders, no names over the telephone."

"So?"

"Suppose I go down to the clinic and ask her in person."

"Why don't you take no for an answer, junior? You had a nice little idea that died. Bury it."

Smedler came out of his office. He showed no signs of having spent a night involving any physical or emotional discomfort. He was freshly shaved and impeccably groomed. Even the frown he aimed at his secretary was normal for the time of day.

"I tried to use the phone, Miss Nelson, and it was tied up by a bunch of foreigners."

"Sorry," Aragon said. "I was one of them."

Smedler ignored him. "I don't like foreign languages spoken on my telephone, Miss Nelson. What if the CIA is listening? They might think I'm selling secrets to Cuba or something."

"We don't have any secrets to sell to Cuba, Mr. Smedler."

"You and I know that but *they* don't . . . Did you get the kind of doughnuts I asked for?"

"With jelly inside," Charity said. "Mr. Aragon has a theory about Mrs. Shaw's disappearance."

"Cherry?"

"Yes, sir. It's an interesting theory."

"The strawberry ones have those irritating little things in them."

"Seeds. Shall I authorize him to pursue it?"

"Use your judgment, Miss Nelson. You've shown excellent judgment in the past. Nothing has happened to warp it, surely? Then carry on."

Smedler disappeared with the bag of doughnuts, two fresh pears and a can of tomato juice.

Aragon said, "Well, has it?"

"Has what?"

"Anything happened to warp your judgment?"

"It gets warped every hour on the hour," Charity said with a kind of grim satisfaction. "What's on your calendar for the next few days?"

"Nothing I can't clean up by this afternoon or push off on someone else."

"Will your car make it as far as Pasoloma?"

"Probably."

"Then a couple of hundred dollars should do it."

"Make it three."

"The plants you see growing around here are not money trees, junior."

"Okay, I'll settle for two. If I run short I can always sell a few secrets to Cuba."

"This is highway robbery," Charity said and made out a check for three hundred dollars. "And listen, junior, you'd better get going first thing tomorrow morning before Smedler finds out how really warped my judgment has become."

Part III

THE HIGHWAY WAS known on both sides of the border as Numero Uno.

The border with its twenty-four gates was the busiest in the world, but most of the cars and vans and buses going into Mexico stopped at Tijuana or some sixty miles further south at Ensenada. Beyond Ensenada the speed and volume of traffic decreased and Aragon was able to slow down enough to decipher an occasional weather-beaten sign along the road. Dr. Ortiz evidently didn't believe in encouraging visitors. The word Pasoloma and an arrow pointing west toward the sea was painted on a shingle nailed to the prostrate trunk of an elephant tree.

Aragon turned right on a narrow dirt road oiled just enough to settle the top layer of dust and coat the sides of his old Chevy with a kind of black glue. The road ended abruptly on a curve with the Pacific Ocean about twenty yards ahead, and Aragon realized he'd arrived in Pasoloma. What Laurie had described on the telephone as a small seaside village was in fact a gas pump, some dilapidated wooden shacks and a dozen kids accompanied by some dogs, chickens and a burro. One of the chickens flew up and landed on the burro's back and the reluctant host was trying to dislodge it with a series of kicks. It was the only activity in the entire village.

The clinic itself was at the top of a newly surfaced driveway curving up a hill between boulders and paloverde trees—the original ranchhouse now serving, according to a sign on the door, as the main office; a number of outbuildings remodeled as staff residences; a cluster of modern cottages with attached carports, most of them occupied by large American cars. In addition to the cottages, two other structures were new—a rectangular one with small high windows obviously meant to discourage sightseers and another that looked like a small hospital, with a late-model station wagon and a jeep parked outside. Both vehicles were identified by the lettering on their sides as belonging to Dr. Manuel Ortiz, Clinica Pasoloma.

It was early afternoon, siesta time. Hardly anyone was in sight. A nurse in uniform was walking slowly toward the hospital, a gardener was clipping a mangy-looking hedge, leaf by leaf, and half a dozen people sat around the swimming pool. Only one was in the pool, an enormously fat man lying on his back with his belly protruding from the water like the carcass of a sea lion bloated with decomposing gases.

Aragon parked his car in front of the ranchhouse and went into the door marked *Oficio*.

153

A middle-aged woman sat behind the reception desk reading a newspaper. She had Indian features, eyes flat and expressionless as pennies, straight black hair and lips that moved only enough to permit limited conversation. Though her language was Spanish, she used no exaggerated gestures or inflections.

"The office is closed."

"Oh, sorry," Aragon said. "I didn't see any sign to that effect."

"Something happened to it."

"Perhaps you could answer one simple question?"

She looked him over carefully. His youth pegged him as a non-customer, his accent as American, his car as poor. There was no use wasting energy on him.

"The office is closed until three o'clock."

"It's two now. Let's pretend we're on daylight-saving time, that way we wouldn't be breaking any rules, would we?"

"I think yes, we would." She folded the newspaper and put it on the desk. "Dr. Ortiz is my sister's son-in-law. We make the rules together, the whole family, and we keep them together."

"I'm sure you do. You look like the kind of person who would make a good rule and stick to it."

"This is a family enterprise."

"And very successful, I hear."

"Where do you hear that?"

"Santa Felicia, California," Aragon said. "I just drove down today to see Mrs. Shaw."

"Who?"

"Miranda Shaw. Mrs. Neville Shaw. Or perhaps Mrs. Grady Keaton."

"Why do you want to see somebody whose name you don't even know?"

"I represent her lawyer."

"Our patients are not allowed to have visitors," said Dr. Ortiz's mother-in-law's sister. "We make that very clear in the instructions they're sent before they arrive for treatment. The only exceptions permitted are that a wife may bring her husband, or vice versa, if they choose to rent one of our cottages."

He asked the price of a cottage and she mentioned a figure that would have rented half a hotel in Santa Felicia.

"It is the sea," she added, observing his shock. "One must pay for the sound of waves and the bracing salt air."

Aragon went down to the beach for a free trial of the waves and the bracing salt air. There was a south swell with sets of eight to ten feet and almost no wind to rough them. In California on such a day, at Hammond's Reef, Malibu, Zuma, Huntington Beach, the water would be swarming with surfers in wet suits maneuvering for position or sitting on their boards like rows of cormorants. At Pasoloma there were only three surfers, young men wearing swim trunks instead of wet suits because the water was still summer-warm.

A purple van carrying Oregon license plates was parked nearby on a patch of sea daisies, its roof draped with jeans and T-shirts drying in the sun. Beside the van a blonde girl lay on her back, nude, sleeping.

Aragon said, tentatively, "Hello?"

She twitched as though an insect had buzzed her ear. Aragon repeated the greeting a little louder and this time she opened one eye. It was blue and bored. "What?"

"I said hello."

"So hello. If you're from the Federales, we're not carrying any grass. Cross my heart. In fact, you can search me if you like, as long as Mike doesn't see you. He's the jealous type and I'm his lady."

"You could have fooled me."

She sat up, shaking the sand out of her hair. "If you're such a gentleman, stop looking." Aragon tried. "Is that Mike out there?"

"Him and his friend, Carl."

"There are three of them."

"The other one's just a guy who was on the beach when we got here."

"Does he have a name?"

"I didn't ask him. Names don't matter anymore. I mean, nobody cares. My old lady had a neat system, she called all her guys the same name. Ed."

"Why Ed?"

"Why not? What's wrong with Ed?"

Aragon had never before argued the merits of the name Ed with a naked girl and it seemed a poor time to start. Besides, she had already lost interest. Her mind was on food.

"Is there any place around here where I could get a hamburger? We've had nothing to eat but fish all the way down the coast. I'm afraid my face will start to break out. Have you heard that too much fish will make your face break out?"

"I haven't heard that, no."

"Maybe it's not true. I hope not. It wouldn't be fair to have your face break out for eating something you don't even like . . . Mike's watching us. I better put some clothes on. Oh Christ, he's coming in."

All three surfers were heading for shore. The waves were still high but they'd started breaking too fast, so that ebb and flow met at an impasse in a wall of water. The girl had pulled a pair of jeans and a T-shirt off the roof of the van and was putting them on. The jeans fitted like hand-me-ups from a younger, thinner sister and the front of the white flimsy T-shirt was somewhat inaccurately labeled Out of Sight.

"Mike believes in nudity," the girl explained. "But not mine. He wants I should be bundled up like an Eskimo all the time."

"Maybe you should."

"Really? I look that good?"

"I think so. The trouble is, the Federales might think so, too, which could cause problems. Officially, they're pretty stuffy about women wearing enough clothing. Unofficially—well, you'd better be more careful."

"No kidding, I look that good? Wait'll I tell Mike. He'll freak out."

The three men emerged from the surf. Aragon picked Grady out immediately. The other two were younger, not yet out of their teens, and they'd had their hair cut for the trip across the border, so that their foreheads and the backs of their necks were several shades lighter than the rest of their bodies. Grady was deep brown all over except for the permanent sun scars across his cheekbones and the bridge of his nose.

Mike escorted his lady into the van in spite of her protests—"Every girl's got two of those and one of them, so what's the big deal?"—and his friend Carl took the hint and began jogging up the beach.

Grady sat down in the sand, shaking his head to get the water out of his ears and off his hair. His movements were violent, as if he were trying to rid himself of something more adhesive than water.

Aragon said, "Are you Grady Keaton?"

"Good question." The gaze he directed at Aragon was without interest and his eyes had a frosted look like starboard lights seen through fog. "I used to be."

"What changed you?"

"I came here. In these parts I'm addressed as Mr. Shaw on account of the lady I'm with is Mrs. Shaw and the Mexicans are very, very square. The real Mr. Shaw doesn't give a damn because he's dead. He died of old age, which is not something I expect to do. How about you?"

"I haven't thought about it."

"Sure you have. Everybody thinks about dying. It's the normal thing. Or is it? What the hell, who elected me judge of normal?" He transferred his gaze to the sea. "Every wave is different, did you know that? I mean every single one of them. Like if an experienced surfer sees a photograph of a wave in a magazine, he can usually tell where the photograph was taken—Pismo, Hollister, Huntington, any top spot on the coast."

"I've heard that but never believed it."

"It's true."

"So Miranda Shaw is with you."

"No."

"You said—"

"I said *I* was with her. There are a few small differences, like who's picking up the tab, who invited who, who gives the orders and makes the decisions. I never even heard of this place until I was on my way. And the kind of salary I make I couldn't afford to stay here for a day. I wouldn't want to, anyway. The surfing's nothing special and I'm usually the only one in the water, so what's the fun? Surfing isn't just riding waves on a board, it's a whole way of life, like those kids in the van surfing from Oregon to La Paz. If I had the money— and I might someday, free money, no strings attached—that's what I'd do. Except I'd start further north at Vancouver and go down to San Lucas and take the ferry that runs over to Puerto Vallarta."

"It doesn't sound like the kind of trip she'd enjoy."

"Who?"

"Miranda Shaw."

"I wasn't thinking of inviting her."

Up to this point Aragon had been standing, shifting his weight from one foot to another until both his shoes were filled with sand. He sat down and removed them and his socks and finally his shirt. The sun struck his chest like a branding iron and he put the shirt back on.

"I'm Tom Aragon, an attorney from Santa Felicia. I was sent to find Miranda Shaw."

"I figured you weren't here on my account."

"In a way I am. I bring greetings from a young friend of yours in Santa Felicia, Frederic Quinn. He asked me to look you up. You're one of his heroes."

"So is Bingo Firenze's uncle, hit man for the Mafia, so I'm not exactly flattered . . . Why do you want to see Miranda?"

"It concerns her husband's will."

"I thought that had all been settled. Shaw left everything to her, didn't he?"

"The question is, what's everything?"

"What's everything? What in hell would it be? It's stocks, bonds, real estate, cars, bank accounts, jewelry, the works. He was a very rich man. Wasn't he?"

"Yes." It was true enough. Shaw was once a very rich man and he left everything to his wife. Aragon didn't consider it his duty to explain that everything was not only bank accounts and stocks and bonds and real estate, it was also debts.

"Something's funny the way you're talking," Grady said. "Was he or wasn't he a rich man?"

"I repeat, he was."

"And he willed his estate to Miranda?"

"She's his sole beneficiary."

"Then what's this about?"

"Shaw's will hasn't gone through probate yet. There are some papers which have to be signed by Mrs. Shaw."

"Well, that's easy." For a moment Grady looked almost friendly. "She's over in the cottage lying down. She sleeps a lot. They all do around here, the place is like a morgue."

The fatigue which Dr. Ortiz claimed was normal for people under treatment seemed to spread from the point of injection throughout her entire body, leaving her simultaneously light-headed and lead-footed. She had giddy spells, and once she had fallen when Grady wasn't there and she couldn't even recall the incident until the soreness of her wrist and the bruises on her arm reminded her. Grady thought she'd been drinking and she let him think it.

She lay drowsy-eyed on the bed, wearing the white chiffon nightgown she'd purchased at a bride boutique in San Diego. She didn't feel like a bride. The injections weren't as painful as they'd been in previous years because Dr. Ortiz had added what he described as a secret new ingredient, but the numbness was almost worse than pain. She'd expected a surge of vitality and youth. Instead she felt shriveled, as though she were gradually being mummified. She had no appetite, for food or life or even Grady.

"Go and surf, dear."

"But you said—"

"Run along without me. I'll come down later and watch you."

Then suddenly it was later and Grady was back.

"Where were you, Miranda?"

"I must have dozed off."

"It's six o'clock."

"I'm sorry, dear. I meant to—"

"There wasn't a soul in sight the whole damn afternoon."

"I thought that's what you wanted, a beach where you didn't have to fight for every good wave."

"Well, I got it, I sure as hell got it."

Always, after one of her long sleeps, she was jittery. "Go and tell Dr. Ortiz I don't feel well. I need something to calm me."

"You've started pill-popping, you know that? Pills and booze and goat glands—Christ, what a combo."

"Please, Grady. I'm quite nervous."

"Let's get out of here, Miranda. Pack your stuff right now and we'll take off."

"I can't. Dr. Ortiz warned me that I must complete the course of treatments or the effect will be lost."

"What effect?"

"Don't I look . . . younger, Grady?"

"You look okay. You looked okay before."

"I feel younger. I really do." She giggled. It was a terrible effort.

The room was like that in any second- or third-rate motel back home. The furnishings were new but already showing signs of wear—a double bed with a forty-watt lamp on each bedside table, a bureau topped by a mirror and a small electric fan, a desk scarred by cigarette burns, a standing ashtray advertising Tío's Tequila, a dressing alcove behind a wooden screen, a shoebox-sized kitchenette off the bathroom. An air-conditioning unit bore a sign *Fuero de Servicio,* Out of Order, and the atmosphere was hot and humid.

Insects droned and buzzed and whirred and ate each other and ate Miranda, too, when they discovered a way into the room through a hole in a screen. Her thin delicate skin was easy to penetrate, and the scent of her perfume was irresistible to bees in the daytime and mosquitoes at night, and to fleas and no-see-ums at any hour. There were clusters of fleabites across her abdomen and under her breasts. Her feet and ankles were covered with tiny red lumps like miniature pimples, which sometimes itched so terribly she scratched them until they bled. On her head, hidden by her hair, were curious welts oozing a colorless liquid that crystallized. When the fragile crystals broke under her comb, the oozing started all over again.

She dreamed of being consumed, of calling to Grady for help, and he came knocking at the door.

"Miranda?"

She opened her eyes.

"Are you awake, Miranda?"

She said, "No," not to be funny but because it was the truth. She was not awake, not hungry, not thirsty, not cold or hot, not in pain, not even itchy from the insect bites.

"Miranda, someone's here to see you from Santa Felicia."

She sat up on the bed, suddenly and fully awake. "I am not receiving visitors this afternoon. Who—who is it?"

"A lawyer named Aragon. Some legal technicality has come up and you've got to sign a few papers."

"Wait a minute, please."

She put on the robe that matched her gown and ran a brush quickly through her hair. With the blinds drawn, the room was nearly dark. When she passed the mirror on her way to the door her image was a white shadow, like the ectoplasm of a bride.

"Hey, Miranda, hurry up."

"All right."

She unbolted the door. Grady came in with a towel wrapped around his waist and immediately turned on the fan and began opening blinds and windows. The fan whined and whirred like a superinsect, scattering its inferiors across the room, muffling their sounds of protest.

Miranda shielded her eyes from the sudden sun. For a whole minute she could see nothing but a moving red blaze. Then gradually the stranger emerged from the blaze, a young man wearing college-style cords and a Hawaiian shirt and horn-rimmed glasses that gave him a rather shy look. He carried a briefcase.

"Mrs. Shaw? I'm Tom Aragon."

"I don't believe we've met."

"No, we haven't. I work for Mr. Smedler."

"Smedler." She repeated the name as if she was honestly trying to remember the man who went with it. "I can't quite . . ."

"Smedler, Downs, Castleberg, McFee, Powell."

"Oh, of course. That's the firm handling my husband's estate."

Or lack of it. He resisted an impulse to say the words, though he was pretty sure they wouldn't have shocked her. She didn't fit Smedler's description of her as a nice well-bred little woman who'd been insulated and protected from the world.

"I'm afraid this is not a very good place to entertain," she said carefully. "Or to do business, Mr. Aragon. There's a café in the main building but it's closed during the afternoon."

"I won't take much of your time."

"It will seem long to Grady. He's easily bored . . . Grady, would you mind? This promises to be a very dull session and you might as well be doing something interesting. Go and surf, dear."

Grady minded. "I surfed already."

"It's a private matter, Grady."

"We're not supposed to have secrets from each other," Grady said.

"Well, we do. Hundreds."

"He knows we're here as man and wife. I don't see what's to hide. I've got a right to be in on—"

"We'll discuss it later." *Go and surf you bastard.*

As soon as he'd gone, Miranda switched off the fan.

"I prefer the heat to the noise, if you have no objection, Mr. Aragon."

"None at all."

"Please sit down."

"Thank you."

He took one of the green vinyl chairs. It had a broken spring in the middle of the seat. He couldn't avoid it, so he tried to sit as lightly as he could, keeping some of his weight on his thigh, a posture that made him look as if he were waiting for the starting gun of a race. He thought about what kind of race it would turn out to be—low or high hurdles, quarter-mile, marathon—and how he wasn't ready for any of them.

She sat in the other vinyl chair. If it had a broken spring, she showed no sign of it. She seemed composed, almost regal, a great lady willing to donate time to the problems of the little people, even in her nightclothes in a hot dingy little room in a foreign country.

"I find these circumstances quite extraordinary, Mr. Aragon. To begin with, no one is supposed to know where I am."

"Someone guessed."

"Smedler, I presume. It's rather bad form for him to send someone after me like this. One would think that he, of all people, would understand, since he's been married three times and heaven knows what else how many times. This is an affair of the heart."

"It is also an affair of the California judiciary."

"The California judiciary can wait. *I've* certainly been kept waiting long enough. Neville died last spring, leaving a legal and uncomplicated will which should have been settled months ago."

"Probate is often a long procedure," Aragon said. "You could have shortened it somewhat by cooperating with Smedler. Why these delaying tactics, Mrs. Shaw?"

"I was in a hurry. Some things can't be postponed. I was due for another treatment at the clinic and Grady needed a holiday. I thought it was possible to combine the two."

"And was it?"

The slight movement of her head didn't indicate yes or no.

"In practical terms, Mrs. Shaw, all you've gained is a couple of weeks and the money Tannenbaum paid you."

"How did you find that out?"

He told her about the Admiral's daughters and the ruby necklace and bracelet. As she listened her eyes narrowed and her jaw tightened as though she was resisting the idea of Juliet and Cordelia wearing her jewelry.

He added, "Disposing of items belonging to a frozen estate is against the law."

"The jewelry belonged to me and was not part of the estate."

"What about the other things you sold?"

"I'm the sole beneficiary, so they were mine, too."

"Unfortunately, you're legally obliged to share them with Mr. Shaw's creditors . . . You knew about the creditors, of course."

Again the slight noncommittal movement of her head. "I didn't *know*."

"You suspected."

"I was aware of odd things happening, phone calls at all hours, strangers at the door. And Neville acted so different, secretive one minute, talking a blue streak the next, never letting me open the mail. I didn't understand what was happening."

"Do you understand now?"

"I'm beginning to," she said with a grim little smile. "He was making sure I didn't inherit anything. If he changed his will, I could fight it in court. If he simply left me nothing but debts, it would be legal and I'd be safe from fortune hunters. He kept referring to fortune hunters as though there was one behind every tree. He took it for granted that I was too stupid to protect myself so he had to do it. Well, he protected me all right. From fortune hunters, if not from anything else."

"He wasn't acting rationally, whatever his motives. Smedler believes you should have demanded a conservator for the estate."

"I'm not the kind of woman who demands. I guess I'm not sure enough of myself to tell other people what to do."

"You seem to me to be quite sure of yourself, Mrs. Shaw. You've made some bold decisions in the past three weeks."

"Yes."

"Perhaps too bold."

She shrugged and turned away. Her movements were graceful but a little contrived, as though they'd been practiced for years in front of mirrors. "If I broke the law and a few conventions, I suppose I'll be sorry eventually. Right now I'm not, I'd do the same thing again. It's going to sound very silly coming from a grown woman, but I couldn't help myself. I fell in love. It never happened to me before, even when I was young. The other girls at school were continually in love, they took it for granted as an everyday thing. For me it was a miracle and still is . . . You look impatient. Am I boring you?"

"No."

"But you would prefer not to hear it."

"Happy beginnings are a dime a dozen. I like happy endings."

"There'll be a happy ending, I intend it that way."

He almost believed her. She seemed to be putting it all together, the strength and power she'd never used, the will she'd never exerted, the determination she'd been afraid to show.

"Fine," he said. "Great. Now let's get the business over with and I can leave." He opened the briefcase and took out a sheaf of papers. "I'll need your initials at the bottom of each page—after you've read it, of course—and your signature at the conclusion."

"I'm not signing."

"You'd better think this through, Mrs. Shaw."

"I already have. If Neville could play his little game, I can play mine."

Aragon sat with the briefcase across his lap. The blinding sun had given him a headache, the heat was unbearable, the broken spring of the chair was sticking into his flesh like a spur. "I told you I liked happy endings, Mrs. Shaw. Especially my own. I am, as Smedler's secretary keeps reminding me, a junior junior employee of the firm. It's not a secure position. Neither is yours. Whatever you got from Mr. Tannenbaum isn't going to last, so you have to consider the possibility that Grady and the money might run out simultaneously."

"I'm buying time, Mr. Aragon."

"Time can't be bought, it can only be spent."

"You don't understand. Grady is starting to love me, really *love* me. I'm becoming indispensable to him. When you're indispensable to someone he *has* to love you."

"My wife is indispensable to me, but so is my auto mechanic and him I'm not too crazy about."

"You're not even trying to understand."

"Look, Mrs. Shaw, sign the papers and I'll get out of here and you can tell Grady only whatever you think he'll believe."

"He'll believe anything I say. He's a beautiful person."

"Glad to hear it. In my line of work I don't meet too many beautiful persons."

She got up suddenly, and forgetting all the lessons she'd learned in mirrors, flung herself down on the bed and began to weep. She wept silently, barely moving a muscle of her face. It was a half-comic, half-sinister sight, like a wax-museum figure rigged to spout tears at the press of a button.

Aragon looked away from her, toward the sea. The purple van was gone and the wide stretch of beach was empty. In the water a solitary swimmer who had to be Grady was heading free-style straight out to sea as if his life depended on it. The next land in that direction was Hawaii, but maybe Grady figured it was worth a try.

"I mustn't cry," she said in a whisper. "Dr. Ortiz won't allow it."

"He's not here, so go right ahead."

"No. It's not good for me. Dr. Ortiz says I have to avoid bad emotions. I must think only of pleasant things."

"I hope he remembers that when he's making out his bill."

"You're a cruel, cynical man."

"I'm an errand boy for Smedler, Downs, Castleberg, McFee, Powell. This isn't a personal matter between you and me, so let's not get nasty."

As he spoke he saw the swimmer turn suddenly, as if he'd heard his name called, and head back for shore. *You should have kept going, Grady.*

Miranda was dabbing away tears with the sleeve of her robe, but new ones kept coming and her eyes were starting to turn red. "I need something to calm me."

Aragon wasn't sure what she meant but he hoped it was pharmaceutical. "I have some aspirin in my car. If you like, I can—"

"Aspirin. Aspirin, for God's sake. I'm dying and you offer me aspirin."

"It's all I've got."

"Call Grady. He can tell Dr. Ortiz to come and give me a shot."

"Grady went for a swim."

"Swim, that's the only thing he ever does, the only thing he ever thinks about."

"Beautiful persons need a lot of exercise," Aragon said.

When Grady returned to the cottage he stopped for a minute at the carport to admire the Porsche that was parked inside. It was a yellow Carrera with gold mag wheels and beige glove-leather seats. Every time he looked at it he felt a little light-headed, he had to convince himself that it was really his and Miranda was going to give him the pink ownership slip as soon as it arrived from the Department of Motor Vehicles. He called it Goldfinger, not out loud in front of anybody, but very softly and secretly as part of a pact between him and the car.

It was the only perfect thing he had ever owned and he felt personally insulted when Miranda criticized it: "Why can't we simply get in it and go? Why do we have to sit here for half an hour with the engine running?" "Not half an hour," he told her. "Just five minutes." For her it was ugly time, full of noise and smell and vibration. He loved every minute of it, it was like waiting for an orgasm.

He entered the cottage without knocking and went into the alcove behind the wooden screen to dress. A white T-shirt, a pair of shorts, the wristwatch Miranda had given him before they left Santa Felicia, the huaraches he'd picked up in Tijuana.

Nobody said anything. The loudest sounds in the room were insects humming and Grady slapping the sand off his legs with a towel. He began to whistle the song "Goldfinger" but stopped almost immediately because he was afraid someone might recognize it and guess it was the name he'd given the Porsche. He felt that in some crazy way this could ruin things. He didn't know how, he only knew things ruined easy.

He came out from behind the screen, still holding the sandy towel. "It's four o'clock, the café should be open by now. I'm going over for a can of beer. Anyone care to join me?"

No one did.

Miranda was sitting at the desk and there were a lot of papers spread out in front of her. She wore a pair of half-glasses he'd never seen before, and when she peered at him over the top of them she looked like an old woman.

"Hey, what is this, Halloween? Take those things off."

"I can't read the fine print without them."

"Fine print. Okay, I get it. This is private business and you want me to split."

"No, I think you should stay." She began gathering up the papers and putting them in numerical order. She moved slowly, as she always did, but Grady saw that this was a different kind of slowness, clumsy and reluctant. "Mr. Aragon has brought us some bad news, Grady. Nothing we can't handle, the two of us together, but—"

"It's about the will," Grady said.

"Yes."

"He didn't leave you everything, after all."

"Yes, he did."

"Then why is the news bad?"

"'Everything' includes his mistakes. Neville made some reckless financial deals during the last year or two of his life."

"How reckless?"

"I'd rather not go into it now, Grady. I don't feel very well. My head—"

"How reckless?"

"Very," she said. "Very reckless."

"So he didn't leave you any money?"

"No."

"But there's the house."

"It has three mortgages on it. Among other things, Neville bought a stud farm in Kentucky."

Aragon, putting the papers back in his briefcase, wondered how she'd found out about the stud farm in Kentucky. If Shaw had told her that, he'd probably told her a lot of other things she'd been pretending not to know. Whatever her reason for the pretense, she had gained nothing from it but a small delay. *I'm buying time, Mr. Aragon . . . Grady is starting to love me, really love me. I'm becoming indispensable to him.*

"What about the car?" Grady said, "My Porsche."

"It's paid for, if that's what you mean. I traded in the Continental and the Mercury." She took off her glasses and hid them away in a needlepoint case. The fine print had been read, all of it bad. "It's really *our* car, isn't it, Grady?"

"Sure. Naturally. I call it mine because you promised to give me the pink slip on it—"

"Whatever is left of the estate we'll share, the two of us. We don't need a fortune to be happy together."

"—and because I do all the driving. You can't even shift gears."

"Shut up," she said. "Shut up about that stupid car."

"Stupid car? Now wait a minute, you can't talk like that about a turbo Carrera."

"I can if I paid for it."

"That's a bitchy remark."

"I have more of the same if you care to hear them."

"Say, what's the matter with you, anyway? I never saw you like this before."

"I have had bad news, terrible news, and all you can do is stand there blabbering about a car while I . . . while my whole world falls apart."

"Since we're supposed to be sharing everything, let's call it *our* world," Grady said. "So *our* world is falling apart. You're right, that's terrible news. But what I want to know is how new is this news?"

"What do you mean?"

"When did you find out?"

"Just now, from Mr. Aragon. He told me about the—the stud farm in Kentucky. And other things."

Aragon didn't deny it, but he glanced toward the door as though he wished he were on the other side of it.

"I had no idea Neville liked horses," she said. "He never let me keep any pets, not even goldfish." She thought of the aquarium in their bedroom at home, the dead fish floating in the murky water that smelled of Scotch. "I would have liked a dog, someone to talk to. Everything was always so quiet. I used to look forward to the gardener cutting the grass or clipping the hedges. He was a funny little man. I forget his name, or perhaps I never knew it. His lawn mower sounded very loud, worse than the Porsche. I have this—this awful headache, Grady. Could you get something for me from Dr. Ortiz?"

"No."

"But I hurt, I hurt all over."

"Sure you hurt. A needle in the butt every morning and a bunch of goats surging around in your bloodstream, what the hell do you expect?"

"I'm only doing it for you, Grady."

"Crap. You've been here two or three times before. Who were you doing it for then?"

"You're cruel, you're so cruel to me."

"I've never lied." He threw the towel into a corner as if he were trying to discard a piece of the past. It lay in a dirty heap. "You must have known Neville had blown away every bill he owned. Why didn't you tell me?"

"I didn't know. Ask Mr. Aragon."

In spite of the mention of his name, neither of them turned to look at Aragon. He picked up his briefcase and took a step toward the door. When this didn't attract attention he took several more steps until he was close enough to put his hand on the doorknob. *Goodbye, Miranda. Nice meeting you. Once.*

Miranda had started crying again. Her tears dropped on the burn-scarred desk, little crystal bombs iridescing in the sun for a moment before they exploded into words: people were cruel to her, they accused her of things, they picked on her. She hated Grady, Smedler, Aragon, all lawyers, lifeguards, nurses, doctors and the California judiciary. She was innocent, her butt hurt and she was going to throw up. She also had a terrible headache but nobody cared, nobody cared about anything except their damned Porsches and everyone should get the hell out of there.

"I was just leaving," Aragon said.

"Take Grady with you. He can show you his turbo Carrera."

Grady stood with his arms crossed on his chest, motionless, expressionless, like a cut-rate Midas turned to bronze instead of gold.

"Do you hear me, Grady? I want you to leave."

"Everybody hears you," Grady said. "You're screaming."

"Not yet. I'm working up to it, though."

"You're making an ass of yourself, Miranda."

"Get out of here."

"All right, all right. Like the man said, I was just leaving."

The café had been opened only a few minutes before and none of the tables was occupied. Two waiters were more or less on duty, an elderly man sitting on a stool picking his teeth and a teenager who bore a strong resemblance to the woman who'd greeted Aragon at the reception desk in the office, thin straight lips and nose, eyes cool as coins. When he saw Grady his face seemed to splinter with excitement.

"Mr. Shaw, Mr. Shaw, sir . . ."

"Bring us a couple of beers, Pedro."

"What kind?"

"You've only got one kind."

"My uncle says to ask. It sounds good."

"I'm buying," Grady told Aragon. "Or rather, Miranda's buying. All I do is write the magic name Shaw on the bill and everything is taken care of."

"Was taken care of."

"That's definite, is it? I mean you weren't trying to scare her to force her to economize, or something along those lines?"

"No."

Grady rubbed his eyes. The pupils were red from the salt water and sand and sun. "She conned me."

"Maybe you con easy."

"It's not just the money I'm talking about. It's the whole deal. I didn't go *after* her, man. She was *there*, I couldn't get past her. So I thought, why not? I was figuring on a little fling, a couple of months, three at the most, and I thought that's what she wanted, too. But then she began using words like commitment and marriage and forever. Forever. Can you beat that? I'm not a forever guy."

Pedro returned, swinging a bottle of beer in each hand.

"Mr. Shaw, sir, I'm ready."

"So am I," Grady said. "What are we ready for?"

"The ride. Tomorrow."

"Oh. Sure."

"Very early before the traffic. How about seven o'clock?"

"You like seven o'clock, Pedro?"

"You bet."

"I don't like seven o'clock. But then, I don't like six or eight o'clock either, so let's make it seven. We'll race the wind, you and me."

"You and me will win. You bet?"

"I bet," Grady said. After the boy left he poured the beer himself. It gushed out over the tops of the bottles like used soapsuds and he sat staring at the foam as though he saw his fortune in it, brief as bubbles and a little dirty. "Here's to Miranda."

"To Miranda."

"Long may she live. Alone."

The beer was too warm and too sweet.

"Christ, I need something stronger than this," Grady said. "You don't have grass on you, do you?"

"No."

"Those kids in the van had some, I could smell it, but they weren't sharing . . . Listen, about Miranda and me, it wasn't working. It wouldn't have worked even if you hadn't shown up with the news about the money."

"I'm glad I didn't ruin anything good."

"Maybe she thinks so. I don't. Like I said, I'm not a forever guy. I feel trapped half the time and guilty the rest. She's so dependent. When I do some perfectly innocent little thing like taking the kid for a ride in my Porsche, she makes out like I abandoned her. It's kind of crazy anyone being dependent on me. Nobody ever was before. It gives me the creeps."

"About the Porsche," Aragon said. "I gather you don't have the pink slip for it."

"The car's mine. She gave it to me. I'm not conceited enough to claim I earned it, but it's *mine.* Hell, she can't even drive it, she doesn't know how to shift gears."

"All that has no bearing on the ownership of the car. As of now it may be the only thing she has left."

"Then how could she afford to come to an expensive place like this?"

"She sold some of her jewelry and other things to a dealer in Santa Felicia."

"Then she's honest-to-God broke."

"Yes."

"And it's a whole new ball game, with me stuck out here in left field."

"She's out there with you. She didn't plan it that way, it's not her fault."

"She shouldn't have lied to me."

"There are people who lie," Aragon said, "and people who want to be lied to. They're often the same people."

Grady drained his glass and put it down on the multicolored tile table. The tiles looked handmade. None of them matched and none of them came out even at the corners. Aragon wondered which of Dr. Ortiz's relatives had worked on it, perhaps a third-cousin-by-marriage who was considered too artistic for one of the menial jobs like Pedro's.

Without being asked, Pedro brought two more beers, wiped off the table with the hem of his apron and reminded Grady of their date to race the wind at seven in the morning.

"The essential thing now," Aragon said, "is to get her back home under the care of her own doctor. She looks pretty spaced-out. What kind of stuff has Ortiz been giving her?"

"It's powerful, I can tell you that much. Knocks her for a loop. Also, she's beginning to ask for it too damn often. She uses the slightest excuse to send me over to get a capsule from Ortiz. He won't let her have more than one at a time."

"How long is she scheduled to stay here?"

"Another two weeks."

"I don't think that would be wise."

"Then you tell her," Grady said. "I already have, for all the good it did. Every time I try to tell her anything she gets a pain in her stomach, her head, her appendix, her butt, you name it. Then she takes one of Ortiz's capsules and conks out. When she wakes up she can't remember what I told her. Half the time I can't either. She has me confused. She always makes me feel I'm in the wrong even when there's no right or wrong involved, just ordinary things."

"Equal alternatives."

"Yeah, that's it, equal alternatives. I'm beginning to think she's a little crazy. She even talked once about having a child. It was grotesque. She's fifty-two. She admitted it, but I knew anyway. Ellen Brewster, the secretary of the club, told me, she looked it up in the files."

"Why would Ellen do that?"

"She wanted to clue me in. For my own good."

"That was kind of Ellen as far as you're concerned. Miranda might feel somewhat different about it."

"It was the truth. I had the right to be told the truth."

"Knowing the truth obviously didn't alter your course of action."

"It never has." Grady's voice was somber. "Maybe I'm crazier than she is. Give me your honest opinion, do you think it's possible?"

"Lots of things are," Aragon said. He didn't give the rest of his honest opinion, that this was more possible than most.

It was after seven and almost dark when Aragon reached the outskirts of Tijuana. He had intended, if all went well, to stay on the freeway and drive right through to Santa Felicia, reaching there about midnight. But he was getting tired and the afternoon had been depressing. He checked in at an American franchise motel, had tostadas and beer at a nearby café and returned to his room.

He closed the windows to block out the noises of the street, which was just coming alive for the night. Then he called Charity Nelson at her apartment and told her he wouldn't be in the office the next morning.

"Where are you, junior?"

"Tijuana."

"What are you doing there?"

"Nothing."

"Nobody does nothing in Tijuana."

"Okay, I'm boozing it up with a couple of hookers."

"That's more like," Charity said. "Did you find Mrs. Shaw?"

"Yes."

"Can't you say anything more than plain ordinary *yes*?"

"I can but you might not want to hear it."

"Try me."

"She's at Dr. Ortiz's rejuvenation clinic in Pasoloma with her friend Grady Keaton."

"The lifeguard?"

"Yes."

"Is he cute?"

"What do you mean by cute?"

"Cute is cute. You know, like Robert Redford."

"He is not like Robert Redford."

"Oh, I wonder what she sees in him, then. To me Robert Redford is—"

"You can tell me about your fantasy life some other time, Miss Nelson," Aragon said. "I'm reporting in that the documents are ready and I'll have them at the office by late tomorrow afternoon."

"You don't sound very happy about it, considering you might even get a bonus if I play your cards right."

"Ha ha ha. Is that better?"

"What's bugging you, junior?"

"This is a dirty business. The lady is doped up and a little crazy, maybe a lot crazy, and I walked out of there and left her."

"You couldn't very well bring her along. The lifeguard wouldn't like it, would he?"

Aragon didn't respond.

"Junior?"

"I'd rather not discuss it."

"I never figured you for the emotional type. This isn't such a dirty business when you look at other dirty businesses."

"Thanks for helping me see things in a new light, Miss Nelson."

"That's my specialty."

"I can believe it. Goodbye."

"Wait a minute. I haven't finished."

"I have," Aragon said and hung up.

He left a wake-up call with the operator for five thirty the next morning.

His return to Pasoloma was slowed by fog and by an unexpectedly heavy procession of vehicles heading into Baja, mostly vans and campers and motor homes with California license plates. The fog started to lift when he reached Pasoloma and the clinic was emerging from its shroud. There was activity around the main office and the hospital building, though it wasn't the kind of activity seen around an ordinary hospital or clinic. People seemed to move very slowly, as though they had—courtesy of Dr. Ortiz—all the time in the world.

Aragon drove directly to the cottage shared by Miranda and Grady. The yellow Porsche was missing from the carport. In its place was Pedro, the boy from the café, talking to a stout middle-aged woman with a cartful of cleaning equipment. Pedro nodded good-morning but he didn't smile or speak. As for the woman, she ducked around the side of the building in a surprising show of speed, pushing the cart in front of her. It sounded as if it had a square wheel.

Aragon said, "That cart could use some oil."

The boy shrugged. "It's old. My mother used to push me around in it when I was little."

"How old are you now?"

"Thirteen. Next year me and my brother are going to the U.S. to get a job, make lots of money." He glanced back at Aragon's Chevy. "You don't make lots of money like Mr. Shaw does."

"Not like Mr. Shaw does, no."

"He's pretty important, I bet. He can't waste time taking people for rides. Racing the wind, that's a crazy idea. Nobody can race something they can't see."

"I'm sorry you missed your ride, Pedro."

"I don't care," the boy said. "I never expected nothing anyway."

Aragon knocked on the door of the cottage, softly at first, then more loudly when there was no response. The windows were closed and the blinds shut as if the people inside were trying to avoid the light and noise of morning.

He knocked again. "Mrs. Shaw?"

Another two or three minutes elapsed before Miranda's voice answered, hoarse and sleepy. "Who is it?"

"Tom Aragon."

"Go away."

"I went away. Now I'm back."

She opened the door. She wore a large loose pink-and-orange-striped robe that made her look as though she'd taken shelter in a tent that wasn't quite tall enough and she'd had to cut a hole in the top for her head.

Her eyelids were swollen and blistered by the heat of her tears. She said, almost literally, "I'm not seeing anyone."

"Are you feeling all right, Mrs. Shaw?"

"Close the door. I'm cold."

"Let me order you some breakfast."

"No, thank you. I know you're trying to be kind but it's quite unnecessary. I'm quite—quite fine."

"Where is Grady?"

"Grady is fine, too, thank you."

"I asked where."

"Where? Well, I'm not really sure. He took one of the boys from the café for a ride in the Porsche. I wish he wouldn't get so friendly with the hired help, it's not dignified. He must learn to—"

"The boy is still waiting for him, Mrs. Shaw."

She sat down on the edge of the bed, her tent collapsing around her. "So am I," she said in a whisper. "But he won't be back. He left in the middle of the night. I'd been very upset by the news you brought me, so Dr. Ortiz gave me a capsule and I went to sleep. When I woke up Grady was gone. There was a note on the desk."

The note was still there. Though it had been crumpled and partly torn and marked by tears, it remained legible. The letters were large and uneven, the lines slanted downward:

> *Miranda*
>
> *Things are beginning to close in on me and I need to get away fast and figure it all out how to do something and be somebody. I thought it was funny at first being called Mr. Shaw but then suddenly it wasn't. Maybe I'll see you in the U.S. after I get established and no more of that Mr. Shaw crap.*
>
> *Please don't go to pieces over my leaving so sudden. We both agreed it wasn't going to be permanent, nothing is, how can we beat odds like that.*
>
> *Take care Miranda and maybe I'll see you in the U.S. and we can have fun like we use to.*
>
>

Your friend
Grady Keaton

*P.S. Don't let the doc pump any more of that junk in you. You look OK as is.
Why do you want to be young again anyway. Being young is hell.*

The note ran true to form. Grady had told no lies, made no promises, expressed no regrets.

"Let me take you home, Mrs. Shaw," Aragon said. "We can leave as soon as you're packed."

"Dr. Ortiz won't like it."

"Did you pay in advance?"

"Yes."

"What about refunds?"

"He doesn't give any."

"Then he'll probably be able to absorb the shock of your departure."

"But what if—what if Grady comes back and I'm not here?"

Aragon didn't want to play any what-if games, but he said, "It would serve him right, wouldn't it, to find you gone? Now pull yourself together and we'll head for home."

"No."

"I can't leave you here, Mrs. Shaw. I feel responsible for what happens to you."

"Why? You only met me yesterday afternoon."

"Some people you get to know very fast." *Much too fast, Miranda.*

He waited outside while she packed her bags. Fog still clung to the beach, so he couldn't see the surf. But he heard it, loud and with a slow steady rhythm. Grady claimed every wave was different, every single one, but these sounded exactly alike.

Miranda came out of the cottage in about twenty minutes. She'd put on a white straw hat, oversized sunglasses and a sleeveless blue shift. Her arms were very thin and pale, as though they'd been tucked away in some dark place, unused.

"I'll call a boy to bring out my luggage," she said. "There are two suitcases and a garment bag."

"Don't bother calling anybody. I can do it."

"I hate to put you to any trouble."

"No trouble."

She didn't travel light. The suitcases were the size of trunks and too heavy to manage more than one at a time. There was no place in the Chevy to hang the garment bag, so he laid it across the back seat. It looked disturbingly human, like someone stuffed, head and all, into a sleeping bag.

She said, "Grady is very strong."

"Is he."

"He can lift almost anything."

Including a Porsche. He almost said it. There was a possibility that she was thinking the same thing and being deliberately ironic, but he couldn't tell for sure. Her expression was hidden by the brim of her hat and the dark glasses and a layer of pride thicker than her makeup.

When he turned the Chevy around he saw the boy, Pedro, watching from the corner of the carport. He waved goodbye. Pedro didn't wave back.

For the first few miles she sat tense and silent, her hands folded tightly in her lap. But gradually she began to relax. She took off her hat and ran her fingers through her hair, she removed her glasses and rubbed her eyes, and now and then she spoke.

"It's awfully hot. Could you turn on the air conditioner?"

"I don't have one."

"I thought all cars came with air conditioners."

In her world they probably did.

Later she talked of Grady. "He left his toothbrush behind. Not that he'll miss it, he's quite careless about personal hygiene. Did you know that?"

"No."

"It didn't seem to matter. Every female in the club had a crush on him anyway, even Ellen, who's a cold fish where men are concerned."

He didn't know that either.

"I wonder what's going to become of me. I can't earn a living. All I ever learned at boarding school was French and ballet and etiquette."

She seemed to have forgotten some of the etiquette. While he was explaining the workings of the probate court she went to sleep, her head resting between the doorframe and the back of the seat.

She woke up at the border to answer questions put to her by an immigration official. Yes, she was a United States citizen, born in Chicago, Illinois. She had nothing to declare. She'd gone to Mexico for treatment at a health resort and was now returning home to Santa Felicia.

"That was a lie," she told Aragon afterward. "I'm not going home. I don't have a home anymore."

"Certainly you do."

"No. The house is mortgaged, it belongs to strangers."

"Not yet. The law moves very slowly. You can continue living in the place until everything is settled."

"I refuse to accept the charity of strangers."

"The strangers are a couple of banks, they're not in the habit of offering charity."

"It makes no difference. Kindly don't pursue the subject, Mr. Aragon. When I left the house I decided that I would never return to it no matter what happened."

"What will you do?"

"Rent a small apartment, perhaps take a course and learn to perform salaried duties, the kind of thing Ellen does at the club."

"Do you have any cash?"

"A little."

"How long will it keep you going?"

"I don't know. I've never had to keep going on my own before. It should—should be an interesting challenge. Don't you agree?"

"Yes." He agreed about the challenge. Whether it would be interesting, or even possible, would depend on Miranda.

They had a late lunch in San Diego. She ordered a double martini and a green salad with white wine. The combination wasn't as potent as one of Dr. Ortiz's capsules but it had its effect. She lost some more of her boarding-school etiquette.

"He stole my car," she said. "That son of a bitch stole my car."

"I believe he was under the impression that you gave it to him, Mrs. Shaw."

"I gave it to him only if I went with it. It was supposed to be *ours*. Gave it to him, my foot. Do you know how much that thing cost?"

"You can get it back."

"How?"

"Tell the police it's been stolen."

"What police? I don't know what state, even what country he's in by this time."

"Maybe he'll return it voluntarily," Aragon said. "I don't know much about Grady, but I got the impression he's not a bad guy even if he's not the beautiful person you thought he was."

She began to cry, using the paper napkin for a handkerchief. "I thought he was—I thought he was such a beautiful person."

"We all make mistakes."

"Oh, shut up."

He shut up. Back in the car so did she. She went to sleep again, this time with her head pressed against Aragon's shoulder. For a small woman she felt very heavy.

She woke up as he slowed for the off ramp into Santa Felicia. It wasn't a gentle and gradual awakening. She was instantly alert as if an alarm had gone off in her brain.

"Why are you leaving the highway? Where are we?"

"Home."

She shook her head, repudiating the word. "I have an earache and my neck is stiff."

"You look fine." It was true. After her long sleep—plus, or in spite of, the last dose of Dr. Ortiz's goat glands—she seemed oddly young.

"Not really," she said. "You're just being kind."

"No. You look great, Miranda."

She checked for herself, staring into a small mirror she took out of her purse, but she didn't indicate who was staring back at her. "Where are you taking me?"

"To your house."

"It's not my house. It never was. Neville paid for it, I only lived there . . . Why did you call me by my first name?"

"I felt like it."

"You really mustn't. It's not proper."

She had remembered her etiquette. Maybe the French and ballet would come later.

Encina Road was only a couple of miles from the freeway, but it was difficult to find and Miranda offered no help. She sat gazing out of the window like a visitor seeing this part of the city for the first time: stone walls covered with ivy and bougainvillea, ancient oak trees draped with moss, rows of spiked cassias more treacherous than barbed wire, high impenetrable hedges of pittosporum and eugenia.

The ten-foot iron gate at the bottom of the Shaws' driveway was closed, and when Aragon pressed the buzzer of the squawk box connecting it to the main residence, nothing happened. He tried the door of the gatehouse. It was locked and the Venetian blinds were closed tight. He waited a minute, almost expecting the old man, Hippollomia, to appear suddenly and explain the situation: *There is no electric . . . Missus forgot to pay.*

He returned to the car.

Miranda looked at him solemnly. "You see? The house will not accept me any more than I will accept it."

"Nonsense. The electricity was turned off because nobody paid the bill."

"That is only the obvious external reason."

"What's the subtle internal one?"

"I already told you. Not that it matters," she added. "I could never stay here again under any circumstances."

"Where will you stay?"

"There must be places for homeless deserted women like me."

"The situation is bad enough without your dramatizing it," he said. "Now let's talk straight. Do you have anyone who can put you up temporarily, relatives, friends, neighbors—"

"No."

"What about members of your club?"

"No. The only person at the club I consider my friend is Ellen. She's been very kind."

"Has she." If that's the best you can do, you're in trouble, Miranda. Ellen's no friend of yours.

A gust of wind blew through the canyon, pelting the roof of the car with eucalyptus pods. Miranda winced as if each one of them had been aimed directly at her. "Please take me away from here. There's a santana coming up, I can sense it all over my body. My skin feels tight."

"I thought that's what you went down to the clinic for, tighter skin. You could have stayed here and gotten the same results cheaper."

170

"That was a boorish remark. What makes you so cranky?"

"I'm tired."

"Why should you be tired? *I'm* the one who's suffered."

"You slept most of the afternoon."

"Surely you don't begrudge me a little sleep after what I've been through."

"No." He didn't begrudge her anything except his time, two days of it so far. Two days of Miranda seemed a lot longer. Three would be more than he could bear. He said, "Suppose we drive to the club and see if Ellen's still there. She might have some advice to offer."

It was a dirty trick to play on Ellen but he couldn't think of anything else to do. At least Ellen was used to her and would know what to expect and maybe even how to deal with it.

Walter Henderson, the manager, was in the office but he looked ready to leave. He wore an after-hours outfit, jogging shoes, a striped warm-up suit and a navy-blue yachting cap. A copy of the *Racing Form* was tucked under one arm in case he stopped to rest while jogging or was becalmed while sailing or got caught in a traffic jam on the way to his bookie's.

"Sorry, we're about to close," he told Aragon. "Seven o'clock, you know. That's our winter schedule except on weekends and special occasions. It was clearly stated in our last newsletter. Didn't you read our last newsletter?"

"No."

"Too bad. I had something rather clever in it."

"Drat, I'm always missing clever things," Aragon said. "Is Miss Brewster still here?"

"She's around some place making a last-minute check with the security guard. Two dead stingrays were tossed in the pool last night. We suspect some Mexican boys. These minority groups have become very bold."

"So I've heard. Shocking."

"Today stingrays, tomorrow great white sharks. Well, we'll cross that bridge when we come to it . . . I'm locking the office now. You can wait for Miss Brewster in the corridor. There's a bench to sit on."

He sat on it. Except for a janitor mopping the tiled terrace, no one was in sight. But he could hear voices in the distance, and they sounded angry. After about five minutes he got up and walked around the pool a couple of times to stretch his legs.

There was no trace of the santana that had been blowing in the foothills or the sea winds which almost always began in the afternoon and stopped abruptly at sundown. The water was so smooth that at the far end where it was eighteen feet deep it looked shallow as a reflection pool, mirroring the lifeguard towers, the flagpole, the diving platform and Aragon himself, foreshortened to child size. Along the walls and floor of the pool every mark was clearly defined, the water-depth signs and the racing lanes. He wondered if anyone ever raced here or whether all the winning and losing was done on deck.

The voices were getting louder. It sounded like an argument between two women and a man, but when the trio appeared at the bottom of the steps coming down from the south row of cabanas one of the women turned out to be little Frederic Quinn. He was staggering under the weight of a sleeping bag, a portable television set and a six-pack of 7-Up. Ellen carried the rest of his supplies—a partly eaten pizza, a box of cheese crackers, a package of bologna and another of frankfurters.

Frederic had been planning a big evening, but the security guard caught him in the middle of the pizza and a rerun of *Star Trek*. The security guard, a pear-shaped divinity student working his way toward a pulpit, might have joined the party if Ellen hadn't shown up. For her benefit he put on a show of doing his duty.

"I'm telling you for the last time, young man, you can't spend the night in a cabana."

"Why not?"

"It's against the rules."

"How am I supposed to know the rules? I'm only a kid."

"You are also," Ellen said, "a pain in the neck."

"I can't help it. I didn't ask to be born. Nobody else asked for me to be born either. My father had a vasectomy but it was bungled. He would have sued except he didn't need the money."

"I do not want to talk about your father's vasectomy, Frederic."

"Yeah? What do you want to talk about?"

"Stingrays," the security guard said. "Dead ones. Two of them. In the pool."

"I don't know a thing about stingrays, dead or alive. I can't be expected to know everything, I'm not a genius."

"Any kid that knows about vasectomies must know about stingrays."

"Not necessarily. I specialize, see?"

"No, I don't see."

"Don't argue with the child, Sullivan, it's a waste of time. Just be clear and be firm." Ellen looked down at Frederic, who had put the sleeping bag on the floor and was sitting on it drinking a can of 7-Up. "Now, Frederic, let's get this straight. Nobody, absolutely nobody's ever allowed to stay in the cabanas after the club is closed."

"That's what you think. Last week I saw Mr. Redfern making macho with Amy Lou Worthington in the Worthingtons' cabana. He's a real pro."

"You watched them, Frederic?"

"Well, sure. There they were and there was I."

"There you *shouldn't* have been."

"There *they* shouldn't have been either."

"In a minute I'm going to lose my temper with you, Frederic."

"Everybody does. No big deal." It was at this point that Frederic spotted Aragon and let out a whoop of recognition. "There's my lawyer. Hey! Hey, Aragon, come here a minute. Remember me? We made a pact in the parking lot, remember?"

As Aragon approached, the guard watched him suspiciously. "A pact in the parking lot, that sounds like the devil's work to me. And since when do nine-year-old boys have lawyers?"

"Since you cops started pushing us around, that's when," Frederic said. "Tell him, Aragon."

"You do that, Aragon," the guard said. "Tell me."

"What do you want to know?"

"You can start with the pact in the parking lot."

"All right. As I was about to leave the lot a few days ago I ran into Frederic. He gave me some information about a person I was looking for and in return I agreed to act as his attorney when the time came."

"The time has come."

"In that case I'll have to talk to my client alone for a few minutes. If you'll excuse us, Mr. Sullivan—"

"You mean this boy is really your client?"

"Yes."

"It sounds like the devil's work, for a certainty."

"Go and finish your rounds, Sullivan," Ellen said. "And leave the theology to us."

As soon as the guard left, Frederic opened another can of 7-Up, switched on the television set and tuned in on a science-fiction movie. Several prehistoric or posthistoric monsters were emerging from a swamp to the sound of some very loud contemporary music.

Ellen spoke above it. "What are you doing here, Mr. Aragon?"

"I found Mrs. Shaw."

"That's fine. It's what you wanted to do, isn't it?"

"Yes."

"Was she alone?"

"Not at first. She is now. In fact, she's out in my car and she'd like to see you."

"Why?"

"You're her friend."

"I'm not. I never was, never will be. I don't see how she can consider me a friend."

"Obviously it's a case of mistaken identity," Aragon said. "So forget it."

"You make it sound as if I'm cruel and unfeeling."

"Are you?"

"I never thought so. I'm kind to animals and I help old ladies across the street. But I don't owe Miranda Shaw anything. She's had the whole bit from the time she was born, money and beauty and being taken care of and cherished."

"All of that's gone now, including Grady. He walked out on her last night. Or rather, he drove out in the Porsche she bought him."

"She bought him a Porsche? My God, what an idiot that woman must be, what a complete— All right, all right, I'll go out and talk to her. Or listen to her, or whatever. I won't be her friend," she added distinctly, "but I'll come as close to it as I can without upchucking."

"You're all heart, Miss Brewster."

On the television screen one of the monsters reared up on its hind legs, bellowing in triumph. Aragon watched for a minute. The limited human imagination which had created a God and a devil in its own image hadn't done much better with monsters. No matter how obviously grotesque they were with their warty skins, pinheads and three eyes, all had four limbs, voices like French horns and 20/20/20 vision.

Aragon went over and turned the set off.

Frederic let out a squawk of protest. "Hey, what'd you do that for? The monsters were just going to take over the world."

"They already have," Aragon said. "It must be a rerun."

"It is. I've seen it before. I've seen everything before."

"You're pretty young for that. How old are you?"

"Nine and seven-twelfths. But when the country switches to the metric system I'm going to add on a couple of years."

"What's the metric system got to do with your age?"

"Nothing. But everybody will be so confused by grams and kilometers and liters they won't notice the difference. In a flash I'll be eleven and seven-twelfths and Bingo Firenze's only eleven, ha ha."

"What if Bingo Firenze has the same idea?"

"He won't. He's too stupid."

"Or too smart."

"No, he's not. His family has to pay extra so the school will keep him. Whose side are you on, anyway? I thought you were *my* lawyer."

"I am," Aragon said. "And indications are that you'll need one."

"The stingray bit, huh? Okay. I found them on the beach where some guy had been practicing spearfishing and I thought I could resuscitate them by throwing them in the pool. It was my good deed for the week—"

"Bad choice of good deed, Frederic. They didn't resuscitate."

"It wasn't my fault. My intentions were pure as snow."

"Have you ever seen snow?"

"No."

"Sometimes it's pretty dirty."

"Well, it starts out clean." Frederic gazed wistfully at the blank television screen as though hoping the monsters would reappear and come charging out to be on his side. "A good lawyer is supposed to trust his client."

"A good client is supposed to tell his lawyer the truth."

"Wheezing Jesus, it was only a joke. I wanted to see the expression on Henderson's face when he walked in the front door and saw creepy crawly things on the bottom of the pool. How was I to know he was going to overreact? Nobody has a sense of humor around this place. When I get old enough I plan to split like Grady, maybe with a chick the way he did, maybe not. Probably not. The only chicks I know are my sister Caroline's friends and they're all fat and hate me."

"I talked to Grady yesterday."

Frederic's face, under the sun scars and freckles and flea-bite scabs, turned a mottled pink. "Grady? Honest, no kidding?"

"No kidding."

"Where is he?"

"He was in Mexico when I saw him."

"Isn't he coming home?"

"I don't think so. Not for a while anyway."

"He's on the lam, I bet. I bet the Federales are after him, or the Mexican Mafia. I bet—"

"You'd lose," Aragon said. "Nobody's after him. He's running because that's the way he is. He gets into things and then wants out."

"What kind of things?"

"Relationships."

The boy took a deep breath and held it, preparing himself for a blow. "Relationships like him and me?"

"No, not like him and you. More complicated ones. You—well, he's still your friend."

"How do you know?"

"He asked after you."

"What were his exact words?"

Aragon made some tactful changes in Grady's exact words. "He said, 'How's my weird little pal Frederic?'"

Frederic let out his breath and the color of his face gradually returned to normal. "Yeah, that sounds like Grady, all right. Did he send me any message?"

"Just to stay out of trouble."

"Man, has he got a lot of nerve. Man oh man, look who's talking about trouble. Hey, you know what I'm going to tell Bingo Firenze? I'm going to tell him my best friend is tooling around Mexico with the Federales after him. Bingo will curl up and blow away."

"May I add good riddance."

"Oh, Bingo's not so bad," said the premature convert to the metric system, "for a kid."

It was arranged, via the pay phone in the corridor, that one of Frederic's brothers would come and take him home. Then Frederic settled down to wait under a palm tree, lying on top of his sleeping bag with the television set balanced on his stomach. The monsters returned and took over the world and everybody lived happily ever after.

Aragon went back to his car. Ellen was in the driver's seat talking to Miranda Shaw. When Ellen saw him approaching she got out and came to meet him. She looked cool but the ring of club keys in her hand was clanking a little too vigorously.

"Mrs. Shaw is going to stay with me temporarily until other arrangements can be made." There was a distinct accent on the words *temporarily* and *other*. "Wait till I lock up, and you can follow me to my apartment."

"Thanks, Miss Brewster."

"This is not going to be a long visit. I hope I've made that clear."

"Absolutely. As soon as the office opens in the morning I'll try to get her some emergency funds from my boss. Then you can whisk her to a motel or something."

"*You* can whisk her to a motel or something. I'm going to be working and I don't get whisking breaks . . . I presume she has luggage."

"A couple of suitcases." He didn't mention that together they were heavy enough to contain Grady's dismembered torso.

While Miranda showered, Ellen prepared a light meal of omelet and green salad. Afterward the two women sat at the kitchen table drinking tea. The room which Ellen had always thought of as neat and compact now seemed cluttered and much too small and intimate to be shared with a stranger.

If Miranda felt any similar tension, she didn't show it. She did most of the talking, mixing past and present in her soft high-pitched voice. She spoke of her gratitude to Ellen for her kindness, and to Aragon for his—"Such a nice young man but rather odd because one can't tell for sure what he's thinking"—and of the clinic in Pasoloma, with its tethered goats, pregnant and reproachful. She told of the happy times in her childhood when she was allowed to have supper in the kitchen with the cook—"Cook and I drinking tea just like this and Cook would read our fortunes in the tea leaves, the larger leaves indicating a trip, the specks that meant money and the little twigs that were tall dark strangers who always turned out to be the postman or the plumber or Cook's boyfriend, who was short and fat."

She talked of her first meeting with Grady. "You introduced us, Ellen. Do you remember? It was in the office. I told him there was a child screaming and asked him if he could do anything about it. And he said probably not. That day is so vivid in my mind I could repeat every word, describe every gesture and expression. Grady looked at me very seriously but in a sort of questioning way. You know?"

"Yes." Ellen knew. Grady looked at every woman the same way and it was always the same question and he didn't wait around very long for an answer.

"I keep thinking of him coming back to the clinic—perhaps now, this very minute—and finding me gone and being terribly sorry. Perhaps I should have stayed and waited for him. After all, he was just as upset as I was by the news Mr. Aragon brought us. Once the first shock of it is over he'll see that nothing has changed between us, we can still get married and be happy together."

"I didn't realize you were intending to be married."

"Of course. Of course we were, Ellen. Otherwise I would never have—I mean, I'm not a slut. Grady's the only man I've ever been intimate with except Neville, and that was different. Neville mostly liked to look at me and watch me brush my hair and things like that. He almost never touched me. Grady was different."

"I'm sure he was."

"Oh, I wish Cook were here to read the tea leaves. All of a sudden I feel so hopeful, yes, and determined, too, as if I can make everything work out for Grady and me to be together again. I'll start by being realistic. Money is important to him. All right, I'll get some. A lot, I'll get a lot of money and buy him back."

"You're tired. Don't think about it now."

"But I must begin planning right away, right here." She surveyed the room as though she were memorizing every detail of it: the bird prints on the wall, the porcelain kettle on the stove, the bread box and matching canister set on the counter, the bouquet of yellow plastic flowers and the ceramic owl cookie jar on top of the refrigerator. She said solemnly, "I will never forget this room and sitting here like this with you, planning a whole new future for myself. Will you ever forget it, Ellen?"

"No," Ellen said. "Probably not."

She stared into her cup. There were no leaves indicating a trip, no specks that meant money, no twigs that were tall dark strangers. There was only a soggy tea bag.

Part IV

IN NOVEMBER, DR. Laurie MacGregor flew down from San Francisco to spend the Thanksgiving holiday with her husband, Tom Aragon. Considerable time was wasted on the problem of what to do with the live twenty-five-pound turkey which Smedler had sent to each of his employees from his brother-in-law's turkey farm. The turkey, after a tranquilizing meal of grain sprinkled with vodka, was taken to the local children's zoo, having lost no more than a few feathers and two friends.

At the club Mr. Henderson decorated the dining room with life-sized plastic skeletons, thus cutting some of the losses entailed by the Halloween Hoedown. People who questioned the propriety of the decorations were given an explanation which Henderson had cunningly devised to foil his critics. The skeletons were reminders of death and hence of the resurrection, for which everyone should be thankful on Thanksgiving. Little Miss Reach, who was ninety and closer to the subject than most, suggested that it would have been better to wait until Easter. Henderson made a note of this for future reference. There was a chance, however slight, that he and maybe even Miss Reach would still be around by Easter.

For Christmas, Cordelia Young received a new Mercedes from her parents. Her thank-you speech was brief:

"Oh, dammit, I wanted a Ferrari."

During the same week Mr. and Mrs. Quinn were sent official notice from Mr. Tolliver, Headmaster, that their son Frederic would not be welcome back for the spring term or any period thereafter. Frederic's speech was also brief: "Hurray!" Mrs. Quinn told Frederic her heart was broken. Mr. Quinn said his was, too, but Mrs. Quinn said hers was more broken than his. During the ensuing argument Frederic was forgotten. He went up to his room, retrieved his Hate List from under the desk blotter where it was hidden and crossed off Mr. Tolliver's name. It was silly to waste a lot of good clean Hate.

On New Year's Eve, Charles Van Eyck attended the Regimental Ball to keep alive his contempt for the military in general and his brother-in-law, Admiral Young, in particular. He went through the receiving line three times, audibly noting the amount of gold braid and ornamental hardware and estimating their cost to the taxpayer. His sister, Iris, struck him on the shin with her cane. The Admiral was more tactful: "My dear Charles, I'm afraid you've had too much to drink. You mustn't make an ass of yourself."

"Why not?" Van Eyck said amiably. "All you fellows are doing it."

Van Eyck was also busy during February.

Amy Lou Worthington received anonymous and somewhat belated acknowledgment of her deflowering in the form of a sympathy card: "Sorry to Hear of Your Loss."

Ellen Brewster found on her desk an old-fashioned lace-and-satin valentine with an old-fashioned message:

> Roses are red
> Violets are blue,
> Sugar is sweet
> And so are you.

Van Eyck had brought it up to date and more in line with his sentiments by penciling out the last line.

Ellen went out to the terrace to thank him in person, but Van Eyck was having one of his sudden and mysterious attacks of deafness. He cupped his right ear and said, "Eh? What's that? Speak up."

"The valentine."

"Eh?"

"Thank you for the valentine."

"Eh?"

"An earthquake has struck Los Angeles and the entire city is in ruins."

"It's about time," Van Eyck said. "I predicted this forty years ago."

At intervals throughout the fall and winter Aragon thought of Miranda Shaw. He'd heard nothing about her at the office, and when he remembered to ask, it was always at an inconvenient time—the middle of the night or over the weekend when the office was closed or during Smedler's and Charity's separate but equal vacations.

It was in April that he saw her on the street, waiting outside the entrance to an underground garage that served a block of stores downtown. Whatever had happened to her during the past months, she had kept up appearances. She was perfectly groomed, her hair in a French twist at the nape of her neck, her dress a flowered silk with a voluminous pleated skirt and scarf. Though she was small, and standing very quietly, she couldn't help being conspicuous among the housewives hurrying to sales and the clerks and secretaries to their jobs. The dress was too fancy and her makeup too theatrical for nine o'clock in the morning.

At closer range he noticed the subtle changes in her. Her red-gold hair seemed a little brassier and there were blue circles under her eyes and lines around her mouth that the makeup didn't hide.

"Good morning, Mrs. Shaw."

"Why, Mr. Aragon. How nice to see you again."

They shook hands. Hers was thin and dry as paper.

"You're looking very well, Mrs. Shaw."

"I'm surviving. One mustn't be greedy." She hesitated, glancing over her shoulder as though checking for eavesdroppers. "I suppose you know my husband's will went through probate in February and the bad news became official. He spent all of his own money and a great deal of other people's."

"How have you been living?"

"Strangely."

"Strangely?"

"I believe that's a fair way to describe it," she said with a faint smile. "I have a job. It's not exactly what I would have chosen but it makes me self-supporting for the first time in my life. I even have a social security number. Yes, it's all quite official, I'm a working woman. Surprised, aren't you?"

"A little."

"The salary isn't much but I get room and board and I won't starve. Do you remember Ellen Brewster at the Penguin Club?"

"Oh yes."

"It was her idea. I never thought I had anything worth teaching anyone, but apparently I do . . . Here they come now. Pretend we're not talking about them."

He didn't have a chance to wonder who "they" were. Cordelia and Juliet were emerging from the underground garage, blinking in the sun like giant moles. They looked at Aragon without recognition or interest. He had no part in their world, there was only room for two.

"Cordelia rammed a concrete pillar," Juliet said. "But it wasn't her fault. There was an arrow pointing left and an arrow pointing right and she couldn't make up her mind, so she hit the pillar which was in the middle."

"An honest mistake," Cordelia admitted cheerfully. "It could happen to anyone."

"But especially you," Juliet said.

"We learned a lesson from it, though."

"It's a dumb way to learn a lesson. Which I didn't anyway."

"You did so. You found out a Mercedes is no better than any other car when it comes up against concrete. Crash, bang, crunch, just like an ordinary Cadillac."

"Pops won't care but Mrs. Young will be furious."

"Girls," Miranda said. "Girls, please. Forget the car for a moment and pay attention to your manners. I've told you repeatedly not to refer to Admiral Young as Pops. He is your father. Wouldn't it sound better to call him that?"

Cordelia shook her head. "Father is what you call somebody with his collar on backwards. Or like in our father who art in heaven. That kind of father belongs to everybody."

"Our *personal* father is Pops," Juliet said. "His wife is Mrs. Young."

"Girls, please. I don't want to be harsh with you but I must ask you not to call your mother Mrs. Young."

"Why not? You do."

"She's not my mother."

"She may not be ours either," Cordelia said. "We have no proof. Anyway, she'd just as soon not be."

"She hates us," Juliet explained. "We don't mind. We hate her back. She hates you, too, but you can't hate her back because you're a lady and ladies never get to do anything they want to."

Both girls thought this was extremely funny. Cordelia screamed with laughter and Juliet's face turned bright pink and she had to wipe her eyes and nose on the sleeve of her wool sweater, which was very absorbent and ideal for the purpose.

Miranda stood quietly, her only sign of emotion a deepening of the lines around her mouth. "You are attracting attention. I want it stopped immediately or I'll report every word of this conversation to your mother. Now run along and start your shopping and I'll meet you at Peterson's in the shoe department in half an hour. I have to go and check how much damage was done to the car."

Cordelia had the last word. "Not enough."

Miranda watched them walk briskly down the street arm in arm and still laughing. Then she turned back to Aragon. "I told you I've been living strangely. This is it. I'm supposed to teach the girls etiquette and the social graces. As you must have observed, I'm not a very good teacher."

"They're not very good students," Aragon said. "Hang in there anyway."

"I don't have a choice."

"Not now. But perhaps eventually . . ."

"Eventually sounds so far in the future. I'm not sure I can wait."

He didn't ask about Grady and she didn't volunteer any information. Grady seemed as far in the past as "eventually" seemed in the future.

A few weeks later, returning to his office after lunch, he found a message on his desk from Ellen Brewster asking him to drop by the Penguin Club on a personal matter. He went as soon as he'd finished work for the day.

It was five thirty, cold and overcast, as it often was in May. The club had made the transition from fall to spring with only minor adjustments—a fresh coat of paint on the walls, a change of greenery in the redwood planters, different pads on the chairs and chaises, and a new lifeguard, a short, stocky young man with a blanket draped over his head and shoulders. He appeared ready and willing to save lives, but the pool was unoccupied.

The seasonal changes in Ellen were more obvious. She had shorter hair, curled and frosted at the tips, and she wore oversized sunglasses and lipstick so glossy it made her mouth look like wet vinyl. He wondered about the sunglasses. There hadn't been any sun for a week.

"I'm glad you came," she said, sounding glad. "Would you like some coffee?"

"Fine."

"Let's go in the snack bar. No one will be there at this time of day."

She was almost right. The only customer was an old man with a copy of *Fortune* open on the table in front of him. His eyes were closed and his chin rested on his collarbone. He was either asleep or dead; no one seemed interested in finding out which.

A fat pink-cheeked blonde stood behind the counter filing her nails. She gave Ellen a bored look.

"The snack bar's closed. I'm just waiting for my ride."

"Isn't there some coffee left?"

"It's stale."

"We'll take it."

"You'll have to pour it yourself and drink it black. I'm off duty and we're out of cream."

The verbal exchange or the sudden honking of an automobile horn outside the rear door had wakened the old man.

"What's happening around here? Can't a man read in peace?"

"It's time to go home, Mr. Van Eyck," Ellen said. "The snack bar is closed."

"No, it's not. *I'm* here."

"You shouldn't be."

"I don't see any Closed sign posted on the door."

"I'm posting it in a minute."

"What about that fellow with you? Wait till Henderson hears about this, you sneaking young men into the snack bar after hours."

"Mr. Aragon is my lawyer."

"Have you done something illegal?"

"Not yet," Ellen said. "But I'm thinking of committing a murder."

"Think again. You'd never get away with it. You lack the finesse, the savoir-faire, and you have childish fits of temper."

"Please go home, Mr. Van Eyck."

"If you insist. Though I resent being evicted in order that you may conduct a rendezvous with a young man who doesn't look any more like a lawyer than I do. Where did he go to law school?"

"Hastings," Aragon said.

"Never heard of it." Van Eyck picked up his magazine and left. In spite of his shuffling gait and a pronounced list to starboard he moved with considerable speed.

Aragon tasted the coffee. The fat blonde had been right. It was stale and bitter and lukewarm. He couldn't do anything about the age and temperature but he added a pinch of salt to take away the bitterness.

"I can get you a year's honorary membership in the club," Ellen said.

"Why would you want to do that?"

"I can't afford to pay you and it wouldn't be fair for me to ask your advice for nothing."

"This coffee ought to cover two cents' worth. Ask ahead."

"I had a letter from Grady yesterday."

"Where is he?"

"Las Vegas." She took off her sunglasses and he saw why she'd worn them in the first place. Her eyes were red and slightly swollen. "He wants to come back here."

"It's a free country. He doesn't need your permission or mine."

"No, but he needs money and a job, so it's not all that free, is it . . . ? Here, I'd like you to read it."

She took a small envelope from her pocket and handed it to Aragon. It had been postmarked five days previously in Las Vegas and in the upper left corner was the address of a motel chain that showed porn films. Grady might have worked there, stayed there, or simply borrowed its writing paper.

> *Dear Ellen*
> *I guess you heard about me and Mrs. Shaw and all that water under the bridge. I hope she's doing OK with no hard feelings etcetra.*
> *I ran into lousy luck which put me in bad with some of the pit bosses and I would like to get out of this freaky place. I feel bad vibes coming at me. What I really wish is I had my old job back. Is there any chance of getting a break from Mr. Henderson. If you think so would you send me an application form to fill out right away. Thanks, you are a real peach.*
> *Best regards from your old friend Grady Keaton*

"'Mrs. Shaw and all that water under the bridge,'" Aragon repeated. "Grady has such a sensitive nature."

"He feels guilty, I'm sure he does. It's just—he doesn't express himself on paper very well."

"Oh, I don't know. I think that's rather a cute way of saying he ran off in her thirty-thousand-dollar car and left her broke in a foreign country."

She rubbed the sunglasses up and down the lapel of her jacket a few times before putting them back on. It was either a stall or an attempt to clear up the view she had through them.

"That's what I need your advice about. Suppose he comes back to Santa Felicia. Whether or not he gets a job at the club, Miranda is bound to find out about it. Can she prosecute him?"

"Without knowing all the details of the case, I'd say she could at least sue him for the return of the car."

"He probably doesn't have it anymore."

"Then she can be a good sport and forgive and forget," Aragon said. "If I were Grady, though, I wouldn't depend on Miranda being a good sport. She's not built for it."

"Could she have him put in jail?"

"Judges and juries decide things like that, lawyers don't."

"If there's any chance he'll be punished, I've got to warn him to stay away."

"Why?"

"You read the letter," she said with a wry little smile. "He's an old friend and I'm a real peach. Aren't us real peaches expected to do things like that?"

"I guess you are."

"Well?"

"Check with Miranda. She might not want him punished any more than you do. Ask her."

"I can't ask her without letting on that I've heard from him and know where he is."

"Make it a hypothetical question."

"I don't believe I could fool her. We've become pretty well acquainted during the past six months."

"How?"

"Seeing each other here at the club. She isn't a member anymore, she can't afford the dues, but she comes in with Admiral Young's daughters. While they swim and have lunch she talks to me in the office. She could swim and have lunch if she wanted to—Mr. Henderson would be glad to bend the rule about employees of members not being allowed the privileges of members. She won't accept any favors, though. Or maybe she just likes to get away from the girls whenever she can . . . Did you know she was working?"

"I met her on the street a couple of weeks ago. She told me you'd gotten her a job."

"Not really. It was my suggestion, that's all. She wasn't trained for anything except being a lady, and there's not much demand for teaching ladyness or ladyship or whatever. Then I thought of Admiral Young's daughters and I suggested to him one day that perhaps Miranda Shaw could teach the girls some of the social graces they lacked. He approved of the idea."

"The girls were with Miranda when I saw her," Aragon said. "I didn't notice much improvement in their ladyshipness."

"No results were guaranteed. I doubt that the Admiral expected any. He's a wise man, he was probably only trying to help Miranda."

"And you?"

"What do you mean *and me?*"

"What was your motive?"

"I'm a nice girl," she said. "Haven't you noticed?"

"Yes. I also noticed you'd been crying. Why?"

"I went to a sad movie. Or I saw a little dog that looked like one I had when I was a kid. Or I remembered my favorite aunt who died last year. Check one of the above."

"Check none of the above. And you mustn't add your tears to 'all that water under the bridge' Grady mentioned."

"How can I avoid it?"

"Don't answer his letter. Don't tell him to come, don't warn him to stay away. Just stay out of it."

"That's a lot of advice in return for a stale cup of coffee."

"I drank the coffee. Are you going to take the advice?"

"Sorry, it's too late," she said. "I sent him the application form yesterday afternoon."

The girls liked to put on their pajamas and eat dinner in the upstairs sitting room with their cat, Snowball, while watching television. Miranda's arrival had changed all that. She insisted they appear at the table properly dressed, on their best behavior and without the cat. This rule applied especially when guests were expected.

Retired military friends of the Admiral stopped on their way through town now and then, and once a month Charles Van Eyck came to see his sister, Iris, motivated not so much by duty as by expedience. Iris possessed a great deal of money which she would one day have to abandon for more spiritual satisfactions. Though considerably younger than he, she was unwell and unhappy and the combination gave him hopes of outliving her. These hopes changed daily like the stock market, gaining a few points here, losing a few there. As an investment the monthly dinner was becoming more and more speculative. Iris seemed to thrive on adversity. Arthritis and a recent heart attack gave her an excuse to do only what she wanted to do, and unhappiness made her oblivious to the needs and desires of other people and the fact that blood was thicker than water.

By his own standards Van Eyck was not greedy but he liked to think about money and he enjoyed its company. He studied his savings-account books and various senior citizens' publications. He visited his safety-deposit boxes and later he would sit in the lobby eating the free cookies and drinking the free coffee. He knew that the cookies and coffee were not actually free, that he was paying for them one way or another, so he ate and drank as much as he could before bank employees started giving him dirty looks. The dirty looks were free.

Lately Van Eyck had another reason for his regular visits to his sister. He distrusted all women, especially the pretty ones like Miranda Shaw. When she was first hired he wrote an anonymous letter to his sister which began *You have taken a Jezzebel into your home . . .* For several days he carried the letter around in his pocket in a sealed stamped correctly addressed envelope, afraid to post it. Iris with her sharp mind and suspicious nature might trace it back to him, and besides, he had a nagging doubt about the spelling of Jezebel. Jezebelle was more literal, Jezebell had a ring to it, Jezebel looked somehow unfinished. He thought of burning the letter but he hated to waste the stamp and some of the clever descriptive material about Miranda Shaw, so he sent it anyway.

To Miranda herself, who opened the door for him, he was polite, even gallant.

"Ah, my dear, how elegant you look this evening."

"Thank you, Mr. Van Eyck. Mrs. Young and the Admiral will be down shortly. May I pour you a drink?"

"Pour ahead."

"Your usual Scotch on the rocks?"

"One rock. I'm very Scotch."

It was his favorite joke and entirely original, but all Miranda did was smile with one side of her mouth as if she were saving the other side for a later and a better joke. He changed the subject abruptly. There was no use aiming his best shots into a wilderness.

"What are we having for dinner?"

"Beef Wellington."

"Why can't we ever have something tasty like pot roast or chicken stew with dumplings?"

"The housekeeper received a French cookbook for Christmas."

"Wellington was an English duke. Very cheeky of them to name a French dish after him. I intend to pour ketchup all over it."

"I do wish you wouldn't, Mr. Van Eyck. The housekeeper was very perturbed last time."

"I'll go out to the kitchen, find the ketchup wherever she's hidden it and bring it right to the table. Beef Wellington indeed. The poor man is probably turning over in his grave smothered in all that greasy foreign pastry."

"Please reconsider about the ketchup," Miranda said. "It will set a bad example for the girls."

The girls were all ready for a bad example. Inside the confines of their best dresses they squirmed and sighed and made faces. Cordelia's lime-green silk had a sash so tight it divided her in two like an egg-timer, and Juliet wore her tattletale dress, a bouffant taffeta that responded noisily to the most discreet movement, crackling, rustling, complaining, almost as though it had a life of its own.

The girls sat side by side at the mahogany table across from Van Eyck and Miranda, who had done the setting herself—silver bowls floating camellias and miniature candles, and crystal bird vases with sprigs of daphne that scented the whole room. The Admiral at the head of the table complimented Miranda on the decorations, but Iris, opposite him, said she hated candles, flickering lights always gave her a migraine. She asked Cordelia to blow out the candles.

"I can't," Cordelia said.

"Why not?"

"I haven't enough breath. My dress is too tight. I think I'm going to faint."

"So am I," Juliet said loyally.

Their mother didn't seem particularly interested. She had the little poodle, Alouette, on her lap and was feeding it bits of shrimp from her seafood cocktail.

The sight infuriated Cordelia. "I don't see why you can bring that dog to the table and we're not allowed to bring Snowball, who loves shrimp. Shrimp is his very favorite thing."

"What were you saying about your dress, Cordelia?"

"It's too tight. I can't breathe. I'm going to faint."

"Don't be tiresome."

"I mean it. I'm going . . . here I go . . . one, two—"

"Well, hurry up and get it over with so the rest of us can eat. The food will be cold."

"You don't *care*."

"Of course I do," Iris said. "I'm hungry."

Frustrated, Cordelia turned her wrath on her uncle. "It's all your fault. We had to dress like this just for you."

Van Eyck looked surprised. "Like what?"

"This."

"Up." Juliet said. "We had to dress up like this just for you."

"Really? Whose bizarre idea was that?"

"Hers." Both girls answered simultaneously, scowling at Miranda across the table.

"She said well-bred young ladies always dress up for company," Cordelia explained. "And I said Uncle Charles isn't company, he's only a relative. And Juliet said you wouldn't notice anyway because you'd be three sheets to the wind."

"You said that about me, Juliet?"

"I may have," Juliet said. "But she's a pig to bring it up."

"Unfortunately, my dear nieces, I am not three sheets to the wind. I am not even one sheet or two, let alone three. But I'm certainly working on it . . . Cooper, let's have some of that special stuff you've been hoarding. I understand that when a military man retires he commandeers all the booze he can lay his hands on. Why not share it with us common folk who paid for it in the first place?"

Cooper Young had learned many years ago at Annapolis to eat quietly and quickly whatever was placed in front of him and retained this habit throughout his life. As a consequence, eating was not enjoyable but it was also not unbearable. He could listen without heartburn while Iris and the girls bickered during the salad course, and his brother-in-law, over the beef and asparagus, delivered a lecture on the sinful extravagances of the Pentagon. Cooper did not answer, did not argue. Now and again he glanced at Miranda, who was equally silent, and he noticed how skillfully she pretended to eat while only rearranging the food on her plate and raising an empty fork to her mouth.

Cherries jubilee.

Cordelia was allowed to flame the cherries as a reward for not fainting, and everyone was quiet while they burned. Then it was time for Miranda to provide the evening's entertainment, a report on the girls' progress since the last family dinner.

"This week," Miranda said, "we have been concentrating on attitudes that affect behavior, for example, self-fulfillment as opposed to selfish fulfillment. We made a list of questions to ask ourselves at the end of each day. We gave them a special name, didn't we, Juliet?"

"Yes, but—"

"What was it?"

"Questions for a summer night. But—"

"Can you recite them?"

"*I* can," Cordelia said, still basking in the warmth and glory of the cherries jubilee. "Questions for a summer night. Here they are:

"Have I earned something today?

"Have I learned something today?

"Have I helped someone?

"Have I felt glad to be alive?"

"How poetic," Iris said. "And what are the answers for a summer night?"

Juliet and her dress complained in unison. "I didn't know we were expected to have the answers, too. Memorizing the questions is hard enough. Anyway, it isn't even summer yet. By the time it comes, maybe I can think of some answers."

"Don't be an ass, there aren't any," Cordelia said crisply. "It's only a game."

"It can't be. A game is where somebody wins and somebody loses. I should know, I'm the one who always loses."

"No, you don't. You only remember the times you lose because you're such a rotten sport. I often let you win to avoid the sight of you bawling and blabbering."

Juliet appealed to Miranda, wistfully, "Is it only a game?"

"No indeed," Miranda said. "I believe they're very important questions."

"But how can I earn anything? I don't work."

"You could earn someone's respect and admiration. Any job well done is worthy of respect. Can you think of a job you did today?"

"I washed the cat, Snowball. He had fleas."

"You see? That's something you earned today, Snowball's gratitude."

"No. He hates being washed and he still has fleas. I got seven more bites on the belly."

"I've got at least twenty-five," Cordelia said.

"Not on the belly."

"I haven't searched there yet. Most of mine are on the wrists and ankles. They itch furiously but I don't dare scratch because Mrs. Young is looking."

Iris was listening as well as looking. "If you girls have fleas, I don't want you coming anywhere near my dog."

"We never do. *He* comes near *us.*"

"Then run away from him."

"He can run faster than we can. And also, he cheats by taking shortcuts under tables and things."

"I suggest," Miranda said, "that we consider the second question. Have you learned something today?"

Cordelia related what she'd learned, that the Pentagon was spending billions of dollars each year on uniforms and pensions while the average citizen was being taxed into oblivion. Van Eyck, with his second sheet to the wind and going for three, applauded vigorously and said by God, at least there was one sensible person in the family besides himself.

Juliet couldn't think of anything she'd learned for the first time, though she had learned for the fourteenth or fifteenth time that cats didn't like to be bathed and neither did fleas but it wasn't fatal to either.

In spite of her makeup Miranda was beginning to look pale. "Perhaps we should go on to the third question. Have you helped someone today?"

"They have helped me decide to go to bed," Iris said and slid the little dog off her lap and onto the floor. "Miranda, I'd like to speak to you privately up in my room . . . Cooper, show Charles to his car and don't give him any more to drink . . . Goodnight, Charles. It was good of you to come. Take care of your liver."

She was tired. Her thin yellowing face sagged with fatigue and she had to use the table and her cane to hoist herself to her feet. It was a heavy antique cane she'd brought from Africa, where it had once been part of a tribal chiefs ceremonial uniform. Iris continued to think of it like that, as an adjunct to her costume, and she refused even to try the lightweight aluminum crutches prescribed by her doctor. Crutches were for cripples. Her cane was a piece of history and a symbol of command, not dependence.

The procession moved up the staircase, slow and solemn as a funeral march, Iris leaning on the banister and her cane, taking one step at a time. Miranda walked behind her, then the two girls, and finally the little dog, Alouette. The shrimp and cherries had given Alouette the hiccups and their rhythmic sound accompanied the procession like the beat of a ghostly drum.

The Admiral escorted his brother-in-law to the front door.

"Iris is damned rude," Van Eyck said, straightening his tie and brushing off his coat as if he'd been physically ejected. "*She's* the one who should be taking lessons in the social amenities, though it's about fifty years too late."

"I'm sorry you feel insulted."

"My liver is a very personal thing. I may never return to this house."

"We shall miss you, Charles."

"Don't be in such a hurry to miss me. I haven't left yet. I might change my mind and take that nightcap you offered me."

"I didn't offer you one."

"Why not?"

"Iris told me not to."

"But she's gone to bed. This is between you and me."

"I'm afraid not," the Admiral said. "Now do you think you'll be able to get home all right? If there's any doubt, I can drive you or call a cab."

"Don't worry about me, old boy. Just take care of yourself."

"What do you mean, Charles?"

"She's a sleek little filly, that Miranda, with plenty of mileage left in her. And don't tell me you didn't notice. I saw you staring at her."

"I don't believe we should refer to a lady in terms of horseflesh."

"You didn't stare at her as if she was a lady," Van Eyck said. "You old Navy men never change. Girl in every port, that sort of thing."

"I never had a girl in every port. Hardly any port, as a matter of fact."

"Why not? I understand the military feel that it's their prerogative to—"

"Go home, Charles."

"That's damned rude."

"Yes."

"I'm a taxpayer."

"Yes."

"You'll rue the day."

"I've lost count of the days I'm going to rue," the Admiral said, opening the door. "Probably up in the thousands by this time . . . Goodnight, Charles. Drive carefully. The Pentagon can't afford to lose a taxpayer."

The girls listened at the door of Iris's room on the second floor. They could hear her talking to Miranda in the loud firm voice that was stronger than the rest of her and needed no support from cane or crutches. The words were too fast to be intelligible. They crashed into each other and splintered into sharp angry syllables.

"She's mad," Cordelia said. "Well, for once *we* didn't do anything."

Juliet wasn't so sure. "Maybe we did, unbeknownst."

"We never do anything unbeknownst. It's always spelled right out. She's probably mad at *her.*"

"I wonder why."

"Maybe it was those questions for a summer night. The whole thing's pretty silly when you think of it. Why not a winter night? Or autumn?"

"Summer sounds better."

"But it's not sensible. On summer nights people are outside barbecuing steaks or playing tennis. It's on winter nights they have nothing to do but sit around making up dumb questions."

"I hate those questions," Juliet said. "I just hate them. They give me the glooms."

"Don't be an ass. They're only words."

"No. She means them. 'Have I earned something today?' How can I earn something when I don't have a job? Maybe we should run away and get jobs, Cordelia. Do you think we could?"

"No."

"Not even a lowly type like washing dishes in a restaurant?"

"They don't wash dishes in restaurants. They toss them into a machine."

"Someone has to toss them. We could be tossers."

"I don't want to be a tosser," Cordelia said. "Now wake up and smell the coffee. We're not good for anything, so we might as well enjoy it."

The heavy oak door of Iris's room opened and Miranda came into the hall with the poodle, Alouette, on a leash beside her. The girls hid behind a bookcase and watched her go down the stairs. She moved very slowly, as if she was tired, while the little dog strained at the leash trying to pull her along.

"We never get to walk the dog anymore since *she* came," Cordelia said. "It's not fair."

"We could walk the cat."

"No, we can't. We tried that once and Snowball just sat down and wouldn't budge. We had to drag him around the block and someone reported us to the Humane Society and they sent a man out to investigate."

Juliet's memory was soft and warm as a pillow. She remembered the Humane Society incident as a nice young man stopping his truck to make complimentary remarks about the cat; and the Singapore incident, which Cordelia frequently referred to in a sinister manner, Juliet couldn't remember at all. She took her sister's word that it had happened (whatever it was) because Cordelia had more sophistication and experience than she did, being two years older. By virtue of this age gap, and the phenomenal number of things that must have occurred during it, Cordelia had become an authority who dispensed information and advice like a vending machine.

"In fact," Cordelia said, "we're not allowed to do practically anything since she came. We may have to get rid of her. It shouldn't be too hard if we plan ahead."

"I'm sick of always talking about her. I want to talk about us for a change. You and me."

"What about us."

"Do you think we'll ever get a second chance?"

"To do what?"

"Be born. Will we ever be born again?"

"I hope to Christ not," Cordelia said. "Once was bad enough."

"But it might be different if we had a second chance. We might be good for something. We might even be pretty. And something else. This time *I* might be born first, two years ahead of *you*."

Juliet knew immediately that she'd gone too far. She turned and ran down the hall to her room, locking the door behind her and barricading it with a bureau in case Cordelia decided to pick the lock with one of her credit cards.

She took a shower and before putting on her pajamas she counted her fleabites. Twenty-eight. A record. She scratched them all until they bled. If she bled to death, right then and there, she would speed up her chances of being born again, brilliant, beautiful and two years ahead of Cordelia.

At ten thirty the Admiral began closing up the house for the night, checking each room for security purposes, making sure that windows were locked and no intruders lurked in closets or behind doors. The job took a long time partly because he enjoyed it and partly because there were so many rooms, some of them never or hardly ever used.

The drawing room, off the foyer, was opened only for formal entertaining. Its elegant little gold chairs looked too fragile to hold a sitter and its Aubusson rugs too exquisite to be stepped on. The walls were hung with gilt-framed family portraits which had, like most of the furniture, been included in the purchase price of the house. For reasons of her own, Iris allowed visitors to think the pictures were of her ancestors, but in fact the amply proportioned ladies and the men with their muttonchop whiskers were as unknown as the artists who painted them. The thrifty Dutchmen who were Iris's real ancestors would have considered such portraits a sinful extravagance.

Next to the living room was the conservatory, which contained an old rosewood grand piano with a broken pedal and ivory keys yellow as saffron. Now and then the Admiral would sit down at the piano and try to pick out melodies he'd learned in his youth: "Shenandoah," "The Blue Bells of Scotland," "Poor Wayfaring Stranger," "Flow Gently, Sweet Afton." But no matter how softly he played, how tightly the doors and windows were closed, Iris always heard and thumped with her cane or sent the housekeeper or the girls to tell him to stop. He opened the lid of the piano, played the first few bars of Brahms' "Lullaby" and replaced the lid almost before any of the notes had a chance to climb the stairs. Then he went on with his job of checking the house.

The solarium, facing south, had an inside wall faucet and a tile floor that slanted down to a screened hole in the middle in order to allow the draining of plants after they were watered. There was only one plant left in the place, a weeping fig which had grown too large to move. The Admiral watered it every night, knowing that at some time, perhaps quite soon, the fig would break out of its clay prison. He usually stayed in this room longer than in any of the others, as though he wanted to be a witness to the plant's exact moment of escape, to hear the noise (big or small? he had no idea) and see a crack in the clay (perhaps a series of cracks, a shattering, an explosion, a room full of shards).

Across the hall the game room had walnut-paneled walls and a billiard table with a rip in it. Year after year the Admiral postponed having the rip repaired. It unnerved the very good players, thus giving the poorer ones like himself a psychological advantage. Beside the library there was a sewing room where no one sewed. Perhaps when the house had been built it was the custom for the women to do petit point or embroidery while the men played billiards. Now the space was a catchall for steamer trunks and suitcases, the housekeeper's reducing machine, a pair of carved teakwood chests Iris had carted halfway around the world, a vacuum cleaner that didn't work, the ski equipment the girls had used at their school in Geneva. Though the equipment was well worn, the boots scuffed, the webs of the poles bent out of shape, he was amazed that the girls had ever skied. Juliet seemed too timid to try, Cordelia too reckless to survive. No matter how hard he attempted to picture them skiing in a nice average way down a nice average slope, he could only imagine Cordelia plunging headlong from Mt. Blanc like an avalanche and Juliet having to be dragged up the smallest knoll and pushed down screaming. Perhaps there never were any nice average slopes in the girls' lives.

The library was in another wing of the house. It had brown leather chairs that smelled of saddle soap. The floor-to-ceiling shelves of books were behind glass and the mantel of the fireplace was decorated with ceramic songbirds. It was a comfortable room, but the Admiral rarely sat there to read or to watch the fire. The bookshelves were locked and he could never remember where he'd put the key; and because of a defective damper the fireplace smoked badly and all the birds had turned grey as if from old age.

The adjoining room was where Iris spent most of her time. Here, too, there was a fireplace, but its logs were artificial and its flames gas. Iris wasn't strong enough to handle real logs in a real grate. Sometimes she couldn't even light the gas without help from Miranda or the housekeeper. The Admiral turned off the gas and the lamp by Iris's reading chair and the other lamp that lit the table where half a dozen miniature chess sets were laid out, each with a game in progress. These were the games Iris was playing by mail with people in other parts of the world. To the Admiral it seemed a little like war to have unseen opponents in foreign countries planning strategic moves against you. But no blood was shed, nothing was lost but prestige.

The kitchen and the rooms beyond it he left alone. They were the working and living quarters of Mrs. Norgate, the housekeeper, and he depended on her as he would have depended on a chief petty officer to keep her part of the ship tight and tidy.

He returned to the front of the house at the same time as Miranda was coming in the door with the little poodle. She'd put a coat over the formal dress she'd worn at dinner, but it offered little protection from the spring fog. She looked cold and damp and her voice was hoarse.

"Alouette wanted to come home. He acts afraid of the dark lately."

"He might have trouble with his vision," the Admiral said. "I understand poodles often do as they get older. Perhaps I should take him to the vet."

"What happens to their vision?"

"Cataracts, I believe."

"Like people."

"Yes. Like people."

She let the dog off the leash and it bounded up the stairs. "He seems all right now. Maybe he simply wanted to get back to his mistress."

"Miranda—"

"I'd better go upstairs and open the door for him so that Mrs. Young won't be disturbed."

"Miranda, I'm sorry about the dinner tonight."

"*You're* sorry?" she repeated. "That's funny, I was just going to tell you that *I* was sorry. It was my responsibility. I should have made better plans."

"No, no. Your plans were fine. Those 'questions for a summer night,' I thought that was an excellent idea."

"Mrs. Young didn't."

"Mrs. Young's illness makes her hard to please. You mustn't take her opinions too seriously. She doesn't mean to disparage your abilities."

"She means to and she's right. I'm not qualified for a position like this, I'm not qualified for anything. It's useless for me to keep on pretending."

"Sit down, Miranda. I'll get you a drink to warm you up."

There was a bench along one wall that looked as if it had once been a pew in a small church. She sat down, shivering, pulling the coat around her. It was several sizes too large. The poodle had been in such a hurry to go out that she'd grabbed the coat out of the hall closet without knowing or caring whom it belonged to.

"A drink won't change how I feel," she said.

"It might. Let me—"

"Those questions for a summer night, what a joke. Hundreds of summer nights have passed, and fall and winter and spring, and I couldn't answer one of those questions positively. I haven't earned or learned or helped or felt glad to be alive."

"You've made me feel glad to be alive."

"You mustn't say nice things like that. You'll make me cry."

"Please don't. I insist you don't, Miranda."

Her face was hidden in the collar of the coat, her voice barely audible. "All right."

"You won't cry."

"No."

"Promise?"

"I promise."

"Thank you." He cleared his throat as if it were his voice, not hers, being muffled in the folds of the coat. "Actually you're the best thing that's happened to this household for a long time and we're all grateful to you. I hope you're not planning to leave."

"I'm not accomplishing anything here."

"But you are. There's a definite improvement in the girls' behavior. They're less self-centered, more responsive to other people. At dinner, for instance, they talked directly to their Uncle Charles instead of around him to each other. Did you notice that?"

"Everyone noticed," she said. "Especially Uncle Charles."

"It was a step up from ignoring him, as they're in the habit of doing. But I'm not only thinking of the girls when I ask you to stay with us. I'm being quite selfish. In fact—well, you must be aware of how happy I am in your presence, Miranda."

"No." She'd hardly been aware of him at all except as a figure in the background, like one of Iris's ivory and wooden chess pieces. Now suddenly he was stepping off the board alive, making sounds, having feelings, being happy and unhappy. It frightened her. She wanted him to step back on the chessboard where he belonged.

The girls, reconciled by this time, were hiding behind the railing at the top of the stairs.

"He said he was happy with her presents," Juliet whispered. "I've never seen her give him any presents. I wonder what kind they are."

"Use your imagination, stupid."

"You mean hanky-panky? Surely they wouldn't commit hanky-panky with Mrs. Young right in the house."

"They wouldn't have to. Pops has tons of room in the back seat of the Rolls."

"Do you think we should tell Mrs. Young?"

"My God, no," Cordelia said. "She'd probably blame us. Let her find out for herself."

Miranda stayed for two months.

During this time the weather remained cold and Van Eyck blamed it on the environmentalist members of the municipal government, accusing them of trying to limit the city's growth by controlling the weather. He wasn't sure how this was being done, but he wrote letters to alert the daily newspaper, the Chamber of Commerce and, in case more inspired revelations and clout were necessary, the bishop of the Episcopalian diocese.

At the beginning of June, Frederic Quinn was released from the high-priced detention facility Sophrosune School, and before being transported to the high-priced detention facility Camp Sierra Williwaw, he had a whole month of freedom. He intended to make the most of it.

He collected a dozen starfish from the wharf pilings and put them in the ovens at the club to dry out. The ensuing stench permeated the ballroom, drifted through the corridors into the cabanas, hung over the pool and terrace. The entire staff was pressed into service to track down the source, but no one thought of opening the ovens until it was time to start cooking for the Saturday night banquet.

Mr. Henderson immediately blamed Frederic, who had made the common criminal mistake of hanging around to see how things turned out.

"By God, this time you've gone too far, you bastard."

"I didn't do it, I didn't, I didn't!"

He swore his innocence on the small Bible which he carried around in his pocket for this very purpose. It was one of the more useful things he had learned at Sophrosune School.

Some of his exploits were more or less in the interests of science. He jumped off the thirty-three-foot diving platform holding a beach umbrella to see if it could be used as a parachute. It couldn't. After that, the cast on his left wrist curtailed his activities to a certain extent but he was still able to let the air out of Mr. Henderson's tires and to put red dye into the Jacuzzi when little Miss Reach was dozing. She woke up, assumed she was bleeding and began to scream to the full capacity of her ninety-year-old lungs. When a stem to stern, inch by inch examination by a number of bystanders proved that she wasn't bleeding, she was rather disappointed. Her whole life had been passing before her eyes and she was just coming to an interesting part.

That same week Charity Nelson reached retirement age. She didn't tell her boss, Smedler, or anyone else at the office, since she had no intention of retiring. Instead she celebrated by herself with two bottles of Cold Duck. Halfway through the second bottle she became quite sentimental and decided to phone her first husband, who lived somewhere in New Jersey. By the time she'd tracked him down to Hackensack and learned his phone number she couldn't remember why she was calling him.

"Hello, George. How are you?"

"It's three o'clock in the morning, that's how I am."

"Your clock must be wrong. Mine says twelve."

"Who is this?"

"Oh, George, how could you forget our anniversary?"

"I'm not having an anniversary. You sound stinko."

"George, I *am* stinko."

"Who the hell is this, anyway?"

"This is me," Charity said. "Me."

She hung up. Men were beasts.

In mid-June, Grady Keaton returned to work at the Penguin Club. The girls brought the news home as their contribution to the dinner entertainment that night, but the Admiral was dining out and Iris was confined to her room, so they had only Miranda to contribute it to.

"That lifeguard is back again," Cordelia said. "The one who locked Frederic Quinn in the first aid room. Remember, Miranda?"

"No." Miranda raised an empty fork to her mouth, chewed air, swallowed. "No."

"You were there."

"I don't remember."

"*I* do," Juliet said. "All hell broke loose. And afterwards Frederic threw up all over your dress and everybody could see what he'd been eating, ugh."

"This isn't a very appetizing subject for the dinner table, Juliet."

"It doesn't bother me."

"Or me," Cordelia agreed. "I don't see why it's all right to talk about food while you're eating it but not when you throw it up."

"Stop it, girls, this very minute . . . Now let's start over on a more civilized level. Tell me what you did today that was interesting."

"We already told you about seeing the lifeguard who's back working at the club. We forget his name."

"Grady," Miranda said. "I think that was his name—Grady."

She went down to the club the next afternoon while the girls were at a movie. She stood outside looking in at the pool through the glass door. Grady was leaning against the steel frame of the lifeguard tower, his arms crossed on his chest, an orange-colored visor shading his face. He seemed smaller than she remembered, as though someone had located a vital plug and let some of the air out of him. He had shaved off his mustache—some girl probably asked him to or asked him not to. She wondered how many girls there'd been in the eight months and three days since Pasoloma.

She wanted to leave, to go back to the Admiral's house and hide in her room, but she couldn't force her limbs to move. She stood there for such a long time that one of the porters came out of the club and asked her if she needed help. He was a young Mexican who spoke the Spanglish of the barrio.

She said, "No, I'm fine. I was just about to leave."

"Okay?"

"Yes. *Thank you.* Muchas gracias."

"Por nada."

He reminded her of the boy in the dining room of the clinic, Pedro. Grady had promised him a ride in the Porsche, but Grady wasn't very successful at keeping promises. The instant they rolled off his tongue they rolled out of his head and heart. "*I never said anything about marriage or commitment or forever . . . Jeez, I'm not a forever-type guy, Miranda.*"

Poor Grady, he didn't recognize what was good for him, he would have to be forced into doing the right thing.

As soon as she returned home she called Ellen. She used the kitchen phone because it was the only one in the house not connected to any of the others and nobody could listen in.

Ellen answered. "Penguin Club."

"Ellen?"

"Yes."

"Why didn't you tell me Grady is back?"

"I wasn't sure how you'd take it."

"I'm taking it very well, thank you. How long has he been here?"

"A week."

"A whole week and you never said a word to me."

"I intended to, but—"

"Are you trying to keep us apart?"

"You are apart, Miranda. You've been apart for a long time."

"No," Miranda said. "Not for a minute. Perhaps Grady doesn't realize it yet, but I do. He came back here to see me."

"He needed a job and Mr. Henderson agreed to rehire him."

"That's simply a cover-up."

"Miranda, please—"

"Oh, I won't rush him. I'll give him a little time to adjust and then I'll arrange a meeting. I've saved enough money to buy a whole new outfit. Grady likes soft silky things."

"Stop it, Miranda. He hasn't even asked after you."

"Of course not. He's too subtle for that. He wouldn't ask you anyway. It's been obvious from the beginning that you've had a hopeless crush on him."

"You just won't listen to reason, will you?"

"Not yours," Miranda said. "You're not my friend anymore."

To celebrate the July Fourth holiday Mr. Henderson planned a special event for the club. It was his most inspired idea since the Easter Egos costume ball where everybody came dressed as the person they would most like to be resurrected as. (Toward the end of the evening two of the resurrectees, Héloïse and Abelard, staged a knockdown drag-out fight. This didn't spoil the party, since it was generally viewed as part of the entertainment, especially the choking scene. A number of volunteers gave Héloïse artificial respiration, but she survived anyway and a good time was had by nearly all.)

The July celebration, which Henderson called a Wing Ding, was given the theme Unidentified Flying Objects. Denied a special permit for a fireworks display on the beach in front of the club—fireworks were illegal throughout the state—Henderson rented a barge and had it anchored offshore as a base for the *fuegos artificiales* he'd brought across the border from Tijuana. The display was a great success until the Coast Guard literally cast a damper on it by dousing the barge with a firehose.

Henderson wasn't the only miscreant. The police and sheriff's deputies were busy all over town trying to enforce the ban on fireworks. From the barrio along the railroad tracks to the elegant old streets which zigzagged up through the foothills the night was alive with the explosions and flashes of homemade bombs and mail-order or under-the-counter shooting stars and Roman candles and whiz-bangs.

An extra loud explosion at 1220 Camino Grande attracted no special attention until a passing motorist saw flames shooting out of a window and called the fire department. By the time the flames were extinguished Iris Young was dead.

Part V

IRIS'S SITTING ROOM was officially sealed off and both the damaged wall and the door were boarded up to prevent further collapse.

Police poked around in the rubble, carrying away boxes of ashes and shattered glass, burned sections of tables and window frames and splinters of lamps, the disemboweled chair where Iris normally sat, her record albums melted now into masses of black glue, the charred remnant of the cane she always used, her mutilated chess pieces blown around the room like men in war.

The people living in the house were questioned and requestioned, separately and together, and bit by bit the circumstances of Iris's final hours emerged. During the afternoon she listened to a new album of *Tosca* while paying some bills and balancing her checkbook. She did some typing. She finished a mystery story she'd been reading. She executed her next moves in the chess game she was playing by mail with the professor in Tokyo and the medical missionary in Jakarta and gave both letters to Miranda to mail.

In the evening she was alone in the house. At her urging the Admiral took the girls to the fireworks display at the club. The housekeeper, Mrs. Norgate, went to babysit her infant grandson. And Miranda was out walking the dog, who had suffered a digestive upset after eating a chocolate éclair.

It was a warm night, but Iris's poor circulation made her susceptible to cold and even in summer she frequently used the gas log in her sitting room downstairs. Miranda offered to light it for her before she left the house. Iris refused. She was in a bad mood as well as in pain. She had appeared at dinner only long enough to complain that the vegetables were overcooked, the beef roast tough and the candles gave her a migraine.

Miranda took the dog to Featherstone Park, half a mile down the hill toward the sea. He seemed to feel better out in the open air, so they stayed for quite a while, the dog lying beside her while she sat on a bench listening to the night explode around her. When she returned to the house the driveway was blocked by police cars and fire engines and a small crowd of curiosity seekers being held back by men in uniform.

"What's happened? Let me past. I live here. Mrs. Young . . . I've got to see if Mrs. Young is all right."

As in all cases of violent death under unusual circumstances, an autopsy was performed. Though the body was severely burned, enough blood and tissue samples were recovered to confirm that the actual cause of death was smoke inhalation. The evidence indicated that while Iris was attempting to light the gas log she'd lost her balance and fallen. A frontal head injury rendered her unconscious and unable to escape the subsequent explosion and fire.

When the body was finally released for burial a memorial service was held in the chapel of the mortuary. The Admiral kept his head bowed throughout the proceedings. Charles Van Eyck, lulled by the minister's voice and three double martinis, drifted into sleep. Now and then Miranda dabbed at her eyes with a lace handkerchief very carefully to avoid smudging her mascara. The girls kept staring at the closed coffin as though they half expected it might open and out would pop Iris, having decided she didn't like being dead.

Cordelia was openly critical of the nature and length of the service. "It's so silly, the minister yapping away about God and heaven when Mrs. Young didn't believe a word of that stuff."

"It's better to be on the safe side," Juliet said. "Just in case."

"In case what?"

"In case it's all true. Besides, it's not hurting anyone."

"It's hurting me. I'm hungry."

"Shut up. I want to hear about heaven."

Even after Iris's burial the damaged door of her sitting room remained boarded up and no workmen were allowed in to start cleaning up and rebuilding. A guard was kept in the hall to enforce the rule.

The girls, perturbed not so much by the death of their mother as by the disruption of their normal routine, hung around the hall trying to get answers and assurances, especially from the day guard, a red-haired young man named Grella.

"We thought the investigation was over and done with," Cordelia said. "Why are you still here?"

"Orders."

"That's not a real answer."

"Best I can do," Grella said. "The fact is, the reports haven't come back from Sacramento yet, and until then—"

"Why Sacramento?"

"That's where the crime lab is."

"What do they do there?"

"Analyze evidence to try and find out exactly what happened."

"It's perfectly clear what happened. Mrs. Young fell while she was lighting the gas log and hit her head. I'm not a bit surprised. She was always bumping into things and getting mad about it and cussing to beat hell."

"We're Navy, you know," Juliet explained, "we learned all the cuss words years ago. But we're not allowed to use them except in the privacy of our own rooms, like chewing gum. You're chewing gum right now, aren't you?"

"Yeah, I guess I am."

"Are you allowed?"

"I think so. I never asked."

"You'd better ask."

"Let's stick to the subject," Cordelia said sharply. "Why is the lab in Sacramento taking such a long time?"

"They're busy. They test evidence sent to them from every place in California."

"That's just physical evidence. Somebody should test the other more important kind of evidence, like what such and such a person said to so-and-so. We know plenty of that stuff."

"No kidding."

"Only nobody will listen."

"I'll listen," Grella said. He didn't have much else to do anyway except, as Juliet had observed, chew gum.

The girls conferred in whispers behind cupped hands, Juliet frowning and looking worried. She would rather have limited the conversation to nice friendly things like gum and the weather and the Navy, which wouldn't offend anyone, with the possible exception of Uncle Charles, who didn't care very much for the Navy. But Cordelia wasn't passing up her chance at an audience.

"Well, first of all," she said, "Mrs. Young had a terrible temper. And every year it got worse. When she went on a rampage she yelled and screamed and threw things. One day she even hit Miranda on the arm with her cane and Pops had to raise Miranda's salary two hundred dollars a month so she wouldn't quit."

"No kidding," Grella said. "Who's Miranda?"

"Oh, you've seen her floating and fluttering around the house. Mrs. Shaw. She's supposed to be teaching us etiquette, which is really dumb because we never go any place we can use it."

"What happened after she got the two-hundred-a-month raise?"

"She stayed. And she used the extra money to buy him presents."

"Mrs. Shaw bought your father presents?"

"Yes."

"Like what?"

"We don't know."

"You didn't see them?"

"No. But we heard him thank her for them. It was one night after Uncle Charles had been here for dinner. Miranda and Pops were standing right in this very hall."

"And where were you?"

Cordelia indicated the railing at the top of the stairs. "Up there. It's our favorite place for finding out what's going on when nobody will tell us."

"So what went on?"

"It was a kind of a mushy scene, with her playing the little woman and him apologizing for the way Mrs. Young treated her and saying don't cry, please don't cry. Sickening. Nobody ever asks *me* not to cry, let alone tacking a please onto it."

"Then what?"

"He thanked her for the presents, said he was very happy with them."

"Your father and Mrs. Shaw, were they chummy? That is, did they . . . ?"

"We think so," Juliet said a little sadly. "Probably in the back seat of the Rolls-Royce."

Blushing, Grella looked down at his feet, which were still there, and then at the door of Iris's sitting room, which wasn't. "Did you witness this—ah, this—"

"Hanky-panky," Cordelia said. "That's what we call it. Everyone knows what we're talking about but it's not vulgar. No, we didn't actually witness it. There were signs though, plenty of them, smiles and stares, touchings that might have looked accidental but weren't."

"Did your mother suspect what was going on?"

"Maybe. She couldn't hear very well but she had eyes like a hawk. Of course, *we* didn't say a word to her about it. She'd have gotten mad at *us*."

"Why?"

"Everyone does."

"This is a very interesting development," Grella said. "I'm not sure what I ought to do about it."

"You ought to tell that lab up in Sacramento there are lots of things they won't find out in test tubes."

Grella didn't tell the lab but he told his sergeant and the sergeant told his lieutenant. There was general agreement that the hanky-panky in the Rolls-Royce put a different light on the case.

On a morning in mid-July, Aragon was summoned to Smedler's office.

Charity was waiting for him when he stepped out of Smedler's private elevator. She had just finished misting her plants and the room was as hot and wet as an equatorial jungle. Beads of moisture clung to her red wig, which was draped over a life-sized bust of President Kennedy.

Charity saw him staring at it. "A work of art, isn't it? I got it at a swap meet over the weekend in exchange for my old muskrat jacket. I was passionately in love with Jack Kennedy, still am after all these years."

"It might cool your ardor if you turned on the air conditioning."

"My plants wouldn't like it."

"Don't tell them."

She wiped some of the moisture off the wig with a piece of Kleenex. "Better not come on funny today, junior. Boss man had another bash with his wife and now he's feeling guilty because he won. Guilt always gives him a migraine."

"What's he want from me?"

"How should I know? Maybe he wants to give you something."

"Like what?"

"His migraine."

Smedler was sitting behind his desk reading the morning mail. The bash with his wife had resulted in no visible scars, but even now his face was flushed and his hands had a very slight tremor.

He wasted only two words—"Sit down"—before coming to the point. "I saw in the newspaper a couple of weeks ago that Admiral Young's wife was killed in a fire. Know anything about it?"

"Only what I read in the newspaper account."

"Sketchy. Very sketchy. Makes me wonder . . . You aren't privy to any off-the-record stuff, are you?"

"No."

Smedler rubbed the left side of his neck and the area behind his left ear, which was a deeper color than the other ear. "I've played golf with the Admiral a couple of times. Nice quiet chap, hardly the type you'd suspect of fooling around."

"Who suspects him of fooling around?"

"My wife heard it on the grapevine at the country club. The rumor is that Miranda Shaw has been working at the Admiral's house in some capacity, and one capacity led to another capacity. I've instructed my wife not to repeat a story like that unless she's sure of the facts. It would be damned embarrassing for a man in my position to be sued for slander. Women don't realize the possible consequences of this gossip. Of course, it may not be gossip. Give me your personal opinion, Aragon. Does a relationship between the two of them seem feasible, considering his age, et cetera, et cetera?"

"The feasibility of a relationship depends on the number of et ceteras."

"Oh, for God's sake, don't talk like a lawyer. Are they sleeping together?"

"I don't know."

"Find out."

"How?"

"Miranda's a friend of yours."

"I spent a day and a half with her," Aragon said. "Most of the time I was driving and she was unconscious. That hardly adds up to a friendship."

"It's possible."

"It didn't happen. What's more, I don't consider it part of my job to pry into the love affairs of admirals."

"It's one admiral, not the whole U.S. Navy, and one love affair, not a history of Hollywood. All I'm asking is that you and Miranda should have a nice cozy talk over a couple of drinks.

If she indicates no personal interest in the Admiral, I'll muzzle my wife and that'll be the end of that . . . It's funny she was left alone in the house that night."

"Who?"

"Iris Young. As I understand it she was crippled. A wealthy woman like that would surely have someone around to look after her or at least to keep her company."

"She had Miranda."

"Yes," Smedler said dryly. "She had Miranda."

The death of Iris had dealt a fatal blow to Charles Van Eyck's social life. Her house was the last place in town where he was more or less welcome for dinner, and in spite of the mediocrity of the food, drink and conversation, he missed the invitations. To his surprise he also missed Iris. She'd been his last surviving relative—if he didn't count the girls, and he didn't—and he felt quite depressed at the idea of being the final Van Eyck, with nothing to leave behind as a memorial except his correspondence. Since most of this was unsigned, it didn't constitute much of a memorial.

Iris had found out about the anonymous letters when he made the mistake of writing one to her about Miranda, and the even worse mistake of not checking the spelling of the word Jezebel. She wasn't taken in by his denials. "People who live in glass houses," Iris had said, "should learn to spell. I can only guess you've been scattering these around the landscape like confetti. Do try not to get caught, Charles. It would embarrass the family."

He had not been caught. Concerned Citizen, One Who Knows, a Word to the Wise, Irate Taxpayer, Member of Loyal Opposition, Awake and Aware, Cassandra and Pentagon Pauper continued their correspondence.

It was a warm sunny afternoon. At the club Van Eyck sat in a deck chair under the twisted old cypress tree. He wore his writing costume: flowered Hawaiian shirt, walking shorts, a tennis visor and bifocals. He had a new refill in his pen and plenty of paper, which he'd snatched from the office while Ellen was on a coffee break. The tide was high but the waves gentle, so there was minimal noise to distract him. Still he was distracted. The pain in his left hip worried him. He thought of a mare he'd ridden as a child which had to be shot when she broke her leg. He wondered where he was going to spend Christmas Day now that Iris was dead. Finally he dozed off for an hour or so, and when he woke up he felt refreshed and the mare and the hip pain and Christmas were going out with the tide. Charles Van Eyck went with them and Seeker of Truth got down to business.

> *To the District Attorney of Santa Felicia County:*
> *Are the police deaf to the voice of a woman crying out from her grave for Justice?*
> *The fire which killed Iris Young was no ordinary fire, her husband no ordinary man, his employee, Miranda Shaw, no ordinary servant. One of these 3 people is dead.*
> *3-1 = 2*
> *2 = a pair*
> *Is this what the anguished voice from the grave is trying to tell you?*
> *Listen! Heed!*
> *This alert comes from:*
>
> *A Seeker of Truth*

As a precaution Seeker inked out the club name and address at the top of the page and the left-hand corner of the envelope. Truth didn't necessarily mean the Whole Truth.

Switching identities, Fair Play wrote a short note to the Admiral advising him to reject further pension payments now that he was a wealthy man, and to consider reimbursing the taxpayers for previous payments.

He lay back in the chair and closed his eyes. Righteousness flowed through his system like a spring tonic. The pain in his hip had disappeared, the broken-legged mare had been old anyway, and he would go to Waikiki for Christmas and eat poi and drink mai tais.

When Aragon phoned the Admiral's house a woman with an English accent told him Mrs. Shaw had taken the girls to the Penguin Club for lunch and a swim and would probably be gone all day. He called the club and talked to Ellen.

"She's here," Ellen said. "She's been showing up with the girls every day lately. The Ingersolls are letting her use their cabana while they're in South America and she just sits in it by herself."

"Why?"

"She wants to avoid people. Most people."

"Who's the exception?"

"Grady. He came back to work about a month ago."

"You don't sound very happy about it. Isn't that what you wanted?"

"Not like this." There was a short silence. "She's still crazy about him, sick-crazy. She sits up in that cabana posing and preening and staring down at him. He can't stand to look at her and she never takes her eyes off him."

"I heard it different. The rumors going the rounds of the country club are about her and the Admiral. What do you think of that?"

"Nothing. He's an old man."

"A rich old man."

"Forget it. I see her every day and I'm telling you the way she watches Grady is—How rich?"

"A whole bunch rich, you should know that."

"I knew his wife was rich, which isn't necessarily the same thing."

"There's no reason to believe he won't inherit a large part of her estate."

"But suppose—Oh, never mind. It was just a thought. I have to hang up now anyway. Henderson has an errand for me in town."

"I'd like to come down and talk to Miranda. Is that okay?"

"With me it is. With her maybe not."

"I can try."

"Try ahead," Ellen said. "If I'm not here, go right on up to cabana number twenty-one."

He left his car in the club parking lot. As he was walking across the street to the front door he saw Grady about fifty yards away heading for the employees' entrance at the back. Aragon waved at him but got no response. Either Grady didn't recognize him or didn't want to.

A wide thickly carpeted staircase led to the row of cabanas on the second floor. The impression of opulence ended abruptly at the top. The corridor was a kind of long dark tunnel dimly lit at each end by a sixty-watt bulb suspended from the ceiling. The brown wooden floor was strewn with swimmers' towels like mounds of dirty snow on a mud road.

He knocked on the door of 21 and Miranda's voice responded immediately.

"Who's there?"

"Tom Aragon."

"Aragon?" She opened the door. "My goodness, this *is* a surprise."

She sounded as though it was a pleasant one. Too pleasant. It made him vaguely uncomfortable.

She wore a pink and yellow silk caftan and her long hair hung loose over her shoulders. It was a couple of shades lighter than when he'd last seen her on the street with the two girls in April. Her hair wasn't the only change. In April she'd been a little depressed, resigned to her fate and not expecting any change for the better. Now she seemed in high spirits. Her eyes sparkled and she had an almost feverish color in her cheeks.

"Come in, Mr. Aragon, come in."

"Thank you."

"How did you find me? Oh—Ellen, of course. Dear little Ellen, she knows everybody's secrets, doesn't she?"

He considered the reference to Ellen inaccurate on all counts but he didn't challenge it.

The cabana was a small three-sided room furnished with webbed plastic chairs and chaise and a glass-topped table. The fourth side had a half-railing which showed the pool below, and beyond it the sea, and twenty miles to the southwest the hazy blue offshore island, a piece of mountain caught and held. Between the island and the shore were the oil platforms like isolated steel prisons built for incorrigibles.

After a few amenities—she was fine, he was fine, the weather was fine—she changed the subject abruptly.

"Grady's back," she said. "Did you know that?"

"I had a glimpse of him outside."

"Doesn't he look beautiful?"

"I—well, he was pretty far away. I'll take your word for it."

"You're probably laughing at me because men aren't supposed to be described as beautiful. Only what if they *are!* You might as well admit the truth."

"All right, I admit the truth," Aragon said. "Grady is a beautiful man."

She smiled. "That's better. He really *is,* believe me. You didn't see him at his best when you came down to Pasoloma with those papers for me to sign. He was in shock."

"I can understand why. Has he gotten over it?"

"Of course. He needed a little time to think, that's all. The instant we met again when he came back here to work I knew nothing had changed between us, that we were as much in love as ever. Naturally, he can't be obvious about it, but I catch him watching me out of the corner of his eye. It's so cute . . . Glance over the railing and see if he's down there now on the lifeguard tower."

"Yes."

"Is he staring up here?"

"No."

"He's very good at pretending to ignore me."

"Is that how you want it?"

"Of course it is. We can't afford to be seen together just yet. The police are everywhere. Fortunately Grady understands, he's being extremely tactful about the situation. He disappears the minute I enter the club and stays out of sight until I'm settled up here in the cabana. But it will be nice when we can act natural again."

"You claim the police are everywhere," Aragon said. "What are they doing?"

"Asking questions about Iris Young, every conceivable sort of question. And I'm sure they're getting every conceivable sort of answer, especially from the girls. Juliet and Cordelia are like children, they'll say anything to draw attention to themselves. I expect some of their statements will be critical of me. They've never liked me, they're not used to anyone giving them orders or even advice, but that's what I'm paid to do and I do it."

"According to the newspaper report, Iris Young was alone in the house the night she died."

"Yes."

"Why?"

"She wanted to be."

"I understand she was crippled."

"She wasn't helpless. She could walk with the aid of a cane, and God knows she could talk, or rather scream. When she got mad you could hear her for miles. Believe me, whatever happened in the house happened because she wanted it to, whether it was being left alone or being waited on hand and foot."

"What was her state of mind that night?"

"The same as it always was—selfish, mean, arrogant."

He hoped, for her sake, that this wasn't an example of her conversations with the police. "Did she seem depressed?"

"Why should she be depressed, with all that money and power? *I'm* the one who should be depressed."

"And are you?"

She gazed at him somberly for a minute, then one corner of her mouth twitched in a demure smile. "What do you think? How do I look?"

"You look very pretty." *And a little wacky.*

"I'm deliriously happy, if you want the truth. Everything's working out the way I planned. May I tell you something in confidence?"

"Yes, but I'd prefer—"

"Absolute confidence, like between lawyer and client, I forget the legal term for it."

"Privileged information."

"Let's call this privileged information."

She was smiling fully now, as if something was turning out to be a great joke. He hoped he wasn't it.

"I'd ask you to cross your heart," she said, "except I've always been told lawyers don't have one."

"I hear beating inside my chest. Maybe I'm an exception."

"Then cross your heart."

He did. Miranda liked games and he didn't mind as long as they were as innocent as this one.

It didn't remain innocent very long. She said, "I'm going to be married within two or three months. Surprised?"

"Yes. I didn't peg Grady as the marrying type."

"I'm not marrying Grady, I'm marrying Cooper."

"Cooper?"

"The Admiral. I expect him to set the date when this business about his wife is all settled. Oh, it will be nice having money again, being able to afford things."

"Things like what?"

"Like Grady."

He knew then why she looked a little wacky. She was.

He said, "You can't buy people, Mrs. Shaw."

"Most people you can't, some you can. Grady's one of the some. Of course, it will take a lot of money and I could never manage it on my own. Cooper is going to help me."

"Is he aware of this?"

"No."

"Is Grady?"

"No. Just you and I. And you can't tell because it's privileged information and you crossed your heart."

Behind the boiler room, which contained the heating and filtering tanks for the pool, there was a small tool shed with a padlock on the door. The lock had been broken so often that no one bothered replacing it anymore and employees had access to the shed for whatever purpose they had in mind. Grady's purpose was lunch. He'd purchased it at a taco stand a couple of blocks up the street, and he sat now on a wooden chest among the rakes and shovels and hedge clippers, the ants and pill bugs, the lengths of piping and coils of rope.

The shed smelled of paint thinner and fertilizer and the cooking fumes from the snack-bar grill, but it was peaceful and quiet except for the sound of the waves. Grady liked to listen to them, trying to estimate their size and shape and whether the tide was coming in or going out. Usually he checked his tide book as soon as he reported to work and then chalked the numbers up on the blackboard beside the pool. High 10:25 p.m. 5.7 Low 5:41 p.m. -0.5. He hadn't done this yet today because he'd seen Miranda arriving with the girls and he wanted to stay out of sight until she went up to the cabana. Avoiding Miranda was easy. Avoiding certain other people wasn't.

"So there you are," little Frederic said. He carried a skateboard and was wearing protective equipment—knee and elbow pads and a red plastic helmet. In spite of these precautions he was plastered with an assortment of grimy bandages on his hands, nose and legs. "I've been looking all over the place for you."

"Now you found me," Grady said. "Bug off."

"What are you hiding in here for?"

"Who says I'm hiding?"

Frederic fitted his skinny little rump snugly into the center of a coil of rope. Then he removed his lunch, a package of bologna, from underneath his helmet. "What's it worth to you if I don't tell?"

"Nothing."

"Take your time. Think it over."

"There's no one to tell."

"Sure there is. You don't happen to have a dill pickle on you, do you? There's this kid at school who wraps a piece of bologna around a dill pickle and he calls it—"

"I don't give a goddamn if he calls it mother. Who is there to tell?"

"The chick you went to Mexico with." Since no dill pickle was available, Frederic didn't bother separating the slices of bologna. He took a bite out of all eight at once. "She's always asking people where you are—the porters, Henderson, Ellen, even me. How come you don't want her to find you?"

"Listen, Frederic. Let's talk this over man to man."

"Hell no. That palsy-walsy stuff just means you're not going to pay me."

"I can't, I don't have the money. Anyway, you're my friend. Aren't you?"

"What gives you a dumb idea like that? I don't have friends. I get shut up in some crazy school that teaches Greek—and who rescues me? Nobody. And where am I going to spend the rest of the summer? A prison camp in the boonies, only they call it an outdoor learning experience in the Sierra wilderness."

"Stop it, kid. I cry easy."

"You might."

"What does that mean?"

Frederic ate the last chunk of bologna, then he tucked the empty container under one of his knee pads beside a gum wrapper and a soggy piece of Kleenex. He disapproved of littering. "You want to know what she's doing up in the cabana right this minute? Wow, you'll throw a fit when I tell you."

"Try me."

"She's talking to her lawyer. His name's Aragon. The reason I'm sure is he's my lawyer, too. Him and me, we're going to sue people together when I grow up, maybe sooner. I'm keeping a list."

Grady didn't throw a fit but he drew in a quick breath and held it as though he'd been knocked over by a wave he didn't see coming. "What are they talking about?"

"Search me."

"I'm searching you."

"I don't know what they're talking about, man. I stood in the hall and listened but I couldn't hear a thing."

"Suppose you got in the cabana next door," Grady said. "You might be able to hear something from there."

"Might. How do I get in?"

"Ellen has a set of master keys."

"She wouldn't give them to me for a million dollars."

"She might give them to me."

Frederic's eyes widened. "Oh, now you're going to turn on the old macho, right? Can I come along and watch?"

"No."

"I haven't seen you in action since—"

"No. Stay here and I'll be back soon."

"If you change your mind, send me some kind of signal, like whistling three times."

"Sure, kid. Sure."

After Grady's departure Frederic amused himself by catching a spider that had spun a web between two of the crooked rust-stained teeth of a rake. For a while he had hopes that it was a black widow and he could train it to bite people to death, a reasonable alternative to suing them, but the creature didn't have the black widow's distinguishing red hourglass on its abdomen. Nor did it seem to want to bite anything, not the ant Frederic offered it, or the scab from his thumb, or a shred of the bandage dangling from his left wrist. He replaced the spider in the teeth of the rake.

During these maneuvers he kept listening hard, but nobody whistled three times or even once and Grady was still missing. Frederic waited another five minutes, then he picked up his skateboard and went back into the boiler room. He kicked a couple of pipes and tried to turn a wheel marked Do Not Touch and to remove a High Voltage sign from the fuse box. But everything was sealed, padlocked, clamped, welded.

Through the kitchen (Private, Keep Out) he left the club by the rear door (Employees Only), where he had a view of the parking lot. Grady and Aragon were standing beside Aragon's old Chevy, right in the very center of the lot without any trees or shrubbery around to provide coverage. There was no possible way of approaching them without being seen. They were out of reach, twenty years and a thousand miles away, and he could never catch up with them.

He had made a secret pact with his best friend, Henry, not to cry under any circumstances. But Henry was in Philadelphia visiting his parents and Frederic was here and now, hurting inside and outside.

Tears rolled down his cheeks like leaden bubbles.

"You got it all wrong," Grady said. He had pulled a pair of jeans on over his trunks because it was against the rules for any employee to enter or leave the club wearing only swimming attire. Aragon noticed that the jeans were too tight around the waist—Grady was eating regularly again.

"I swear to God, Aragon, I haven't even spoken to her since I came back."

"Why not?"

"I tried to, I wanted to be friendly, but she avoided me. I thought she was sore at me and I didn't blame her. I just felt grateful she hadn't put the cops on me about the Porsche. So while she was avoiding me I was avoiding her and it was working out fine. Then suddenly zap, I get this letter."

He handed Aragon a piece of pale blue paper that had obviously been unfolded and refolded a number of times. It was soiled at the crease lines and damp from moisture seeping from his swim trunks into the pockets of his jeans but the ink hadn't smudged. The writing, neat boarding- school backhand, was embellished with a few touches of Miranda's own, extra-large capitals and circles over the i's instead of dots.

> *Beloved:*
> *I want to write that word over and over again because it is beautiful like you. Beloved, beloved, beloved.*
> *Oh, how hard this masquerade has been on both of us, acting like strangers when all we can think about is lying in each other's arms. But be patient, my dearest. I have made my plans very carefully, and though they may seem strange to you at first, please trust me. We must live as well as love. This is the only way we can do both.*
>
> > *Your own*
> > *Miranda*

"I couldn't believe it at first," Grady said. "I thought she was putting me on. But she's not the type, she's deadly serious about everything." He read the note again before he replaced it in his pocket. "That's a lot of crap how all we can think about is lying in each other's arms. Jeez, I never even thought about it when I was doing it, and that was a year ago."

"Eight months."

"Close enough. I don't sit around staring at calendars."

"In the note she refers to plans," Aragon said. "What plans?"

"You're the one who talked to her, not me. I told you before, I haven't even spoken to her since I got back. Now suddenly she's writing stuff about lying in each other's arms. For all I know, she's got a church and preacher lined up. I feel trapped, man. Trapped." He thumped the hood of the car with his fist. It left an imprint in the dust like an animal track.

"Why did you come back here, Grady?"

"I needed the job and the surfing's good. I never dreamed Miranda would be waiting for me with a bunch of crazy ideas. Maybe I should run away. What do you think?"

"You're pretty good at it," Aragon said. "Maybe you should."

"I mean it. She might be really far out. She might try something wild, like taking a shot at me or sticking a knife in my back, especially if she finds out I'm interested in someone else."

"Are you?"

"Sort of."

"Explain 'sort of.'"

"Well, Ellen and me, we got something going. She's a nice girl with class and a steady job. It might work out okay. I could do worse."

"Could she?"

Grady thumped the hood of the car again but there was no force behind it. It was like a gesture he'd seen done in a movie by someone he identified with. "Stop coming down hard on me because of that business in Mexico. It wasn't my fault. None of it was my idea in the first place, not her and me, not the trip, not even the Porsche, which never did me any good anyway. You know what happened to it?"

"You sold it and lost the money in a crap game."

"I parked it in a garage in Phoenix and it got ripped off," Grady said. "How's that for a laugh?"

"Fair."

"You still think I'm a louse, huh?"

"Close enough. I don't sit around staring at dictionaries."

"Well, I'm not so crazy about you either, you self-righteous bastard. You probably never had to do a day's work in your life, everything handed to you on a platter, college, law school, the whole bit. Me, I ran away from home when I was thirteen, they were going to kick me out anyway. Want to know why? I stole a car. How's that for laugh number two?"

"About as funny as laugh number one."

"It was my uncle's car and I didn't mean to steal it, I only wanted to go for a ride. But once I started driving I couldn't stop. I kept right on going until the gas tank was empty. I ended up near a ball park in Visalia. I watched the game for a while, then I hitchhiked home and got the hell beat out of me. I left again the next day, this time with the money my aunt kept hidden under her mattress . . . So there you have it, the story of my life, chapter one."

"The lady, the mattress, the money," Aragon said. "You started early and learned fast."

"I found out where it's at and how to get there. Sure. Why not?"

"Is the word out about you and Ellen?"

"We haven't done any advertising, but I guess Mr. Henderson has caught on and some of Ellen's neighbors in the apartment building, people like that. Ellen's got a lot of friends, and friends talk."

"Are you living in her apartment?"

"Not technically, no. I rent a room on Quinientos Street."

"Does Miranda know about it?"

"I don't see how, unless she followed me home from work one night, and she wouldn't do that. She's always got those two crazies with her. They tag along after her like she's their mother."

"Or stepmother."

From Grady's lack of reaction to the word, Aragon was certain that he wasn't aware of Miranda's plans for his future and her own, via the Admiral.

"What do you think I should do?" Grady said.

"What do you want to do?"

"Sit tight, keep things alive with Ellen, pretend I never got the letter."

"When did you get it?"

"Three days ago. It was slipped under the door of the guard shack with my name on the envelope."

"So you can't very well pretend you didn't get it."

"I guess not."

"Have you showed it to Ellen?"

"No."

"Do you intend to?"

"No. It's strictly between Miranda and me, or rather between Miranda and Miranda. I can't be held responsible for what's cooking inside her head."

Frederic slalomed across the parking lot on his skateboard between parked cars and lampposts and concrete markers. When he reached Aragon's Chevy he came to a stop by jumping off the skateboard. The board kept right on going, under a BMW and a Lincoln and ending up against the front tire of a Ford van. Frederic retrieved it, spun the wheels to make sure they weren't damaged and approached the two men. His recent tears had cleared little paths through the dirt on his cheeks.

"Bug off," Grady said.

Frederic shook his head. "Can't."

"Try."

"Can't. Your girlfriend sent me here on an errand."

"What girlfriend?"

"Don't rush me, man." Frederic took off his plastic helmet, releasing a squashed yogurt carton and two sticks of gum now soft as putty and molded to the shape of his head. He looked up at Grady, red-eyed and reproachful. "I waited a long time in that stinky shed for you to come back with the keys."

"The situation changed," Grady said.

"You never meant to come back."

"Sure I did."

"No, you didn't."

"Have it your way. What's the errand and who sent you?"

"Maybe I won't tell you."

Grady put his hands on the boy's shoulders and squeezed. "Then again, maybe you will, right?"

"Sure. Right. Lay off the rough stuff. I was only kidding. Can't you take a joke? Ellen sent me to tell Mr. Aragon to come back to the club and call his office. A lady wants to talk to him."

"Thanks, Frederic," Aragon said.

"You don't have to thank me," Frederic said. "A small tip will be enough."

"I've only got two dimes. You can have one."

"One skinny little dime. There ought to be a minimum-tip law like the minimum-wage law. Say, how's that for a new political idea?"

"Great. In another twelve years you can run for Congress." It was a sobering thought.

Aragon used the other dime on the public telephone in the corridor. Only one lady was likely to know where he was, and the switchboard transferred the call to her office.

"Miss Nelson? It's me."

"Who's me?"

"Tom."

"Tom who?"

"Aragon."

Charity tapped the phone sharply with a pencil by way of reprimand. "I'm beginning to wonder if you'll ever make the big time in this business, junior. An attorney headed for the larger life doesn't say it's me. He says this is Tomás Aragon of Smedler, Downs, Castleberg, McFee and Powell."

"You already know that."

"It won't kill you to practice a little."

"All right. This is Tomás Aragon of Smedler, Downs, Castleberg, McFee and Powell. So what's new?"

"Plenty. Smedler just came from the courthouse and the whole place was buzzing with rumors. The report on Iris Young's death arrived from the crime lab last night by special messenger and the word is she was murdered."

"Whose word?"

"There's an old babe in the D.A.'s office who has a crush on Smedler—he's fairly attractive if you squint a little and the light's not too good—and she's always getting him in a corner and feeding him goodies to arouse his interest. Verbal goodies, I mean. He's on a diet. Anyway, she told him that the D.A.'s in seventh heaven."

"What does it take to put a D.A. in seventh heaven, or even fifth or sixth?"

"Evidence for a case that will make him look good to the voters in the next election," Charity said. "You saw Iris Young once, didn't you?"

"Briefly."

"Was she using a cane?"

"Yes. It was burned in the fire."

"Wrong. There was a lot of intricate metalwork on the head of it which didn't burn. Where the metal joined the wood some blood seeped into the cracks. It matched the blood taken from Mrs. Young's body, but there was a difference in the two samples that's supposed to be very significant."

"In what way?"

"Smedler's snitch didn't know."

"Why are you telling me all this, Miss Nelson?"

"Smedler asked me to clue you in. He thought maybe you could find out more by sort of hanging around the sheriff's department."

"If I sort of hang around the sheriff's department, somebody's going to sort of wonder why."

"Tell them you work for Smedler, Downs, Castleberg, McFee and Powell. After all, Miranda Shaw is one of our clients, or used to be, and she was living in the Youngs' house when the murder occurred and we have a right to—Oh my God, you don't suppose she's actually *involved*. Yes, you do. I can tell by your silence."

"I—"

"And so does Smedler. And that's why he's so curious about the report from the crime lab. Well, if he really wants to find things out, I wish he'd pick somebody more competent than you."

"So do I," Aragon said and hung up.

Ellen Brewster was standing outside the door of her office waiting for him. She wore a short sleeveless white dress which showed off her newly acquired tan but made her look as if she was trying too hard to be like one of the teenagers herded in flocks on the beach and in the snack bar and around the lifeguard towers.

Her voice was strained. "Do you have time to come in for a minute, Mr. Aragon?"

"I think so."

He went in and she closed the door behind him. The room was still noisy. There was shouting and laughing from the pool area, and outside by the roadway some men were pruning a eucalyptus tree with a power saw.

She said, "Did you talk to Miranda?"

"Yes."

"It wouldn't be fair for me to ask what she told you, would it?"

"No."

"I can't help it, I have to ask one question anyway. Does she know that Grady and I—that we—"

"No."

"I was pretty sure she didn't but I had to be positive."

"Why?"

"I guess I'm afraid of her."

"She's not exactly formidable—twice your age, about half your size and a little nuts."

"She isn't a little nuts," Ellen said. "Where Grady's concerned she's totally irrational. She hasn't changed since the night you dumped her on me when you drove her here from that clinic in Mexico. She told me then that she'd do anything to make it possible for her and Grady to be together again. She said if he needed money to be happy, no matter how much money, she'd get it somehow and buy him back. Can you believe it?"

"Yes." They were the same words Miranda had used in the cabana half an hour ago. "So what are you afraid of, that he can be bought?"

"I don't know whether he can or not. I just don't want her to try. It's not fair."

"Don't worry. She hasn't a nickel."

He sounded more confident than he felt.

"Nothing," he told Charity when he returned to the office later in the day.

"Nothing?" she repeated. "You've been gone all afternoon, and *nothing?*"

"Nothing definite. I did what you told me to—hung around here and there, kept my ears open, asked subtle questions like how are you, got subtle answers like fine. There are the usual rumors which a case of this kind inspires. But one of them may possibly be worth something."

"What is it?"

"That the D.A. has enough evidence to ask the grand jury for an indictment."

"An indictment against whom?"

"I don't know."

"Probably the husband," Charity said. "It usually is in this day and age. Nobody keeps a butler anymore."

Part VI

Let the record show that all nineteen members of the grand jury are present and have been sworn and the District Attorney is ready to continue the presentation of his case.

"MR. FOREMAN AND ladies and gentlemen of the grand jury. During the morning session I outlined the general procedure I would follow, since this is the first homicide brought before you. In the course of the afternoon I will deal more with specifics. But first I would like to state that I am aware, as you must be, that the grand jury system has recently been criticized in the media on several grounds: the manner in which jurors are selected, the secrecy of the proceedings, the absence of any attorney to represent the defense and of a judge to rule on what is or isn't permissible, and the fact that only twelve votes are required to issue an indictment, which allows for seven dissenters if the full jury of nineteen is present, as it is now. It is not my business to answer these criticisms. The system exists and we must operate within it. I have complete faith in your ability to reach a fair and impartial decision and I believe it will be a unanimous one."

The District Attorney stopped to wipe his forehead with a handkerchief. The courthouse air conditioning was on the blink again and the chamber, in spite of its size and high ceiling, was hot. All the windows had to be closed to shut out traffic noises. A fan droned at the back of the room, pushing the air around without cooling it.

The District Attorney's name was Zachary Tilford and he was in his early thirties, an age considered by many to be too young for the job. He knew this and in order to counteract it he spoke in an aggressively sharp staccato voice. His words bounced off the walls like ping-pong balls.

"The house at 1220 Camino Grande is a mansion by today's standards. Purchased about a dozen years ago by Vice-Admiral Cooper Young, USN, Retired, and his wife, Iris Van Eyck Young, it has been occupied since then by the Admiral and his wife and their two unmarried daughters, Cordelia and Juliet. A housekeeper, Mrs. Paulette Norgate, joined the household a short time later, and last year Miranda Shaw, a well-bred attractive widow, then fifty-two, was hired to act as a kind of social governess for the daughters. These five people lived in the house. During the day other employees came to assist with the cleaning and cooking and general household chores, but for purposes of this hearing we will not concern ourselves with the latter group.

211

"Iris Young was sixty-two and in poor health. A chronic arthritic, she had suffered two heart attacks. She lived the life of a semi-recluse, spending most of her waking hours in her sitting room on the main floor, occupied with her business interests—she was a wealthy woman—as well as her books and music. For a hobby she played chess by mail with various people around the world. This was among her activities on the afternoon of July the fourth. We know that because she gave Mrs. Shaw two letters to post, one addressed to a professor at the University of Tokyo, the other to a missionary in Jakarta. The rest of the time she spent finishing a book she'd been reading and listening to an opera. For Mrs. Young it was a typical afternoon, except for one thing. It was her last.

"Shortly after nine o'clock that night Iris Young died. Preliminary reports indicated that she was attempting to light the gas log in the fireplace when she fell forward, struck her head and lost consciousness. The escaping gas exploded and set fire to the room and everything in it, but an autopsy proved that Mrs. Young's death was actually due to smoke inhalation. I want to bring to your attention at this point that the official temperature reading in Santa Felicia at nine o'clock on the night of July the fourth was seventy-two degrees after a daytime high of eighty-one. The temperature in Iris Young's sitting room must have been somewhere between those two extremes, probably about seventy-six degrees, warm even for someone who was an invalid. Yet she allegedly tried to light the gas log. I call this curious circumstance number one.

"Curious circumstance number two: Mrs. Young was alone in the house. As I promised this morning, I will not waste the jury's time and the taxpayers' money bringing in witnesses to testify to evidence already well-documented in the investigative reports which are included in the exhibits.

"Where was her family and the other people who lived in the house? The Admiral had escorted his two daughters to a fireworks display at the Penguin Club; Miranda Shaw was out walking the dog; and the housekeeper, Mrs. Norgate, had gone to babysit her grandson. The last person to see Mrs. Young alive was Miranda Shaw. I want to bring to your attention at this point that it was Mrs. Shaw's habit to walk the dog before she retired between ten thirty and eleven o'clock. On the night in question she left the house at eight thirty, claiming the dog suffered a digestive upset. This may be true. Certainly, neither Iris Young nor the dog is in a position to deny it.

"At any rate, our list of curious circumstances continues to grow. Number three: Miranda Shaw left the house with the dog a couple of hours earlier than usual. Number four: she was the last person to see Iris Young alive."

The District Attorney paused again to wipe the sweat off his forehead and take a drink of water from the pitcher on the table in front of him. He was suffering from a sudden attack of nerves in addition to the heat. Although he'd reminded the grand jury—somewhat unnecessarily—that this was the first case of homicide to be brought before them, he had neglected to inform them that it was also his first. Since grand jury proceedings were always secret, and the transcripts often sealed afterward by order of a judge, he was more or less flying blind. It was small consolation that the jurors were in the same plane.

"Most of you, if you have heard at all of the crime lab in Sacramento, may think of it as a remote place where obscure research is carried on which has no connection with you personally. Well, it is no longer remote and its work no longer obscure. The lab, in fact, has moved right into your lives in the form of the document I am now holding in my hand. It contains the results of the tests made on the material taken from the scene of Iris Young's death. This covered a wide range of things, the most important being the blood and tissue samples from Iris Young's body. Among the items salvaged from the ruins—the wood splinters and pieces of glass and other rubble—two specific items stand out, a cane and a candlestick.

"Each of you has been furnished with a list of exhibits I will offer you in support of my case. The first is the document I'm now holding in my hand. Many people, scientists and lab technicians, contributed to it, but it's signed by Dr. Gustave Wilhelm, acting head of the arson division. Dr. Wilhelm cannot be here to testify until later in the week, so I will take the liberty of presenting to you an outline of his report in order to answer the first of the three significant questions in this case: Was a murder committed? What were the reasons behind it? Who had these reasons? It would be illogical to proceed with the last two questions until we've established a definite answer to the first. Was a murder committed? Yes. This document in my hand is, in fact, the story of a murder, written in the language of science instead of literature and having as its leading character not a person but a cane.

"The cane belonged to Iris Young. According to a statement by her husband, she purchased it merely as an artifact used by an African chieftain in certain tribal rites. Later it became her constant companion. It is made of zebrawood with an ornamental head of copper and the remnants of it are on the table to your left wrapped in plastic and identified by a red tag. Even without my unwrapping it you can see that it's been badly burned. What you can't see is that at the head, where the copper has been hammered into the wood, there are bloodstains. The fact that any of Iris Young's blood was found on this cane is enough to suggest foul play. Microscopic tests have made the suggestion a fact. Let me clarify.

"A by-product of any fire is carbon monoxide, a colorless, odorless gas which has a strong affinity for the red blood cells of the body. Its presence is easily detected not only in the bloodstream but in the respiration passages and the lungs, where small granules of carbon can be found if a person has breathed in smoke. Tissues taken from Iris Young's nasal and bronchial passages and lungs contained such granules. Also, samples of her blood indicate that carbon monoxide had forced the vital oxygen out of her red cells and caused death by asphyxiation. So what she died of is clear. How it happened is another matter.

"It was at first believed that Iris Young while leaning over in the act of lighting the gas log lost her balance and fell, that she struck the upper area of her face hard enough to cause bleeding and to render her unconscious. But now let's ask some basic questions:

"Was blood found on the gas log? No.

"Anywhere near it? No.

"Any place in the room at all? Yes. On the head of the cane.

"What type of blood was it? AB negative.

"Did it, in fact, come from Iris Young's body? Yes.

"Did it contain evidence of carbon monoxide? No. I repeat, no. The blood on the cane came from a woman who had not breathed in any smoke at all.

"Is it possible that Iris Young's head wound was the result of her falling on her own cane? No. The force of such a fall would not have been enough to cause the kind of injury she sustained.

"How, then, did she die? She was struck. She did not fall and strike anything, she was struck with her own cane.

"Could this blow have been an act of impulse and the fire a desperate attempt to cover up the attack? No. I believe that the fire was, in fact, the main event, premeditated, carefully planned even down to the date, July Fourth, when the sound of an explosion would be nothing unusual. The holiday also made it easier to get the other people out of the house— Admiral Young to watch a fireworks display with his daughters, and the housekeeper to babysit her grandson while his parents went out celebrating. Oh yes, it was carefully planned, all right, except that explosions and fires are not predictable whether they're arranged by an amateur or a professional. As many prisoners are painfully aware, arson doesn't necessarily burn up evidence of itself.

"Iris Young was meant to be cremated in that fire. Perhaps that would have happened if she'd been fatter, since body fat acts as a fuel, but Iris Young was a thin woman. Her cane was meant to be destroyed and it was, but only partially. The part that was left provided the blood samples to compare with those taken from her body.

"There is still another object which was intended for destruction, or at least for damage enough to render it useless as evidence."

He walked over to the table where the exhibits were displayed and picked up a candlestick wrapped, like the cane, in transparent plastic.

"Here it is. An antique silver candlestick, ten inches high, bent, as you can see, by the force of the explosion and somewhat discolored by smoke. According to the housekeeper and the members of the family, it's one of a set of four always kept on the buffet in the dining room. How did it get from the buffet in the dining room to the floor of Iris Young's sitting room? The obvious explanation is that she took it there herself. But let me read a couple of sentences from a statement given to one of my deputies by the housekeeper, Mrs. Norgate:

"'Miranda Shaw liked to use candles on the dinner table because she thought they made her look more youthful. But lately Mrs. Young had gotten so she couldn't stand them. She said flickering lights gave her a headache.' There's no reason to doubt Mrs. Norgate's word. More-over, the same observation has been made by other members of the household, that Mrs. Young hated candles. Yet this candlestick was found in her room. Without her fingerprints on it, without, in fact, any fingerprints on it at all. I have lost count of the curious facts in this case but this must be number five or six. Or ten. Or fifteen. More questions arise:

"What was the candlestick doing in Iris Young's room? It was doing what came naturally, holding a candle.

"And what was the candle doing? Committing a murder.

"And what does all this add up to? The following sequence of events: Iris Young was struck with her own cane, the candle was lit and its holder wiped clean, the gas was turned on and the murderer left the house."

The District Attorney paused again, not for effect but because one of the jurors, a retired librarian, had raised her hand.

"Yes, Mrs. Zimmerman?"

"Why don't you bring in some witnesses?"

"I will, of course. But in order to save both time and the taxpayers' money—two important advantages of the grand jury system—I'm calling only enough witnesses to present my case without the kind of detail and repetition necessary in a criminal trial."

"I'm sorry. I didn't—"

The foreman intervened. "The calling of witnesses—who, when, how many—is up to the District Attorney, Mrs. Zimmerman."

"But he's just standing there telling me what to think."

"He's giving you material for thought. That's an entirely different matter . . . Please con-tinue, Mr. District Attorney."

"Thank you, Mr. Foreman. I would like to go back for a minute to the results of the autopsy performed on Iris Young. Tissue removed from her air sacs and breathing passages showed carbon particles which indicated that she died of asphyxiation caused by the inhalation of smoke. Tissue removed from other areas, especially the abdominal cavity, showed traces of other chemicals, in particular flurazepam hydrochloride. This is a crystalline compound readily soluble in either alcohol or water and rapidly absorbed and metabolized by the body. It's a commonly used sedative sold, by prescription only, under the name Dalmane. That Iris Young, a semi-invalid, should have taken something to induce sleep is not surprising. But the circumstances are peculiar. Dalmane is a very quick-acting drug meant to be administered only after the patient has retired or is about to retire. Iris Young was in her sitting room, fully clothed. So we have another curious fact to add to our growing list.

"And on the heels of that one we come to still another. Dalmane, as I said before, is available by prescription only in fifteen-milligram orange and ivory capsules or thirty-milligram red and ivory. Dr. Albert Varick, Mrs. Young's personal physician, is attending a medical conference in Puerto Rico this week but we have his sworn statement available for you to read. The gist is as follows: From time to time Dr. Varick has prescribed various medications for Iris Young, mainly Indocin, to alleviate the pain of her chronic arthritis. But according to his records and Iris Young's medical file, Dr. Varick never issued her a prescription for Dalmane. Yet there was such a prescription in that house. A police sergeant will give you the details about it later.

"Now, before calling my first witness, Admiral Cooper Young, I feel you should be told in advance that Admiral Young did not wish to testify and so stated when he was served with a subpoena. He cannot by any means be called a hostile witness, but he is a reluctant one, agreeing to testify only because he believes it's his duty to assist in the enforcement of the law. Please bear this in mind as you listen to him."

The Admiral moved to the witness stand with the brisk no-nonsense walk he'd learned at Annapolis fifty years previously. He gave the appearance of wearing a uniform, though it was only a dark grey suit with a white cuff-linked shirt and black tie and shoes. His face had the slightly jaundiced color that accompanies a fading suntan.

His reluctance to testify would have been apparent to the jury without any previous warning. He glanced at them with obvious distaste before responding to the District Attorney's first question.

"Will you state your name and address for the record, please?"

"Cooper Randolph Young, 1220 Camino Grande, Santa Felicia."

"And your occupation?"

"Vice-Admiral, United States Navy, Retired."

"What was the nature and duration of your relationship with Iris Van Eyck Young?"

"She was my wife for thirty-five years."

"Was it a happy relationship?"

"Yes."

"Would you say that your household was, by and large, a congenial one?"

"Yes."

"I realize this must be a painful experience for you. I wouldn't have asked you to go through it if it weren't necessary. Do you understand that?"

"I hear you talking."

"I can't very well apologize for doing my duty, Admiral."

"No. Such an apology would not be accepted anyway."

"Very well, let's proceed. Would you tell the jury where you were in the late afternoon and early evening of July the Fourth of this year?"

"At home with my family—my wife and my two daughters."

"Anyone else in the house?"

"Mrs. Norgate, our housekeeper, who was cooking dinner."

"And Mrs. Shaw?"

"Yes."

"What was Mrs. Shaw doing?"

"I'm not sure, but she was probably fixing the table for dinner, arranging the centerpiece, the flowers, and so on."

"And candles?"

"And candles, yes."

"Were your dinners usually formal?"

"Yes, as part of my daughters' social education."

"Was there anything different about the dinner that night?"

"It was quite a bit earlier than usual because Mrs. Norgate had an engagement and I had promised my daughters to take them to a display of fireworks at the club. Mrs. Shaw was invited to go along but she refused."

"She refused on what grounds?"

"She didn't want to leave Mrs. Young alone."

"But she *did* leave her alone."

"Only to walk the dog."

"That was long enough, wasn't it?" The D.A. glanced pointedly at the table of exhibits. "Wasn't it?"

"Mrs. Shaw is not responsible for what happened. She was always very gentle and kind to my wife."

"And vice versa?"

"And vice versa, yes."

The District Attorney had been sitting back in his chair until this point in the questioning. Now he leaned forward and wrote on the legal pad in front of him *And vice versa?!*

"Did you know Mrs. Shaw before you hired her, Admiral?"

"Yes. She and her husband were members of the same beach club my wife and I belonged to. All four of us knew each other, though not very well."

"What was the name of the club?"

"The Penguin Club."

"That's pretty well restricted to people in the upper financial brackets, isn't it?"

"Yes."

"Was Mrs. Shaw still a member when she came to you seeking employment?"

"She was not a member and she didn't come to me seeking employment. The possibility of such a job was suggested to her by Miss Brewster, the club secretary, who then spoke to me about Mrs. Shaw's predicament."

"Predicament?"

"Her husband had died leaving a great many debts."

"And so you took her into your house, like a good Samaritan?"

"No, not like that at all. My wife and I needed help with our daughters."

"Would you care to elaborate on that?"

"No."

"All right. Now—"

"Am I permitted to make a statement?"

"Go ahead."

"I want to protest my two daughters' being given subpoenas to testify."

"Do you have any reason to *object* to their testimony, Admiral?"

"I simply feel they're not equipped to deal with stressful situations like this."

"They're of legal age, are they not?"

"Yes."

"And represented by legal counsel?"

"Yes, but they won't listen to his advice."

"I talked personally with both your daughters and they exhibited no signs of stress and no aversion to testifying. Your paternal concern is admirable but perhaps not justified in this instance."

"I have registered my protest."

"It will be on the record, Admiral . . . Now, when did Mrs. Shaw start working for you?"

"Sometime in January."

"Did she fit in well with the other members of your household?"

"Yes."

"Right from the start?"

"There was the usual period of adjustment under such circumstances."

"What was your own relationship with Mrs. Shaw?"

"Relationship?"

"Was it strictly one of employer and employee?"

"She was an employee certainly but I considered her more like a friend. And vice versa, I believe."

"You were friends?"

"Yes."

"More than casual friends?"

"We were friends."

"Close friends?"

"No, I wouldn't say we were—look, she lived in my house, we saw each other every day, we talked, we ate at the same table. What does that make us?"

"A good question, Admiral."

Once again the District Attorney leaned forward to write on the yellow pad in front of him *What does that make us?* He didn't hurry. He wanted to be sure the jury had plenty of time to supply their own answer to the Admiral's question.

"Tell me, Admiral, did Mrs. Shaw go out socially?"

"What exactly do you mean?"

"Did she have dates?"

"I don't know."

"What percentage of her evenings would you say she spent at home? Fifty percent?"

"I didn't keep track."

"Seventy-five percent? Ninety percent?"

"She spent most of her evenings in the house with the family. Dinners usually lasted until quite late because they were, as I said before, part of my daughters' social education."

"You and your wife, your two daughters and Mrs. Shaw, was this a happy group?"

"Happy is a pretty strong word."

"I agree, happy is a pretty strong word. I'll amend the question. Did the five of you get along in a reasonably civilized manner?"

"Yes."

"That will be all, Admiral."

"I beg your pardon?"

"I have no more questions. You're free to leave."

The old man didn't move.

"Admiral? You may step down now."

"Before I do I would like to make another statement."

"Go ahead."

"If this is all you wanted from me, you might have spared me the embarrassment of a subpoena. I haven't told you anything you didn't already know and I haven't cast any new light on the situation . . ."

"Perhaps you have, Admiral. Thank you very much."

"You didn't even ask me about my wife's death, how it must have happened."

"We know how it happened, Admiral. Please step down."

It was the second most important occasion in Cordelia's life—the first being the Singapore incident—and she had prepared for it by buying a new outfit, a red and white polka-dot pantsuit and genuine red snakeskin shoes. ("Whoever heard of a genuine red snake?" Juliet said. "You were *had.*") She put on her best wristwatch, three rings, a bracelet made of carved ivory elephants and as a last-minute addition the ruby necklace, formerly Miranda's, which she'd bought from Mr. Tannenbaum a year ago. She hadn't worn it since Miranda moved into the house and she didn't know why she suddenly decided to wear it today, keeping it hidden under the collar of her jacket until she got into her car and on her way to the courthouse.

No one had clearly explained to Cordelia the actual function of the grand jury, but she wasn't nervous. She had, in fact, the pleasant feeling that she was doing her duty, and she spoke in a loud distinct voice, giving her name, Cordelia Catherine Young, and her address, 1220 Camino Grande, and her occupation, none.

"Miss Young, have you discussed the testimony you're about to give with any members of your family?"

"You asked me not to."

"I'm asking you now whether you did."

"Maybe I exchanged a few words with Juliet. I couldn't very well *not*. The subpoenas arrived at the same time and there she was and there I was. We could hardly pretend nothing was happening."

"Did you discuss with her in detail what you were going to say before this jury?"

"No." Cordelia kept her hands in the pockets of her jacket, fingers crossed to protect her from a perjury charge, but in case crossed fingers had no legal significance she added, "Not really."

"Do you know Miranda Shaw, Miss Young?"

"Naturally. She lives in the same house, day and night."

"What is her job?"

"She's supposed to teach me and Juliet things like etiquette, which we already know and anyway we're never invited any place where we can use it. Mrs. Young just couldn't get that through her head."

"Mrs. Young is—was—your mother?"

"I assume she was. That's what it says on my passport."

"Did you get along well with your mother?"

"Nobody got along well with her. She was too hard to please and she had a terrible temper."

The District Attorney stood up and walked around the table, partly to stretch his legs, partly to give the jury a chance to examine this new picture of Iris Young, considerably different from the one presented by the Admiral.

He returned to face the witness chair. "Miss Young—may I call you Cordelia?"

"I don't mind if you think it's etiquette."

"We make our own rules of etiquette in this courtroom. Now, you said a moment ago, Cordelia, that nobody got along well with your mother."

"It's true."

"If Mrs. Shaw, for instance, didn't have a fairly pleasant relationship with her, what made her stay in the house?"

"Money."

"Will you explain that?"

"Mrs. Shaw intended to leave after Mrs. Young hit her with the cane but Pops gave her a raise so she'd stay."

"How much of a raise?"

"Two hundred dollars a month."

"Do you know how Mrs. Shaw received the extra money? Was it added to her salary?"

"Good lord, no. That way Mrs. Young would have found out about it because she paid all the bills and salaries and stuff."

"Then where did this extra two hundred a month come from?"

"Pops gave it to her. It worked out fine because she gave some of it right back."

"How?"

"She bought him presents."

"Mrs. Shaw bought your father presents?"

"Yes."

"Did you ever see any of them?"

"No. But Juliet and I heard him thanking her one night in the hall. He said her presents had made him very happy."

"What did you think when you heard this?"

"Exactly what you're thinking," Cordelia said. "Hanky-panky."

"Hanky-panky?"

"That's Juliet's expression for it. She hates to say dirty words when she doesn't have to. Of course, I can spell it out for you if you—"

"No, no. Hanky-panky is fine." The District Attorney sat down again, heavily, as though the pressure of gravity on him had suddenly increased. "I'd like you now to go back to the early evening of July the Fourth. Where were you and Cordelia?"

"Home."

"Doing what?"

"Helping Miranda get the table ready for dinner. The sun was still shining but she made me pull the drapes so we could eat by candlelight. It's supposed to be more civilized, that's what *she* says."

"Did your mother come to the table for dinner?"

"Long enough to gripe about the food and take her medicine. The doctor made her take a capsule for her arthritis at every meal."

"And you distinctly recall her doing so?"

"Yes. She took one of the same capsules she always did."

"What color was it?"

"One end was white and the other end blue."

"The colored end couldn't have been orange?"

"No."

"Or red?"

"No. I was sitting right beside her. She took one of her ordinary blue and white capsules and after that she got up and left without finishing her food."

"Where did she go?"

"Where she always went to escape from the rest of us, her sitting room. She even had a lock put on it to keep us out."

"When?"

"About a month before she died. It worried the doctor because he was afraid something might happen to her and nobody would be able to get in to help her. But I told him not to fret, I could always pick the lock with one of my credit cards."

"You could pick the lock?"

"It's easy. Even Juliet can do it."

"Getting back to dinner on the night of July the fourth, why did your mother leave the table before finishing her food?"

"She said the meat was tough and the candles had given her a migraine. Even though Miranda took the candles off the table right away, she left anyway."

"Evidently she didn't share Mrs. Shaw's feeling that eating by candlelight was more civilized?"

"She never liked anything Miranda did."

"Why didn't she fire her?"

"Because Miranda took us off her hands, out of the house. Mrs. Young hated having us around but she worried about us when we weren't. We spent a lot of time down at the beach club. I swam a lot but Juliet mostly ate because she had a crush on one of the waiters. It wasn't very romantic. She got fat as a pig and then she found out he was married and had five children. It was a shattering blow plus having to go on a diet."

"I'm sure it was. Thank you, Cordelia. I have no more questions."

Cordelia stepped down from the stand with some reluctance. The second biggest occasion of her life was over and she didn't know for sure what it was all about. In addition, the red snakeskin shoes were beginning to pinch and the ruby necklace felt quite heavy around her neck, as if Miranda herself had somehow become entangled in the silver clasp.

In comparison with her sister, Juliet was conspicuously dowdy. She'd inherited the frugal nature of her mother's Dutch ancestors, and all her clothes came from Salvation Army and Humane Society thrift stores, and out-of-the-way little shops with names like New to You or Practically Perfect or Born Again Bargains.

The beige chiffon dress she wore had a pleated bodice which moved in and out like an accordion with every breath she took. She took a great many because ever since breakfast she'd been having an attack of nerves. People had urged her to tell the truth but nobody had defined what the truth was except Uncle Charles Van Eyck, and his advice was diluted with alcohol: "Truth is a matter of opinion. So opine, Juliet. Opine."

She wished that Cordelia could be on the stand beside her encouraging her to opine, but the District Attorney explained that this was against the rules of a grand jury hearing, and like it or not, she was on her own. It gave her a creepy feeling having no Cordelia to watch for guidance, a frown, a nod, a shrug. When she walked to the front of the room her knees shook and the accordion pleats kept going in and out very rapidly. She could feel her lips quivering in the anxious little smile Cordelia hated— "You look like an idiot when you do that"—and her mind was an absolute blank—"Opine, Juliet, opine."

She knew the grand jury was supposed to consist of nineteen people, but there seemed to be at least fifty and she noticed that the District Attorney, who previously seemed rather nice, had very cruel eyebrows. She gave her name and address in a whisper, as if the information were top secret being dragged out of her under duress: Juliet Ariel Young, 1220 Camino Grande.

The District Attorney's eyebrows jumped at her. "I must ask you to speak louder, Miss Young."

"I . . . can't."

"Please try. Would you like a glass of water?"

Even the mention of water made her want to go to the bathroom, and she said "No" quite firmly.

"That's better, Miss Young. Perhaps you'd feel more at ease if I called you Juliet. Let's give it a try anyway . . . Now tell me, Juliet, were you living at 1220 Camino Grande the first week of June, approximately a month before your mother died?"

"Yes."

"On the afternoon of June the sixth was a package delivered to the house for Miranda Shaw?"

"Yes. She wasn't home, so the deliveryman asked me to sign for it."

"And did you?"

"Yes."

"Would you describe the package?"

"It was a huge silver box tied with white satin ribbon. There was a fancy label on it, The Ultimate in Intimate, which is the name of a bridal boutique downtown."

"What did you do with the box?"

"Left it on the hall table. Miranda got very excited when she came and saw it. She took it right up to her room and locked the door."

"Did she mention it to anyone?"

"No."

"Were you curious?"

"I guess I must have been."

"Please speak up, Juliet. Did your curiosity prompt you to take any action?"

"You know it did. I told you all about it."

"Now tell the jury."

"It was Cordelia's turn to help Miranda fix the table for dinner, so while they were busy downstairs I went upstairs and sort of let myself into Miranda's room."

"You picked the lock?"

"I guess you could call it that."

"Did you find the box?"

"I didn't have to find it. It was in plain sight on the floor, empty."

"What about its contents?"

"There was an expensive-looking nightgown made of some white filmy material trimmed with lace and little pink rosebuds. A robe made of the same material was draped over a chair."

"Where was the nightgown?"

"On the bed, lengthwise, as if someone invisible was lying inside it. The wig made it worse."

"Wig?"

"She had put one of her wigs on the pillow. It made me feel qualmsy. I got out of there in a hurry."

"Did you talk to anyone about it?"

"No."

"Not even your sister?"

"Expecially not her. She would have wanted to go and see it for herself and drag me along and I was scared we'd be . . . that Miranda would catch us and . . . well, you know."

"I don't know. Tell me."

"I was scared if Miranda caught us she'd take steps. That was the way she threatened us, saying she'd take steps if we didn't listen to her and obey her. She never explained what she meant, but she meant something not very nice. If my father marries her it'll be murder. She can twist him around her little finger."

"Wait. Hold on a minute, Juliet. You said if your father *marries* her?"

"Yes."

"Let's put things in perspective here. The clothes which Mrs. Shaw bought at the bridal boutique were delivered on June the sixth, is that right?"

"Yes."

"That was a month before your mother died."

"Yes."

"Do you think there's something peculiar about this order of events?"

"I don't . . . can't think anything."

"Why not?"

"I live in the same house with her."

"Are you afraid, Juliet?"

Juliet didn't answer. She had her hands clasped together very tightly, as though someone had threatened to separate them by force.

"Let the record show," the District Attorney said, "that the witness is nodding her head affirmatively."

From the moment Charles Van Eyck walked into the courtroom it was obvious to the District Attorney that the old man had primed himself for the occasion with alcohol. He thanked the bailiff effusively for escorting him to the witness stand, bowed to the members of the jury, shook hands with the District Attorney and swore to tell the truth, the whole truth and nothing but the truth.

"Are you feeling all right, Mr. Van Eyck?"

"Yes, indeed. Never better. And yourself?"

"Please sit down, if you don't mind."

"Oh, I don't mind. Not at all. A pleasure to be here. Didn't have anything else to do anyway."

"Will you state your name and address for the record?"

"Charles Maas Van Eyck, 840 Camino Azur, the azur referring to the jacaranda trees planted along the road, though the blossoms are actually more purplish than bluish, wouldn't you say so?"

"You're retired, are you not, Mr. Van Eyck?"

"Dear me, no. I'm a monitor of government waste. Can't afford to retire from a job like that when there are so few of us and millions of them. Even *you* are one of *them* because you're a county employee."

"Then I suggest we get down to business immediately and avoid further waste. You were related to the deceased woman, Iris Young?"

"She was my sister."

"Was it a close relationship?"

"Close as either of us could stand."

"When was the last time you saw her?"

"Towards the end of June, shortly before she died. She called and asked me to come over, she had something important to talk to me about while the Admiral and the girls were out of the house. Very odd. We never had much to say to each other."

"Did you go?"

"Hard to say no to Iris. She's always been a forceful woman. Kicked and screamed when she was a baby and much the same sort of thing when she got older."

"Who let you into the house?"

"Miranda Shaw. She was on her way to the garden to cut some flowers."

"Did you exchange any words?"

"I asked her about the possibility of a small drink before I talked to Iris. But she said no because Iris had seen my car coming up the driveway and was waiting. In fact, the music was already playing."

"Music?"

"People like Iris who are getting deaf often use the trick of playing loud background music so that other people will have to shout above it. Most irritating. An ordinary conversation turns into a shouting match."

"Do you remember what the weather was like?"

"It's always pretty much the same at that time of year, warm, sunny, rather monotonous."

"Were the windows open in your sister's room?"

"Yes, I distinctly recall sitting beside one to get away from the music. Never cared much for Mozart, same damn thing over and over. He probably started too young, should have been booted out to play cricket like the rest of the boys."

"Can you give me the gist of the conversation you had with your sister, Mr. Van Eyck?"

"She was in the process of drawing up a new will and she wanted to warn me not to expect anything, since I already had an adequate income. I objected to the idea of being cut off without a penny—the principle of the thing, her own flesh and blood and all that—so she said very well, she would leave me a penny. Iris had a rather crude sense of humor."

"Did she tell you anything else about the will?"

"Its main purpose was to set up trusts for the two girls so they'd be well provided for during their lifetime but unable to throw money around. The capital would eventually go to various institutions and foundations."

"What did she intend to leave to Admiral Young, her husband?"

"The house."

"Just the house?"

"Probably its contents, too."

"No cash, stocks, bonds?"

"He has a sizable pension. Iris thought anything more would simply make him a target for some predatory woman."

"Did she mention anyone in particular?"

"She didn't have to. Cooper never got much chance to meet other women, predatory or not, and Miranda was right there in the house all the time. I said, 'Cooper's too old for Miranda.' And she said, 'He's also going to be too poor.'"

"Let's recapitulate for a minute, Mr. Van Eyck. This discussion about your sister's new will took place in a room with the windows open and music playing so loud that you had to shout in order to be heard."

"Yes."

"Did the possibility of an eavesdropper occur to you?"

"Certainly. I'm sure it occurred to her, too. I'd say she probably depended on it to get her message across."

"By that you mean she expected and wanted to be overheard?"

"I think so."

"You may step down now, Mr. Van Eyck. Thank you very much."

"It was no trouble, not a bit. I didn't have anything else to do anyway."

Once again Van Eyck shook hands with the District Attorney and bowed to the members of the jury. Then the District Attorney sat back in his chair and watched the members while they watched the old man leave. They looked a little uneasy, as though they'd just caught the first real scent of blood in the air.

It was time to call in the police.

Sergeant Reuben Orr of the sheriff's department testified that in the early hours of July the fifth—"as soon as we could wake up the judge"—he had obtained a search warrant to enter the premises at 1220 Camino Grande.

"And did you search the premises, Sergeant?"

"Yes, sir. I and my partner, Ernesto Salazar, spent the next two days going through the house room by room except for the burned area, which was left to an arson specialist."

"Did you find anything which has a particular bearing on this case?"

"Yes, sir, several items."

"Are they in this courtroom now?"

"Yes, sir, on the table with the other exhibits. They've been marked 15 A, 15 B, 15 C, and 16."

"Let's consider 15 A first. Would you go over and pick it up and show it to the jury?"

"Yes, sir."

"Now describe it, please."

"It's a piece of pale blue notepaper which has been crumpled and then straightened out and placed between sheets of heavy plastic for safekeeping. The paper is of good quality, made of rags instead of wood pulp, and there are words on it written with a felt-tipped black pen."

"Where did you find it?"

"In a trash bin outside the door of the main kitchen."

"What condition was it in at that time?"

"Crumpled."

"What is it?"

"A letter or note, at least the beginning of one."

"We'll return to that in a moment. I direct your attention to exhibit 15 B. What is it, Sergeant?"

"A half-empty box of pale blue stationery."

"Could the sheet of paper marked 15 A have come from this box?"

"Not only could, it did."

"Where was the box found?"

"In the room occupied by Mrs. Miranda Shaw."

"What about exhibit 15 C?"

"I found that in the same place, on the desk in her room. It's an address book bound in blue leather which has faded and turned greenish from overexposure to light. There are gold initials on the front, M.W.S."

"What does the book contain?"

"Names, addresses and phone numbers, dates of anniversaries and birthdays, and a Christmas card list going back several years."

"All in what appears to be the same handwriting?"

"Yes, sir, even though the entries were made at different times with different writing instruments—pencil, metal nib and ballpoint pens, and in the case of the most recent entries, a black felt-tipped pen."

"Was this handwriting similar in any way to that of the unfinished letter or note found in the trash bin?"

"It was similar in all ways, including the instrument used, a black felt-tipped pen."

"So 15 A was written on a sheet of paper from 15 B, the box of stationery found in Miranda Shaw's room, in the same handwriting as in 15 C, Miranda Shaw's address book."

"Yes, sir."

"Would you read to the jury the words written on 15 A?"

"Yes, sir . . . 'Dearly Beloved: I don't expect you to approve of my plan. It must seem drastic to you but please, please realise that it is the only way we can be together. This is the important thing, being together, you and I, now and always . . .' The word realise, spelled with an S, has been stroked out and realize, spelled with a Z, written above it. Possibly on this account the note was crumpled up and thrown away."

"Does the phrase 'dearly beloved' have any connotation in your mind?"

"Those are the words that usually begin a marriage ceremony."

"A marriage ceremony?"

"Yes, sir."

At the back of the room the fan, as if it had been waiting for the right moment, made a few gasping noises and expired. The District Attorney poured himself another glass of water.

"Sergeant Orr, which of the exhibits 15 A, B and C did you find first?"

"We started our search on the ground floor, so we found the note in the trash bin first, 15 A. It sounded peculiar in view of what had happened, so I was on the lookout for any clue as to who wrote it. When I found the box of stationery and then the address book containing the same handwriting, I became interested in everything else in Mrs. Shaw's room which might possibly have some bearing on the case."

"Such as exhibit 16?"

"Yes, sir."

"Show it to the jury and explain what it is and where you found it."

"Yes, sir. It's a bottle of red and ivory capsules prescribed by Dr. Michael Lane for Mrs. Miranda Shaw on June the twentieth of this year. I found it in the medicine cabinet of Mrs. Shaw's bathroom. Each capsule contains thirty milligrams of Dalmane, which is a fast-acting sedative. The dosage on the bottle is given as one capsule at bedtime for sleep."

"How many capsules are left in this bottle?"

"Six."

"How many were in it originally?"

"According to the pharmacist's label, thirty."

"Now, if Mrs. Shaw took one every night as prescribed, beginning June the twentieth until July the fourth when you picked this up in her medicine cabinet, how many should there be left in the bottle?"

"Fifteen."

"Are there fifteen left?"

"No, sir. As I said before, there are six."

"So nine are unaccounted for."

"They're missing, yes, sir."

"Thank you, Sergeant. That will be all."

It was enough.

On October the fourteenth the grand jury of the county of Santa Felicia returned an indictment of willful homicide against Miranda Waring Shaw in the death of Iris Van Eyck Young, a human being.

Part VII

SHORTLY AFTER MIRANDA Shaw was arrested Aragon went out to the county jail to see her. He was escorted to one of the consulting rooms, which was the size of a shoebox and smelled of disinfectant flowing in through the air conditioner along with cold dry air and the inescapable noises of an institution.

A policewoman brought Miranda as far as the door and then left, or appeared to leave. Aragon had the feeling she was standing just outside in the corridor.

He said, "Hello, Mrs. Shaw," but she didn't answer or even glance at him.

She had changed during the weeks since he'd talked to her in the cabana at the Penguin Club. The makeup around her eyes only emphasized their dullness and her face seemed frozen under its layers of pink and ivory. She'd been allowed to wear her own clothes instead of the cotton dress which was the women's uniform. She had on a blue faille suit that made her look as if she were on her way to a cocktail party and had just dropped in at the jail for a visit with some erring relative.

"I'm sorry," he said. "I'm very sorry."

"Are you. Well, that doesn't change a thing, does it?"

"I thought you'd like to be told anyway."

"Thanks."

They sat down on steel and plastic chairs riveted to the floor.

"Smedler sent me," he said. "He wanted you to know that Admiral Young is arranging bail for you. It's taking time because of the amount of money involved, a hundred thousand dollars. Though that's much too high under the circumstances, there's nothing we can do about it, the judge has an ulcer and quotes Scripture. However, you should be out of here by tomorrow morning."

"Then what?"

"A trial date will be set, which won't be definite because there'll probably be a number of postponements. You can figure on three or four months minimum."

"And where do I spend these three or four months?"

"Not here, that's the important thing."

"I have nowhere to go. I can't very well return to the Admiral's house. It wouldn't look right and I wouldn't feel right with those girls following me around, spying on me. They'd enjoy that, it would be like a new game to them."

227

"Or not so new."

She clutched the steel arms of the chair. He noticed that most of the coral polish on her nails had been chipped or peeled off and the nails themselves bitten. "Did they say evil things about me to the grand jury?"

"Evil? No."

"Why does Cooper want to bail me out?"

"He thinks you're innocent. A lot of people do."

"It's too bad some of them weren't on the grand jury."

"Some of them were," Aragon said. "The vote of fourteen to five means that five people were against the indictment. After going over the transcript, Smedler agrees with them and so do I. Not only is the D.A.'s case weak, he broke half the rules of evidence in presenting it. He won't be able to get away with that kind of stuff when the actual trial comes up . . . Do you feel like answering some questions?"

"I'm not sure."

"Suppose we find out."

"Go ahead."

"Did you ever buy the Admiral any presents?"

"Of course not."

"Both the girls claim they overheard him thanking you."

"They're mistaken. Surely nobody believed them. Why should I, living on a pitifully small salary, buy presents for Cooper with all his money? It's ridiculous."

"People do ridiculous things."

"In this case two people *heard* ridiculous things. Surely nobody believed them," she said again.

"The fact that both girls claim to have overheard it may make it twice as believable."

"But the two of them are always in cahoots about everything."

"I think we can find ways to establish that when the time comes." He consulted the page of notes Smedler had made when he read the transcript of the hearing. "One of the points brought up was that you refused an invitation to go to a fireworks display at the club on the grounds that you didn't want to leave Mrs. Young alone. Yet you left her alone anyway."

"I walked the dog."

"A couple of hours earlier than usual."

"Yes. She asked me to. She said Alouette was acting sick. Heaven knows, that was nothing unusual. She fed the poor creature absurd things like chocolate éclairs and cheesecake."

"At dinner that night you removed the candlesticks from the table because the flickering lights were giving Mrs. Young a migraine. Where did you put them?"

"On the buffet."

"Then at that time both candlesticks would have had your fingerprints on them. Did you handle either of them again?"

"No. I had no reason to."

Aragon felt encouraged. Though she couldn't, under the circumstances, have been enjoying herself, at least she was coming to life. Her eyes were getting brighter and a trace of animation showed on her face.

He said, "A bottle of Dalmane was found in your medicine cabinet. Do you take it regularly?"

"No. Hardly ever. I've been afraid of drugs ever since that clinic in Mexico."

"There were only six capsules left."

"Six? That's impossible. The bottle was nearly full the last time I noticed it."

"And you don't know what happened to the rest?"

"No."

"Did anyone have access to your room?"

"It was cleaned twice a week by one of the day staff. Otherwise I kept it locked. I'm not positive, but I suspect the girls had learned some method of unlocking it. Occasionally items would be in a slightly different place from where I'd left them, or a drawer would be partly open."

"They picked the lock with a credit card," he said. "That's how they knew about the lingerie from the bridal shop."

"I see."

"You bought it on June the sixth."

"Around then, yes."

"Why?"

"For my marriage to Cooper. I had to have a decent trousseau."

"Mrs. Young was still alive at the time."

"Yes, but she didn't *stay* alive. Wasn't it a nice coincidence that she—"

"Be quiet. I mean, for God's sake, don't say things like that. It wasn't nice and a lot of people think it wasn't a coincidence."

"Well, you don't have to be so mean about it. I see things from my standpoint and you see them from yours."

"For the next few months we're going to be sharing a standpoint. Mine." In spite of the air conditioning he had begun to sweat. He loosened his tie and opened the top button of his shirt. "In fact, from now on you've got to consider yourself on trial. Watch what you say, what you do. Be careful where you go and with whom."

"It would be simpler if I just stayed here in jail," she said bitterly. "I might as well if I have no rights left, if I can't even see the people I want to."

"That depends on what people you want to see."

"I won't tell you. You'll only get mean again if I do."

"Grady Keaton. Is he one of them?"

"Yes."

"Why?"

"*Why?* Because we love each other. And I must explain to him that whatever I did was for the two of us, so we could be together."

"I think we should avoid bringing Grady into the case if we can," Aragon said.

"What difference does it make?"

"It may seem peculiar in this day and age, but juries are more likely to vote for a conviction if sexual misconduct is involved. The events leading up to and down from Pasoloma—or down to and up from if you want to be geographical—can do you a lot of harm."

"I want to see Grady."

"I'm advising you not to, for the time being anyway. If you have a message for him, let me deliver it."

She was silent for a long time, staring at the blank grey wall as though it were her window on the world.

"I love him," she said finally. "Tell him I love him and when all this silly fuss is over we'll be together again."

The front doors of the club were propped open with rubber wedges and taped with Fresh Paint signs. There was no one in the office. Aragon walked in unchallenged.

Under a shroud of late-summer fog the terrace was deserted and in the pool only one swimmer was visible, a large woman moving slowly through the water like an overloaded barge.

In the corridor Walter Henderson, the manager, was occupied at the bulletin board tacking up some of the pictures from the last party, a backgammon and bingo tournament. By Henderson's standards it had been a dull affair, with a great deal of confusion about who was playing what, and he was trying to plan something more dynamic for the next theme party, which would fall on Halloween. Since the social-events committee had vetoed any more money for decorations, he was working on a clever way to use the life-sized plastic skeletons from the previous Halloween. A Gallows Gala might be effective, with each of the skeletons dressed as a famous murderer or murderee and strategically placed throughout the club and its grounds, hanging from the diving tower and from a limb of the cypress tree (very effective if there was a decent wind), peeking into the ballroom windows from the oleander hedge, even sitting on one of the toilets in the ladies' powder room. (What delicious screams—he could hear them now: *Help, help!*)

". . . could help me," Aragon said.

Henderson was jolted back to reality as the skeletons fell from the diving tower and out of the tree and off the toilet. "Oh, damn. What do you want?"

"I'm looking for Ellen Brewster."

"She's in the office."

"No."

"Well, she's *supposed* to be in the office. But of course, that doesn't mean a thing around here. Try the snack bar. She's been drinking coffee by the gallon lately."

"Thanks."

Aragon went down the corridor to the snack bar. A couple of the tables were occupied by boys and girls in tennis costume. Little Frederic Quinn was among them, his tennis racket stuck in the back of his sweater in order to leave his hands free for shooting straws out of their paper sheaths. He acknowledged Aragon's presence by shooting a straw at him. It missed.

Ellen was sitting at a corner table with a pot of tea in front of her and a doughnut with a bite taken out of it. She looked cold.

He said, "May I sit down?"

"I guess."

"Anything the matter?"

"I hate the summer fogs. They depress me. Winter fogs are natural, you expect them and you're depressed anyway and—Oh hell, the fog has nothing to do with it. I feel lousy, that's all."

"Sorry."

"Why did you come here?"

"To see Grady," Aragon said. "I have a message for him."

"Really? Well, you're about forty-eight hours too late. He took off as soon as he heard the news about Miranda. Oh, I think he wanted to leave anyway, I could see him getting restless, bored. Miranda's arrest simply brought it to a head. He was afraid she'd drag him into it and the whole business about the Porsche would come out and maybe a lot of other stuff as well."

"Do you know where he went?"

"He didn't leave a forwarding address. He just patted me on the head, told me I was a nice girl and packed his bags." She had begun crumbling the doughnut and rolling the pieces into greasy little pills. "Want to hear something funny? I lent him fifty dollars."

Frederic aimed a straw in her direction. It hit her on the side of the head but she paid no attention.

"Tell Miranda," she said, "tell her he wanted to say goodbye to her but he had to leave right away because a chance for a decent job came up very suddenly. In Oklahoma."

"A chance for a job came up very suddenly in Oklahoma."

"Yes."

"She won't believe it."

"Why not?" Ellen said. "I did."

The indictment and arrest of Miranda also led to some less predictable events.

In early fall Cordelia, free of the restraint of her mother and to a large extent of the Admiral, who was preoccupied, bought an Aston-Martin guaranteed by the dealer to go one hundred and thirty miles an hour. Anxious to determine the accuracy of this claim, Cordelia chose for the test a side road that was practically deserted. When she floored the accelerator, only one other car was in sight, but unfortunately it belonged to an off-duty patrolman.

Cordelia's defense was that nearly everything in the Aston-Martin was computerized and something must have gone wrong with the circuits controlling the speedometer. Her driver's license was revoked anyway and she took up bicycling. Clad in matching jogging suits and plastic helmets the girls pedaled around town on a bright red tandem equipped with a horn on the main handlebars for Cordelia and a bell at the rear for Juliet.

Juliet had some criticism of this arrangement, which pretty well limited her view: "Your behind is enormous."

"What do I care," Cordelia said. "I'm in front."

In late September, Frederic Quinn was, for a price, reinstated at Sophrosune School. For his first report in Social Studies class he chose a black widow spider. After spending two days (and a hundred and fifty demerits) in the search he found a specimen underneath a gopher trap in the garage and brought it to school in his sister April's Lucite earring box. By this time the spider had lost a couple of legs and considerable *joie de vivre* as well as *joie de tuer.* However, the red hourglass on its abdomen was still visible, identifying it as dangerous.

"Get that damn thing out of here," the teacher said. "You're supposed to be making your report on a current event from the newspaper."

"I am. It was in all the newspapers how a woman I know personally was arrested for murder just like a black widow spider stinging her mate to death, only it wasn't her mate—"

"Put it in the wastebasket."

"This is my sister's best earring box. She'll kill me."

"You have a choice," the teacher said. "Her or me."

It was in mid-November, after Miranda's trial had been postponed for a third time, that Charles Van Eyck received the letter from Tokyo. He didn't know anyone in Tokyo, and those of his acquaintances financially able to travel in the Orient were no longer physically able.

There was no doubt, however, that the letter was meant for him. The envelope was neatly typed Charles Maas Van Eyck, 840 Camino Azur, Santa Felicia, California, and even the zip code was correct. Still he hesitated to open it. At his age bad news outnumbered good by a considerable margin and he felt it would be wise to prepare himself for the worst with a glass of the best. He poured himself half a tumbler of Scotch from the decanter in his den.

It was a cold drizzly day, exactly the kind he remembered from his trips to Scotland— hardly any wonder the natives had invented Scotch, it was a simple matter of survival—so he lit the logs laid tepee style in the grate, avocado prunings, grey and smooth and no bigger than a child's arm. Then, using his thumbnail as a paper knife, he slit open the envelope.

> *Dear Charles:*
>
> *I don't know when or if you will receive this. I am enclosing it in my chess move to Professor Sukimoto in Tokyo, asking him to stamp and post it for me. I have addressed the outside envelope to his office at the university as usual but this time I marked it Hold for Return. I know he is on a research leave in Paris and won't be back for several months. This fits in perfectly with the plans I've made for Miranda.*
>
> *It won't surprise you to learn that I've worked things out as carefully as my limited mobility allowed. What will surprise you is that you were actually present when the idea took shape in my mind. It was the last time you came to this house*

for dinner. Miranda, acting out her role of governess, had given the girls some questions to answer, questions for a summer night she called them. Juliet protested that it wasn't summer yet, so she didn't have the answers. But I had mine, right away, then and there.

Do you remember those questions? I can never forget them:

Have I earned something today?

Have I learned something today?

Have I helped someone?

Have I felt glad to be alive?

In my case the answers were easy: no, no, no and no. I added one more question. Did I have a reason to go on living? No.

You were right, Charles, in that anonymous letter you wrote warning me about taking a Jezebel into my home. She is exactly what you claimed, a Jezebel. And Cooper is what he always has been, a nice gullible fool. And the girls, my daughters, they will be the victims unless I act to stop it.

I must protect my girls. They will never marry, never create, never be employed. (What happened? Why are they like this? I've blamed myself a thousand times and Cooper a thousand more, though the blame game is useless.) But within their limits they can be quite happy if they aren't criticized or ridiculed, if they're not at the mercy of a woman like Miranda.

So I have made my plans and I think they'll work. Even some of the things I didn't really plan may implicate her in my death. The Dalmane is an example. I took a dozen or so capsules from her medicine chest—I learned from watching Cordelia how easily a lock can be picked—to alleviate some of the suffering which is inevitable. I have endured a great deal of suffering and I can endure more, but I hope the Dalmane capsules will help. I will swallow them after the candle is lit and before I turn on the gas and strike myself on the head with my cane, not hard, just enough to cause bleeding. Heads bleed easily, more easily than hearts, perhaps.

I expect the handle of the cane and the candlestick, both being metal, to survive the fire to some extent. There will be blood on the cane, which should start the police wondering, and no fingerprints on the candlestick because I will have wiped it clean, and that will keep them wondering. Probably none of them will even think of suicide because the whole thing is too bizarre. That's why I planned it the way I did.

I intend to get Miranda to mail this to Professor Sukimoto, a grotesque little touch I can't resist. I'll also see that she walks the dog early. She's bound to tell the police I asked her to, but will they believe her? Will anyone believe anything she says? Cooper, perhaps. No one else.

Poor Cooper. I feel sorry for him, but he'll get over my death pretty quickly even without Miranda around to help him. And she won't be around. She won't be marrying my husband, spending my money, managing my daughters.

I have unloaded all this on you, Charles, because I have a notion you'd rather not think of me as a victim. I have been a victim of some cruel things in my life but I am in full charge of my own death.

It's a victory of sorts.

Iris

The receptionist in the District Attorney's office wore a uniform of a mustard color which made Van Eyck quite nauseated.

He said faintly, "Some time ago, July, I believe it was, I wrote the D.A. a letter about the Iris Young case."

"What is the name, please?"

"My name or the name on the letter?"

"I thought you said you wrote it."

"I did. But I didn't sign it. I never do. I mean, there are so many things one can express better without signing a name."

"I'm sure one can," the woman said. "But when you do sign a name, what do you sign?"

"I believe in this case it was Fair Play. That's not important, however. I mentioned my letter to the D.A. merely to introduce—or rather to let it be known that my interest in the case is—"

"Wait here a moment, Mr. Play."

"No, no. I'm not Mr. Play."

"But you just said—"

"Forget about the name. The important thing is that I've just had a revelation, a most astonishing revelation."

"We don't have time for revelations in this department, especially those induced by alcohol. And you have been drinking, haven't you, Mr. Play?"

"I told you I'm *not* Mr. Play. I don't even *know* anybody called Mr. Play."

"Then why did you sign his name to a letter?"

"Oh God," Van Eyck said and turned and ran.

Back home he poured himself another tumbler of Scotch. Then he threw some more avocado logs in the grate and put the letter from Tokyo on top of them.

It flamed briefly, turned black, turned grey, and rode the updraft into the chimney.

Dear me, he thought with a little twinge of surprise. *I believe I've just murdered Miranda.*

MERMAID

to Eleanor McKay Van Cott

CONTENTS

1

CHILD

1

THE GIRL WAS conspicuous even before she entered the office. It was a windy day and everything was in motion except her face. Her coat beat against her legs like captive wings and her long fair hair seemed to be trying to tie itself into knots. The sign above the door, SMEDLER, DOWNS, CASTLEBERG, MACFEE, POWELL, ATTORNEYS AT LAW, twisted and turned as if the partners were struggling among themselves.

Charity Nelson, Mr. Smedler's private secretary, was taking the receptionist's place during the lunch hour because she herself was on a diet and didn't want to see or think of food.

The front door opened and the wind pushed the girl into the office. She looked surprised at what had happened. She was very thin, which made Charity think about food and sent nasty little pains up and down and around her stomach.

She said irritably, "What can I do for you?"

"I like the little cage."

"Little cage?"

"The one outside . . . the one at the back."

"That's Mr. Smedler's own elevator. It leads to his private office."

"Do you think he'd give me a ride in it?"

"No."

"Not even one?"

"Only if you were a client."

The girl didn't look like a client, at least not the kind who paid. She was quite pretty, with high cheekbones and large brown eyes as bright and expressionless as glass.

"Do you wish to see Mr. Smedler?" Charity said.

"I don't know."

She took a seat at the corner window and picked up a magazine. It lay on her lap unopened and, Charity noticed, upside down.

"Are you sure you came to the right office?" Charity said.

"Yes, I took a taxi. The driver knew just where to go."

"I didn't mean how did you get here. I meant did you have a specific reason for coming. You realize this is a law firm."

"I'm bothering you, aren't I? My brother Hilton is always telling me I mustn't bother people, but how can I help it if I don't know what bothers them?"

"Would you care to make an appointment with one of our attorneys?"

"I think I'll just sit here for a while and look around."

"Everyone's out to lunch."

"I don't mind," the girl said. "I'm not in a hurry."

At 1:25 they began returning to the office: two typists, a file clerk, Mr. MacFee with a client, Mr. Powell and his secretary, a junior member of the firm and the receptionist, who looked, Charity noted bitterly, well-fed and contented.

The girl showed her first sign of excitement. She rose suddenly, dropping the magazine on the floor.

"That's him," she said. "He's who I want to see, the one wearing the glasses. He has a nice face. What's his name?"

"Tom Aragon. What's yours?"

"Cleo."

"Cleo what?"

"The same as my brother Hilton's. Jasper, Cleo Jasper. It's awfully ugly, don't you think?"

"I'll check and see if Mr. Aragon will have time to talk to you." She told Aragon on the intercom: "Some chick is waiting to see you because you have a nice face. Can you buy that?"

"Sure. Send her in."

"Better come out and get her, junior. She looks like she couldn't find her way out of a wet paper bag."

Aragon shared an office with another junior member of the firm. It was furnished as if no clients were expected, and in fact few came. Aragon's duties were mostly confined to legwork for the senior lawyers, especially Smedler, whose cases often involved rich women. Cleo Jasper wasn't yet a woman and she didn't look rich. The straight-backed chair she sat down on seemed to suit her better than the overstuffed leather surrounding Smedler. Her clothes were oddly childish, a navy-blue jumper over a white blouse, white knee socks and shoes that looked like the Mary Janes of another era. She wasn't carrying a handbag, but one of the pockets of her jumper bulged as though it contained a coin purse.

"What can I do for you, Miss Jasper?"

"I've never been to a lawyer before. You have a nice face—that's why I picked you."

"I suppose it's as good a reason as any other," Aragon said. "Why do you need a lawyer?"

"I want to find out my rights. I have a new friend. He says I have some rights."

"Who claims you don't?"

"Nobody exactly. Except that I never get to do what I want to do, what other people do."

"Like what?"

"Vote. Not that I specially want to vote, not knowing anything about Presidents and things, but I didn't even know I could."

"How old are you?"

"Twenty-two. My new friend says I could have voted four years ago and nobody even told me."

"Wasn't the subject brought up in school?"

"I can't remember. I have foggy times. Hilton says voting is just for responsible people, who don't have foggy times."

"Are you an American citizen?"

"I was born right here in Santa Felicia." The girl frowned. "It was a terrible occasion. Hilton and his wife, Frieda, often talk about how it was such a terrible occasion."

"Why?"

"My mother died. She was too old to have a baby but she had one anyway and I'm it. Hilton says she almost got into the record book because she was forty-eight. Hilton was already grown up and married when I was born. But I didn't go to stay with him and Frieda until I was eight. I lived with my grandmother before that. She was very nice, only she died. Hilton says she wore herself out worrying over me. She left me a lot of money. I never get to use it, though."

"Why not?"

"I'm exceptional."

"I see."

"Well, are you surprised or aren't you?"

"Not particularly. All people are exceptional in one way or another."

"You don't understand. I'm . . . My new friend has lots of fun ways of saying it, like I have a few marbles missing or I've only got one oar in the water or I'm not playing with a full deck. It sounds better like that than spelling it right out that I'm . . . you know, retarded."

He was, in fact, surprised. She had none of the Down's syndrome physical features and she spoke well, expressing herself quite clearly. She even wanted to vote. Whether or not she was simply echoing the ideas of her new friend, it seemed an unusual desire on the part of a retarded girl.

Not girl, he thought. She was a woman of twenty-two. That's where the retardation was more obvious. If she'd claimed to be fourteen or fifteen he would have believed her.

"Can you read and write?"

"Some. Not very much."

"What about your new friend? Does he read and write very well?"

"Oh, gosh yes. He's one of the . . ." She slapped her left hand over her mouth so quickly and decisively it must have hurt her. "I'm not supposed to talk about him to anyone."

"Why not?"

"It would spoil things. He's my only friend except for the gardener and his dog, Zia. Zia is a basset hound. Do you like basset hounds?"

"Yes."

"I just love them."

"Getting back to your new friend . . ."

"No. No, I really mustn't."

"All right. We'll talk about the voting. I believe the only requirements are that you be an American citizen, at least eighteen years old, not on parole or confined to a mental institution and that you sign an affidavit to that effect. You are, of course, expected to be able to read the affidavit before signing."

"I could practice ahead of time, couldn't I?"

"Of course."

Her lips began to move as though she was already practicing in silence. She had a small, well-shaped mouth with prominent ridges between the upper lip and the nose. According to old wives' tales, when this area was clearly defined it indicated strength of character. Aragon looked at the timid, underdeveloped girl in front of him and decided the old wives must have been wrong.

She said finally, "Tell me about my other rights."

"Which ones?"

"Suppose I just wanted to get on a bus and go somewhere . . . oh, somewhere like Chicago. Could I do that?"

"It depends on whether you have sufficient funds and whether you feel capable of looking after yourself in a large city. It would be a good idea to talk it over first with your brother and his wife."

"No way."

"Why not?"

"They wouldn't let me go. I've never been anyplace except once last Easter on a boat. Me and some of the other students at Holbrook were taken on a cruise to Catalina on Donny Whitfield's father's yacht."

Holbrook Hall was known throughout Southern California as a school for the troubled and troubling offspring of the very wealthy. In the more expensive magazines it was advertised as "a facility designed to meet the special needs of exceptional teenagers and young adults."

"How long have you been at Holbrook Hall, Cleo?"

She blushed very faintly. "You called me Cleo. That's nice. It's friendly, you know."

"How long?"

"Forever."

"Come on, Cleo."

"A year, maybe longer. I always had a governess before that. Also Hilton and Frieda gave me lessons in things. He's really smart and she used to be a schoolteacher. Ted goes to college. He's their son. He drinks and smokes pot and . . . well, lots of things like that. Imagine him being my nephew and he's only a year younger than I am. He tells everybody I'm a half-wit that his parents found in an orphanage."

"So you want to get away from Ted and your brother and sister-in-law."

"Mainly I only want to know my rights."

"Is there money available to you?"

"I have charge cards. But if I used any of them to do something Hilton disapproved of he would probably cancel them. At least that's what my new friend says."

"Your new friend seems to have quite a few opinions about your affairs."

"Oh my, yes. Some I don't understand. Like he says we are all in cages and we must break out of them. I thought if I could get inside the cage that goes up and down your building and then out by myself again I would sort of understand what he's talking about."

"Why not ask him?"

"I'm supposed to try and figure things out by myself. He says I'm not as dumb as I act. I don't understand that part either and I try. I try real, real hard."

"I'm sure you do," Aragon said. Cleo's new friend, whatever his motive, was feeding her stuff she couldn't digest. "What else does your friend advise you to do?"

"He thinks I should take some money from my savings account and spend it on whatever I want, without Hilton's permission."

"Could you do that?"

"I guess. If I wasn't scared."

"Does your friend ever bring up the subject of borrowing any of this money?"

"Oh, no. He hates money. He says it's rotten, only that's not the word he used."

"'The love of money is the root of all evil.' Is that what he said?"

"Why, yes." She looked pleased. "So you know him, too."

"No. We've both read some of the same books. The quotation is from the Bible."

"Is that what the Bible really says about money?"

"One of the things."

"Then I suppose it's true. It's funny, though, because Hilton is very Christian, yet he works all the time to make more of it."

"People often do."

"Hilton quotes the Bible quite a bit. Ted says it's a bunch of—he used a bad word. Ted knows more bad words than anyone in the world except Donny Whitfield at school. Donny talks so dirty hardly anybody can understand him. He's fat. On our free afternoons from school we each get five dollars to spend and Donny spends his all on ice cream. His afternoons are never really free, he has to have a counselor with him every minute to keep him out of trouble. He's a bad boy. Why are there good boys and bad boys?"

"No one can answer that, Cleo."

"You'd think if God was going to the trouble of making boys in the first place he'd just make good ones."

Charity Nelson, Mr. Smedler's secretary, stuck her head in the door. When she saw that the girl was still there she raised her eyebrows until they almost disappeared under her orange wig.

"Mr. Smedler wants to see you, junior."

"Tell him I have a client."

"I told him. He didn't believe me."

"Tell him again."

"You're playing with fire, junior. Smedler had a big weekend."

When Charity closed the door again the girl said, "That woman doesn't like me."

"Miss Nelson doesn't like many people."

"I'd better leave now." She glanced uneasily at the door as if she were afraid Charity might be hiding behind it. "I took too much of your time already."

"Fifteen minutes."

"Hilton says every second counts. He says time and tide wait for no man, whatever that means. It must mean something or Hilton wouldn't say it."

"What brought you to this office in the first place?"

"Nothing. I mean I pass here every day on my way to Holbrook Hall. Frieda and Hilton drive me mostly but sometimes Ted when he's home from college. That's scary but sort of fun, too. Anyway, that's how I saw the little cage moving up and down and wanted a ride in it and . . . and . . ."

She had begun to stammer and he couldn't understand her words. He waited quietly until she calmed down. He didn't know what had excited her, all the talking she'd done or memories of riding scarily with Ted or something deeper and inexplicable.

She pressed her fists against the sides of her mouth as if to steady it. "Also I wanted to see a lawyer about my rights. I thought if I came here I'd get to ride in the little cage."

"Sorry. That's not possible today."

"Some other time?"

"Maybe."

"Maybes never happen," she said. "Not the nice ones anyway."

"This one will."

She stood up and removed the coin purse from her pocket. "I'll pay you now." She emptied the contents of the purse on his desk: three one-dollar bills, two quarters and a nickel. "I hope this is enough. I had to pay the taxi to bring me here and this is all that's left of my free-afternoon money."

"Let's make the charge one dollar. This is your first visit and I haven't helped you very much."

"You tried," she said softly. "And you have a nice face."

"Shall I call you a taxi?"

"No, I can walk. I think I'll go to the museum. The staff likes us to go to the museum on free days. They think we're learning something. How far is it from here?"

"About a mile and a half. Do you know the way?"

"Oh sure. I've been there millions of times . . ."

He watched from the window as she left the building. The museum was due north. She walked rapidly and confidently south.

2

THE TABLE WAS long and dark walnut, carved in the intricate Georgian style and designed for an elegant English dining room. But Hilton sat at the head of it as though he were a captain instructing his crew on how to maneuver through stormy seas, which to Hilton meant taxes, Democrats, inflation, undercooked lamb and bad manners.

The crew wasn't paying much attention. His wife, Frieda, had brought a copy of *TV Guide* to the table and was surveying the evening's listings. She was a pretty woman given to fat and to peevish little smiles when she was annoyed and didn't want to admit it. They appeared frequently during mealtime when she was struck by the gross unfairness of Hilton being able to eat everything in sight and never gain an ounce, while she couldn't even walk past a chocolate éclair without putting on a pound or two.

The rest of the crew was equally inattentive. Lisa, the college student who served dinner every night because the cook refused to work after seven o'clock, moved rhythmically in and out and around and about as if she had an invisible radio stuck in her ear. Her skintight jeans and T-shirt were partly hidden by an embroidered white bib apron, the closest thing to a uniform that Frieda could coax her into wearing. She was the same age as Cleo but the two seldom had any personal communication except for occasional shrugs and eye rollings when Hilton was being particularly boring.

Cleo sat with her left hand propping up her head, her eyes fixed on the plate in front of her.

Frieda had come to depend on television for company. Hilton was often away on business, and even when he was at home the conversation was kept on Cleo's level so Cleo wouldn't feel excluded. It was Frieda herself who felt excluded.

"Please remove your elbow from the table, Cleo," Hilton said. "And eat your soup like a good girl."

"I can't. It's got funny things in it like shells."

"They *are* shells. It's bouillabaisse."

"And bones, too."

"Well?"

"The gardener won't even give his dog bones. He says they might make holes in his bowels."

"I don't consider this a suitable subject for dinner conversation. Now eat your soup. Cook makes excellent bouillabaisse. Waste not, want not."

"Oh, for heaven's sake," Frieda said. "Don't eat the soup if you don't like it . . . Now tell us what you did today."

"I went to the museum."

"You were gone all afternoon."

"I saw lots and lots of pictures."

"Did you meet anyone?"

"There were lots and lots of people."

"I meant, did you talk to anyone?"

"One person."

"Was it a man or a woman?"

"A man."

"Cleo, dear, we're not trying to pry," Hilton said. "But what did you and this man talk about?"

"I asked him where the ladies' room was. And he told me, and then he said, 'Have a nice day,' so I did."

There was a brief silence, then Hilton's voice sounding worried: "I thought the museum was closed on Mondays."

The girl sat mute and pale, staring down at the bones and shells in front of her until Lisa came to take them away.

A twitch appeared at the corner of Hilton's right eye, moving the lid like an evil little wink. "Of course you know how important it is to tell the truth, don't you, Cleo?"

"I went to the museum. There were lots and lots of pictures. I saw lots and lots of people . . ."

"I care about you very deeply, Cleo. Your welfare was entrusted to me. I have to know where you go and what company you keep."

"I go to Holbrook Hall. I have lots of company at Holbrook Hall."

"Leave the girl alone for now," Frieda said sharply.

"Obviously this is one of her foggy times. We can't expect her to behave like a normal person."

"I am exceptional," Cleo said.

"Certainly you are, dear. And it's not your fault you're different. Everyone's different. Look at Lisa. She's different from other people."

"In what way?" Lisa said, putting the gravy boat on the table, spilling a dollop and wiping it up with her forefinger.

"You wear awfully tight pants," Cleo said. "I don't see how you can go to the . . . well, you know, the ladies' room if you're in a hurry."

"Practice."

Hilton sat in gloomy silence. He had felt for some time now that things were getting out of hand, that he had no control over Cleo or Frieda or the servants. Even the gardener's dog, Zia, didn't acknowledge his presence when he walked down the driveway to get the paper in the morning.

Bad manners and taxes and crime and Democrats and unsuitable subjects for dinner conversation were sweeping the country. He was only forty-five and he wanted to stop the world and get off.

"I would rather be exceptional wearing tight pants," Cleo said.

Hilton sighed and served the scrawny rock hens which reminded him of Cleo, and the wild rice which was only grass from Minnesota, and the asparagus which he hated.

"Why couldn't I be exceptional wearing tight pants? Why not?"

"Please don't argue with me, Cleo."

"Why can't I wear . . ."

"Because that style of dress is not suitable for you."

"Why isn't it?"

"There's a stranger in our house. We don't air our personal problems in front of . . ."

"I'm going to tell on you. I'm going to tell everybody."

"They won't listen to you."

"Oh, yes, they will. I have rights."

Hilton ate the scrawny little hen that reminded him of Cleo, and the wild rice which was really grass and the asparagus which he hated. His hands shook.

"I have rights," the girl said again softly.

Later that night Ted came home on his semester break from college. He'd hoped to arrive in time to make a pass at Lisa but she'd already left and he went up to his room alone. He rolled a joint with some pot he'd bought from an assistant professor who'd allegedly smuggled it in from Jakarta. More likely it was grown in somebody's backyard, but he lit up anyway, stripped to his shorts and lay down on the bed.

He was a good-looking young man, tall and heavyset like his father. His long brown hair reached almost to his shoulders in spite of Hilton's attempts to get him to cut it. He wore a beard which his parents hadn't seen yet and were certain to squawk about. But after the first couple of puffs he didn't care.

He was only halfway through the joint when there was a knock on the door.

"Who is it?"

"Me. Let me in."

He opened the door and Cleo came into the room. She was wearing a pink nightgown, not quite transparent.

"Hey, go and put some clothes on," Ted said by way of greeting. "The old boy will have a fit. He thinks I'm a sex maniac."

"Are you?"

"Sure."

"What do sex maniacs do?"

"Oh, Christ, beat it, will you?"

"You're smoking that funny stuff again, aren't you? I could smell it all the way down the hall."

"So?"

"Give me a puff."

"Why?"

"Donny Whitfield says it makes you feel keen. I want to feel keen."

"Well, at least you don't have to worry that it will damage your brain."

She took a puff and immediately let the smoke out again, then sat down on the bed. "I don't feel keen."

"You should inhale and hold it. Like this."

"Okay." She made another attempt. "Your beard looks awful."

"Thanks."

"May I touch it?"

"If you're that hard up for a thrill, go ahead."

She touched his beard, very gently. "Oh. Oh, it's soft. Like a bunny."

"That's me, *Playboy* bunny of the year. Now haul your ass out of here."

"You talk dirty," she said. "Give me another puff."

"I will if you promise to leave right afterwards."

"I promise."

She inhaled the smoke, holding it in her lungs for a few seconds. "I think I'm beginning to feel keen. But I'm not sure—I never felt keen before."

"You promised to leave."

"In a minute. I haven't had a chance to ask you the question I came to ask you."

"Go ahead."

"Do you think I'd look good in tight pants, the kind Lisa wears?"

"How the hell would I know?"

"I could show you my figure."

"Hey, wait a minute. For Christ's sake, don't . . ."

But she'd already taken off the pink nightgown and was standing naked, pale and shivering as though she had a chill. She didn't have a chill.

Ted closed his eyes.

"Ted, are you sleeping?"

"Yeah."

"You didn't even look at me."

"I looked enough."

"Well, what do you think?"

"About what?"

"Gosh, you must have foggy moments like me. You haven't paid any attention. I asked you a question."

He sat up on the bed. Sweat was pouring down the back of his neck.

"Are you having a foggy moment, Ted?"

"Yeah."

"You're not sleeping, are you, Ted?"

"No."

"You haven't even looked at me yet."

"I looked enough."

"I like being here with you, Ted, you know? It's cozy. Do you like it, too?"

"Yeah."

She sat down on the bed beside him. Their thighs were touching and he could feel the quiver of her body and her warm breath against his neck.

"Cleo . . . listen. You better . . ."

"Now I've even forgotten the question I was going to ask you and it was terribly important. Oh, now I remember. Do you think I should wear tight pants like Lisa?"

"Not now," he said in a whisper. "Not for a while."

"You're feeling real keen, aren't you, Ted?"

"Lie down."

"What if I don't want to?"

"You want to."

He put one hand between her legs. She let out a squeal and fell back on the bed.

Hilton was awakened by the sound of a car. He thought it must belong to a neighbor, since Ted wasn't due to arrive until the following morning and his arrival was usually accompanied by the blare of a stereo and the whine of tires.

Hilton lay for a long time listening to the night sounds, the ones he hated: Frieda snoring in the adjoining room, the dog Zia barking at a stray cat; and the one he liked: the song of the mockingbird which could begin any time of the day or night. During the day it seemed a medley of all the noises in the neighborhood, coos and rattles and squawks and shrieks, but at night it was mainly a pure clear whistle, the same phrase repeated over and over again, like an impressionist revealing his true self only after the audience had left.

There were other sounds, too: a cricket in the rosebush outside Hilton's room and the rolls and gurgles of hunger inside his stomach. He got up, put on a robe and slippers and went out into the hall intending to go down to the kitchen for some milk and crackers. Before he reached the top of the stairs he saw a light shining under the door of Ted's room at the end of the hall.

Hilton stood listening. Ted's presence was always accompanied by noise of one kind or another, but tonight there was none, not even faint music from a radio. He thought Frieda or the day maid had left a light on after cleaning the room to have it ready for Ted.

He opened the door. Two people were lying across the bed, their bodies so closely entwined they looked like one, a monster with two heads. It wasn't the first time Ted had sneaked a girl into his room, and Hilton had started to close the door before he realized the girl was Cleo.

A scream formed in his throat, froze, melted, trickled back down into his chest. The two bodies separated and became two.

"God almighty," Ted said and sat up on the bed.

"Get dressed," his father said, "and get out."

"Oh, for Christ's sake, this is some homecoming."

"Put your robe on, Cleo."

"I don't have a robe," Cleo said. "Only that pink nightie Frieda gave me for my birthday."

"Here." Hilton took off his own robe and covered her with it.

"Are you mad at me, Hilton?"

"No."

"Cross your heart and hope to . . ."

"Please be quiet."

"He's mad at me," Ted said. "I'm the villain."

"You are a despicable cad," Hilton said. "And I want you out of this house tonight."

"I've been driving all day. I'm tired."

"Not too tired, I notice. Now move. And don't come back to this house, ever."

"Well, for Christ's sake, how do you like that," Ted said. "This crazy kid comes in here naked and flings herself at me and . . ."

"Shut up. Get moving and don't come back to this house. Ever."

"This is crazy, I tell you."

"Cleo, go to your room. I want to talk to you."

"You are mad at me. I," the girl said, "I knew it, I just knew it. And I didn't come in here naked. I had my nightie on and I took it off to show Ted what my figure looked like, in order to get his opinion."

"It seems to have been favorable." Hilton walked out into the hall and after a minute the girl followed him, dragging the pink nightgown on the floor behind her like a guilty conscience.

In the blue and white room whose furnishings had not been altered since she was a child, Cleo sat in a white wicker rocking chair that creaked and squawked with every move she made. Hilton stood with his back to her, facing the wallpaper Cleo had been allowed to choose for herself: masses of white flowers and green leaves and blue-eyed kittens.

"Stop that," he said. "Stop that rocking."

"You are mad at me."

"I'm disappointed."

"It's the same thing."

"No."

"Is Ted going away?"

"Yes."

"Forever and ever?"

"He won't be living in this house anymore." His voice shook. "Are you sorry for what you did?"

"I guess. If you want me to be."

"I want you to be sorry."

"Okay, I am."

He knew he might as well be talking to one of the blue-eyed kittens romping across the wallpaper, but he couldn't stop trying. "I love you. You realize that, don't you, Cleo?"

"Oh, sure. You're always telling me."

"Do you love me in return?"

"Sure."

"No, you don't," he said in a harsh whisper. "You care about nothing."

"Oh, I do so. I love Zia and ice-cream cones and T. V. and flowers and strawberries . . ."

"And where do I rate on that scale—somewhere between ice-cream cones and strawberries?"

She'd begun to rock again, very fast, as if to outdistance his voice, and muffle the funny little sounds that were coming from her mouth. These were the sounds of her foggy moments. After a time they would go away.

"Cleo, answer me. Where do I fit on that scale of yours?"

"I have to love Zia best," she said slowly, "because he never gets mad and when I talk to him he always listens like I was a real person."

He turned and grabbed the back of the wicker chair to keep it quiet. "You *are* a real person, Cleo."

"Not like the others. You said I didn't care about things. Real people care about things."

"I didn't mean that. I'm sorry. I'm terribly sorry."

"That's all right."

"Cleo." He fell on his knees beside her, and began stroking her hair. "Promise me something. You must never let another man touch you. Will you promise me that?"

"Sure," she said. He smelled nice, nicer than Ted.

In the morning Ted's BMW was missing and the only sign he'd come and gone was a pair of skis taken from the roof rack and thrown alongside the driveway.

The ski season was over.

From the breakfast room the sounds of quarreling began as soon as it was light outside. Loud sounds, soft sounds, then loud again, depending on who was talking, Frieda or Hilton.

Cleo stared up at the ceiling and listened. Frieda was such a good screamer that every word was clear: Ted was her son as well as Hilton's . . . Hilton had no right to kick him out so cruelly, his very own son . . . It wasn't even Ted's fault, it was hers, that damned girl, spoiled, spoiled rotten . . . She didn't know right from wrong and had no intention of learning . . . It was Hilton who spoiled her, letting her twist him around her little finger, setting him against his own son . . . And what if she had a baby? . . . All these damned morons should be sterilized . . .

Cleo put her hands over her ears but the sounds sifted in through the open window, seeped up through the floorboards and under the cracks of doors like poison gas . . . your fault . . . sacrificed the whole family . . . damn morons should be sterilized . . . spoiled brat . . . one bad apple spoils the whole barrel . . .

She rolled her head back and forth on the pillow, smothering the words in feathers. She wasn't an apple, a brat, a moron. She was Cleo.

"I am Cleo," she said aloud. "I got rights."

2

WOMAN

3

DURING THE NEXT few days Aragon thought of the girl off and on in a desultory way. It wasn't until Thursday that he had reason to remember her more vividly. A card was brought into his office by the receptionist: Hilton W. Jasper. The card made him think of the girl's high, thin voice repeating, "Hilton says . . . Hilton says."

He told the receptionist, "Send him in here."

"Here?"

"It's the only place I have."

"It's a mess. This man looks important, you know, like in M-O-N-E-Y."

"Send him in anyway. He might enjoy slumming."

Hilton Jasper wasn't quite what Aragon expected. A tall, well-built man in his forties, he was almost handsome except for the puffiness around his eyes and the thin, tight mouth.

"Mr. Aragon?"

"Please sit down, Mr. Jasper."

"Thank you." He sat in the same straight-backed cane chair his sister had occupied. "We haven't met, Mr. Aragon. I didn't even know of your existence until an hour ago. Now it seems you may be very important to me."

"In what way?"

"I have a young sister, Cleo. Her welfare is of prime concern to me." He paused. "I have reason to believe she came here the day before she disappeared."

"She came to my office on Monday afternoon."

"Why? Oh, I'm aware of the confidentiality between lawyers and clients but I can hardly consider my sister a client. She had no reason to seek legal advice. Everything has always been taken care of for her. The idea of her coming to a law office is quite incomprehensible to me. Unless—and I'm forced to consider this possibility—she was interested in you personally."

"No."

"You're young, I thought there was a possibility . . . She's so innocent. She has this habit of taking a fancy to people, of trusting them."

251

"I saw her Monday the first and last time. Her visit lasted fifteen minutes approximately. And that's just what it was, a visit. She didn't seem to be in any kind of trouble that would require the services of an attorney."

"Thank God for that."

"Would you like a glass of water, Mr. Jasper?"

"No."

Aragon poured one anyway from the pitcher on his desk into a paper cup. Jasper drank it.

"Did she appear normal to you, Mr. Aragon?"

"Normal is a pretty big word."

"Not big enough to include Cleo, I'm afraid."

"While she was here she behaved in a responsible manner. I don't give I.Q. tests."

"What brought her here?"

"What brought you, Mr. Jasper?"

"A private detective I hired traced her movements on the day before she disappeared. He found out she took a taxi from the school during the lunch hour. She told my wife and me that she'd spent the afternoon at the museum. I didn't believe it. The museum's closed on Mondays. Anyway, the taxi driver said he drove her to this office. So here I am . . . The school knows nothing, or so they claim. These places never know anything except about collecting money. In that field they're experts."

"You've been to the police?"

"Yes. They were polite, no more."

"They don't get very excited about missing persons because they usually turn up safe and sound. Do you think she ran away, Mr. Jasper?"

"I've had no ransom demands," Jasper said grimly. "Also, she withdrew her entire savings account from the bank, a matter of a thousand dollars. The money won't do her any good, may even make things worse. She's so vulnerable, at the mercy of anyone, anything." He wiped his forehead with the back of his hand. "It never occurred to me she'd draw the money out. I gave her everything she needed, everything she wanted. The account was in her name because I was trying to encourage her to be responsible about money, to save. And she did save, money she got for birthdays, Christmas, things like that."

"Then it was her own money?"

"Yes."

"She committed no crime to get it?"

"No."

"And she's over twenty-one?"

"Yes."

"Are you her legal guardian?"

"Yes."

"You signed a document to that effect?"

"Yes."

"Have you checked it recently?"

"No. It's in one of my safe-deposit boxes. I'm not even sure which one."

"Legal guardianships usually terminate at twenty-one."

"But she's not . . . not competent."

"A judge would have to decide that."

"It's common knowledge."

"Common knowledge is not a term recognized by the courts," Aragon said. He felt uncomfortable with the man, more uncomfortable than he had with Cleo. "I'm not sure what you want from me, Mr. Jasper."

"Help. I must get Cleo back to the safety and security of her own home. But first I have to find her. Where could she have gone, where in God's name could she have gone? We have relatives here and there throughout the country but none of them would take her in. They wouldn't want to be held responsible for her. They know what she is." His voice rose. "No, she's out there alone someplace, probably telling everyone she meets how much money she's carrying, inviting disaster, asking for it. You don't understand how easily a girl like that can be taken in, a mere smile or a kind word. I have to find her."

"You told me you hired a detective."

"Yes, when it became clear the police weren't interested. The detective traced Cleo as far as your office, then he had to fly to Houston to testify in a custody case. It was a poor start. I anticipated a poorer finish and fired him."

"And came here."

"I had you checked out by one of my secretaries. You've looked for missing people before. And you have an additional advantage. You've seen my sister, talked to her, noticed the extent of her incapacity. You know her."

"You don't get to know someone in fifteen minutes."

"Perhaps she told you things."

Aragon thought of all the times he'd heard 'Hilton says, Hilton says.' "A great deal of her conversation consisted of quotes from you, Mr. Jasper. Your opinions seemed very important to her."

"I thought they were, until last week." A film of moisture appeared in the man's eyes. "I need your help, Aragon. I can pay any amount you ask for."

"It's not up to me. I work for a law firm, and I do what the head of that firm, Mr. Smedler, tells me to do."

"Smedler can be handled." There was a note of contempt in his voice, as though handling people like Smedler was simply routine. "Are you interested in the assignment?"

"Yes. As long as you realize that the girl cannot be forced to return."

"Even if she's mentally and emotionally unstable?"

"I doubt you could prove that. The laws protecting the rights of individuals have become very strict."

"I have never forced her to do anything," he said, but he looked oddly disturbed, as though something he thought hidden had been discovered. "Force is not part of my nature. When you find her you will simply persuade her to come home, where she is loved and safe."

"What caused her to leave. Mr. Jasper?"

"I don't know."

"There were no quarrels?"

"No."

"Even a small disagreement might provoke—"

"I told you, no."

"May I talk to your wife?"

"I think not. She's easily upset. It would be preferable if you dealt entirely with me."

"Cleo mentioned your son, Ted. He might have some information not available to you, Mr. Jasper."

"That's impossible. He's away at college."

"What college?"

"It would be a waste of time to question Ted. Anyway, why she left isn't the issue. It's where she went that must concern you."

"The two are usually connected."

"Find her," Jasper said. "Just find her."

He made it sound more like an order than a plea.

"Has she ever run away before?"

"No."

"Talked about it?"

"No."

"When was the last time you saw her?"

"Monday night. Cleo and my wife and I had dinner together. During the course of it I asked her how she'd spent her afternoon and she said she had gone to the museum. I was pretty sure the museum was closed on Mondays but she spoke of seeing lots and lots of pictures. I didn't argue. After dinner she went to her room to watch T. V. Frieda and I retired early. It's a large house with thick, solid walls that muffle sounds. Perhaps Cleo stayed up late watching T. V. At any rate, she didn't appear for breakfast and we didn't waken her. I left for the office and Frieda went to a meeting. We assumed that when the school bus came to pick her up she would board it as usual. The cook says she saw the bus waiting in the driveway when she arrived for work but didn't see Cleo get on it. That's all."

It didn't sound like all, or even like half. Jasper seemed to realize this, too.

"I can't tell you everything," he said, "because I don't know everything. I've acted *in loco parentis* for fourteen years, ever since Cleo was eight, and I thought I understood the girl. It appears now I was wrong. The lie about how she'd spent the afternoon may not have been the first, perhaps only one of a hundred. I say perhaps. Again I don't know."

The admission was obviously difficult for Jasper. Though the room was chilly, he wiped his forehead as if being wrong or even doubtful gave him a fever.

"The school called Tuesday afternoon to see if Cleo had stayed home because of illness. They keep close watch on these matters because many of the students are highly susceptible to contagious diseases. So that's how we discovered she had gone."

"Did she take anything with her?"

"Yes."

"Clothes? Suitcase?"

"The dog," Jasper said. "She took the dog, Zia."

He pressed a handkerchief against his mouth and the noise it stifled could have been a cough, a laugh, a cry of rage.

"The dog," he repeated. "It's a basset hound belonging to our gardener, Trocadero. The old man's heartbroken. He saw her leave the grounds with the dog at midmorning and thought she was going to take a run on the beach, which is only three blocks away. He spent the afternoon searching for the dog, calling the Humane Society, the Animal Shelter, even the police. After the school called in the late afternoon I did some searching myself, but not for the dog. I drove around to various neighbors, called friends, checked the bus station, the airport, even the two local car rentals, though I knew Cleo couldn't drive. Finally I went to Troc's apartment over the garage and told him Cleo had run away and taken Zia with her. He didn't believe me."

"What did he believe?"

"That someone had picked them up in a car. He had no proof, nothing to go on but a hunch. He claims Zia weighs sixty-five pounds, much too heavy for Cleo to lift, let alone smuggle aboard a bus or plane. Troc placed an ad in the lost-and-found column of the local paper offering a fifty-dollar reward for the return of the dog, no questions asked. The ad appeared in this morning's paper. So far there have been no answers."

He paused, staring out the window with its view of the city. Every day it seemed to be crawling farther up the mountain that separated it from the desert beyond. It was a small city but it looked suddenly enormous, capable of hiding hundreds of lost dogs and young girls.

Jasper turned back to face Aragon. "Do you recall the three girl hitchhikers who were murdered here last year?"

"Yes."

"So do I." The bodies of two of the girls had been found at the bottom of a wooded canyon, partially decomposed. The third body was picked up by a fishing boat beyond the kelp line, bloated by decomposing gases and mangled by sharks.

"Don't borrow trouble," Aragon said. "The interest is too high."

"Have you any more concrete advice?"

"You might follow up on that ad. Increase its size, change the wording from *return of the dog* to *leading to the return*. And increase the reward to five hundred dollars."

"I can pay more. Any amount."

"Try it this way first."

"I considered inserting an ad for Cleo herself, with a picture and description and so on, but Frieda vetoed the idea. She has too much of what she terms pride. I'm not sure that's the right word. At any rate I didn't go against her wishes. Things are bad enough without that."

"There's a hotline for runaways that pretty well covers the country. If she changes her mind and wants to come home, you'll hear about it."

"She wouldn't know about such a thing as a hot line. She's very unworldly."

"You said she watches T. V."

"Yes."

"A lot?"

"Yes."

"Maybe she's not as unworldly as you think, Mr. Jasper."

Jasper stirred in his chair like a boxer evading a punch. "I'd better be leaving. I'm already late for an appointment . . . Are you going to help me find her, Aragon?"

"I have to wait for orders."

"They'll come."

When he went out to the parking lot at five thirty he found Charity Nelson waiting beside his old Chevy. For purposes of shade, the space with his name on it was the best in the lot, but the shade was provided by a eucalyptus tree and the owners of newer vehicles took pains to avoid it. The Chevy stood in splendid isolation, its already pockmarked finish immune to the tree's oily drippings.

Charity was leaning against the hood, fanning herself with an envelope.

"When are you going to get rid of this old heap, Aragon?"

"When somebody gives me a new heap."

"Maybe this is a down payment." She patted her handbag. "Want to guess what's in here?"

"A love letter."

"Close. Love and money are like ham and eggs in Smedler's mind . . . Here. Better cash it, junior, before the old boy discovers he's flipped."

Aragon opened the envelope she gave him. It contained a check for two weeks' salary and a note in Smedler's handwriting: *Giving you 2 wks leove of obsence. Don't blob. WHS.*

"Blob?" Aragon said. "Is this in code?"

"Smedler makes his o's and a's alike. He's giving you two weeks' leave of absence and doesn't want you to blab to the others in the office . . . Why did you ask him for a leave of absence?"

"I've contracted an obscure tropical disease which requires prolonged—"

"Come off it. Why did you ask him?"

"I didn't."

"Then he really has flipped. Kind of a shame. He's not actually a bad guy underneath all that evil."

He got in the car and turned on the ignition but Charity didn't take the hint.

"I bet I know just where you're heading, junior," she said. "To San Francisco to see your wife."

"Mr. Smedler orders me not to blob, I don't blob."

"He didn't mean me. He couldn't. I'm his confidential secretary."

"You are a blobbermouth and he knows it."

"Oh come on, junior. Just give me a hint."

"I'm going back to school," Aragon said with some truth. "I need a refresher course."

4

HOLBROOK HALL WAS located on the former estate of a turn-of-the-century cattle baron. Its stone walls were part of a government work project of the thirties but the main gate with its electronic eye was strictly modern and so were the outbuildings scattered here and there throughout the grounds. They were redwood structures that looked like bungalows.

The atmosphere was strangely quiet for a school. There was no shouting, no laughter, only the noise of a power mower and the whinnying of horses. As he passed the corral Aragon saw that two of the horses were under saddle and had recently been ridden too hard and too fast. A moment later the riders came into view, a pair of adolescent boys wearing western boots and cowboy hats pulled down over their foreheads. At the sound of the car they raised their thumbs for a ride.

Aragon opened the door and they both got in the front. They were about fourteen years old, dirty, tired and morose. Tears mingled with sweat, and water leaked from the canteens they carried.

"What are you guys up to?"

"Nothing."

"Not a thing."

"We took a ride."

"We got caught."

"We going to visit my mom in New York."

"We forgot the sandwiches."

"We going to surprise her."

"My mom, too."

"She's not your mom. We're not brothers."

"My mom's right tight close by in New Orleans."

"We forgot the sandwiches."

The boys were let out at one of the bungalows and Aragon proceeded on up the driveway to the main house of the estate, a Mediterranean-style classic. Its tile-floored foyer served as the school's reception room.

At one of the desks a young man sat typing, slowly and thoughtfully, as though he was writing his memoirs. The other desk was empty except for a large blue bird eating peanuts. The nuts were being shelled for him by a teenaged girl with the slant-eyed, sweet-tempered look of a Down's syndrome child.

The man said, "Knock it off, Sandy. We have company."

"A friend?"

"Sure."

The girl rose, the bird flew out the window, and the young man turned back to Aragon.

"Are you Mr. Aragon?"

"Yes."

"Mrs. Holbrook's expecting you. Lovely morning. Nothing beats spring. Come this way."

Mrs. Holbrook's office with its red leather upholstery and semicircular desk was more imposing than its occupant. She was a tiny woman with short curly white hair and dimples and soft blue eyes that appeared somewhat baffled.

"Please sit down, Mr. Aragon."

"Thanks."

"This is a distressing situation. A school like ours is hard hit by any scandal. We are dependent on grants and donations. Our fees are high but they simply don't cover our costs and we need benefactors like Mr. Jasper. He's been very generous in the past . . . And there's Cleo herself, of course. She must be considered."

"Yes." He wondered how far down on the consideration list Cleo rated.

"The other students don't know, naturally. I let it out that she was suffering from chicken pox—I picked something contagious just in case any of them thought of going to visit her . . . I must say I'm surprised at Cleo. It's not like her to do something like this."

"What is like her?"

"To withdraw when things don't suit her, to refuse food and wander by herself down to the stable or the poultry pens. These young people often have a strong rapport with animals. She's a timid girl, overindulged, overprotected. A positive step like running away and being able to stay away this long is quite amazing. Nothing has prepared me for it. Well, practically nothing."

"Does 'practically nothing' mean a little something?"

She hesitated before replying. "At the last staff meeting Cleo's name came up. One of the counselors reported that she seemed to be gaining self-confidence, was even getting a little feisty. He felt it was a step forward and the others agreed."

"By others, are you referring to teachers or counselors?"

"Here they're the same thing. We avoid the word *teacher* because it sometimes has a negative connotation these days."

"What counselor made the observation about Cleo at the staff meeting?"

"Roger Lennard."

"Did he have a special interest in Cleo?"

"Not in the way you might mean," she said dryly. "We hire as counselors for the girls men who are not—ah, interested in women. And vice versa for the boys. It minimizes staff-student romances, which can be a problem even in a place like this. Some of the parents refuse to admit that these young people have the same sexual drives as other young people. We deal with them as best we can."

"There's no chance that Cleo was romantically involved with Mr. Lennard?"

"None."

"None?"

"He's gay as a goose."

She walked to the other end of the room, pausing to straighten one of the class pictures hanging on the wall. She had a small, neat figure and her yellow linen suit looked expensive. She wore no jewelry except a wedding band.

"Exactly what's the matter with Cleo, Mrs. Holbrook?"

"Most likely a combination of things. It's hard to separate mental retardation from emotional retardation. Cleo's a dependent, passive little creature. She's never made a decision in her life, never been expected to, wouldn't be allowed to, probably. So we can't tell for sure how she'd act on her own. I myself suspect that among other factors she has a mild form of epilepsy. But our attempts to get an electroencephalogram were unsuccessful. As soon as she saw the needles she became hysterical and the Jaspers took her home. For accurate results, the patient's cooperation in an EEG is necessary, so no further attempts were made. What a pity. Because if epilepsy should turn out to be part of her problem, it can be treated. Another method of treatment, of course, would be complete separation from her brother and his wife . . . Here I go again, speaking out of turn, diagnosing, practicing medicine without a license. But when you've been in a place like this for over thirty years you see so much repetition it tends to make you oversimplify. Cleo is, like all of us, complex. As we say, exceptional."

She glanced at the door. It was as definite a dismissal as if she had pointed at it and ordered him to leave.

Aragon said, "Let's review briefly, Mrs. Holbrook. In your opinion, it was unusual for Cleo to take a direct action like running away, and even more unusual for her to stay away this long."

"Yes."

"Yet there is some evidence, according to counselor Roger Lennard, that she was becoming more self-sufficient."

"That's right."

"Are you quite sure that Mr. Lennard and Cleo—"

"Quite, quite sure. Roger was the one who brought her name up at the staff meeting. If there was any relationship between them, he certainly wouldn't have advertised it."

"How do you feel about Cleo, Mrs. Holbrook?"

"I can't afford to get personally involved with any one student. It diminishes my ability to deal with the others." The telephone on her desk rang and she went to answer it. "Yes? . . . Lund and Johnston, that's a first, isn't it? . . . Are the horses all right? . . . Send the boys in. *After* they've showered." She hung up and turned back to Aragon. "I hope Cleo's little caper hasn't started a trend."

"I thought the students hadn't found out about it."

"They found out," she said with a sigh. "Somehow they always do. One way or another, they always do."

Under the oak tree where Aragon had left his car a young man was sitting eating out of a giant bag of corn chips. He was about eighteen, very fat and red-faced, and there was an asthmatic wheeze in his voice when he spoke:

"Hey, man."

"Yes?"

"Want a chip?"

"No, thanks."

"Hear anything from Cleo?"

"Cleo who?"

"Cleo who, that's a hot one. Who you trying to kid? Cleo who. That chicken pox story is a riot. They must think we're a bunch of kooks. Want to hear my opinion?"

"I do, yes."

"She's been kidnapped. The reason the kidnappers haven't asked for ransom yet is they're giving old man Jasper time to get all shook up. The more shook up he gets the more he'll be ready to kick in with a bunch of bucks to get her back. Think about it."

Aragon thought. "Is your name Donny Whitfield?"

"Yeah. How'd you know?"

"Cleo mentioned you."

"Yeah? What'd she say? She kinda likes me, wants to share my space?"

"We didn't discuss that. She talked about the school cruise to Catalina on your father's yacht."

"Oh, that. Big deal. The old boy likes to dress up and play captain." The corn chips were all gone. Donny began on a package of M&M's. "What a clown."

"Were you on that cruise, Donny?"

"Sure. Me and the first mate, we used to do business together."

"What kind of business?"

"What makes you think I'd tell you? You're probably a narc."

"No."

"I'm not telling anyway. It might spoil future deals."

"Where did you go on that Easter cruise, Donny?"

"Just Catalina. Dragon Lady Holbrook didn't trust us any further. In fact, she wouldn't have trusted us that far except my old man told her we couldn't get into any trouble because there was no trouble to get into. Not that Cleo would anyway. She's more goody-goody than the rest of us. Most of us aren't. What a square. She's afraid to breathe unless her old man tells her to. Pitiful."

"He's not her old man, Donny. He's her brother."

"Same diff. He's the boss, he calls the shots." The boy coughed, aiming some chocolate spit at the oak tree. It dribbled down the bark like tobacco juice. "You headed for town?" he said, wiping his mouth with his forearm.

"Yes."

"I know where they sell some pretty good grass. You buying?"

"No."

"Aw come on, man. Let's go. I can ride in the trunk as far as the gate, then I'll sit up front with you."

"I don't think so," Aragon said. "The trunk's locked and I lost the key."

"Man oh man, that's another chicken pox story. What do you think I am, some nut like the rest of them? You just don't want to give me a ride, right?"

"Right."

"Screw you." The boy stared morosely into the now empty bag of M&M's. "I bet if I was kidnapped my old man wouldn't pay a dime to get me back."

"I bet he would."

"Naw. He keeps me shut up in this dump so I won't interfere with his chicks. Got any gum?"

"Sorry, no."

"Screw you."

5

ARAGON SPENT THE rest of the day at the public library and in the microfilm department of the local newspaper. Hilton Wilmington Jasper was listed as an oil executive and a bank director, born in Los Angeles to Elliot and Lavinia Jasper, a graduate of Cal Tech in Pasadena, married to Frieda Grant, one son, Edward.

The same reference volume listed Peter Norman Whitfield, philanthropist, graduate of Princeton, married five times, one son, Donald Norman Whitfield, and a daughter, deceased.

Ted Jasper was found among the seniors of an old Santa Felicia high school yearbook. The picture showed a smiling blond youth whose sports were listed as tennis and soccer, hobby as girls, and ambition, to attend Cal Poly and become a veterinarian. A current Cal Poly student directory gave his address as 207 Almond Street. When Aragon called the number listed he was told Ted had gone home on the semester break.

An educational journal rated Holbrook Hall as a superior facility for exceptional students. Both boarding and day arrangements. Fees high. Well endowed, established 1951.

No information was available on Roger Lennard.

After a T. V. dinner and a bottle of beer Aragon phoned his wife. She was a doctor specializing in pediatrics and completing her residency requirements at a hospital in San Francisco. It wasn't an ideal arrangement for a marriage, but it was working and it wouldn't last forever. They planned on living together in Santa Felicia within a year.

Laurie sounded tired but cheerful. "I'm so glad you called, Tom. I get sick of kids. I want to talk to a nice sensible adult."

"What's this, my dedicated wife sick of kids?"

"I'm entitled to a moment of undedication now and then. How about you?"

"Smedler is working in mysterious ways again. I'm expected to track down a runaway re-tarded girl who maybe isn't so retarded and maybe didn't run away. I have a hunch she might have been coaxed, possibly promised something. She's not a girl, either. She's twenty-two."

"That's a bit old for a runaway."

"She doesn't look her age."

"You know her?"

"I met her once."

"Pretty?"

"Very."

"That complicates matters."

"I'm afraid so."

"A lot of runaways are picked up while trying to hitchhike. We get quite a few in here. They don't always come out. How are her parents taking it?"

"Coolly. They're both dead. She was raised by a brother at least twenty years older. He's the one who commissioned me to look for her."

"Commissioned? That sounds lucrative."

"Two weeks' pay in advance. More later, perhaps. Very perhaps."

"You don't have a contract?"

"No."

"Really, Tom, who's the lawyer in this family? You should have a contract."

"I don't think Mr. Jasper expects much from me. And he's not the type to pay for what he doesn't get. No little sister, no big bucks."

"How come you bought a deal like that?"

"I didn't buy it. I was sold . . . Laurie, why do we have to spend all our time talking about other people when we have so much to say about just the two of us?"

"You started it."

"I had all these great things I was going to say to you—"

"Well, it's too late now. Someone wants me in the operating room."

"*I* want you in the operating room," Aragon said. "Or any other room."

"I love you, too. Bye."

"Laurie—"

But she'd hung up, and he swallowed all the great things he had to say to her with the aid of another bottle of beer. Then he called Charity Nelson at her apartment on the West Side. When she answered the phone there were loud staccato noises in the background.

"Hello. I'm too busy to talk. Call back."

"What's all the hubbub?"

"I'm watching an educational program."

"It sounds more like a shoot-em-up western."

"All right." She turned down the sound. "What do you want?"

"Is there any connection between Smedler and Mr. Jasper?"

"How would I know?"

"I have a notion you might have looked it up."

"Of course I looked it up. They're not friends really but they both belong to the Forum Club and serve on a couple of the same boards of directors, the Music Academy and Holbrook Hall. And they have this bond between them that rich men develop—you put your money in my bank and I'll buy stock in your copper mine. It's a great system if you own a bank or a copper mine. The best way to get rich is to start rich."

"Don't let it depress you," Aragon said. "Go back to your shoot-em-up."

"If I had a million dollars—"

"You'd blow it."

"By God, I believe you're right," she said thoughtfully. "But what a blow, junior, what a blow."

"Am I invited?"

"I'll consider it. First, I'd buy me a racehorse. Not one of your ordinary nags but a real thoroughbred with class and guts and stamina. Boy, he'd leap out of that starting gate like a bullet."

"There goes your million."

"You're a wet blanket, junior, a killjoy, a—"

"Okay, okay, with my million I'll buy a house in the country where you can keep the horse between races."

"Do you know anything about feeding horses?"

"I thought they fed themselves."

"You're not taking me seriously, junior. Go to bed and have a nightmare."

He went to bed. If he had a nightmare he couldn't remember it when he woke the next morning to the ringing of the phone. A woman identifying herself as Frieda Jasper spoke in a sharp, brittle voice. Making no apology for the earliness of the hour and giving no reason, she asked him to come immediately to 1200 Via Vista.

6

THE HOUSE, BUILT on a hill overlooking the Pacific, was a two-story adobe with a red tile roof and iron grilling across the lower-floor windows. It looked as though it had been there for a hundred years through a succession of earthquakes, fires and floods. It was a California house, with ice plant covering the ground instead of grass, and landscaped with drought-resistant native plants like ceanothus and sugar-bush.

The woman who crossed the patio to meet him was tall and sturdily built, with a mass of curly red hair just beginning to turn grey. She held a newspaper in one hand, clutching it as though she intended using it to swat a fly or discipline a dog. There were no flies or dogs in sight.

"Mr. Aragon? Please sit down. I thought we'd talk out here on the patio. It's such a pleasant morning."

It was lightly foggy and the wind blowing in from the sea was cold. He buttoned his coat.

"Unless, of course, you would prefer to go inside?"

"Oh, no." The way she was holding the newspaper made him think she would have used it on him if he'd disagreed.

They sat on cushioned redwood chairs with a small redwood table between them.

"My husband was called to Sacramento by the governor for an emergency meeting on offshore oil leases. Only such an important matter would have taken him away from the house at a time like this. He left me with instructions on what to do if anything new developed. The first was to call you immediately. He's taken a liking to you. Hilton does things like that—perhaps every good executive has to." One corner of her mouth curled up in a small, unamused smile. "I know what every executive's wife has to do, and that is obey orders. So here we are, you and I." She made it sound like the opposite of a fun date.

"Has anything new happened, Mrs. Jasper?"

"I think it's going to. Have you seen the morning paper?"

"Not yet."

"It contains the advertisement about the dog. I didn't even have a chance to check it out before the phone began to ring. A man who said he was on welfare described a dog he'd found on his front porch. It was obviously a beagle, not a basset, and I advised him to ask the Animal Shelter to pick it up. The second call was more interesting. A woman with an accent, perhaps Irish, told me that one of her tenants had brought home a dog. She manages an apartment house where dogs are not allowed and she's bringing the dog here in about an hour. It's undoubtedly Zia. She spoke of a small shaved area on the dog's chest where he'd been treated for a hot spot. I'd like you to stay and meet her, Mr. Aragon."

"Did she give a name?"

"Griswold. Mrs. Griswold."

"And address?"

"I forgot to ask. I was terribly rattled. I even had the wild idea that it might be Cleo herself playing a trick on us. She likes to play tricks, but of course anything that elaborate is way beyond her ability."

"Did Mrs. Griswold seem eager to collect the reward?"

"She never mentioned it."

"Not a word?"

"No. I'm prepared to hand it over to her, of course. Hilton left me five one-hundred-dollar bills in case something like this happened. I don't think he expected it though." She glanced at her wristwatch. It was large and serviceable-looking, like Frieda Jasper herself. "We have at least forty-five minutes to wait, assuming Mrs. Griswold arrives on time. I have some coffee made. Would you like some?"

"I would, yes."

The fog was lifting. Steam rose from the swimming pool and the heavy shake roof of the house next door. The sea shone like a bright new revelation. In the distance Mexican palm trees, skinny and shaggy-topped, stood like a row of upside-down dust mops.

She returned carrying a tray with a glass pot of coffee and two ceramic mugs.

"Cream? Sugar?"

"Black."

"Troc's working in the citrus grove out back. I haven't told him yet about the dog. He's old and very emotional and I would be afraid of the consequences if the woman doesn't show up." She sat down again. "We have well over half an hour to wait. I suppose you'll want to ask questions about Cleo."

"Yes."

"The second of the instructions Hilton left me was to be discreet. I'm not sure I can talk about Cleo and be discreet at the same time. I'll try."

She didn't try very hard. After a swallow of coffee and a couple of deep breaths of air she was off:

"I didn't want to take the girl in. She was eight, a year older than my son, Ted, already fixed in her ways and spoiled by a half-crazy grandmother. But there was no one else willing and able to do it, so she came here. At first Hilton couldn't stand the sight of her because he'd always blamed her for his mother's death. When he came to realize her innocence and her vulnerability, he felt terribly guilty, to blame a child for being born. He gave her everything, everything he had, and unfortunately everything *I* had, too. Ted was sent away to school so I could spend more time educating her."

"What did she learn?"

"She learned," Mrs. Jasper said grimly, "whatever she damned well wanted to. Reading? She read quite well indeed if it involved the captions on the pictures in a movie magazine and not a newspaper or book. A selective learner, the educators might call her now. No matter how little she accomplished, Hilton praised her, or rather over-praised her. I went along with it. He was on a guilt trip, you see, and I was his passenger. A fourteen-year guilt trip. God knows how many times I felt we'd come to the end of the line. Maybe this is it."

She finished her coffee and looked into the empty cup as if she hoped to find in it tea leaves that would foretell the end of the line. There was only a coffee stain and a thirsty buffalo fly on the cup's rim.

"I never knew Hilton's mother. Hilton and I didn't meet until after she died. In my high moments I like to think he swept me off my feet and we got married and had a child. My low moments are more realistic. He was grief-stricken and lonely and I was available, the motherly type five years his senior. If there was any sweeping off of feet, I did it. He was smart, handsome and destined for big things."

There was no mention of love, either on his part or hers, either for each other or for the girl. There was only duty, guilt, sacrifice, anger.

"If Hilton's business associates were told some of the things I've told you, Mr. Aragon, they wouldn't believe them. Hilton has a reputation as a cool, unsentimental, hardheaded, hard-driving executive. Our close friends know about Cleo, of course, but we don't have many. I've never had the time for them. Up until this past year, when Hilton agreed to send Cleo to Holbrook Hall, I've been a full-scale babysitter."

"What did Cleo take with her when she left here, Mrs. Jasper?"

"As far as I can tell, nothing. She wore the clothes she usually wore to school."

"In addition to the thousand dollars she withdrew from the bank, did she carry a charge card?"

"Yes, at Drawford's department store."

"Was she accustomed to using it?"

"For Christmas gifts, birthdays, occasions like that. Usually when she shopped I went with her and she used my cards."

She described what Cleo had been wearing on the morning she left with the dog. It was the same kind of outfit Aragon remembered from Cleo's visit to his office, a navy blue jumper with white blouse and knee socks and black shoes.

"She picked her own clothes," Mrs. Jasper added. "Mostly little-girl stuff. That was partly because she was so small we often had to buy things in the teen department of the store, but it was also her own choice. That is, until recently."

"What happened recently?"

"We hired a new girl to come in and serve dinner every night—Lisa, a college senior. Cleo decided she wanted to dress more like Lisa." She rubbed her left temple with her fingertips as though she were trying to erase a new headache or an old memory. "I guess Hilton's little sister finally decided to become a woman."

From the driveway came the unmistakable noise of an old Volkswagen, followed by the crunch of metal. There were a hundred yards of parking space available, but the VW had chosen to park directly behind Aragon's Chevy.

A short, stout middle-aged woman wriggled out of the front seat and stooped to examine the two bumpers. Her frown and the way she stood with her hands on her hips indicated that in her opinion Aragon's Chevy had willfully and deliberately backed into her VW. When she satisfied herself that no damage had been done she opened the front door of the car and a dog jumped out, dragging a length of rope. She attempted to grab the rope but the dog was too fast for her. He made a beeline for the garage, nose to the ground and tail wagging so furiously it was going in a circle. His legs were so short his stomach barely cleared the grass. A loud, full-throated bark announced to the world that Zia was home and in charge.

The woman puffed her way across the patio, trying to explain simultaneously that the dog was a holy terror, wouldn't obey, dragged her every which way, and she hoped it was the right dog because she certainly didn't intend to take it back, not on your life.

Frieda Jasper assured her it was the right dog. "I'm Frieda Jasper, Mrs. Griswold."

"Thank heaven for that. About the dog, I mean. The strength of that mite of a creature you wouldn't believe."

"And this is Mr. Aragon, who is representing my husband in this matter."

Mrs. Griswold, in the act of offering her stubby, sunburned hand to Aragon, suddenly withdrew it. "Representing, what's that mean?"

"I'm one of Mr. Jasper's lawyers."

"A lawyer? Well, if that isn't one for the books, dragging a lawyer into the case of a lost dog. Rich folks sure live different. I wouldn't pay no lawyer for a commonsense thing like a lost dog." Her sharp little eyes focused accusingly on Aragon. "Well, whatever commission you're supposed to get, it's not coming out of my share of the reward."

"I'm on salary, not commission," Aragon said. "You'll receive the reward in full, Mrs. Griswold."

"Oh, no, I won't. I'm only getting fifty dollars for delivering the dog. It's not much, but fair is fair. I didn't find it and I didn't see the ad. It was my tenant, Timothy North. His car's on the blink."

"Can you tell me the circumstances under which he found the dog?"

"He didn't. A man gave it to him. He was in the bar where he works when a man came in and he had this dog with him."

"Can you tell us the name of the bar or its location?"

"No. But it probably was one of those peculiar places, if you catch my gist. Mr. North is a pleasant young man, eats healthy, never touches a drop of booze, but he's—well, peculiar."

"It was a gay bar?"

"I guess that's what they call it."

"Did the man come in alone?"

"My goodness, I wasn't there. They don't like women coming into those places. Anyway, you've got the dog back, so what difference does it make?"

"Perhaps a great deal."

"It said in the ad, 'no questions asked,' and here I am faced with a whole bunch of them. Fraud, that's what it is, fraud, and you a lawyer, too. You ought to be ashamed."

"The dog was stolen, Mrs. Griswold, and I'm trying to locate the young woman who stole it."

"My goodness, don't you lawyers have more important things to do than tracking down a dog thief? . . . Now I'll take my money if you don't mind, and be on my way."

"I prefer to hand the money over to Mr. North personally . . ."

"That sounds like you don't trust me."

"Of course we trust you," Frieda Jasper said. "You volunteered the information that you didn't either find the dog or see the advertisement. Only an honest woman would have done that."

Mrs. Griswold was partly mollified. "Even my worst enemies never called me dishonest."

"However, Mr. Aragon feels he must talk to your tenant because he might have some vital information. Much more is at stake than a stolen dog."

"It's the girl," Mrs. Griswold said. "It's the girl you're after. Well, like I told you before, no girl would have any business going into that bar."

"These places usually have a pretty steady clientele, like an unofficial club," Aragon said. "Perhaps Mr. North knew the man who brought the dog in, or at least could give me a description. Would I find him at home now?"

"He was there when I left. I'm going right back and you can follow me in your car if you want to."

"I'll do that."

Mrs. Griswold's driving proved to be as unorthodox as her parking. She raced through the city streets as though they were roped off for a Grand Prix, and when she hit the freeway she slowed to forty miles an hour and cars honked and passed her on both sides. She finally turned into a driveway without making a signal and Aragon had to slam on his brakes to avoid hitting her.

"You almost hit me," she said when she got out of her VW. "You're certainly not much of a driver. Are you just learning?"

"I've learned quite a lot in the last fifteen minutes."

"I like to set a good example to young people," Mrs. Griswold said virtuously. "I'll be up front in the office if you need me. Mr. North's is number ten, at the far end. You may have to pound pretty hard. He's a bit deaf, being exposed to all that loud music night after night." She turned to go, then suddenly wheeled around to face Aragon again. "What about my reward?"

"Mr. North hired you. I expect he'll pay you."

"He bloody well better or I'll double his rent."

The apartment house was more like a motel, a series of small pink stucco buildings with a carport separating each pair. The inner courtyard contained a live oak tree that looked dead, and a fountain with a bronze dolphin prepared to spout water when someone remembered to turn it on. Number ten was at the rear of the courtyard. Its windows were open and music was playing inside, not the kind of loud rock or disco that Mrs. Griswold had referred to but a soft, melancholy Russian nocturne.

Mr. North's quick response was also unexpected. The door opened before Aragon had a chance to knock.

"Mr. Timothy North?"

"You know it. I saw you out back with Griswold."

The young man's eyes went with the music. They were sad and grey and remote. But he had the body of a weight lifter, overdeveloped chest and biceps that looked ready to burst through his skin as well as his T-shirt. His voice seemed, like his muscles, to have been overused.

He said hoarsely, "The basset was yours, huh?"

"I'm prepared to pay the reward."

"Fine. I'm prepared to accept it." He turned off the music. "I hope it's in cash. What did you say your name was?"

"Tom Aragon."

"And I'm Tim. Tom and Tim. Cute. We could be twins. How about that?"

"If you don't mind, I'd like to ask you a few questions, Mr. North."

"Tim."

"Tim."

"Questions weren't part of the deal, Tom," North said reproachfully. "But you're calling the shots, amigo. You got the dog, you got the money. All I got is egg on my face. Or what might look like egg to somebody suspicious."

"I don't see any egg."

"Okay, come in."

About half of the small room was taken up by an expensive-looking exercise machine. The cologne North had sprayed on himself wasn't quite strong enough to cover the smell of sweat that hung in the air.

North gazed at the machine with parental pride. "Some little contraption, huh? It's a killer. You wouldn't last a minute on it."

"Probably not," Aragon said. "What's the name of the bar where you work, Mr. North?"

"Phileo's. *Phileo,* that's the Greek word for *I love.* Cute, huh?"

"Real cute."

"It's not the kind of place where you'd bring your mother, but we got plenty of action. You ought to drop in sometime."

"Sorry, my mother never lets me go anywhere without her."

"We might make an exception in her case."

"Neither does my wife."

"So you have a wife. You're not wearing a wedding band."

"When we were married we couldn't afford two wedding bands, so we flipped for it. She won. Cute, huh?"

North's shrug indicated that other people's cutes weren't as amusing as his own. Leaning against the exercise machine, he waved his hand in the direction of the couch. "Sit down."

The couch needed cleaning and reupholstering but Aragon sat. "When did you acquire the dog, Mr. North?"

"Night before last. This man comes into Phileo's with a basset hound on a leash. He wasn't one of our regulars. As far as I know I never saw him before. Or since."

There was something bitter in North's voice that puzzled Aragon. "Would you describe him?"

"Medium height, a bit paunchy around the middle. Wavy brown hair thinning on top. I'd guess he was in his middle thirties. Not bad-looking but he had a bad case of the glooms. Nothing like the glooms to kill off a guy's looks. Me, when I feel them coming on I mount Baby here and sweat them away." He patted the machine on what was more or less its rear end. "Anyway, the guy sits down at the table nearest the door and he and the dog are real quiet, minding their own business. As far as I was concerned they could have stayed there. But the boss spotted them right away and sends me right over. I had to tell the guy that dogs weren't allowed in there. He apologized. He said dogs didn't seem to be welcome anyplace anymore, that his landlord had told him to get rid of it or else, and he was looking for someone to take it off his hands. The fact is, I've always been a pushover for dogs and I think he guessed this. I said I'd consider it. I went back to the bar and made some customer a margarita—I distinctly remember it was a margarita—and went back and told the guy okay, I'd take it. It was a real cute dog. I kidded myself that Griswold's little heart would melt at the sight of it. It didn't."

"You said the dog was on a leash?"

"A thin brown leather leash and collar with metal tags."

"It was on a rope when Mrs. Griswold delivered it."

"That was a funny thing. When he gave me the dog he removed its collar with the leash attached, said he wanted something to remember it by. It didn't occur to me until I read the ad in the paper that he didn't want me to see the dog's tags because it was stolen. Was it?"

"Yes, but not by him—by a young woman."

"You can bet the rent it wasn't his woman," North said with a sardonic smile. "Ordinary people don't just drop by Phileo's for a drink. We're out of the way. You have to come looking for us and know what you're looking for. This guy belonged there. He didn't look happy about it. Maybe he was still in the closet or just coming out because he'd discovered closets have glass doors. No matter. He belonged at Phileo's. Taking the dog there with him, that part was unusual. We don't run any far-out joint that involves animals. Besides, he wasn't the type."

"How could you tell?"

"I got X-ray eyes when it comes to people's weaknesses. This guy was depressed, real depressed. I don't say he was sick. He probably had plenty to be depressed about." Once again there was a curiously bitter note in his voice: *so the guy was depressed—serves him right.*

"Would you recognize the man if you saw him again?"

"Bet the rent I would. Faces are my business." North's own face was beginning to show signs of impatience. "Now I think I've answered enough questions for five hundred dollars minus fifty for Griswold. I could slit my throat for offering her fifty. She'd probably have taken twenty. Well, next time I'll know better. Not much chance of that, though, is there?"

"No."

The envelope changed hands. North folded the five crisp new hundred-dollar bills and put them in the back pocket of his jeans. Then he picked up the morning newspaper opened to the want-ad section and kissed it vigorously. "Thank you, *Daily Press* . . . Maybe I should have it framed. On second thought, maybe I should give it to you for good luck. Here you are, Tom. Good luck."

It didn't turn out that way.

From a public phone booth in the nearest gas station he called the number given in the lost-and-found ad. A woman answered in a heavy Spanish accent:

"This is the Jasper residence. Hello."

"Is Ted there?"

"Just a min—No, no. No, no, no."

There were too many no's. "This is a friend of his from school. I just wanted to say hello."

"He not here. Mr. Jasper not here. Mrs. Jasper not here. Nobody. Nobody home. Ted say nobody home."

"Tell him a friend of his from Cal Poly is passing through town and wants to buy him a drink."

There were sounds of a slight scuffle, a barely audible "Goddam you, Valencia, when are you *going* to learn?" Then a man's voice:

"Who is this?"

"We were in the same lab last semester."

"I didn't have a lab last semester."

"Maybe I have the wrong Jasper. Theodore?"

"Edward."

"Wrong Jasper, obviously. Sorry. It was a natural mistake."

"Not so natural," Ted said. "We're not listed in the phone book . . . Who is this anyway? And what do you want?"

Aragon hung up. It was a stupid error, not checking the telephone directory. But he had the notion that Ted wouldn't have been of much help under any circumstances. He sounded like a very angry and suspicious young man.

7

IT WAS STILL morning, though it felt later. The hours spent with Frieda Jasper, Mrs. Griswold and Timothy North seemed to have spread across a whole day like an oil spill, leaving black stains and the smell of tar.

He drove to Holbrook Hall for his second visit of the week. Halfway up the long steep driveway, two older students were preparing to have a picnic lunch under an enormous fig tree. A third was in the tree itself—Donny Whitfield, his fat, sunburned legs dangling like meat on a hook. He let out a yell when he saw Aragon's car.

"Hey. Hey, wait up!"

Aragon stopped. The boy dropped out of the tree and came stumbling across the lawn. He got in the car, breathing noisily.

"Jeez, am I glad to see you."

Aragon wished he could say the same, but everything about Donny seemed swollen—his short puffy fingers, his cheeks distended like those of a squirrel storing food for winter, his thighs bulging out of the cutoff jeans. Even his eyelids looked blistered from the heat of either tears or sun.

He said, "I forget your name."

"Tom Aragon."

"Listen, man, I got to split this dump. They put me on a diet, me and those two back there. All we're allowed for lunch is lettuces and cottage cheese, rabbit food, yuck. They even locked the candy machine. How's that for a low blow? You don't happen to have a chocolate bar on you?"

"No."

"Pack of Life Savers?"

"No. Sorry."

"Screw you."

"You told me that yesterday."

"So? It still goes. If you help me get out of here, I bet I could help you find Cleo. I know about chicks from all my dad's chicks. They're the same, even a nut like Cleo. How about it, do we have a deal?"

"What happened to the kidnapping theory you had yesterday?"

"Down the drain, I figure, now that she flew the coop. A lot of my dad's chicks did the same." Donny removed the huge wad of chewing gum from his mouth, examined it critically and put it back in. "Look, man, I'm ready to deal. I can lay my hands on some money. You must need money or you wouldn't be driving this hunk of rust. How about it?"

"You're not actually a prisoner here, are you, Donny?"

"You want to know what would happen if I walked out without one of those dimwit counselors tagging along? They'd call the cops."

"Why?"

"I'm on probation. If I stick around here, I stay out of the slammer. It was a bum rap. I don't belong with the crazies you see in this joint. I'm not retarded either. I got an A in school once. Want to guess what in?"

"Tell me."

"Eating," the boy said somberly. "It was a joke, ha ha."

"What bum rap did they pin on you, Donny?"

"That was long ago and far away, man. Anyway, my dad fixed it. He's a great fixer, dear old dad, specially when it leaves him free to mess around with the chicks without competition from me. Maybe you think I'm not much competition, right?"

"I'm not a chick," Aragon said. "I have to go up and see Mrs. Holbrook now. Want to come along for the ride?"

"Naw. She makes me puke."

Waiting in the small reception room outside Mrs. Holbrook's office, Aragon wondered what the charge against the boy had been. Donny wasn't likely to talk, Mrs. Holbrook probably even less so, and juvenile records were often ordered sealed by the judge in the case.

Mrs. Holbrook greeted him with a neat professional smile. She did not sit down or ask him to sit down. The omissions seemed a neat professional way of informing him that she was busy and suggesting that, even if she weren't, his presence wouldn't be welcome. It was evident that she sensed trouble.

She said, "I gather nothing's been heard from Cleo?"

"Nothing."

"I'm afraid I can't be of any further help, Mr. Aragon. I gave you all the information you asked for yesterday."

"Perhaps not quite all, Mrs. Holbrook. I'd like to speak to Roger Lennard."

"He hasn't been at work most of this week."

"That was one of the things you didn't tell me yesterday."

"You didn't ask yesterday."

"How long has he been absent from the school?"

"He called in last Wednesday morning and said he had the flu. We have to be extremely cautious, since some of our students are very susceptible to such contagions, so I told him to stay home until he felt better. He did. There's no mystery about Mr. Lennard's absence. I hope you've abandoned that silly idea of any romantic attachment between Mr. Lennard and Cleo."

"I may have other silly ideas," Aragon said. "How long has he worked here?"

"Since last Christmas, when one of our regular counselors left for Europe on a Fulbright scholarship."

"Can you give me Lennard's address and phone number?"

She opened a drawer of one of the maroon-painted filing cabinets that lined the rear wall.

"His address and phone number are still the same as these on his application form. Four hundred Hibiscus Court, Space C, telephone 682-3380. I still don't understand why you insist on dragging Mr. Lennard into this. Roger is a conscientious young man, totally dedicated to his students. He tries to make them feel normal, human, not social outcasts."

"Is there a picture of him in his file, Mrs. Holbrook?"

"Yes."

"May I see it, please?"

The picture was almost as vague in detail as the description Timothy North had provided of the man with the basset. It could have been almost any dark-haired youngish man trying to look earnest on an application form for an earnest-type job.

"Do you mind if I borrow this?"

"It's beginning to look," Mrs. Holbrook said grimly, "as though you're determined to discredit our school. I've a good notion to call Roger right this minute and let him speak for himself."

"That would suit me fine."

She pressed the numbers on the phone and waited a full minute before hanging up. "He's probably asleep," she said.

"Suppose I check that out."

"Go ahead. You will anyway."

"I have to, Mrs. Holbrook."

Timothy North was still working out on his exercise machine in the small stucco bungalow. The pink sweat band around his head had turned dark with moisture. He wiped his face and hands on a towel before glancing at the picture.

"Sure, that's him all right. Not a happy chappy, is he? Well, maybe he has reasons."

"Bet the rent on it," Aragon said.

Hibiscus Court was a mobile-home park separated from the luxury condos along the beachfront by the railroad track, and from the city proper by the rickety old frame houses and buckling sidewalks of the barrio where Aragon had spent his youth.

Space C was occupied by one of the smaller units. It was well-kept, its handkerchief-size lawn trimmed, the azaleas in ceramic pots carefully shaped. The window frames and the posts of the carport were newly painted in light green. A card on the main door bore the name Roger E. Lennard. The Venetian blinds on the windows were closed tight and the carport was empty. Aragon knocked anyway. There was no answer.

After a time he became aware of someone watching from the rear of the building. He turned and said, "Hello? Hello there."

A man stepped out briskly and started walking toward him. There was nothing furtive or guilty in his manner. He gave the impression that spying on a neighbor was merely part of his lifestyle. The straw sombrero he wore emphasized his shortness. His face was deeply tanned and creased like a piece of paper that had been scorched by the sun and folded and refolded a hundred times.

"Looking for Mr. Lennard?"

"Yes. I'm Tomás Aragon."

"Spanish?"

"Yes."

"Spanish, Latino, Hispanic, Mexican, Chicano—what do you fellows like to be called, anyway?"

"Fellows is good enough."

"No slur intended and none taken, I hope. After all, I'm used to being called a few things myself." He pushed back his sombrero and revealed a head as brown and hairless as a basketball. "Baldy. Curly. Kojak. Don't bother me a bit being called names like that. The real one's Abercrombie."

They shook hands. Then the old man took out a pouch of tobacco and a package of cigarette papers and began rolling himself a cigarette with the clumsiness of a novice. "Trying to save a bit of money, but I can't seem to get the hang of this. I see it done in old movies all the time, slick as a whistle, but it never works out like that for me. Must be trick photography."

"Are you the manager of this place, Mr. Abercrombie?"

"Not exactly. I get a little something off my space rental if I go around making sure the rules are obeyed. No parties or loud television after ten. No dogs or cats or birds that talk."

"Mr. Lennard had a dog, did he not?"

"Not for long, he didn't. To tell the truth, I was surprised at him trying to break the rules like that. Then I found out he was only keeping it for a friend. Mr. Lennard's the quiet type who don't have many friends, so I told him the dog could stay for a day or two until he found another home for it. He must have found one pretty quick because I never heard the dog after that. I haven't seen Mr. Lennard either. Matter of fact, I don't see much of him anyway. During the day he works at that peculiar-like school and at night he often goes out by himself, to the movies or library—that's what I used to think anyway. Like I said, Mr. Lennard's not the type to have a lot of friends. He just came to town last winter from Utah. His car had Utah plates on it, a red Pinto wagon."

Abercrombie lit the cigarette. Some of the burning tobacco fell down the front of his shirt, adding two or three more holes to the dozen already there.

"I got it too loose this time," he explained. "Sometimes it's so tight I can hardly get a drag out of it. Trick photography, that's how they do it in the movies, trick photography. Anyhow, when I went over to tell Mr. Lennard he had to find another place for the dog he handed me a real surprise. He asked me if it was all right if he got married and his wife moved in with him. How's that for a kicker?"

It was a kicker, all right, Aragon thought. And the kickees included himself, the Jaspers, Mrs. Holbrook and her school, and probably most of all, Cleo. "Did Lennard announce the date of his wedding?"

"Right away. 'The sooner the better'—those were his very words."

"Did he appear happy?"

"Excited, more like. And scared, too. Marriage is a big step. I never took it myself. Maybe my legs were too short."

Abercrombie paused, obviously expecting a laugh. Aragon obliged. It wasn't very convincing but it seemed to satisfy the old man. He went on:

"I told Mr. Lennard he could bring his bride to live here as long as they didn't have any children. That's another of our rules, no children. Well, sir, you should have seen him blush, just like some pimply little teenager. I said, you'll have to bring the lady around and introduce her to the other people in the court. He said he would but he never did."

"When did this conversation take place?"

"About the middle of the week. I'm not sure what day."

"And where?"

"Right here where we're standing, under the carport."

"You didn't go inside?"

"He never invited me inside. It's not my business to go where I'm not wanted."

"Were the Venetian blinds closed, the way they are now?"

"He kept them that way." The old man squinted as he took another puff of the cigarette. "Are you hinting the woman might have been in there all the time I was talking to him?"

"Possibly."

"That's no normal behavior, an engaged man hiding his intended like she had two heads. Unless she's the real shy type. There are a few shy women, I guess. I never get to meet any of them . . . I didn't think to ask if you were a friend of Mr. Lennard's."

"No."

"You're not a bill collector, are you?"

"Not exactly," Aragon said. But it was time for Roger Lennard to start paying his debts.

It was mid-afternoon when he finally stopped for lunch at a taco stand near his apartment. The early morning mist had long since been driven out to sea by a hot dry wind blowing in from the desert on the other side of the mountain. He sat under the thick shade of a laurel tree, sipping iced tea and thinking of Cleo. The evidence was circumstantial but there seemed little doubt that she had run away to marry Roger Lennard. He tried to imagine Cleo as a bride in long white gown and veil or even an ordinary dress, but all he could conjure up was the picture of a skinny, blank-eyed girl wearing a navy-blue jumper and white blouse and knee socks. According to Frieda Jasper, Cleo hadn't taken any clothes with her, so she would probably use the thousand dollars from her bank account to buy a trousseau of some kind. Perhaps, however, she had enough business sense—or Roger Lennard had it for her—to have saved the cash and made any purchases for her wedding at the department store where she held a charge card.

Cleo and Roger. A bride and groom as unreal as the plastic figures on top of a wedding cake, standing on ground no more stable than sugar frosting.

Aragon finished his tea, fed the remaining ice cubes to the laurel tree and the plastic cup to the trash bin and went back to his car. He knew that he had to tell the Jaspers and that the rest of the day would be all uphill. He felt the need to touch home base before going off into another game, so he drove to his office.

Charity Nelson must have been watching the world as she often did from the windows of Smedler's quarters on the top floor. The steel cage of the outside elevator descended the wall and she came charging out, hanging on to her wig so it wouldn't blow off in the wind.

He was glad to see her and told her so.

She looked shocked. "My God, junior, you having a heat stroke or something? Come on up and I'll put a cold pack on your head."

"Where's the boss?"

"Smedler had a very important client who wanted to play golf. Smedler, of course, wanted to stay here and work like a beaver but he forced himself to go to the country club. A man of sacrifice, not so?"

"Not so."

"Come along."

They took the elevator up to Charity's office. It was filled with the plants that were her children, raised from infancy, nurtured, nursed tenderly through diseases: the dieffenbachia whose scale she scraped off with her fingernails, the marantas and crotons she misted night and morning to discourage red spider mites, the coleus whose mealybugs she treated with Q-Tips dipped in alcohol, the Hawaiian elf which required a drink of warm unchlorinated water every noon, the aphelandra which kept losing its limbs to aphids, these were her special darlings. To the hardier plants that could pretty well fend for themselves she gave a good home but little real love.

She perched on the edge of her desk, swinging her legs and examining them critically as they swung. "My legs are the only vestiges of my youth. They're still pretty good, don't you think?"

"Do you want me to tell you you've got great gams?"

"I wouldn't mind."

"You've got great gams."

"Thank you, junior. Now I suppose you want a compliment in return."

"It might be a nice switch."

"Okay. Smedler says you're a young man who's going places. Of course he didn't specify what places—that's a lawyer for you, can't make a statement without leaving himself an out . . . Want some orange juice?"

"Please."

She poured the juice not into the small plastic cups beside the water cooler but into the crystal stemware she reserved for special occasions. He wondered what the occasion was and if he had, however reluctantly, played a part in it.

She raised her glass. "Here's to the twenty-third anniversary of my first divorce. His name was Harold and he was a teetotaler. You ever been married to a teetotaler?"

"No."

"It's like being married to an aardvark. It's okay if you're another aardvark. Harold never drank anything but orange juice. It's weird, every time I drink the stuff I think of him. Memories can be a real drag. Anyway, here's to Harold, if he isn't dead of an overdose of vitamin C."

She made a face when she drank the orange juice as if it tasted of Harold.

"Sit down, junior, and tell all."

"Sorry, I have orders from Smedler not to blob, as you may recall."

"I've done a little detective work of my own and found out what you're working on anyway. This man Jasper has big bucks in oil and copper. He's going to be deep-down-in-the-pocket grateful if you find his sister. You could be rich."

"Money can't buy happiness."

"You got that mixed up, junior. Happiness can't buy money, though God knows I keep trying."

"When Mr. Jasper hears what I've got to tell him," Aragon said, "I'll be lucky to get out of this with two cents and a handshake."

"You found her? You actually *found* her?"

"Not exactly. But I know why she went away. It's not the kind of information Mr. Jasper will be happy to hear."

"What happened?"

"She eloped with one of her counselors."

"What's the matter with that? I think it's romantic."

"He's gay."

"Well," Charity said, and again, "well. That's not quite so romantic, is it?"

"No."

"However, maybe he's only half gay, or three fifths. Or even seven tenths. That would leave—"

"I don't know the exact percentage."

"To a normal woman even a little is too much."

Charity poured another round of orange juice. She was beginning to feel more kindly toward the long-gone Harold. A teetotaler, yes, but he sure as hell wasn't a pansy.

She went on to tell Aragon more about Harold than he wanted to know and certainly more than Harold would have wanted him to know. He listened patiently until, having finished off Harold, she started in on George. George, it seemed, was not a teetotaler. In fact, he drank like a fish.

"But he was not a pansy," Charity said solemnly. "None of my husbands has been a pansy."

"Glad to hear it. Now I have to—"

"George's weakness was blondes. Any size, any age."

"—leave. Goodbye. Keep up the good work."

"What good work? What's the matter with you, junior?"

He stepped into the elevator and the door clanged shut.

"Don't you want to hear about George?"

"Later," Aragon said. Much much later.

When he returned to his car he saw that the lid of the trunk was not completely closed. There were no signs of forced entry and everything was still inside: a box of tools; a nylon jacket belonging to his wife, Laurie; a first aid kit; his beach shoes, the soles encrusted with tar; and an orange that had rolled out of its bag when he'd bought groceries a few nights before. That was the last time he'd had occasion to use the trunk.

He tried unsuccessfully to close the lid. Then he saw what was keeping it partly open. A large wad of chewing gum had been pushed into the lock.

Aragon thought of the desperation on Donny Whitfield's face when they met at Holbrook Hall that morning and it was suddenly clear what had happened. Donny had used the keys, inadvertently left in the ignition, to open the trunk. Then he'd replaced the keys and hidden himself in the trunk. The wad of chewing gum forced into the lock kept the lid from closing tightly and allowed Donny to escape.

Some people would do anything to get off their diets.

8

THE PLANE FROM Sacramento arrived at twilight. Though Hilton Jasper sat in one of the rear seats, he let all the other passengers get off before him. He didn't want to go back to a house without Cleo, without Ted. From the window he could see Frieda waiting for him at the gate, pacing up and down with quick little steps that indicated her impatience. She was always impatient, impatient for night to fall, impatient for morning to begin, impatient to drive him to the airport, to drive him home again. The world moved too slowly for Frieda. She wore herself out trying to hurry it along.

The flight attendant handed him his briefcase. "We're here, Mr. Jasper."

"Yes. Thanks."

"Unless you want to go back to Sacramento with us—"

"I think not."

He stepped out of the plane and Frieda came hurrying to meet him. She took the briefcase out of his hand. It was probably meant to be a loving gesture but there was no love in it. She said, "Everyone got off before you. I thought you might have missed the plane."

"Someone has to be last."

She frowned, as though she was trying to understand this odd bit of philosophy. Frieda was always the first on a plane and the first off. It was as natural to her as any ordinary bodily function.

"You look tired," she said. "Cook made you a lovely dinner. It will take only three or four minutes to heat it up in the microwave."

"I'm not really hungry, Frieda."

"Of course you're hungry," Frieda said in a tone that meant he damned well better be hungry because she was. "And it's especially important that you have a good meal tonight."

"Why?"

"Mr. Aragon is coming over at nine. He has something to tell you . . . Now please don't get excited, Hilton. The doctor warned you to take it easy. Cleo is all right. She's not dead or injured or any of the dozen things you imagined. I repeat, she's all right. Apparently she just doesn't want to come home."

"Because of Ted—that terrible scene—"

"For God's sake, let's not go into that again. Her decision to leave very likely had nothing to do with Ted. Perhaps she's been planning it for a long time. The girl never confided in me. I never knew what was going on in that head of hers. When I asked her anything personal she'd just stare at me with those funny eyes—"

"Be quiet, Frieda."

They drove home in silence, and they ate in silence in a small alcove off the kitchen which had a view of the mountains. As the sun set each night the mountains gradually turned from violet to midnight blue and finally disappeared. Lights were springing up along the foothills like strings of Christmas decorations.

Frieda served the meal herself. The only live-in maid, Valencia, had gone to her room to watch television, or whatever maids called Valencia did in their rooms. Frieda had never bothered to find out. She felt reasonably sure, however, that the woman, who spoke little English, would not be eavesdropping like the cook or intruding to express an opinion like Lisa, the college girl who served dinner.

"I hate these silences," she said finally. "They're mean, hostile. Can't you think of anything to say?"

"Nothing you'd want to hear."

"All right, I'll say something and you won't want to hear it either. Ted came to pick up his things this morning. I gave him some money. Don't worry, it was from my own bank account."

"Your own bank account came from my own bank account. And I specifically asked you not to give him any money."

"You commanded me not to."

"But you did anyway."

"He's my son. You treated him unfairly, cruelly."

"He did something unforgivable. If it weren't for that, Cleo would be at home right now, safe and secure."

"And you know where *we'd* be, Hilton? Right here with her for the next ten, twenty, thirty years like the last fourteen, babysitting a girl who's never shown the slightest shred of gratitude, who doesn't even like us."

He dropped his fork on the plate and spit the food from his mouth into a napkin. She knew she had hit him hard and she was almost but not quite sorry that she was going to hit him again.

"If Cleo walked in the front door this very minute," she said, "I'd walk out the back. And you and Cleo could live happily ever after."

"What are you implying, you bitch?"

"I'm not implying anything. I'm stating it outright. You and Cleo can live happily ever after as far as I'm concerned. I don't want to be around."

"By God, you are a bitch."

"It took fourteen years of Cleo to make me one."

Outside, the dog Zia had begun to bark, a deep-throated menacing bark incongruous for his size. He paused now and then as if to gauge the effect of his threats, and during these pauses a car engine could be heard.

Hilton got up so fast he almost knocked the table over, and he reached the front door at the same time as Aragon.

"Have you found her?"

"No," Aragon said. "But I'm pretty sure she's all right."

"Thank God for that. Come in. Come in and tell me about it."

They went down the long galleria to the kitchen. Frieda had cleared the dishes off the table and was pouring herself a cup of coffee. She didn't offer any to either of the men.

Aragon sat across the table from Hilton Jasper and began to talk. "For the past few months Cleo has been counseled at school by a man named Roger Lennard. He's in his early thirties and has the reputation of being very conscientious in his work. He evidently gave Cleo some new ideas about herself and indicated some possibilities for her future. At any rate, he and Cleo became involved emotionally. I won't say romantically, because Lennard is a homosexual."

Jasper made a strange choking noise as if he had something stuck in his throat. "And she's with *him*?"

"They're going to be married. Perhaps they already are."

"Cleo doesn't even know what a homosexual is," Jasper said. "She doesn't really know what marriage is."

Frieda spoke for the first time. "She's not the innocent little angel my husband imagines she is. He never let me tell her the facts of life. He said she was too young, too simple-minded. I didn't insist. I assumed they took care of these matters at school. She was certainly no innocent. I know that from"—she gave Hilton a long meaningful stare—"from experience . . . Don't we, Hilton?"

"Please don't interrupt, Frieda." And to Aragon: "Tell me more about this Roger Lennard. Where does he live?"

"In a mobile-home court down near the beach. It was one of his neighbors who told me about the impending marriage. Lennard asked permission to have his wife come to live in the unit he rented."

"He must be a real prize, a counselor in a school like Holbrook making a play for one of his students."

"Mrs. Holbrook thinks very highly of him."

"Then she's evidently a poor judge of people."

"Just who made a play for whom?" Frieda said. "That's what I'd like to know."

Jasper went over and put his hand on her shoulder. "You appear tired, Frieda. Perhaps you should go to bed."

"I don't want to go to bed."

"I suggest you reconsider." He pressed his hand down hard on her shoulder. "You want to appear all bright-eyed and bushy-tailed tomorrow at breakfast the way you usually are, don't you?"

"I'm glad she's gone. You hear that, Hilton? I'm glad. She's ruined enough of my life."

"You'd better go to bed."

"Let her ruin somebody else's."

Aragon watched her leave, her heels clicking decisively on the tile floor. It was the first time he'd thought of Cleo as a ruiner, a destructive force, more of a victimizer than a victim.

"Forgive my wife," Jasper said quietly. "This business has put a severe strain on both of us. Frieda is just as devoted to the girl as I am."

He didn't sound convinced or convincing and seemed to realize it. He let the subject drop abruptly, as though he'd picked up a rock too hot and heavy to handle.

Aragon rose, ready to leave. "I'm sorry I haven't been able to solve your problem, Mr. Jasper, but this is the end of the line for me."

"Where's Cleo?"

"I made it clear that I don't know."

"Then you haven't done what you were hired to do," Jasper said. "Cleo must be found and rescued."

"By 'rescued' you mean brought back here?"

"Yes."

"The law is pretty specific about kidnapping."

"Use persuasion."

"I'm afraid Roger Lennard has already used persuasion."

"She must be rescued," Jasper repeated. "It's not the homosexual part that worries me most. It's the fact that he's a fortune hunter. Cleo will come into her grandmother's full estate when she's twenty-five. A great deal of money is involved. Cleo is vaguely aware of this, certainly aware enough to have told Roger Lennard about it. But I'm sure she has no idea about the California community property laws or anything involving money. A million dollars in the bank isn't as real to her as a crisp new ten-dollar bill. If someone grabbed the ten-dollar bill from her, she'd resent it and try to get it back or else come crying to me for another one. But a million dollars that she can't see or feel or buy candy with is nothing to her. To Roger Lennard it's everything. He may even be faking a few love scenes. The thought of it makes me sick."

He looked sick. His face had a waxen pallor and there was a fringe of moisture across the top of his forehead. Aragon had acquired a minimal knowledge of medicine from his wife, Laurie, and Jasper appeared to him like a man set up for a heart attack. A big man, an ex-athlete, overweight, with a sedentary job and under a heavy strain, he was programmed for one. Whether it happened or not was a matter of luck, good or bad.

Jasper said, "That bastard Lennard is going to regret this. He'll wish he had stayed in the closet with the door deadlocked!"

"I advise you to wait for the facts before you take any action."

"Then get the facts."

"I'm not trained in police work, or psychology either, for that matter. I don't know where to go from here."

"You got this far. Keep going. If you won't, I will."

"Stay out of it personally, Mr. Jasper, at least until you—"

"Cool down? I don't cool easily."

It wasn't exactly news. The blood had come rushing back into Jasper's face and he looked ready to burst his skin. He slapped his hand flat against the table.

"When I get through with that bastard," he said, "he'll be lucky to get a job as a dishwasher. He's contemptible, a man without moral decency, to take advantage of a girl like Cleo entrusted to his care. God knows what romantic notions he put into her head."

Aragon knew of only one notion, and not by the wildest stretch of the imagination could it be called romantic. He remembered almost precisely the words she'd used on her visit to his office: "My new friend says I got rights, I can do what other people do, like vote." Vote. Lennard's approach was certainly unique.

"I'll do the best I can, Mr. Jasper. But don't expect miracles. Both people involved, Lennard positively, Cleo probably, must be aware that they've asked for trouble."

"I don't expect miracles. I expect results. Go back to where Lennard's been living, examine his personal effects, his correspondence, bank accounts if any, even the books he reads."

"You're asking me to break in."

"No. We won't call it that."

"Others will. Gaining entry to Lennard's place would require a search warrant issued by a judge to a policeman under circumstances strongly suggesting a crime. I don't meet any of these conditions."

"I have connections."

"Don't try to use them. You'll cause difficulty for both of us if you do."

"Very well."

"I take that as a promise, Mr. Jasper."

"It's a promise I may not be able to keep. If I should happen to see them walking past my office building, I'll knock the hell out of—"

"It's a long way from Hibiscus Court to the Jasper building. However, I think they're still in the city. Otherwise Lennard wouldn't have asked permission for his bride to come and live in the court with him. There's another fact: Lennard has a job to keep."

"That's what he thinks," Jasper said. "As of tomorrow morning Lennard's name will be off the school payroll and the salary for the two weeks' notice he's entitled to will be mysteriously delayed or lost in the mails. The facts surrounding his dismissal will be available to any prospective employer. Let's see how romance thrives on a little adversity."

"Sometimes it does, Mr. Jasper."

Jasper refused to consider this. "It will be three years before Cleo comes into her fortune. I confidently predict that by that time Roger Lennard will be long gone and forgotten and Cleo's estate will have a conservator."

"Your second prediction may come true but I wouldn't bet on the first one."

"He will be gone and forgotten," Jasper repeated with grim satisfaction.

When the two men parted, Jasper didn't offer to shake hands. It was a bad sign, a symptom, Aragon thought, of the paranoia often afflicting rich men, that people who didn't agree with them were against them.

Aragon unlocked the door of his car. Donny Whitfield's morning escapade had taught him to take more sensible precautions against chewing gum in the trunk lock. The gum was still there. He was about to get into the car when he heard a soft, tentative voice from the other side of the eugenia hedge:

"Señor?"

He replied in Spanish. "What are you doing over there?"

"Waiting to talk to you. Most privately."

"All right, get in and we'll go to the end of the driveway. The Jaspers are probably waiting to hear my car leave."

She got into the front seat, a short, plump woman wearing what seemed to be several layers of dark clothing. She smelled of oregano.

He said, "You're Valencia?"

"Yes. Valencia Ybarra."

"I'm Tomás Aragon. I'm looking for Cleo."

"I know. I heard. I hear things they don't want me to. They think because I don't speak good English I don't understand, so they ignore me like a dog."

He parked on the street below and turned off his headlights.

"It's not so good talking here. The police are always driving past. I'm afraid they might arrest us."

"What for?"

"They don't need a reason when you're Chicano in a rich neighborhood. Chicanos are suspicious characters. How about we go and get some pizza?"

"Pizza?"

"Pepperoni. The food they serve in the house is so tasteless I am always hungry. Are you hungry?"

"Yes." He couldn't remember eating dinner.

"The pizza parlor is nearby, only about five blocks. I'm not dressed to go in but you could go in and bring something out for me."

If pepperoni pizza was the asking price for some inside information, he was willing to pay it.

As they ate he thought of Donny Whitfield. The boy had had nearly twelve hours of non-diet by this time and had probably used every minute to advantage.

"So you hear things, Valencia?"

"Many."

"Why did Cleo run away?"

She was amazed by the question. "To get a man. Why not? That is natural. They would never allow her to get a man, especially the señor. He treated her like a little girl and she behaved like a little girl. But not always. Ho, ho, not always."

"What's the 'ho, ho' about?"

"I am thirsty. A large Coke would soothe my throat."

Aragon provided the large Coke and waited.

"The night before she left," Valencia said, "Ted came home. It was late, everybody was in bed. She and Ted got together."

"What do you mean, they got together?"

"You don't know? How old are you anyway?"

"All right, all right, I know. But Ted is her nephew. They're blood relatives."

"Ah yes, they make such a fuss about things like that in this country. Is it so odd, two young people going to bed together? But the fussing that went on when the señor discovered them, oh, oh, you wouldn't believe it. Ted was forced to leave in the middle of the night. And the next morning the señor and his wife screamed at each other all through breakfast. Such language."

"And you think that's why Cleo ran away?"

"She went to find a man. She liked that business with Ted. She's ready to get married and have children. In Mexico, pretty soon she'd be an old maid."

The news about Ted and Cleo had caught Aragon by surprise but he had little doubt of its validity. It fitted in with Jasper's reluctance to have his wife questioned and with Ted's suspicious reaction to the phone call Aragon had made to the house that morning. He asked Valencia about the call.

"Ted was at my elbow telling me what to say. He pinched my arm so hard it left a bruise."

"Where was Mrs. Jasper at this time?"

"She went to the bank to get Ted the money he wanted and wasn't supposed to have . . . That was you on the other end of the line?"

"Yes."

"You don't go to school with Ted."

"No."

"You tell lies."

"When I have to."

"That's no excuse. I hope you confess to the priest."

She was sucking noisily the last drops of Coke from the bottom of her cup.

He said, "Shall I drive you home now?"

"I haven't finished yet. There are still things to tell."

"All right. Go on."

"Perhaps another Coke?"

Another Coke was provided. She was clearly enjoying the scene—the food and drink, the attention, the activity going on around her—and seemed in no hurry to end it.

"I should come here more often," she said. "The Jasper house is so quiet, like someone died. I like a bit of noise, people laughing and music playing, even babies crying. Sometimes it's a relief to hear the dog barking or Trocadero mowing the lawn or clipping hedges."

"Quit stalling, Valencia."

"Do you think we could come here another time?"

"Maybe."

"That means no, doesn't it?"

"It probably does."

"Oh well, you're too young for me anyway. And too Anglo. You even look Anglo with those horn-rimmed glasses of yours. Who ever heard of a Chicano wearing horn-rimmed glasses?"

"You're stalling again, Valencia. Get back to the subject, whatever it is."

"It's Ted, of course. You weren't the only one who telephoned him before he left the house. After lunch he had another call. I put him on and then I heard him say, 'All right, I'll be right there.' Those were his words: 'All right, I'll be right there.'"

"That doesn't sound very sinister."

"Maybe not, unless you know who the caller was, or you think you know. It was her voice, Cleo's."

"Cleo's?"

"Aha, surprised you, didn't I? You didn't believe me before when I said she liked that business with Ted. Now you've changed your mind, eh? She's young and hungry, why should she not eat?"

"Did you inform Mrs. Jasper about this phone call from Cleo or a girl you thought was Cleo?"

"Never. It would start another big fuss. They treat me like a dog, I behave like a dog, I say nothing."

"The rumor is that Ted has a number of girlfriends. It would be quite natural for him to move in with one of them after being kicked out of his own house."

"The voice was Cleo's. She asked him to meet her someplace and he said all right, he would. His car was already packed with his clothes and things because he had to leave before his father got home. The señora stood at the door, waving goodbye and crying. Silly woman. What's there to cry about when a baby bird flies out of the nest? If he stayed on, now *that* would be good cause for crying."

"What time did Ted leave?"

"Between one thirty and two."

He recalled the picture of Ted as a senior in his high school yearbook, a baby bird already out of the nest even then. "Did he seem happy about going?"

"Why not? He's a fine-looking young man with a fine car and money in his pocket. He's a bit on the heavy side for my taste. I prefer the lean type like you. Lean men are often stronger."

"I'm extremely weak," Aragon said.

He figured it was time to drive Valencia home.

He let her off at the bottom of the Jaspers' driveway. Through the trees he could see the house at the top of the hill. The main floor was dark but lights showed in some of the second-floor windows.

"If I were you, Valencia, I wouldn't mention any of this to the Jaspers. It will only increase their burden."

"It could very well increase mine, too. They might fire me. Chicanos are blamed for everything."

"Things are changing."

"Not for me."

"You have a comfortable place to stay, don't you?"

"Yes."

"You have a room of your own, a radio and T. V. perhaps, regular meals."

"The meals are tasteless," she said. "And the room is lonely without a man. Perhaps you have an older brother? An uncle?"

"I come from a very small family of very weak men."

"Now you're making fun of me."

"I'd like to see you smile."

"I never smile. I have a crooked tooth at the front. Besides, who's there to smile at? Trocadero? He's over seventy. The grocery boy goes to high school and the garbage man is black as coal."

"When the right man comes along you'll smile without even thinking of your crooked tooth. And the right man won't even see it."

"What a liar you are," Valencia said, sounding pleased. "You'd better go see your priest."

9

DRAWFORD'S DEPARTMENT STORE catered to the young ladies and the old money of the city's North Side. Located at the head of a recently constructed shopping mall, it was built in the style of the string of old missions along the southern California coast. There were differences. Its bell tower clanged the hours only when the store was open for business, the taped music was soft and secular except at Christmas, and the thickly carpeted floors were not meant for the bare feet of padres. Bare feet were not, in fact, allowed at all. There was a sign to that effect on each of the four entrance doors.

The credit department was on the third floor. Its manager was on vacation but the assistant manager agreed to see Aragon.

She was a young woman who looked as if she'd been born and brought up in the store itself, nurtured on the skinny sandwiches of its tearoom, coiffed in its beauty salon, clothed in its designer dresses, perfumed and made up in the cosmetics section, educated in the pages of its chic, glossy catalogues. Aragon would scarcely have been surprised if she'd introduced herself as Ms. Drawford.

"I'm Mrs. Flaherty," she said. "May I help you?"

Aragon gave her his card and she read it through jewel-trimmed glasses from the optometry department.

"Drawford's is always happy to welcome an attorney," she said with a well-practiced smile. "Especially if he's on our side."

"Thank you."

"What can we do for you?"

"I'm trying to find out if the holder of a certain credit card purchased anything here during the past week."

"I'm sorry but we cannot give out that information." It sounded like a line from Drawford's Training Manual for New Personnel.

"Does that mean under any circumstances, Mrs. Flaherty?"

"Almost any. It would be advisable if you'd wait for Mr. Illings to get back from his fishing trip in British Columbia. That will be in another week and a half."

"That might be a week and a half too late. This is really important."

Mrs. Flaherty threw away the manual. "Oh damn, I knew something like this was going to happen the minute he left. Right off the bat someone waltzes in, a lawyer yet, and asks for confidential information. What am I supposed to do?"

"Use your own judgment."

"Okay. What's the name of the credit card holder, the billing address and the number of the card?"

"Cleo Jasper. The bills are probably sent to her brother, Hilton Jasper, on Via Vista."

"And the number of the card?"

"I don't have it, sorry."

"I'd really like to know what this is all about."

"And I'd really like to tell you. But as any employee of Drawford's must realize, rules are rules."

"All right, I'll see what I can do. I'll have to get her credit card number from our files, then run it through the computer and see what comes out."

She was gone for five minutes, during which Aragon had time to examine her office. It was mostly chrome and glass, very neat and almost devoid of personal touches except for two small framed photographs on the desk, one of a baby and the other of a young man in football uniform who looked like Joe Namath. Drawford's would probably not approve of an assistant credit manager having a photograph of Joe Namath on her desk, so Aragon assumed the picture was of Mrs. Flaherty's husband, and the baby their joint effort.

Mrs. Flaherty returned carrying a sheet of paper. "The computer indicates that Miss Jasper made some purchases two days ago."

"What were they?"

"We don't know yet. When a purchase is made, the slip contains the name of the credit card holder and the number of the associate. When we check that number we'll have the name of the associate and thus the department in which she or he works."

"By 'associate' you mean sales clerk?"

"If you insist. Drawford's believes that *associate* sounds better and improves morale. Now then, we'll find out whether that associate is working today and after that you can do—well, whatever it is that people like you do."

"They work," Aragon said, " . . . and when do I get the names of the associates?"

"My secretary's checking that now."

The secretary turned out to be not a clone of Mrs. Flaherty but a close copy. She had the same hairdo and wore an almost identical expression and dress. She said that one of the numbers belonged to Mrs. deForrest of the shoe salon and the other to Miss Horowitz of the better jewelry department. Miss Horowitz had sold Miss Jasper a set of rings and Mrs. deForrest had sold her two pairs of shoes.

This was Miss Horowitz's day off but Mrs. deForrest was on duty in the shoe salon, having clocked in at 9:07 that morning.

Mrs. deForrest was not a product of Drawford's catalogues or training manual. She looked like a grandmother who'd had to go back to work in order to pay her bills.

"Cleo Jasper," she said, frowning. "Let me think a minute. I'm pretty good at names."

While Mrs. deForrest thought, Aragon watched the other customers: a middle-aged woman surrounded by piles of boxes which indicated she was either hard to please or hard to fit, two teenagers pooling their finances to pay for a pair of sandals, an elegantly dressed woman in a wheelchair examining a display of matching shoes and handbags.

"Yes," Mrs. deForrest said. "Yes, I recall now. A young woman, who had trouble signing her name. In fact she didn't sign her first name. She used only the initial."

Aragon showed her one of the pictures Mrs. Jasper had given him of Cleo.

"Of course this is the girl," Mrs. deForrest said. "Why didn't you show it to me in the first place?"

"I thought she might have changed her appearance and seeing the picture would only put you off."

"Well, she did not change it. The picture's exactly her. Cute little thing. Bought a pair of Italian sandals with very high heels. She could hardly walk in them. She looked comical, like a little girl dressed up in her mother's clothes. I urged her to buy a more sensible pair of shoes for walking, with a special non-slip sole. We sell a lot of them to people who want to be sure of their footing on slippery surfaces. And that's especially important for someone in Mrs. Jasper's condition."

"Miss Jasper."

"Miss? Dear me, that's getting so common these days but I still can't help being shocked."

"What is common?"

"Going right ahead and having children without bothering to get married. Why, she looked barely out of high school and she had that eight-month waddle if I ever saw one. That's why the non-slip shoes were so important, to avoid a fall that might cause a premature birth."

"Would you take another look at this picture, Mrs. deForrest?"

"Sure." She studied the picture again, more carefully. "I certainly think it's the same girl. I wouldn't want to swear on a stack of Bibles. If I had to do that, swear to it in court or anything, I really couldn't. I'd hate to get involved in anything messy."

"So would I," Aragon said. But he knew he had.

Contacted by phone at her apartment, Miss Horowitz confirmed the sale of a pair of rings to Cleo Jasper. Sales were never brisk in the better jewelry department, Miss Horowitz explained, except when there was a special sale on such things as diamonds and jade, so individual customers were easy to recall. The girl had bought a set of wedding bands. The girl's band was too big for her but she said she would grow into it. She didn't want to wait for a special order . . . "I don't wonder she was in a hurry. She was conspicuously pregnant."

"Was she happy about it?"

"Quite. In fact, very. I honestly can't understand the present generation. Can you?"

"No."

He understood even less Cleo's apparently imminent contribution to the next generation.

When Aragon reached the parking lot of his apartment building he could hear a phone ringing from one of the open windows. He didn't hurry. If the ringing came from his apartment he couldn't reach the phone in time anyway. He locked his car, counting the rings of the phone automatically at first, then, as they continued, deliberately: ten . . . twelve . . . sixteen . . . They stopped for about half a minute, then began again. When he went up the steps to the second floor he realized the ringing was coming from his own apartment.

He let himself in, breathing deeply to expel the sense of impending disaster he felt. The call must be very urgent or the ringing would have stopped at the usual six or seven.

He said, "Hello?"

"Mr. Aragon?"

"Yes."

"This is Rachel Holbrook. I'm in a café across the street. I saw your car drive up. I've been waiting for you."

"How did you know where to wait?"

"A girl in your office gave me your address and told me you usually came home at noon to pick up your mail in case there was a letter from your wife."

"They're a chatty group."

"A bit unprofessional, yes. Would you come over and have a cup of coffee with me? It's very important."

"About Cleo?"

"It's a related matter. Can you come?"

He didn't want to and she must have sensed it. Her voice hardened.

"You owe me one, Mr. Aragon. Don't you pay your debts?"

"When I know what they are."

"Come on over and I'll tell you about this one, such as how to pay it."

"All right."

She sat in the front booth, looking out of place in the dingy blue-collar café with its cigarette-scarred tables and splitting vinyl seats. She wore a white-brimmed hat and a dark-red suit with white collar and cuffs. He didn't like the color, which reminded him not of burgundy or plums but of raw liver or yesterday's blood.

There was a glass of water in front of her, untouched. The water looked murky and the table was marked with the rings of other glasses from other meals.

"This isn't a nice place," she said abruptly.

"I didn't pick it."

"I've become spoiled. All through college I worked in joints like this and it didn't bother me. Now I feel—well, frightened, uneasy. Those men eating lunch at the counter, I'm sure they have no evil intentions toward me. And yet . . . and yet, perhaps they do."

"Their only intention is to eat their food." And keep it down, he added silently. "What's happened, Mrs. Holbrook?"

"Donny Whitfield has been missing since yesterday morning. That's the one you owe me, Mr. Aragon."

"I see."

"You don't appear surprised."

"No."

"He escaped in your car."

"I believe so."

"The evidence I have doesn't indicate any actual complicity on your part, Mr. Aragon. Just stupid negligence, leaving your car keys in the ignition. Nothing goes unnoticed around Holbrook Hall. One of our students saw the whole thing but she didn't report it until the search for Donny began last night. She had the make and model of your car, even the license number." Mrs. Holbrook took a sip of water. "Although the search was as quiet and unobtrusive as possible, I knew I'd have to make up some plausible story about Donny to stop the speculations. I told two of the key students of the school grapevine—key for keyhole— that Donny's father had decided to send him to a fat camp for the summer. So far, my version has been accepted."

"Does Mr. Whitfield know about Donny?"

"I was unable to reach him. He has a house in Palm Springs, a condominium near the harbor and a yacht moored at the marina, but he wasn't at any of those places."

A waiter approached the table and Mrs. Holbrook ordered a cup of coffee and Aragon a bowl of soup. He knew the soup came from a can and nothing much could be done to ruin it.

"Donny's a wild boy," Mrs. Holbrook said. "I had a great many misgivings about accepting him at the school. But he put on a good show during our initial talks. He was sweet, contrite, eager to please, ready to cooperate. I bought the whole act. His first violent rage came as a shock to me. I didn't report it to his father. Donny himself was the victim of violence. It was almost inevitable that he'd pass it on."

"He told me he was on probation. What for?"

"Assault with a deadly weapon."

"Then you'll have to call the police in on this."

"I will, of course. I'm stalling, trying to give him a chance to come back of his own accord. If he doesn't, his probation will be revoked and he'll be sent God knows where. I would like to prevent that. Donny's a victim. His father is what is politely called a wealthy playboy, meaning a rich man without discipline, morals or responsibility. His mother was a bit actress who took to booze and barbiturates and eventually overdosed when Donny was five. A succession of stepmothers and live-ins weren't much improvement."

"Where do I fit into this?" Aragon said. "You didn't go to the trouble of coming here in order to discuss Donny Whitfield's case history."

"No, I didn't."

"The boy's escape is the one I owe you. How do you want it paid?"

"Let me state my position, not as a person, but as the head of a school which serves an important purpose in the community."

"Go ahead."

The soup arrived, overwatered and underheated, but Aragon ate it anyway while Mrs. Holbrook watched him with the ill-concealed irritation of someone who is not hungry.

"You pay me back," she said finally, "by keeping silent."

"About what?"

"Donny Whitfield. His disappearance is not yet generally known and I'd like to keep it that way as long as possible. He may come back of his own volition. Meanwhile something else has happened. Mr. Jasper has called a meeting of the board of directors for this afternoon at two o'clock at the school. Each member of the board contributes heavily to our endowment fund, so it doesn't function merely as an advisory committee. I wasn't invited as I usually am, and Mr. Jasper didn't tell me the reason for the sudden meeting, but I think something more is involved than just Cleo running away from home. My efforts to contact Roger Lennard have failed and I've begun to suspect the worst."

"What's your idea of the worst, Mrs. Holbrook?"

"What you mentioned as a possibility the first time we met, that Cleo and Roger are together somewhere. Even worse than worst, that Mr. Jasper has found out about it. Mr. Jasper has never called a meeting of the board before, in fact has seldom attended one. He must have discovered something linking Cleo and Roger, and he's going to blame the school for it."

"He didn't discover it," Aragon said. "I did."

"I can't believe it. Roger's not a bisexual, or a promiscuous homosexual. He's had the same lover ever since he came to town last December. I've seen him when he's come to pick Roger up at the school several times. A man about Roger's age, a muscle-beach type, evidently the macho partner in the marriage. That's what Roger called it—a marriage."

"Do you know his friend's name?"

"We were never introduced, but in our conversations Roger referred to him as Timothy."

Timothy North, of the pink bungalow and the exercise machine and the cock-and-bull story about a stranger coming into the bar with a lost basset hound. The story had been crazy enough to be true. And Aragon had accepted it because there seemed to be no reason for him to lie.

"One of the factors in my hiring Roger in the first place was his steady relationship with this man Timothy. Call it a marriage, a pair bond, whatever. They were like an ordinary couple searching for a house to buy which they could afford. Because of the strength of this relationship, I felt Roger could be completely trusted with both the male and female students. I'm at a loss to explain what could have happened."

"No one is asking you to explain."

"No?" She stared into the cup of coffee as though she could see its bitterness without bothering to taste it. "Do you know how the board of directors will regard this? They will question my judgment, my hiring practices, my character, perhaps even my sanity. The school will be found guilty, its administration, its faculty, its policies, all guilty as charged. They must not be given an additional count against me, like Donny's running away."

"I don't intend to tell anybody, Mrs. Holbrook."

"Oh, they'll find out anyway, of course. But meanwhile Donny might decide to return voluntarily. It's quite possible."

But her troubled eyes indicated she didn't think so. Neither did Aragon.

"It was a mistake to put him on that diet," Mrs. Holbrook said. "I argued with the dietitian about it but she insisted it would improve Donny's self-image if he lost some weight. It's frightening how logical theories and good intentions can blow up in your face. I wonder— I've often wondered—are the Donnys and Cleos worth the trouble they cause? Twenty years ago if I'd heard myself asking a question like that I would have been appalled. Now I simply grope for answers and come up with more questions. How many lives should be warped for the sake of one disturbed child? If it's true about Roger and Cleo, why in God's name didn't he have sense enough to realize what he was getting into and back out of it? Couldn't he see what a dismal future was in store for him?"

"Cleo will inherit a million dollars when she's twenty-five," Aragon said. "That might make his future less dismal."

"Roger doesn't care about money. His work, his books, his music, these are the things he values."

"A million dollars will buy a lot of books and music. Even if Cleo could be found mentally incompetent to handle her own affairs, once she's married to Roger he will be her guardian, not Jasper, no matter what legal maneuvers he goes through."

"You wouldn't be so cynical about Roger if you met him."

"I intend to do just that."

"I can't believe that Roger would—I just can't believe—"

"Yes, you can, Mrs. Holbrook," Aragon said. "You've already started."

He paid the bill and walked her back to her car, a black Seville parked about a block away. The front bumper overlapped the parking space marker by at least two feet, a fact that did not go unnoticed. A handwritten note pushed under the windshield wiper read *Lern To Park*. Although she smiled slightly as she crumpled the note in her hand she didn't look amused. To people in her profession reprimands were to give, not to take.

"I'd like to think quite a few of my pupils can spell better than this," she said dryly. "Well, thank you for your time, Mr. Aragon. I appreciate your promise to keep quiet about Donny Whitfield. Things are already bad enough. The Cleo story won't look very pretty in the newspaper: *School Counselor Elopes with Retarded Heiress.*"

"The local paper is usually more tactful than that."

"Not where Mr. Jasper is concerned. He's for oil-drilling in the channel. They stand opposed. They wouldn't pass up a chance like this to get at him, perhaps at me as well. Some people resent having a school like ours in their vicinity. They consider our students dangerous. They're not, of course."

Neither of them mentioned the name of the exception.

He told her he would be interested in hearing the outcome of the board of directors' meeting and wrote down on his card the telephone number of his apartment and of his office, which had a twenty-four-hour answering service.

As he watched her pull away from the curb he hoped her driving was a little better than her parking and a lot better than that of Mrs. Griswold, who'd returned the basset hound to the Jaspers.

He remembered his wild ride through the city streets following Mrs. Griswold to her tenant's bungalow to pay the reward money.

Timothy North must have laughed all the way to the bank.

10

SHORTLY BEFORE TWO o'clock the members of the board of directors began arriving. From the north windows of her office Mrs. Holbrook could have watched them, noting which ones had found time to come to a meeting so suddenly arranged. She stood instead at the south window, surveying the grounds of her school. She knew every square foot of its acreage, the tennis and basketball courts, the pool enclosed by an eight-foot chain-link fence with its gate double-padlocked, the picnic grounds, the corral and dog runs; she knew how much the new roof for the stable had cost; she knew the names of every horse and dog, of every shrub and tree on the property. It was her small kingdom and for thirty years she had lived in it and for it.

Tears stung her eyes and blurred her vision. Everything seemed to be moving, as if the first tremor of an earthquake had struck. There was a knock on the door. She blinked away the tears and said, "Come in."

A girl entered, carrying an oversized canvas tote bag with the name Gretchen printed on it. She was sixteen, large and sturdy, with a moon face and round eyes and the faint trace of a mustache.

"I came to clean," Gretchen said.

"You cleaned yesterday, Gretchen. Things haven't had a chance to get dirty."

"I see dirt that other people can't."

"All right. Go ahead."

The girl began her work at the bottom shelf of one of the bookcases. She sat on the floor, removed a dustcloth from the tote bag and started wiping each book individually. She hummed tunelessly as she worked. The noise didn't bother Mrs. Holbrook. Gretchen was happy at these times and Mrs. Holbrook was happy for her.

Her gaze returned to the school grounds. A picnic was in progress and a group of boys was playing basketball, coached by their athletic director, Miss Trimble. A girl was working a quarter horse in the training ring but the pool and the tennis courts were empty. Only one student was using the playground. He was swinging on a tire suspended from a limb of a huge cypress tree.

His name was Michael and he was new and very quiet and Mrs. Holbrook was worried about him. She went down the hall and out the back door and crossed the lawn to the cypress tree. The boy didn't turn his head or indicate in any way that he was aware of her.

"Hello, Michael," she said. "Do you like swinging?"

His eyes were closed and he might have been asleep except for the movement of his legs.

"Have you had lunch, Michael?"

He made a sound that could have been yes or no. She was quite sure it was no. The dietitian had already discussed Michael's case with her. A problem eater given to hunger strikes, he was at least twenty pounds underweight.

"I have a bowl of very nice apples in my office," she said. "Or perhaps you and I could walk down to the grove and pick some oranges. Would you like that?"

He spoke without opening his eyes.

"I hate you."

"I don't hate you back, Michael. I think you and I can become good friends. Your mother's driving down to see you next month. Did you know that?"

"I hate you."

She felt the sting of tears again. She would have liked to hate him back but . . . Instead, she wanted to hold him in her arms and comfort him. He was helpless and possibly hopeless. There was no apparent cause for his condition. He had loving parents, three sisters and a brother, all normal, and no history of childhood illnesses or accidents. He was probably, as one of the counselors had pointed out, the victim of the commonest and most mysterious cause of all, a failure of genetic programming, a fancy name for rotten luck. She tried to remember which counselor had said it. Perhaps it was Roger Lennard and perhaps he was talking about himself, not this quiet boy on the swing with his eyes closed to the world.

"You can't see anything unless you open your eyes, Michael," she said gently. "It's like being blind, and you wouldn't like to be blind, would you? . . . I know. I bet someone has glued your eyelashes together. Let's go to the tap over there and wash away the glue, and presto, your eyes will pop open again. How about it?"

"I hate you."

"That's okay. I'm not so crazy about me, either."

She turned and went back to her office, pausing only to pick up some bark that had peeled off the lemona eucalyptus tree and toss it in the trash bin. A failure in genetic programming. Rotten luck. She was almost sure now those were Roger's words and that he'd been talking about himself. Though he had never openly indicated dissatisfaction with his role in life, she sometimes sensed his uneasiness, his awareness that he was out of sync, out of tune.

In the office Gretchen was still at work on the bottom shelf of books, still humming, still happy. Mrs. Holbrook picked up the phone and called Roger's number as she had done a dozen times in the past two days. She was about to hang up when she heard the click of a receiver being lifted.

"Roger? Is that you, Roger?"

The only answer was a whimpering animal sound followed by the thud of something falling, or being thrown.

"Roger, it's Rachel Holbrook. Are you drunk? Answer me."

She waited for a full minute before hanging up. She felt dizzy with anger, days, weeks, years of anger, at the Rogers and Cleos and Donnys and Michaels and boards of directors, years of anger she had never shown, never even realized she felt.

She spoke as quietly and as calmly as possible to the girl sitting on the floor. "I have an important errand, Gretchen. Perhaps we'd better postpone the rest of the cleaning to another day."

"No, I can't. Everything's terribly dirty. It's going to take me six months to finish up."

"I need your cooperation, Gretchen. My secretary had to go to the dentist. When he returns I want you to give him a message for me. Can you do that?"

"No. I'm very busy."

"Gretchen, for God's sake—"

"You told us not to swear," Gretchen said. "God is a dirty word."

The carport beside Space C of Hibiscus Court was occupied by a car Mrs. Holbrook recognized as Roger Lennard's, a red Pinto station wagon with Utah license plates.

She stopped her Seville behind it and was about to get out when a man came hurrying toward her. He was an old man, so brown and wrinkled he looked as though he'd been hung out to dry in the California sun like a string of chili peppers.

"You can't stop there, lady," he said.

"Why not?"

"These are single units, one parking space apiece, no exceptions." The old man removed his straw hat. "My name's Abercrombie. I make sure the rules are followed."

"I'm in a hurry."

"Everybody's in a hurry. When everybody's in a hurry nobody gets anywhere. It's like all the people wanting to drive in the fast lane when the other lanes are open."

"Where do I leave my car?"

"You can go back to the street or you can follow this road to the guest parking lot at the rear."

She went back to the street. She had the impression that Mr. Abercrombie's rules would cover every inch, every nook and cranny, every leaf and blade of grass on the premises. When she returned he had disappeared.

She knocked on Roger Lennard's door and said in the voice she reserved for students who were being deliberately malicious, "Roger, it's Rachel Holbrook. I want to talk to you. Open this door."

If there was any response she couldn't hear it above the sounds of traffic on the street and in the air.

She knocked again, waited, then tried the door. It was locked. She'd come prepared for that. Now and then one of the students would lock himself in a dorm or lavatory or classroom and she would have to call in a locksmith to extricate him. After a number of these occasions the locksmith had provided her with a piece of metal, one of the tools of his trade called a picklock, and taught her how to use it. She carried it in her purse as casually as she did her wallet and lipstick. She used it now expertly, her body screening her movements from the possible gaze of Mr. Abercrombie.

The door opened. The first thing she saw was a kitchen table containing a salt shaker, a bottle of ketchup and a typewriter. There was a sheet of paper in the typewriter and a white envelope beside it. The kitchen chair was overturned and the telephone was on the floor beside it. It was a child's phone in the form of Mickey Mouse and she couldn't imagine Roger owning such a thing unless it had been given to him by a practical joker.

"Roger?"

She took a tentative step into the room. It was only then that she saw him lying on his side on a couch, his partly open mouth revealing bright red stains.

She forced herself to go over and touch his forehead. It was warm, but not warm enough. She picked up the telephone and called the emergency number printed on the front of it. Then she righted the kitchen chair and sat down to wait for the police and paramedics. She knew what the red stains in his mouth meant: There was nothing that could be done for Roger except by experts.

Even in the dim light she could make out the words on the page in the typewriter.

She picked up the white envelope and saw with a shock that it was addressed to her at Holbrook Hall. It was ready to be mailed, sealed and stamped with an extra stamp because of its bulk. Impulsively, without even thinking of any consequence of her action, she put the envelope in her purse. Then she called one of the numbers Aragon had written on his card.

He answered on the second ring. "Yes?"

"This is Rachel Holbrook," she said. "I'm at Roger Lennard's place. I think he's dead."

"Dead?"

"Yes. Pills."

"How did you get in?"

"I used a picklock."

"Surely you know that's illegal."

"Yes."

"What else have you done?"

"I took an envelope from the table. It was addressed to me, sealed and stamped. I consider it my property."

"What you consider and what the police consider may be quite different. You've called them, haven't you?"

"Yes."

"Put the letter back. Stay cool. I'll be right over."

He hung up.

She opened her purse to put the letter back, then closed it again. It was her property, Roger wanted her to have it, no one had any right to take it from her. Clutching the purse under her arm, she went out the door into the afternoon sun.

Mr. Abercrombie was leaning against the hood of Roger's car, watching her.

"I saw what you did," he said. "Picked the lock like an old pro."

"I had to. I thought he might be drunk."

"And is he?"

"No. I think he's dead."

Abercrombie made a snorting little noise. "You women are always exaggerating. A man takes a drink, he's drunk. He lies down for a nap, he's dead."

"I called the police and paramedics."

"For crying out loud, you crazy lady. What did you do that for? Why didn't you come to me? We can't have police and paramedics cluttering up the property for no reason except your imagination."

Two sounds were audible now: the full-scale siren of the police and the two-note electronic whelper of the paramedics.

"Crazy lady," Abercrombie said again. But he unfolded a canvas chair for her to sit on and began fanning her with his straw hat.

"Mr. Lennard had a row," he said. "You know, a quarrel. A man came to see him around lunchtime and I could hear their voices real loud until someone closed the windows. I saw the man leave, walk toward the street. He was a big fellow, heavyset, wearing a light grey suit and a Panama hat. Of course there's no chance of foul play or anything like that," he added anxiously. "Is there?"

"I can't answer that."

"Do you think I should tell the police about Mr. Lennard quarreling with that man?"

"Yes."

"Should I tell him about you picking the lock to get in?"

"No," Mrs. Holbrook said. "I'll tell them myself."

The paramedics arrived, four young men so quick and precise that their movements seemed choreographed. Abercrombie held the door open for them and they all went inside, filling the tiny room to capacity. People were already coming out of the other housing units, some curious, some frightened, some annoyed. They were quiet, listening to the paramedics' radio.

"This is Medic Two calling Santa Felicia Hospital . . . We have a cardiac arrest, a man about thirty, no pulse, no respiration . . . We're applying CPR, no luck so far . . . We have him now on the scope, getting only a straight line . . . Adrenalin intravenous started . . . We're moving right out . . ."

Roger was carried out, strapped to a stretcher. In the sunlight Mrs. Holbrook saw what she had missed previously: that his right eye and the whole right side of his face were badly swollen and discolored.

The police arrived as the emergency vehicle was pulling away, two black-and-whites and an unmarked car. The man who got out of the unmarked car looked like an ordinary middle-aged businessman on his way to his job at a bank or insurance office. He introduced himself to Abercrombie as Lieutenant Peterson, while three of the other men went inside.

"*She* discovered him," Abercrombie said, pointing to Mrs. Holbrook. "I don't know her. I never saw her before. She picked the lock. Go ahead, ask her."

"What is your name, sir?"

"Abercrombie."

"I'd like your full name and address, please."

Abercrombie told him and the lieutenant wrote down the information on a note pad.

"And the victim's name, please?"

"Victim?" Abercrombie repeated. "How do you know he's a victim?"

"Well, he was certainly the victim of something or we all wouldn't be here. Right?"

"His name was Roger Lennard."

"And his occupation?"

"A schoolteacher, something like that. He didn't call it a schoolteacher."

"Mr. Lennard was one of the counselors at my school," Mrs. Holbrook said.

"And your name is?"

"Rachel Holbrook."

"Address?"

"I live at the school, Holbrook Hall. Mr. Lennard called in sick a few days ago and I've been trying to get in touch with him on a certain matter. When I couldn't, I drove down here to see him, thinking he might be quite sick."

"Or drunk," Abercrombie said. "But *I* knew he couldn't be drunk. He was a Mormon—they're not supposed to drink. He wasn't sick, either. He was messing around with some girl, told me he was going to be married and wanted to bring the bride here until they could find a nice apartment. This is a single unit, see, and we don't allow—"

"You and I will talk later, Mr. Abercrombie," the lieutenant said. "I'd like to question Mrs. Holbrook alone for a few minutes, if you don't mind."

They sat in the back seat of Lieutenant Peterson's car. He closed the windows and turned on the air-conditioner.

"I called my lawyer," Mrs. Holbrook said. "I believe I should wait for him before answering any questions."

"That's your privilege, ma'am."

There was a silence. It didn't seem to bother the lieutenant. He leaned back and closed his eyes, as if he'd been waiting for a chance to take a nap.

"I've never been in a situation like this before," she said.

He didn't find the statement interesting enough to make him open his eyes.

"I mean, this sort of thing doesn't happen to a woman like me."

"Women like you don't usually go around picking locks either."

"I've never done it before except at school when I've had to free some student who'd been locked in a room."

"What did you use?"

"A picklock."

"Show it to me."

She opened her purse, taking no pains to hide the large envelope from Roger's kitchen table. It bore no sender's name or address; there was nothing to connect it with its source. She showed him the picklock.

"This belongs in a burglar's tool kit," he said, "not a lady's handbag."

"I gave you my reason for having it and my reason for using it. When you're trying to extricate a wildly hysterical child from a locked room you don't question the legality of what or how you do it. You just do it. On the last occasion it was a girl, fifteen. She wasn't hysterical. She was unconscious from an overdose of Seconal. Her mouth and tongue and throat were bright red the way Roger's were. The girl lived. I don't think Roger will."

"Why not?"

"I've had some experience with death. Roger's body was already cooling." Her voice shook in spite of her efforts to control it. "I'm—I was very fond of Roger. His work with the students was so positive, he emphasized what they had, not what they didn't have. He gave them a sense of identity."

"What about his identity?"

"I can't answer that."

"You've done pretty well so far."

He gave her back the picklock and she returned it to her purse.

"Was Mr. Lennard depressed lately?" he said.

"No."

"Did he say anything to you about getting married?"

"No."

"Did you know he was having a love affair?"

"Yes."

"Were you acquainted with the girl?"

"It wasn't a girl."

She could see Aragon's old Chevy trying to get into the road that bisected the court. A patrolman waved him away and he backed up into the street.

"What's his name?" the lieutenant said.

"Whose name?"

"The man you just recognized."

"He's my lawyer, Tomás Aragon."

"Never heard of him."

"I never heard of him either until a few days ago," she said. "As a matter of fact, he doesn't even know yet that he's my lawyer."

"You have surprises for everyone, Mrs. Holbrook."

"I've been getting quite a few myself lately."

"Well, let's see how Mr. Aragon reacts to his new client."

The lieutenant helped her out of the car and they stood waiting for Aragon's approach. After the shade and coolness of the air-conditioned car the sun was blinding and the heat oppressive, but the lieutenant neither blinked nor unbuttoned his coat. He said to Aragon, "Mrs. Holbrook's lawyer, I presume?"

Aragon acknowledged his sudden appointment with a somewhat baffled smile and the two men exchanged names as they shook hands.

"Mrs. Holbrook and I have just concluded a pleasant little chat," the lieutenant said. "She has an interesting new hobby you should discuss with her some time. You might want to encourage her to take up something more conventional, like needlepoint."

Aragon looked at Mrs. Holbrook. "You told him about the picklock?"

"I had to. Abercrombie saw me use it."

"You wouldn't make a very good criminal, Mrs. Holbrook."

"Don't sell her short," the lieutenant said. "She may be telling me a little so I won't ask her for a lot." Then to Mrs. Holbrook: "I'd like you to stick around for a while until I talk to Mr. Abercrombie and get a report from the hospital on Mr. Lennard. Does that suit you?"

"It will have to, I guess."

"You guessed right."

He didn't offer them the use of his car to wait in, so they walked back and sat on a bus stop bench under an oak tree.

"Did you tell him I was your lawyer?" Aragon asked.

"Yes. Aren't you?"

"I don't know. If anything comes up which makes you and Mr. Jasper adversaries, my prior commitment is to him."

"Nothing has come up. Perhaps nothing will."

"I'd like to find out a little bit more about what I'm getting into. Did you put the envelope back as I asked you to?"

"No."

"No? That's it, no?"

"That's it."

He said a word in Spanish that he hadn't spoken since he was a teenager.

She looked at him curiously. "So what does that mean?"

"It means, what am I going to do with this dame and how did I get into a crazy situation like this?"

"It means all that?"

"To me it does."

"You'll have to spell it for me some time."

"I don't think so," Aragon said. "Where's the envelope now?"

"In my purse."

"Will you let me see it?"

"What good would that do? It's still sealed. I don't intend to open it until I'm alone."

"What have you got to lose?"

"It's what Roger has to lose that concerns me. There might be something in here that, if he survives, he wouldn't want people to know, things he might regret having written. The envelope is full and carries an extra stamp. There's more to it than just a simple suicide note."

"It may be more than just a simple suicide," Aragon said. "When I came in I heard a couple of policemen talking about an attack. Someone hit Roger a hard blow on the right side of his face. His hands were unmarked, so apparently he didn't put up much of a fight, either because he was knocked unconscious or because he didn't want to."

"Abercrombie told me Roger had a visitor around lunchtime, a big man wearing a grey suit and Panama hat. Abercrombie heard them quarreling."

"Timothy North is a big man, and in view of Roger's impending marriage he and Roger had a lot to quarrel about. But I somehow doubt that he owns any suits. They're not part of his lifestyle . . . Mr. Jasper is also a big man."

"Yes."

"He probably owns a couple of dozen suits."

"Very likely."

"What's more, he's left-handed."

"What does that have to do with it?"

"The injuries to Roger's face were on the right side, one of the policemen said."

She touched her own face as though it hurt and she expected to find it bleeding. "Roger—Mr. Jasper—these are not violent people. How did all this happen to them? And to me? I'm a respectable woman. I don't go around breaking into people's houses or picking up things I'm not supposed to touch. Yet I did."

"It's not too late to correct one of those mistakes. Return the letter."

"It's my property."

"As long as it was on Roger Lennard's table, it belongs to him. If he had posted it, it would be yours on delivery."

He didn't realize her intention until she was already in the street, darting between the cars. She must have been sixty or more, but she moved with the speed of a natural athlete and luck was with her. He didn't catch up with her until the letter was in the mailbox, beyond the reach of everyone except the U.S. Postal Service.

"Roger intended to mail it," she said calmly. "I simply did it for him."

They returned to Hibiscus Court, walking in silence like strangers. The lieutenant was sitting in the front seat of his unmarked car, talking on a radiotelephone. He got out when he saw them coming.

His face remained impassive but he sounded rather amused. "You two look as if you've been playing games. A little hot for that, isn't it?" He didn't wait for an answer. "One of my men tells me you talked for a while at the bus stop, then Mrs. Holbrook suddenly dashed across the road and mailed something in the postbox. Is that right, Mrs. Holbrook?"

"Quite right," she said. "I remembered a letter I'd forgotten to post earlier."

"Memories like that pop up at the darnedest times, don't they? I mean, one minute you're sitting calmly talking to your lawyer and the next minute you're tearing across the road waving your purse to stop traffic."

"Things happen like that sometimes."

"Was it an important letter?"

"It was to me."

"Don't you have a secretary who handles that sort of chore?"

"He had to go to the dentist."

Because it was true it sounded true. He let the subject drop. To Aragon he said, "By the way, I didn't ask you how you managed to arrive here so fast. You got ESP? Listen to police calls?"

"I answer my telephone."

"Oh, never mind. I don't expect the truth anyway. I haven't met a lawyer yet who told the truth the first time around."

"I'm sorry your experience has been so limited."

"That could be taken as a hostile remark."

"Yours wasn't very friendly either, lieutenant."

"Maybe not, but this is my show. You're the guest. When the time comes and it's your show I'll be just as polite as I have to be."

"I look forward to that."

The lieutenant returned his attention to Mrs. Holbrook. "Is this your first visit to Mr. Lennard's place?"

"Yes."

"Abercrombie tells me Lennard had another visitor around lunchtime."

"He told me that, too."

"Can you guess who it might have been? Any ideas on the subject?"

"His description was very vague."

"That's not an answer to my question, Mrs. Holbrook. You said previously you were fond of Roger Lennard, very fond—I believe that was how you phrased it. If you were all that fond of him, you must know something about his private life."

"We had many conversations, but they were mostly about his work with the students."

"Do you know his friends?"

"Some of them."

"One in particular?"

"I knew Roger had one in particular but I wasn't personally acquainted with him. I only saw him when he came to pick Roger up at school occasionally."

"What's his name?"

"Timothy North."

"Is he locally employed?"

"He's a bartender. He's not in Roger's social class at all. I can't understand how the two of them—"

"Where does he tend bar?"

Mrs. Holbrook appealed to Aragon. "Do I have to answer all these questions?"

"He'll get the answers anyway," Aragon said. "If you save him time he might save you trouble."

"It's called Phileo's," Mrs. Holbrook said. "I believe it's a—well, a strange place. I'm sure Roger didn't go there habitually. He might have dropped in now and then. But Roger was a very idealistic young man."

"You keep referring to him in the past tense, Mrs. Holbrook."

"I'm sorry. I wasn't aware of doing it."

"You happen to be correct. Roger never regained consciousness. They've pulled the plugs."

She stood very straight and stiff. The lieutenant had seen other people do this when they were stretched too taut and getting ready to snap. "Let's stop the questioning for now."

"My God," she said. "What if I had come sooner? Could I have saved him? What if—"

"Look, this job is tough enough without the what-ifs. You go home and take a stiff drink. Or a couple of aspirin. To each his own."

"Did he kill himself?"

"He might have had a little help. However, there was a piece of paper in his typewriter that might have been the beginning of a suicide note. But we have no proof that it was or that he wrote it. You go home," he repeated. "Hit the booze or the aspirin and take a rest."

"I don't want—"

"You don't want," the lieutenant said. "But I want. Good day, Mrs. Holbrook."

She refused Aragon's offer to drive her back to the school, but she let him walk her to her car which she'd left at a gas station. She didn't move like the woman who'd run across the street to post the letter. Her gait was slow and awkward, as if she had, within the hour, grown years older and pounds heavier. She rested her head against the steering wheel for a moment before putting the keys in the ignition.

"Are you sure you can make it?" Aragon said.

"I have to," she said simply. "This has just been a preliminary event. The main bout's coming up now."

The scarcity of cars in the Privileged Parking zone made it apparent that the board of directors' meeting was over. She expected nothing further for the present than an informal note or a message from her secretary. Instead, her secretary had gone home and Hilton Jasper was sitting in the office, waiting.

In spite of the NO SMOKING PLEASE sign on her desk and the absence of ashtrays, he was smoking a cigarette. When she entered he crushed the cigarette in the wastebasket with obvious reluctance and rose to his feet.

"I've been waiting for you"—he consulted his wristwatch—"for over an hour."

"Punching a time clock isn't part of my job. This is my private office. Who let you in?"

He indicated the girl Gretchen, who was in the opposite corner of the room, still dusting books but no longer humming. "She's not much of a talker but she's a very good worker. I could use her in my business."

Gretchen gave no real sign that she heard or understood or cared, but she increased her pace and Mrs. Holbrook knew she had done all three.

She said, "You'd better stop for the day, Gretchen."

"I'm not finished."

"If you finish all the books today, you won't have any left to do tomorrow."

"I can do them again."

"That's nonsense, Gretchen. Now you hurry along and get into your swimsuit. It's almost pool time. You're such a strong swimmer, the timid students need your good example. Then afterwards maybe John will let you help him clean the pool."

The girl hesitated. She wanted to stay and dust the rest of the books but she also wanted to set a good example. Then suddenly she made up her mind, stuffed all the dustcloths into the tote bag and trudged across the room and out into the hall.

Mrs. Holbrook closed the door behind her and bolted it. "I suspect Gretchen of being one of the main stems of the school grapevine. By dinnertime everyone in the school will know that Cleo's brother was in my office and that he broke the no-smoking rule."

"She doesn't know I'm Cleo's brother."

"That's what you think. There are very few secrets around here. It's often wise to act as if every room was bugged." Though the smell of smoke was making her slightly ill, she closed the three windows that were open, then went back and sat at her desk, her hands folded in front of her. "Did the directors reach a conclusion?"

"Yes. In the best interest of the school, you are to ask Roger Lennard for his immediate resignation."

"That won't be easy."

"It might be simpler than you think."

"Indeed?"

"He won't be surprised, believe me. He's expecting it. I talked to him late this morning. He refused to admit he'd done anything wrong. In fact, he wouldn't even tell me where Cleo is. He lied, said he didn't know. I tried friendly persuasion to get the truth out of him. When that didn't work I hit him. He still wouldn't drop his injured innocence act, so I hit him again. He didn't even have guts enough to fight back."

"Roger didn't believe in violence."

"Well, maybe he does now." But the satisfaction in his voice had undertones of guilt. "I haven't hit anyone since I was a kid."

"Really? I hope you didn't hurt your hand. I notice you've been keeping it in your pocket. Let me see."

He took his left hand out of his pocket and she saw with pleasure it was almost as swollen and discolored as Roger's face.

She feigned surprise. "My goodness. Does it hurt?"

"Yes."

"You should have this examined."

"I haven't time to see a doctor."

"I didn't mean a doctor. I meant the police."

"Police? Are you telling me that little pipsqueak called the police because I hit him, after what he did to my sister, enticed her away from home, seduced her with promises—"

"No, that little pipsqueak didn't call the police," she said quietly. "I did."

"You did? Why?"

"I was the one who found him dead. I phoned the police and then Aragon."

For a few moments he was stunned and speechless. Then: "I didn't hit him that hard. I swear I didn't."

"Don't swear it to me. I have no jurisdiction."

"It's impossible to kill a man with your fist unless you're a professional boxer."

"Perhaps you missed your calling, Mr. Jasper."

Deliberately, almost maliciously, she withheld the information about the pills.

"Another tenant heard you quarreling with Roger and saw you leave," she said. "From his description and my own background knowledge I suspected it was you. But I didn't tell the police. Perhaps I would have if I'd been absolutely sure."

"Now that you're sure, what are you going to do?"

"Nothing. I expect you to do it yourself. Just phone and inform them that you hit Roger twice with your fist because he intended to marry, or had already married, your sister. Does that sound to you like a good story?"

"Not when you put it like that, when you leave out all the details."

"The details will come out later."

"For God's sake," he said, "I never meant—"

"That's irrelevant, isn't it?" She took a certain pleasure in watching him suffer. "The policeman I talked to this afternoon was a Lieutenant Peterson. I asked him what if I'd come sooner, and he stopped me. He said his job was tough enough without the what-ifs. Well, mine is tough enough without the I-never-meants."

"I went there only to reason with him. But he wouldn't be reasonable."

"If you're setting out to hit all the people who aren't reasonable, you're going to be a very busy man, Mr. Jasper."

"I didn't intend to kill him."

"Perhaps you didn't," she said. "He took some pills also. The actual cause of death won't be known until after an autopsy."

"Damn you, why didn't you tell me about the pills sooner?"

"Because I don't like bullies," she said. "And Roger was my friend."

11

FRIEDA SPENT THE afternoon sorting through clothes and bric-a-brac and books to be donated to the Assistance League rummage sale. The clothing would be sent to the cleaners, the bric-a-brac washed or polished, the books dusted. She carefully avoided Cleo's room and Ted's. Ted's would be half-empty and Cleo's exactly the way she'd left it when she walked away with the dog.

The house was quiet and orderly without the two of them. Each hour came in a neat little package and piled up in corners unopened.

When Hilton arrived home for dinner she went downstairs to meet him.

"You're late," she said.

"I can tell time."

"Oh, we're in a mood, are we? You must have had a bad day."

"It was—interesting."

"That's more than mine was." She noticed his hand when he put his hat away in the hall closet. "What's the matter with your hand?"

"I hurt it."

"That's obvious. Let me take a look at it."

"Stop fussing. It doesn't suit you. Is dinner ready?"

It was ready. Cook had left some time ago and Lisa, the college girl who did the serving, was waiting in the kitchen. Someone—the cook? Valencia? Lisa?—had removed one or two of the extension boards of the dining room table, so it was smaller and appeared less deserted.

"If you're going to have difficulty handling a soup spoon with your right hand," Frieda said, "we can skip that course and go on to the salad."

"Get rid of the girl."

"What do you mean, get rid of her? Fire her?"

"Tell her we won't need her for tonight."

"Why?"

"I have something important to discuss with you in private."

"That sounds ominous. I don't like it. You're frightening me, Hilton."

"I can't help it."

"Is it about Cleo?"

"It's about me."

Lisa came in wearing her usual uniform: skintight jeans and T-shirt partly covered by an apron. She carried two bowls of soup, hot consommé floating sprigs of parsley on lemon rafts.

Frieda spoke in the too-bright voice she used as a cover-up. "Lisa, we've decided to have dinner alone tonight. You're free to leave."

Lisa put the soup bowls on the table in a manner that clearly indicated her displeasure. "I don't want to leave just yet. My boyfriend's not picking me up until eight o'clock."

"Where is he now?"

"The university library."

"Suppose you go and meet him. I'll give you five dollars for cab fare."

"That might not cover it and I'm broke."

"All right. Ten dollars."

"I still think it'd be simpler if I just stayed and served dinner as usual. A cab might get caught in a traffic jam. Or Brent might finish his term paper early and we'd miss each other. I don't see why I can't sit quietly in the kitchen and watch television until Brent comes."

"I don't want to hear any television sounds coming out of the kitchen," Jasper said. "And I don't want any dining room sounds going into the kitchen. Have I spelled that out clearly enough for you?"

"Okay, okay. But I don't like having my plans screwed up like this."

"Here." He took a twenty-dollar bill from his wallet and shoved it at her. She stared at it a moment before accepting it. Then she folded it and tucked it into the rear pocket of her jeans. "I see you hurt your hand."

"Yes. Good night."

She phoned for a cab in the kitchen, speaking in a very loud, distinct voice to make sure they overheard. Then she went out the back door, slamming it behind her.

"Twenty dollars was too much," Frieda said.

"I didn't have a ten."

"You could have asked me."

"I could have, yes." *I could have . . . I never meant . . . what if . . .* Useless phrases belonging only to the past.

"What happened to your hand?"

"I hit a man."

"Oh, I don't believe it. You'd never do anything so primitive."

"Well, I did."

"What on earth for?"

"I wanted to make him tell me where Cleo is. I was sure he knew. She probably went directly to him the morning she left here. He refused to admit anything."

"You should have tried to bribe him. God knows that's not above you. We just had an example of it a minute ago."

"I wanted to hit him."

"That's always been the governing principle of your life. You wanted to do something, so you did it . . . Do you want to eat your soup? If you don't, I'll take it back to the kitchen and we'll go on with the rest of the meal."

He looked at her bitterly. "There's no sympathy in you, is there, Frieda?"

"I'm reserving mine for the man who was hit."

"Don't waste your time. He's dead."

She tried to cover her alarm with a show of cynicism. "If this is one of your attempts to build yourself a macho image, forget it."

"I'll have to go to the police. I've been trying to get in touch with some of the company's lawyers but they're in Washington or L.A. or Sacramento. One is even hunting capercaillie in Scotland. They're everyplace but here. And they're not accustomed to dealing with cases like this anyway. It's a criminal matter."

"Roger Lennard," she said. "You killed Roger Lennard?"

"I'm not sure. He took some pills. Maybe he'd already taken them when I arrived. He made no attempt to fight back. I thought it was because he didn't have the guts, but maybe he was already dying. We have to wait for the results of an autopsy."

"How long will that take?"

"I don't know."

She sat twisting the soup spoon around and around between her fingers as though she was trying to wring its neck. "Chalk another one up to Cleo. She'll beat us all before she's through."

"Don't blame Cleo. It's my fault. Cleo wouldn't hurt a fly."

"No, she wouldn't hurt a fly. Or a dog or a horse. But what about the rest of us? We're the ones who get our wings pulled out, our paws stepped on."

"Please, let's not argue about Cleo. We have to decide what to do next."

"We? You mean I now have a part in the decision making?"

"You always did."

He was down and she would have liked to kick him a few more times to make sure he remembered after he got up again. But she was a reasonable woman with a keen sense of survival. He was down. That was enough.

"Give me the whole picture," she said. "You knocked at his door. Was it locked?"

"Yes."

"Did you tell him who was there?"

"Yes."

"And he unlocked the door and let you in?"

"Yes, right away. I had the peculiar feeling that he might even have been expecting me. He seemed almost resigned. He knew who I was, of course. Cleo probably talked about me to him the way she does to everyone."

"All right, he let you in. Then what?"

Her husband stared into his soup bowl. The little lemon raft with its cargo of parsley had floated to one side as if his breath had provided enough wind to move it. "He lives—lived— in a mobile home, a very small one where everything is wall-to-wall. There was a typewriter on the table, I remember, and a magazine on the couch. I asked him right away where Cleo was and he claimed he didn't know, that she'd walked out on him. He talked very slowly and calmly and that made me even angrier. I began to yell at him. One of the neighbors overheard me and reported it later to the police."

"When you hit him, did he fall down?"

"No. I hit him again."

"Then did he fall down?"

"No."

"How could you have killed him when he wasn't even knocked over by the force of the blows?"

"The effects of head injuries aren't always immediately apparent."

"But he was still standing up when you left?"

"Yes."

"Then the chances are that you had nothing to do with his death?"

"I made it clear to him that he didn't have much of a future in this town or in his profession or with Cleo. If that caused him to take an overdose of pills, then I have some moral responsibility for his death."

"A man doesn't commit suicide because of a few words spoken in anger. He may have been planning it for weeks, months, even years. He had many personal problems, according to Aragon." She paused. "What about Aragon? He might be able to help you."

"He's too young and inexperienced."

"At least he's not hunting capercaillie in Scotland," she said sharply. "Whatever the hell capercaillie is. Shall I call him?"

"If you like."

"If I like? What I'd like is a nice peaceful life without a husband who goes around slugging people."

She had hit him once too often while he was down. He was getting up now, and it showed in his face and his voice.

"The person I should have slugged is you, Frieda."

"It's a bit late for that. It would cost you too much, especially where it hurts, in the pocketbook."

"You intend to leave me, don't you?"

"If Cleo comes back, yes. I can't face another year like the past fourteen."

"Have things been that bad?"

"Worse. You don't realize that because you were away most of the time, at the office or at meetings out of town, while I was stuck at home watching her every minute, trying to teach her to talk properly and to read, looking after the succession of stray animals and birds she dragged home only to lose interest in them almost immediately, the way she lost interest in the dog Zia. She took him with her that morning and then she must have simply left him somewhere, forgot all about him."

"Why do our conversations always revert to Cleo?"

"Because she's been the focus of our lives, not you or I or Ted."

He said, "Here I am, in serious trouble, sitting in front of a bowl of cold soup, across the table from a wife who hates me, talking about a sister who ran away from me."

"At least we can take care of the cold soup part."

She carried the soup bowls back to the kitchen and returned with two plates of salad. "I repeat the question, Hilton. Shall I call Aragon? You don't have to take his advice, just see what he has to say."

"Go ahead."

"You might want to do it yourself."

"No. You handle these things very well, Frieda. It's one of your talents."

She used the wall phone in the kitchen. There was no answer from Aragon's apartment, so she left a message with the answering service at his office for him to call back. She saw the headlights of a car coming up the driveway and she thought at first what a nice coincidence it was, to have Aragon show up at the very time she was trying to get in touch with him. But as she listened she knew the car couldn't be his. The engine sounded too quiet and smooth.

She went to the front door and opened it at the first ring of the chime. The overhead light that switched on automatically when the door opened revealed a tall middle aged man with a deeply tanned face and bright, expressionless eyes that reminded her of Cleo's.

"Mrs. Hilton Jasper?"

"Yes."

"You shouldn't open the door like that without first asking who is there."

"All right, who is here?"

"Lieutenant Peterson of the Police Department."

"This is an inconvenient time to receive you," she said coolly. "We're in the middle of dinner."

"Really? Funny thing, I was in the middle of dinner myself when the desk sergeant played me a tape of a message that had just come in from a woman. Sounded like a girl, actually. It seems she'd been listening to the six o'clock news and heard about the death of a man she knew, Roger Lennard. Is that name familiar to you?"

"Vaguely."

"Perhaps your husband might find it less vague."

Her response was to open the door a little farther to allow him to step inside. When she closed it again the overhead light went off and Lieutenant Peterson's face was in shadow. It looked better that way, more expressive, kinder, with the disturbing brightness of his eyes obscured.

"Let's not beat around the bush, Lieutenant," she said. "We've called our attorney and until he arrives my husband isn't going to make any statement."

"That's fine. I'll wait."

"I'm not sure when he's coming. I left a message with his answering service but he may not even get it tonight."

"I'll still wait. I presume you have a spare bedroom."

She let out a gasp of surprise.

"Now, now, don't get shook. That was just a little joke to lighten up the atmosphere."

"It wasn't very successful."

"Many of my jokes aren't. Win a few, lose a few. I'd like to see Mr. Jasper, all jokes aside."

"As I told you, we're in the middle of dinner. Would you mind waiting for him?"

"I wouldn't mind, no. But I'd prefer to come and sit at the table with you. What are you serving, by the way? I hope you don't mind my asking. You see, I was in the middle of dinner myself."

"Avocado and grapefruit salad and seafood Newburg."

"Sounds great. Did you make the seafood yourself?"

"We have a cook."

"Congratulations. Good cooks are hard to find these days."

"I didn't say she was a good cook . . . Are you by any chance inviting yourself for dinner?"

"The thought crossed my mind."

"This is—this is really extraordinary."

"I don't agree. Put a hungry man on the trail of seafood Newburg and what he does is quite ordinary."

"I don't know what Mr. Aragon will say when he gets here if you're sitting having dinner with us."

"Aragon? Now, he's pretty small potatoes for a big man like your husband. Potatoes. There goes my mind again, back to food."

"I've never been in a situation like this before in my life."

"As a matter of fact, neither have I. But we mustn't shut ourselves off from new experiences, must we?"

"Come this way."

It wasn't the most gracious invitation he'd ever received but it was the only one for dinner that night, so he followed her down the hall.

Jasper was standing at the head of the dining room table, his left hand in his pocket.

"Hilton, this is Lieutenant Peterson," Frieda said. "He has kindly consented to join us for dinner."

The lieutenant nodded. "Glad to meet you, Mr. Jasper. I don't imagine the feeling is mutual."

"No, it's not."

"Ah well, suppose we forget business for a while and act like new friends about to break bread together for the first time."

Jasper's only reply was to pull out a chair and then put his own plate of salad, which he hadn't touched, in front of the lieutenant. Frieda turned up the heat under the silver chafing dish that contained the seafood.

She said, "My husband and I aren't having wine with dinner tonight but I'll open a bottle for you if you like."

"Not while I'm on duty."

The lieutenant ate quickly and quietly with only an occasional remark about the weather, the food, the state of the nation. Neither of the Jaspers made any attempt to converse. Frieda served the food and Jasper pushed it around on his plate in a pretense of eating.

Afterward, the lieutenant said, "Excellent, excellent. I truly appreciate having a home-cooked meal now and then. Since my wife died I've probably eaten more Big Macs and fries than any man in town."

Jasper took a deep breath and held it for a moment before speaking. "Why are you here, Lieutenant?"

"As I told your wife, the desk sergeant received a phone call about six thirty. He played the tape of it for me. It was the voice of a young woman, a girl probably, who'd been listening to the six o'clock news and heard about Roger Lennard's death. A man named Abercrombie had spoken rather freely to the press describing someone who'd visited Lennard in the late morning. She claimed the description fitted you."

"I see."

"A lot of policemen would like people to believe that we go around solving crimes by taking fingerprints and making plaster casts and ballistics tests. Now these things all look good in a courtroom once the criminal is on trial. But how he's caught is usually a different story. Somebody squealed, a disgruntled employee or partner, a jealous lover, a cast-off wife. These are the people who solve crimes. If it weren't for the young woman's phone call I wouldn't be here. Tall man in a grey suit and Panama hat—that's not much to go on. Add a name and address, and the picture changes. Did you go to see Roger Lennard this morning?"

"I'd like to hear that tape."

"That's not an answer to my question, Mr. Jasper."

"I'll answer your questions if you let me listen to the tape."

"No," Frieda said. "No, you won't. You're not to say anything until Mr. Aragon—"

"Be quiet, Frieda. What about it, Lieutenant? Do we have a deal?"

"Sounds fair to me."

"I want to hear the tape first."

"Now that part isn't so fair," the lieutenant said. "Maybe you think you might recognize the voice?"

"I might."

"We'll have to go out to my car. I brought the tape with me. I intended to play it for you anyway."

Frieda made one more attempt to stop him but he pushed her aside. "Let me handle my own affairs," he said. "I'm a big boy now."

"You don't eat like one. You're a stupid, pigheaded little boy."

"I hate to break up a good old-fashioned family row," the lieutenant said. "But sometimes I have to. Let's go, Mr. Jasper. Would you like to come along too, Mrs. Jasper? It's the least I can do in return for the excellent meal."

"I hope you get indigestion," Frieda said.

The tape was brief:

"Police Department, Sergeant Kowalski speaking."

"Hello. Is this the right place to phone to tell you something?"

"Yes ma'am, if you've got something to tell."

"I heard it on the radio about Roger Lennard being dead. Is it true? I guess it must be true or they wouldn't say it to everybody like that."

"Yes ma'am."

"They said a man quarreled with Roger. I know who it was. He's mean, he's a mean old man."

"Just a minute and I'll transfer this—"

"His name is Hilton Jasper and he lives at twelve hundred Via Vista."

"Would you give me your name please, ma'am?"

The tape ended with a click. The voice was Cleo's.

The lieutenant said, "Think that might be someone you know, Mr. Jasper?"

"No."

"Maybe you'd care to hear it again?"

"No, thanks," Jasper said. "I had an idea it might be a secretary I had to fire last week."

"Disgruntled employee, right?"

"Yes."

"I didn't think a man in your position had much to do with the hiring and firing of secretaries."

"There are exceptions."

"I'm sure there are. Let's play it again to make sure it wasn't your disgruntled employee, shall we?"

"No. *No.*"

"Usually when we're having somebody try to identify a voice, we play the tape several times."

"There's no need for that. It wasn't my former secretary."

"I know that, Mr. Jasper. Who was it?"

Jasper shook his head.

"You won't identify the caller?"

"I can't."

"Can't, won't, same difference as far as I'm concerned. I don't get an answer . . . It sounded like a girl to me. Would you agree with that?"

"I guess so."

"Perhaps it was one of those girls at the special school where Roger Lennard worked."

"Perhaps."

"Well, you've heard the tape. Now I'd like to hear your answers to a few questions. Shall we go back into the house?"

"I'd prefer to stay here."

"Mrs. Jasper?"

"Mrs. Jasper."

"Feisty woman. I like the type but they're tough to live with. Any kids?"

"We have a son, Edward. He'll be a senior at Cal Poly this fall."

"No daughters?"

"No."

"Once in a while our crimes are solved for us by disgruntled daughters as well as employees . . . How long have you known Lennard?"

"Not long."

"What made you decide to call on him this morning?"

"I prefer not to answer that."

"Your prefers and my prefers aren't going to jibe, are they?"

"I'll make a simple statement about my actions this morning without going into motives. I quarreled with Lennard, I hit him twice, he didn't fall down, I left. Those are the facts. I can't tell you any more at this time."

"You haven't told me anything I didn't know."

"I confessed to hitting him. That will have to be enough for now."

The lieutenant rewound the tape and played it through again. "You'll notice, Mr. Jasper, that the girl refers to Mr. Lennard as Roger."

"Yes, I noticed."

"She was evidently a friend of his."

"Yes."

"And you evidently were not a friend either of his or of hers. She called you a mean old man."

"So I heard."

"How old are you?"

"Forty-four."

"That's not old," the lieutenant said. "Is her other claim also exaggerated?"

"Am I mean? Apparently someone thinks so."

"Some secret enemy?"

"You might say that."

"Oh, no, I wouldn't say that at all, Mr. Jasper. I'm convinced you know this girl, perhaps very well. Have you been fooling around?"

"No."

"I believe you. She didn't sound like the kind of person who'd appeal to a man of your social status. She's definitely lower class, don't you agree?"

"I'm not in the habit of judging a person's social position by listening to a few sentences on tape," Jasper said stiffly. "Now if you'll excuse me, I'll—"

"Who was the girl, Jasper?"

"I can't say."

"Okay. That's all for now. You're free to go back in the house, watch T. V. or go to bed, or finish the argument with your wife, whatever."

"Aren't you going to wait for Aragon?"

"Why should I?" the lieutenant said. "I'd probably get even less information with him around . . . Thank your wife again for the dinner. And tell her I never get indigestion from food, only from people."

The lieutenant returned to headquarters. Kowalski, the desk sergeant who'd played him the tape on the radiophone, was still on duty. He was eating a ham sandwich that oozed the bilious yellow of mustard. A young woman in uniform was sitting at a desk with a typewriter in front of her, scratching her head with a pencil. Nothing much seemed to be happening, except possibly inside the young woman's head.

"Quiet night," Kowalski said. "Anything we can do for you, lieutenant?"

"I'd like to see the city directory."

"Sarah will get it for you. Hey, Sarah."

The young woman dropped her pencil. "Don't you hey-Sarah me or I'll report you to the National Organization for Women."

"You reported me twice this month."

"Three times and out."

"All right, all right. Sarah, honorable policeperson, would you please drag your beautiful butt over to the shelf and get the lieutenant the city directory?"

"That 'beautiful butt' remark could be construed as sexual harassment."

"Get the directory, kiddo," the lieutenant said.

He took the directory back to his office, a small room, hardly more than a cubicle, sparsely furnished with two straight-backed chairs in addition to the swivel chair behind his desk. There was also a filing cabinet, and a water cooler used mainly to water the Boston fern on a five-foot stand in the corner, its fronds reaching all the way to the floor. Except for the standard electronic equipment, the desk was almost bare: no heavy paperweight that could be used as a weapon and no papers that could be spied on. On one side there was a small graceful porpoise carved out of ironwood and on the other a photograph of three people in tennis clothes: a fair-haired woman and two teenaged boys.

The house at 1200 Via Vista was listed in the directory as jointly owned by Frieda and Hilton Jasper, with Edward Jasper, Cleo Jasper, Paolo Trocadero and Valencia Ybarra as residents. Trocadero and Ybarra were probably servants and Jasper had mentioned his son Edward, but claimed to have no daughters. So who was Cleo and why hadn't her name come up in the conversation?

He called the record room and asked for any recent information on Hilton or Cleo Jasper. Ten minutes later Sarah appeared with a card bearing the name Hilton Jasper, the time of his arrival at the police station, the nature of his complaint, a missing person described as his sister, Cleo, a student at Holbrook Hall. Attached to the card was a passport-size picture of an unsmiling pretty girl with long straight hair. The absence of any further information indicated that no action had been taken on the case.

The lieutenant leaned back in his chair, his hands clasped behind his head. His eyes moved back and forth as if he were watching a computer readout on the ceiling.

Cleo Jasper. Runaway. Student at Holbrook Hall. Victim of some degree of mental or emotional impairment. Member of a wealthy family. Alive as of six thirty. Still in town, since a nonlocal radio station wouldn't bother to report the death of someone as unimportant as Lennard.

No indication even of Cleo's existence had been given by the Jaspers, Mrs. Holbrook, or Aragon. What were they protecting—the girl's future? Their own pride? The reputation of the school?

The lieutenant yawned, stretched, studied the picture on the card again.

"Cleo," he said aloud. "Where the hell are you?"

12

THE MAIL WAS delivered to Holbrook Hall the following morning at ten o'clock. Rachel Holbrook had been waiting for it, pacing around her office as if she were measuring its precincts, glancing at her wristwatch every few minutes. When she saw the truck coming up the driveway she went to meet the postman at the front door.

He was a plump, cheerful young man who felt it was part of his job to give his important customers a preview of the day's haul.

"Lots of throwaway stuff this morning, Mrs. Holbrook. And bills—I guess you can't run a place like this without a bunch of bills."

"Thank you, Harry, I'll just take it and—"

"New issues of *Reader's Digest, Psychology Today, Audiovisual Journal.* Letters for the kids, naturally. I always wondered, do they read their own letters or are they read to them?"

"A catalogue of playground equipment. I'd like to borrow that when you've finished, if you don't mind, Mrs. Holbrook. My kids are getting old enough now to use things like that in the yard."

"I'll save it for you, Harry. Goodbye."

The box of mail was so heavy she could hardly carry it back to her office. The job of separating it was usually left to her secretary but this morning she did it herself. She found the letter from Roger Lennard almost immediately. It looked like any other letter, but it was the first she'd ever received from a dead man and it seemed to give off a faintly sour odor.

She called Aragon at his apartment.

"Roger's letter has arrived," she said. "I think you should be here when I open it."

"Why?"

"I'm beginning to wonder if I did the correct thing. Yesterday it seemed so logical and right. Now I don't know. I'm frightened."

He hesitated. Then: "I should be there in about twenty minutes. Take it easy."

"Roger meant me to have it. It's not as though I took something that didn't belong to me, do you think?"

"I think you should stop second-guessing until I get there."

He came within twenty minutes.

It was a cool morning, with the sun just starting to break through the low overcast of clouds. Along the driveway up to the school there were patches of moisture under the big trees where the night fog had condensed and dripped from the leaves, the grey lace of the acacias, the leathery loquats, the prickly oaks and feathery pepper trees. It would be another three months before the rains started, and these night fogs were what kept the trees alive.

Rachel Holbrook was standing on the front steps talking to two girl students. When she saw Aragon she dismissed the girls with a smile and a gesture. They walked away, giggling, whispering behind their hands, glancing back at the new arrival.

"Good morning, Mr. Aragon," she said formally and loud enough for the girls to overhear. "You've come about the accounting, of course."

"Yes. It's a good morning for accounting."

"Come in." She added, after she closed the door, "The whole school knows something is up. I don't want to add any fuel to the fire."

The drapes in her office were closed. Light came from the fluorescent fixtures in the ceiling and the draftsman's lamp on her desk, angled to shine directly on the letter from Roger Lennard. The setting looked a little too theatrical. Aragon was not sure what role he was expected to play in the production.

She handed him the letter and told him to open it.

"Why me?" he said.

"It will prove that I haven't already done so, for one thing."

"And for another?"

She didn't answer directly. "I've had a chance to appraise the situation and I realize now that I might have done something quite criminal."

"There's no such thing as quite criminal, Mrs. Holbrook. It is or it isn't."

"Very well. I removed evidence from the scene of a possible crime. But you will be my witness to the fact that I didn't know what was in here and my motive in taking it was solely to spare Roger in case he survived."

"That sounds very noble. But I don't think Lieutenant Peterson is much of a believer in nobility."

"Are you?"

"Sometimes." This wasn't one of the times. He had driven to L.A. the previous night on business for Smedler and hadn't arrived home until three o'clock in the morning. He felt tired and hungry and irritable.

"I don't claim that my motives were noble, Mr. Aragon. They were human, that's all."

"It's your letter, Mrs. Holbrook. You open it."

She slit the envelope with her thumbnail and shook the contents out on her desk. There were almost a dozen sheets of paper. Some appeared to be completed letters, some were half-finished and some sheets bore only a few words. One of the completed letters began *Dear Mrs. Holbrook.* She read it aloud in a low, cautious voice.

> *Dear Mrs. Holbrook:*
>
> *You have been more like a mother to me than my own mother. You have respected my work, which is all I'm good for, maybe not even that anymore. You have encouraged me and given me your friendship.*
>
> *I am writing this to say goodbye and to thank you for your kindness and generosity. I know you will not judge this as an act of cowardice on my part. It is, quite simply, inevitable, something I have been considering for a long time.*
>
> *Last year when I was excommunicated from the church you took me in and gave me back some of my self-confidence.*
>
> *Since I have been a practicing homosexual I will not be able to join my family in the afterworld. I can only hope that there is another place, perhaps a better place, where I can be with truly good people like you. I go to my death believing there must be such a place.*

I have been writing off and on all morning and now I don't know what to do with the stuff. I just don't think people will want to read what I have to say. I am putting it all into this envelope and you can do with it whatever you think best. I've always trusted your judgment.

Please remember me as someone who has felt blessed by your friendship.

Roger

Mrs. Holbrook got up and walked to the window as though she were about to look out through the closed drapes. She made no sound, but Aragon knew she was weeping.

"I'm sorry," he said. "I'll read the rest if you like." She nodded and he sat down at her desk and picked up one of the other sheets of paper.

To Whom It May Concern If Anybody:

I tried, I really tried. I prayed to God but he turned out to be a cruel old man in the sky who knows more about hate than about love. I tried, everyone laughed but I tried. And failed. Failed failed failed. Let that be my epitaph, Roger Lennard, he tried, he failed.

What message do I want to leave to the world? A curse on all pious bigots everywhere.

Another letter was to his parents.

Dear Mom and Dad:

It was good to hear your voices on the phone the other night. You sounded so happy, Mom, when I told you the news about my getting married. And I was happy too. I really thought it would work out. Cleo admires me and respects me.

I can almost hear you saying, the girl must be crazy. Well, she is, sort of. But she wants to have a family and so do I. I've always loved kids. My head was filled with hope. But all the time I had this terrible turmoil inside me, despair, hate, rage. It is impossible for me to make a family, impossible. Oh, how I can picture Dad scowling over that because he thinks that men are first and foremost created to make families. But what if they can't? Can't can't can't what if they can't?

Another unfinished letter was addressed to Cleo.

Dear little Cleo, you should never have come to me with your troubles. I often told you at school that you could, but when you did, when you suddenly appeared out of the blue, I got carried away. I forgot I was supposed to be objective. I thought, why not? Why can't Cleo and I have children like normal people? All of a sudden I had real hope for the future. I would change, you would change, we would change each other. We would have a family, I could be a good Mormon again.

I liked the feel of you in my arms. Your skin was so soft you seemed made of silk and flowers. Then you began to talk about Ted. Ted did this, Ted did that. You never meant to tease me, you had no idea how much I was suffering. Then you said, Oh Roger, are you one of those funny people? And I said yes. Yes, I'm one of the funnies, funny ha ha, funny peculiar, funny split your sides. I'm one of the funnies, so please laugh, Cleo, don't lie there like a stone flower.

I have written a poem about us, Cleo.

Funny sky
Funny sea,
Funny I,
Funny me.
Funny me
Funny us,
Funnily
Oblivious.
Oblivious. I like that word. It sounds like a nice place to go.
Forgive me, Cleo, if I have harmed you in any way, if I have given you ideas beyond your grasp. You were so anxious to become what you called a real person. And I was so anxious to help you become one. We had high hopes and high failures. This is how the world ends.

Some of the other sheets of paper contained only a few words.

Cruel. All around me is cruel. I am afraid. Nightmare, daymare, morningmare, afternoonmare. What is it all about? It is too late. It is too late for anyone to tell me.

Tim, Tim my beloved, please forgive me. I had to choose between you and the church. What else could I do, what other decision could I make with the family on my back like that? Please, Tim. Please don't judge me harshly.

To the Probate Court:
I, Roger Lennard, mens sana in corpore sano, would like my worldly possessions distributed as follows:
My books to Holbrook Hall
My classical records to the Public Library.
All other possessions to my dear friend, Timothy North.

Roger Lennard

Mom, Mom I can't stand never seeing you again

Slowly and carefully Aragon put the papers back in the envelope. "I'm sorry," he said again.

"Yes."

"Lieutenant Peterson will have to be informed of this right away. What are you going to tell him?"

"That it came in the mail."

"That's all?"

"That's all."

"He won't be satisfied," Aragon said. "He'll want to know, for instance, if this is the same envelope you were seen posting yesterday."

"On the other hand," she said, "he might be so happy at having Roger's death proved a suicide that he'll let the matter drop."

"I don't think the lieutenant will ever be that happy."

"We'll have to wait and see."

She unlocked the drawer where she kept her personal belongings during office hours and placed the envelope in her purse. "I suppose I should deliver it to him myself."

"Yes."

"It would be kind of you to come along for moral support."

"Better if I don't," Aragon said. "Lawyers aren't very high on the lieutenant's popularity poll."

The red light on the intercom had started to blink and Mrs. Holbrook switched on the speaker. "Yes, Richie?"

"The captain is here to see you, Mrs. Holbrook."

"But I didn't— I wasn't exp— Wait a minute." She turned to Aragon. "Captain? Isn't that a higher rank than lieutenant?"

"Yes."

"Please wait. I'm not sure how to handle this. The entire school will be aroused if he arrived here in a police car."

But he hadn't come in a police car. The captain's hat he wore could have been purchased in any maritime shop along the coast, and his well-tailored navy-blue blazer and white slacks weren't the kind of clothing found in a policeman's locker.

The man was about fifty, with a round red face and bushy sun-bleached eyebrows that seemed to have a life of their own, like blond caterpillars. He gave off an odor of cologne and bourbon and cigar smoke.

"Well, well, what's going on here?" he said jovially. "A séance?"

"You might call it that," Mrs. Holbrook replied.

"Include me in. I've never been to a séance. But first let's get a little light in here." He went over to the windows and began pulling open the drapes. "If I'm going to see ghosts I want the genuine article that'll stand up to daylight."

"Mr. Whitfield, this is Mr. Aragon."

Whitfield's handshake was firm and hearty. "I was in a town in Spain once called Aragon. Not much of a place but it had some pretty girls. You couldn't get near them, though. There were a dozen old crones surrounding each one."

Aragon couldn't think of a suitable comment, so he kept quiet.

"I have nothing against Spain," Whitfield added. "The fact is, I'm not at home on land. Any land, anywhere. The sea's where I live. I'm heading for Ensenada tomorrow. One of my crewmen wants to check on his wife and I figure, why not? Some of the *muchachas* in these Mexican ports can be pretty lively."

Failing for the second time to get a response from Aragon, he turned his attention to Mrs. Holbrook. "I came as soon as I got your message."

Mrs. Holbrook looked surprised. She had been trying to contact him for two days but she had left no message and no name. "I don't quite understand, Mr. Whitfield."

"The girl in your office caught me as I was leaving my condo. In fact, the phone rang as I was going out the door. She told me to come to the school to discuss Donny's curriculum. She didn't sound too sure of the word *curriculum*. Maybe you'd better tell her what it means."

"When a call is made from this office concerning a student I handle it personally or through my secretary. His name is Richard. I have no female employees authorized to perform such duties, and if I had she would certainly be familiar with words like curriculum."

"What's going on around here? I tell you, I had this phone call from some girl at the school and she said I was to come right over and discuss Donny's curriculum. Hell, it was that word that brought me over here so fast. I thought maybe the kid was finally straightening out. Any other time I've heard from the school it's been about one of Donny's famous emergencies, like when he stole the laundry truck and rammed it into a tree."

Aragon spoke for the first time since Whitfield's arrival. "What else did the girl say, Mr. Whitfield?"

"Nothing much. She emphasized that I was to come here immediately. I failed to understand the reason for the big hurry but I went along with the request. So here I am—at considerable loss of time, if I may add—and no one's even expecting me."

"Did she give a name?"

"No."

"Do you remember her exact words?"

"Well, she just said, 'This is Mrs. Holbrook's office at Holbrook Hall.' No, wait a minute. She sort of slurred the name of the school. It almost sounded like Holy Hall."

"The students often call it that," Mrs. Holbrook said.

"So it was one of those damn little half-wits playing a joke on me. That's the thanks I get for practically supporting this so-called school."

"It is more than so-called, Mr. Whitfield. It's a real school which takes students the other schools don't want, can't manage, can't teach."

"Hell, I don't want Donny to learn Latin and a lot of crap like that. I just want him to learn to behave himself, keep his nose clean."

"We don't guarantee results. And we don't teach Latin. We try to teach acceptable social behavior such as the avoidance of profanity."

"Well, goddamn it, I'm sorry. But the trouble I've had with that kid—"

"You're going to have more, Mr. Whitfield."

"What does that mean?"

"We'd better sit down and discuss it." To Aragon she said, "I was about to deliver this envelope. I wonder if you'd be so kind as to do it for me. It's a rush job and I may be occupied here for some time."

Aragon had no choice. He took the envelope and departed. There was no exchange of goodbyes.

As he was walking toward the parking lot he looked back and saw Whitfield through the window, slumped in one of the leather chairs. His right leg was slung over the arm of the chair and his chin was resting on his fist. Upside down on the desk was his captain's hat, a symbol of his store-bought authority.

Aragon left the envelope at Police Headquarters and drove down to the harbor. The harbormaster's office was on the second floor of a small building beside the yacht club. From it the entire coastline could be seen for miles in either direction, as well as everything that was happening on the breakwater and the wharf and at the marina. The entrance to the harbor lay between the end of the wharf and the breakwater. Almost every day its depth varied according to the movement of sand by the tides and currents. In spite of almost continual dredging, the channel was sometimes blocked entirely for the larger craft. On many occasions the commercial fishing fleet had to wait at anchor outside the harbor while the other half was trapped inside like grounded whales.

Today the entrance was navigable. A ketch, still under power, was heading for the open sea, raising its mainsail. A boat that serviced the oil platforms was picking up speed as it left the five-mile-an-hour limit of the harbor.

The harbormaster, Sprague, an ex-Seabee, had had an indoor job for half a dozen years but it was too late to prevent the sun damage that mottled his face in the form of skin cancers. Now in his sixties, he had difficulty remembering names and faces but he never forgot a boat and he considered all the craft tied up in the harbor as his personal fleet. Only God and the weather outranked him.

He was on the phone when Aragon entered.

"Hold it, Wavewalker. I've had two more complaints against you for littering."

"Hell, a few beer cans ain't littering. They sink to the bottom."

"Sure, and pretty soon you'll be trying to float on a pile of rust. So clean up your act. Where are you heading?"

"*The Ruby*. She's laying in her usual supply of caviar and Chivas Regal."

"When will you be back?"

"As soon as possible. You think we like rolling around on this tub?"

"Get a horse."

Sprague motioned Aragon to sit down. "What's on your mind?"

Aragon offered one of his business cards. Sprague studied it for a moment, then dropped it on his desk.

"I'm interested in Peter Whitfield's yacht," Aragon said.

"Interested in what way?"

"I hear it's heading for Ensenada tomorrow."

Sprague raised his binoculars. They were very powerful and heavy and his hands shook as he adjusted the focus. When they steadied he said, "It looks as if they're getting ready for something. They've taken off the sail covers."

"May I see?"

"Go ahead. It's the blue ketch *Spindrift*, Marina J, port side."

Aragon took the binoculars. He had more trouble steadying them than Sprague had had, but eventually he could make out the large boat that bore the name *Spindrift*. Two men were on deck, dressed like twins in dark blue pants and blue-and-white diagonally striped T-shirts. One was folding the dark-blue covers that protected the sails from the weather; the other was sitting astride the boom.

He said, "What's the little flag at the top of the mast?"

"That's the burgee indicating the captain's on board."

"Who is the captain?"

"Whitfield likes to take the wheel but he doesn't have his captain's papers. The boat's actually run by Manny Ocho and a couple of permanent crewmen. Whitfield calls himself captain. A lot of people do who hang around here. It's a case of more captains than boats."

"Would the burgee be flying if Ocho was on board without Whitfield?"

"No, no. Whitfield couldn't allow that."

"Can you get me in touch with the boat?"

"No problem."

There was some delay in getting through to the *Spindrift*, then a man's voice answered, "Yes."

"Hi, Manny. What's up?"

"Oh, Mr. Sprague. We pretty soon get under way."

"No goodbyes, no farewell party?"

"Not this time, no sir."

"Is the captain on board?"

"No. Wait—wait a minute—"

Another man's voice came on the line. "You're damn tootin' the captain's on board. Who wants to know?"

"Sprague. I'm just checking."

"Yeah? Well, everything's A-OK, Sprague, old boy. We're off and running."

"Where to?"

"The moon, man, the moon."

"Hold it, please." Sprague put his hand over the mouthpiece and said to Aragon, "You want to talk to Whitfield? He sounds drunk."

"I saw Whitfield less than half an hour ago and he wasn't drunk," Aragon said. "I'd better go out there and check things out."

"Sure. I'd go with you but I can't leave my post. Take the ramp nearest the breakwater. The gate's open. These guys are always squawking about security but they leave the gates open for convenience."

"Thanks, Mr. Sprague."

"Sure. Tell Manny, next time I want a party."

Some of the boats were owned by people who lived out of town. These seldom left the harbor. Others were used only on weekends and for the sailing races on Wet Wednesdays. A few were permanent residences, as permanent as the city's bylaws allowed. A Monterey seiner was coming in loaded with fish, moving low and slow in the water, surrounded by a noisy tangle of gulls.

A lone pelican, sitting aloof and self-sufficient on the breakwater railing, viewed these barbarous antics with contempt. He didn't need handouts, though he was not above accepting offerings from the fishermen who lined the breakwater. A pelican had occupied that same spot for years. Aragon and his school friends used to come down to the harbor on Saturdays and fish solely in order to feed the bird, flattered by its friendship. Perhaps it was the same pelican, or a son or grandson.

There wasn't enough activity in Marina J for Aragon's approach to go unnoticed. When he reached the *Spindrift* there was nobody on deck. The boat seemed suddenly deserted, though a radio was playing rock music in one of the cabins.

He called out, "Whitfield?"

He knew there were at least four people on board—Manny Ocho, the two crewmen and the man who had claimed to be Captain Whitfield—but none of them responded to his call. There was further evidence that the *Spindrift* wasn't expecting visitors. The gangplank had been drawn up. When he'd first seen the ketch from the harbormaster's office the gangplank had been down like a welcome mat.

"Captain Whitfield?"

There was a slight response this time. Someone turned off the radio. A dark-winged gull perched on the bowsprit let out a raucous laugh, then went back to his task of cleaning the oil off his breast feathers.

"Manny Ocho?" Aragon switched to Spanish. "What's going on down there? Are you in trouble?"

Ocho started to reply but someone yelled, "Speak English, you bastard."

"*Chinga tu madre,*" Ocho said.

"I told you, speak English." The voice rose hysterically. "What's that mean, that *chinga* business?"

"Guess."

"I am guessing, you bad-mouthed little creep. I ought to kill you."

"You need me, I not need you."

Aragon was forgotten for the moment as the argument continued. Only a couple of feet of water separated the ramp from the deck of the *Spindrift*. He jumped it easily and landed on the deck. The door was closed to the forward cabin where the argument was taking place. Aragon pounded on it with his fist and there was immediate silence. Then the door was jerked open so violently that he almost fell down the steps into the cabin. After the glare of the sun it was dark and he could see very little at first. But the voice was recognizable, half whine, half bluster:

"Well, well, look who's dropped in, my old pal that leaves his car keys in the ignition."

3

MERMAID

13

WHEN CLEO WOKE up, the boat was rocking slightly with the rising tide. She wasn't ready to wake up yet, so she kept her eyes closed and rolled her head back and forth on the pillow and thought of the baby inside her rolling back and forth, too, rocking, rocking, rock-a-bye baby. She held another pillow clasped tight against her belly. This second one was made of foam rubber and it felt smooth and yielding like flesh. Sometimes, in a foggy moment, she believed it was real flesh, her own real baby. But usually she knew it wasn't, that her real baby was deep down inside her, very tiny, hardly bigger than a grain of sugar.

Once she tied the pillow around her waist inside her dress and went downtown, walking along the streets and into the stores. People looked at her oddly.

Some were pitying: "Why, you poor child, you're scarcely more than a child yourself. How far gone are you?"

"Quite," Cleo said solemnly. "Quite far gone."

Some were contemptuous. "Don't they teach about contraceptives in school? Look at her. Probably on welfare. That brat of hers will probably be on welfare, too. And *we'll* be picking up the bills."

One woman reached out and touched Cleo on the stomach.

Cleo drew back, surprised and frightened. "What did you do that for?"

"For luck. Didn't you ever hear that?"

"No."

"Whenever you see a woman big with child you touch her on the stomach for luck."

She went back to the motel near the beach and told Roger about the woman who touched the baby for luck, only it wasn't the baby.

"Why did you do a thing like that?" he said, turning red with anger. "People will think you're crazy."

"But there really is a baby deep inside. And you're going to be the father and I'm going to be the mother. You promised, Roger. That very first day when I came to you and told you what happened with Ted and me, you said you would take care of me. You said you would

311

see to it that Hilton wouldn't take the baby away and have me fixed like he did our cat. You promised, Roger."

"Yes."

"And after this one, we'll have some more. Boy, girl, boy, girl, or two boys and two girls, whichever you think is best. It wouldn't be fair to have just one child. It would always be lonely, the way I am."

"What if we can't make it, Cleo, if things don't work out?"

"You're always telling me that people can work anything out if they really try, that people can *make* things work out. You told me that."

"Yes."

"You weren't lying?"

"I didn't intend to lie, Cleo. Perhaps I only spoke too soon, too optimistically."

She began to cry then, and Roger held her in his arms, trying to soothe her, stroking her hair, brushing her tears away with his mouth.

"Come inside, Roger," she said. "Come in and visit our baby. Come inside."

"Not now."

"Why not?"

"The dog," he said. "The dog wants out. I have to go and walk him."

"Oh, I'm sick of that dog. He's always interfering like this. He's not my friend anymore . . . Will you come back soon?"

"Yes."

Roger was gone a long time. When he came back he told her he'd arranged to have the dog returned to the Jaspers. He was very pale and smelled of liquor.

"Are you going to visit the baby now, Roger?"

"I want to."

They lay down again and she clasped her legs around his and held him tight against her. She could feel him struggling to get away and pretty soon he began to cry.

"God forgive me. I'm sorry, Cleo. Sorry, sorry, sorry."

Roger always said things three times when he really meant them, so that was the night she found out that things sometimes didn't work out no matter how hard people tried.

This time when Roger left he took his clothes with him and that was the end of the marriage.

She phoned Ted at the house the next morning and told him a sort of lie. She said Hilton had kicked her out just the way he had kicked Ted out and she was staying at a motel because she had nowhere to go. She asked him to help her find a place to live. He said he'd be right down, though he sounded rather peculiar.

She waited for him outside the motel.

His first words were, "That story you gave me on the phone was a lot of bull, wasn't it?"

"A little," she said. "Not a whole lot."

"So what actually happened?"

"I ran away. I ran away because they kicked you out and I didn't think it was fair."

"Why'd you do that?"

"Because I like you."

"Oh, come off it, kid." But he sounded flattered. "You shouldn't have run away. You know you can't look after yourself. What do you intend to do?"

"I was going to get married."

"What changed your mind?"

"I found out he was already married."

"Hang in there. He might divorce her."

"It's not a her."

"So why did you drag me into this?"

"I don't know."

She did know, though she hadn't known for long. When she telephoned him for help she had only a vague idea in her mind, but now she was perfectly sure. Ted had nice features, he laughed easily, he played games well, he surfed and skied, and he could teach all these things to a son the way a good father should.

They walked along the waterfront. Ted told her his mother had given him enough money to live on for the summer, and that if his father hadn't relented by next fall she intended to sell some bonds to finance his senior year in college. Cleo asked him where he was going for the summer. He wasn't certain.

"Aspen, maybe," he said. "It's not as lively as it is in the winter but there's still plenty of action if you look for it."

"I was in Catalina once." She recalled the trip vividly because it had been the only real experience in her life, with no Hilton or Frieda around, no Mrs. Holbrook or counselors, just the waves and the sea birds and a pleasant little man who ran the boat. She even remembered his name, Manny Ocho, because there weren't many names in her life to remember. She saw the little man once in a while because on her free afternoons she sometimes took a bus down to the harbor and looked for the boat. If it was there she waved to the skipper or whoever was on board. But usually it was gone and the space where it was supposed to be was empty. She felt left out, like a little girl not invited to a party.

She said, "Do you think I'd like Aspen?"

"Sure. Why not?"

"I've got a thousand dollars."

Ted laughed. "That's about four days' worth in Aspen."

This was a shock. She thought a person could live for a whole year on a thousand dollars. "Where is Aspen?"

"In the mountains in Colorado."

"Is it healthful?"

"In some ways, I guess. In others, no."

"I mean, does it have a healthful climate? I need a healthful climate."

"Look, kid, the most healthful climate for you is right here. You'd better call my parents and tell them you'll be home pretty soon. Will you do that?"

"If you want me to, Ted."

"Listen, what I want has nothing to do with anything. It's simple logic. You know what logic is, common sense."

"If you're driving alone someplace and I wanted to go to the very same place, wouldn't it be common sense to take me along?"

"No," he said. "No, no."

"Why do men always say things three times? Why not two or four?"

"Okay, well make it four. *No.*"

"I didn't really ask anyway. I just said, wouldn't it be common sense?"

"Listen, you wanted me to help you find an apartment or someplace to live. I can drive you around and we'll look for vacancy signs. And that'll be the end of it. Understand?"

"Yes."

"You're sure?"

"Yes. But let's keep walking. It's such a neat day and you and I haven't ever really talked before."

"All right. We'll walk and talk. But don't start getting any funny ideas. You and I are going our separate ways."

She gazed up at him wistfully. "But Aspen sounds so pretty."

"It's not that pretty. Besides, I may not go there. It's the first name that occurred to me, is all. I may go to Borneo."

"I never heard of Borneo. Does it have a healthful climate?"

"Jeez," Ted said. "Let's walk."

"But does it have a healthful climate?"

"It's a jungle infested with giant snakes and rodents."

"Then why are you going there?"

"To get away from people who ask dumb questions."

"I have to ask dumb questions," she said. "I'm dumb, aren't I?"

"Come on, come on, come on."

She didn't move.

"Now what's the matter?"

"You did it again, Ted."

"Did what?"

"Said something three times, instead of two or four."

Ted said, "Move it, kid," and gave her a little push. They began walking out toward the breakwater, past the Coast Guard headquarters, the marine accessories store and yacht brokers' offices, a fish market, and finally the breakwater itself. The tide was low and a small group of children were picking up mussels off the rocks on the sea side. On the other side, between two rows of marinas, a western grebe was diving for dinner. It came up with a fish in its beak and maneuvered it around until the fish could be swallowed headfirst. The bird's long thin neck bulged for a moment or two. Cleo didn't like to see creatures eating other creatures, so she closed her eyes and clung to Ted's arm to help keep her balance.

When she opened her eyes again, there was the *Spindrift,* sky-blue and white, with dark blue sail covers. At first she thought there was no one on deck; then she saw Manny Ocho about three quarters of the way up the mainmast, inspecting some rigging.

She called to him and waved. "Manny, it's me, Cleo."

He waved back. "Hey, Cleo, why you not in school?"

"I'm on vacation."

"Pretty soon, I'm on vacation, too."

"Where are you going?"

"Ensenada, see my wife and kids, make sure everything's okey doke. Who's your friend?"

"Ted."

"Want to come aboard?"

"Oh, yes, I'd love to."

"Better go the long way round. Too far to jump, too dirty to swim."

They walked back to the entrance ramp of the marina, with Cleo pulling Ted by the hand to hurry him along.

"Who the hell wants to go on a boat?" he said. "I thought I was supposed to help you find an apartment."

"That can wait. I still have the room at the motel where Roger and I were going to spend our honeymoon."

"Has it occurred to you that I might have affairs of my own to settle?"

"Oh, Ted, you don't really want to go to Borneo, do you? Maybe Manny might let us ride along with him to Ensenada. Wouldn't that be fun?"

"I doubt it."

"I bet it's a lot nicer than Borneo," Cleo said. "I bet it's not infected with snakes."

When they reached the *Spindrift* the gangplank was down, and they went on board as Manny Ocho slid down from the mast on a rope like a circus performer.

"I show off," he said, examining the palms of his hands. "Hurts like hell. Cleo, you looking good, happy. This your young man?"

"She's my aunt," Ted said.

"Your aunt, ho, ho. A joke, no?"

"It's no joke."

"You're a big boy to have such a cute little aunt. Me, I got nine, ten aunts, all old and fat and ugly."

Cleo giggled, hiding her face against Ted's sleeve. He didn't seem to mind. She really was cute.

Manny showed them around the *Spindrift* with great pride. In a sense it belonged more to him than to Whitfield, who merely held the owner's papers and couldn't have taken the boat out of the harbor by himself.

The captain's quarters occupied the entire forward cabin. It was spacious and luxuriously furnished, but its teak paneling was marred by Whitfield's collection of pinups, some of them signed, and its thick, red wool carpeting bore the stains of too many spilled drinks. A television set that projected its picture on a large screen was turned on to a baseball game, and a crewman was sitting in the captain's swivel chair, watching the game and sipping Coke out of a can.

Manny explained the crewman. "Mr. Whitfield, he at his place in Palm Springs, not expected for a couple more days. Maybe sooner, maybe longer. I think he looking for a new chick."

"I wish Donny could get away from school and come down here," Cleo said. "We could have a party. Wouldn't that be fun?"

Manny laughed. "Aunts not supposed to like parties. And why you want Donny?"

"You need a lot of people to have a real party and I hardly know any."

"Donny not a real people. He a pig."

"He gives me chocolate bars and imitates Mrs. Holbrook and makes me laugh."

Manny moved his mouth around as if he intended to spit in the ocean. Then he remembered he was below deck and he swallowed instead.

"Besides," Cleo added, "if we were having a party and Mr. Whitfield suddenly appeared, it would be okay because Donny would be here . . . Don't you think so, Ted?"

Ted didn't even hear the question. He was busy examining the pictures on the wall with the air of a connoisseur.

"Okey doke," Manny said, and showed her how to open the red leather case where the phone was concealed. Then he and Ted went to see the boat's navigation room.

It took about five minutes and considerable lying to reach Donny at Holbrook Hall.

"Hey, Donny, it's me."

"Who's me?"

"Cleo. Guess what. I'm on the *Spindrift*."

"What are you doing there?"

"I'm with Ted. You remember Ted, who picks me up at school sometimes. He's the one that drives the car you like, the kind your dad's going to buy you if you ever get off probation."

"That'll be in about a million years," Donny said bitterly. "Maybe more."

"Oh, don't be so gloomy. Come on down and we'll celebrate."

"Celebrate what?"

"I'm getting married."

"Why?"

"Because of the baby."

"No kidding, you're going to have a real baby?"

She didn't like the question. "Of course it's real, dummy. And I'm sailing to Ensenada on my honeymoon. You can come along if you want to."

"Sure I want to. A lot of good that does. You know how they watch me around this joint, like I was public enemy numero uno."

"Dream up something. Like the laundry truck. Remember when you stole the laundry truck?"

"I got caught."

"That was just bad luck, hitting the tree," Cleo said. "Why don't you try again?"

"I'll think about it."

He didn't have to think about it very long. That was the morning Aragon left his car keys in the ignition.

The party had all the elements of success, beginning with the people: Manny Ocho and the crewmen about to visit their families for the first time in weeks, Cleo ready for her honeymoon, Donny, who'd finally escaped from Holbrook Hall and didn't intend to go back—"If dear old dad shows up we'll throw him overboard"—and a footloose young man who'd been kicked out of his house. In addition, the *Spindrift* carried plenty of booze, and one of the crewmen, Velasco, had purchased a quantity of hashish from a lower State Street bar, using money he had collected from the others on board.

The party began with lunch: guacamole prepared by Velasco and served with corn chips, and beluga caviar which Whitfield kept in a supposedly foolproof safe. None of them actually liked caviar but it had such an impressive price they felt duty bound to eat it. Cleo tried to pretend it was black tapioca but Velasco kept talking about "feesh eggs. Nearly three hundred dollars a pound for feesh eggs," and Ted sang a song about virgin sturgeon needing no urging. Ocho sprinkled his share with Tabasco sauce and rolled it up in a tortilla.

When the others had finished eating, Donny scooped up everything that was left on their plates and piled it on his own—guacamole, corn chips, caviar—until it looked like a heap of dog vomit. Eventually he had to go on deck to throw up. Cleo went with him, and being very suggestible, she threw up, too.

Then she and Donny sat side by side in the bow, watching the gulls quarreling and listening to the music coming from the cabin, Velasco playing the harmonica and Ted singing dirty fraternity songs. Cleo couldn't make out the words of all the songs because the cabin was tightly closed to prevent the odor of hashish from reaching the wrong noses. Donny was sweating so much his hair was wet and water rolled down from his forehead onto his cheeks like tears.

"Your face is very red," Cleo said.

"What do I care? I can't see it."

"Is my face red?"

"I dunno. I can't see that either."

This was such a hilarious joke that Donny doubled up with laughter. Cleo wasn't amused. Throwing up had made her feel quite sober.

"Donny," she said. "Do you ever have foggy moments?"

"Foggy? Naw. I get flashes, great big bright white flashes. I see things never been seen before. It's a blast, man."

"Why do you call me man?"

"It's just an expression. Besides, you got no boobs."

"I'm going to grow some when the baby comes."

"Naw. You're built like a man."

"Oh, I am not. Look."

Cleo took off her T-shirt.

"Pimples," Donny said. "Just a couple of pimples."

"Roger liked them."

"He would. He's gay, stupid." Donny looked at her sharply. "Don't tell me you ever made it with that creep."

"Practically. We were even supposed to be married, but suddenly it wasn't such a good idea. I'm going to marry Ted instead."

"When?"

"I don't know. I haven't told him yet."

"Oh, wow. You really are a kook. I thought you were related to him."

"We're only sort of related. Anyway, he was away at school most of the time and I was at home so we hardly knew each other so we're practically strangers. He's the father."

"Father?"

"Of my baby." She giggled. "Me and Ted, we made it, right down the hall from where Hilton was sleeping. Only it turned out he wasn't sleeping. He came charging in and made a horrible fuss."

Donny threw up again over the railing. This seemed to give him extra insight into the situation. "You can't have the kid. There's no such thing as being sort of related. If you and Ted are related, the kid will be even more half-witted than you are."

"I'm not half-witted," Cleo said obstinately. "And I also got boobs."

"You should have an abortion."

"Well, I won't, so there."

"Okay, but don't say I didn't warn you. Wait'll the kid comes out with two heads and one leg . . . Oh, for Christ's sake, don't start crying. I'm just trying to get you to face facts. If Ted doesn't want to marry you he won't, and you can't force him." Donny had one of his bright white flashes. "Unless he's stoned. That's it. We can get him stoned and drag him to a preacher."

"We don't need a preacher," Cleo said. "I saw this television movie where as soon as the boat left the dock the captain began marrying two people."

"My old man wouldn't go for that. He's against marriage."

"Then how about Manny? Or you?"

"Me?" The idea had instant appeal to Donny but he refused at first to admit it. "I couldn't do that. I'm not the captain."

"You're the owner's son, you could just make yourself the captain. You could proclaim it. You got rights, Donny. As soon as the boat leaves the dock you can say, 'I proclaim myself captain.'"

"'I proclaim myself captain.' Hey, I like that." Donny stood up straight and assumed a Napoleonic pose. "I proclaim myself captain."

"Aye, aye, sir," Cleo said.

The party ended early, with everyone going to bed wherever they lost consciousness. Festivities were resumed the following morning when Ted and Velasco went ashore for fresh supplies. They didn't bother with caviar or more avocados for guacamole; they went directly to the bar on lower State Street where Velasco had purchased the hashish. It was closed, so they made a buy from a man standing outside a pawnshop and then returned to the boat.

Throughout the day Cleo tried to persuade Manny Ocho to cast off without waiting for the arrival of Donny's father. Ocho, who despised Whitfield, would have liked to oblige, but he had too strong a sense of survival. Jobs like his didn't come along very often. Rich men were getting stingier, learning to skipper their own craft and picking up unpaid crews here and there, mostly teenagers and restless young men like Ted who wanted travel and adventure more than wages.

That night Ocho had a telephone call from Palm Springs. Whitfield said he would drive up the next morning, check in at his condo for an hour or so, then come aboard ready to sail.

Ocho broke the news to the others that this was to be the last night of the party. They cheered themselves up by opening a case of Johnny Walker and starting a series of toasts: to the Presidents of the United States and Mexico, the Los Angeles Dodgers, the man who invented scotch, and the *Spindrift*, "the greatest ketch ever caught." This was Ted's contribution.

"When you catch a ketch," he said. "The ketch is caught."

Donny laughed, but neither Cleo nor the three Mexicans understood the pun, even when Ted repeated it with emphasis and gestures.

"When you catch a ketch, the ketch is caught."

"Aw, the hell," Velasco said, and proposed a toast of his own, to Señora Pinkass and her girls of Tijuana.

The final toast was proposed by Ocho to Whitfield, or rather to "his money, which keeps us all afloat."

But the party lacked the festive spirit of the previous day and night. The imminent arrival of Whitfield cast a pall over the deck as thick as a summer fog. In addition, the stuff that Ted and Velasco had purchased from the man outside the pawnshop turned out not to be hashish but ordinary marijuana mixed with tea leaves.

They smoked it anyway, of course, and eventually Velasco played his harmonica, though Ted declined to sing. He was pretty confused by this time and wanted to go ashore. But Cleo sat on his lap and Donny brought him another tumbler full of Johnny Walker.

"Come on, Ted," Cleo said. "You'll spoil the party if you don't sing."

"I don't remember the words."

"Sure you do. What about that one, 'Dirty Gertie from Bizerte'?"

"Madame," he said with great dignity, "I am not accepting any requests from the audience."

"Not even from me?"

"And who are you?"

"Me. Cleo."

"Aw, leave him alone," Donny said. "He's got a lousy voice anyway."

Donny remained the soberest of the partygoers. He dreaded meeting his father and trying to explain how he'd gotten away from Holbrook Hall. He might be able to convince him that Mrs. Holbrook had given him special permission to go to Ensenada on the *Spindrift*. But then his father might remember that the school wasn't allowed to do anything like that without an investigation and report by the probation department and a lot of other crap. No, words weren't going to work, none that he'd thought of so far.

At six o'clock Manny Ocho turned on the radio to get the news and the weather report. It was then that Cleo found out about Roger Lennard's death. Roger Lennard, thirty-three, had been found dead, possibly a victim of foul play. A description was given of Lennard's visitor, who had been heard quarreling with him. Cleo knew at once it had to be Hilton and she phoned the police and told them. Then she went back to sit on Ted's lap again.

But there was no lap. Ted had passed out on a couch and was lying on his back with his mouth open, snoring. Cleo listened to him for a few minutes, frowning. She wasn't sure she wanted a husband who snored; it might keep her and the baby awake.

Manny Ocho and the two crewmen watched an old movie on television which Cleo had seen half a dozen times before. She went up to join Donny, who was sitting on the bowsprit, brooding.

"Do you snore, Donny?"

"You ask the stupidest questions. How the hell would I know?"

"You don't have to shout."

"You don't have to listen. Go away and leave me alone."

"I have nowhere to go. Ted's asleep and the others are watching a movie with a lot of cowboys which I don't like in the first place."

It was dark by this time and everything on board was wet, even Cleo's hair. She shivered with cold and sadness.

"Poor Roger," she said. "He wouldn't be dead if it wasn't for me. Does that make me a sort of murderer?"

"You did the poor slob a favor."

"Maybe they'll put me on probation like they did you."

"Lay off, will you? I'm trying to think."

"I hate to be alone."

"You're not alone—you got the baby. So why don't you and the kid go below and have a nice heart-to-heart talk?"

"You can be real nasty, Donny."

"Bug off."

She watched the rest of the movie with Ocho and the crewmen. Then all four of them went to bed after a final nightcap.

Donny sat on the bowsprit for a long time trying to straighten out his head. He feared his father's power but he wanted the same thing for himself. He despised Whitfield's collection of young women, yet he lusted after every one of them. He hated the sound of his father's voice, but he wanted to hear it.

He watched a lone star trying to break through the overcast. When it was no longer visible Donny went below to the captain's cabin and took the phone out of the red leather case and called the house in Palm Springs.

It was eleven o'clock. Donny let the phone ring a dozen times in case his father was drunk or in bed with some chick or asleep.

Eventually Whitfield answered and he didn't sound drunk or sleepy. "Who the hell's this?"

"Donny."

"Donny? What are you doing up so late?"

"I couldn't sleep. Anyway, I wanted to talk to you."

Whitfield was immediately suspicious. "Listen, son. You know the school has a limit on spending money."

"I don't want any money."

"Well, that's a switch. Don't tell me you simply wanted to hear my voice."

This was so close to the truth that Donny couldn't speak for a minute. No sound could get past the sudden lump in his throat.

"Son? What's the matter, son?"

"Nothing."

"How's school going?"

"Fine. I'm even taking stuff like—ah, Latin."

"Latin? That's terrific. *Amo, amas, amat*, right?"

"Listen, Dad, I heard the *Spindrift* is going to Ensenada."

"Now where did you hear—?"

"I'd like to go along. The school will give me special permission because I'm doing so well in my studies like, you know, Latin, I'm working real hard."

"Yes. Well, you realize I'd like to take you, son, but the fact is I've invited other company."

"You wouldn't have to tell them I was your son. I could pretend to be one of the crew."

"You're putting me in a bind, son. I'd certainly like to reward you for your change in attitude and behavior but I honestly can't. This is very special company, if you know what I mean."

"Sure. It's okay."

"Donny, you remember that BMW you wanted me to buy you as soon as you get your driver's license back? I'll get one for you, how about that?"

"Thanks."

"Now Donny, it's obvious that you're disappointed. But be patient. Wait a few more years until you're off probation and you and I will take the *Spindrift* all around the world. Tahiti, Bora Bora, Fiji. How's that for a deal?"

"Screw you," Donny said and hung up. By the time he got off probation he'd be an old man.

He went to bed alone in the captain's quarters. Getting up at dawn the next day he showered and dressed for the new role he was about to assume. The clothes came from his father's mahogany wardrobe.

The white tailored slacks were too small, so he wore his own jeans, threadbare at the knees and seat. The navy-blue blazer didn't come close to buttoning but he put it on anyway. The captain's hat was too large, so he stuffed some toilet tissue in the back to make it fit. Then he opened one of the drawers of the rolltop desk and took out the two guns his father always kept there, a Smith & Wesson .22 and a German Luger. Donny used his limited knowledge of firearms, gained during a short session at a military academy, to make sure the guns were loaded and the safeties in order. Then he dropped the .22 into the pocket of the blazer and tucked the Luger in the waistband of his jeans. Already he felt like a new person, and the image in the mirror beside the wardrobe reaffirmed the feeling. It was a captain who stared back at him, a commander, a leader of men.

He went back to the galley.

Velasco was at the stove, mixing up a batch of *huevos rancheros* in a large iron frying pan. "Hey, Donny. You looking good all dressed up."

"I am your new captain," Donny said.

"By golly, no kidding. You hear that, Gomez? We got a new captain."

Gomez, who had gone back to sleep with his head on the table, was not impressed. Donny kicked him on the butt and Gomez woke up with a moan of pain.

"Salute me, you bastard. Salute your new captain."

"What the hell, by golly," Velasco said. "What you doing, Donny?"

"Call me captain and salute me."

"Maybe later. The eggs, they burn if I don't stir."

"Screw the eggs."

Donny went over and pulled the iron frying pan off the stove and dumped its contents on the floor. The mixture oozed red like a fresh kill.

"Hey, Donny, what the hell, Jesus Christ, what you doing?"

"Salute me, *pachuco*."

"Not *pachuco*. Last night you and me, all of us, amigos. Amigos forever."

"Forever just ended," Donny said. "You got that?"

"Sure, sure."

"Mix up another batch of eggs and serve them to me in my quarters."

"Okay, Donny."

"You don't say 'okay' to a captain. Say it right, dammit."

"Aye, aye, sir."

"That's better."

He went in search of Cleo and found her in one of the guest cabins, lying on a bunk with a blanket pulled up to her chin. The outlines of her thin body could hardly be seen under the blanket, so she appeared to be a severed head.

"Cleo, wake up."

"How can I wake up when I'm not asleep?"

"Then open your eyes."

She opened her eyes and saw Donny looking terribly funny in an oversized hat. "What are you all dressed up like that for?"

"I was thinking over what you said last night, about how I got rights, so I'm proclaiming myself captain."

"That's nice."

"Being as I'm now captain, I can marry you."

"I thought I was going to marry Ted."

"Sure you are. But I'm going to be like the minister as soon as we leave shore."

Cleo threw off the blanket and sat up. "Then this is my wedding day."

"Yeah. You got anything to wear besides those crummy jeans?"

"No."

"Come on and we'll search through my dad's— that is, *my* quarters and see if some chick left a fancy robe, you know, something flimsy."

Ted was asleep on the opposite bunk, lying on his stomach with his arms at his sides and his head twisted to one side. His mouth was open and he was making snorting and whistling sounds.

They both watched him for a minute. Then Donny said, "Are you sure you want to marry *that?*"

"I guess so. I mean, he looks better when he's awake."

"Give me your shoelaces."

"Why should I?"

"Follow orders."

"But my shoes are the only decent thing I have on. They're practically new from Drawford's."

"I need the laces to tie his hands in case he wakes up and tries to mutiny." Donny showed her the Luger he had tucked in his waistband and the .22 in his pocket. "There'll be no mutiny on my ship."

"Where did you get those?"

"From my dad's— from *my* quarters."

"Are you going to shoot somebody?"

"Maybe. If I have to."

"Even me?"

"We'll see. Give me your shoelaces."

She took the laces out of her shoes and Donny tied Ted's hands behind his back. At one point Ted's snoring changed pitch and rhythm as if he was about to wake up, but he didn't. Cleo watched in silence, deriving some satisfaction from the fact that Ted didn't look like a bridegroom any more than she looked like a bride.

She followed Donny back to the captain's quarters, where they had breakfast served by a mute and sullen Velasco. The change in Velasco and in Donny made Cleo uneasy.

"Maybe this isn't such a good idea," she said when Velasco had left. "Maybe we don't have all those rights Roger said people had."

"We got rights same as everybody else. Now we have to make plans. You know how to use a gun?"

"Point it at somebody and press the trigger."

"No. First you fix the safety." He gave her the .22 and showed her how to do it. "There. Now you're ready to shoot someone."

"What if I don't really want to?"

"You obey orders. On a ship the captain is God."

"You don't look like God to me. He doesn't wear a hat."

"How do you know? Nobody's ever seen him. Maybe he looks exactly like me, fat as a pig."

"Well, I bet when you pass people on the street they don't say, 'There goes God.'"

"Oh, cut that crap and listen. The crew might try to jump ship or sound an alarm. It's up to you to keep them quiet by holding the gun on them."

"What if they won't keep quiet?"

"You shoot them."

"I don't think I'm going to like that part. I've never shot anyone."

"You won't have to. It's nothing but a threat, see? If they try to pull anything, you shoot a hole in the floor to warn them."

"That might make the boat leak."

"It won't make the boat leak, stupid," Donny said. "Now there's one more thing you got to do. I could have saved us a lot of trouble if I'd decided to take over the ship last night. We'd be far at sea by this time. But I didn't, so here we are, no use crying."

"You can't anyway," Cleo said reasonably. "God never cried."

"Oh, can the God bit and let me think a minute." He pushed the cap back from his forehead and the toilet paper padding fell out on the floor. His face was very red and all screwed up like a fretful baby's. "Now here's the problem. When my dad drives up from Palm Springs he usually leaves very early to avoid the desert heat, so he may be arriving at his condo any minute. If he should look out the window and see the *Spindrift* missing, he'll call the Coast Guard and they'll send the cutter after us right away. So we have to buy time, an hour at least, more if we can get it."

"I've got an idea. Why don't we wait for him and invite him to come along?"

"You loony, don't you know the first thing he'd do? Send for the cops to take me back to that goddamn school. Yes, and you, too. You got that? *You, too.*"

"I don't want to go back. I want to get married."

"Then cooperate. As soon as he arrives he'll check in at his condo. It's on the beach and you can see it from the bridge through binoculars. I'll stand watch, and the minute he arrives I want you to make a call to the condo. I'll give you the number."

"What am I supposed to say?"

"Tell him that you're Mrs. Holbrook's secretary. Then you ask him to come to Holbrook Hall in order to discuss his son's curriculum."

"Curliculum. What's that mean?"

"Never mind what it means. Just say it right. Cur-ri-culum."

"Curriculum. Okay, then what?"

"Then he goes to the school and I order the crew to cast off."

"What if the crew won't listen to you?"

"They'll listen." Donny patted the Luger in his waistband and laughed. "We're all amigos, all of us. Amigos forever."

Manny Ocho knocked on the door and entered without waiting for permission. Though he had a well-deserved hangover, he was freshly shaved and uniformed.

"Hey, Donny, what's going on? What you say to my crew? And what you doing wearing your father's clothes?"

"They're my clothes. I'm your new captain. Be ready to cast off when I say the word."

"You don't give me orders."

"I give you orders." Donny took the Luger out of his waistband. "And you obey them."

"You crazy boy, Donny. You mixed up in the *cabeza.*"

"Don't bother rolling your eyes at Cleo for help. She's on my side and she has a gun, too. How do you like that?"

"It's bad," Manny said. "Very bad."

"So don't make it worse by trying anything funny. You stay down here with Cleo while I go up on the bridge. Cleo will entertain you. She does a great striptease. She has nothing much to show, but she shows it anyway."

"This very bad, Donny."

"I'm not Donny. I'm your captain."

After Donny left, Cleo picked up the .22 from the table and began clicking the safety catch off and on for practice. She forgot about Ocho until he spoke to her in the voice he used to shout orders to his crew:

"Stop that."

Cleo was so surprised by his tone that she almost dropped the gun. "I'm not doing anything."

"Maybe by accident."

"No. Donny showed me how to use it."

"You going to use it?"

"Not really. I mean, I guess not unless Donny wants me to."

"You reaching for big trouble, Cleo," Ocho said. "This Donny, he a bad boy, you a nice little girl. You stay nice, you stay away from him."

"I can't. I want to get married."

"You going to marry *Donny?*"

"No. It's—well, it's like this."

She tried to reconstruct the movie she'd seen where the captain married two people as soon as the boat left the dock. But Ocho kept shaking his head and muttering to himself.

Up on the bridge Donny kept the binoculars focused on his father's condominium on the beach. The binoculars were too heavy to allow continual observation, so he raised them every three or four minutes on the lookout for his father's silver-grey Cadillac. He spotted it shortly before ten o'clock, parked in its slot beside the condo. There was no sign of his father or his companion, if any.

He hurried down to the cabin where Ocho and Cleo had turned on the television set and were watching a children's cartoon, Ocho from the captain's swivel chair, Cleo from the table with the gun in front of her.

Ocho switched off the television set and stood up. "Hey, Donny, you listen to me."

"You got nothing I want to hear," Donny said. "Cleo, make that call now."

"I can't remember the number."

"Jeez, I've told you twice: 9694192. Now have you got it?"

"I guess so."

"You remember what to say?"

"Sure. I'm the secretary and then that business about Donny's curliculum."

"Cur-ri-cu-lum."

"Okay, don't scream. Curriculum."

"You listen now, Donny," Ocho said again. "This Cleo, she a nice little girl, you leave her alone, you put her ashore."

Donny turned to Cleo. "You want to go ashore, kid?"

"No, I don't."

"In fact, you invited me here, didn't you? You phoned Holbrook Hall and told me to come down. We were going to have a party, right?"

"Yes."

"So you're not such a nice little girl after all, are you?"

"I didn't mean any harm, Donny."

"I want Manny clued in on what actually happened. You started the whole damn thing, didn't you?"

"Sort of."

"You hear that, Manny? You're not a hero trying to rescue a poor, innocent girl. She's none of those things: not poor, not innocent, not a girl. She's a rich woman, five years older than I am. So I'm the one you ought to feel sorry for."

"I do," Ocho said. "I feel very sorry for you, Donny."

"Then get ready to cast off. As soon as my father leaves his condo we're moving. *We're moving.*"

Ocho shook his head. "I got my family to think of, my job—"

"You got your own hide to think of first." Donny patted the Luger in his waistband. It was beginning to feel uncomfortable poking into his stomach, so he transferred the gun to his coat pocket. "Look at it this way. It's your hide against my hide and I like my hide better. Isn't that reasonable?"

"Yes, sir."

"And you'll spell it out to the crew?"

"Yes, sir."

Donny returned to the bridge to watch the condo for any further signs of activity. As soon as he saw the silver Cadillac leave its parking slot he called Ocho, and the two of them went to the navigation room.

The engine wouldn't start.

"Good," Ocho said. "Stiff. Not used for a whole month."

"Goddamn it, you're supposed to keep the thing ready to go at any time."

"You goddamn it yourself. I keep it good. I keep it the best."

"Then start it the best."

On the second attempt the engine turned over, but almost immediately Donny reached out and switched it off.

"The phone's ringing. Answer it."

"What you want me to say?"

"Just answer it."

The call was from the harbormaster's office and they both knew trouble was coming. That it came in the form of Aragon was the only surprise.

"Well, well," Donny said when he jerked open the door and Aragon almost fell into the cabin. "Look who's dropped in, my old pal that leaves his car keys in the ignition."

14

It took a moment for Aragon to regain his balance and somewhat longer for his eyes to adjust after the brilliance of the morning sun. The curtains were closed and the cabin seemed relatively gloomy. Donny Whitfield sat at a rolltop desk with a gun in his hand, and standing near him was a short, wiry-looking Mexican wearing a blue-and-white diagonally striped shirt and a light-blue peaked cap. Aragon assumed this was Manny Ocho who had answered the phone.

He started to address Ocho in Spanish but was immediately interrupted.

"Only English spoken here," Donny said. "Well, nice of you to drop in, pal. Now suppose you drop out."

"Is the girl here?"

"What girl?"

"You know what girl."

"Oh, her. Yeah, sure. She's around someplace trying to find the bridegroom. You walked into a wedding. How's that for luck?"

"The wedding had better be postponed," Aragon said. "I intend to take Cleo back to her family."

"You're going to poop the party, right?"

"Right."

"Uh uh. Wrong . . . Manny, you have your orders. Obey them."

"Please, you wait," Ocho said. "Donny, you listen a minute."

"Hurry up."

Ocho turned to leave, shaking his head. As he passed Aragon he muttered a warning about a gun.

"You can be best man," Donny told Aragon. "Or Cleo might even want to change bridegrooms. You're not bad-looking and at least you aren't related. What's your name?"

"Tom Aragon."

"Cleo Aragon. Hmmmm, sort of a nice ring to it. Not that Cleo's particular. She'd marry any guy that's still breathing. Weird thing is, I never knew she was like that when we were at school together. Maybe it's the sea air." Donny laughed. "How's the sea air affecting you, Aragon?"

"Who's the bridegroom?"

"She calls him Ted."

"You've got to stop this crazy thing, Donny. She's his aunt."

"If that doesn't bother Cleo, why should it bother me?"

"Who's going to perform the ceremony? Did they have the necessary blood tests? Did they take out a license?"

"Details. Screw details."

"And did you know that you're violating the terms of your probation by having a gun?"

"Screw probation," Donny said. "Probation is for landlubbers. At sea it's only a word."

"What kind of stuff are you on, Donny? What did you take?"

"Nothing. I smoked a little pot last night and had a few drinks, but since then, nothing. Nothing from outside anyway. It's the inside stuff that I'm on. It's all coming from inside. There's some pretty strong stuff in there, man, stronger than anything you can buy on the street."

Aragon believed him. Whatever Donny's body was manufacturing, it seemed as powerful and unpredictable as the animal tranquilizer the kids called angel dust.

He said, "Show me where Cleo is and I'll take her home."

"Home? Where the hell's home for people like Cleo and me? A lousy detention school? Juvenile Hall or the slammer? Where the hell is home?"

"Drop the self-pity kick for a minute and pay attention. I want you and Cleo to come with me, and we'll try to straighten out this whole business. I'll even forget about the gun. I didn't see it."

"You saw it and you better not forget it. That's my best friend. Him and me, we can go anywhere we want to, do anything we want to—"

"Cut the crazy talk, Donny."

"Okay, suppose I buy that crap about you trying to straighten things out for me and Cleo. What then? We get sent back to Holbrook Hall or worse, so the rest of you can live happily ever after."

"I can't perform miracles, Donny."

"No? Well, I won't settle for less."

"Is that your final word?"

"You got it. Come on, we'll go up on deck. There might be someone you want to wave bye-bye to." Donny laughed again. "Or didn't you know we've left the dock?"

"No."

"That's the trouble with you brainy guys—you start concentrating on something so hard you're not aware of an earthquake until a brick hits you on the head. We're under way, man. We're off and running."

"There are a lot of serious charges against you already, Donny. Don't add kidnapping."

"Kidnapping? Nobody forced you to come along. Nobody even invited you. You jumped on board. You know what that makes you? A stowaway. I could file a few charges of my own."

"The punishment for kidnapping can be life imprisonment."

"So? With any luck I'll get the death penalty. Meanwhile you and I are going for a little sail. Come on, we don't want to keep Cleo and the bridegroom waiting."

They went up on deck.

Manny Ocho was at the helm. He had the *Spindrift* going several times faster than the harbor speed limit of five miles an hour, and Aragon knew from the glance Ocho gave him that he was doing it in the hope of attracting the attention of the harbor patrol boat. But there was no sign of Sprague or the boat. The only protest came from a small sloop the *Spindrift* passed in the channel.

"Slow down," a man yelled through a megaphone. "You damn near hit me."

Ocho made an obscene gesture and yelled back, "Report me. Call Sprague."

But the sloop merely rolled and pitched in the *Spindrift's* wake, and the harbor patrol boat remained at its mooring in front of the office and the Coast Guard cutter was still tied up at the Navy pier.

Traffic was light. The fishing fleet had departed hours ago and the pleasure boaters seldom went out before the afternoon winds began. Even when the *Spindrift* reached the open sea there wasn't enough wind to take over the job of moving the boat. Donny ordered the sails raised anyway.

Working silently and swiftly, Velasco and Gomez raised the sails and Donny pronounced the boat now ready for the wedding ceremony. It was a picturesque setting, but the bride and groom were missing.

"Cleo," Donny shouted. "Where the hell are you? Time to get married."

Cleo appeared on the starboard deck wearing a white chiffon nightgown she'd found in one of the cabin drawers. The gown was too long and she had to hold it up with her left hand while she carried the .22 in her right. Her hair was combed but she'd forgotten to wash her face and her cheeks were still tear-stained.

"I don't feel like a bride," she told Donny.

"You don't look like one either," Donny said. "Where's Ted?"

"I couldn't get his hands untied. You made the knots too tight."

"Oh for chrissake, can't you do anything right? You don't have to untie them. Cut them with a knife."

"I don't want to cut them. They're my shoelaces. They're practically brand-new."

"All right, all right, you hold the gun on our guest here and I'll go and get Ted."

"Hello, Cleo," Aragon said. "Do you remember me?"

She stared at him, frowning. "No."

"You came to my office not too long ago."

"Why?"

"To ask me about your rights—how to register to vote, for instance. You told me about your brother and his wife and about your counselor, Roger Lennard."

"Poor Roger is dead."

"Yes."

"I mustn't think about that now. I'm supposed to be happy. It's my wedding day."

"No, it isn't, Cleo. There's no one on board qualified to perform the ceremony and you don't have the necessary blood tests or license. And even if you had all these things, the marriage wouldn't be legal anyway because you and Ted are related."

"I won't listen to you," she said. "I think you're a nasty man."

Donny came back with Ted. Ted's hands were free and he was rubbing his wrists where the nylon laces had bitten into his skin. He looked angry and confused and he'd wet his pants.

"What's happening around here? I wake up and my hands are tied. My hands are tied, for chrissake. What for? I thought we were having a party."

"That party's over," Donny said. "We're about to start another one. Cleo has decided she wants to get married, and since she's a little short of bridegrooms since Roger died, she picked you."

"Me? For chrissake, why would she pick me?"

"Because she says you're the father of her baby."

"That's impossible. There isn't any baby."

"Oh, Ted, there is so," Cleo said reproachfully. "It's still very tiny, maybe like sort of a grain of sugar or a grape seed."

"There isn't any baby, dammit. We had only started to make love when my father barged in. I didn't even penetrate. You're still a virgin."

"Ted, you know that's not true. We were doing it exactly like in the movies, no clothes and everything. So now we have to get married."

Ted appealed to Aragon. "Whoever you are, they're both crazy. We have to get out of here."

"Stay cool, and play along," Aragon said quietly. "That's our only chance."

"Why should I marry some half-wit because she thinks she's pregnant? Whatever happened—and God knows it wasn't much—happened just a few days ago. I tell you, she's still a virgin. And even if she weren't she'd have no way of knowing so soon that she was pregnant."

Cleo was crying again. She cried as easily as a plastic doll with a water-filled syringe in her head. "He doesn't want to marry me, Donny. What should I do now?"

"Ask him again, real sweet and polite."

"Nobody wants to marry me."

"Maybe he'll change his mind." Donny pointed the Luger directly at Ted's chest. "Go on, ask him again, Cleo."

"Ted, will you marry me?"

"No. Get it through your thick head, we didn't have complete intercourse. You are not pregnant. You're still a virgin."

"But we had all our clothes off and everything exactly like the movies."

"You're crazy," Ted screamed. "The whole damn bunch of you are crazy."

The first bullet from the Luger grazed his right shoulder. He turned and ran toward the railing. As he jumped overboard a second bullet struck him on the left arm.

Two more struck the water at the same time that Ted did. Cleo began screaming with excitement and jumping up and down until she tripped on the hem of the white nightgown that was her bridal costume. The .22 fell out of her hand and slid across the deck in Aragon's direction.

"Don't move," Donny told Aragon. "It's a bad year for heroes." And to Ocho, who was turning the boat around and heading back toward Ted, "Keep on course. Let the bastard drown."

"Throw him a life jacket," Aragon said.

"Why? A dip in the ocean will cool him off. Maybe he'll have a change of heart and decide Cleo isn't so bad after all."

"He might be seriously injured. And if there are any sharks in the area, the blood will attract them."

"I bet those sharks would be pleasantly surprised to find two guys instead of one," Donny said. "Suppose you go in after him, amigo."

"We're at least a mile from shore. I can't swim very well."

"Learn by experience. That's what they're always telling us at school—learn by experience."

"Give us a sporting chance," Aragon said. "We need two life jackets."

Donny took two life jackets from a forward hatch and threw them at Aragon. After removing his shoes and pants Aragon put one of the life jackets on over his shirt. Then, holding the other jacket in his hand, he jumped into the water.

Ted was some hundred yards from the boat, not yelling for help or trying to swim. His eyes were closed and Aragon thought he was unconscious until he saw that Ted's legs were moving slightly to keep him from rolling over on his stomach.

The water temperature at this distance from shore and beyond the thick kelp beds that paralleled the coast was still well below sixty degrees. This might be low enough to slow the bleeding of Ted's arm and help numb his pain. But it might also be low enough to cause both men to suffer from exposure unless they were picked up within an hour or so. Even without the complication of Ted's wounds, hypothermia could be fatal without quick treatment.

The *Spindrift* was turning away, its engine accelerating as it headed southwest. Watching it pull away, Aragon had a moment of panic. He knew he would be unable to drag Ted over the kelp beds and in to shore, and their only hope was to be spotted by a passing boat or one of the low-flying helicopters that serviced the oil platforms.

Both were possible. The sea was calm, with a long smooth swell and no whitecaps to hide any floating object.

This was Aragon's first attempt to swim while wearing a life jacket and he found it difficult to move his arms. He rolled over on his back and used his legs as propellants.

He shouted, "Ted, can you hear me?"

Ted opened his eyes. He looked dazed and terrified. "Shot me—arm—"

"I want you to help me get this life jacket on you."

Ted kept saying, "Shot me—shot me—" as if he was more overcome by surprise than by a sense of danger or by pain.

"Put your injured arm through here first. Then I'll pull the jacket around your back and get the other arm through. It may hurt but it has to be done."

"Shot me—shot me—"

"Stop that. You have to cooperate. Understand?"

It took several minutes for the life jacket to be put on and fastened. Ted was gradually becoming more rational and more aware of the danger they were in. He asked about the *Spindrift*.

"It's gone," Aragon said. "Move your right arm and your legs as much as possible to keep your blood circulating."

"Didn't know—had any left."

"You have lots left." He wasn't sure whether this was true or even whether he'd given the correct advice to Ted to keep moving. He only knew that the water was incredibly cold. His original estimate of being able to survive an hour or two without much damage now seemed ridiculous. He was already numb below the ankles and suffering from what was called in his boyhood an ice-cream headache. He'd never taken a lifesaving course or even one in first aid, and he wished now he had paid more attention to some of his wife's lectures on practical medicine.

Ted said, "You shot?"

"No."

"What are you doing here?"

"I wanted to cool off."

"You got it."

A great blue heron flew overhead, his neck folded, his long legs stretched out stiffly behind him like a defeathered tail.

Ted had closed his eyes again and the wind was picking up. These were both bad omens. The rougher the sea, the more difficult it would be for anyone to spot them, and the greater the chances of Ted choking on salt water.

"Ted, keep moving."

"Can't—tired."

"A boat will come along any minute."

"Tired. Leave me alone."

Ted's youth was a plus factor. But there were too many minuses. Before he was shot he'd spoken of a party on board, and it was obvious then that he was suffering a hangover from alcohol or drugs or both. Also, he probably hadn't eaten in many hours and his resistance was lowered.

"A boat will come along any minute," Aragon repeated. "We'll be rescued. Do you hear me, Ted?"

If Ted heard, he didn't believe it or didn't care enough to open his eyes.

"Are you listening, Ted? By this time Whitfield will have gone back to the harbor and found his boat missing. He'll send the Coast Guard out after it right away. They should be passing us any minute. Hear that, Ted? Any minute. Hang on. Don't give up, Ted. Move. Try harder. Move."

He kept saying the same things over and over like a coach pep-talking one of his players during a game.

The wind was still rising, and now and then his voice was choked off as a wave slapped his face. The increase in wind velocity would have the effect of luring the Lasers and Mercuries and Lidos and Victories, the Hobie Cats and Alpha Cats and Nacras. But these smaller craft usually stayed inside the kelp line. The larger craft, like the fishing fleet, had departed much earlier in the day, going out under power, some as far as the Island twenty-five miles offshore, to return in the afternoon under sail.

Aragon continued talking, using both his hands to hold Ted's head as far out of the water as possible. The numbness had spread through his whole body and he was feeling hardly any discomfort. He remembered reading that people who froze to death didn't suffer pain the way people did who burned to death.

He heard his own voice coaxing, ordering, questioning, demanding, and he wondered if it was all being wasted on a dead man.

"Cut it out, Ted. Now open your eyes. You've got to cooperate. Get in there and pitch. Keep kicking your legs. We're going to be rescued. Any minute. Any minute. You hear? Open your eyes, dammit, open your eyes."

But his voice was getting weaker and the numbness seemed to have reached his brain like a dose of Pentothal. When he finally heard the engine he was only mildly interested, and the men yelling at him seemed to be making a fuss over nothing. One of them had orange hair and looked a little like some woman, someone he'd known a long time ago. A long long time ago . . .

The orange hair emerged from the fog like a sunrise. It had a face in the middle, not a young face or a pretty one, but familiar and reassuring.

"You really blew it this time, junior," Charity Nelson said. "I brought you some carnations. That's how I know you're awake. I put one under your nose and your nostrils twitched."

He struggled to speak. His voice sounded as if it were coming from under water. "How— Ted?"

"Hush. The doctor told me not to let you talk when you woke up. How's Ted Jasper? Still alive in the Intensive Care Unit and his mother's with him. That's all I know."

He turned his head to one side and saw the cot beside the window, looking as if it had been slept in.

"Your doctor's been with you all night," Charity said. "I sent her out to get some breakfast. How are you feeling?"

"All right."

"Smedler gave me the whole day off to help look after you. I was a nurse once. I don't remember much about it but I can still plump pillows, give a bath and hold your hand. Want me to hold your hand?"

"More than I want you to give me a bath."

"I'll overlook that remark, junior. Are you hungry? Of course you are. How about something revolting like poached eggs and mashed potatoes? You're supposed to be on a soft diet."

"Why?"

"Beats me. If I were in charge of your case I'd give you steak and french fries. There's nothing like a long cold swim to sharpen the appetite." Charity leaned over and peered into his face. "Everything considered, you don't look so bad. Maybe your doctor will let you have steak and french fries after all. She's very sympathetic. Cute, too. In fact, a real knockout, with blue eyes and black hair and dimples. Dimples yet. I've always wanted dimples. When I was in high school I sent away for something advertised in *True Romances* guaranteed to make dimples. For one buck I received a little piece of metal I was supposed to stick in my cheek with adhesive plaster every night. I used it and in the morning I'd have a dimple for fifteen minutes. That's the story of my life—none of my dimples lasted more than fifteen minutes."

"Laurie," he said. "You were describing my wife, Laurie."

"Of course I was. I called her yesterday afternoon as soon as I heard what had happened. Smedler himself went to pick her up at the airport. How's that for a first?"

"Laurie." He put his arm over his forehead so Charity wouldn't see the tears welling in his eyes.

She saw them anyway. "Now don't get sloppy and sentimental. Here's some Kleenex. Or maybe you'll need a towel if you're going to pull out all the stops. Incidentally she seems crazy about you, too. She doesn't see as much of you as I do—that may explain why."

He wiped his eyes with the piece of Kleenex she handed him. "Who rescued—?"

"Don't ask questions and I'll tell you what I know. The harbormaster became suspicious when you didn't come back from the *Spindrift.* He tried to contact the boat by phone and couldn't. Then he saw it speeding out of the harbor and he notified the Coast Guard. They sent the cutter after you. Ted Jasper was in bad shape by that time, suffering from loss of blood and shock and hypothermia. You had some degree of hypothermia but they warmed you up and stuck a few needles into you and here you are."

"What about Cleo and Donny?"

"They've both been arrested. That's all I was able to find out."

Donny Whitfield. He thought of the fat, morose boy he'd first seen outside Holbrook Hall. If it wasn't for one small mistake, Donny might still be there, sitting under the oak tree eating corn chips and chocolates. *It's my fault. I made the mistake. I left the keys in the ignition. My fault—*

"My fault," he said and began shaking his head back and forth as if to shake off his guilt.

"Stop that," Charity said, readjusting the oxygen mask none too gently. "Any more acting up and I'll call the nurse to jab you with another needle."

"Car key—"

"What do you want your car keys for? You're not going anyplace. Now shut up or I'll resign from your case. This Florence Nightingale bit is a drag. Where do you want me to put the flowers I brought you?"

He told her.

"Junior, that's not nice. But since irritability is one of the first signs of convalescence, I'll overlook it this time. I may, however, bring it up in the future when you're asking for a favor at the office. By the way, congratulations."

"What for?"

"You were hired to find Cleo. You found her."

There was a knock on the door. Charity said, "Come in . . . Oh, he's doing fine. Weepy, hungry, crabby. Can't ask for better signs."

"Thank you, Miss Nelson."

The voice was pleasant and cool; the hand that touched his forehead was soft, the fingers on his pulse gentle.

"I'm Dr. MacGregor," she said. "I'm in charge of your case and I don't believe you need that oxygen mask on anymore. Mind if I remove it?"

"Laurie. *Laurie.* It's really you."

"Please don't get emotional—Tom, you might have died. You might have *died.*"

They held each other close for a long time, unaware that Charity was watching from the doorway. She would be expected to describe the scene later to all the girls in the office and she wanted to make sure she didn't miss any details.

Rachel Holbrook knew what was coming but she was not sure when or what form it would take: perhaps an invitation to appear at the next board of directors meeting in two or three weeks, or a formal letter from the executive committee, or a long-winded legal document full of whereases and therefores. What she didn't expect was a phone call from Smedler, her only longtime friend among the directors.

Smedler didn't waste time on amenities. "Have you seen today's papers, Rachel?"

"No."

"The reporters and photographers are having a field day with this. The *L.A. Times* has it featured as their leading story, and in the local paper there's a whole page of pictures, a rundown on everyone involved and even a history of the school. There'll undoubtedly be an editorial within the next few days crying for blood. Some of it is bound to be yours, Rachel."

"That's understandable."

"For sure they'll demand an investigation of the school and its policies. There'll be suggestions ranging from your resignation to the complete closure of the school, all from outraged citizens, many of whom have wanted to close the place for years."

"What do you propose that I do?"

"Anticipate. Get your licks in first and fast. Write a letter requesting an indefinite leave of absence until the matter has been fully investigated and steps are taken to prevent further incidents."

"Indefinite," she said. "That could mean a long time."

"Yes."

"I can't be held responsible for what happened."

"Whether you can be or can't be, you will be. Harsh criticism is inevitable, perhaps a drop in enrollment and some defections among the faculty. There may also be a decrease in donations and bequests. You're in for a lot of flak, Rachel. The only way you can avoid it is by leaving town for a while."

"Perhaps I should change my name and assume a disguise."

"Don't be bitter, Rachel. This thing has affected a great number of people. Some of them will want your hide. So put it out of reach. Take a holiday."

"Is that your legal advice?"

"It's my advice as a friend. I hope it will be accepted in the same spirit."

"Thanks. I'll think about it."

"Pack first, think later," Smedler said. "There's only one hitch to the plan. Should the police ask you to stick around, you'll have to stick. You may be subpoenaed if and when the Whitfield boy comes to trial and there's some kind of hearing concerning Cleo. But if I were you, right now I'd sit down and write a letter requesting an indefinite leave of absence. Bring it to my office and I'll have copies made and hand-delivered to all the members of the board. Your request will be immediately accepted."

"Thanks for your advice."

"Honestly, Rachel, you don't know how much I hate to do this to you."

"Not as much as I hate to have it done."

She hung up and reached for a sheet of the school's best stationery.

I hereby request an indefinite leave of absence from my duties as principal of Holbrook Hall.

She signed her name, put the sheet of paper in an envelope and addressed the envelope to the president of the board of directors. Then she went outside by the back door.

Nothing seemed to have changed. There were the usual sounds: screams and laughter from the pool area, the whinnying of a horse, the excited barking of dogs.

Gretchen was polishing the leaves of a camellia planted in a redwood tub. Only such sturdy leaves as a camellia's could have withstood her loving attack.

"Good morning, Gretchen. I see you're working hard."

"I always do," Gretchen said brusquely, as if she'd been accused of laziness. "*Somebody* has to."

The fig tree was dropping its fruit like small brown eggs onto the grass. As they fell, two boys wearing cowboy boots were squashing the eggs into little yellow omelets.

The round-eyed girl, Sandy, was shelling peanuts to feed to the scrub jay watching impatiently from the edge of the roof. Sandy would place a peanut on her head and the bird would swoop down, grab it with his beak and fly off to hide it. There were pounds and pounds of nuts scattered throughout the grounds, buried in the grass or the vegetable garden, stuffed in the crevices between flagstones and the hollows of trees and underneath the shingles of the roof, dropped into chimneys and even into the goldfish pond. The bird always tired of the game before the girl did and flew off to seek more challenging pastimes.

In the playground the quiet boy, Michael, sat in the middle of the teeter-totter, using his feet to pump it up and down. Bang thump. Bang thump. He wore a knitted headband which had fallen or been pulled down over his eyes.

"Michael, I'm going away. I wanted to say goodbye to you. I probably won't be seeing you for a long time."

Bang thump. Bang thump.

"Michael?"

"I hate you."

"I know you do. I thought you might say goodbye to me anyway."

"Goodbye," Michael said. "Goodbye. Goodbye. Goodbye. Goodbye. Goodbye. Goodbye."

"Thank you, Michael. That's enough."

"Goodbye. Goodbye. Goodbye."

She walked away as fast as possible. But she couldn't get out of earshot. The others had taken up Michael's chant. Sandy and the two boys under the fig tree and Gretchen were all chanting in unison with Michael.

"Good . . . bye . . . good . . . bye . . . good . . ."

When she reached the corner of the building Rachel Holbrook turned and waved. They waved back, Gretchen and the two boys and Sandy and even Michael. It was an encouraging sign that Michael had responded at all. Perhaps as he grew older, under the guidance of a new principal . . . *No, I really mustn't think about any of them. I must go away and forget them for a long time . . .*

"Goodbye," she said firmly.

The room was small and bare except for three steel chairs and a table, all bolted to the floor. The door had a barred window through which a uniformed policeman glanced every few minutes.

A previous occupant had damaged the thermostat and the air-conditioning couldn't be regulated. Cold air kept blasting in from a vent high in the wall, making the room as cold as a walk-in refrigerator. Donny sat on the table dangling his legs.

"How about that," he said, gesturing toward the door. "My own personal guard. Man oh man, they must think I'm public enemy numero uno. Did you bring me any money?"

Whitfield shook his head. "They wouldn't let me hand you any, so I tried to deposit some in an account at the commissary. But they don't have that system at Juvenile Hall, just at the adult—ah, facility."

"So what system are us poor jerks in here stuck with?"

"You have to earn points."

"How?"

"Good behavior, doing work, et cetera. You earn so many points by doing such and such a job and then you can spend the points like money. If you work and behave yourself you'll be able to get candy bars and cigarettes, things like that. The idea is to treat rich and poor alike."

"Jee-sus."

"Well, goddammit, son, this isn't a hotel. And I didn't put you here."

"You sent the cops after your precious boat."

"I didn't," Whitfield said. "I swear I didn't. I would have let you take a little cruise, knowing you'd come back."

"So you think I'd come back. Don't kid yourself. I was heading for the moon, man, straight for the moon."

Whitfield focused his eyes on a spot on the bare grey wall. This was his son, his only child, and he couldn't bear to look at him, to touch him, even to be in the same room with him. "I didn't put you here, Donny."

"But I bet you don't mind if they keep me here. It's cheaper than Holbrook Hall."

"Listen, son. I've hired a lawyer from L.A., the best money can buy. But he can't get you out on bail. There's no bail for juveniles, especially ones with a record like yours. And the charges against you are pretty bad."

"Like how bad?"

"I don't even know if I can remember them all. Kidnapping—that's the worst. Then there's grand theft, assault with a deadly weapon, assault with intent to do great bodily harm, assault with intent to commit murder—"

"Okay, okay."

"Although you were brought here to Juvenile Hall because you're not yet eighteen, the chances are ninety-nine to a hundred that you'll be tried as an adult. That makes things even worse." The room was so cold that Whitfield's voice was trembling. "Donny, if you could only show remorse, if you could convey to the authorities that you're sorry for what you've done, that you didn't mean to—"

"I meant to," Donny said. "And I'm not sorry."

"Son, please."

"Screw the son bit. It makes me puke . . . You got any chocolate bars on you?"

"I brought you two pounds of See's candies but they wouldn't let me bring them in."

"Those stinking cops are probably gobbling them up right now." Donny slid off the table. He looked impassive except for a tic in his left eyelid which he concealed by averting his face. "Well, I guess that's all. You might as well leave. You'll be late getting to Ensenada."

Whitfield once more studied an invisible spot on the wall. "I was going to cancel the trip to make sure I'd be here for your trial. But the lawyer told me not to bother. He said there'd probably be one delay after another, so your case might not come up for as long as a year, and it would be a waste of time for me to wait around and . . ." His voice faded as if suddenly he knew he'd hit the wrong note but there was no right one. "I'm sorry. I'm doing everything I can, everything I possibly can."

"Yeah. Sure."

"Donny. Donny, couldn't you at least *pretend* to be remorseful?"

"I'm remorseful all right when I think of those damn cops gobbling up all my candies. What kind were they? Any marshmints? Chocolate cherries? Peanut butter crackle?"

"For God's sake, Donny, haven't you anything else to say to me?"

"Marshmints are my favorites," Donny said.

Cleo was still wearing the stained jeans and T-shirt and sneakers without laces when Hilton went to the county jail to take her home.

Bail had been set high, at twenty-five thousand dollars, because she would be charged as a principal in the case, which one of the lawyers said was the new term used for accessory to a crime. Hilton tried to explain this to her on the way home.

"You will be accused of helping Donny do some of the things he's charged with. Do you understand?"

"All I did was hold the gun."

"Did he force you to? Were you acting under duress?"

"It was hardly even a gun. It was only an itty-bitty thing."

"Guns kill. That's what they're made for. Did you obey Donny because you were afraid for your life?"

"Heavens, no. Who could be afraid of Donny? He's so silly."

She sat beside him in the front seat, her legs drawn up and her chin resting on her knees. Her face was almost hidden by a beige curtain of hair.

"Where are your shoelaces?" he said.

She told him about Donny tying Ted's hands behind his back as he lay on the bunk. Hilton listened, feeling the blood flow out of him as if each word she spoke was a puncture wound in his heart.

He ached with fatigue. He had been up all night, contacting lawyers, the judge who set bail, a medical doctor and a psychiatrist recommended by a bail bondsman. Every half hour he phoned the hospital for a report on Ted's condition. He knew that whether Ted lived or died, Frieda would hold him responsible. His marriage had ended and his son was listed in very critical condition, yet he still knew almost nothing of what had happened since Cleo had walked away from the house with the basset hound on a leash. The psychiatrist had urged him not to question Cleo too closely. What good would it do anyway? A gun was an itty-bitty thing and Donny was merely silly.

"There was a nasty old doctor at the jail," Cleo said. "He told me I'm not going to have a baby. How does *he* know anyway? He can't see it if it's no bigger than a grain of sugar."

"It's his job to know. He's a gynecologist."

"Long words don't mean anything. Curriculum. Curriculum—what is that anyway? Donny had one at the school . . . Will I be going back there, to Holbrook Hall?"

"I don't think so."

"Oh, well, I don't care. It wasn't all that much fun." She hesitated. "Will I be staying at home all the time like I used to?"

"That depends."

"What on?"

"The judge will have to decide to what extent you were responsible for your actions."

"I didn't do anything wrong, Hilton. I just held that little wee gun."

"Stop it. I prefer not to hear any more about it."

"Oh, Hilton, you're mad at me." She peeked at him around the curtain of hair, wet-eyed and wistful. "Aren't you?"

"No."

"I'm glad. I didn't really do anything much."

His hands gripped the steering wheel as if they were trying to squeeze the life out of it. Nothing much. Roger Lennard was dead and Ted on the point of death. Rachel Holbrook's life work was in ruins and Donny Whitfield would almost certainly be sent to the penitentiary. Nothing much.

"Everything can be the same as it was before," Cleo said. "Frieda will read to me, and we'll go shopping and to the movies, and maybe Frieda will teach me how to drive. Roger said that was one of my rights, to learn to drive."

"Frieda won't be living with us anymore."

"Why not?"

"She doesn't want to."

The simple explanation satisfied her because she understood it. If you wanted to do something, you did it. If you didn't, you didn't.

"You can hire somebody to take her place, can't you?" Cleo said. "Somebody like her, only nicer and more understanding."

"I'm afraid I couldn't find such a person."

"That means there'll just be the two of us, you and me? It doesn't sound like much fun."

"No, I don't suppose it will be."

"Valencia hardly speaks any English and Cook always chases me out of the kitchen because I interfere with the T. V. game shows. I won't have anyone to talk to unless you stay home."

"I can't, Cleo. I have a job."

"We have lots of money already, don't we?"

"Quite a bit, yes."

"Why do you want more?"

"To provide for your future. You're only twenty-two. You may live another fifty or sixty years. You'll require a great deal of money."

"No, I won't, Hilton. I'll have a husband to take care of me. Won't I?"

He didn't answer.

"Won't I, Hilton? Won't I have a husband?"

"I don't know."

"I bet you don't want me to. I bet you're jealous. Look what you did to Roger."

"You mustn't talk like that, Cleo. There's nothing in this world I'd like better than to see you married to a decent young man who will love you for your—your good qualities."

"I don't believe it. You told me I was never to let another man touch me. Don't you remember, it was the night Ted and I—"

"I spoke during an emotional reaction. I didn't mean it. After you're married you will have an intimate relationship with your husband like any other girl."

"But I'm not like any other girl, am I?"

"No."

"I wonder why not."

He turned into the long, winding driveway that led to the house. About halfway up, Trocadero was putting the finishing touches on a juniper sculpture, cutting the tiny needles as precisely as a barber. The basset hound Zia sat at his feet but came bounding out to bark at the car. Troc whistled him back and pretended not to see Cleo.

"Zia doesn't like me anymore," Cleo said. "I can tell. He wasn't even wagging his tail."

"We'll buy you a dog of your own, any kind you like."

"No thanks."

"Don't you want one?"

"I'd rather have a husband and babies."

"Of course you would. But in the meantime—"

He couldn't finish the sentence. It would be a long meantime, impossible to fill with dogs and movies and shopping.

He stopped the car in front of the house. "You'd better go up to your room and take a shower and put on some clean clothes."

"I don't want to. I like these ones."

"They're dirty. Valencia will wash and dry them for you while we're having lunch. Please don't argue with me, Cleo. I'm terribly tired."

"I'm just as tired as you are. The jail was so noisy I couldn't sleep."

"Then we'll both take a long nap after lunch. Right now I have to call the hospital again."

She went up to her room and showered and shampooed her hair. Then she stood in front of the full-length mirror in her bedroom, letting the water drip down her body, tickling her skin. She liked the way she looked, a mermaid escaped from the sea.

Valencia came in without knocking to pick up Cleo's clothes and take the wet towels away. Valencia said, *"Hija mala."*

"You're mean to say things I can't understand."

"Wicked girl. You done wicked."

"No, I didn't."

"Troc say you wicked. Cook say you loco."

"What do they know? They're only servants."

She put on one of the bathrobes Frieda had given her and went downstairs to have lunch with Hilton. But he was lying on the couch in his den, his face to the wall. She wondered if he was dead, so she touched him on the shoulder. It was like switching on one of the mixing machines Cook kept in the kitchen. Hilton began to shake all over as if he were being ground up inside, his liver and heart and stomach and appendix, all ground up into hamburger. It took away her appetite.

She went into the kitchen to see if Cook would let her watch television with her. But Cook shooed her away like a chicken, flapping her apron at her and making chicken sounds. So she sat at the long dining room table by herself, thinking about Hilton's insides being all ground up. She left most of the food on her plate untouched and ate only a muffin. Then she went back into the den.

"Hilton?"

"Go away."

"I have nowhere to go."

He was still shaking but not nearly so much, and his voice had no tremor at all. He just sounded very tired.

"Ted died," he said. "The bullet taken out of him was a twenty-two. It came from your gun."

"I don't believe it. You're trying to scare me."

"You shot him. You shot my son, Ted."

"Honestly I didn't. I only held the gun. I only held that teeny little gun. You can't blame me."

"I don't blame you. I blame myself."

"That's silly. You weren't even there."

"Go away," Hilton said. "Go away."

She returned to her room, thinking that Hilton's brain, not merely his liver and stomach and heart, had been ground up in the mixer because he was imagining that Ted had died and that he himself was to blame. It was too bad. Hilton used to be awfully smart.

She brushed her hair, still wet, and put on the freshly laundered jeans and T-shirt, and wondered where mermaids went when they came up from the sea. There didn't seem to be a place for them.

She asked Valencia, who didn't understand the word, and Cook, who said, "Never you mind about mermaid. March back in there and finish your vegetables."

Then she walked down to where Troc was barbering the juniper and she asked him about mermaids.

Troc gave her a peculiar look. "Are you having one of them foggy moments of yours?"

"All I did was ask you a question."

"I'll go fetch the boss. You wait here, girl. You wait right here."

She waited only long enough for him to disappear around the bend. Then she ran down the rest of the driveway to the street. She felt very light and airy, moving with the wind like a silk sail. And suddenly, magically, she knew what mermaids did when they came up from the sea. They went down to it again.

She could see the harbor in the distance and she kept running toward it. Everyone on the *Spindrift* would be very surprised to see her and they would all have a party to celebrate, Manny Ocho and the crew, and Donny and Ted and the young man who told her about voting and some of her other rights.

None of that seemed important anymore. She was going to a party.

ABOUT THE AUTHOR

Margaret Millar (1915–1994) was born in Ontario, Canada, and was educated at Kitchener-Waterloo Collegiate Institute and the University of Toronto, majoring in classics. In 1938, she married Kenneth Millar (who wrote under the name Ross Macdonald). She published her first novel, *The Invisible Worm*, in 1941 and she worked as a screenwriter for Warner Brothers. She was active in the conservation movement in California in the 1960s and was named a Woman of the Year by the *Los Angeles Times* in 1965, and in 1983, she became a Grand Master of the Mystery Writers of America.

COLLECTED MILLAR

The Complete Writings of Margaret Millar in Seven-Volumes

Collect all seven to complete the illustration on the spine!

THE FIRST DETECTIVES
ISBN: 978-1-68199-031-6
$19.99

The Paul Prye Mysteries
The Invisible Worm (1941)
The Weak-Eyed Bat (1942)
The Devil Loves Me (1942)

Inspector Sands Mysteries
Wall of Eyes (1943)
The Iron Gates [*Taste of Fears*] (1945)

DAWN OF DOMESTIC SUSPENSE
978-1-68199-030-9
$19.99

Fire Will Freeze (1944)
Experiment in Springtime (1947)
The Cannibal Heart (1949)
Do Evil in Return (1950)
Rose's Last Summer (1952)

THE MASTER AT HER ZENITH
978-1-68199-027-9
$17.99
Vanish in an Instant (1952)
Wives and Lovers (1954)
Beast in View (1955)
An Air That Kills (1957)
The Listening Walls (1959)

LEGENDARY NOVELS OF SUSPENSE
978-1-68199-028-6
$17.99
A Stranger in My Grave (1960)
How Like an Angel (1962)
The Fiend (1964)
Beyond This Point Are Monsters (1970)

THE TOM ARAGON NOVELS
978-1-68199-029-3
$17.99
Ask for Me Tomorrow (1976)
The Murder of Miranda (1979)
Mermaid (1982)

FIRST THINGS, LAST THINGS
978-1-68199-032-3
$19.99
Banshee (1983)
Spider Webs (1986)
Collected Short Fiction (2016)
It's All in the Family (1948) (semi-autobiographical children's book)

MEMOIR
978-1-68199-033-0
$16.99
The Birds and the Beasts Were There (1968)

THE COMPLETE WRITINGS OF
MARGARET
MILLAR
AVAILABLE AS EBOOKS FOR THE FIRST TIME

NOVELS OF SUSPENSE
continued

The Cannibal Heart
ISBN: 978-1-68199-024-8

An Air That Kills
ISBN: 978-1-68199-013-2

The Listening Walls
ISBN: 978-1-68199-014-9

A Stranger in My Grave
ISBN: 978-1-68199-015-6

How Like an Angel
ISBN: 978-1-68199-016-3

The Fiend
ISBN: 978-1-68199-017-0

Beyond This Point Are Monsters
ISBN: 978-1-68199-018-7

Banshee
ISBN: 978-1-68199-019-4

Spider Webs
ISBN: 978-1-68199-020-0

OTHER NOVELS

Experiment in Springtime
ISBN: 978-1-68199-022-4

Wives and Lovers
ISBN: 978-1-68199-025-5

STORIES

The Collected Short Stories
ISBN: 978-1-68199-021-7

CHILDREN'S BOOKS

It's All in the Family
ISBN: 978-1-68199-023-1

NONFICTION

The Birds and the Beasts Were There
ISBN: 978-1-68199-026-2

www.syndicatebooks.com

3 1170 01027 7121